P9-ECN-366

THE PILGRIM'S PROGRESS AND THE HOLY WAR

THE PILGRIM'S PROGRESS AND THE HOLY WAR

By JOHN BUNYAN

PURITAN PUBLISHING COMPANY, INC.

Chicago, Illinois

PRINTED IN THE UNITED STATES OF AMERICA
AMERICAN BOOK—STRATFORD PRESS, INC., NEW YORK

CONTENTS

The Author's Apology 1
The Pilgrim's Progress 7
The Second Part 111
The Holy War 201

THE AUTHOR'S APOLOGY

FOR HIS BOOK

When at the first I took my Pen in hand,
Thus for to write; I did not understand
That I at all should make a little Book
In such a mode; Nay, I had undertook
To make another, which when almost done,
Before I was aware, I this begun.
And thus it was: I writing of the Way
And Race of Saints, in this our Gospel-Day,
Fell suddenly into an Allegory
About their Journey, and the way to Glory,
In more than twenty things, which I set down;
This done, I twenty more had in my Crown,
And they again began to multiply,
Like sparks that from the coals of fire do fly.
Nay then, thought I, if that you breed so fast,
I'll put you by yourselves, lest you at last
Should prove ad infinitum, *and eat out*
The Book that I already am about.
Well, so I did; but yet I did not think
To show to all the World my Pen and Ink
In such a mode; I only thought to make
I knew not what: nor did I undertake
Thereby to please my Neighbor; no not I;
And did it mine own self to gratify.
Neither did I but vacant seasons spend
In this my Scribble; nor did I intend
But to divert myself in doing this,
From worser thoughts, which make me do amiss.
Thus I set Pen to Paper with delight,
And quickly had my thoughts in black and white.
For having now my Method by the end,
Still as I pull'd, it came; and so I penn'd
It down; until at last it came to be,
For length and breadth the bigness which you see.

Well, when I had thus put mine ends together,
I shew'd them others, that I might see whether
They would condemn them, or them justify:
And some said, let them live; some, let them die.
Some said, John, *print it; others said, Not so:*
Some said, It might do good; others said, No.
Now was I in a strait, and did not see
Which was the best thing to be done by me:
At last I thought, Since you are thus divided,
I print it will; and so the case decided.
For, thought I, Some, I see, would have it done
Though others in that Channel do not run;
To prove then who advised for the best,
Thus I thought fit to put it to the test.
I further thought, if now I did deny
Those that would have it thus, to gratify,
I did not know but hinder them I might
Of that which would to them be great delight.
For those which were not for its coming forth,
I said to them, Offend you I am loth;
Yet since your Brethren pleased with it be,
Forbear to judge, till you do further see.
If that thou wilt not read, let it alone;
Some love the meat, some love to pick the bone:
Yea, that I might them better palliate,
I did too with them thus expostulate.
May I not write in such a stile as this?
In such a method too, and yet not miss
Mine end, thy good? why may it not be done?
Dark Clouds bring Waters, when the bright bring none;
Yea, dark, or bright, if they their Silver drops
Cause to descend, the Earth, by yielding Crops,
Gives praise to both, and carpeth not at either,
But treasures up the Fruit they yield together:
Yea, so commixes both, that in her Fruit
None can distinguish this from that, they suit
Her well, when hungry: but if she be full,
She spues out both, and makes their blessings null.
You see the ways the Fisherman doth take
To catch the Fish; what Engins doth he make?
Behold how he ingageth all his Wits,
Also his Snares, Lines, Angles, Hooks and Nets.
Yet Fish there be, that neither Hook, nor Line,
Nor Snare, nor Net, nor Engine can make thine;
They must be grop't for, and be tickled too,
Or they will not be catcht, what e're you do.

How doth the Fowler seek to catch his Game,
By divers means, all which one cannot name?
His Gun, his Nets, his Limetwigs, light, and bell:
He creeps, he goes, he stands; yea who can tell
Of all his postures, Yet there's none of these
Will make him master of what Fowls he please.
Yea, he must Pipe, and Whistle to catch this;
Yet if he does so, that Bird he will miss.
If that a Pearl may in a Toads-head dwell,
And may be found too in an Oystershell;
If things that promise nothing, do contain
What better is than Gold; who will disdain,
(That have an inkling of it,) there to look,
That they may find it. Now my little Book,
(Tho' void of all those paintings that may make
It with this or the other Man to take),
Is not without those things that do excel
What do in brave, but empty notions dwell.
Well, yet I am not fully satisfied,
That this your Book will stand when soundly try'd;
Why, what's the matter! it is dark, what tho?
But it is feigned. What of that I tro?
Some men by feigning words as dark as mine,
Make truth to spangle, and its rays to shine.
But they want solidness: Speak man thy mind,
They drown'd the weak; Metaphors make us blind.
Solidity, indeed becomes the Pen
Of him that writeth things Divine to men:
But must I needs want solidness, because
By Metaphors I speak; Was not Gods Laws,
His Gospel-Laws, in older time held forth
By Types, Shadows and Metaphors? Yet loth
Will any sober man be to find fault
With them, lest he be found for to assault
The highest Wisdom. No, he rather stoops,
And seeks to find out what by pins and loops,
By Calves, and Sheep, by Heifers, and by Rams;
By Birds, and Herbs, and by the blood of Lambs,
God speaketh to him. And happy is he
That finds the light, and grace that in them be.
Be not too forward therefore to conclude,
That I want solidness, that I am rude:
All things solid in shew, not solid be;
All things in parables despise not we,
Lest things most hurtful lightly we receive,
And things that good are, of our souls bereave.

My dark and cloudy words they do but hold
The Truth, as Cabinets inclose the Gold.
The Prophets used much by Metaphors
To set forth Truth; Yea, who so considers
Christ, his Apostles too, shall plainly see,
That Truths to this day in such Mantles be.
Am I afraid to say that holy Writ,
Which for its Stile, and Phrase puts down all Wit,
Is every where so full of all these things,
(Dark Figures, Allegories) yet there springs
From that same Book that lustre, and those rays
Of light, that turns our darkest nights to days.
Come, let my Carper to his Life now look,
And find There darker lines than in my Book
He findeth any. Yea, and let him know,
That in his best things there are worse lines too.
May we but stand before impartial men,
To his poor One, I durst adventure Ten,
That they will take my meaning in these lines
Far better than his Lies in Silver Shrines.
Come, Truth, although in Swadling-clouts, I find
Informs the Judgment, rectifies the Mind,
Pleases the Understanding, makes the Will
Submit; the Memory too it doth fill
With what doth our Imagination please;
Likewise, it tends our troubles to appease.
Sound words I know Timothy *is to use,*
And old Wives Fables he is to refuse;
But yet grave Paul, *him no where doth forbid*
The use of Parables; in which lay hid
That Gold, those Pearls, and precious stones that were
Worth digging for; and that with greatest care.
Let me add one word more, O man of God!
Art thou offended? dost thou wish I had
Put forth my matter in another dress,
Or that I had in things been more express?
Three things let me propound, then I submit
To those that are my betters, as is fit.
1. *I find not that I am denied the use*
Of this my method, so I no abuse
Put on the Words, Things, Readers, or be rude
In handling Figure, or Similitude,
In application; but, all that I may,
Seek the advance of Truth, this or that way:
Denied, did I say? Nay, I have leave,
(Example too, and that from them that have

God better pleased by their words or ways,
Than any man that breatheth now a-days),
Thus to express my mind, thus to declare
Things unto thee, that excellentest are.
2. *I find that men (as high as Trees) will write*
Dialogue-wise; yet no man doth them slight
For writing so: Indeed if they abuse
Truth, cursed be they, and, the craft they use
To that intent; But yet let Truth be free
To make her Sallies upon Thee, and Me,
Which way it pleases God. For who knows how,
Better than he that taught us first to Plough,
To guide our Mind and Pens for his Design?
And he makes base things usher in Divine.
3. *I find that holy Writ in many places,*
Hath semblance with this method, where the cases
Doth call for one thing, to set forth another:
Use it I may then, and yet nothing smother
Truths golden Beams; Nay, by this method may
Make it cast forth its rays as light as day.
And now, before I do put up my Pen,
I'll shew the profit of my Book, and then
Commit both thee, and it unto that hand
That pulls the strong down, and makes weak ones stand.
This Book it chalketh out before thine eyes
The man that seeks the everlasting Prize:
It shews you whence he comes, whither he goes,
What he leaves undone; also what he does:
It also shews you how he runs and runs,
Till he unto the Gate of Glory comes.
It shews too, who sets out for life amain,
As if the lasting Crown they would attain:
Here also you may see the reason why
They lose their labour, and like Fools do die.
This Book will make a Traveller of thee,
If by its Counsel thou wilt ruled be;
It will direct thee to the Holy Land,
If thou wilt its Directions understand:
Yea, it will make the slothful, active be;
The Blind also, delightful things to see.
Art thou for something rare, and profitable?
Wouldest thou see a Truth within a Fable?
Art thou forgetful? wouldest thou remember
From New-year's-day *to the last of* December?
Then read my fancies, they will stick like Burs,
And may be to the Helpless, Comforters.

This Book is writ in such a Dialect,
As may the minds of listless men affect:
It seems a Novelty, and yet contains
Nothing but sound, and honest Gospel-strains.
Would'st thou divert thyself from Melancholy?
Would'st thou be pleasant, yet be far from folly?
Would'st thou read Riddles, & their Explanation?
Or else be drowned in thy Contemplation?
Dost thou love picking meat? Or would'st thou see
A man i'th Clouds, and hear him speak to thee?
Would'st thou be in a Dream, and yet not sleep?
Or wouldest thou in a moment laugh, and weep?
Wouldest thou lose thyself, and catch no harm?
And find thyself again without a charm?
Would'st read thyself, and read thou know'st not what
And yet know whether thou art blest or not,
By reading the same lines? O then come hither,
And lay my Book, thy Head, and Heart together.

JOHN BUNYAN.

THE PILGRIM'S PROGRESS:

IN THE SIMILITUDE OF A DREAM

As I walk'd through the wilderness of this world, I lighted on a certain place, where was a Den; and I laid me down in that place to sleep: and as I slept I dreamed a Dream. I dreamed, and behold *I saw a man cloathed with Rags, standing in a certain place, with his face from his own House, a Book in his hand, and a great burden upon his back.* I looked, and saw him open the Book, and read therein; and as he read, he wept and trembled: and not being able longer to contain, he brake out with a lamentable cry; saying, *what shall I do?*

In this plight therefore he went home, and refrained himself as long as he could, that his Wife and Children should not perceive his distress; but he could not be silent long, because that his trouble increased: wherefore at length he brake his mind to his Wife and Children; and thus he began to talk to them, *O my dear Wife,* said he, *and you the Children of my bowels, I your dear friend, am in myself undone, by reason of a burden that lieth hard upon me: moreover, I am for certain informed that this our City will be burned with fire from Heaven, in which fearful overthrow, both myself, with thee, my Wife, and you my sweet babes, shall miserably come to ruin; except (the which, yet I see not) some way of escape can be found, whereby we may be delivered.* At this his Relations were sore amazed; not for that they believed that what he had said to them was true, but because they thought that some frenzy distemper had got into his head: therefore, it drawing towards night, and they hoping that sleep might settle his brains, with all haste they got him to bed; but the night was as troublesome to him as the day: wherefore instead of sleeping, he spent it in sighs and tears. So when the morning was come, they would know how he did; he told them, worse and worse. He also set to talking to them again, but they began to be hardened; they also thought to drive away his distemper by harsh and surly carriages to him: sometimes they would deride, sometimes they would chide, and sometimes they would quite neglect him: wherefore he began to retire himself to his Chamber to pray for, and pity them; and also to condole his own misery: he would also walk solitarily in the Fields, sometimes reading, and sometimes praying: and thus for some days he spent his time.

Now, I saw upon a time, when he was walking in the Fields, that he was (as he was wont) reading in his Book, and greatly distressed in his mind;

and as he read, he burst out, as he had done before, crying, *What shall I do to be saved?*

I saw also that he looked this way, and that way, as if he would run; yet he stood still, because as I perceived he could not tell which way to go. I looked then, and saw a Man named *Evangelist* coming to him, and asked, *Wherefore doest thou cry?* He answered, Sir, I perceive, by the Book in my hand, that I am condemned to die, and after that to come to Judgement; and I find that I am not willing to do the first, nor able to do the second.

Then said *Evangelist*, Why not willing to die? since this life is attended with so many evils? The Man answered, Because I fear that this burden that is upon my back, will sink me lower than the Grave; and I shall fall into *Tophet*. And Sir, if I be not fit to go to Prison, I am not fit (I am sure) to go to Judgement, and from thence to Execution; and the thoughts of these things make me cry.

Then said *Evangelist*, If this be thy condition, why standest thou still? He answered, Because I know not whither to go. Then he gave him a *Parchment Roll*, and there was written within, *Fly from the wrath to come.*

Conviction of the Necessity of Flying

The Man therefore read it, and looking upon *Evangelist* very carefully; said, Whither must I fly? Then said *Evangelist*, pointing with his finger over a very wide Field, Do you see yonder *Wicket-gate?* The Man said, No. Then said the other, Do you see yonder shining light? He said, I think I do. Then said *Evangelist*, Keep that light in your eye, and go up directly thereto, so shalt thou see the Gate; at which when thou knockest, it shall be told thee what thou shalt do.

So I saw in my Dream, that the Man began to run; now he had not run far from his own door, but his Wife and Children perceiving it, began to cry after him to return: but the Man put his Fingers in his Ears, and ran on crying, Life, Life, Eternal Life: so he looked not behind him, but fled towards the middle of the Plain.

The Neighbors also came out to see him run, and as he ran, some mocked, others threatned; and some cried after him to return. And among those that did so, there were two that were resolved to fetch him back by force: the name of the one was *Obstinate*, and the name of the other *Pliable*. Now by this time the Man was got a good distance from them; But however they were resolved to pursue him; which they did, and in a little time they overtook him. Then said the Man, Neighbors, *Wherefore are you come?* They said, To perswade you to go back with us; but he said, That can by no means be: You dwell, said he, in the City of *Destruction* (the place also where I was born), I see it to be so; and dying there, sooner or later, you will sink lower then the Grave, into a place that burns with Fire and Brimstone; Be content good Neighbors, and go along with me.

What! said *Obstinate*, *and leave our Friends, and our comforts behind us!*

Yes, said *Christian* (for that was his name), because that *all* is not worthy to be compared with a *little* of that that I am seeking to enjoy, and if you will go along with me, and hold it, you shall fare as I myself; for there where I go, is enough, and to spare; Come away, and prove my words.

OBS. *What are the things you seek, since you leave all the World to find them?*

CHR. I seek an *Inheritance, incorruptible, undefiled, and that fadeth not away;* and it is laid up in Heaven, and safe there, to be bestowed at the time appointed on them that diligently seek it. Read it so, if you will, in my Book.

OBS. *Tush,* said *Obstinate, away with your Book; will you go back with us, or no?*

CHR. No, not I, said the other; because I have laid my hand to the Plough.

OBS. *Come then, Neighbor* Pliable, *let us turn again, and go home without him; There is a Company of these Craz'd-headed Coxcombs, that when they take a fancy by the end, are wiser in their own eyes than seven men that can render a Reason.*

PLI. Then said *Pliable,* Don't revile; if what the good *Christian* says is true, the things he looks after are better than ours: my heart inclines to go with my Neighbor.

OBS. *What! more Fools still? be ruled by me and go back; who knows whither such a brainsick fellow will lead you? Go back, go back, and be wise.*

CHR. Nay, but do thou come with me Neighbor *Pliable;* there are such things to be had which I spoke of, and many more Glories besides. If you believe not me, read here in this Book; and for the truth of what is exprest therein, behold all is confirmed by the blood of him that made it.

PLIABLE TO GO WITH CHRISTIAN

PLI. *Well Neighbor* Obstinate (*said* Pliable), *I begin to come to a point; I intend to go along with this good man, and to cast in my lot with him: But my good Companion, do you know the way to this desired place?*

CHR. I am directed by a man whose name is *Evangelist,* to speed me to a little Gate that is before us, where we shall receive instruction about the way.

PLI. *Come then good Neighbor, let us be going.* Then they went both together.

OBS. And I will go back to my place, said *Obstinate.* I will be no Companion of such misled fantastical Fellows.

Now I saw in my Dream, that when *Obstinate* was gone back, *Christian* and *Pliable* went talking over the Plain; and thus they began their discourse.

CHR. Come Neighbor *Pliable,* how do you do? I am glad you are perswaded to go along with me; and had even *Obstinate* himself but felt what I have felt of the Powers and Terrors of what is yet unseen, he would not thus lightly have given us the back.

PLI. *Come Neighbor* Christian, *since there is none but us two here, tell me now further what the things are, and how to be enjoyed, whither we are going?*

CHR. I can better conceive of them with my Mind, than speak of them with my Tongue: But yet since you are desirous to know, I will read of them in my Book.

PLI. *And do you think that the words of your Book are certainly true?*

CHR. Yes verily, for it was made by him that cannot lye.

PLI. *Well said; what things are they?*

CHR. There is an endless Kingdom to be inhabited, and everlasting life to be given us, that we may inhabit that Kingdom for ever.

PLI. *Well said; and what else?*

CHR. There are Crowns of Glory to be given us; and Garments that will make us shine like the Sun in the Firmament of Heaven.

PLI. *This is excellent; and what else?*

CHR. There shall be no more crying, nor sorrow; For he that is owner of the place, will wipe all tears from our eyes.

PLI. *And what company shall we have there?*

CHR. There we shall be with *Seraphims*, and *Cherubins*, Creatures that will dazzle your eyes to look on them: There also you shall meet with thousands, and ten thousands that have gone before us to that place; none of them are hurtful, but loving, and holy: every one walking in the sight of God, and standing in his presence with acceptance for ever. In a word, there we shall see the Elders with their Golden Crowns: there we shall see the Holy Virgins with their Golden Harps: there we shall see Men that by the World were cut in pieces, burned in flames, eaten of Beasts, drowned in the Seas, for the love that they bare to the Lord of the place, all well, and cloathed with Immortality as with a Garment.

PLI. *The hearing of this is enough to ravish ones heart; but are these things to be enjoyed? How shall we get to be Sharers hereof?*

CHR. The Lord, the Governor of that Country, hath recorded *that* in this Book: the substance of which is, If we be truly willing to have it, he will bestow it upon us freely.

PLI. *Well, my good Companion, glad am I to hear of these things: Come on, let us mend our pace.*

CHR. I cannot go so fast as I would, by reason of this burden that is upon my back.

Now I saw in my Dream, that just as they had ended this talk, they drew near to a very *Miry Slough*, that was in the midst of the Plain, and they being heedless, did both fall suddenly into the bog. The name of the Slough was *Dispond*. Here therefore they wallowed for a time, being grievously bedaubed with the dirt; and *Christian*, because of the burden that was on his back, began to sink in the Mire.

PLI. *Then said* Pliable, *Ah, Neighbor* Christian, *where are you now?*

CHR. Truly, said *Christian*, I do not know.

IT IS NOT ENOUGH TO BE PLIABLE

PLI. At that *Pliable* began to be offended; and angerly said to his Fellow, *Is this the happiness you have told me all this while of? If we have such ill speed at our first setting out, what may we expect, 'twixt this and our Journeys end? May I get out again with my life, you shall possess the brave Country alone for me.* And with that he gave a desperate struggle or two, and got out of the Mire, on that side of the Slough which was next his own House; so away he went, and *Christian* saw him no more.

Wherefore *Christian* was left to tumble in the Slough of *Dispond* alone; but still he endeavoured to struggle to that side of the Slough that was still further from his own House, and next to the Wicket-gate; the which he did, but could not get out, because of the burden that was upon his back. But I beheld in my Dream, that a Man came to him, whose name was *Help*, and asked him, *What he did there?*

CHR. Sir, said *Christian*, I was directed this way, by a man called *Evangelist;* who directed me also to yonder Gate, that I might escape the wrath to come: And as I was going thither, I fell in here.

HELP. *But why did you not look for the steps?*

CHR. *Fear* followed me so hard, that I fled the next way, and fell in.

HELP. *Then*, said he, *Give me thy hand!* So he gave him his hand, and he drew him out, and set him upon sound ground, and bid him go on his way.

Then I stepped to him that pluckt him out, and said, Sir, wherefore, since over this place is the way from the City of *Destruction* to yonder *Gate*, is it that *this* Plat is not mended, that poor travellers might go thither with more security? And he said unto me, This *Miry slough* is such a place as cannot be mended. It is the descent whither the scum and filth that attends conviction for sin doth continually run, and therefore it is called the *Slough of Dispond:* for still as the sinner is awakened about his lost condition, there ariseth in his soul many fears and doubts and discouraging apprehensions, which all of them get together, and settle in this place: And this is the reason of the badness of this ground.

What Makes the Slough of Dispond

It is not the pleasure of the King that this place should remain so bad. His Laborers also have, by the direction of His Majestye's Surveyors, been for above this sixteen hundred years imployed about this patch of ground, if perhaps it might have been mended: yea, and to my knowledge, said he, *Here* hath been swallowed up at least twenty million Cart Loads; yea millions, of wholesome Instructions, that have at all seasons been brought from all places of the Kings Dominions (and they that can tell, say, they are the best Materials to make good ground of the place); if so be it might have been mended; but it is the *Slough of Dispond* still, and so will be, when they have done what they can.

True, there are by the direction of the Lawgiver, certain good and substantial Steps, placed even through the very midst of this *Slough;* but at such time as this place doth much spue out its filth, as it doth against change of Weather, these steps are hardly seen; or if they be, Men through the dizziness of their heads, step besides; and then they are bemired to purpose, notwithstanding the steps be there; but the ground is good when they are once got in at the Gate.

Now I saw in my Dream, that by this time *Pliable* was got home to his House again. So his Neighbors came to visit him; and some of them called him wise Man for coming back; and some called him Fool, for hazarding himself with *Christian;* others again did mock at his Cowardliness; saying, Surely since you began to venture, I would not have been so base to have given out for a few difficulties. So *Pliable* sat sneaking among them. But at last he got more confidence, and then they all turned their tales, and began to deride poor *Christian* behind his back.

And thus much concerning *Pliable.*

Mr. Worldly-Wiseman Meets Christian

Now as Christian was walking solitary by himself, he espied one afar off come crossing over the field to meet him; and their hap was to meet just as they were crossing the way of each other. The Gentleman's name was Mr. *Worldly-Wiseman;* he dwelt in the Town of *Carnal-Policy,* a very great Town, and also hard by from whence Christian came. This man then meeting with Christian, and having some inkling of him,—for Christian's setting forth from the City of *Destruction* was much noised abroad, not only in the Town where he dwelt, but also it began to be the *Town*-talk in some other places.—Master *Worldly-Wiseman* therefore, having some guess of him, by beholding his laborious going, by observing his sighs and groans, and the like, began thus to enter into some talk with *Christian.*

World. *How now, good fellow, whither away after this burdened manner?*

Chr. A burdened manner indeed, as ever I think poor creature had. And whereas you ask me, *Whither away,* I tell you, Sir, I am going to yonder Wicket-gate before me; for there, as I am informed, I shall be put into a way to be rid of my heavy burden.

World. *Hast thou a Wife and Children?*

Chr. Yes, but I am so laden with this burden, that I cannot take that pleasure in them as formerly: methinks, I am as if I had none.

World. *Wilt thou harken to me, if I give thee counsel?*

Chr. If it be good, I will; for I stand in need of good counsel.

World. *I would advise thee then, that thou with all speed get thyself rid of thy burden; for thou wilt never be settled in thy mind till then: nor canst thou enjoy the benefits of the blessing which God hath bestowed upon thee till then.*

Chr. That is that which I seek for, even to be rid of this heavy burden; but get it off myself I cannot: nor is there a man in our Country that can take it off my shoulders; therefore am I going this way, as I told you, that I may be rid of my burden.

World. *Who bid thee go this way to be rid of thy burden?*

CHR. A man that appeared to me to be a very great and honorable person; his name, as I remember, is *Evangelist.*

WORLD. *I beshrow him for his counsel; there is not a more dangerous and troublesome way in the world than is that unto which he hath directed thee; and that thou shalt find if thou wilt be ruled by his counsel. Thou hast met with something (as I perceive) already; for I see the dirt of the* Slough of Dispond *is upon thee; but that Slough is the beginning of the sorrows that do attend those that go on in that way. Hear me, I am older than thou! thou art like to meet with in the way which thou goest, Wearisomness, Painfulness, Hunger, Perils, Nakedness, Sword, Lions, Dragons, Darkness; and in a word, death, and what not? These things are certainly true, having been confirmed by many testimonies. And why should a man so carelessly cast away himself, by giving heed to a stranger?*

CHR. Why, Sir, this burden upon my back is more terrible to me than all these things which you have mentioned: nay, methinks I care not what I meet with in the way, so be I can also meet with deliverance from my burden.

WORLD. *How camest thou by thy burden at first?*

CHR. By reading this Book in my hand.

WORLD. *I thought so; and it is happened unto thee as to other weak men, who meddling with things too high for them, do suddenly fall into thy distractions; which distractions do not only unman men (as thine I perceive has done thee) but they run them upon desperate ventures, to obtain they know not what.*

CHR. I know what I would obtain; it is ease for my heavy burden.

WORLD. *But why wilt thou seek for ease this way, seeing so many dangers attend it, especially, since (hadst thou but patience to hear me) I could direct thee to the obtaining of what thou desirest, without the dangers that thou in this way wilt run thy self into: yea, and the remedy is at hand. Besides, I will add, that instead of those dangers, thou shalt meet with much safety, friendship, and content.*

CHR. Pray, Sir, open this secret to me.

WORLD. *Why in yonder Village (the Village is named* Morality) *there dwells a Gentleman, whose name is* Legality, *a very judicious man (and a man of a very good name) that has skill to help men off with such burdens as thine are from their shoulders: yea, to my knowledge he hath done a great deal of good this way: Aye, and besides, he hath skill to cure those that are somewhat crazed in their wits with their burdens. To him, as I said, thou mayest go, and be helped presently. His house is not quite a mile from this place; and if he should not be at home himself, he hath a pretty young man to his Son, whose name is* Civility, *that can do it (to speak on) as well as the old Gentleman himself: There, I say, thou mayest be eased of thy burden, and if thou art not minded to go back to thy former habitation, as indeed I would not wish thee, thou mayest send for thy Wife and Children to thee to this Village, where there are houses now stand empty, one of which thou mayest have at reasonable rates: Provision is there also cheap and good, and that which will make thy life the more happy, is, to be sure there thou shalt live by honest neighbors, in credit and good fashion.*

Now was *Christian* somewhat at a stand, but presently he concluded; if this be true which this Gentleman hath said, my wisest course is to take his advice; and with that he thus farther spoke.

CHR. Sir, which is my way to this honest man's house?

WORLD. *Do you see yonder high hill?*

CHR. Yes, very well.

WORLD. By that *Hill* you must go, and the first house you come at is his.

Christian Afraid of Mount Sinai

So *Christian* turned out of his way to go to Mr. *Legality's* house for help; but behold, when he was got now hard by the *Hill*, it seemed so high, and also that side of it that was next the way side did hang so much over, that Christian was afraid to venture further, lest the *Hill* should fall on his head: wherefore there he stood still, and he wot not what to do. Also his burden, *now*, seemed heavier to him than while he was in his way. There came also flashes of fire out of the Hill, that made *Christian* afraid that he should be burned. Here therefore he sweat, and did quake for fear. And now he began to be sorry that he had taken Mr. *Worldly-Wisemans* counsel; and with that he saw *Evangelist* coming to meet him; at the sight also of whom he began to blush for shame.

Evangelist Findeth Christian

So *Evangelist* drew nearer and nearer, and coming up to him, he looked upon him with a severe and dreadful countenance: and thus began to reason with *Christian.*

EVAN. What doest thou here? *Christian*, said he? at which word *Christian* knew not what to answer: wherefore, at present he stood speechless before him. Then said *Evangelist* farther, *Art not thou the man that I found crying without the walls of the City of* Destruction?

CHR. Yes, dear Sir, I am the man.

EVAN. *Did not I direct thee the way to the little Wicket-gate?*

CHR. Yes, dear Sir, said *Christian.*

EVAN. *How is it then that thou art so quickly turned aside? for thou art now out of the way.*

CHR. I met with a Gentleman, so soon as I had got over the *Slough of Dispond*, who perswaded me that I might, in the *Village* before me, find a man that could take off my burden.

EVAN. *What was he?*

CHR. He looked like a Gentleman, and talked much to me, and got me at last to yield; so I came hither: but when I beheld this Hill, and how it hangs over the way, I suddenly made a stand, lest it should fall on my head.

EVAN. *What said that Gentleman to you?*

CHR. Why, he asked me whither I was going, and I told him.

EVAN. *And what said he then?*

CHR. He asked me if I had a Family, and I told him: but, said I, I am so loaden with the burden that is on my back, that I cannot take pleasure in them as formerly.

EVAN. *And what said he then?*

CHR. He bid me with speed get rid of my burden, and I told him, 'twas ease that I sought: And said I, I am therefore going to yonder *Gate* to receive further direction how I may get to the place of deliverance. So he said that he would shew me a better way, and short, not so attended with difficulties, as the way, Sir, that you set me: which way, said he, will direct you to a Gentleman's house that hath skill to take off these burdens: So I believed him, and turned out of that way into this, if haply I might be soon eased of my burden: but when I came to this place, and beheld things as they are, I stopped for fear (as I said) of danger: but I now know not what to do.

EVAN. *Then* (said Evangelist) *stand still a little, that I may shew thee the words of God.* So he stood trembling. *Then* (said Evangelist) *See that ye refuse not him that speaketh; for if they escaped not who refused him that spake on Earth, much more shall not we escape, if we turn away from him that speaketh from Heaven.* He said moreover, *Now the just shall live by faith; but if any man draws back, my soul shall have no pleasure in him.* He also did thus apply them, *Thou art the man that art running into this misery, thou hast began to reject the counsel of the most high, and to draw back thy foot from the way of peace, even almost to the hazarding of thy perdition.*

Then *Christian* fell down at his foot as dead, crying, Woe is me, for I am undone: at the sight of which *Evangelist* caught him by the right hand, saying, all manner of sin and blasphemies shall be forgiven unto men; be not faithless, but believing; then did *Christian* again a little revive, and stood up trembling, as at first, before *Evangelist.*

Then *Evangelist* proceeded, saying, *Give more earnest heed to the things that I shall tell thee of.* I will now shew thee who it was that deluded thee, and who 'twas also to whom he sent thee. The man that met thee, is one *Worldly-Wiseman*, and rightly is he so called; partly, because he savoureth only the Doctrine of this world (therefore he always goes to the Town of *Morality* to Church) and partly because he loveth that Doctrine best, for it saveth him from the Cross; and because he is of this carnal temper, therefore he seeketh to prevent my ways, though right. Now there are three things in this mans counsel that thou must utterly abhor:

1. His turning thee out of the way.
2. His labouring to render the Cross odious to thee.
3. And his setting thy feet in that way that leadeth unto the administration of Death.

First, Thou must abhor his turning thee out of the way; yea, and thine own consenting thereto: because this is to reject the counsel of God, for the sake of the counsel of a *Worldly-Wiseman.* The Lord says, *Strive to enter in at the strait gate*, the gate to which I sent thee; *for strait is the gate that leadeth unto life, and few there be that find it.* From this little wicket-gate, and from the way thereto hath this wicked man turned thee, to the bringing of thee almost to destruction; hate therefore his turning thee out of the way, and abhor thyself for hearkening to him.

Secondly, Thou must abhor his labouring to render the Cross odious unto thee; for thou art to *prefer it before the treasures of Egypt:* besides, the King of Glory hath told thee, that he that will save his life shall lose it: *and he that comes after him, and hates not his father, and mother, and wife, and children, and brethren, and sisters; yea, and his own life also, he cannot be my Disciple*. I say therefore, for a man to labour to perswade thee, that that shall be thy death, without which the truth hath said, thou canst not have eternal life, This Doctrine thou must abhor.

Thirdly, Thou must hate his setting of thy feet in the way that leadeth to the ministration of death. And for this thou must consider to whom he sent thee, and also how unable that person was to deliver thee from thy burden.

He to whom thou wast sent for ease, being by name *Legality*, is the Son of the Bond-woman which now is, and is in bondage with her children, and is in a mystery this Mount *Sinai*, which thou hast feared will fall on thy head. Now if she with her children are in bondage, how canst thou expect by them to be made free? This *Legality* therefore is not able to set thee free from thy burden. No man was as yet ever rid of his burden by him, no, nor ever is like to be: ye cannot be justified by the Works of the Law; for by the deeds of the Law no man living can be rid of his burden: therefore Mr. *Worldly-Wiseman* is an alien, and Mr. *Legality* a cheat: and for his son *Civility*, notwithstanding his simpering looks, he is but an hypocrite, and cannot help thee. Believe me, there is nothing in all this noise, that thou hast heard of this sottish man, but a design to beguile thee of thy Salvation, by turning thee from the way in which I had set thee. After this *Evangelist* called aloud to the Heavens for confirmation of what he had said; and with that there came words and fire out of the Mountain under which poor Christian stood, that made the hair of his flesh stand. The words were thus pronounced, *As many as are of the works of the Law, are under the curse; for it is written, Cursed is every one that continueth not in all things which are written in the Book of the Law to do them.*

Now *Christian* looked for nothing but death, and began to cry out lamentably, even cursing the time in which he met with Mr. *Worldly-Wiseman*, still calling himself a thousand fools for hearkening to his counsel; he also was greatly ashamed to think that this Gentleman's arguments, flowing only from the flesh, should have that prevalency with him to forsake the right way. This done, he applied himself again to *Evangelist* in words and sense as follows.

CHR. Sir, what think you? is there hopes? may I now go back, and go up to the *Wicket-gate?* Shall I not be abandoned for this, and sent back from thence ashamed? I am sorry I have hearkened to this man's counsel, but may my sin be forgiven?

EVAN. Then said *Evangelist* to him, Thy sin is very great, for by it thou hast committed two evils; thou hast forsaken the way that is good, to tread in forbidden paths: yet will the man of the Gate receive thee, for he has good will for men; only, said he, take heed that thou turn not aside again, lest thou perish from the way when his wrath is kindled but a little. Then did *Christian* address himself to go back, and *Evangelist,* after he had kist him, gave him one smile, and bid him God speed: so he went on with haste, neither spake he to any man by the way; nor if any man asked him, would he vouchsafe them an answer. He went like one that was all the while treading on forbidden ground, and could by no means think himself safe, till again he was got into the way which he left to follow Mr. *Worldly-Wiseman's* counsel. So in process of time, *Christian* got up to the Gate. Now over the Gate there was written, *Knock and it shall be opened unto you.* He knocked therefore, more than once or twice, saying,

May I now enter here? will he within
Open to sorry me, though I have been
An undeserving Rebel? then shall I
Not fail to sing his lasting praise on high.

At last there came a grave Person to the Gate, named *Good Will,* who asked *Who was there? and whence he came? and what he would have?*

CHR. Here is a poor burdened sinner. I come from the City of *Destruction,* but am going to Mount *Zion,* that I may be delivered from the wrath to come. I would therefore, Sir, since I am informed that by this Gate is the way thither, know if you are *willing* to let me in.

GOOD WILL. I am *willing* with all my heart, said he; and with that he opened the Gate.

SATAN ENVIES THOSE THAT ENTER THE STRAIGHT GATE

So, when *Christian* was stepping in, the other gave him a pull; Then said *Christian,* What means that? The other told him, A little distance from this Gate, there is erected a strong Castle, of which *Beelzebub* is the Captain: from thence both he, and them that are with him shoot Arrows at those that come up to this Gate; if haply they may die before they can enter in. Then said *Christian,* I rejoice and tremble. So when he was got in, the Man of the Gate asked him, Who directed him thither?

CHR. *Evangelist* bid me come hither and knock (as I did); And he said, that you, Sir, would tell me what I must do.

GOOD WILL. *An open Door is set before thee, and no man can shut it.*

CHR. Now I begin to reap the benefits of my hazards.

GOOD WILL. *But how is it that you came alone?*

CHR. Because none of my Neighbors saw their danger, as I saw mine.

GOOD WILL. *Did any of them know of your coming?*

CHR. Yes, my Wife and Children saw me at the first, and called after me to turn again: Also some of my Neighbors stood crying, and calling after me to return; but I put my Fingers in my Ears, and so came on my way.

GOOD WILL. *But did none of them follow you, to perswade you to go back?*

CHR. Yes, both *Obstinate*, and *Pliable:* But when they saw that they could not prevail, *Obstinate* went railing back; but *Pliable* came with me a little way.

GOOD WILL. *But why did he not come through?*

CHR. We indeed came both together, until we came at the Slough of *Dispond*, into the which we also suddenly fell. And then was my Neighbor *Pliable* discouraged, and would not adventure further. Wherefore getting out again, on that side next to his own House, he told me, I should possess the brave Country alone for him: So he went *his* way, and I came *mine. He* after *Obstinate*, and I to this Gate.

GOOD WILL. Then said *Good Will*, Alas poor Man, is the Cœlestial Glory of so small esteem with him, that he counteth it not worth running the hazards of a few difficulties to obtain it.

CHR. Truly, said *Christian*, I have said the truth of *Pliable*, and if I should also say the truth of myself, it will appear there is no betterment 'twixt him and myself. 'Tis true, he went back to his own house, but I also turned aside to go in the way of death, being perswaded thereto by the carnal arguments of one Mr. *Worldly-Wiseman*.

GOOD WILL. Oh, did he light upon you? what, he would have had you a sought for ease at the hands of Mr. *Legality;* they are both of them a very cheat: But did you take his counsel?

CHR. Yes, as far as I durst: I went to find out Mr. *Legality*, until I thought that the Mountain that stands by his house, would have fallen upon my head: wherefore there I was forced to stop.

GOOD WILL. That Mountain has been the death of many, and will be the death of many more: 'tis well you escaped being by it dasht in pieces.

CHR. Why, truly I do not know what had become of me there, had not *Evangelist* happily met me again as I was musing in the midst of my *dumps:* but 'twas Gods mercy that he came to me again, for else I had never come hither. But now I am come, such a one as I am, more fit indeed for death by that Mountain, than thus to stand talking with my Lord: But O, what a favour is this to me, that yet I am admitted entrance here.

GOOD WILL. We make no objections against any, notwithstanding all that they have done before they come hither, they in no wise are cast out, and therefore, good *Christian*, come a little way with me, and I will teach thee about the way thou must go. Look before thee; dost thou see this narrow way? THAT is the way thou must go. It was cast up by the Patriarchs, Prophets, Christ, and his Apostles; and it is as straight as a Rule can make it: This is the way thou must go.

CHRISTIAN DIRECTED ON HIS WAY

CHR. But said *Christian, Is there no turnings nor windings by which a Stranger may lose the way?*

Good Will. Yes, there are many ways *butt* down upon this; and they are crooked, and wide: But *thus* thou may'st distinguish the right from the wrong, *That* only being straight and narrow.

Then I saw in my Dream, That *Christian* asked him further, If he could not help him off with his burden that was upon his back; for as yet he had not got rid thereof, nor could he by any means get it off without help.

He told him; As to thy burden, be content to bear it, until thou comest to the *place* of Deliverance; for there it will fall from thy back itself.

Then *Christian* began to gird up his loins, and to address himself to his Journey. So the other told him, that by that he was gone some distance from the Gate, he would come at the House of the *Interpreter;* at whose Door he should knock; and he would shew him excellent things. Then *Christian* took his leave of his Friend, and he again bid him God speed.

Christian Comes to the House of the Interpreter

Then he went on, till he came at the House of the *Interpreter,* where he knocked over and over: at last one came to the Door, and asked *Who was there?*

Chr. Sir, here is a Traveller, who was bid by an acquaintance of the Good-man of this House, to call here for my profit: I would therefore speak with the Master of the House. So he called for the Master of the House; who after a little time came to *Christian,* and asked him what he would have?

Chr. Sir, said *Christian,* I am a Man that am come from the City of *Destruction,* and am going to the Mount *Zion,* and I was told by the Man that stands at the Gate, at the head of this way, That if I called here, you would shew me excellent things, such as would be an help to me in my Journey.

Inter. Then said the *Interpreter,* Come in, I will shew thee that which will be profitable to thee. So he commanded his Man to light the Candle, and bid *Christian* follow him; so he had him into a private Room, and bid his Man open a Door; the which when he had done, *Christian* saw the Picture of a very grave Person hang up against the Wall, and this was the fashion of it. *It had eyes lift up to Heaven, the best of Books in his hand, the Law of Truth was written upon his lips, the World was behind his back; it stood as if it pleaded with Men, and a Crown of Gold did hang over his head.*

Chr. *Then said* Christian, *What means this?*

Inter. The Man whose Picture this is, is one of a thousand; he can beget Children, travel in birth with Children, and nurse them himself when they are born. And whereas thou seest him with his eyes lift up to Heaven, the best of Books in his hand, and the Law of Truth writ on his lips: it is to shew thee, that his work is to know and unfold dark things to sinners; even as also thou seest him stand as if he pleaded with Men: And whereas thou seest the World as cast behind him, and that a Crown hangs over his head; that is, to shew thee that slighting and despising the things that are present, for the love that he hath to his Masters service, he is sure in the World that comes next to have Glory for his Reward. Now, said the *Interpreter,* I have shewed thee this Picture first, because the Man whose Picture this is, is the only Man, whom the Lord of the Place whither thou art going, hath authorized to be thy Guide in all difficult places thou mayest meet with in the way: wherefore take good heed to what I have shewed thee, and bear well in thy mind what thou hast seen; lest in thy Journey thou meet with some that pretend to lead thee right, but their way goes down to death.

Then he took him by the hand, and led him into a very large *Parlour* that was full of dust, because never swept; the which, after he had reviewed a little while, the *Interpreter* called for a man to *sweep*. Now when he began to sweep, the dust began so abundantly to fly about, that *Christian* had almost therewith been choaked. Then said the *Interpreter* to a *Damsel* that stood by, Bring hither the Water, and sprinkle the Room; which when she had done, it was swept and cleansed with pleasure.

CHR. *Then said* Christian, *What means this?*

INTER. The *Interpreter* answered; this Parlour is the heart of a Man that was never sanctified by the sweet Grace of the Gospel: the *dust* is his Original Sin, and inward Corruptions that have defiled the whole Man. He that began to sweep at first is the Law; but She that brought water, and did sprinkle it, is the Gospel. Now, whereas thou sawest that so soon as the first began to sweep, the dust did so fly about that the Room by him could not be cleansed, but that thou wast almost choaked therewith: this is to shew thee, that the Law, instead of cleansing the heart (by its working) from sin, doth revive, put strength into, and increase it in the soul, even as it doth discover and forbid it, but doth not give power to subdue.

Again, as thou sawest the *Damsel* sprinkle the Room with Water, upon which it was cleansed with pleasure; this is to shew thee, that when the Gospel comes in the sweet and precious influences thereof to the heart, then, I say, even as thou sawest the Damsel lay the dust by sprinkling the Floor with Water, so is sin vanquished and subdued, and the soul made clean, through the faith of it, and consequently fit for the King of Glory to inhabit.

I saw moreover in my Dream, that the *Interpreter* took him by the hand, and had him into a little Room, where sate two little Children, each one in his Chair. The name of the eldest was *Passion*, and of the other *Patience*. *Passion* seemed to be much discontent, but *Patience* was very quiet. Then *Christian* asked, What is the reason of the discontent of *Passion?* The *Interpreter* answered, The Governor of them would have him stay for his best things till the beginning of the next year; but he will have all now: But *Patience* is willing to wait.

Then I saw that one came to *Passion*, and brought him a Bag of Treasure, and poured it down at his feet; the which he took up, and rejoiced therein; and withal, laughed *Patience* to scorn. But I beheld but a while, and he had lavished all away, and had nothing left him but Rags.

CHR. *Then said* Christian *to the* Interpreter, *Expound this matter more fully to me.*

INTER. So he said, These two Lads are Figures; *Passion*, of the Men of *this* World; and *Patience*, of the Men of *that* which is to come. For as here thou seest, *Passion will have all now*, this year; that is to say, in *this* World; *So* are the Men of this World: they must have all their good things now, they cannot stay till next *Year;* that is, until the *next* World, for their Portion of good. That Proverb, *A Bird in the Hand is worth two in the Bush*, is of more Authority with them, than are all the Divine Testimonies of the good of the World to come. But as thou sawest, that he had quickly lavished all away, and had presently left him, nothing but Rags; so will it be with all such Men at the end of this World.

CHR. *Then said* Christian, *Now I see that* Patience *has the best Wisdom; and that upon many accounts.* 1. *Because he stays for the best things.* 2. *And also because he will have the glory of his, when the other hath nothing but Rags.*

INTER. Nay, you may add another; to wit, the Glory of the *next* World will never wear out; but these are suddenly gone. Therefore *Passion* had not so much reason to laugh at *Patience*, because he had his good things first, as *Patience* will have to laugh at *Passion*, because he had his best things *last;* for *first* must give place to *last*, because *last* must have his time to come, but *last* gives place to *nothing;* for there is not another to succeed. He therefore that hath his Portion *first*, must needs have a time to spend it; but he that has his Portion *last*, must have it lastingly. Therefore it is said of *Dives*, *In thy life-time thou receivedest thy good things, and likewise* Lazarus *evil things; But now he is comforted, and thou art tormented.*

CHR. *Then I perceive, 'tis not best to covet things that are* now; *but to wait for things to* come.

INTER. You say Truth; *For the things that are seen, are* Temporal; *but the things that are not seen, are* Eternal. But though this be so; yet since things present, and our fleshly appetite, *are such near Neighbors one to another;* and again, because things to come, and carnal sense, are such strangers one to another: therefore it is, that the first of these so suddenly fall into *amity*, and that *distance* is so continued between the second.

Then I saw in my Dream, that the *Interpreter* took *Christian* by the hand, and led him into a place where was a Fire burning against a Wall, and one standing by it always, casting much Water upon it to quench it: yet did the Fire burn higher and hotter.

Then said Christian, *What means this?*

The *Interpreter* answered, This fire is the work of Grace that is wrought in the heart; he that casts Water upon it, to extinguish and put it out, is the *Devil:* but in that thou seest the fire notwithstanding burn higher and hotter, thou shalt also see the reason of that: So he had him about to the back side of the Wall, where he saw a Man with a Vessel of Oil in his hand, of the which he did also continually cast (but secretly) into the fire. Then said *Christian, What means this?* The *Interpreter* answered, This is *Christ*, who continually, with the Oil of his Grace, maintains the work already begun in the heart; by the means of which, notwithstanding what the Devil can do, the souls of his People prove gracious still. And in that thou sawest that the Man stood behind the Wall to maintain the fire; this is to teach thee, that it is hard for the tempted to see how this work of Grace is maintained in the soul.

I saw also that the *Interpreter* took him again by the hand, and led him into a pleasant place, where was builded a stately Palace, beautiful to behold; at the sight of which, *Christian* was greatly delighted; he saw also upon the top thereof, certain Persons walked, who were cloathed all in Gold. Then said *Christian*, May we go in thither? Then the *Interpreter* took him, and led him up toward the door of the Palace; and behold, at the door stood a great Company of men, as desirous to go in, but durst not. There also sat a Man, at a little distance from the door, at a Table-side, with a Book, and his Inkhorn before him, to take the Name of him that should enter therein: He saw also that in the doorway, stood many Men in Armor to keep it; being resolved to do to the Man that would enter, what hurt and mischief they could. Now was *Christian* somewhat in a maze: at last, when every Man started back for fear of the armed men; *Christian* saw a Man of a very stout countenance come up to the Man that sat there to write; saying, *Set down my name, Sir;* the which when he had done, he saw the Man draw his Sword, and put an Helmet upon his Head, and rush toward the door upon the armed men, who laid upon him with deadly force; but the Man, not at all discouraged, fell to cutting and hacking most fiercely; so, after he had received and given many wounds to those that attempted to keep him out, he cut his way through them all, and pressed forward into the Palace; at which there was a pleasant voice heard from those that were within, even of those that walked upon the top of the Palace, saying,

Come in, Come in;
Eternal Glory thou shalt win.

So he went in, and was cloathed with such Garments as they. Then *Christian* smiled, and said, I think verily I know the meaning of this.

The Man in an Iron Cage

Now, said *Christian*, let me go hence: Nay stay (said the *Interpreter*,) till I have shewed thee a little more, and after that thou shalt go on thy way. So he took him by the hand again, and led him into a very dark Room, where there sat a Man in an Iron Cage.

Now the Man, to look on, seemed very sad: he sat with his eyes looking down to the ground, his hands folded together; and he sighed as if he would break his heart. Then said *Christian*, What means this? At which the *Interpreter* bid him talk with the Man.

Chr. Then said *Christian* to the Man, *What art thou?* The Man answered, *I am what I was not once.*

Chr. *What wast thou once?*

Man. The *Man* said, I was once a fair and flourishing Professor, both in mine own eyes, and also in the eyes of others: I once was, as I thought, fair for the Cœlestial City, and had then even joy at the thoughts that I should get thither.

CHR. *Well, but what art thou now?*

MAN. I am *now* a Man of Despair, and am shut up in it, as in this Iron Cage. I cannot get out; O *now* I cannot.

CHR. *But how camest thou in this condition?*

MAN. I left off to watch, and be sober; I laid the reins upon the neck of my lusts; I sinned against the light of the Word, and the goodness of God: I have grieved the Spirit, and he is gone; I tempted the Devil, and he is come to me; I have provoked God to anger, and he has left me; I have so hardened my heart, that I *cannot* repent.

Then said *Christian* to the *Interpreter*, But is there no hopes for such a Man as this? Ask him, said the *Interpreter*.

CHR. Then said *Christian, is there no hope but you must be kept in the Iron Cage of Despair?*

MAN. No, none at all.

CHR. *Why? The Son of the Blessed is very pitiful.*

MAN. I have crucified him to myself, afresh. I have despised his Person, I have despised his Righteousness, I have counted his Blood an unholy thing, I have done despite to the Spirit of Grace: Therefore I have shut myself out of all the Promises; and there now remains to me nothing but threatnings, dreadful threatnings, faithful threatnings of certain Judgment, which shall devour me as an Adversary.

INTER. *For what did you bring yourself into this condition?*

MAN. For the Lusts, Pleasures, and Profits of this World; in the enjoyment of which, I did then promise my self much delight; but now every one of those things also bite me, and gnaw me like a burning worm.

INTER. *But canst thou not now repent and turn?*

MAN. God hath denied me repentance; his Word gives me no encouragement to believe; yea, himself hath shut me up in this Iron Cage; nor can all the men in the World let me out. O Eternity! Eternity! how shall I grapple with the misery that I must meet with in Eternity!

INTER. Then said the *Interpreter* to *Christian*, Let this mans misery be remembered by thee, and be an everlasting caution to thee.

CHR. Well, said *Christian*, this is fearful; God help me to watch and be sober; and to pray, that I may shun the causes of this mans misery. Sir, is it not time for me to go on my way now?

INTER. Tarry till I shall shew thee one thing more, and then thou shalt go on thy way.

So he took *Christian* by the hand again, and led him into a Chamber, where there was one rising out of Bed; and as he put on his Raiment, he shook and trembled. Then said *Christian*, Why doth this man thus tremble? The *Interpreter* then bid him tell to *Christian* the reason of his so doing. So he began, and said: This night as I was in my sleep, I Dreamed, and behold the Heavens grew exceeding black; also it thundered and lightned in most fearful wise, that it put me into an Agony. So I looked up in my Dream, and saw the Clouds rack at an unusual rate; upon which I heard a great sound of a Trumpet, and saw also a Man sit upon a Cloud, attended with the thousands of Heaven; they were all in flaming fire, also the Heavens were on a burning flame. I heard then a voice, saying, *Arise ye Dead, and come to Judgment;* and with that, the Rocks rent, the Graves opened, & the Dead that were therein, came forth; some of them were exceeding glad, and looked upward; and some sought to hide themselves under the Mountains. Then I saw the Man that sat upon the Cloud, open the Book; and bid the World draw near. Yet there was by reason of a fierce flame that issued out and came from before him, a convenient distance betwixt him and them, as betwixt the Judge and the Prisoners at the Bar. I heard it also proclaimed to them that attended on the Man that sat on the Cloud; *Gather together the Tares, the Chaff, and Stubble, and cast them into the burning Lake;* and with that, the bottomless pit opened, just whereabout I stood; out of the mouth of which there came in an abundant manner Smoke, and Coals of fire, with hideous noises. It was also said to the same persons; *Gather my Wheat into the Garner.* And with that I saw many catch'd up and carried away into the Clouds, but I was left behind. I also sought to hide myself, but I could not; for the Man that sat upon the Cloud, still kept his eye upon me: my sins also came into my mind, and my Conscience did accuse me on every side. Upon this I awaked from my sleep.

CHR. *But what was it that made you so afraid of this sight?*

MAN. Why I thought the day of Judgement was come, and that I was not ready for it: but this frighted me most, that the Angels gathered up several, and left me behind; also the pit of Hell opened her mouth just where I stood: my Conscience too afflicted me; and as I thought, the Judge had always his eye upon me, shewing indignation in his countenance.

Then said the *Interpreter* to *Christian, Hast thou considered all these things?*

CHR. Yes, and they put me in *hope* and *fear.*

INTER. Well, keep all things so in thy mind, that they may be as a *Goad* in thy sides, to prick thee forward in the way thou must go. Then *Christian* began to gird up his loins, and to address himself to his Journey. Then said the *Interpreter*, The Comforter be always with thee good *Christian,* to guide thee in the way that leads to the City.

So *Christian* went on his way, saying,

Here have I seen things rare and profitable;
Things pleasant, dreadful; things to make me stable
In what I have began to take in hand:
Then let me think on them, and understand
Wherefore they shewed me was, and let me be
Thankful, O good Interpreter, to thee.

Now I saw in my Dream, that the highway up which *Christian* was to go, was fenced on either side with a Wall, and that Wall is called *Salvation.*

Up this way therefore did burdened *Christian* run, but not without great difficulty, because of the load on his back.

He ran thus till he came at a place somewhat ascending; and upon that place stood a *Cross,* and a little below in the bottom, a Sepulchre. So I saw in my Dream, that just as *Christian* came up with the *Cross*, his burden loosed from off his Shoulders, and fell from off his back, and began to tumble; and so continued to do, till it came to the mouth of the Sepulchre, where it fell in, and I saw it no more.

Then was *Christian* glad and lightsome, and said with a merry heart, *He hath given me rest, by his sorrow; and life, by his death.* Then he stood still a while, to look and wonder; for it was very surprising to him, that the sight of the Cross should thus ease him of his burden. He looked therefore, and looked again, even till the springs that were in his head sent the waters down his cheeks. Now as he stood looking and weeping, behold three shining ones came to him, and saluted him, with *Peace be to thee:* so the first said to him, *Thy sins be forgiven.* The second, stript him of his Rags, and cloathed him with change of Raiment. The third also set a mark in his forehead, and gave him a Roll with a Seal upon it, which he bid him look on as he ran, and that he should give it in at the Cœlestial Gate; so they went their way. Then *Christian* gave three leaps for joy, and went on singing,

Thus far did I come loaden with my sin;
Nor could ought ease the grief that I was in,
Till I came hither: What a place is this!
Must here be the beginning of my bliss?
Must here the burden fall from off my back?
Must here the strings that bound it to me crack?
Blest Cross! blest Sepulchre! blest rather be
The Man that there was put to shame for me.

I saw then in my Dream that he went on *thus,* even until he came at a bottom, where he saw, a little out of the way, three Men fast asleep with Fetters upon their heels. The name of the one was *Simple,* another *Sloth,* and the third *Presumption.*

Christian then seeing them lie in this case, went to them, if peradventure he might awake them. And cried, You are like them that sleep on the top of a Mast, for the dead Sea is under you, a Gulf that hath no bottom. Awake therefore and come away; be willing also, and I will help you off with your Irons. He also told them, If he that goeth about like a *roaring* Lion comes by, you will certainly become a prey to his teeth. With that they lookt upon him, and began to reply in this sort; *Simple* said, *I see no danger; Sloth* said, *Yet a little more sleep:* and *Presumption* said, *Every Fatt must stand upon his own bottom.* And so they lay down to sleep again, and *Christian* went on his way.

Yet was he troubled to think that men in that danger should so little esteem the kindness of him that so freely offered to help them; both by awakening of them, counseling of them, and proffering to help them off with their Irons. And as he was troubled thereabout, he espied two Men come tumbling over the Wall, on the left hand of the narrow way; and they made up apace to him. The name of the one was *Formalist*, and the name of the other *Hypocrisy*. So, as I said, they drew up unto him, who thus entered with them into discourse.

CHR. *Gentlemen, Whence came you, and whither do you go?*

FORM. and HYP. We were born in the land of Vain-glory, and are going for praise to Mount *Zion.*

CHR. *Why came you not in at the Gate which standeth at the beginning of the way? Know you not that it is written, That he that cometh not in by the door, but climbeth up some other way, the same is a thief and a robber?*

FORM. and HYP. They said, That to go to the Gate for entrance, was by all their Countrymen counted too far about; and that therefore their usual way was to make a short cut of it, and to climb over the wall as they had done.

CHR. *But will it not be counted a Trespass against the Lord of the City whither we are bound, thus to violate his revealed will?*

FORM. and HYP. They told him, That as for that, he needed not to trouble his head thereabout: for what they did, they had custom for; and could produce, if need were, Testimony that would witness it, for more than a thousand years.

CHR. *But, said* Christian, *will your practice stand a Trial at Law?*

FORM. and HYP. They told him, That Custom, it being of so long a standing, as above a thousand years, would doubtless now be admitted as a thing legal, by an Impartial Judge. And besides, said they, if we get into the way, what's matter which way we get in? If we are in, we are in: thou art but in the way, who, as we perceive, came in at the Gate; and we are also in the way, that came tumbling over the wall. Wherein now is thy condition better than ours?

CHR. I walk by the *Rule* of my Master, you walk by the rude working of your fancies. You are counted thieves already, by the Lord of the way; therefore I doubt you will not be found true men at the end of the way. You come in by yourselves without his direction, and shall go out by yourselves without his mercy.

To this they made him but little answer; only they bid him look to himself. Then I saw that they went on every man in his way, without much conference one with another; save that these two men told *Christian,* That, as to *Laws and Ordinances,* they doubted not but they should as conscientiously do them as he. Therefore said they, We see not wherein thou differest from us, but by the Coat that is on thy back, which was, as we tro, given thee by some of thy Neighbors, to hide the shame of thy nakedness.

CHR. By Laws and Ordinances, you will not be saved, since you came not in by the door. And as for this Coat that is on my back, it was given me by the Lord of the place whither I go; and that, as you say, to cover my nakedness with. And I take it as a token of his kindness to me, for I had nothing but rags before. And besides, thus I comfort myself as I go: Surely, think I, when I come to the Gate of the City, the Lord thereof will know me for good, since I have his Coat on my back; a Coat that he gave me freely in the day that he stript me of my rags. I have moreover a mark in my forehead, of which perhaps you have taken no notice, which one of my Lords most intimate Associates, fixed there in the day that my burden fell off my shoulders. I will tell you moreover, that I had then given me a Roll sealed to comfort me by reading, as I go in the way; I was also bid to give it in at the Cœlestial Gate, in token of my certain going in after it: all which things I doubt you want, and want them because you came not in at the Gate.

To these things they gave him no answer, only they looked upon each other and *laughed*. Then I saw that they went on all, save that *Christian* kept before, who had no more talk but with himself, and that sometimes sighingly, and sometimes comfortably: also he would be often reading in the Roll that one of the shining ones gave him, by which he was refreshed.

Christian Comes to the Hill Difficulty

I beheld then, that they all went on till they came to the foot of the Hill *Difficulty*, at the bottom of which was a Spring. There was also in the same place two other ways besides that which came straight from the Gate; one turned to the left hand, and the other to the right, at the bottom of the Hill: but the narrow way lay right up the Hill (and the name of the going up the side of the Hill, is called *Difficulty*). *Christian* now went to the Spring and drank thereof to refresh himself, and then began to go up the Hill; saying,

This Hill, though high, I covet to ascend;
The difficulty will not me offend;
For I perceive the way to life lies here;
Come, pluck up, Heart; lets neither faint nor fear:
Better, tho' difficult, th'right way to go,
Than wrong, though easy, where the end is wo.

The other two also came to the foot of the Hill. But when they saw that the Hill was steep and high, and that there was two other ways to go; and supposing also, that these two ways might meet again with that up which *Christian* went, on the other side of the Hill; therefore they were resolved to go in those ways (now the name of one of those ways was *Danger*, and the name of the other *Destruction*). So the one took the way which is called *Danger*, which led him into a great Wood; and the other took directly up the way to *Destruction*, which led him into a wide field full of dark Mountains, where he stumbled and fell, and rose no more.

I looked then after *Christian*, to see him go up the Hill, where I perceived he fell from running to going, and from going to clambering upon his hands and his knees, because of the steepness of the place. Now about the midway to the top of the Hill, was a pleasant *Arbor*, made by the Lord of the Hill, for the refreshing of weary Travellers. Thither therefore *Christian* got, where also he sat down to rest him. Then he pull'd his Roll out of his bosom and read therein to his comfort; he also now began afresh to take a review of the Coat or Garment that was given him as he stood by the Cross. Thus pleasing himself a while, he at last fell into a slumber, and thence into a fast sleep, which detained him in that place until it was almost night, and in his sleep his Roll fell out of his hand. Now as he was sleeping, there came one to him, and awaked him saying, *Go to the Ant, thou sluggard, consider her ways and be wise*. And with that *Christian* suddenly started up, and sped him on his way, and went apace till he came to the top of the Hill.

Now when he was got up to the top of the Hill, there came two men running against him amain; the name of the one was *Timorous,* and the name of the other *Mistrust,* to whom *Christian* said, Sirs, what's the matter you run the wrong way? *Timorous* answered, That they were going to the City of *Zion,* and had got up that *difficult* place; but, said he, the further we go, the more danger we meet with, wherefore we turned, and are going back again.

Yes, said *Mistrust,* for just before us lie a couple of Lions in the way, (whether sleeping or waking we know not); and we could not think, if we came within reach, but they would presently pull us to pieces.

Chr. Then said *Christian,* You make me afraid, but whither shall I fly to be safe? If I go back to mine own Country, *That* is prepared for Fire and Brimstone; and I shall certainly perish there. If I can get to the Cœlestial City, I am sure to be in safety there. I must venture. To go back is nothing but death; to go forward is fear of death, and life everlasting beyond it. I will yet go forward.

Christian Shakes Off Fear

So *Mistrust* and *Timorous* ran down the Hill; and *Christian* went on his way. But thinking again of what he heard from the men, he felt in his bosom for his Roll, that he might read therein and be comforted; but he felt and found it not. Then was *Christian* in great distress, and knew not what to do, for he wanted that which used to relieve him, and that which should have been his Pass into the Cœlestial City. Here therefore he began to be much perplexed, and knew not what to do; at last he bethought himself that he had slept in the *Arbor* that is on the side of the Hill: and falling down upon his knees, he asked God forgiveness for that his foolish Fact; and then went back to look for his Roll. But all the way he went back, who can sufficiently set forth the sorrow of *Christians* heart? somtimes he sighed, somtimes he wept, and often times he chid himself, for being so foolish to fall asleep in that place which was erected only for a little refreshment from his weariness. Thus therefore he went back; carefully looking on this side and on that, all the way as he went, if happily he might find his Roll, that had been his comfort so many times in his Journey. He went thus till he came again within sight of the *Arbor*, where he sat and slept; but that sight renewed his sorrow the more, by bringing again, even afresh, his evil of sleeping into his mind. Thus therefore he now went on bewailing his sinful sleep, saying, *O wretched Man that I am,* that I should sleep in the day-time! that I should sleep in the midst of difficulty! that I should so indulge the flesh, as to use *that* rest for ease to my flesh, which the Lord of the Hill hath erected only for the relief of the spirits of Pilgrims! How many steps have I took in vain! (Thus it happened to *Israel* for their sin, they were sent back again by the way of the Red-Sea.) And I am made to tread those steps with sorrow, which I might have trod with delight, had it not been for this sinful sleep. How far might I have been on my way by this time! I am made to tread those steps thrice over, which I needed not to have trod but once: Yea now also I am like to be benighted, for the day is almost spent. O that I had not slept! Now by this time he was come to the *Arbor* again, where for awhile he sat down and wept, but at last (as *Christian* would have it) looking sorrowfully down under the Settle, there he espied his Roll; the which he with trembling and haste catch'd up, and put it into his bosom. But who can tell how joyful this Man was, when he had gotten his Roll again! For this Roll was the assurance of his life and acceptance at the desired Haven. Therefore he laid it up in his bosom, gave thanks to God for directing his eye to the place where it lay, and with joy and tears betook himself again to his Journey. But Oh how nimbly now did he go up the rest of the Hill! Yet before he got up, the Sun went down upon *Christian;* and this made him again recall the vanity of his sleeping to his remembrance, and thus he again began to condole with himself: *Oh thou sinful sleep! how for thy sake am I like to be benighted in my Journey! I must walk without the Sun, darkness must cover the path of my feet, and I must hear the noise of doleful Creatures, because of my sinful sleep!* Now also he remembered the story that *Mistrust* and *Timorous* told him of, how they were frightened with the sight of the Lions. Then said *Christian* to himself again, These Beasts range in the night for their prey, and if they should meet with me in the dark, how should I shift them? how should I escape being by them torn in pieces? Thus he went on his way, but while he was thus bewailing his unhappy miscarriage, he lift up his eyes, and behold there was a very stately Palace before him, the name of which was *Beautiful,* and it stood just by the Highway side.

The Lions in the Way

So I saw in my Dream, that he made haste and went forward, that if possible he might get Lodging there; now before he had gone far, he entered into a very narrow passage, which was about a furlong off of the Porter's Lodge, and looking very narrowly before him as he went, he espied two Lions in the way. Now, thought he, I see the dangers that *Mistrust* and *Timorous* were driven back by. (The Lions were chained, but he saw not the Chains.) Then he was afraid, and thought also himself to go back after them, for he thought nothing but death was before him. But the *Porter* at the Lodge, whose Name is *Watchful,* perceiving that *Christian* made a halt, as if he would go back, cried unto him, saying, Is thy strength so small? fear not the Lions, for they are chained: and are placed there for trial of faith where it is; and for discovery of those that have none: keep in the midst of the Path, and no hurt shall come unto thee.

Then I saw that he went on, trembling for fear of the Lions; but taking good heed to the directions of the *Porter;* he heard them roar, but they did him no harm. Then he clapt his hands, and went on, till he came and stood before the Gate where the *Porter* was. Then said *Christian* to the *Porter*, Sir, What house is this? and may I lodge here to night? The *Porter* answered, This House was built by the Lord of the Hill, and he built it for the relief and security of Pilgrims. The *Porter* also asked whence he was, and whither he was going?

CHR. I am come from the City of *Destruction*, and am going to Mount *Zion*, but because the Sun is now set, I desire, if I may, to lodge here to night.

POR. *What is your name?*

CHR. My name is now *Christian;* but my name at the first was *Graceless:* I came of the race of *Japhet*, whom God will perswade to dwell in the Tents of *Shem.*

POR. *But how doth it happen that you come so late? the Sun is set.*

CHR. I had been here sooner, but that, wretched man that I am! I slept in the *Arbor* that stands on the Hill side; nay, I had notwithstanding that, been here much sooner, but that in my sleep I lost my evidence, and came without it to the brow of the Hill; and then feeling for it, and finding it not, I was forced with sorrow of heart to go back to the place where I slept my sleep, where I found it, and now I am come.

POR. Well, I will call out one of the Virgins of this place, who will, if she likes your talk, bring you in to the rest of the Family, according to the Rules of the House. So *Watchful* the *Porter* rang a Bell, at the sound of which came out at the door of the House a grave and beautiful Damsel, named *Discretion*, and asked why she was called.

The *Porter* answered, This Man is in a Journey from the City of *Destruction* to Mount *Zion*, but being weary, and benighted, he asked me if he might lodge here to night; so I told him I would call for thee, who, after discourse had with him, mayest do as seemeth thee good, even according to the Law of the House.

Then she asked him whence he was, and whither he was going, and he told her. She asked him also, how he got into the way, and he told her. Then she asked him, What he had seen, and met with in the way, and he told her; and last, she asked his name, so he said, It is *Christian;* and I have so much the more a desire to lodge here tonight, because, by what I perceive, this place was built by the Lord of the Hill, for the relief and security of Pilgrims. So she smiled, but the water stood in her eyes: and after a little pause, she said, I will call forth two or three more of the Family. So she ran to the door, and called out *Prudence*, *Piety*, and *Charity*, who after a little more discourse with him, had him in to the Family; and many of them meeting him at the threshold of the house, said, Come in thou blessed of the Lord; this

House was built by the Lord of the Hill, on purpose to entertain such Pilgrims in. Then he bowed his head, and followed them into the House. So when he was come in, and set down, they gave him something to drink; and consented together that until supper was ready, some of them should have some particular discourse with *Christian*, for the best improvement of time: and they appointed *Piety*, and *Prudence*, and *Charity*, to discourse with him; and thus they began.

How Christian Was Driven Out of His Own Country

Pi. *Come good* Christian, *since we have been so loving to you, to receive you into our House this night; let us, if perhaps we may better ourselves thereby, talk with you of all things that have happened to you in your Pilgrimage.*

Chr. With a very good will, and I am glad that you are so well disposed.

Pi. *What moved you at first to betake yourself to a Pilgrims life?*

Chr. I was driven out of my Native Country, by a dreadful sound that was in mine ears, to wit, That unavoidable destruction did attend me, if I abode in that place where I was.

Pi. *But how did it happen that you came out of your Country this way?*

Chr. It was as God would have it, for when I was under the fears of destruction, I did not know whither to go; but by chance there came a man, even to me (as I was trembling and weeping), whose name is *Evangelist*, and he directed me to the Wicket-Gate, which else I should never have found; and so set me into the way that hath led me directly to this House.

Pi. *But did you not come by the House of the Interpreter?*

Chr. Yes, and did see such things there, the remembrance of which will stick by me as long as I live; specially three things, *to wit*, How Christ, in despite of Satan, maintains his work of Grace in the heart; how the Man had sinned himself quite out of hopes of Gods mercy; and also the Dream of him that thought in his sleep the day of Judgment was come.

Pi. *Why? Did you hear him tell his Dream?*

Chr. Yes, and a dreadful one it was. I thought it made my heart ake as he was telling of it; but yet I am glad I heard it.

Pi. *Was that all that you saw at the House of the Interpreter?*

Chr. No, he took me and had me where he shewed me a stately Palace, and how the People were clad in Gold that were in it; and how there came a venturous Man, and cut his way through the armed men that stood in the door to keep him out; and how he was bid to come in, and win eternal Glory. Methought those things did ravish my heart; I would have stayed at that good Mans house a twelvemonth, but that I knew I had further to go.

Pi. *And what saw you else in the way?*

Chr. Saw! Why I went but a little further, and I saw one, as I thought in my mind, hang bleeding upon the Tree; and the very sight of him made my burden fall off my back (for I groaned under a heavy burden) but then it fell down from off me. 'Twas a strange thing to me, for I never saw such a thing before: yea, and while I stood looking up (for then I could not forbear looking) three shining ones came to me: one of them testified that my sins were forgiven me; another stript me of my rags, and gave me this broidered Coat which you see; and the third set the mark which you see, in my forehead, and gave me this sealed Roll (and with that he plucked it out of his bosom).

PI. *But you saw more than this, did you not?*

CHR. The things that I have told you were the best: yet some other matters I saw, as namely I saw three Men, *Simple*, *Sloth*, and *Presumption*, lie asleep a little out of the way as I came, with Irons upon their heels; but do you think I could awake them? I also saw *Formalist* and *Hypocrisy* come tumbling over the wall, to go, as they pretended, to *Sion*, but they were quickly lost; even as I myself did tell them, but they would not believe. But, above all, I found it *hard* work to get up this Hill, and as *hard* to come by the Lions mouth; and truly if it had not been for the good Man, the Porter that stands at the Gate, I do not know but that, after all, I might have gone back again: but now I thank God I am here, and I thank you for receiving of me.

Then *Prudence* thought good to ask him a few questions, and desired his answer to them.

PRU. *Do you not think sometimes of the Country from whence you come?*

CHR. Yes, but with much shame and detestation; *Truly, if I had been mindful of that Country from whence I came out, I might have had opportunity to have returned, but now I desire a better Country, that is, an Heavenly.*

PRU. *Do you not yet bear away with you some of the things that then you were conversant withal?*

CHR. Yes, but greatly against my will; especially my inward and carnal cogitations; with which all my Country-men, as well as myself, were delighted; but now all those things are my grief: and might I but chuse mine own things, I would chuse never to think of those things more; but when I would be doing of that which is best, that which is worst is with me.

PRU. *Do you not find sometimes, as if those things were vanquished, which at other times are your perplexity?*

CHR. Yes, but that is but seldom; but they are to me golden hours, in which such things happen to me.

PRU. *Can you remember by what means you find your annoyances at times, as if they were vanquished?*

CHR. Yes, when I think what I saw at the Cross, that will do it; and when I look upon my broidered Coat, that will do it; also when I look into the Roll that I carry in my bosom, that will do it; and when my thoughts wax warm about whither I am going, that will do it.

PRU. *And what is it that makes you so desirous to go to Mount* Zion?

CHR. Why, there I hope to see him *alive*, that did hang *dead* on the Cross; and there I hope to be rid of all those things, that to this day are in me an annoyance to me; there they say there is no death, and there I shall dwell with such Company as I like best. For to tell you truth, I love him, because

I was by him eased of my burden, and I am weary of my inward sickness; I would fain be where I shall die no more, and with the Company that shall continually cry, *Holy, Holy, Holy.*

Then said *Charity* to *Christian, Have you a family? are you a married man?*

CHR. I have a Wife and four small Children.

CHA. *And why did you not bring them along with you?*

CHR. Then *Christian* wept, and said, Oh how willingly would I have done it, but they were all of them utterly averse to my going on Pilgrimage.

CHA. *But you should have talked to them, and have endeavoured to have shewen them the danger of being behind.*

CHR. So I did, and told them also what God had shewed to me of the destruction of our City; but I seemed to them as one that mocked, and they believed me not.

CHA. *And did you pray to God that he would bless your counsel to them?*

CHR. Yes, and that with much affection; for you must think that my Wife and poor Children were very dear unto me.

CHA. *But did you tell them of your own sorrow, and fear of destruction? for I suppose that destruction was visible enough to you?*

CHR. Yes, over, and over, and over. They might also see my fears in my countenance, in my tears, and also in my trembling under the apprehension of the Judgment that did hang over our heads; but all was not sufficient to prevail with them to come with me.

CHA. *But what could they say for themselves why they came not?*

CHR. Why, my Wife was afraid of losing this World; and my Children were given to the foolish delights of youth: so what by one thing, and what by another, they left me to wander in this manner alone.

CHA. *But did you not with your vain life, damp all that you by words used by way of perswasion to bring them away with you?*

CHR. Indeed I cannot commend my life; for I am conscious to myself of many failings: therein, I know also that a man by his conversation, may soon overthrow what by argument or perswasion he doth labour to fasten upon others for their good: Yet, this I can say, I was very wary of giving them occasion, by any unseemly action, to make them averse to going on Pilgrimage. Yea, for this very thing, they would tell me I was too precise, and that I denied myself of sins (for their sakes) in which they saw no evil. Nay, I think I may say, that, if what they saw in me did hinder them, it was my great tenderness in sinning against God, or of doing any wrong to my Neighbor.

CHA. *Indeed,* Cain *hated his Brother, because his own works were evil, and his Brother's righteous; and if thy Wife and Children have been offended with thee for this, they thereby shew themselves to be implacable to good; and thou hast delivered thy soul from their blood.*

What Christian Had for Supper

Now I saw in my Dream, that thus they sat talking together until supper was ready. So when they had made ready, they sat down to meat; Now the Table was furnished with fat things, and with Wine that was well refined; and all their talk at the Table, was about the Lord of the Hill: As namely, about what HE had done, and wherefore HE did what HE did, and why HE had builded that House: and by what they said, I perceived that HE had been a *great Warrior*, and had fought with and slain him that had the power of Death, but not without great danger to himself, which made me love him the more.

For, as they said, and as I believe (said *Christian*) he did it with the loss of much blood; but that which put Glory of Grace into all he did, was, that he did it of pure love to his Country. And besides, there were some of them of the Household that said they had seen and spoke with him since he did die on the Cross; and they have attested, that they had it from his own lips, that he is such a lover of poor Pilgrims, that the like is not to be found from the East to the West.

They moreover gave an instance of what they affirmed, and that was, He had stript himself of his glory that he might do this for the Poor; and that they heard him say and affirm, That he would not dwell in the Mountain of *Zion* alone. They said moreover, That he had made many Pilgrims Princes, though by nature they were Beggars born, and their original had been the Dunghil.

Thus they discoursed together till late at night, and after they had committed themselves to their Lord for Protection, they betook themselves to rest. The Pilgrim they laid in a large upper Chamber, whose window opened towards the Sunrising; the name of the Chamber was *Peace*, where he slept till break of day; and then he awoke and sang,

Where am I now! is this the love and care
Of Jesus for the men that Pilgrims are!
Thus to provide! That I should be forgiven!
And dwell already the next door to Heaven!

So in the Morning they all got up, and after some more discourse, they told him that he should not depart, till they had shewed him the *Rarities* of that place. And first they had him into the Study, where they shewed him Records of the greatest Antiquity; in which, as I remember my Dream, they shewed him first the Pedigree of the Lord of the Hill, that he was the Son of the Ancient of Days, and came by an eternal Generation. Here also was more fully recorded the Acts that he had done, and the names of many hundreds that he had taken into his service; and how he had placed them in such Habitations that could neither by length of Days, nor decays of Nature, be dissolved.

Then they read to him some of the worthy Acts that some of his Servants had done. As how they had subdued Kingdoms, wrought Righteousness, obtained Promises, stopped the mouths of Lions, quenched the violence of Fire, escaped the edge of the Sword; out of weakness were made strong, waxed valiant in fight, and turned to flight the Armies of the *Aliens*.

Then they read again in another part of the Records of the House, where it was shewed how willing their Lord was to receive into his favour any, even any, though they in time past had offered great affronts to his Person and proceedings. Here also were several other Histories of many other famous things, of all which *Christian* had a view. As of things both Ancient and Modern; together with Prophecies and Predictions of things that have their certain accomplishment, both to the dread and amazement of enemies, and the comfort and solace of Pilgrims.

The next day they took him and had him into the Armory; where they shewed him all manner of Furniture, which their Lord had provided for Pilgrims, as Sword, Shield, Helmet, Breast plate, *All Prayer*, and Shoes that would not wear out. And there was here enough of this to harness out as many men for the service of their Lord, as there be Stars in the Heaven for multitude.

They also shewed him some of the Engines with which some of his Servants had done wonderful things. They shewed him *Moses's* Rod, the Hammer and Nail with which *Jael* slew *Sisera*, the Pitchers, Trumpets, and Lamps too, with which *Gideon* put to flight the Armies of *Midian*. Then they shewed him the Ox's goad wherewith *Shamgar* slew six hundred men. They shewed him also the Jaw bone with which Samson did such mighty feats; they shewed him moreover the Sling and Stone with which *David* slew *Goliath* of *Gath:* and the Sword also with which their Lord will kill the Man of Sin, in the day that he shall rise up to the prey. They shewed him besides many excellent things, with which *Christian* was much delighted. This done, they went to their rest again.

Christian Sees the Delectable Mountains

Then I saw in my Dream, that on the morrow he got up to go forwards, but they desired him to stay till the next day also, and then said they, we will (if the day be clear) shew you the delectable Mountains, which they said, would yet further add to his comfort, because they were nearer the desired Haven than the place where at present he was. So he consented and staid. When the Morning was up they had him to the top of the House, and bid him look South, so he did; and behold at a great distance he saw a most pleasant Mountainous Country, beautified with Woods, Vineyards, Fruits of all sorts; Flowers also, with Springs and Fountains, very delectable to behold. Then he asked the name of the Country, they said it was *Immanuels Land;* and it is as common, said they, as this *Hill* is, to and for all the Pilgrims. And when thou comest there, from thence, said they, thou mayest see to the Gate of the Cœlestial City, as the Shepherds that live there will make appear.

Now he bethought himself of setting forward, and they were willing he should: but first, said they, let us go again into the Armory. So they did; and when he came there, they harnessed him from head to foot with what was of proof, lest perhaps he should meet with assaults in the way. He being therefore thus accoutred walketh out with his friends to the Gate, and there he asked the *Porter* if he saw any Pilgrims pass by, Then the *Porter* answered, Yes.

CHR. Pray did you know him? said he.

POR. I asked his name, and he told me it was *Faithful.*

CHR. O, said *Christian,* I know him, he is my Townsman, my near Neighbor, he comes from the place where I was born: how far do you think he may be before?

POR. He is got by this time below the Hill.

CHR. Well, said *Christian,* good Porter, the Lord be with thee, and add to all thy blessings much increase, for the kindness that thou hast shewed to me.

Then he began to go forward, but *Discretion, Piety, Charity,* and *Prudence,* would accompany him down to the foot of the Hill. So they went on together, reiterating their former discourses till they came to go down the Hill. Then said *Christian,* As it was *difficult* coming up, so (so far as I can see) it is *dangerous* going down. Yes, said *Prudence,* so it is; for it is an hard matter for a man to go down into the Valley of *Humiliation,* as thou art now, and to catch no slip by the way; therefore, said they, are we come out to accompany thee down the Hill. So he began to go down, but very warily, yet he caught a slip or too.

Then I saw in my Dream, that these good Companions (when *Christian* was gone down to the bottom of the Hill) gave him a loaf of Bread, a bottle of Wine, and a cluster of Raisins; and then he went on his way.

But now in this Valley of *Humiliation* poor *Christian* was hard put to it, for he had gone but a little way before he espied a foul *Fiend* coming over the field to meet him; his name is *Apollyon.* Then did *Christian* begin to be afraid, and to cast in his mind whether to go back, or to stand his ground. But he considered again, that he had no Armor for his back, and therefore thought that to turn the back to him might give him greater advantage with ease to pierce him with his Darts; therefore he resolved to venture, and stand his ground. For thought he, had I no more in mine eye than the saving of my life, 'twould be the best way to stand.

CHRISTIAN MEETS APOLLYON

So he went on, and *Apollyon* met him. Now the Monster was hideous to behold, he was cloathed with scales like a Fish (and they are his pride) he had Wings like a Dragon, feet like a Bear, and out of his belly came Fire and Smoke, and his mouth was as the mouth of a Lion. When he was come up to *Christian,* he beheld him with a disdainful countenance, and thus began to question with him.

APOL. *Whence come you, and whither are you bound?*

CHR. I am come from the City of *Destruction*, which is the place of all evil, and am going to the City of *Zion*.

APOL. *By this I perceive thou art one of my Subjects, for all that Country is mine; and I am the Prince and God of it. How is it then that thou hast ran away from thy King? Were it not that I hope thou mayest do me more service, I would strike thee now at one blow to the ground.*

CHR. I was born indeed in your Dominions, but your service was hard, and your wages such as a man could not live on, *for the wages of Sin is death;* therefore when I was come to years, I did as other considerate persons do, look out if perhaps I might mend my self.

APOL. *There is no Prince that will thus lightly lose his Subjects, neither will I as yet lose thee. But since thou complainest of thy service and wages be content to go back; what our Country will afford, I do here promise to give thee.*

CHR. But I have let myself to another, even to the King of Princes, and how can I with fairness go back with thee?

APOL. *Thou hast done in this, according to the Proverb, changed a bad for a worse: but it is ordinary for those that have professed themselves his Servants, after a while to give him the slip, and return again to me: do thou so too, and all shall be well.*

CHR. I have given him my faith, and sworn my Allegiance to him; how then can I go back from this, and not be hanged as a Traitor?

APOL. *Thou didst the same to me, and yet I am willing to pass by all, if now thou wilt yet turn again, and go back.*

CHR. What I promised thee was in my nonage; and besides, I count that the Prince under whose Banner now I stand, is able to absolve me; yea, and to pardon also what I did as to my compliance with thee: and besides, (O thou destroying *Apollyon*) to speak truth, I like his Service, his Wages, his Servants, his Government, his Company, and Country better than thine: and therefore leave off to perswade me further, I am his Servant, and I will follow him.

APOL. *Consider again when thou art in cool blood, what thou art like to meet with in the way that thou goest. Thou knowest that for the most part, his Servants come to an ill end, because they are transgressors against me, and my ways. How many of them have been put to shameful deaths! and besides, thou countest his service better than mine, whereas he never came yet from the place where he is, to deliver any that served him out of our hands; but as for me, how many times, as all the World very well knows, have I delivered, either by power or fraud, those that have faithfully served me, from him and his, though taken by them, and so I will deliver thee.*

CHR. His forbearing at present to deliver them, is on purpose to try their love, whether they will cleave to him to the end: and as for the ill end thou sayest they come to, that is most glorious in their account. For for present deliverance, they do not much expect it; for they stay for their Glory, and then they shall have it, when their Prince comes in his, and the Glory of the Angels.

APOL. *Thou hast already been unfaithful in thy service to him, and how doest thou think to receive wages of him?*

CHR. Wherein, O *Apollyon,* have I been unfaithful to him?

APOL. *Thou didst faint at first setting out, when thou wast almost choked in the Gulf of Dispond; thou didst attempt wrong ways to be rid of thy burden, whereas thou shouldest have stayed till thy Prince had taken it off: thou didst sinfully sleep and lose thy choice thing: thou wast also almost perswaded to go back, at the sight of the Lions; and when thou talkest of thy Journey, and of what thou hast heard, and seen, thou art inwardly desirous of vain-glory in all that thou sayest or doest.*

CHR. All this is true, and much more, which thou hast left out; but the Prince whom I serve and honour, is merciful, and ready to forgive: but besides, these infirmities possessed me in thy Country, for there I suckt them in, and I have groaned under them, been sorry for them, and have obtained pardon of my Prince.

APOL. Then *Apollyon* broke out into a grievous rage, saying, *I am an Enemy to this Prince: I hate his Person, his Laws, and People: I am come out on purpose to withstand thee.*

CHR. *Apollyon,* beware what you do, for I am in the King's Highway, the way of Holiness, therefore take heed to your self.

APOL. Then *Apollyon* straddled quite over the whole breadth of the way, and said, I am void of fear in this matter, prepare thy self to die, for I swear by my Infernal Den, that thou shalt go no further, here will I spill thy soul; and with that, he threw a flaming Dart at his breast, but *Christian* had a Shield in his hand, with which he caught it, and so prevented the danger of that. Then did *Christian* draw, for he saw 'twas time to bestir him; and *Apollyon* as fast made at him, throwing Darts as thick as Hail; by the which, notwithstanding all that *Christian* could do to avoid it, *Apollyon* wounded him in his head, his hand and foot; this made *Christian* give a little back: *Apollyon* therefore followed his work amain, and *Christian* again took courage, and resisted as manfully as he could. This sore combat lasted for above half a day, even till *Christian* was almost quite spent. For you must know that *Christian* by reason of his wounds, must needs grow weaker and weaker.

Then *Apollyon* espying his opportunity, began to gather up close to *Christian,* and wrestling with him, gave him a dreadful fall; and with that, *Christian's* Sword flew out of his hand. Then said *Apollyon, I am sure of thee now;* and with that, he had almost prest him to death, so that *Christian* began to despair of life. But as God would have it, while *Apollyon* was fetching of his last blow, thereby to make a full end of this good Man, *Christian* nimbly reached out his hand for his Sword, and caught it, saying, *Rejoice not against me, O mine Enemy! when I fall, I shall arise;* and with that, gave him a deadly thrust, which made him give back, as one that had received his mortal wound: *Christian* perceiving that, made at him again, saying, *Nay, in all these things we are more than Conquerors, through him that loved us.* And with that, *Apollyon* spread forth his Dragon's wings, and sped him away, that *Christian* saw him no more.

In this Combat no man can imagine, unless he had seen and heard as I did, what yelling, and hideous roaring *Apollyon* made all the time of the fight, he spake like a Dragon: and on the other side, what sighs and groans brast from *Christian's* heart. I never saw him all the while give so much as one pleasant look, till he perceived he had wounded *Apollyon* with his two edged Sword, then indeed he did smile, and look upward: but 'twas the dreadfullest sight that ever I saw.

Christian Gives God Thanks

So when the Battle was over, *Christian* said, I will here give thanks to him that hath delivered me out of the mouth of the Lion; to him that did help me against *Apollyon:* and so he did, saying,

> *Great* Beelzebub, *the Captain of this Fiend,*
> *Design'd my ruin; therefore to this end*
> *He sent him harnest out, and he with rage*
> *That Hellish was, did fiercely me engage:*
> *But blessed* Michael *helped me, and I*
> *By dint of Sword, did quickly make him fly:*
> *Therefore to him let me give lasting praise,*
> *And thank and bless his holy name always.*

Then there came to him an hand, with some of the leaves of the Tree of Life, the which *Christian* took, and applied to the wounds that he had received in the Battle, and was healed immediately. He also sat down in that place to eat Bread, and to drink of the Bottle that was given him a little before; so being refreshed, he addressed himself to his Journey, with his Sword drawn in his hand, for he said, I know not but some other Enemy may be at hand. But he met with no other affront from *Apollyon,* quite through this Valley.

Now at the end of this Valley, was another, called the Valley of the *Shadow of Death,* and *Christian* must needs go through it, because the way to the Cœlestial City lay through the midst of it. Now this Valley is a very solitary place. The Prophet *Jeremiah* thus describes it, *A Wilderness, a Land of Deserts, and of Pits, a Land of Drought, and of the shadow of death, a Land that no man* (but a Christian) *passeth through, and where no man dwelt.*

Now here *Christian* was worse put to it than in his fight with *Apollyon,* as by the sequel you shall see.

I saw then in my Dream, that when Christian was got to the Borders of the Shadow of Death, there met him two Men, Children of them that brought up an evil report of the good Land, making haste to go back: to whom *Christian* spake as follows,

Chr. *Whither are you going?*

Men. They said, Back, back; and we would have you to do so too, if either life or peace is prized by you.

CHR. *Why? what's the matter? said* Christian.

MEN. Matter! said they; we were going that way as you are going, and went as far as we durst; and indeed we were almost past coming back, for had we gone a little further, we had not been here to bring the news to thee.

CHR. *But what have you met with, said* Christian?

MEN. Why we were almost in the Valley of the Shadow of Death, but that by good hap we looked before us, and saw the danger before we came to it.

CHR. *But what have you seen, said* Christian?

MEN. Seen! why the Valley itself, which is as dark as pitch; we also saw there the Hobgoblins, Satyrs, and Dragons of the Pit: we heard also in that Valley a continual howling and yelling, as of a People under unutterable misery, who there sat bound in affliction and Irons: and over that Valley hangs the discouraging Clouds of confusion; death also doth always spread his wings over it: in a word, it is every whit dreadful, being utterly without Order.

CHR. *Then said* Christian, *I perceive not yet, by what you have said, but that this is my way to the desired Haven.*

MEN. Be it thy way, we will not chuse it for ours. So they parted, and *Christian* went on his way, but still with his Sword drawn in his hand, for fear lest he should be assaulted.

I saw then in my Dream, so far as this Valley reached, there was on the right hand a very deep Ditch; that Ditch is it into which the blind have led the blind in all Ages, and have both there miserably perished. Again, behold on the left hand, there was a very dangerous Quag, into which, if even a good man falls, he can find no bottom for his foot to stand on. Into that Quag *King* David *once did fall*, and had no doubt therein been smothered, had not He that is able, pluckt him out.

The path-way was here also exceeding narrow, and therefore good *Christian* was the more put to it; for when he sought in the dark to shun the ditch on the one hand, he was ready to tip over into the mire on the other; also when he sought to escape the mire, without great carefulness he would be ready to fall into the ditch. Thus he went on, and I heard him here sigh bitterly: for besides the dangers mentioned above, the pathway was here so dark, that ofttimes when he lift up his foot to set forward, he knew not where, or upon what he should set it next.

About the midst of this Valley, I perceived the mouth of Hell to be, and it stood also hard by the wayside. Now thought *Christian*, what shall I do? And ever and anon the flame and smoke would come out in such abundance, with sparks and hideous noises (things that cared not for *Christians* Sword, as did *Apollyon* before) that he was forced to put up his Sword, and betake himself to another weapon called *All-Prayer*, so he cried in my hearing, *O Lord I beseech thee deliver my Soul.* Thus he went on a great while, yet still the flames would be reaching towards him: also he heard doleful voices, and rushings to and fro, so that sometimes he thought he should be torn to pieces, or trodden down like mire in the Streets. This frightful sight was seen, and these dreadful noises were heard by him for several miles together: and coming to a place, where he thought he heard a company of *Fiends* coming forward to meet him, he stopt, and began to muse what he had best to do. Sometimes he had half a thought to go back. Then again he thought he might be half way through the Valley; he remembred also how he had already vanquished many a danger: and that the danger of going back might be much more than for to go forward; so he resolved to go on. Yet the *Fiends* seemed to come nearer and nearer; but when they were come even almost at him, he cried out with a most vehement voice, *I will walk in the strength of the Lord God;* so they gave back, and came no further.

One thing I would not let slip, I took notice that now poor *Christian* was so confounded, that he did not know his own voice; and thus I perceived it. Just when he was come over against the mouth of the burning Pit, one of the wicked ones got behind him, and stept up softly to him, and whisperingly suggested many grievous blasphemies to him, which he verily thought had proceeded from his own mind. This put *Christian* more to it than any thing that he met with before, even to think that he should now blaspheme him that he loved so much before; yet could he have helped it, he would not have done it: but he had not the discretion neither to stop his ears, nor to know from whence those blasphemies came.

When *Christian* had travelled in this disconsolate condition some considerable time, he thought he heard the voice of a man, as going before him, saying, *Though I walk through the valley of the shadow of death, I will fear none ill, for thou art with me.*

Then was he glad, and that for these reasons:

First, Because he gathered from thence that some who feared God were in this Valley as well as himself.

Secondly, For that he perceived God was with them, though in that dark and dismal state; and why not, thought he, with me? though by reason of the impediment that attends this place, I cannot perceive it.

Thirdly, For that he hoped (could he overtake them) to have company by and by. So he went on, and called to him that was before, but he knew not what to answer, for that he also thought himself to be alone. And by and by, the day broke: then said *Christian, He hath turned the shadow of death into the morning.*

Christian Glad at Break of Day

Now morning being come, he looked back, not of desire to return, but to see, by the light of the day, what hazards he had gone through in the dark. So he saw more perfectly the Ditch that was on the one hand, and the Quag that was on the other; also how narrow the way was which lay betwixt them both; also now he saw the Hobgoblins, and Satyrs, and Dragons of the Pit, but all afar off; for after break of day, they came not nigh; yet they were discovered to him, according to that which is written, *He discovereth deep things out of darkness, and bringeth out to light the shadow of death.*

Now was *Christian* much affected with his deliverance from all the dangers of his solitary way, which dangers, though he feared them more before, yet he saw them more clearly now, because the light of the day made them conspicuous to him. And about this time the Sun was rising, and this was another mercy to *Christian:* for you must note, that though the first part of the Valley of the Shadow of death was dangerous, yet this second part which he was yet to go, was, if possible, far more dangerous: for from the place where he now stood, even to the end of the Valley, the way was all along set so full of Snares, Traps, Gins, and Nets here, and so full of Pits, Pit-falls, deep Holes and Shelvings down there, that had it now been dark, as it was when he came the first part of the way, had he had a thousand souls, they had in reason been cast away; but as I said, just now the Sun was rising. Then said he, *His candle shineth on my head, and by his light I go through darkness.*

In this light therefore he came to the end of the Valley. Now I saw in my Dream, that at the end of this Valley lay blood, bones, ashes, and mangled bodies of men, even of Pilgrims that had gone this way formerly: And while I was musing what should be the reason, I espied a little before me a Cave, where two Giants, *Pope* and *Pagan*, dwelt in old time, by whose Power and Tyranny the Men whose bones, blood, ashes, &c. lay there, were cruelly put to death. But by this place *Christian* went without much danger, whereat I somewhat wondered; but I have learnt since, that *Pagan* has been dead many a day; and as for the other, though he be yet alive, he is by reason of age, and also of the many shrewd brushes that he met with in his younger days, grown so crazy, and stiff in his joints, that he can now do little more than sit in his Cave's mouth, grinning at Pilgrims as they go by, and biting his nails, because he cannot come at them.

So I saw that *Christian* went on his way, yet at the sight of the *old Man*, that sat in the mouth of the *Cave*, he could not tell what to think, specially because he spake to him, though he could not go after him; saying, *You will never mend, till more of you be burned:* but he held his peace, and set a good face on't, and so went by, and catcht no hurt. Then sang *Christian*,

O world of wonders! (I can say no less)
That I should be preserv'd in that distress
That I have met with here! O blessed be
That hand that from it hath delivered me!
Dangers in darkness, Devils, Hell, and Sin,
Did compass me, while I this Vale was in:
Yea, Snares, and Pits, and Traps, and Nets did lie
My path about, that worthless silly I
Might have been catch't, intangled, and cast down:
But since I live, let JESUS *wear the Crown.*

CHRISTIAN OVERTAKES FAITHFUL

Now as *Christian* went on his way, he came to a little ascent, which was cast up on purpose that Pilgrims might see before them: up there therefore

Christian went, and looking forward he saw *Faithful* before him, upon his Journey. Then said *Christian* aloud, Ho, ho, So-ho; stay and I will be your Companion. At that *Faithful* looked behind him, to whom *Christian* cried again, Stay, stay, till I come up to you. But *Faithful* answered, No, I am upon my life, and the Avenger of Blood is behind me. At this *Christian* was somewhat moved, and putting to all his strength, he quickly got up with *Faithful*, and did also overrun him, so the *last was first*. Then did *Christian* vain-gloriously smile, because he had gotten the start of his Brother: but not taking good heed to his feet, he suddenly stumbled and fell, and could not rise again, until *Faithful* came up to help him.

Then I saw in my Dream, they went very lovingly on together; and had sweet discourse of all things that had happened to them in their Pilgrimage; and thus *Christian* began.

CHR. *My honoured and well beloved Brother* Faithful, *I am glad that I have overtaken you; and that God has so tempered our spirits, that we can walk as Companions in this so pleasant a path.*

FAITH. I had thought dear friend, to have had your company quite from our Town, but you did get the start of me; wherefore I was forced to come thus much of the way alone.

CHR. *How long did you stay in the City of* Destruction, *before you set out after me on your Pilgrimage?*

FAITH. Till I could stay no longer; for there was great talk presently after you was gone out, that our City would in short time with Fire from Heaven be burned down to the ground.

CHR. *What! Did your Neighbors talk so?*

FAITH. Yes, 'twas for a while in every body's mouth.

CHR. *What, and did no more of them but you come out to escape the danger?*

FAITH. Though there was, as I said, a great talk thereabout, yet I do not think they did firmly believe it. For in the heat of the discourse, I heard some of them deridingly speak of you, and of your desperate Journey (for so they called this your Pilgrimage), but I did believe, and do still, that the end of our City will be with Fire and Brimstone from above: and therefore I have made mine escape.

CHR. *Did you hear no talk of Neighbor* Pliable?

FAITH. Yes *Christian*, I heard that he followed you till he came at the Slough of *Dispond*, where, as some said, he fell in; but he would not be known to have so done: but I am sure he was soundly bedabbled with that kind of dirt.

CHR. *And what said the Neighbors to him?*

FAITH. He hath, since his going back, been had greatly in derision, and that among all sorts of People: some do mock and despise him, and scarce will any set him on work. He is now seven times worse than if he had never gone out of the City.

CHR. *But why should they be so set against him, since they also despise the way that he forsook?*

FAITH. O, they say, Hang him, he is a Turn-Coat, he was not true to his profession. I think God has stirred up even his Enemies to hiss at him, and make him a Proverb, because he hath forsaken the way.

CHR. *Had you no talk with him before you came out?*

FAITH. I met him once in the Streets, but he leered away on the other side, as one ashamed of what he had done; so I spake not to him.

CHR. *Well, at my first setting out, I had hopes of that Man; but now I fear he will perish in the overthrow of the City, for it is happened to him, according to the true Proverb, The Dog is turned to his Vomit again, and the Sow that was washed to her wallowing in the Mire.*

FAITH. They are my fears of him too. But who can hinder that which will be?

CHR. Well Neighbor *Faithful*, said *Christian*, let us leave him; and talk of things that more immediately concern ourselves. *Tell me now, what you have met with in the way as you came; for I know you have met with some things, or else it may be writ for a wonder.*

FAITH. I escaped the Slough that I perceive you fell into, and got up to the Gate without that danger; only I met with one whose name was *Wanton*, that had like to have done me a mischief.

CHR. *'Twas well you escaped her Net;* Joseph *was hard put to it by her, and he escaped her as you did, but it had like to have cost him his life. But what did she do to you?*

FAITH. You cannot think (but that you know something) what a flattering tongue she had, she lay at me hard to turn aside with her, promising me all manner of content.

CHR. *Nay, she did not promise you the content of a good conscience.*

FAITH. You know what I mean, all carnal and fleshly content.

CHR. *Thank God you have escaped her: The abhorred of the Lord shall fall into her Ditch.*

FAITH. Nay, I know not whether I did wholly escape her, or no.

CHR. *Why, I tro you did not consent to her desires?*

FAITH. No, not to defile myself; for I remembered an old writing that I had seen, which saith, *Her steps take hold of hell.* So I shut mine eyes, because I would not be bewitched with her looks: then she railed on me, and I went my way.

CHR. *Did you meet with no other assault as you came?*

FAITH. When I came to the foot of the Hill called *Difficulty*, I met with a very aged Man, who asked me, *What I was, and whither bound?* I told him, That I was a Pilgrim, going to the Cœlestial City. Then said the Old Man, *Thou lookest like an honest fellow; Wilt thou be content to dwell with me, for the wages that I shall give thee?* Then I asked him his name, and where he dwelt? He said his name was *Adam the first, and I dwell in the Town of Deceit.* I asked him then, What was his work? and what the wages that he would give? He told me, That his work was *many delights; and his wages, that I should be his Heir at last.* I further asked him, What House he kept, and what other Servants he had? So he told me, *That his House was maintained with all the dainties in the world, and that his Servants were those of his own begetting.* Then I asked, if he had any children? He said that he had but three Daughters, *The lust of the flesh, the lust of the eyes, and the pride of life;* and that I should marry them all, if I would. Then I asked, how long time he would have me live with him? And he told me *As long as he lived himself.*

CHR. *Well, and what conclusion came the* Old Man *and you to, at last?*

FAITH. Why, at first, I found myself somewhat inclinable to go with the Man, for I thought he spake very fair; But looking in his forehead as I talked with him, I saw there written, *Put off the old Man with his deeds.*

CHR. *And how then?*

FAITH. Then it came burning hot into my mind, whatever he said, and however he flattered, when he got me home to his House, he would sell me for a Slave. So I bid him forbear to talk, for I would not come near the door of his House. Then he reviled me, and told me that he would send such a one after me, that should make my way bitter to my Soul. So I turned to go away from him: but just as I turned myself to go thence, I felt him take hold of my flesh, and give me such a deadly twitch back, that I thought he had pull'd part of me after himself. This made me cry, *O wretched Man!* So I went on my way up the Hill.

Now when I had got about half way up, I looked behind me, and saw one coming after me, swift as the wind; so he overtook me just about the place where the Settle stands.

CHR. *Just there,* said Christian, *did I sit down to rest me; but, being overcome with sleep, I there lost this Roll out of my bosom.*

FAITH. But good Brother hear me out: So soon as the Man overtook me, he was but a word and a blow: for down he knockt me, and laid me for dead. But when I was a little come to myself again, I asked him wherefore he served me so? he said, Because of my secret inclining to *Adam the first;* and with that, he strook me another deadly blow on the breast, and beat me down backward, so I lay at his foot as dead as before. So when I came to myself again, I cried him mercy; but he said, I know not how to show mercy, and with that knockt me down again. He had doubtless made an end of me, but that one came by, and bid him forbear.

CHR. *Who was that, that bid him forbear?*

FAITH. I did not know him at first, but as he went by, I perceived the holes in his hands, and his side; then I concluded that he was our Lord. So I went up the Hill.

CHR. *That Man that overtook you, was* Moses. *He spareth none, neither knoweth he how to shew mercy to those that trangress his Law.*

FAITH. I know it very well, it was not the first time that he has met with me. 'Twas he that came to me when I dwelt securely at home, and that told me, He would burn my House over my head if I staid there.

CHR. *But did not you see the House that stood there on the top of that Hill, on the side of which* Moses *met you?*

FAITH. Yes, and the Lions too, before I came at it; but for the Lions, I think they were asleep, for it was about Noon; and because I had so much of the day before me, I passed by the Porter, and came down the Hill.

CHR. *He told me indeed that he saw you go by; but I wish you had called at the House; for they would have shewed you so many Rarities, that you would scarce have forgot them to the day of your death. But pray tell me, Did you meet nobody in the Valley of* Humility?

FAITH. Yes, I met with one *Discontent*, who would willingly have perswaded me to go back again with him: his reason was, for that the Valley was altogether without *Honour*. He told me moreover, that there to go was the way to disobey all my Friends, as *Pride, Arrogancy, Self-Conceit, Worldly Glory*, with others, who he knew, as he said, would be very much offended, if I made such a Fool of myself as to wade through this Valley.

CHR. *Well, and how did you answer him?*

FAITH. I told him, That although all these that he named might claim kindred of me, and that rightly (for indeed they were my Relations, *according to the flesh*), yet since I became a Pilgrim, they have disowned me, as I also have rejected them; and therefore they were to me now no more than if they had never been of my Lineage. I told him moreover, that as to this Valley, he had quite mis-represented the thing: *for before Honour is Humility, and a haughty spirit before a fall.* Therefore said I, I had rather go through this Valley to the Honour that was so accounted by the wisest, than chuse that which he esteemed most worth our affections.

CHR. *Met you with nothing else in that Valley?*

FAITH. Yes, I met with *Shame*. But of all the Men that I met with in my Pilgrimage, he I think bears the wrong name: the other would be said nay, after a little argumentation (and somewhat else), but this boldfaced *Shame*, would never have done.

CHR. *Why, what did he say to you?*

FAITH. What! why he objected against Religion itself; he said it was a pitiful low sneaking business for a Man to mind Religion; he said that a tender conscience was an unmanly thing, and that for a Man to watch over his words and ways, so as to tye up himself from that hectoring liberty that the brave spirits of the times accustom themselves unto, would make me the Ridicule of the times. He objected also, that but few of the Mighty, Rich, or Wise, were ever of my opinion; nor any of them, neither, before they were perswaded to be Fools, and to be of a voluntary fondness to venture the loss of all, *for no body else knows what.* He moreover objected the base and low estate and condition of those that were chiefly the Pilgrims of the times in which they lived: also their ignorance, and want of understanding in all natural Science. Yea, he did hold me to it at that rate also about a great many more things than here I relate; as, that it was a *shame* to sit whining and mourning under a Sermon, and a *shame* to come sighing and groaning home. That it was a shame to ask my Neighbor forgiveness for petty faults, or to make restitution where I had taken from any. He said also that Religion made a man grow strange to the great, because of a few vices (which he called by finer names) and made him own and respect the base, because of the same Religious Fraternity. And is not this, said he, a shame?

CHR. *And what did you say to him?*

FAITH. Say! I could not tell what to say at the first. Yea, he put me so to it, that my blood came up in my face, even this *Shame* fetch'd it up, and had almost beat me quite off. But at last I began to consider, *That that which is highly esteemed among Men, is had in abomination with God.* And I thought again, This *Shame* tells me what men are, but it tells me nothing what *God*, or the *Word* of God is. And I thought moreover, that at the day of doom, we shall not be doomed to death or life, according to the hectoring spirits of the world; but according to the Wisdom and Law of the Highest. Therefore thought I, what God says is best, is best, though all the Men in the world are against it. Seeing then, that God prefers his Religion, seeing God prefers a tender Conscience, seeing they that make themselves Fools for the Kingdom of Heaven are wisest; and that the poor man that loveth Christ is richer than the greatest Man in the world that hates him; *Shame* depart, thou art an Enemy to my Salvation: shall I entertain thee against my Soveraign Lord? How then shall I look him in the face at his coming? Should I now be *ashamed* of his Ways and Servants, how can I expect the blessing? But indeed this *Shame* was a bold Villain; I could scarce shake him out of my company; yea, he would be haunting of me, and continually whispering me in the ear, with some one or other of the infirmities that attend Religion: but at last I told him, 'Twas but in vain to attempt further in this business; for those things that he disdained, in those did I see most glory. And so at last I got past this *importunate* one. And when I had shaken him off then I began to sing:

The trials that those men do meet withal,
That are obedient to the Heavenly call,
Are manifold, and suited to the flesh,
And come, and come, and come again afresh;
That now, or sometime else, we by them may
Be taken, overcome, and cast away.
O let the Pilgrims, let the Pilgrims then,
Be vigilant, and quit themselves like men.

CHR. *I am glad, my Brother, that thou didst withstand this Villain so bravely; for of all, as thou sayst, I think he has the wrong name: for he is so bold as to follow us in the Streets, and to attempt to put us to shame before all men; that is, to make us ashamed of that which is good: but if he was not himself audacious, he would never attempt to do as he does, but let us still resist him: for notwithstanding all his Bravadoes, he promoteth the Fool, and none else.* The Wise shall Inherit Glory *said* Solomon, but shame shall be the promotion of Fools.

FAITH. I think we must cry to him for help against shame, that would have us be valiant for Truth upon the Earth.

CHR. *You say true. But did you meet nobody else in that Valley?*

FAITH. No, not I, for I had Sunshine all the rest of the way, through that, and also through the Valley of the Shadow of Death.

CHR. *'Twas well for you, I am sure it fared far otherwise with me.* I had for a long season, as soon almost as I entred into that Valley, a dreadful Combat with that foul Fiend *Apollyon:* yea, I thought verily he would have killed me; especially when he got me down, and crusht me under him, as if he would have crusht me to pieces. For as he threw me, my Sword flew out of my hand; nay he told me *He was sure of me:* but *I cried to God, and he heard me, and delivered me out of all my troubles.* Then I entred into the Valley of the Shadow of Death, and had no light for almost half the way through it. I thought I should have been killed there, over, and over. But at last day brake, and the Sun rose, and I went through that which was behind with far more ease and quiet.

Moreover, I saw in my Dream, that as they went on, *Faithful,* as he chanced to look on one side, saw a Man whose name is *Talkative,* walking at a distance besides them (for in this place, there was room enough for them all to walk). *He was a tall Man, and something more comely at a distance than at hand.* To this Man *Faithful* addressed himself in this manner.

FAITH. *Friend, Whither away? Are you going to the Heavenly Country?*

TALK. I am going to that same place.

FAITH. *That is well; then I hope we may have your good Company.*

TALK. With a very good will will I be your Companion.

FAITH. *Come on then, and let us go together, and let us spend our time in discoursing of things that are profitable.*

TALK. To talk of things that are good, to me is very acceptable, with you, or with any other; and I am glad that I have met with those that incline to so good a work. For to speak the truth, there are but few that care thus to spend their time (as they are in their travels), but chuse much rather to be speaking of things to no profit, and this hath been a trouble to me.

FAITH. *That is indeed a thing to be lamented; for what things so worthy of the use of the tongue and mouth of men on Earth, as are the things of the God of Heaven?*

TALK. I like you wonderful well, for your saying is full of conviction; and I will add, What thing so pleasant, and what so profitable, as to talk of the things of God?

What things so pleasant? (that is, if a man hath any delight in things that are wonderful) for instance, if a man doth delight to talk of the History or Mystery of things, or if a man doth love to talk of Miracles, Wonders, or Signs, where shall he find things recorded so delightful, and so sweetly penned, as in the holy Scripture?

FAITH. *That's true: but to be profited by such things in our talk should be that which we design.*

TALK. That is it that I said: for to *talk* of such things is most profitable, for by so doing, a Man may get knowledge of many things, as of the vanity of earthly things, and the benefit of things above: (thus in general) but more particularly, by this a man may learn the necessity of the New-birth, the insufficiency of our works, the need of Christs righteousness, etc. Besides, by this a man may learn by *talk*, what it is to repent, to believe, to pray, to suffer, or the like: by this also a Man may learn what are the great promises and consolations of the Gospel, to his own comfort. Further, by this a Man may learn to refute false opinions, to vindicate the truth, and also to instruct the ignorant.

FAITH. *All this is true, and glad am I to hear these things from you.*

TALK. Alas! the want of this is the cause that so few understand the need of Faith, and the necessity of a work of Grace in their Soul, in order to eternal life; but ignorantly live in the works of the Law, by which a man can by no means obtain the Kingdom of Heaven.

FAITH. *But by your leave, Heavenly knowledge of these, is the gift of God; no man attaineth to them by human industry, or only by the talk of them.*

TALK. All this I know very well, for a man can receive nothing except it be given him from Heaven; all is of Grace, not of works: I could give you an hundred Scriptures for the confirmation of this.

FAITH. *Well, then, said* Faithful, *what is that one thing, that we shall at this time found our discourse upon?*

TALK. What you will: I will talk of things Heavenly, or things Earthly; things Moral, or things Evangelical; things Sacred, or things Prophane; things past, or things to come; things foreign, or things at home; things more Essential, or things Circumstantial; provided that all be done to our profit.

FAITH. Now did *Faithful* begin to wonder; and stepping to *Christian* (for he walked all this while by himself), he said to him (but softly), *What a Brave Companion have we got! Surely this man will make a very excellent Pilgrim.*

CHR. At this *Christian* modestly smiled, and said, This man with whom you are so taken, will beguile with this tongue of his, twenty of them that know him not.

FAITH. *Do you know him then?*

CHR. Know him! Yes, better than he knows himself.

FAITH. *Pray what is he?*

CHR. His name is *Talkative*, he dwelleth in our Town; I wonder that you should be a stranger to him, only I consider that our Town is large.

FAITH. *Whose son is he? And whereabout doth he dwell?*

CHR. He is the son of one *Saywell*, he dwelt in *Prating-row;* and he is known of all that are acquainted with him, by the name of *Talkative* in *Prating-row:* and notwithstanding his fine tongue, he is but a sorry fellow.

FAITH. *Well, he seems to be a very pretty man.*

CHR. That is, to them that have not thorough acquaintance with him, for he is best abroad, near home he is ugly enough: your saying, That he is a *pretty man*, brings to my mind what I have observed in the work of the Painter, whose Pictures shew best at a distance; but very near, more unpleasing.

FAITH. *But I am ready to think you do but jest, because you smiled.*

CHR. God forbid that I should *jest* (though I smiled) in this matter, or that I should accuse any falsely; I will give you a further discovery of him: This man is for any company, and for any *talk;* as he *talketh now* with you, so will he *talk* when he is on the *Ale-bench:* and the more drink he hath in his crown, the more of these things he hath in his mouth. Religion hath no place in his heart, or house, or conversation; all he hath, lieth in his *tongue,* and his Religion is to make a noise *therewith.*

FAITH. *Say you so! Then am I in this man greatly deceived.*

CHR. Deceived! you may be sure of it. Remember the Proverb, *They say and do not; but the Kingdom of God is not in word, but in power.* He *talketh* of Prayer, of Repentance, of Faith, and of the New Birth: but he knows but only to *talk* of them. I have been in his Family, and have observed him both at home and abroad; and I know what I say of him is the truth. His house is as empty of Religion, *as the white of an Egg is of savour.* There is there neither Prayer, nor sign of Repentance for sin: yea, the brute in his kind serves God far better than he. He is the very stain, reproach, and shame of Religion to all that know him; it can hardly have a good word in all that end of the Town where he dwells, through him. Thus say the common People that know him, *A* Saint *abroad, and a* Devil *at home.* His poor Family finds it so, he is such a *churl,* such a railer at, and so unreasonable with his Servants, that they neither know how to do for, or speak to him. Men that have any dealings with him, say 'tis better to deal with a Turk than with him, for fairer dealing they shall have at their hands. This *Talkative,* if it be possible, will go beyond them, defraud, beguile, and overreach them. Besides, he brings up his Sons to follow his steps; and if he findeth in any of them *a foolish timorousness* (for so he calls the first appearance of a tender conscience) he calls them fools and blockheads; and by no means will employ them in much, or speak to their commendations before others. For my part I am of opinion, that he has by his wicked life caused many to stumble and fall; and will be, if God prevent not, the ruin of many more.

FAITH. *Well, my Brother, I am bound to believe you; not only because you say you know him, but also because like a Christian, you make your reports of men. For I cannot think that you speak these things of ill will, but because it is even so as you say.*

CHR. Had I known him no more than you, I might perhaps have thought of him as at the first you did. Yea, had he received this report at *their* hands only that are enemies to Religion, I should have thought it had been a slander (a Lot that often falls from bad mens mouths upon good mens Names and Professions): But all these things, yea and a great many more as bad, of my own knowledge I can prove him guilty of. Besides, good men are ashamed of him, they can neither call him *Brother* nor *Friend;* the very naming of him among them, makes them blush, if they know him.

FAITH. *Well, I see that* Saying *and* Doing *are two things, and hereafter I shall better observe this distinction.*

CHR. They are *two* things indeed, and are as diverse as are the Soul and the Body: for as the Body without the Soul, is but a dead Carcass; so, *Saying,* if it be alone, is but a dead Carcass also. The Soul of Religion is the practick part: *Pure Religion and undefiled, before God and the Father, is this, To visit the Fatherless and Widows in their affliction, and to keep himself unspotted from the World.* This *Talkative* is not aware of, he thinks that *hearing* and *saying* will make a good Christian, and thus he deceiveth his own Soul. Hearing is but as the sowing of the Seed; talking is not sufficient to prove that fruit is indeed in the heart and life; and let us assure ourselves, that at the day of Doom men shall be judged according to their fruits. It will not be said then, *Did you believe?* but, were you *Doers*, or *Talkers* only? and accordingly shall they be judged. The end of the World is compared to our Harvest, and you know men at Harvest regard nothing but Fruit. Not that any thing can be accepted that is not of Faith; but I speak this to show you how insignificant the profession of *Talkative* will be at that day.

FAITH. *This brings to my mind that of* Moses, *by which he describeth the beast that is clean. He is such an one that parteth the Hoof, and cheweth the Cud: not that parteth the Hoof only, or that cheweth the Cud only. The Hare cheweth the Cud, but yet is unclean, because he parteth not the Hoof. And this truly resembleth* Talkative; *he cheweth the Cud, he seeketh knowledge, he cheweth upon the Word, but he divideth not the Hoof, he parteth not with the way of sinners; but as the Hare, retaineth the foot of a Dog, or Bear, and therefore he is unclean.*

CHR. You have spoken, for ought I know, the true Gospel sense of those Texts, and I will add another thing. *Paul* calleth some men, yea and those great Talkers too, sounding Brass, and Tinkling Cymbals; that is, as he expounds them in another place, *Things without life, giving sound.* Things without life, that is, without the true Faith and Grace of the Gospel; and consequently, things that shall never be placed in the Kingdom of Heaven among those that are the Children of life: Though their *sound*, by their *talk*, be as if it were the *Tongue* or voice of an Angel.

FAITH. *Well, I was not so fond of his company at first, but I am as sick of it now. What shall we do to be rid of him?*

CHR. Take my advice, and do as I bid you, and you shall find that he will soon be sick of your Company too, except God shall touch his heart and turn it.

FAITH. *What would you have me to do?*

CHR. Why, go to him, and enter into some serious discourse about *the power of Religion:* And ask him plainly (when he has approved of it, for that he will) whether this thing be set up in his Heart, House, or Conversation.

FAITH. Then *Faithful* stepped forward again, and said to *Talkative: Come, what chear? how is it now?*

TALK. Thank you, Well. I thought we should have had a great deal of *Talk* by this time.

FAITH. *Well, if you will, we will fall to it now; and since you left it with me to state the question, let it be this: How doth the saving grace of God discover itself, when it is in the heart of man?*

TALK. I perceive then that our talk must be *about the power of things;* Well, 'tis a very good question, and I shall be willing to answer you. And take my answer in brief thus. First, *Where the Grace of God is in the heart, it causeth there a great outcry against sin.* Secondly,—

FAITH. *Nay hold, let us consider of one at once: I think you should rather say, It shows itself by inclining the Soul to abhor its sin.*

TALK. Why, what difference is there between crying out against, and abhoring of sin?

FAITH. *Oh! a great deal; a man may cry out against sin, of policy; but he cannot abhor it, but by vertue of a Godly antipathy against it: I have heard many cry out against sin in the Pulpit, who yet can abide it well enough in the heart, house, and conversation.* Joseph's *Mistris cried out with a loud voice, as if she had been very holy; but she would willingly, notwithstanding that, have committed uncleanness with him. Some cry out against sin, even as the Mother cries out against her Child in her lap, when she calleth it Slut and naughty Girl, and then falls to hugging and kissing it.*

TALK. You lie at the catch, I perceive.

FAITH. *No not I, I am only for setting things right. But what is the second thing whereby you would prove a discovery of a work of grace in the heart?*

TALK. Great knowledge of Gospel Mysteries.

FAITH. *This sign should have been first; but first or last, it is also false;* for, *Knowledge, great knowledge, may be obtained in the mysteries of the Gospel, and yet no work of grace in the Soul: Yea, if a man have* all *knowledge, he may yet be nothing, and so consequently be no child of God. When Christ said,* Do you know all these things? *and the Disciples had answered, Yes: He addeth,* Blessed are ye, if ye do them. *He doth not lay the blessing in the knowing of them, but in the doing of them. For there is a knowledge that is not attended with doing:* He that knoweth his Masters will, and doth it not. *A man may know like an Angel, and yet be no Christian; therefore your sign is not true. Indeed to know, is a thing that pleaseth Talkers and Boasters; but to do, is that which pleaseth God. Not that the heart can be good without knowledge, for without that the heart is naught. There is therefore knowledge and knowledge. Knowledge that resteth in the bare speculation of things, and knowledge that is accompanied with the grace of faith and love, which puts a man upon doing even the will of God from the heart: the first of these will serve the Talker, but without the other the true Christian is not content.* Give me understanding, and I shall keep thy Law, yea, I shall observe it with my whole heart.

TALK. You lie at the catch again, this is not for edification.

FAITH. *Well, if you please, propound another sign how this work of grace discovereth itself where it is.*

TALK. Not I, for I see we shall not agree.

FAITH. *Well, if you will not, will you give me leave to do it?*

TALK. You may use your liberty.

FAITH. *A work of grace in the soul discovereth itself, either to him that hath it, or to standers by.*

To him that hath it, thus. *It gives him conviction of sin, especially of the defilement of his nature, and the sin of unbelief (for the sake of which he is sure to be damned, if he findeth not mercy at God's hand by faith in Jesus Christ.) This sight and sense of things worketh in him sorrow and shame for sin; he findeth moreover revealed in him the Saviour of the World, and the absolute necessity of closing with him for life, at the which he findeth hungerings and thirstings after him, to which hungerings, etc. the promise is made. Now according to the strength or weakness of his Faith in his Saviour, so is his joy and peace, so is his love to holiness, so are his desires to know him more, and also to serve him in this World. But though I say it discovereth itself thus unto him; yet it is but seldom that he is able to conclude that this is a work of Grace, because his corruptions now, and his abused reason, makes his mind to mis-judge in this matter; therefore in him that hath this work, there is required a very sound Judgment, before he can with steadiness conclude that this is a work of Grace.*

To others it is thus discovered.

1. *By an experimental confession of his Faith in Christ.* 2. *By a life answerable to that confession,* to wit, *a life of holiness; heart-holiness, family-holiness (if he hath a Family), and by Conversation-holiness in the World: which in the general teacheth him, inwardly to abhor his Sin, and himself for that in secret, to suppress it in his Family, and to promote holiness in the World; not by talk only, as an Hypocrite or* Talkative *Person may do: but by a practical Subjection in Faith, and Love, to the power of the word. And now Sir, as to this brief description of the work of Grace, and also the discovery of it, if you have ought to object, object; if not, then give me leave to propound to you a second question.*

TALK. Nay, my part is not now to object, but to hear; let me therefore have your second question.

FAITH. It is this, *Do you experience the first part of this description of it? and doth your life and conversation testify the same? or standeth your Religion* in Word or in Tongue, *and not in* Deed *and* Truth? *pray, if you incline to answer me in this, say no more than you know the God above will say* Amen *to; and also, nothing but what your Conscience can justify you in:* For, not he that commendeth himself is approved, but whom the Lord commendeth. *Besides, to say I am thus, and thus, when my Conversation, and all my Neighbors tell me I lye, is great wickedness.*

TALK. Then *Talkative* at first began to blush, but recovering himself, Thus he replyed, You come now to Experience, to Conscience, and God: and to appeal to him for justification of what is spoken: This kind of discourse I did not expect, nor am I disposed to give an answer to such questions, because, I count not myself bound thereto, unless you take upon you to be a *Catechiser;* and, though you should so do, yet I may refuse to make you my Judge. But I pray will you tell me, why you ask me such questions?

FAITH. *Because I saw you forward to talk, and because I knew not that you had ought else but notion. Besides, to tell you all the Truth, I have heard of you, that you are a Man whose Religion lies in talk, and that your Con-*

versation gives this your Mouth-profession the lye. They say You are a spot among Christians, and that Religion fareth the worse for your ungodly conversations that some already have stumbled at your wicked ways, and that more are in danger of being destroyed thereby; your Religion, and an Ale-House, and Covetousness, and uncleanness, and swearing, and lying, and vain Company-keeping, etc. will stand together. The proverb is true of you, which is said of a Whore, to wit, *That she is a shame to all Women; so you are a shame to all Professors.*

TALK. Since you are ready to take up reports, and to judge so rashly as you do, I cannot but conclude you are some peevish, or melancholy Man, not fit to be discoursed with, and so adieu.

CHR. Then came up *Christian,* and said to his Brother, I told you how it would happen, your words and his lusts could not agree; he had rather leave your company, than reform his life. But he is gone as I said; let him go; the loss is no man's but his own; he has saved us the trouble of going from him; for he continuing, as I suppose he will do, as he is, he would have been but a blot in our Company: besides, the Apostle says, *From such withdraw thyself.*

FAITH. *But I am glad we had this little discourse with him, it may happen that he will think of it again; however, I have dealt plainly with him, and so am clear of his blood, if he perisheth.*

CHR. You did well to talk so plainly to him as you did, there is but little of this faithful dealing with men now a days; and that makes Religion to stink in the nostrils of many, as it doth: for they are these *Talkative* Fools, whose Religion is only in word, and are debauched and vain in their Conversation, that (being so much admitted into the Fellowship of the Godly) do stumble the World, blemish Christianity, and grieve the Sincere. I wish that all men would deal with such as you have done, then should they either be made more conformable to Religion, or the company of Saints would be too hot for them.

How Talkative *at first lifts up his Plumes!*
How bravely doth he speak! how he presumes
To drive down all before him! but so soon
As Faithful *talks of* Heart-work, *like the Moon*
That's past the full, into the wane he goes;
And so will all, but he that Heart-work *knows.*

Thus they went on talking of what they had seen by the way, and so made that way easy, which would otherwise, no doubt, have been tedious to them: for now they went through a Wilderness.

Now when they were got almost quite out of this Wilderness, *Faithful* chanced to cast his eye back, and espied one coming after them, and he knew him. Oh! said *Faithful* to his Brother, who comes yonder? Then *Christian* looked, and said, It is my good friend *Evangelist.* Ay, and my good friend too, said *Faithful;* for 'twas he that set me the way to the Gate. Now was *Evangelist* come up unto them, and thus saluted them.

EVAN. Peace be with you, dearly beloved, and, peace be to your helpers.

CHR. *Welcome, welcome, my good* Evangelist, *the sight of thy countenance brings to my remembrance thy ancient kindness, and unwearied laboring for my eternal good.*

FAITH. *And, a thousand times welcome*, said good Faithful; *Thy company, O sweet* Evangelist, *how desirable is it to us, poor Pilgrims!*

EVAN. Then, said *Evangelist*, How hath it fared with you, my friends, since the time of our last parting? *what* have you met with, and *how* have you behaved your selves?

Then *Christian* and *Faithful* told him of all things that had happened to them in the way; and *how*, and with *what* difficulty they had arrived to that place.

EVAN. Right glad am I, said *Evangelist;* not that you met with trials, but that you have been victors, and for that you have (notwithstanding many weaknesses) continued in the way to this very day.

I say, right glad am I of this thing, and that for mine own sake and yours; I have sowed, and you have reaped, and the day is coming, when both he that sowed, and they that reaped shall rejoice together; that is, if you hold out: for, in due time ye shall reap, if you faint not. The Crown is before you, and it is an incorruptible one; so run that you may obtain it. Some there be that set out for this Crown, and after they have gone far for it, another comes in, and takes it from them; hold fast therefore that you have, let no man take your Crown. You are not yet out of the gun-shot of the Devil. You have not resisted unto blood, striving against sin. Let the Kingdom be always before you, and believe stedfastly concerning things that are invisible. Let nothing that is on this side the other world get within you; and above all, look well to your own hearts, and to the lusts thereof; for they are deceitful above all things, and desperately wicked: set your faces like a flint, you have all power in Heaven and Earth on your side.

CHR. *Then* Christian *thanked him for his exhortation, but told him withal, that they would have him speak farther to them for their help, the rest of the way; and the rather, for that they well knew that he was a Prophet, and could tell them of things that might happen unto them; and also how they might resist and overcome them. To which request* Faithful *also consented. So* Evangelist *began as followeth.*

EVAN. My Sons, you have heard in the words of the truth of the Gospel, that you must through many tribulations enter into the Kingdom of Heaven. And again, that in every City, bonds and afflictions abide in you; and therefore you cannot expect that you should go long on your Pilgrimage without them, in some sort or other. You have found something of the truth of these testimonies upon you already, and more will immediately follow: for now, as you see, you are almost out of this Wilderness, and therefore you will soon come into a Town that you will by and by see before you: and in that Town you will be hardly beset with enemies, who will strain hard but they will kill you: and be you sure that one or both of you must seal the testimony which you hold, with blood: but be you faithful unto death, and the King will give you a Crown of life. He that shall die there, although his death will be unnatural, and his pain perhaps great, he will yet have the better of his fellow; not only because he will be arrived at the Cœlestial City soonest, but because he will escape many miseries that the other will meet with in the rest of his Journey. But when you are come to the Town, and shall find fulfilled what I have here related, then remember your friend, and quit your selves like men; and commit the keeping of your souls to your God in well-doing, as unto a faithful Creator.

Vanity-Fair

Then I saw in my Dream, that when they were got out of the Wilderness, they presently saw a Town before them, and the name of that Town is *Vanity;* and at the town there is a *Fair* kept, called *Vanity-Fair*. It is kept all the Year long: it beareth the name of *Vanity-Fair*, because the Town where 'tis kept, *is lighter than* Vanity; and also, because all that is there sold, or that cometh thither, is *Vanity*. As is the saying of the wise, *All that cometh is Vanity*.

This Fair is no new erected business, but a thing of ancient standing; I will shew you the original of it.

Almost five thousand years agone, there were Pilgrims walking to the Cœlestial City, as these two honest persons are; and *Beelzebub*, *Apollyon*, and *Legion*, with their Companions, perceiving by the path that the Pilgrims made, that their way to the City lay through *this Town* of *Vanity*, they contrived here to set up a Fair; a Fair wherein should be sold of *all sorts of Vanity*, and that it should last all the year long. Therefore at *this Fair* are all such Merchandize sold, as Houses, Lands, Trades, Places, Honors, Preferments, Titles, Countries, Kingdoms, Lusts, Pleasures and Delights of all sorts, as Whores, Bawds, Wives, Husbands, Children, Masters, Servants, Lives, Blood, Bodies, Souls, Silver, Gold, Pearls, Precious Stones, and what not.

And moreover, at this Fair there is at all times to be seen Jugglings, Cheats, Games, Plays, Fools, Apes, Knaves, and Rogues, and that of every kind.

Here are to be seen too, and that for nothing, Thefts, Murders, Adulteries, False-swearers, and that of a blood-red colour.

And as in other fairs of less moment, there are the several Rows and Streets, under their proper names, where such and such Wares are vended: So here likewise, you have the proper Places, Rows, Streets, (*viz.* Countreys and Kingdoms) where the Wares of this Fair are soonest to be found: Here is the *Britain* Row, the *French* Row, the *Italian* Row, the *Spanish* Row, the *German* Row, where several sorts of Vanities are to be sold. But as in other *fairs*, some one Commodity is as the chief of all the *fair*, so the Ware of *Rome* and her Merchandize is greatly promoted in *this fair:* Only our *English* Nation, with some others, have taken a dislike thereat.

Now, as I said, the way to the Cœlestial City lies just through *this Town*, where this lusty Fair is kept; and he that will go to the City, and yet not go through this Town, *must* needs *go out of the World.* The Prince of Princes himself, when here, went through *this Town* to his own Country, and that upon a *Fair-day* too: Yea, and as I think, it was *Beelzebub* the chief Lord of this *Fair,* that invited him to buy of his Vanities; yea, would have made him Lord of the *Fair,* would he but have done him Reverence as he went through the *Town.* Yea, because he was such a person of Honour, Beelzebub had him from *Street* to *Street,* and shewed him all the Kingdoms of the World in a little time, that he might, if possible, allure that Blessed One, to *cheapen* and *buy* some of his *Vanities.* But he had no mind to the Merchandize, and therefore left the *Town,* without laying out so much as one Farthing upon these *Vanities.* This *Fair* therefore is an Ancient thing, of long standing, and a very great *Fair.*

The Pilgrims Enter the Fair

Now these Pilgrims, as I said, must needs go through this *fair.* Well, so they did; but behold, even as they entred into the *fair,* all the people in the *fair* were moved, and the Town it self as it were in a Hubbub about them; and that for several reasons: For,

First, the Pilgrims were cloathed with such kind of Raiment as was diverse from the Raiment of any that Traded in that *fair.* The people therefore of the *fair* made a great gazing upon them. Some said they were Fools, some they were Bedlams, and some they are Outlandish-men.

Secondly, And as they wondred at their Apparel, so they did likewise at their Speech, for few could understand what they said; they naturally spoke the Language of *Canaan,* but they that kept the *fair,* were the men of this World: so that from one end of the *fair* to the other, they seemed *Barbarians* each to the other.

Thirdly, But that which did not a little amuse the Merchandizers, was, that these Pilgrims set very light by all their Wares, they cared not so much as to look upon them: and if they called upon them to buy, they would put their fingers in their ears, and cry, *Turn away mine eyes from beholding vanity;* and look upwards, signifying that their Trade and Traffic was in Heaven.

One chanced mockingly, beholding the carriages of the men, to say unto them, What will ye buy? But they, looking gravely upon him, said, *We buy the Truth.* At that, there was an occasion taken to despise the men the more; some mocking, some taunting, some speaking reproachfully, and some calling upon others to smite them. At last things came to an hubbub and great stir in the *fair,* in so much that all order was confounded. Now was word presently brought to the *Great One* of the *fair,* who quickly came down, and deputed some of his most trusty friends to take these men into examination, about whom the *fair* was almost overturned. So the men were brought to examination; and they that sat upon them asked them whence they came, whither they went, and what they did there in such an unusual Garb? The men told them, that they were Pilgrims and Strangers in the

World, and that they were going to their own Country, which was the Heavenly *Jerusalem;* and that they had given none occasion to the men of the Town, nor yet to the Merchandizers, thus to abuse them, and to let them in their Journey. Except it was for that, when one asked them what they would buy, they said they would *buy the Truth.* But they that were appointed to examine them did not believe them to be any other than Bedlams and Mad, or else such as came to put all things into a confusion in the *fair.* Therefore they took them and beat them, and besmeared them with dirt, and then put them into the Cage, that they might be made a Spectacle to all the men of the *fair.* There therefore they lay for some time, and were made the objects of any mans sport, or malice, or revenge. The Great One of the *fair* laughing still at all that befel them. But the men being patient, and not rendering railing for railing, but contrarywise blessing, and giving good words for bad, and kindness for injuries done, some men in the *fair* that were more observing, and less prejudiced than the rest, began to check and blame the baser sort for their continual abuses done by them to the men. They therefore in angry manner let fly at them again, counting them as bad as the men in the Cage, and telling them that they seemed confederates, and should be made partakers of their misfortunes. The others replied, That for aught they could see, the men were quiet, and sober, and intended nobody any harm; and that there were many that traded in their *fair,* that were more worthy to be put into the Cage, yea, and Pillory too, than were the men that they had abused. Thus, after divers words had passed on both sides (the men behaving themselves all the while very wisely and soberly before them), they fell to some Blows, and did harm one to another. Then were these two poor men brought before their Examiners again, and there charged as being guilty of the late Hubbub that had been in the *fair.*

The Pilgrims in Chains

So they beat them pitifully, and hanged irons upon them, and led them in chains up and down the *fair,* for an example and a terror to others, lest any should further speak in their behalf, or join themselves unto them. But *Christian* and *Faithful* behaved themselves yet more wisely, and received the ignominy and shame that was cast upon them, with so much meekness and patience, that it won to their side (though but few in comparison of the rest) several of the men in the *fair.* This put the other party yet into a greater rage, insomuch that they concluded the death of these two men. Wherefore they threatned that the Cage nor irons should serve their turn, but that they should die, for the abuse they had done, and for deluding the men of the *fair.*

Then were they remanded to the Cage again until further order should be taken with them. So they put them in, and made their feet fast in the Stocks.

Here also they called again to mind what they had heard from their faithful friend *Evangelist,* and was the more confirmed in their way and sufferings, by what he told them would happen to them. They also now comforted each other, that whose lot it was to suffer, that even he should have the best on't; therefore each man secretly wished that he might have that preferment; but committing themselves to the All-wise dispose of him that ruleth all things, with much content they abode in the condition in which they were, until they should be otherwise disposed of.

Then a convenient time being appointed, they brought them forth to their Tryal in order to their Condemnation. When the time was come, they were brought before their Enemies and arraigned; The Judge's name was Lord *Hate-good*. Their indictment was one and the same in substance, though somewhat varying in form; the Contents whereof was this.

The Indictment

That they were enemies to, and disturbers of their Trade; that they had made Commotions and Divisions in the Town, and had won a party to their own most dangerous opinions, in contempt of the Law of their Prince.

Then *Faithful* began to answer, That he had only set himself against that which had set itself against him that is higher than the highest. And said he, As for disturbance, I make none, being myself a man of Peace; the Parties that were won to us, were won by beholding our Truth and Innocence, and they are only turned from the worse to the better. And as to the King you talk of, since he is *Beelzebub*, the Enemy of our Lord, I defy him and all his Angels.

Then Proclamation was made, that they that had aught to say for their Lord the King against the Prisoner at the Bar, should forthwith appear and give in their evidence. So there came in three Witnesses, to wit, *Envy*, *Superstition*, and *Pickthank*. They were then asked, If they knew the Prisoner at the Bar? and what they had to say for their Lord the King against him?

Then stood forth *Envy*, and said to this effect; My Lord, I have known this man a long time, and will attest upon my Oath before this honourable Bench, That he is—

Judge. Hold, give him his Oath;

So they sware him. Then he said, My Lord, This man, notwithstanding his plausible name, is one of the vilest men in our Country; he neither regardeth Prince nor People, Law nor Custom: but doth all that he can to possess all men with certain of his disloyal notions, which he in the general calls Principles of Faith and Holiness. And in particular, I heard him once myself affirm, *That Christianity and the Customs of our Town of* Vanity, *were Diametrically opposite, and could not be reconciled*. By which saying, my Lord, he doth at once, not only condemn all our laudable doings, but us in the doing of them.

Judge. Then did the Judge say to him, Hast thou any more to say?

Envy. My Lord I could say much more, only I would not be tedious to the Court. Yet if need be, when the other Gentlemen have given in their Evidence, rather than any thing shall be wanting that will dispatch him,

I will enlarge my Testimony against him. So he was bid stand by. Then they called *Superstition,* and bid him look upon the Prisoner; they also asked, What he could say for their Lord the King against him? Then they sware him, so he began.

SUPER. My Lord, I have no great acquaintance with this man, nor do I desire to have further knowledge of him; However this I know, that he is a very pestilent fellow, from some discourse that the other day I had with him in this *Town,* for then talking with him, I heard him say, That our Religion was naught, and such by which a man could by no means please God: which sayings of his, my Lord, your Lordship very well knows, what necessarily thence will follow, *to wit,* That we still do worship in vain, are yet in our Sins, and finally shall be damned; and this is that which I have to say.

Then was *Pickthank* sworn, and bid say what he knew, in behalf of their Lord the King against the Prisoner at the Bar.

PICK. My Lord, and you gentlemen all, This fellow I have known of a long time, and have heard him speak things that ought not to be spoke. For he hath railed on our noble Prince *Beelzebub,* and hath spoke contemptibly of his honourable Friends, whose names are the Lord *Oldman,* the Lord *Carnal-delight,* the Lord *Luxurious,* the Lord *Desire of Vain-glory,* my old Lord *Lechery,* Sir *Having Greedy,* with all the rest of our Nobility; and he hath said moreover, that if all men were of his mind, if possible, there is not one of these Noblemen should have any longer a being in this Town. Besides, he hath not been afraid to rail on you, my Lord, who are now appointed to be his Judge, calling you an ungodly Villain, with many other such like vilifying terms, with which he hath bespattered most of the Gentry of our Town. When this *Pickthank* had told his tale, the Judge directed his speech to the Prisoner at the Bar, saying, Thou Runagate, Heretick, and Traitor, hast thou heard what these honest Gentlemen have witnessed against thee?

FAITH. *May I speak a few words in my own defence?*

JUDGE. Sirrah, Sirrah, thou deservest to live no longer, but to be slain immediately upon the place; yet that all men may see our gentleness towards thee, let us see what thou hast to say.

FAITH. 1. I say then in answer to what Mr. *Envy* hath spoken, I never said aught but this, *That what Rule, or Laws, or Custom, or People, were flat against the Word of God, are diametrically opposite to Christianity.* If I have said amiss in this, convince me of my error, and I am ready here before you to make my recantation.

2. As to the second, to wit, Mr. *Superstition,* and his charge against me, I said only this, *That in the worship of God there is required a divine Faith; but there can be no divine Faith without a divine Revelation of the will of God: therefore whatever is thrust into the worship of God, that is not agreeable to divine Revelation, cannot be done but by an human Faith; which Faith will not be profit to Eternal life.*

3. As to what Mr. *Pickthank* hath said, I say (avoiding terms, as that I am said to rail, and the like), That the Prince of this Town, with all the Rabble-

ment his Attendants, by this Gentleman named, are more fit for a being in Hell, than in this Town and Country; *and so the Lord have mercy upon me.*

Then the Judge called to the Jury (who all this while stood by, to hear and observe), Gentlemen of the Jury, you see this man about whom so great an uproar hath been made in this Town: you have also heard what these worthy Gentlemen have witnessed against him; also you have heard his reply and confession: It lieth now in your breasts to hang him, or save his life, But yet I think meet to instruct you into our Law.

There was an Act made in the days of *Pharaoh* the Great, Servant to our Prince, That lest those of a contrary Religion should multiply and grow too strong for him, their Males should be thrown into the River. There was also an Act made in the days of *Nebuchadnezzar* the Great, another of his Servants, that whoever would not fall down and worship his golden Image, should be thrown into a fiery Furnace. There was also an Act made in the days of *Darius*, That whoso, for some time, called upon any God but him, should be cast into the Lions' Den. Now the substance of these Laws this Rebel has broken, not only in thought (which is not to be borne) but also in word and deed; which must therefore needs be intolerable.

For that of *Pharaoh*, his Law was made upon a supposition, to prevent mischief, no Crime being yet apparent; but here is a Crime apparent. For the second and third, you see he disputeth against our Religion; and for the Treason he hath confessed, he deserveth to die the death.

Then went the Jury out, whose names were, Mr. *Blind-man*, Mr. *No-good*, Mr. *Malice*, Mr. *Love-lust*, Mr. *Live-loose*, Mr. *Heady*, Mr. *High-mind*, Mr. *Enmity*, Mr. *Lyar*, Mr. *Cruelty*, Mr. *Hate-light*, and *Mr. Implacable*, who every one gave in his private Verdict against him among themselves, and afterwards unanimously concluded to bring him in guilty before the Judge. And first Mr. *Blind-man* the Foreman said, *I see clearly that this man is an Heretick.* Then said Mr. *No-good*, *Away with such a fellow from the Earth. Ay*, said Mr. *Malice*, *for I hate the very looks of him.* Then said Mr. *Love-lust*, *I could never endure him. Nor I*, said Mr. *Live-loose*, *for he would always be condemning my way. Hang him, hang him*, said Mr. *Heady. A sorry Scrub*, said Mr. *High-mind. My heart riseth against him*, said Mr. *Enmity. He is a Rogue*, said Mr. *Lyar. Hanging is too good for him*, said Mr. *Cruelty. Lets dispatch him out of the way*, said Mr. *Hate-light.* Then said Mr. *Implacable*, *Might I have all the World given me, I could not be reconciled to him, therefore let us forthwith bring him in guilty of death;* And so they did, therefore he was presently condemned, To be had from the place where he was, to the place from whence he came, and there to be put to the most cruel death that could be invented.

The Cruel Death of Faithful

They therefore brought him out, to do with him according to their Law; and first they Scourged him, then they Buffeted him, then they Lanced his flesh with Knives; after that, they Stoned him with Stones, then prickt him with their Swords, and last of all they burned him to Ashes at the Stake. Thus came *Faithful* to his end. Now, I saw that there stood behind the multitude, a Chariot and a couple of Horses, waiting for *Faithful*, who (so soon as his adversaries had dispatched him) was taken up into it, and straightway was carried up through the Clouds, with sound of Trumpet, the nearest way to the Cœlestial Gate. But as for *Christian*, he had some respit, and was remanded back to prison, so he there remained for a space. But he that over-rules all things, having the power of their rage in his own hand, so wrought it about, that *Christian* for that time escaped them, and went his way.

And as he went he sang, saying,

> *Well,* Faithful, *thou hast faithfully profest*
> *Unto thy Lord: with whom thou shalt be blest;*
> *When* Faithless *ones, with all their vain delights,*
> *Are crying out under their hellish plights.*
> *Sing,* Faithful, *sing; and let thy name survive,*
> *For though they kill'd thee, thou art yet alive.*

Now I saw in my Dream, that *Christian* went not forth alone, for there was one whose name was *Hopeful* (being made so by the beholding of *Christian* and *Faithful* in their words and behaviour, in their sufferings at the *fair*), who joyned himself unto him, and entering into a brotherly covenant, told him that he would be his Companion. Thus one died to make Testimony to the Truth, and another rises out of his Ashes to be a Companion with *Christian*. This *Hopeful* also told *Christian*, that there were many more of the men in the *fair* that would take their time and follow after.

So I saw that quickly after they were got out of the *fair*, they overtook one that was going before them, whose name was *By-ends;* so they said to him, What Country-man, Sir? and how far go you this way? He told them, That he came from the Town of *Fair-speech*, and he was going to the Cœlestial City (but told them not his name).

From Fair-speech, *said* Christian; *is there any that be good live there?*

BY-ENDS. Yes, said *By-ends*, I hope.

CHR. *Pray Sir, what may I call you?*

BY-ENDS. I am a Stranger to you, and you to me; if you be going this way, I shall be glad of your Company; if not, I must be content.

CHR. *This Town of* Fair-speech, *I have heard of it, and, as I remember, they say it's a Wealthy place.*

BY-ENDS. Yes, I will assure you that it is, and I have very many rich Kindred there.

CHR. *Pray, who are your Kindred there, if a man may be so bold?*

BY-ENDS. Almost the whole Town; and in particular, my Lord *Turn-about*, my Lord *Time-server*, my Lord *Fair-speech*, (from whose Ancestors that Town first took its name): Also Mr. *Smooth-man*, Mr. *Facing-bothways*, Mr. *Any-thing*, and the Parson of our Parish, Mr. *Two-tongues*, was my Mother's own Brother by Father's side: And, to tell you the Truth, I am a Gentleman of good Quality; yet my Great-Grandfather was but a Waterman, looking one way, and rowing another; and I got most of my Estate by the same occupation.

CHR. *Are you a married man?*

BY-ENDS. Yes, and my Wife is a very vertuous Woman, the Daughter of a vertuous Woman. She was my Lady *Fainings* Daughter, therefore she came of a very Honourable Family, and is arrived at such a pitch of Breeding, that she knows how to carry it to all, even to Prince and Peasant. 'Tis true, we somewhat differ in Religion from those of the stricter sort, yet but in two small points: First, we never strive against Wind and Tide. Secondly, we are always most zealous when Religion goes in his Silver Slippers; we love much to walk with him in the Street, if the Sun shines, and the people applaud it.

Then *Christian* stept a little a to-side to his fellow *Hopeful*, saying, It runs in my mind that this is one *By-ends* of *Fair-speech*, and if it be he, we have as very a Knave in our Company as dwelleth in all these parts. Then said *Hopeful*, *Ask him; methinks he should not be ashamed of his name.* So *Christian* came up with him again, and said, Sir, you talk as if you knew something more than all the World doth, and if I take not my mark amiss, I deem I have half a guess of you: Is not your name Mr. *By-ends* of *Fair-speech?*

BY-ENDS. That is not my name, but indeed it is a Nickname that is given me by some that cannot abide me, and I must be content to bear it as a reproach, as other good men have borne theirs before me.

CHR. *But did you never give an occasion to men to call you by this name?*

BY-ENDS. Never, never! the worst that ever I did to give them an occasion to give me this name, was, that I had always the luck to jump in my Judgment with the present way of the times, whatever it was, and my chance was to get thereby; but if things are thus cast upon me, let me count them a blessing, but let not the malicious load me therefore with reproach.

CHR. *I thought indeed, that you was the man that I had heard of, and to tell you what I think, I fear this name belongs to you more properly than you are willing we should think it doth.*

BY-ENDS. Well, if you will thus imagine, I cannot help it. You shall find me a fair Company-keeper, if you will still admit me your associate.

CHR. *If you will go with us, you must go against Wind and Tide, the which, I perceive, is against your opinion: You must also own Religion in his Rags, as well as when in his Silver Slippers, and stand by him too, when bound in Irons, as well as when he walketh the Streets with applause.*

BY-ENDS. You must not impose, nor lord it over my Faith; leave me to my liberty, and let me go with you.

CHR. *Not a step further, unless you will do in what I propound, as we.*

Then said *By-ends*, I shall never desert my old Principles, since they are harmless and profitable. If I may not go with you, I must do as I did before you overtook me, even go by myself, until some overtake me that will be glad of my Company.

Christian Has New Companions

Now I saw in my dream, that *Christian* and *Hopeful*, forsook him, and kept their distance before him; but one of them looking back, saw three men following Mr. *By-ends*, and behold, as they came up with him, he made them a very low *Congee*, and they also gave him a *Compliment*. The men's names were Mr. *Hold-the-World*, Mr. *Money-love*, and Mr. *Save-all;* men that Mr. *By-ends* had formerly been acquainted with; for in their minority they were schoolfellows, and were taught by one Mr. *Gripe-man*, a Schoolmaster in *Love-gain*, which is a market town in the County of *Coveting* in the North. This Schoolmaster taught them the art of getting, either by violence, cousenage, flattery, lying, or by putting on a guise of Religion; and these four Gentlemen had attained much of the art of their Master, so that they could each of them have kept such a School themselves.

Well when they had, as I said, thus saluted each other, Mr. *Money-love* said to Mr. *By-ends*, Who are they upon the Road before us? For *Christian* and *Hopeful* were yet within view.

By-ends. They are a couple of far countrymen, that after *their mode*, are going on Pilgrimage.

Money-love. Alas, why did they not stay that we might have had their good company, for *they*, and *we*, and *you* Sir, I hope, are all going on Pilgrimage.

By-ends. We are so indeed, but the men before us are so rigid, and love so much their own notions, and do also so lightly esteem the Opinions of others; that let a man be never so godly, yet if he jumps not with them in all things, they thrust him quite out of their company.

Save-all. That's bad; But we read of some, *that are righteous over-much*, and such men's rigidness prevails with them to judge and condemn all but themselves. But I pray *what* and *how* many, were the things wherein you differed.

By-ends. Why they after their headstrong manner, conclude that it is duty to rush on their Journey *all* weathers, and I am for waiting for *Wind* and *Tide*. They are for hazarding all for God, at a clap, and I am for taking *all* advantages to secure my life and estate. They are for holding *their notions*, though all other men are against them; but I am for Religion in what, and so far as the times, and my safety will bear it. They are for Religion, when in rags, and contempt; but I am for him when he walks in his golden slippers in the Sun-shine, and with applause.

Hold-the-World. Ay, and hold you there still, good Mr. *By-ends*, for, for my part, I can count him but a fool, that having the liberty to keep what he has, shall be so unwise as to lose it. Let us be wise as *Serpents*, 'tis best to make hay when the Sun shines; you see how the Bee lieth still all winter and bestirs her then only when she can have profit with pleasure. God sends sometimes Rain, and sometimes Sun-shine; if they be such fools to go through the first, yet let us be content to take fair weather along with us.

For my part I like that Religion best, that will stand with the security of God's good blessings unto us; for who can imagine that is ruled by his reason, since God has bestowed upon us the good things of this life, but that he would have us keep them for his sake. *Abraham* and *Solomon* grew rich in Religion. And *Job* says, that a good man *shall lay up gold as dust.* But he must not be such as the men before us, if they be as you have described them.

SAVE-ALL. I think that we are all agreed in this matter, and therefore there needs no more words about it.

MONEY-LOVE. No, there needs no more words about this matter indeed, for he that believes neither Scripture nor reason (and you see we have both on our side) neither knows his own liberty, nor seeks his own safety.

BY-ENDS. My Brethren, we are, as you see, going all on Pilgrimage, and for our better diversion from things that are bad, give me leave to propound unto you this question.

Suppose a man, a Minister, or a Tradesman, &c. should have an advantage lie before him to get the good blessings of this life. Yet so, as that he can by no means come by them, except, in appearance at least, he becomes extraordinary Zealous in some points of Religion, that he meddled not with before, may he not use this means to attain his end, and yet be a right honest man?

MONEY-LOVE. I see the bottom of your question, and with these Gentlemen's good leave, I will endeavour to shape you an answer. And first to speak to your question, as it concerns a *Minister* himself. *Suppose a Minister, a worthy man, possessed but of a very small benefice, and has in his eye a greater, more fat, and plump by far; he has also now an opportunity of getting of it; yet so as by being more studious, by preaching more frequently and zealously, and because the temper of the people requires it, by altering of some of his principles; for my part I see no reason but a man may do this (provided he has a call) ay, and more a great deal besides, and yet be an honest man.* For why,

1. His desire of a greater benefice is lawful (this cannot be contradicted) since 'tis set before him by providence; so then, he may get it if he can, *making no question for conscience sake.*

2. Besides, his desire after that benefice makes him more studious, a more zealous preacher, &c. and so makes him a better man. Yea makes him better improve his parts, which is according to the mind of God.

3. Now as for his complying with the temper of his people, by dissenting, to serve them, some of his principles, this argueth, 1. That he is of a self-denying temper. 2. Of a sweet and winning deportment. 3. And so more fit for the Ministerial function.

4. I conclude then, that a Minister that changes a *small* for a *great*, should not, for so doing, be judged as covetous, but rather, since he is improved in his parts and industry thereby, be counted as one that pursues his call, and the opportunity put into his hand to do good.

And now to the second part of the question which concerns the *Tradesman* you mentioned: suppose such an one to have but a poor imploy in the world, but by becoming Religious, he may mend his market, perhaps get a rich wife, or more and far better customers to his shop. For my part I see no reason but that this may be lawfully done. For why,

1. To become religious is a vertue, by what means soever a man becomes so.

2. Nor is it unlawful to get a rich wife, or more custom to my shop.

3. Besides the man that gets these by becoming religious, gets that which is good, of them that are good, by becoming good himself; so then here is a good wife, and good customers, and good gain, and all these by becoming religious, which is good. Therefore to become religious to get all these is a good and profitable design.

This answer, thus made by this Mr. *Money-love* to Mr. *By-ends* question, was highly applauded by them all; wherefore they concluded upon the whole, that it was most wholsome and advantageous. And because, as they thought, no man was able to contradict it, and because *Christian* and *Hopeful* was yet within call, they joyntly agreed to assault them with the question as soon as they overtook them, and the rather because they had opposed Mr. *By-ends* before. So they called after them, and they stopt, and stood still till they came up to them; but they concluded as they went, that not Mr. *By-ends*, but old Mr. *Hold-the-World* should propound the question to them, because, as they supposed, their answer to him would be without the remainder of that heat that was kindled betwixt Mr. *By-ends* and them, at their parting a little before.

So they came up to each other and after a short salutation, Mr. *Hold-the-World* propounded the question to *Christian* and his fellow, and bid them to answer it if they could.

Chr. Then said *Christian*, even a babe in Religion may answer ten thousand such questions. For if it be unlawful to follow Christ for loaves, as it is, *Joh.* 6. How much more abominable is it to make of him and religion a stalking horse to get and enjoy the world. Nor do we find any other than Heathens, Hypocrites, Devils and Witches that are of this opinion.

1. *Heathens*, for when *Hamor* and *Shechem* had a mind to the Daughter and Cattle of *Jacob*, and saw that there was no ways for them to come at them, but by becoming circumcised, they say to their companions; If every male of us be circumcised, as they are circumcised, shall not their Cattle, and their substance, and every beast of theirs be ours? Their Daughter and their Cattle were that which they sought to obtain, and their Religion the stalking horse they made use of to come at them. Read the whole story, *Gen.* 34. 20, 21, 22, 23.

2. The Hypocritical Pharisees were also of this Religion, long prayers were their pretence, but to get widows' houses were their intent, and greater damnation was from God their Judgment, *Luke* 20. 46, 47.

3. *Judas* the Devil was also of this Religion, he was religious for the bag, that he might be possessed of what was therein; but he was lost, cast away, and the very Son of perdition.

4. *Simon* the witch was of this Religion too, for he would have had the

Holy Ghost, that he might have got money therewith, and his sentence from *Peter's* mouth was according, *Acts* 8. 19, 20, 21, 22.

5. Neither will it out of my mind, but that that man that takes up Religion for the world, will throw away Religion for the world; for so surely as *Judas* designed the world in becoming religious, so surely did he also sell Religion, and his Master for the same. To answer the question therefore affirmatively, as I perceive you have done, and to accept of as authentick such answer, is both Heathenish, Hypocritical and Devilish, and your reward will be according to your works. Then they stood staring one upon another, but had not wherewith to answer *Christian. Hopeful* also approved of the soundness of *Christian's* answer, so there was a great silence among them. Mr. *By-ends* and his company also staggered and kept behind, that *Christian* and *Hopeful* might outgo them. Then said *Christian* to his fellow, If these men cannot stand before the sentence of men, what will they do with the sentence of God? & if they are mute when dealt with by vessels of clay, what will they do when they shall be rebuked by the flames of a devouring fire?

Lucre Hill a Dangerous Hill

Then *Christian* and *Hopeful* out-went them, and went till they came at a delicate Plain, called *Ease*, where they went with much content; but that plain was but narrow, so they were quickly got over it. Now at the further side of that plain, was a little Hill called *Lucre*, and in that *Hill* a *Silver-Mine*, which some of them that had formerly gone that way, because of the rarity of it, had turned aside to see; but going too near the brink of the pit, the ground being deceitful under them, broke, and they were slain; some also had been maimed there, and could not to their dying day be their own men again.

Then I saw in my Dream, that a little off the road, over against the *Silver-Mine*, stood *Demas* (*Gentleman*-like) to call to Passengers to come and see: who said to *Christian* and his Fellow; Ho, turn aside hither, and I will shew you a thing.

Chr. *What thing so deserving, as to turn us out of the way?*

De. Here is a Silver-*Mine*, and some digging in it for Treasure; if you will come, with a little pains, you may richly provide for yourselves.

Hope. Then said Hopeful, *Let us go see.*

Chr. Not I, said *Christian;* I have heard of this place before now, and how many have there been slain; and besides, that Treasure is a snare to those that seek it, for it hindreth them in their Pilgrimage. Then *Christian* called to *Demas*, saying, *Is not the place dangerous? hath it not hindred many in their Pilgrimage?*

De. Not very dangerous, except to those that are careless: but withal, he *blushed* as he spake.

Chr. Then said *Christian* to *Hopeful*, Let us not stir a step, but still keep on our way.

Hope. *I will warrant you, when* By-ends *comes up, if he hath the same invitation as we, he will turn in thither to see.*

Chr. No doubt thereof, for his principles lead him that way, and a hundred to one but he dies there.

De. Then *Demas* called again, saying, But will you not come over and see?

Chr. Then *Christian* roundly answered, saying, *Demas,* Thou art an Enemy to the right ways of the Lord in this way, and hast been already condemned for thine own turning aside, by one of his Majesty's Judges; and why seekest thou to bring us into the like condemnation? Besides, if we at all turn aside, our Lord the King will certainly hear thereof; and will there put us to shame, where we would stand with boldness before him.

Demas cried again, That he also was one of their fraternity; and that if they would tarry a little, he also himself would walk with them.

Chr. Then said *Christian,* What is thy name? is it not the same by the which I have called thee?

De. Yes, my name is *Demas,* I am the son of *Abraham.*

Chr. I know you, *Gehazi* was your Great-Grandfather, and *Judas* your Father, and you have trod their steps. It is but a devilish prank that thou usest. Thy Father was hanged for a Traitor, and thou deservest no better reward. Assure thyself, that when we come to the King, we will do him word of this thy behaviour. Thus they went their way.

By this time *By-ends* and his companions was come again within sight, and they at the first beck went over to *Demas.* Now whether they fell into the Pit by looking over the brink thereof; or whether they went down to dig, or whether they were smothered in the bottom, by the damps that commonly arise, of these things I am not certain: But this I observed, that they were never seen again in the way. Then sang *Christian,*

> By-ends *and Silver-*Demas *both agree;*
> *One calls, the other runs, that he may be,*
> *A sharer in his Lucre; so these two*
> *Take up in this World, and no further go.*

Now I saw, that just on the other side of this Plain, the Pilgrims came to a place where stood an old *Monument,* hard by the High-way-side, at the sight of which they were both concerned, because of the strangeness of the form thereof; for it seemed to them as if it had been a *Woman* transformed into the shape of a Pillar: here therefore they stood looking, and looking upon it, but could not for a time tell what they should make thereof. At last *Hopeful* espied written above upon the head thereof, a Writing in an unusual hand; but he being no Scholar, called to *Christian* (for he was learned) to see if he could pick out the meaning: so he came, and after a little laying of Letters together, he found the same to be this, *Remember Lot's Wife.* So he read it to his fellow; after which, they both concluded, that that was the Pillar of Salt into which *Lot's Wife* was turned for looking back with a *covetous heart,* when she was going from *Sodom* for safety, which sudden and amazing sight, gave them occasion of this discourse.

CHR. Ah my brother, this is a seasonable sight, it came opportunely to us after the invitation which *Demas* gave us to come over to view the Hill *Lucre:* and had we gone over as he desired us, and as thou wast inclining to do (my Brother) we had, for aught I know, been made ourselves like this Woman, a spectacle for those that shall come after to behold.

HOPE. I am sorry that I was so foolish, and am made to wonder that I am not now as *Lot's* Wife; for wherein was the difference 'twixt her sin and mine? She only looked back, and I had a desire to go see. Let Grace be adored, and let me be ashamed that ever such a thing should be in mine heart.

CHR. Let us take notice of what we see here, for our help for time to come: *This* woman escaped one Judgment; for she fell not by the destruction of *Sodom,* yet she was destroyed by another; as we see, she is turned into a Pillar of Salt.

HOPE. True, and she may be to us both *Caution* and *Example; Caution* that we should shun her sin, or a sign of what judgment will overtake such as shall not be prevented by this caution. So *Korah, Dathan,* and *Abiram,* with the two hundred and fifty men, that perished in their sin, did also become a sign, or example to others to beware. But above all, I muse at one thing, to wit, how *Demas* and his fellows can stand so confidently yonder to look for that treasure, which this Woman, but for looking behind her, after (for we read not that she stept one foot out of the way) was turned into a Pillar of Salt; specially since the Judgment which overtook her, did make her an example, within sight of where they are: for they cannot chuse but see her, did they but lift up their eyes.

CHR. It is a thing to be wondered at, and it argueth that their heart is grown desperate in the case; and I cannot tell who to compare them to so fitly, as to them that pick Pockets in the presence of the Judge, or that will cut Purses under the Gallows. It is said of the men of *Sodom, that they were sinners exceedingly,* because they were sinners *before the Lord;* that is, in his eyesight; and nothwithstanding the kindnesses that he had shewed them, for the land of *Sodom,* was now, like the Garden of *Eden heretofore.* This therefore provoked him the more to jealousy, and made their plague as hot as the fire of the Lord out of Heaven could make it. And it is most rationally to be concluded, that such, even such as these are, that shall sin in the sight, yea, and that too in despite of such examples that are set continually before them, to caution them to the contrary, must be partakers of severest Judgments.

HOPE. Doubtless thou hast said the truth, but what a mercy is it, that neither thou, but especially I, am not made myself this example: this ministreth occasion to us to thank God, to fear before him, and always to remember *Lot's* Wife.

The River of Life

I saw then, that they went on their way to a pleasant River, which *David the King* called *the River of God;* but *John, the River of the water of life.*

Now their way lay just upon the bank of the River: here therefore *Christian* and his Companion walked with great delight. They drank also of the water of the River, which was pleasant and enlivening to their weary Spirits: besides, on the banks of this River on either side were *green Trees*, that bore all manner of Fruit; and the leaves of the Trees were good for Medicine; with the Fruit of these Trees they were also much delighted; and the leaves they eat to prevent Surfeits, and other Diseases that are incident to those that heat their blood by Travels. On either side of the River was also a Meadow, curiously beautified with Lilies; and it was green all the year long. In this Meadow they lay down and slept, for here they might *lie down safely*. When they awoke, they gathered again of the Fruit of the Trees, and drank again of the Water of the River, and then lay down again to sleep. Thus they did several days and nights. Then they sang:

Behold ye how these Crystal streams do glide
(To comfort Pilgrims) by the Highway side;
The Meadows green, besides their fragrant smell,
Yield dainties for them: And he that can tell
What pleasant Fruit, yea Leaves, these Trees do yield,
Will soon sell all, that he may buy this Field.

So when they were disposed to go on (for they were not, as yet, at their Journey's end) they eat and drank, and departed.

Now I beheld in my Dream, that they had not journied far, but the River and the way, for a time, parted. At which they were not a little sorry, yet they durst not go out of the way. Now the way from the River was rough, and their feet tender by reason of their Travels: *So the soul of the Pilgrims was much discouraged, because of the way*. Wherefore still as they went on, they wished for better way. Now a little before them, there was on the left hand of the Road, a *Meadow*, and a Stile to go over into it, and that *Meadow* is called *By-Path-Meadow*. Then said *Christian* to his fellow, If this Meadow lieth along by our way side, lets go over into it. Then he went to the Stile to see, and behold a Path lay along by the way on the other side of the fence. 'Tis according to my wish said *Christian*, here is the easiest going; come good *Hopeful*, and let us go over.

Hope. *But how if this Path should lead us out of the way?*

Chr. That's not like, said the other; look, doth it not go along by the way side? So *Hopeful*, being perswaded by his fellow, went after him over the Stile. When they were gone over, and were got into the Path, they found it very easy for their feet; and withal, they looking before them, espied a Man walking as they did, (and his name was *Vain confidence*) so they called after him, and asked him whither that way led? he said, *To the Cœlestial Gate*. Look, said *Christian*, did not I tell you so? by this you may see we are right. So they followed, and he went before them. But behold the night came on, and it grew very dark, so that they that were behind lost the sight of him that went before.

He therefore that went before (*Vain confidence* by name) not seeing the way before him, fell into a deep Pit, which was on purpose there made by the Prince of those grounds to catch *vain glorious* fools withal and was dashed to pieces with his fall.

Now *Christian* and his fellow heard him fall. So they called, to know the matter, but there was none to answer, only they heard a groaning. Then said *Hopeful,* Where are we now? Then was his fellow silent, as mistrusting that he had led him out of the way. And now it began to rain, and thunder, and lighten in a very dreadful manner, and the water rose amain.

Then *Hopeful* groaned in himself, saying, *Oh that I had kept on my way!*

CHR. Who could have thought that this path should have led us out of the way?

HOPE. *I was afraid on't at very first, and therefore gave you that gentle caution. I would have spoke plainer, but that you are older than I.*

CHR. Good Brother be not offended, I am sorry I have brought thee out of the way, and that I have put thee into such eminent danger; pray my Brother forgive me, I did not do it of an evil intent.

HOPE. *Be comforted my Brother for I forgive thee; and believe too, that this shall be for our good.*

CHR. I am glad I have with me a merciful Brother. But we must not stand thus; let's try to go back again.

HOPE. *But good Brother let me go before.*

CHR. No, if you please, let me go first; that if there be any danger, I may be first therein, because by my means we are both gone out of the way.

HOPE. *No, said* Hopeful, *you shall not go first, for your mind being troubled, may lead you out of the way again.* Then for their encouragement, they heard the voice of one saying, *Let thine heart be towards the Highway, even the way that thou wentest, turn again.* But by this time the Waters were greatly risen, by reason of which, the way of going back was very dangerous. (Then I thought that it is easier going out of the way when we are in, than going in when we are out.) Yet they adventured to go back; but it was so dark, and the flood was so high, that in their going back, they had like to have been drowned nine or ten times.

THE GIANT DESPAIR

Neither could they, with all the skill they had, get again to the Stile that night. Wherefore, at last, lighting under a little shelter, they sat down there till the day brake; but being weary, they fell asleep. Now there was not far from the place where they lay, a *Castle,* called *Doubting-Castle,* the owner whereof was *Giant Despair,* and it was in his grounds they now were sleeping; wherefore he getting up in the morning early, and walking up and down in his Fields, caught *Christian* and *Hopeful* asleep in his grounds. Then with a *grim* and *surly* voice he bid them awake, and asked them whence they were? and what they did in his grounds? They told him, they were Pilgrims, and that they had lost their way. Then said the *Giant,* You have this night trespassed on me, by trampling in, and lying on my grounds, and therefore you must go along with me. So they were forced to go, because he was stronger than they. They also had but little to say, for they knew themselves in a fault. The *Giant* therefore drove them before him, and put them into his Castle, into a very dark Dungeon, nasty and stinking to the spirit of these two men. Here then they lay, from *Wednesday* morning till *Saturday* night, without one bit of bread, or drop of drink, or any light, or any to ask how they did. They were therefore here in evil case, and were far from friends and acquaintance. Now in this place, *Christian* had double sorrow, because 'twas through his unadvised haste that they were brought into this distress.

Now *Giant Despair* had a Wife, and her name was *Diffidence*. So when he was gone to bed, he told his Wife what he had done, to wit, that he had taken a couple of Prisoners, and cast them into his *Dungeon*, for trespassing on his grounds. Then he asked her also what he had best to do further to them. So she asked him what they were, whence they came, and whither they were bound; and he told her: then she counselled him, that when he arose in the morning, he should beat them, without any mercy. So when he arose, he getteth him a grievous Crab-tree Cudgel, and goes down into the *Dungeon* to them; and there, first falls to rateing of them as if they were dogs, although they gave him never a word of distaste; then he falls upon them, and beats them fearfully, in such sort, that they were not able to help themselves, or to turn them upon the floor. This done, he withdraws and leaves them, there to condole their misery, and to mourn under their distress. So all that day they spent the time in nothing but sighs and bitter lamentations. The next night she talking with her Husband about them further, and understanding that they were yet alive, did advise him to counsel them, to make away themselves. So when morning was come, he goes to them in a surly manner, as before, and perceiving them to be very sore with the stripes that he had given them the day before, he told them, that since they were never like to come out of that place, their only way would be, forthwith to make an end of themselves, either with Knife, Halter, or Poison: For why, said he, should you chuse life, seeing it is attended with so much bitterness. But they desired him to let them go; with that he looked ugly upon them, and rushing to them, had doubtless made an end of them himself, but that he fell into one of his fits; (for he sometimes in sun-shine weather fell into fits) and lost (for a time) the use of his hand: wherefore he withdrew, and left them, (as before) to consider what to do. Then did the Prisoners consult between themselves, whether 'twas best to take his counsel or no: and thus they began to discourse.

CHR. Brother, said *Christian*, what shall we do? the life that we now live is miserable; for my part I know not whether is best, to live thus, or to die out of hand? *My soul chooseth strangling rather than life;* and the Grave is more easy for me than this Dungeon. Shall we be ruled by the Giant?

HOPE. *Indeed our present condition is dreadful, and death would be far more welcome to me than* thus *for ever to abide. But yet let us consider, the Lord of the Country to which we are going, hath said, Thou shalt do no murther, no not to another man's person; much more then are we forbidden to take his counsel to kill ourselves. Besides, he that kills another, cannot but commit murder upon his body; but for one to kill himself, is to kill body and soul at once. And moreover, my Brother, thou talkest of ease in the Grave; but hast thou forgotten the Hell, whither for certain the murderers go? for no murderer hath eternal life,* etc. *And, let us consider again, that all the Law is not in the hand of* Giant Despair. *Others, so far as I can understand, have been taken by him, as well as we; and yet have escaped out of his hand. Who knows but that God that made the world may cause that* Giant Despair *may die; or that, at some time or other he may forget to lock us in; or, but he may in short time have another of his fits before us, and may lose the use of his limbs; and if ever that should come to pass again, for my part, I am resolved to pluck up the heart of a man, and to try my utmost to get from under his hand. I was a fool that I did not try to do it before: but however, my Brother, let's be patient, and endure a while; the time may come that may give us a happy release: but let us not be our own murderers.* With these words, *Hopeful* at present did moderate the mind of his Brother; so they continued together (in the dark) that day, in their sad and doleful condition.

Well, towards evening the Giant goes down into the Dungeon again, to see if his Prisoners had taken his counsel; but when he came there, he found them alive, and truly, alive was all: for now, what for want of Bread and Water, and by reason of the Wounds they received when he beat them, they could do little but breathe. But, I say, he found them alive; at which he fell into a grievous rage, and told them, that seeing they had disobeyed his counsel, it should be worse with them than if they had never been born.

Hopeful Comforts Christian

At this they trembled greatly, and I think that *Christian* fell into a Swound; but coming a little to himself again, they renewed their discourse about the *Giant's* counsel; and whether yet they had best to take it or no. Now *Christian* again seemed to be for doing it, but *Hopeful* made his second reply as followeth.

Hope. *My Brother, said he, remembrest thou not how valiant thou hast been heretofore.* Apollyon *could not crush thee, nor could all that thou didst hear, or see, or feel in the Valley of the Shadow of Death. What hardship, terror, and amazement hast thou already gone through, and art thou now nothing but fear? Thou seest that I am in the Dungeon with thee, a far weaker man by nature than thou art: also this Giant has wounded me as well as thee, and hath also cut off the Bread and Water from my mouth; and with thee I mourn without the light: but let's exercise a little more patience. Remember how they playedst the man at* Vanity Fair, *and wast neither afraid of the Chain nor Cage; nor yet of bloody Death: wherefore let us (at least to avoid the shame, that becomes not a Christian to be found in) bear up with patience as well as we can.*

Now night being come again, and the *Giant* and his Wife being in bed, she asked him concerning the Prisoners, and if they had taken his counsel: To which he replied, They are sturdy Rogues, they chuse rather to bear all hardship than to make away themselves. Then said she, Take them into the Castle-yard to morrow, and show them the *Bones* and *Skulls* of those that thou hast already dispatch'd; and make them believe, e're a week comes to an end, thou also wilt tear them in pieces, as thou hast done their fellows before them.

So when the morning was come, the *Giant* goes to them again, and takes them into the Castle-yard, and shews them as his Wife had bidden him. These, said he, were Pilgrims as you are, once, and they trespassed in my grounds as you have done; and when I thought fit, I tore them in pieces; and so within ten days I will do you. Go get you down to your Den again; and with that he beat them all the way thither. They lay therefore all day on *Saturday* in a lamentable case, as before. Now when night was come, and when Mrs. *Diffidence* and her Husband, the *Giant*, were got to bed, they began to renew their discourse of their Prisoners: and withal, the old *Giant* wondered, that he could neither by his blows, nor counsel, bring them to an end. And with that his Wife replied, I fear, said she, that they live in hope that some will come to relieve them, or that they have pick-locks about them; by the means of which they hope to escape. And, sayest thou so, my dear? said the *Giant*, I will therefore search them in the morning.

Well, on *Saturday* about midnight they began to *pray*, and continued in Prayer till almost break of day.

Now a little before it was day, good *Christian*, as one half amazed, brake out in this passionate Speech, *What a fool*, quoth he, *am I thus to lie in a stinking Dungeon, when I may as well walk at liberty! I have a* Key *in my bosom, called* Promise, *that will, I am persuaded, open any Lock in* Doubting Castle. Then said *Hopeful*, That's good news; good Brother pluck it out of thy bosom and try.

Then *Christian* pulled it out of his bosom, and began to try at the Dungeon door, whose bolt (as he turned the Key) gave back, and the door flew open with ease, and *Christian* and *Hopeful* both came out. Then he went to the outward door that leads into the *Castle-yard*, and with his *Key* opened the door also. After he went to the *Iron* Gate, for that must be opened too, but that Lock went *damnable* hard, yet the Key did open it; then they thrust open the Gate to make their escape with speed, but that Gate, as it opened, made such a creaking, that it waked *Giant Despair*, who hastily rising to pursue his Prisoners, felt his Limbs to fail, for his fits took him again, so that he could by no means go after them. Then they went on, and came to the King's high-way again, and so were safe, because they were out of his Jurisdiction.

Now when they were gone over the Stile, they began to contrive with themselves what they should do at that Stile, to prevent those that should come after, from falling into the hands of *Giant Despair*. So they consented to erect there a Pillar, and to engrave upon the side thereof *Over this Stile is the Way to* Doubting-Castle, *which is kept by* Giant Despair, *who despiseth the King of the Cœlestial Country, and seeks to destroy his holy Pilgrims.* Many therefore that followed after, read what was written, and escaped the danger. This done, they sang as follows.

> *Out of the way we went, and then we found*
> *What 'twas to tread upon forbidden ground:*
> *And let them that come after have a care,*
> *Lest heedlessness makes them, as we, to fare:*
> *Lest they, for trespassing, his prisoners are,*
> *Whose Castle's* Doubting, *and whose name's* Despair.

They went then, till they came to the Delectable Mountains, which Mountains belong to the Lord of that Hill, of which we have spoken before; so they went up to the Mountains, to behold the Gardens and Orchards, the Vineyards, and Fountains of water; where also they drank, and washed themselves, and did freely eat of the Vineyards. Now there was on the tops of these Mountains Shepherds feeding their flocks, and they stood by the highway side.

Talk with the Shepherds

The Pilgrims therefore went to them, and leaning upon their staves (as is common with weary Pilgrims, when they stand to talk with any by the way); they asked, *Whose delectable Mountains are these? and whose be the sheep that feed upon them?*

SHEP. These Mountains are *Immanuel's Land,* and they are within sight of his City, and the sheep also are his, and he laid down his life for them.

CHR. *Is this the way to the Cœlestial City?*

SHEP. You are just in your way.

CHR. *How far is it thither?*

SHEP. Too far for any but those that shall get thither indeed.

CHR. *Is the way safe, or dangerous?*

SHEP. Safe for those for whom it is to be safe, *but transgressors shall fall therein.*

CHR. *Is there in this place any relief for Pilgrims that are weary and faint in the way?*

SHEP. The Lord of these Mountains hath given us a charge, *Not to be forgetful to entertain strangers:* Therefore the good of the place is even before you.

I saw also in my Dream, that when the Shepherds perceived that they were way-faring men, they also put questions to them (to which they made answer as in other places), as, Whence came you? and, How got you into the way? and, By what means have you so persevered therein? For but few of them that begin to come hither, do shew their face on these Mountains. But when the Shepherds heard their answers, being pleased therewith, they looked very lovingly upon them; and said, *Welcome to the delectable Mountains.*

The Shepherds, I say, whose names were *Knowledge, Experience, Watchful*, and *Sincere*, took them by the hand, and had them to their Tents, and made them partake of that which was ready at present. They said moreover, We would that you should stay here a while, to be acquainted with us, and yet more to solace yourselves with the good of these delectable Mountains. They told them, That they were content to stay; and so they went to their rest that night, because it was very late.

Then I saw in my Dream that in the morning the Shepherds called up *Christian* and *Hopeful* to walk with them upon the Mountains. So they went forth with them, and walked a while, having a pleasant prospect on every side. Then said the Shepherds one to another, Shall we shew these Pilgrims some wonders? So when they had concluded to do it, they had them first to the top of an Hill called *Error*, which was very steep on the furthest side, and bid them look down to the bottom. So *Christian* and *Hopeful* lookt down, and saw at the bottom several men dashed all to pieces by a fall that they had from the top. Then said *Christian*, What meaneth this? The Shepherds answered; Have you not heard of them that were made to err, by hearkening to *Hymeneus* and *Philetus*, as concerning the Faith of the Resurrection of the Body? They answered, Yes. Then said the Shepherds, Those that you see lie dashed in pieces at the bottom of this Mountain, *are they:* and they have continued to this day unburied (as you see) for an example to others to take heed how they clamber too high, or how they come too near the brink of this Mountain.

Then I saw that they had them to the top of another Mountain, and the name of that is *Caution;* and bid them look afar off. Which when they did, they perceived as they thought, several men walking up and down among the Tombs that were there. And they perceived that the men were blind, because they stumbled sometimes upon the Tombs, and because they could not get out from among them. Then said *Christian*, *What means this?*

The Shepherds then answered, Did you not see a little below these Mountains a *Stile* that led into a Meadow on the left hand of this way? They answered, Yes. Then said the Shepherds, From that Stile there goes a path that leads directly to *Doubting-Castle*, which is kept by *Giant Despair;* and these men (pointing to them among the Tombs) came once on Pilgrimage, as you do now, even till they came to that same *Stile*. And because the right way was rough in that place, they chose to go out of it into that Meadow, and there were taken by Giant *Despair*, and cast into *Doubting-Castle;* where, after they had a while been kept in the Dungeon, he at last did put out their eyes, and led them among those Tombs, where he has left them to wander to this very day; that the saying of the wise Man might be fulfilled, *He that wandereth out of the way of understanding shall remain in the Congregation of the dead*. Then *Christian* and *Hopeful* looked one upon another, with tears gushing out; but yet said nothing to the Shepherds.

Then I saw in my Dream, that the Shepherds had them to another place, in a bottom, where was a door in the side of an Hill; and they opened the door, and bid them look in. They looked in therefore, and saw that within it was very dark, and smoaky; they also thought that they heard there a rumbling noise as of fire, and a cry of some tormented, and that they smelt the scent of Brimstone. Then said *Christian, What means this?* The Shepherds told them, saying, this is a By-way to Hell, a way that Hypocrites go in at; namely, such as sell their Birth-right, with *Esau:* such as sell their Master, with *Judas:* such as blaspheme the Gospel, with *Alexander:* and that lie and dissemble, with *Ananias* and *Sapphira* his wife.

HOPE. Then said *Hopeful* to the Shepherds, *I perceive that these had on them, even every one, a shew of Pilgrimage as we have now; had they not?*

SHEP. Yes, and held it a long time too.

HOPE. *How far might they go on Pilgrimage in their day, since they notwithstanding were thus miserably cast away?*

SHEP. Some further, and some not so far as these Mountains.

Then said the Pilgrims one to another, *We had need cry to the Strong for strength.*

SHEP. Ay, and you will have need to use it when you have it, too.

By this time the Pilgrims had a desire to go forwards, and the Shepherds a desire they should; so they walked together towards the end of the Mountains. Then said the Shepherds one to another, Let us here shew to the Pilgrims the Gates of the Cœlestial City, if they have skill to look through our Perspective Glass. The Pilgrims then lovingly accepted the motion: so they had them to the top of an high Hill, called *Clear*, and gave them their Glass to look. Then they essayed to look, but the remembrance of that last thing that the Shepherds had shewed them made their hand shake, by means of which impediment they could not look steadily through the Glass; yet they thought they saw something like the Gate, and also some of the Glory of the place.

> *Thus by the* Shepherds, *Secrets are reveal'd,*
> *Which from all other men are kept conceal'd:*
> *Come to the* Shepherds *then, if you would see*
> *Things deep, things hid, and that mysterious be.*

When they were about to depart, one of the Shepherds gave them a *note of the way*, Another of them *bid them beware of the flatterer*, The third, *bid them take heed that they sleep not upon the Inchanted Ground*, and the fourth, *bid them God speed*. So I awoke from my Dream.

The Country of Conceit

And I slept, and dreamed again, and saw the same two Pilgrims going down the Mountains along the High-way towards the City. Now a little below these Mountains, on the left hand, lieth the Country of *Conceit*, from which Country there comes into the way in which the Pilgrims walked, a little crooked Lane. Here therefore they met with a very brisk Lad, that came out of that Country; and his name was *Ignorance*. So *Christian* asked him, *From what parts he came? and whither he was going?*

IGN. Sir, I was born in the Country that lieth off there, a little on the left hand; and I am going to the Cœlestial City.

CHR. *But how do you think to get in at the Gate, for you may find some difficulty there?*

IGN. As other good People do, said he.

CHR. *But what have you to shew at that Gate, that may cause that the Gate should be opened to you?*

IGN. I know my Lords will, and I have been a good liver, I pay every man his own; I Pray, Fast, pay Tithes, and give Alms, and have left my Country for whither I am going.

CHR. *But thou camest not in at the Wicket-Gate, that is at the head of this way; thou camest in hither through that same crooked Lane; and therefore I fear, however thou mayest think of thyself, when the reckoning day shall come, thou wilt have laid to thy charge that thou art a Thief and a Robber, instead of getting admittance into the City.*

IGN. Gentlemen, ye be utter strangers to me, I know you not; be content to follow the Religion of your Country, and I will follow the Religion of mine. I hope all will be well. And as for the Gate that you talk of, all the World knows that that is a great way off of our Country. I cannot think that any man in all our parts doth so much as know the way to it; nor need they matter whether they do or no, since we have, as you see, a fine pleasant green Lane, that comes down from our Country the next way into it.

When *Christian* saw that the man was wise in his own conceit, he said to *Hopeful* whisperingly, *There is more hopes of a fool than of him.* And said moreover *When he that is a fool walketh by the way, his wisdom faileth him, and he saith to every one that he is a fool.* What, shall we talk further with him? or out-go him at present? and so leave him to think of what he hath heard already; and then stop again for him afterwards, and see if by degrees we can do any good of him? Then said *Hopeful:*

Let Ignorance a little while now muse
On what is said, and let him not refuse
Good Counsel to imbrace, lest he remain
Still Ignorant of what's the chiefest gain.
God saith, Those that no understanding have
(Although he made them) them he will not save.

HOPE. He further added, It is not good, I think, to say all to him at once, let us pass him by, if you will, and talk to him anon, *even as he is able to bear it.*

So they both went on, and Ignorance he came after. Now when they had passed him a little way, they entered into a very dark Lane, where they met a man whom seven Devils had bound with seven strong Cords, and were carrying of him back *to the door* that they saw in the side of the Hill. Now good *Christian* began to tremble, and so did *Hopeful* his Companion: yet as the Devils led away the man, *Christian* looked to see if he knew him, and he thought it might be one *Turn-away* that dwelt in the *Town* of *Apostacy.*

But he did not perfectly see his face, for he did hang his head like a Thief that is found. But being gone past, *Hopeful* looked after him, and espied on his back a Paper with this Inscription, *Wanton Professor, and damnable Apostate*. Then said *Christian* to his Fellow, Now I call to remembrance that which was told me of a thing that happened to a good man hereabout. The name of the man was *Little-Faith*, but a good man, and he dwelt in the Town of *Sincere*.

Broad-Way-Gate and Dead-Man's-Lane

The thing was this; at the entering in of this passage there comes down from *Broad-way-gate* a Lane called *Dead-man's-lane;* so called, because of the Murders that are commonly done there. And this *Little-Faith* going on Pilgrimage, as we do now, chanced to sit down there and slept. Now there happened, at that time, to come down that *Lane* from *Broad-way-gate* three Sturdy Rogues, and their names were *Faint-heart*, *Mistrust*, and *Guilt*, (three brothers) and they espying *Little-Faith* where he was, came galloping up with speed. Now the good man was just awaked from his sleep, and was getting up to go on his Journey. So they came all up to him, and with threatening Language bid him *stand*. At this, *Little-Faith* lookt as white as a Clout, and had neither power to fight nor fly. Then said *Faint-heart*, Deliver thy Purse; but he making no haste to do it, (for he was loth to lose his Money,) *Mistrust* ran up to him, and thrusting his hand into his Pocket, pull'd out thence a bag of Silver. Then he cried out, Thieves, thieves. With that, *Guilt* with a great Club that was in his hand, strook *Little-Faith* on the head, and with that blow fell'd him flat to the ground, where he lay bleeding as one that would bleed to death. All this while the Thieves stood by: but at last, they hearing that some were upon the Road, and fearing lest it should be one *Great-grace* that dwells in the City of *Good-confidence*, they betook themselves to their heels, and left this good man to shift for himself. Now after a while, *Little-Faith* came to himself, and getting up, made shift to scrabble on his way. This was the story.

Hope. *But did they take from him all that ever he had?*

Chr. No: the place where his Jewels were, they never ransack'd, so those he kept still; but as, I was told, the good man was much afflicted for his loss. For the Thieves got most of his spending Money. That which they got not (as I said) were Jewels, also he had a little odd Money left, but *scarce* enough to bring him to his Journeys end; nay, (if I was not misinformed) he was forced to beg as he went, to keep himself alive (for his Jewels he might not sell). But beg, and do what he could, *he went* (as we say) *with many a hungry belly*, the most part of the rest of the way.

Hope. *But is it not a wonder they got not from him his Certificate, by which he was to receive his admittance at the Cœlestial gate?*

Chr. 'Tis a wonder, but they got not that: though they mist it not through any good cunning of his, for he being dismayed with their coming upon him, had neither power nor skill to hide any thing: so 'twas more by good Providence than by his endeavour, that they mist of *that good thing*.

HOPE. *But it must needs be a comfort to him, that they got not this Jewel from him.*

CHR. It might have been great comfort to him, had he used it as he should; but they that told me the story, said, That he made but little use of it all the rest of the way; and that because of the dismay that he had in their taking away of his Money: indeed he forgot it a great part of the rest of the Journey; and besides, when at any time, it came into his mind, and he began to be comforted therewith, then would fresh thoughts of his loss come again upon him, and those thoughts would swallow up all.

HOPE. *Alas poor Man! this could not but be a great grief unto him.*

CHR. Grief! Ay, a grief indeed, would it not have been so to any of us, had we been used as he, to be robbed and wounded too, and that in a strange place, as he was? 'Tis a wonder he did not die with grief, poor heart! I was told, that he scattered almost all the rest of the way with nothing but doleful and bitter complaints. Telling also to all that over-took him, or that he over-took in the way as he went, where he was robbed, and how; who they were that did it, and what he lost; how he was wounded, and that he hardly escaped with life.

HOPE. *But 'tis a wonder that his necessities did not put him upon* selling, or pawning *some of his Jewels, that he might have wherewith to relieve himself in his Journey.*

CHR. Thou talkest like one upon whose head is the Shell to this very day: For what should he *pawn* them? or to whom should he sell them? In all that Country where he was Robbed, his Jewels were not accounted of, nor did he want that relief which could from thence be administred to him; besides, had his Jewels been missing at the Gate of the Cœlestial City, he had (and that he knew well enough) been excluded from an Inheritance there; and that would have been worse to him than the appearance and villainy of ten thousand Thieves.

HOPE. *Why art thou so tart my Brother? Esau* sold his Birth-right, *and that for a mess of Pottage; and that Birth-right was his greatest Jewel; and if he, why might not* Little-Faith *do so too?*

CHR. *Esau* did sell his Birth-right indeed, and so do many besides; and by so doing, exclude themselves from the chief blessing, as also that *Caitiff* did. But you must put a difference betwixt *Esau* and *Little-faith*, and also betwixt their Estates. *Esau's Birth-right* was typical, but *Little-faith's* Jewels were not so. *Esau's* belly was his God, but *Little-faith's* belly was not so. *Esau's* want lay in his fleshly appetite, *Little-faith's* did not so. Besides, *Esau* could see no further than to the fulfilling of his Lusts, *For I am at the point to die*, said he, *and what good will this Birth-right do me?* But *Little-faith*, though it was his lot to have but a *little faith*, was by his *little faith* kept from such extravagances; and made to *see* and *prize* his Jewels more, than to sell them, as *Esau* did his Birth-right. You read not any where that *Esau* had *faith*, no not so much as a little. Therefore no marvel, if where the flesh only bears sway (as it will in that Man where *no* faith is to resist) if he sells his *Birth-right*, and his Soul and all, and that to the Devil of Hell; for it is with such, as it is with the Ass, *Who in her occasions cannot be turned away*. When their minds are set upon their Lusts, they will have them whatever they cost. But *Little-faith* was of another temper, his mind was on things Divine; his livelihood was upon things that were Spiritual, and from above. Therefore to what end should he that is of such a temper sell his Jewels, (had there been any that would have bought them) to fill his mind with empty things? Will a man give a penny to fill his belly with hay? or can you perswade the *Turtle-dove* to live upon Carrion, like the *Crow?* Though *faithless* ones, can for carnal Lusts, pawn, or mortgage, or sell what they have, and themselves outright to boot; yet they that have *faith, saving-faith,* though but a *little* of it, cannot do so. Here therefore, my Brother, is thy mistake.

HOPE. *I acknowledge it; but yet your severe reflection had almost made me angry.*

CHR. Why, I did but compare thee to some of the Birds that are of the brisker sort, who will run to and fro in trodden paths with the shell upon their heads: but pass by that, and consider the matter under debate, and all shall be well betwixt thee and me.

HOPE. *But* Christian, *These three fellows, I am perswaded in my heart, are but a company of Cowards: would they have run else, think you, as they did, at the noise of one that was coming on the road? Why did not* Little-Faith *pluck up a greater heart? He might, methinks, have stood one brush with them, and have yielded when there was no remedy.*

CHR. That they are Cowards, many have said, but few have found it so in the time of Trial. As for *a great heart, Little-faith* had none; and I perceive by thee, my brother, hadst thou been the Man concerned, thou art but for a brush, and then to yield. And verily, since this is the height of thy Stomach now they are at a distance from us, should they appear to thee, as they did to him, they might put thee to second thoughts.

But consider again, they are but Journeymen-Thieves, they serve under the King of the Bottomless pit; who, if need be, will come in to their aid himself, and his voice is *as the roaring of a Lion.* I myself have been engaged as this *Little-faith* was, and I found it a terrible thing. These three Villains set upon me, and I beginning like a *Christian* to resist, they gave but a call, and in came their Master. I would, as the saying is, have given my life for a penny; but that, as God would have it, I was cloathed with Armour of proof. Ay, and yet though I was so harnessed, I found it hard work to quit myself like a man; no man can tell what in that Combat attends us, but he that hath been in the Battle himself.

HOPE. *Well, but they ran, you see, when they did but suppose that one* Great-grace *was in the way.*

CHR. True, they have often fled, both they and their Master, when *Great-grace* hath but appeared, and no marvel, for he is *the King's Champion.* But I tro, you will put some difference between *Little-faith* and the *King's Champion;* all the King's Subjects are not his Champions: nor can they, when tried, do such feats of War as he. Is it meet to think that a little child should handle *Goliath* as *David* did? or that there should be the strength of an *Ox* in a *Wren?* Some are strong, some are weak, some have *great* faith, some have *little:* this man was one of the weak, and therefore he went to the walls.

HOPE. *I would it had been* Great-grace, *for their sakes.*

CHR. If it had been he, he might have had his hands full. For I must tell you, That though *Great-grace* is excellent good at his Weapons, and has and can, so long as he keeps them at Sword's point, do well enough with them: yet if they get within him, even *Faint-heart, Mistrust,* or the other, it shall go hard but they will throw up his heels. And when a man is down, you know what can he do.

Whoso looks well upon *Great-grace's* face, shall see those Scars and Cuts there, that shall easily give demonstration of what I say. Yea once I heard he should say, (and that when he was in the Combat) *we despaired even of life:* How did these sturdy Rogues and their Fellows make *David* groan, mourn, and roar? Yea, *Haman,* and *Hezekiah* too, though Champions in their day, were forced to bestir them, when by these assaulted; and yet, that notwithstanding, they had their Coats soundly brushed by them. *Peter* upon a time would go try what he could do; but, though some do say of him that he is the Prince of the Apostles, they handled him so, that they made him at last afraid of a sorry Girl.

Besides, their King is at their Whistle, he is never out of hearing; and if at any time they be put to the worst, he, if possible, comes in to help them. And of him it is said, *The Sword of him that layeth at him cannot hold the Spear, the Dart, nor the Habergeon. He esteemeth Iron as Straw, and Brass as rotten Wood. The Arrow cannot make him flie. Slingstones are turned with him into stubble, Darts are counted as stubble, he laugheth at the shaking of a Spear.* What can a man do in this case? 'Tis true, if a man could at every turn have *Job's* Horse, and had skill and courage to ride him, he might do notable things. *For his neck is clothed with Thunder, he will not be afraid as the Grashopper, the glory of his Nostrils is terrible, he paweth in the Valley, rejoyceth in his strength, and goeth out to meet the armed men. He mocketh at fear, and is not affrighted, neither turneth back from the Sword. The quiver rattleth against him, the glittering Spear, and the shield. He swalloweth the ground with fierceness and rage, neither believeth he that it is the sound of the Trumpet. He saith among the Trumpets, Ha, ha; and he smelleth the Battel afar off, the thundring of the Captains, and the shoutings.*

But for such footmen as thee and I are, let us never desire to meet with an enemy, nor vaunt as if we could do better, when we hear of others that they have been foiled, nor be tickled at the thoughts of our own manhood, for such commonly come by the worst when tried. Witness *Peter,* of whom I made mention before. He would swagger, Ay he would: He would, as his vain mind prompted him to say, do better, and stand more for his Master, than all men: But who so foiled, and run down by these *Villains,* as he?

When therefore we hear that such Robberies are done on the King's Highway, two things become us to do; first to go out Harnessed, and to be sure *to take a Shield with us.* For it was for want of that, that he that laid so lustily at *Leviathan* could not make him yield. For indeed, if that be wanting, he fears us not at all. Therefore he that had skill, hath said, *Above all take the Shield of Faith, wherewith ye shall be able to quench all the fiery darts of the wicked.*

Good to Have a Convoy

'Tis good also that we desire of the King a Convoy, yea that he will go with us himself. This made *David* rejoyce when in the Valley of the Shadow of Death; and *Moses* was rather for dying where he stood, than to go one step without his God. O my Brother, if he will but go along with us, what need we be afraid of ten thousands that shall set themselves against us, but without him, *the proud helpers fall under the slain.*

I for my part have been in the fray before now, and though (through the goodness of him that is best) I am as you see alive: yet I cannot boast of my manhood. Glad shall I be, if I meet with no more such brunts, though I fear we are not got beyond all danger. However, since the Lion and the Bear hath not as yet devoured me, I hope God will also deliver us from the next uncircumcised *Philistine.*

Poor Little-Faith! *Hast been among the Thieves?*
Wast robb'd! Remember this, Who so believes
And gets more faith, shall then a Victor be
Over ten thousand, else scarce over three.

The Pilgrims Taken in a Net

So they went on, and *Ignorance* followed. They went then till they came at a place where they saw a *way* put itself into their *way*, and seemed withal to lie as straight as the way which they should go; and here they knew not which of the two to take, for both seemed straight before them; therefore here they stood still to consider. And as they were thinking about the way, behold a man black of flesh, but covered with a very light Robe, came to them and asked them, Why they stood there? They answered, They were going to the Cœlestial City, but knew not which of these ways to take. Follow me, said the man, it is thither that I am going. So they followed him in the way that but now came into the road, which by degrees turned, and turned them so from the City that they desired to go to, that in little time their faces were turned away from it; yet they followed him. But by and by, before they were aware, he led them both within the compass of a Net, in which they were both so entangled that they knew not what to do; and with that, the *white robe fell off the black man's back;* then they saw where they were. Wherefore there they lay crying sometime for they could not get themselves out.

Chr. Then said *Christian* to his fellow, Now do I see my self in an error. Did not the Shepherds bid us beware of the flatterers? As is the saying of the Wise man, so we have found it this day: *A man that flattereth his Neighbour, spreadeth a Net for his feet.*

Hope. They also gave us a note of directions about the way, for our more sure finding thereof: but therein we have also forgotten to read, and have not kept ourselves from the Paths of the destroyer. Here *David* was wiser than we; for saith he, *Concerning the works of men, by the word of thy lips, I have kept me from the Paths of the destroyer.* Thus they lay bewailing themselves in the Net. At last they espied a shining One coming towards them, with a whip of small cord in his hand. When he was come to the place where they were, He asked them whence they came? and what they did there? They told him, That they were poor Pilgrims going to *Sion*, but were led out of their way, by a black man, cloathed in white, who bid us, said they, follow him; for he was going thither too. Then said he with the Whip, it is *Flatterer*, a false Apostle, that hath transformed himself into an Angel of light. So he rent the Net, and let the men out. Then said he to them, Follow me, that I may set you in your way again; so he led them back to the way, which they had left to follow the *Flatterer*. Then he asked them, saying, Where did you lie the last night? They said, with the Shepherds upon the delectable Mountains. He asked them then, If they had not of them Shepherds *a note of direction for the way?* They answered, Yes. But did you, said he, when you was at a stand, pluck out and read your note? They answered, No. He asked them why? They said they forgot. He asked, moreover, If the Shepherds did not bid them beware of the *Flatterer?* They answered, Yes; But we did not imagine, said they, that this fine-spoken man had been he.

Then I saw in my Dream, that he commanded them to *lie down;* which when they did, he chastised them sore, to teach them the good way wherein they should walk; and as he chastised them, he said, *As many as I love, I rebuke and chasten; be zealous therefore, and repent.* This done, he bids them go on their way, and take good heed to the other directions of the Shepherds. So they thanked him for all his kindness, and went softly along the right way.

Come hither, you that walk along the way;
See how the Pilgrims fare, that go astray!
They catched are in an intangling Net,
'Cause they good Counsel lightly did forget:
'Tis true, they rescu'd were, but yet you see
They're scourg'd to boot: Let this your caution be.

They Meet an Atheist

Now after a while, they perceived afar off, one coming softly and alone, all along the High-way to meet them. Then said *Christian* to his fellow, Yonder is a man with his back toward *Sion*, and he is coming to meet us.

Hope. I see him, let us take heed to ourselves now, lest he should prove a *Flatterer* also. So he drew nearer and nearer, and at last came up unto them. His name was *Atheist*, and he asked them whither they were going?

Chr. *We are going to the Mount* Sion.

Then *Atheist* fell into a very great Laughter.

CHR. *What is the meaning of your Laughter?*

ATHEIST. I laugh to see what ignorant persons you are, to take upon you so tedious a Journey; and yet are like to have nothing but your travel for your pains.

CHR. *Why man? Do you think we shall not be received?*

ATHEIST. Received! There is no such place as you Dream of, in all this World.

CHR. *But there is in the World to come.*

ATHEIST. When I was at home in mine own Country I heard as you now affirm, and, from that hearing went out to see, and have been seeking this City this twenty years: but find no more of it, than I did the first day I set out.

CHR. *We have both heard and believe that there is such a place to be found.*

ATHEIST. Had not I, when at home, believed, I had not come thus far to seek. But finding none, (and yet I should, had there been such a place to be found, for I have gone to seek it further than you) I am going back again, and will seek to refresh myself with the things that I then cast away, for hopes of that which I now see is not.

CHR. Then said *Christian* to *Hopeful*, his Fellow, *Is it true which this man hath said?*

HOPE. Take heed, he is one of the *Flatterers;* remember what it hath cost us once already for our harkning to such kind of Fellows. What! no Mount *Sion!* Did we not see from the delectable Mountains the Gate of the City? Also, are we not now to walk by Faith? Let us go on, said *Hopeful,* lest the man with the Whip overtakes us again.

You should have taught me that Lesson, which I will round you in the ears withal; *Cease, my son, to hear the Instruction that causeth to err from the words of knowledge.* I say, my Brother, cease to hear him, and let us believe to the saving of the Soul.

CHR. *My Brother, I did not put the question to thee, for that I doubted of the truth of our belief myself: but to prove thee, and to fetch from thee a fruit of the honesty of thy heart. As for this man, I know that he is blinded by the god of this World: Let thee and I go on, knowing that we have belief of the Truth, and no lie is of the Truth.*

HOPE. Now do I rejoyce in the hope of the Glory of God: So they turned away from the man; and he, laughing at them, went his way.

I saw then in my Dream, that they went till they came into a certain Country, whose Air naturally tended to make one drowsy, if he came a stranger into it. And here *Hopeful* began to be very dull and heavy of sleep, wherefore he said unto *Christian*, I do now begin to grow so drowsy that I can scarcely hold up mine eyes; let us lie down here and take one Nap.

CHR. *By no means,* said the other, *lest sleeping, we never awake more.*

HOPE. Why my Brother? sleep is sweet to the Labouring man; we may be refreshed if we take a Nap.

CHR. *Do you not remember that one of the Shepherds bid us beware of the Inchanted ground? He meant by that, that we should beware of sleeping; wherefore let us not sleep as do others, but let us watch and be sober.*

HOPE. I acknowledge myself in a fault and had I been here alone I had by sleeping run the danger of death. I see it is true that the wise man saith, *Two are better than one.* Hitherto hath thy Company been my mercy; *and thou shalt have a good reward for thy labour.*

CHR. *Now then,* said *Christian, to prevent drowsiness in this place, let us fall into good discourse.*

HOPE. With all my heart, said the other.

CHR. *Where shall we begin?*

HOPE. Where God began with us. But do you begin, if you please.

When Saints do sleepy grow, let them come hither,
And hear how these two Pilgrims talk together:
Yea, let them learn of them, in any wise,
Thus to keep ope their drowsy slumb'ring eyes.
Saints' fellowship, if it be manag'd well,
Keeps them awake, and that in spite of hell.

CHR. Then *Christian* began and said, *I will ask you a question. How came you to think at first of doing as you do now?*

HOPE. Do you mean, How came I at first to look after the good of my Soul?

CHR. *Yes, that is my meaning.*

HOPE. I continued a great while in the delight of those things which were seen and sold at our *fair;* things which, as I believe now, would have (had I continued in them still) drowned me in perdition and destruction.

CHR. *What things were they?*

HOPE. All the Treasures and Riches of the World. Also I delighted much in Rioting, Revelling, Drinking, Swearing, Lying, Uncleanness, Sabbath-breaking, and what not, that tended to destroy the Soul. But I found at last, by hearing and considering of things that are Divine, which indeed I heard of you, as also of beloved *Faithful,* that was put to death for his Faith and good-living in *Vanity-fair, That the end of these things is death.* And that *for these things' sake, the wrath of God cometh upon the children of disobedience.*

CHR. *And did you presently fall under the power of this conviction?*

HOPE. No, I was not willing presently to know the evil of sin, nor the damnation that follows upon the commission of it, but endeavoured, when my mind at first began to be shaken with the word, to shut mine eyes against the light thereof.

CHR. *But what was the cause of your carrying of it thus to the first workings of God's blessed Spirit upon you?*

HOPE. The causes were, 1. I was ignorant that this was the work of God upon me. I never thought that, by awakenings for sin, God at first begins the conversion of a sinner. 2. Sin was yet very sweet to my flesh, and I was loth to leave it. 3. I could not tell how to part with mine old Companions;

their presence and actions were so desirable unto me. 4. The hours in which convictions were upon me, were such troublesome and such heart-affrighting hours, that I could not bear, no not so much as the remembrance of them upon my heart.

CHR. *Then as it seems, sometimes you got rid of your trouble.*

HOPE. Yes verily, but it would come into my mind again, and then I should be as bad, nay worse, than I was before.

CHR. *Why, what was it that brought your sins to mind again?*

HOPE. Many things, as,

1. If I did but meet a good man in the Streets; or,
2. If I have heard any read in the Bible; or,
3. If mine Head did begin to Ake; or,
4. If I were told that some of my Neighbors were sick; or,
5. If I heard the Bell toll for some that were dead; or,
6. If I thought of dying myself; or,
7. If I heard that sudden death happened to others.
8. But especially, when I thought of myself, that I must quickly come to Judgment.

CHR. *And could you at any time with ease get off the guilt of sin, when by any of these ways it came upon you?*

HOPE. No, not latterly, for then they got faster hold of my Conscience. And then, if I did but think of going back to sin (though my mind was turned against it) it would be double torment to me.

CHR. *And how did you do then?*

HOPE. I thought I must endeavour to mend my life, for else thought I, I am sure to be damned.

CHR. *And did you endeavour to mend?*

HOPE. Yes, and fled from, not only my sins, but sinful Company too; and betook me to Religious Duties, as Praying, Reading, weeping for Sin, speaking Truth to my Neighbors, etc. These things I did, with many others, too much here to relate.

CHR. *And did you think yourself well then?*

HOPE. Yes, for a while; but at the last my trouble came tumbling upon me again, and that over the neck of all my Reformations.

CHR. *How came that about, since you was now Reformed?*

HOPE. There were several things brought it upon me, especially such sayings as these; *All our righteousnesses are as filthy rags. By the works of the Law no man shall be justified. When you have done all things, say, we are unprofitable:* with many more the like. From whence I began to reason with myself thus: If *all* my righteousnesses are filthy rags, if by the deeds of the Law, *no* man can be justified; And if, when we have done *all*, we are yet unprofitable: Then 'tis but a folly to think of Heaven by the Law. I further thought thus: If a Man runs an 100*l.* into the Shop-keepers' debt, and after that shall pay for all that he shall fetch; yet his old debt stands still in the Book uncrossed, for the which the Shop-keeper may sue him, and cast him into Prison till he shall pay the debt.

CHR. *Well, and how did you apply this to yourself?*

HOPE. Why, I thought thus with myself: I have by my sins run a great way into God's Book, and that my now reforming will not pay off that score; therefore I should think still under all my present amendments, But how shall I be freed from that damnation that I have brought myself in danger of by my former transgressions?

CHR. *A very good application: but pray go on.*

HOPE. Another thing that hath troubled me, even since my late amendments, is, that if I look narrowly into the best of what I do now, I still see sin, new sin, mixing itself with the best of that I do. So that now I am forced to conclude, that notwithstanding my former fond conceits of myself and duties, I have committed sin enough in one duty to send me to Hell, though my former life had been faultless.

CHR. *And what did you do then?*

HOPE. Do! I could not tell what to do, till I brake my mind to *Faithful;* for he and I were well acquainted: And he told me, That unless I could obtain the righteousness of a man that never had sinned, neither mine own, nor all the righteousness of the World could save me.

CHR. *And did you think he spake true?*

HOPE. Had he told me so when I was pleased and satisfied with mine own amendments, I had called him Fool for his pains: but now, since I see my own infirmity, and the sin that cleaves to my best performance, I have been forced to be of his opinion.

CHR. *But did you think, when at first he suggested it to you, that there was such a man to be found, of whom it might justly be said, That he never committed sin?*

HOPE. I must confess the words at first sounded strangely, but after a little more talk and company with him, I had full conviction about it.

CHR. *And did you ask him what man this was, and how you must be justified by him?*

HOPE. Yes, and he told me it was the Lord Jesus, that dwelleth on the right hand of the most High: and thus, said he, you must be justified by him, even by trusting to what he hath done by himself in the days of his flesh, and suffered when he did hang on the Tree. I asked him further, How that man's righteousness could be of that efficacy, to justify another before God? And he told me, He was the mighty God, and did what he did, and died the death also, not for himself, but for me; to whom his doings, and the worthiness of them should be imputed, if I believed on him.

CHR. *And what did you do then?*

HOPE. I made my objections against my believing, for that I thought he was not willing to save me.

CHR. *And what said* Faithful *to you then?*

HOPE. He bid me go to him and see. Then I said, It was presumption: but he said, No; for I was invited to come. Then he gave me a Book of *Jesus* his inditing, to encourage me the more freely to come. And he said concerning that Book, That every jot and tittle thereof stood firmer than Heaven and earth. Then I asked him, What I must do when I came? and he told me, I must entreat upon my knees, with all my heart and soul, the Father to reveal him to me. Then I asked him further, How I must make my supplication to him? And he said, Go, and thou shalt find him upon a mercy-seat, where he sits all the year long, to give pardon and forgiveness to them that come.

Hopeful Bid to Pray

I told him that I knew not what to say when I came: and he bid me say to this effect, *God be merciful to me a sinner, and make me to know and believe in Jesus Christ; for I see that if his righteousness had not been, or I have not faith in that righteousness, I am utterly cast away. Lord, I have heard that thou art a merciful God, and hast ordained that thy Son Jesus Christ should be the Saviour of the World; and moreover, that thou art willing to bestow him upon such a poor sinner as I am, (and I am a sinner indeed) Lord take therefore this opportunity, and magnify thy grace in the Salvation of my soul, through thy Son Jesus Christ*, Amen.

Chr. *And did you do as you were bidden?*

Hope. Yes; over, and over, and over.

Chr. *And did the Father reveal his Son to you?*

Hope. Not at the first, nor second, nor third, nor fourth, nor fifth, no, nor at the sixth time neither.

Chr. *What did you do then?*

Hope. What! why I could not tell what to do.

Chr. *Had you not thoughts of leaving off praying?*

Hope. Yes, an hundred times, twice told.

Chr. *And what was the reason you did not?*

Hope. I believed that that was true which had been told me; *to wit*, That without the righteousness of this Christ, all the World could not save me: and therefore thought I with myself, If I leave off, I die; and I can but die at the throne of Grace. And withal, this came into my mind, *If it tarry, wait for it, because it will surely come, and will not tarry*. So I continued praying until the Father shewed me his Son.

Chr. *And how was he revealed unto you?*

Hope. I did *not* see him with my bodily eyes, but with the eyes of mine understanding; and thus it was. One day I was very sad, I think sadder than at any one time in my life; and this sadness was through a fresh sight of the greatness and vileness of my sins. And as I was then looking for nothing but *Hell*, and the everlasting damnation of my Soul, suddenly, as I thought, I saw the Lord Jesus look down from Heaven upon me, and saying, *Believe on the Lord Jesus Christ, and thou shalt be saved.*

But I replied, Lord, I am a great, a very great sinner; and he answered, *My grace is sufficient for thee*. Then I said, But Lord, what is believing? And then I saw from that saying [*He that cometh to me shall never hunger, and he that believeth on me shall never thirst*] that believing and coming was all one; and that he that came, that is, ran out in his heart and affections after salvation by Christ, he indeed believed in Christ. Then the water stood in mine eyes, and I asked further, But Lord, may such a great sinner as I am, be indeed accepted of thee, and be saved by thee? And I heard him say, *And him that cometh to me, I will in no wise cast out.* Then I said, But how, Lord, must I consider of thee in my coming to thee, that my faith may be placed aright upon thee? Then he said, *Christ Jesus came into the World to save sinners. He is the end of the Law for righteousness to every one that believes. He died for our sins, and rose again for our justification. He loved us and washed us from our sins in his own blood. He is Mediator between God and us. He ever liveth to make intercession for us.* From all which I gathered that I must look for righteousness in his person, and for satisfaction for my sins by his blood; that what he did in obedience to his Father's Law, and in submitting to the penalty thereof, was not for himself, but for him that will accept it for his Salvation, and be thankful. And now was my heart full of joy, mine eyes full of tears, and mine affections running over with love to the Name, People, and Ways of Jesus Christ.

CHR. *This was a Revelation of Christ to your soul indeed. But tell me particularly what effect this had upon your spirit.*

HOPE. It made me see that all the World, notwithstanding all the righteousness thereof, is in a state of condemnation. It made me see that God the Father, though he be just, can justly justify the coming sinner. It made me greatly ashamed of the vileness of my former life, and confounded me with the sense of mine own Ignorance; for there never came thought into mine heart before now that shewed me so the beauty of Jesus Christ. It made me love a holy life, and long to do something for the Honour and Glory of the name of the Lord Jesus. Yea I thought, that had I now a thousand gallons of blood in my body, I could spill it all for the sake of the Lord Jesus.

IGNORANCE COMES UP AGAIN

I then saw in my Dream, that *Hopeful* looked back and saw *Ignorance,* whom they had left behind, coming after. *Look,* said he to *Christian, how far yonder Youngster loitereth behind.*

CHR. Ay, Ay, I see him; he careth not for our Company.

HOPE. *But I tro, it would not have hurt him, had he kept pace with us hitherto.*

CHR. That's true, but I warrant you he thinketh otherwise.

HOPE. *That I think he doth, but however let us tarry for him.* So they did.

Then *Christian* said to him, *Come away man; why do you stay so behind?*

IGN. I take my pleasure in walking alone, even more a great deal than in Company, unless I like it the better.

Then said *Christian* to *Hopeful* (but softly) *Did I not tell you, he cared not for our Company. But however, come up, and let us talk away the time in this solitary place.* Then directing his Speech to *Ignorance,* he said, *Come, how do you? how stands it between God and your Soul now?*

IGN. I hope well, for I am always full of good motions that come into my mind to comfort me as I walk.

CHR. *What good motions? pray tell us.*

IGN. Why, I think of God and Heaven.

CHR. *So do the Devils and damned Souls.*

IGN. But I think of them, and desire them.

CHR. *So do many that are never like to come there:* The Soul of the Sluggard desires and hath nothing.

IGN. But I think of them, and leave all for them.

CHR. *That I doubt; for leaving of all is an hard matter, yea a harder matter than many are aware of. But why, or by what, art thou perswaded that thou hast left all for God and Heaven?*

IGN. My heart tells me so.

CHR. *The wise man says,* He that trusts his own heart is a fool.

IGN. This is spoken of an evil heart, but mine is a good one.

CHR. *But how dost thou prove that?*

IGN. It comforts me in hopes of Heaven.

CHR. *That may be through its deceitfulness; for a man's heart may minister comfort to him in the hopes of that thing for which he yet has no ground to hope.*

IGN. But my heart and life agree together, and therefore my hope is well grounded.

CHR. *Who told thee that thy heart and life agree together?*

IGN. My heart tells me so.

CHR. *Ask my Fellow if I be a Thief. Thy heart tells thee so! Except the word of God beareth witness in this matter, other Testimony is of no value.*

IGN. But is it not a good heart that has good thoughts? And is not that a good life that is according to God's Commandments?

CHR. *Yes, that is a good heart that hath good thoughts, and that is a good life that is according to God's Commandments. But it is one thing indeed to have these, and another thing only to think so.*

IGN. Pray what count you good thoughts, and a life according to God's Commandments?

CHR. *There are good thoughts of divers kinds, some respecting ourselves, some God, some Christ, and some other things.*

IGN. What be good thoughts respecting ourselves?

CHR. *Such as agree with the Word of God.*

IGN. When does our thoughts of ourselves agree with the Word of God?

CHR. *When we pass the same Judgment upon ourselves which the Word passes. To explain myself; the Word of God saith of persons in a natural condition,* There is none Righteous, there is none that doth good. *It saith also,* That every imagination of the heart of man is only evil, and that continually. *And again,* The imagination of man's heart is evil from his Youth. *Now then, when we think thus of ourselves, having sense thereof, then are our thoughts good ones, because according to the Word of God.*

IGN. I will never believe that my heart is thus bad.

CHR. *Therefore thou never hadst one good thought concerning thyself in thy life. But let me go on: As the Word passeth a Judgment upon our* HEART, *so it passeth a Judgment upon our WAYS; and when our thoughts of our HEARTS and WAYS agree with the Judgment which the Word giveth of both, then are both good, because agreeing thereto.*

IGN. Make out your meaning.

CHR. *Why, the Word of God saith, That man's ways are crooked ways, not good, but perverse. It saith, They are naturally out of the good way, that they have not known it. Now when a man thus thinketh of his ways, I say when he doth sensibly, and with heart-humiliation thus think, then hath he good thoughts of his own ways, because his thoughts now agree with the judgment of the Word of God.*

IGN. What are good thoughts concerning God?

CHR. *Even (as I have said concerning ourselves) when our thoughts of God do agree with what the Word saith of him. And that is, when we think of his Being and Attributes as the Word hath taught: of which I cannot now discourse at large. But to speak of him with reference to us, then we have right thoughts of God, when we think that he knows us better than we know ourselves, and can see sin in us, when and where we can see none in ourselves; when we think he knows our inmost thoughts, and that our heart with all its depths is always open unto his eyes. Also when we think that all our Righteousness stinks in his Nostrils, and that therefore he cannot abide to see us stand before him in any confidence even of all our best performances.*

IGN. Do you think that I am such a fool, as to think God can see no further than I? or that I would come to God in the best of my performances?

CHR. *Why, how dost thou think in this matter?*

IGN. Why, to be short, I think I must believe in Christ for Justification.

CHR. *How! think thou must believe in Christ, when thou seest not thy need of him! Thou neither seest thy original, or actual infirmities, but hast such an opinion of thyself, and of what thou doest, as plainly renders thee to be one that did never see a necessity of Christ's personal righteousness to justify thee before God: How then dost thou say, I believe in Christ?*

IGN. I believe well enough for all that.

CHR. *How doest thou believe?*

IGN. I believe that Christ died for sinners, and that I shall be justified before God from the curse, through his gracious acceptance of my obedience to his Law. Or thus, Christ makes my Duties that are Religious acceptable to his Father by virtue of his Merits; and so shall I be justified.

CHR. *Let me give an answer to this confession of thy faith.*

1. *Thou believest with a* Fantastical *Faith, for this faith is no where described in the Word.*

2. *Thou believest with a* False *Faith, because it taketh Justification from the personal righteousness of Christ, and applies it to thy own.*

3. *This faith maketh not Christ a Justifier of thy person, but of thy actions; and of thy person for thy actions' sake, which is false.*

4. *Therefore this faith is deceitful, even such as will leave thee under wrath, in the day of God Almighty. For true Justifying Faith puts the soul (as sensible of its lost condition by the Law) upon flying for refuge unto Christ's righteousness: (Which righteousness of* his, *is not an act of grace, by which he maketh for Justification* thy *obedience accepted with God, but* his *personal obedience to the Law in doing and suffering for us, what that required at our hands.) This righteousness, I say, true faith accepteth, under the skirt of which, the soul being shrouded, and by it presented as spotless before God, it is accepted, and acquit from condemnation.*

IGN. What! would you have us trust to what Christ in his own person has done without us! This conceit would loosen the reins of our lust, and tolerate us to live as we list. For what matter how we live, if we may be justified by Christ's personal righteousness from all, when we believe it?

CHR. Ignorance *is thy name, and as thy name is, so art thou; even this thy answer demonstrateth what I say.* Ignorant *thou art of what Justifying righteousness is, and as ignorant how to secure thy Soul through the faith of it, from the heavy wrath of God. Yea, thou also art ignorant of the true effects of saving faith in this righteousness of Christ, which is, to bow and win over the heart to God in Christ, to love his Name, his Word, Ways, and People; and not as thou ignorantly imaginest.*

HOPE. Ask him if ever he had Christ revealed to him from Heaven?

IGN. *What! You are a man for revelations! I believe that what both you, and all the rest of you say about that matter, is but the fruit of distracted brains.*

HOPE. Why man! Christ is so hid in God from the natural apprehensions of all flesh, that he cannot by any man be savingly known, unless God the Father reveals him to them.

IGN. *That is your faith, but not mine; yet mine I doubt not, is as good as yours: though I have not in my head so many whimsies as you.*

CHR. Give me leave to put in a word: You ought not so slightly to speak of this matter: for this I will boldly affirm (even as my good companion hath done) that no man can know Jesus Christ but by the Revelation of the Father: yea, and faith too, by which the soul layeth hold upon Christ (if it be right) must be wrought by the exceeding greatness of his mighty power; the working of which faith, I perceive, poor *Ignorance*, thou art ignorant of. Be awakened then, see thine own wretchedness, and fly to the Lord Jesus; and by his righteousness, which is the righteousness of God, (for he himself is God) thou shalt be delivered from condemnation.

IGN. *You go so fast, I cannot keep pace with you; do you go on before, I must stay awhile behind.*

Then they said,

> *Well* Ignorance, *wilt thou yet foolish be*
> *To slight good Counsel, ten times given thee?*
> *And if thou yet refuse it, thou shalt know*
> *Ere long the evil of thy doing so.*

Remember man in time, stoop, do not fear,
Good Counsel taken well, saves; therefore hear.
But if thou yet shalt slight it, thou wilt be
The loser (Ignorance) I'll warrant thee.

Then *Christian* addressed thus himself to his fellow.

CHR. Well, come my good *Hopeful*, I perceive that thou and I must walk by ourselves again.

So I saw in my Dream, that they went on apace before, and *Ignorance* he came hobbling after. Then said *Christian* to his companion, *It pities me much for this poor man, it will certainly go ill with him at last.*

HOPE. Alas, there are abundance in our Town in his condition; whole Families, yea, whole Streets, (and that of Pilgrims too) and if there be so many in our parts, how many think you, must there be in the place where he was born?

CHR. *Indeed the Word saith,* He hath blinded their eyes, lest they should see, &c. *But now we are by ourselves, what do you think of such men? Have they at no time, think you, convictions of sin, and so consequently fears that their state is dangerous?*

HOPE. Nay, do you answer that question yourself, for you are the elder man.

CHR. *Then I say sometimes (as I think) they may, but they being naturally ignorant, understand not that such convictions tend to their good; and therefore they do desperately seek to stifle them, and presumptuously continue to flatter themselves in the way of their own hearts.*

HOPE. I do believe as you say, that fear tends much to Men's good and to make them right, at their beginning to go on Pilgrimage.

CHR. *Without all doubt it doth, if it be right: for so says the word,* The fear of the Lord is the beginning of Wisdom.

HOPE. How will you describe right fear?

CHR. *True, or right fear, is discovered by three things.*

1. By its rise. It is caused by saving convictions for sin.

2. It driveth the soul to lay fast hold of Christ for Salvation.

3. It begetteth and continueth in the soul a great reverence of God, his word, and ways, keeping it tender, and making it afraid to turn from them, to the right hand, or to the left, to anything that may dishonour God, break its peace, grieve the Spirit, or cause the Enemy to speak reproachfully.

HOPE. Well said, I believe you have said the truth. Are we now almost got past the enchanted ground?

CHR. *Why, are you weary of this discourse?*

HOPE. No verily, but that I would know where we are.

CHR. *We have not now above two miles further to go thereon. But let us return to our matter. Now the Ignorant know not that such convictions that tend to put them in fear, are for their good, and therefore they seek to stifle them.*

HOPE. How do they seek to stifle them?

CHR. 1. They think that those fears are wrought by the Devil (though indeed they are wrought of God) and thinking so, they resist them, as things that directly tend to their overthrow. 2. They also think that these fears tend to the spoiling of their faith (when alas for them, poor men that they are! they have none at all), and therefore they harden their hearts against them. 3. They presume they ought not to fear, and therefore, in despite of them, wax presumptuously confident. 4. They see that these fears tend to take away from them their pitiful old self-holiness, and therefore they resist them with all their might.

HOPE. I know something of this myself; for before I knew myself it was so with me.

CHR. *Well, we will leave at this time our Neighbor* Ignorance *by himself, and fall upon another profitable question.*

HOPE. With all my heart, but you shall still begin.

CHR. *Well then, did you not know about ten years ago, one* Temporary *in your parts, who was a forward man in Religion then?*

HOPE. Know him! Yes, he dwelt in *Graceless*, a Town about two miles off of *Honesty*, and he dwelt next door to one *Turn-back*.

CHR. *Right, he dwelt under the same roof with him. Well, that man was much awakened once; I believe that then he had some sight of his sins, and of the wages that was due thereto.*

HOPE. I am of your mind, for (my House not being above three miles from him) he would ofttimes come to me, and that with many tears. Truly I pitied the man, and was not altogether without hope of him; but one may see it is not every one that cries, *Lord, Lord.*

CHR. *He told me once, That he was resolved to go on Pilgrimage as we go now; but all of a sudden he grew acquainted with one* Save-self, *and then he became a stranger to me.*

HOPE. Now since we are talking about him, let us a little enquire into the reason of the sudden backsliding of him and such others.

CHR. *It may be very profitable, but do you begin.*

HOPE. Well then, there are in my judgment four reasons for it.

WHY SOME GO BACK

1. Though the Consciences of such men are awakened, yet their minds are not changed: therefore when the power of guilt weareth away, that which provoked them to be Religious ceaseth. Wherefore they naturally turn to their own course again: even as we see the Dog that is sick of what he hath eaten, so long as his sickness prevails he vomits and casts up all; not that he doth this of a free mind (if we may say a Dog has a mind) but because it troubleth his Stomach; but now when his sickness is over, and so his Stomach eased, his desires being not at all alienate from his vomit, he turns him about and licks up all. And so it is true which is written, *The Dog is turned to his own vomit again.* This, I say, being hot for heaven, by virtue only of the sense and fear of the torments of Hell, as their sense of Hell and the fears

of damnation chills and cools, so their desires for Heaven and Salvation cool also. So then it comes to pass that when their guilt and fear is gone, their desires for Heaven and Happiness die, and they return to their course again.

2. Another reason is, they have slavish fears that do overmaster them. I speak now of the fears that they have of men: *For the fear of men bringeth a snare*. So then, though they seem to be hot for Heaven, so long as the flames of Hell are about their ears, yet when that terror is a little over, they betake themselves to second thoughts: namely, that 'tis good to be wise, and not to run (for they know not what) the hazard of losing all; or at least, of bringing themselves into unavoidable and unnecessary troubles: and so they fall in with the world again.

3. The shame that attends Religion lies also as a block in their way; they are proud and haughty, and Religion in their eye is low and contemptible. Therefore when they have lost their sense of Hell and wrath to come, they return again to their former course.

4. Guilt, and to meditate terror, are grievous to them, they like not to see their misery before they come into it. Though perhaps the sight of it first, if they loved that sight, might make them fly whither the righteous fly and are safe; but because they do, as I hinted before, even shun the thoughts of guilt and terror, therefore, when once they are rid of their awakenings about the terrors and wrath of God, they harden their hearts gladly, and chuse such ways as will harden them more and more.

CHR. *You are pretty near the business, for the bottom of all is, for want of a change in their mind and will. And therefore they are but like the Felon that standeth before the Judge; he quakes and trembles, and seems to repent most heartily: but the bottom of all is the fear of the Halter, not of any detestation of the offence; as is evident, because, let but this man have his liberty, and he will be a Thief, and so a Rogue still; whereas, if his mind was changed, he would be otherwise.*

HOPE. Now I have shewed you the reasons of their going back, do you show me the manner thereof.

CHR. *So I will willingly.*

1. They draw off their thoughts, all that they may, from the remembrance of God, Death, and Judgment to come.

2. Then they cast off by degrees private Duties, as Closet-Prayer, curbing their lusts, watching, sorrow for sin, and the like.

3. Then they shun the company of lively and warm Christians.

4. After that, they grow cold to publick Duty, as Hearing, Reading, Godly Conference, and the like.

5. Then they begin to pick holes, as we say, in the Coats of some of the Godly, and that devilishly; that they may have a seeming colour to throw Religion (for the sake of some infirmity they have spied in them) behind their backs.

6. Then they begin to adhere to, and associate themselves with carnal, loose, and wanton men.

7. Then they give way to carnal and wanton discourses in secret; and glad are they if they can see such things in any that are counted honest, that they may the more boldly do it through their example.

8. After this, they begin to play with little sins openly.

9. And then, being hardened, they shew themselves as they are. Thus being launched again into the gulf of misery, unless a Miracle of Grace prevent it, they everlastingly perish in their own deceivings.

Now I saw in my Dream, that by this time the Pilgrims were got over the Inchanted Ground, and entering in the Country of *Beulah*, whose Air was very sweet and pleasant, the way lying directly through it, they solaced themselves there for a season. Yea, here they heard continually the singing of Birds, and saw every day the flowers appear in the earth, and heard the voice of the Turtle in the Land. In this Country the Sun shineth night and day; wherefore this was beyond the Valley of the *Shadow of Death*, and also out of the reach of Giant *Despair;* neither could they from this place so much as see *Doubting-Castle*. Here they were within sight of the City they were going to: also here met them some of the Inhabitants thereof; for in this Land the shining Ones commonly walked, because it was upon the Borders of Heaven. In this Land also the contract between the Bride and the Bridegroom was renewed; Yea here, *as the Bridegroom rejoyceth over the Bride, so did their God rejoyce over them.* Here they had no want of Corn and Wine; for in this place they met with abundance of what they had sought for in all their Pilgrimage. Here they heard voices from out of the City, loud voices; saying, *Say ye to the daughter of* Zion, *Behold thy Salvation cometh, behold, his reward is with him.* Here all the Inhabitants of the Country called them, *The holy People*, *The redeemed of the Lord*, *Sought out*, etc.

Now as they walked in this Land, they had more rejoicing than in parts more remote from the Kingdom to which they were bound; and drawing near to the City, they had yet a more perfect view thereof. It was builded of Pearls and precious Stones, also the Street thereof was paved with Gold, so that by reason of the natural glory of the City, and the reflection of the Sun-beams upon it, *Christian*, with desire fell sick, *Hopeful* also had a fit or two of the same Disease. Wherefore here they lay by it a while, crying out because of their pangs, *If you see my Beloved, tell him that I am sick of love.*

But being a little strengthened, and better able to bear their sickness, they walked on their way, and came yet nearer and nearer, where were Orchards, Vineyards and Gardens, and their Gates opened into the High-way. Now as they came up to these places, behold the Gardener stood in the way; to whom the Pilgrims said, Whose goodly Vineyards and Gardens are these? He answered, They are the King's, and are planted here for his own delights, and also for the Solace of Pilgrims. So the Gardener had them into the Vineyards, and bid them refresh themselves with Dainties. He also shewed them *there* the King's walks, and the *Arbors* where he delighted to be. And here they tarried and slept.

Now I beheld in my Dream, that they talked more in their sleep at this time, than ever they did in all their Journey; and being in a muse thereabout, the Gardener said even to me Wherefore musest thou at the matter? It is the nature of the fruit of the Grapes of these Vineyards to go down so sweetly, as to cause the lips of them that are asleep to speak.

So I saw that when they awoke, they addressed themselves to go up to the City. But, as I said, the reflections of the Sun upon the City (for the City was pure Gold) was so extremely glorious, that they could not, as yet, with open face behold it, but through an *Instrument* made for that purpose. So I saw, that as they went on, there met them two men, in Raiment that shone like Gold, also their faces shone as the light.

These men asked the Pilgrims whence they came? and they told them; they also asked them, Where they had lodg'd, what difficulties, and dangers, what comforts and pleasures they had met in the way? and they told them. Then said the men that met them, You have but two difficulties more to meet with, and then you are in the City.

Christian then and his Companion asked the men to go along with them, so they told them they would; but, said they, you must obtain it by your own faith. So I saw in my Dream that they went on together till they came in sight of the Gate.

Now I further saw that betwixt them and the Gate was a River, but there was no Bridge to go over, the River was very deep. At the sight therefore of this River, the Pilgrims were much stounded; but the men that went with them, said, You must go through, or you cannot come at the Gate.

The Pilgrims then began to enquire if there was no other way to the Gate; to which they answered, Yes, but there hath not any, save two, to wit, *Enoch* and *Elijah*, been permitted to tread that path, since the foundation of the World, nor shall, until the last Trumpet shall sound. The Pilgrims, then, especially *Christian*, began to dispond in his mind, and looked this way and that, but no way could be found by them, by which they might escape the River. Then they asked the men, if the Waters were all of a depth? They said, No; yet they could not help them in that Case, for said they: *You shall find it deeper or shallower, as you believe in the King of the place.*

They then addressed themselves to the Water; and entring, *Christian* began to sink, and crying out to his good friend *Hopeful* he said, I sink in deep Waters, the Billows go over my head, all his Waves go over me, *Selah.*

Then said the other, Be of good cheer, my Brother, I feel the bottom, and it is good. Then said *Christian*, Ah my friend, the sorrows of death have compassed me about, I shall not see the Land that flows with Milk and Honey. And with that, a great darkness and horror fell upon *Christian*, so that he could not see before him; also here he in great measure lost his senses, so that he could neither remember nor orderly talk of any of those sweet refreshments that he had met with in the way of his Pilgrimage. But all the words that he spake still tended to discover that he had horror of mind, and hearty fears that he should die in that River, and never obtain entrance in at the Gate: here also, as they that stood by perceived, he was much in the troublesome thoughts of the sins that he had committed, both since and before he began to be a Pilgrim. 'Twas also observed, that he was troubled with apparitions of Hobgoblins and Evil Spirits. For ever and anon he would intimate so much by words. *Hopeful* therefore here had much ado to keep his Brother's head above water, yea sometimes he would be quite gone down, and then ere a while he would rise up again half dead. *Hopeful* also would endeavour to comfort him, saying, Brother, I see the Gate, and men standing by it to receive us. But *Christian* would answer: 'Tis you, 'tis you they wait for, you have been *Hopeful* ever since I knew you. And so have you, said he to *Christian.* Ah Brother, said he, surely if I was right, he would now arise to help me; but for my sins he hath brought me into the snare, and hath left me. Then said *Hopeful,* My Brother, you have quite forgot the Text, where it's said of the wicked, *There is no band in their death, but their strength is firm: they are not troubled as other men, neither are they plagued like other men.* These troubles and distresses that you go through in these Waters, are no sign that God hath forsaken you, but are sent to try you, whether you will call to mind that which heretofore you have received of his goodness, and live upon him in your distresses.

Christian Delivered from His Tears in Death

Then I saw in my Dream, that *Christian* was in a muse a while; to whom also *Hopeful* added this word, *Be of good cheer, Jesus Christ maketh thee whole:* And with that, *Christian* brake out with a loud voice, Oh I see him again! and he tells me, *When thou passest through the waters, I will be with thee, and through the Rivers, they shall not overflow thee.* Then they both took courage, and the enemy was after that as still as a stone, until they were gone over. *Christian* therefore presently found ground to stand upon; and so it followed that the rest of the River was but shallow. Thus they got over. Now upon the bank of the River, on the other side, they saw the two shining men again, who there waited for them. Wherefore being come up out of the River, they saluted them saying, *We are ministring Spirits, sent forth to minister for those that shall be Heirs of Salvation.* Thus they went along towards the Gate. Now you must note that the City stood upon a mighty hill, but the Pilgrims went up that hill *with ease,* because they had these two men to lead them up by the Arms; also they had left their *Mortal* Garments behind them in the River; for though they went in with them, they came out without them. They therefore went up here with much agility and speed, though the foundation upon which the City was framed was higher than the Clouds. They therefore went up through the regions of the Air, sweetly talking as they went, being comforted, because they safely got over the River, and had such glorious Companions to attend them.

The talk they had with the shining Ones, was about the Glory of the place, who told them, that the beauty, and glory of it was inexpressible. There, said they, is the Mount *Sion,* the Heavenly *Jerusalem,* the innumerable company of Angels, and the Spirits of Just men made perfect. You are going now, said they, to the Paradise of God, wherein you shall see the Tree of

Life, and eat of the never-fading fruits thereof: and when you come there you shall have white Robes given you, and your walk and talk shall be every day with the King, even all the days of Eternity. There you shall not see again such things as you saw when you were in the lower Region upon the Earth, to wit, sorrow, sickness, affliction, and death, *for the former things are passed away*. You are going now to *Abraham*, to *Isaac*, and *Jacob*, and to the Prophets; men that God hath taken away from the evil to come, and that are now resting upon their Beds, each one walking in his righteousness. The men then asked, What must we do in the holy place? To whom it was answered, You must there receive the comfort of all your toil, and have joy for all your sorrow; you must reap what you have sown, even the fruit of all your Prayers and Tears, and sufferings for the King by the way. In that place you must wear Crowns of Gold, and enjoy the perpetual sight and Visions of the *Holy One*, *for there you shall see him as he is*. There also you shall serve him continually with praise, with shouting and thanksgiving, whom you desired to serve in the World, though with much difficulty, because of the infirmity of your flesh. There your eyes shall be delighted with seeing, and your ears with hearing the pleasant voice of the mighty One. There you shall enjoy your friends again, that are got thither before you; and there you shall with joy receive even every one that follows into the Holy Place after you. There also you shall be cloathed with Glory and Majesty, and put into an equipage fit to ride out with the King of Glory. When he shall come with sound of Trumpet in the Clouds, as upon the wings of the wind, you shall come with him; and when he shall sit upon the Throne of Judgment, you shall sit by him; yea, and when he shall pass Sentence upon all the workers of Iniquity, let them be Angels or Men, you also shall have a voice in that Judgment, because they were his and your Enemies. Also when he shall again return to the City, you shall go too, with sound of Trumpet, and be ever with him.

Now while they were thus drawing towards the Gate, behold a company of the Heavenly Host came out to meet them: to whom it was said by the other two shining Ones, These are the men that have loved our Lord, when they were in the World; and that have left all for his holy Name, and he hath sent us to fetch them, and we have brought them thus far on their desired Journey; that they may go in and look their Redeemer in the face with joy. Then the Heavenly Host gave a great shout, saying, *Blessed are they that are called to the Marriage supper of the Lamb:*

There came out also at this time to meet them several of the King's Trumpeters, cloathed in white and shining Raiment, who with melodious noises and loud, made even the Heavens to echo with their sound. These Trumpeters saluted *Christian* and his Fellow with ten thousand welcomes from the world: and this they did with shouting, and sound of Trumpet.

This done, they compassed them round on every side; some went before, some behind, and some on the right hand, some on the left (as 'twere to guard them through the upper Regions) continually sounding as they went, with melodious noise, in notes on high; so that the very sight was to them that could behold it, as if Heaven itself was come down to meet them. Thus therefore they walked on together, and as they walked, ever and anon, these Trumpeters, even with joyful sound, would, by mixing their Musick with looks and gestures, still signify to *Christian* and his Brother, how welcome they were into their company, and with what gladness they came to meet them. And now were these two men, as 'twere, in Heaven, before they came at it; being swallowed up with the sight of Angels, and with hearing of their melodious notes. Here also they had the City itself in view, and they thought they heard all the Bells therein to ring, to welcome them thereto: but above all, the warm, and joyful thoughts that they had about their own dwelling there, with such company, and that for ever and ever. Oh! by what tongue or pen can their glorious joy be expressed? And thus they came up to the Gate.

Now when they were come up to the Gate, there was written over it, in Letters of Gold, *Blessed are they that do his commandments, that they may have right to the Tree of life; and may enter in through the Gates into the City.*

Then I saw in my Dream, that the shining men bid them call at the Gate; the which when they did, some from above looked over the Gate, to wit, *Enoch*, *Moses*, and *Elijah*, etc. to whom it was said, These Pilgrims are come from the City of *Destruction*, for the love that they bear to the King of this place: and then the Pilgrims gave in unto them each man his Certificate, which they had received in the beginning. Those therefore were carried in to the King, who when he had read them, said, Where are the men? To whom it was answered, They are standing without the Gate, the King then commanded to open the Gate, *That the righteous Nation*, said he, *that keepeth truth may enter in.*

Now I saw in my Dream, that these two men went in at the Gate; and lo, as they entered, they were transfigured, and they had Raiment put on that shone like Gold. There was also that met them with Harps and Crowns, and gave them to them; the Harp to praise withal, and the Crowns in token of honour. Then I heard in my Dream that all the Bells in the City rang again for joy, and that it was said unto them, *Enter ye into the joy of your Lord.* I also heard the men themselves, that they sang with a loud voice, saying, *Blessing, Honour, Glory, and Power, be to him that sitteth upon the Throne, and to the Lamb for ever and ever.*

Now just as the Gates were opened to let in the men, I looked in after them; and behold, the City shone like the Sun, the Streets also were paved with Gold, and in them walked many men, with Crowns on their heads, Palms in their hands, and golden Harps to sing praises withal.

There were also of them that had wings, and they answered one another without intermission, saying, *Holy, Holy, Holy, is the Lord.* And after that, they shut up the Gates: which when I had seen, I wished myself among them.

Now while I was gazing upon all these things, I turned my head to look back, and saw *Ignorance* come up to the River side; but he soon got over, and that without half that difficulty which the other two men met with.

For it happened that there was then in that place one *Vain-hope* a Ferryman, that with his Boat helped him over: so he, as the other I saw, did ascend the Hill to come up to the Gate, only he came alone; neither did any man meet him with the least encouragement. When he was come up to the Gate, he looked up to the writing that was above; and then began to knock, supposing that entrance should have been quickly administered to him. But he was asked by the men that lookt over the top of the Gate, Whence came you? and what would you have? He answered, I have eat and drank in the presence of the King, and he has taught in our Streets. Then they asked him for his Certificate, that they might go in and shew it to the King. So he fumbled in his bosom for one, and found none. Then said they, Have you none? But the man answered never a word. So they told the King, but he would not come down to see him, but commanded the two shining Ones that conducted *Christian* and *Hopeful* to the City, to go out and take *Ignorance* and bind him hand and foot, and have him away. Then they took him up, and carried him through the air to the door that I saw in the side of the Hill, and put him in there. Then I saw that there was a way to Hell, even from the Gates of Heaven, as well as from the City of *Destruction*. So I awoke, and behold it was a Dream.

FINIS

The Conclusion.

Now Reader, I have told my Dream to thee;
See if thou canst Interpret it to me;
Or to thyself, or Neighbor: but take heed
Of mis-interpreting; for that, instead
Of doing good, will but thyself abuse:
By mis-interpreting evil insues.

Take heed also, that thou be not extream,
In playing with the out-side *of my Dream:*
Nor let my figure, or similitude,
Put thee into a laughter or a feud;
Leave this for Boys *and* Fools; *but as for thee*
Do thou the substance of my matter see.

Put by the Curtains, look within my Vail;
Turn up my Metaphors and do not fail
There, if thou seekest them, such things to find,
As will be helpful to an honest mind.

What of my dross *thou findest there, be bold*
To throw away, but yet preserve the Gold.
What if my Gold be wrapped up in Ore?
None throws away the Apple for the Core.
But if thou shalt cast all away as vain,
I know not but 'twill make me dream again.

THE END.

THE

AUTHOR'S WAY OF SENDING FORTH HIS SECOND PART OF THE PILGRIM

Go, now my little Book, to every place
Where my first Pilgrim *has but shewn his Face:*
Call at their door: If any say, who's there?
Then answer thou, Christiana is here.
If they bid thee come in, *then enter thou*
With all thy boys. And then, as thou know'st how,
Tell who they are, also from whence they came;
Perhaps they'll know them, by their looks, or name.
But if they should not, ask them yet again
If formerly they did not Entertain
One Christian *a Pilgrim; If they say*
They did, and was delighted in his way:
Then let them know that those related were
Unto him, yea, his Wife and Children are.
Tell them that they have left their House and Home,
Are turned Pilgrims, seek a World to come:
That they have *met with hardships in the way,*
That they do *meet with troubles night and Day;*
That they have trod on Serpents, fought with Devils,
Have also overcome a many evils.
Yea tell them also of the next, who have
Of love to Pilgrimage *been stout and brave*
Defenders of that way, and how they still
Refuse this World, to do their Father's will.
Go, tell them also of those dainty things,
That Pilgrimage *unto the* Pilgrim *brings.*
Let them acquainted be, too, how they are
Beloved of their King, under his care;
What goodly Mansions *for them he provides,*
Tho' they meet with rough Winds, and swelling tides.
How brave a calm they will enjoy at last,
Who to *their Lord, and* by *his ways hold fast.*
Perhaps with heart and hand they will embrace
Thee, as they did my firstling, and will grace

Thee, and thy fellows, with such cheer and fair,
As shew will, they of Pilgrims *lovers are.*

1. *Object.*

But how if they will not believe of me
That I am truly thine, cause some there be
That counterfeit the Pilgrim, and his name,
Seek by disguise to seem the very same.
And by that means have wrought themselves into
The hands and houses of I know not who.

Answer.

'Tis true, some have of late, to Counterfeit
My *Pilgrim, to their own, my Title set;*
Yea others, half my name and Title too
Have stitched to their Book, to make them do;
But yet they by their Features *do declare*
Themselves not mine to be, whosee'r they are.
If such thou meet'st with, then thine only way
Before the mall, is, to say out thy say,
In thine own native Language, which no man
Now useth, nor with ease dissemble can.
If after all, they still of you shall doubt,
Thinking that you like Gipsies *go about,*
In naughty-wise the country to defile,
Or that you seek good People to beguile
With things unwarrantable: send for me
And I will Testifie you Pilgrims *be;*
Yea, I will Testifie that only you
My Pilgrims *are: and that alone will do.*

2. *Object.*

But yet, perhaps, I may enquire for him
Of those that wish him damned life and limb.
What shall I do, when I at such a door,
For *Pilgrims* ask, and they shall rage the more?

Answer.

Fright not thyself, my Book, for such Bugbears
Are nothing else but ground for groundless fears:
My Pilgrim's *Book has travell'd Sea and Land,*
Yet could I never come to understand,
That it was slighted, or turned out of Door
By any Kingdom, were they Rich or Poor.

In France *and* Flanders *where men kill each other,*
My Pilgrim *is esteem'd a Friend, a Brother.*
In Holland *too, 'tis said, as I am told,*
My Pilgrim *is with some, worth more than Gold.*
Highlanders, *and* Wild-Irish *can agree*
My Pilgrim *should familiar with them be.*
'Tis in New-England *under such advance,*
Receives there so much loving Countenance,
As to be Trim'd, new-Cloth'd, and Deck'd with Gems,
That it may shew its Features, and its limbs,
Yet more, so comely doth my Pilgrim *walk,*
That of him thousands daily Sing and talk.
If you draw nearer home, it will appear
My Pilgrim *knows no ground of shame, or fear;*
City, and Country will him entertain,
With Welcome Pilgrim. *Yea, they can't refrain*
From smiling, if my Pilgrim *be but by,*
Or shews his head in any Company.
Brave Galants do my Pilgrim *hug and love,*
Esteem it much, yea, value it above
Things of a greater bulk, yea, with delight,
Say my Lark's-leg *is better than a* Kite.
Young Ladies, and young Gentlewomen too,
Do no small kindness to my Pilgrim *shew;*
Their Cabinets, their Bosoms, and their Hearts
My Pilgrim *has, 'cause he to them imparts,*
His pretty riddles, in such wholesome strains
As yields them profit double to their pains
Of reading. Yea, I think I may be bold
To say some prize him far above their Gold.
The very Children that do walk the street,
If they do but my Holy Pilgrim *meet,*
Salute him will, will wish him well, and say,
He is the only Stripling *of the Day.*
They that have never seen him, yet admire
What they have heard of him, and much desire
To have his company, and hear him tell
Those Pilgrim stories *which he knows so well.*
Yea, some who did not love him at the first,
But call'd him Fool, *and* Noddy, *say they must*
Now they have seen *and* heard *him, him commend,*
And to those whom they love, they do him send.
Wherefore my Second Part, *thou need'st not be*
Afraid to shew thy Head: none can hurt thee,
That wish but well to him, that went before;
'Cause thou com'st after with a second store

Of things as good, as rich, as profitable,
For Young, for Old, for Stagg'ring and for Stable.

3. *Object.*

But some there be that say, he laughs too loud;
And some do say his Head is in a Cloud.
Some say, his Words and Stories are so dark,
They know not how, by them, to find his mark.

Answer.

One may (I think) say, both his laughs and cries,
May well be guess't at by his watry Eyes.
Some things are of that Nature as to make
One's fancie Checkle while his Heart doth ake:
When Jacob *saw his* Rachel *with the Sheep,*
He did at the same time both kiss and weep.
Whereas some say a Cloud is in his Head,
That doth but shew how Wisdom's covered
With its own mantles: and to stir the mind
To a search after what it fain would find,
Things that seem to be hid in words obscure,
Do but the Godly mind the more allure,
To study what those Sayings should contain,
That speak to us in such a Cloudy strain.
I also know, a dark Similitude
Will on the Fancie more itself intrude,
And will stick faster in the Heart and Head,
Than things from Similes not borrowed.
Wherefore, my Book, let no discouragement
Hinder thy travels. Behold, thou art sent
To Friends not foes: to Friends that will give place
To thee, thy Pilgrims and thy words embrace.
Besides, what my first Pilgrim *left conceal'd,*
Thou my brave Second Pilgrim, *hast reveal'd;*
What Christian *left lock't up and went his way,*
Sweet Christiana *opens with her Key.*

4. *Object.*

But some love not the method of your first:
Romance they count it, throw't away as dust,
If I should meet with such, what should I say?
Must I slight them as they slight me, or nay?

Answer.

My Christiana, *if with such thou meet,*
By all-means in all loving-wise, them greet;

Render them not reviling for revile;
But if they frown, I prethee on them smile:
Perhaps 'tis Nature, or some ill report
Has made them thus *dispise, or* thus *retort.*
Some love no Cheese, some love no Fish, and some
Love not their Friends, nor their own House or Home;
Some start at Pig, slight Chicken, love not Fowl,
More than they love a Cuckow or an Owl:
Leave such, my Christiana, *to their choice,*
And seek those, who to find thee will rejoyce;
By no means strive, but in all humble wise,
Present thee to them in thy Pilgrim's *guise.*
Go then, my little Book, and shew to all
That entertain, and bid thee welcome shall,
What thou shalt keep close, shut up from the rest,
And wish what thou shalt shew them may be blest
To them for good, may make them chuse to be
Pilgrims, better by far, than thee or me.
Go then, I say, tell all men who thou art;
Say, I am Christiana, *and my part*
Is now with my four Sons to tell you what
It is for men to take a Pilgrim's *lot.*
Go also tell them who, *and what they be,*
That now do go on Pilgrimage *with thee;*
Say, here's my neighbor Mercy, *she is one,*
That has long-time with me a Pilgrim *gone:*
Come see her in her Virgin *Face, and learn*
'Twixt Idle ones and Pilgrims *to discern.*
Yea let young Damsels learn of her to prize,
The world which is to come, in any wise.
When little Tripping *Maidens follow God,*
And leave old doting Sinners to his Rod;
'Tis like those Days wherein the young ones cried
Hosannah *to whom old ones did deride.*
Next tell them of old Honest, *who you found*
With his white hairs treading the Pilgrim's ground;
Yea, tell them how plain-hearted this *man was,*
How after his good Lord he bare his Cross:
Perhaps with some gray Head this may prevail,
With Christ to fall in Love, and Sin bewail.
Tell them also how Master Fearing *went*
On Pilgrimage, and how the time he spent
In Solitariness, with Fears and Cries,
And how at last, he won the Joyful Prize.
He was *a good Man, though much down in Spirit,*
He is *a good Man, and doth Life inherit.*

Tell them of Master Feeblemind *also,*
Who, not before, but still behind would go;
Shew them also how he had like been slain,
And how one Great-Heart *did his life regain:*
This man was true of Heart, tho' weak in grace,
One might true Godliness read in his Face.
Then tell them of Master Ready-to-halt,
A Man with Crutches, but much without fault:
Tell them how Master Feeblemind *and he*
Did love, and in Opinions *much agree.*
And let all know, tho' weakness was their chance
Yet sometimes one could Sing, *the other* Dance.
Forget not Master Valiant-for-the-Truth,
That Man of courage, tho' a very Youth.
Tell every one his Spirit was so stout,
No Man could ever make him face about;
And how Great-Heart *and he could not forbear,*
But put down Doubting Castle, slay Despair.
Overlook not Master Despondancie,
Nor Much-afraid *his Daughter, tho' they lie*
Under such Mantles as may make them look
(With some) as if their God had them forsook.
They softly went, but sure, and at the end,
Found that the Lord of Pilgrims *was their Friend.*
When thou hast told the World of all these things,
Then turn about, my Book, and touch these strings;
Which, if but *touched will such Musick make,*
They'll make a Cripple dance, a Giant quake.
These Riddles that lie couch't within thy breast,
Freely propound, expound: and for the rest
Of thy mysterious lines, let them remain
For those whose nimble Fancies shall them gain.

Now may this little Book a blessing be,
To those that love this little Book and me;
And may its buyer have no cause to say,
His money is but lost or thrown away:
Yea may this Second Pilgrim *yield that Fruit*
As may with each good Pilgrim's *fancie suit;*
And may it perswade some that go astray,
To turn their Foot and Heart to the right way.

Is the Hearty Prayer
of the Author,
JOHN BUNYAN.

THE PILGRIM'S PROGRESS:

IN THE SIMILITUDE OF A

DREAM

THE SECOND PART

Courteous Companions, some-time since, to tell you my Dream that I had of *Christian*, the Pilgrim, and of his dangerous Journey toward the Cœlestial Country, was pleasant to me and profitable to you. I told you then also what I saw concerning his *Wife* and *Children*, and how unwilling they were to go with him on Pilgrimage; insomuch that he was forced to go on his Progress without them, for he durst not run the danger of that destruction which he feared would come by staying with them, in the City of Destruction. Wherefore as I then shewed you, he left them and departed.

Now it hath so happened, thorough the Multiplicity of Business, that I have been much hindred and kept back from my wonted Travels into those Parts whence he went, and so could not till now obtain an opportunity to make further enquiry after whom he left behind, that I might give you an account of them. But having had some concerns that way of late, I went down again thitherward. Now having taken up my Lodgings in a Wood about a mile off the place, as I slept I dreamed again.

And as I was in my Dream, behold, an aged Gentleman came by where I lay; and because he was to go some part of the way that I was travelling, methought I got up and went with him. So as we walked, and as Travellers usually do, it was as if we fell into discourse, and our talk happened to be about *Christian* and his Travels: For thus I began with the old man.

Sir, said I, *what Town is that there below, that lieth on the left hand of our way?*

Then said Mr. *Sagacity*, for that was his name, It is the City of *Destruction*, a populous place, but possessed with a very ill conditioned and idle sort of People.

I thought that was that City, quoth I, *I went once myself through that Town, and therefore know that this report you give of it, is true.*

SAG. Too true, I wish I could speak truth in speaking better of them that dwell therein.

Well Sir, quoth I, *then I perceive you to be a well meaning man: and so one that takes pleasure to hear and tell of that which is good; pray did you never hear what happened to a man some time ago in this Town (whose name was* Christian) *that went on Pilgrimage up towards the higher Regions?*

SAG. Hear of him! Ay, and I also heard of the Molestations, Troubles,

Wars, Captivities, Cries, Groans, Frights and Fears that he met with, and had in his Journey. Besides, I must tell you, all our Country rings of him; there are but few Houses that have heard of him and his doings, but have sought after and got the *Records* of his Pilgrimage; yea, I think I may say, that that his hazardous Journey, has got a many well-wishers to his ways.

Christians Called Fools

For though when he was here, he was *Fool* in every man's mouth, yet now he is gone, he is highly commended of all. For, 'tis said he lives bravely where he is: yea many of them, that are resolved never to run his hazards, yet have their mouths water at his gains.

They may, quoth I, *well think, if they think any thing that is true, that he liveth well where he is, for he now lives at and in the Fountain of Life, and has what he has without labour and sorrow, for there is no grief mixed therewith.*

Sag. Talk! The people talk strangely about him. Some say, that he *now walks in White*, that he has a Chain of Gold about his Neck, that he has a Crown of Gold, beset with Pearls, upon his head. Others say that the shining ones that sometimes shewed themselves to him in his Journey, are become his Companions, and that he is as familiar with them in the place where he is, as here one Neighbor is with another. Besides 'tis confidently affirmed concerning him, that the King of the place where he is, has bestowed upon him already a very rich and pleasant Dwelling at Court, and that he every day eateth and drinketh, and walketh, and talketh with him, and receiveth of the smiles and favours of him that is Judge of all there. Moreover, it is expected of some that his Prince, the Lord of that Country, will shortly come into *these* parts, and will know the reason, if they can give any, why his Neighbors set so little by him, and had him so much in derision when they perceived that he would be a Pilgrim.

For they say, that now he is so in the affections of his Prince, and that his *Sovereign* is so much concerned with the *Indignities* that were cast upon *Christian* when he became a Pilgrim, that he will look upon all as if done unto himself; and no marvel, for 'twas for the love that he had to his Prince, that he ventured as he did.

I dare say, quoth I, *I am glad on it; I am glad for the poor man's sake, for that now he has rest from his labour, and for that he now reapeth the benefit of his Tears with Joy: and for that he has got beyond the Gun-shot of his Enemies, and is out of the reach of them that hate him. I also am glad for that a rumour of these things is noised abroad in this Country. Who can tell but that it may work some good effect on some that are left behind? But, pray Sir, while it is fresh in my mind, do you hear anything of his Wife and Children? poor hearts, I wonder in my mind what they do!*

Sag. Who! *Christiana*, and her Sons! They are like to do as well as did *Christian* himself, for though they all play'd the Fool at the first, and would by no means be perswaded by either the tears or the entreaties of *Christian*, yet second thoughts have wrought wonderfully with them; so they have packt up and are also gone after him.

Better and better, quoth I. *But what! Wife and Children and all?*

SAG. 'Tis true, I can give you an account of the matter, for I was upon the spot at the instant, and was thoroughly acquainted with the whole affair.

Then, said I, *a man it seems may report it for a truth?*

SAG. You need not fear to affirm it, I mean that they are all gone on Pilgrimage, both the good Woman and her four Boys. And being we are, as I perceive, going some considerable way together, I will give you an account of the whole of the matter.

This *Christiana* (for that was her name from the day that she with her Children betook themselves to a *Pilgrim's* life,) after her Husband was gone *over the River*, and she could hear of him no more, her thoughts began to work in her mind. First, for that she had lost her Husband, and for that the loving bond of that Relation was utterly broken betwixt them. For you know, said he to me, nature can do no less but entertain the living with many a heavy Cogitation in the remembrance of the loss of loving Relations. This therefore of her Husband did cost her many a Tear. But this was not all, for *Christiana* did also begin to consider with herself, whether her unbecoming behaviour towards her Husband, was not one cause that she saw him no more, and that in such sort he was taken away from her. And upon this, came into her mind by *swarms*, all her unkind, unnatural, and ungodly Carriages to her dear Friend: which also clogged her Conscience, and did load her with guilt. She was moreover much broken with calling to remembrance the restless Groans, brinish Tears and self-bemoanings of her Husband, and how she did harden her heart against all his entreaties, and loving perswasions (of her and her Sons) to go with him, yea, there was not any thing that *Christian* either said to her, or did before her, all the while that his burden did hang on his back, but it returned upon her like a flash of lightning, and rent the Caul of her Heart in sunder. Specially that bitter outcry of his, *What shall I do to be saved*, did ring in her ears most dolefully.

Then said she to her Children, Sons, we are all undone. I have sinned away your Father, and he is gone; he would have had us with him; but I would not go myself, I also have hindred you of Life. With that the boys fell all into Tears, and cried out to go after their Father. Oh! Said *Christiana*, that it had been but our lot to go with him, then had it fared well with us beyond what 'tis like to do now. For tho' I formerly foolishly imagin'd concerning the troubles of your Father, that they proceeded of a foolish Fancy that he had, or for that he was overrun with Melancholy Humours; yet now 'twill not out of my mind, but that they sprang from another cause, to wit, for that the Light of Light was given him, by the help of which, as I perceive, he has escaped the Snares of Death. Then they all wept again, and cryed out: Oh, Wo worth the day.

The next night, *Christiana* had a Dream, and behold she saw as if a broad Parchment was opened before her in which were recorded the sum of her ways, and the times, as she thought, lookt *very black upon her*. Then she cried out aloud in her sleep, *Lord have Mercy upon me a Sinner*, and the little Children heard her.

After this she thought she saw two very ill-favoured ones standing by her Bed-side, and saying, *What shall we do with this Woman? For she cries out for Mercy waking and sleeping: If she be suffered to go on as she begins, we shall lose her as we have lost her Husband.* Wherefore we must by one way or other, seek to take her off from the thoughts of what shall be hereafter: else all the World cannot help it, but she will become a Pilgrim.

Now she awoke in a great Sweat; also a trembling was upon her, but after a while she fell to sleeping again. And then she thought she saw *Christian* her Husband in a place of Bliss among many *Immortals*, with an *Harp* in his Hand, standing and playing upon it before one that sate on a Throne with a Rainbow about his Head. She saw also as if he bowed his Head with his Face to the Pav'd-work that was under the Prince's Feet, saying, *I heartily thank my Lord and King for bringing of me into this Place.* Then shouted a company of them that stood round about, and harped with their Harps: but no man living could tell what they said, but *Christian* and his Companions.

Next morning when she was up, and prayed to God, and talked with her Children a while, one knocked hard at the door; to whom she spake out saying, *If thou comest in God's name, come in.* So he said *Amen*, and opened the Door, and saluted her with *Peace be to this House.* The which when he had done, he said, *Christiana*, knowest thou wherefore I am come? Then she blusht and trembled, also her heart began to wax warm with desires to know whence he came, and what was his Errand to her. So he said unto her; my name is *Secret*, I dwell with those that are high. It is talked of where I dwell, as if thou had'st a desire to go thither: also there is a report that thou art aware of the evil thou hast formerly done to thy Husband in hardening of thy Heart against his way, and in keeping of these thy Babes in their Ignorance. *Christiana*, the merciful one has sent me to tell thee that he is a God ready to forgive, and that he taketh delight to multiply to pardon offences. He also would have thee know that he inviteth thee to come into his presence, to his Table, and that he will feed thee with the Fat of his House, and with the Heritage of *Jacob* thy Father.

There is *Christian*, thy Husband *that was*, with Legions more his Companions, ever beholding that face that doth minister Life to beholders: and they will be all glad when they shall hear the sound of thy feet step over thy Father's Threshold.

Christiana Is Overcome

Christiana at this was greatly abashed in herself, and bowing her head to the ground, this *Visitor* proceeded and said, *Christiana!* Here is also a Letter for thee which I have brought from thy Husband's King. So she took it and opened it, but it smelt after the manner of the best Perfume, also it was written in Letters of Gold. The contents of the Letter was, *That the King would have her do as did* Christian *her Husband; for that was the way to come to his City, and to dwell in his Presence with Joy, for ever.* At this the good Woman was overcome. So she cried out to her *Visitor, Sir, will you carry me and my Children with you, that we also may go and worship this King.*

Then said the Visitor, *Christiana! The bitter is before the sweet:* Thou must through Troubles, as did he that went before thee, enter this Cœlestial City. Wherefore I advise thee, to do as did *Christian* thy Husband: go to the *Wicket Gate* yonder, over the Plain, for that stands in the head of the way up which thou must go, and I wish thee all good speed. Also I advise that thou put this Letter in thy Bosom. That thou read therein to thyself and to thy Children, until you have got it by root-of-Heart. For it is one of the Songs that thou must Sing while thou art in this House of thy Pilgrimage. Also this thou must deliver in at the *further* Gate.

Now I saw in my Dream, that this Old Gentleman, as he told me this Story, did himself seem to be greatly affected therewith. He moreover proceeded and said, So *Christiana* called her Sons together, and began thus to Address herself unto them. My Sons, I have as you may perceive, been of late under much exercise in my Soul about the Death of your Father; not for that I doubt at all of his Happiness; for I am satisfied now that he is well. I have also been much affected with the thoughts of mine own State and yours, which I verily believe is by nature miserable. My Carriages also to your Father in his distress, is a great load to my Conscience. For I hardened both my own heart and yours against him, and refused to go with him on Pilgrimage.

The thoughts of these things would now kill me out-right; but that for a Dream which I had last night, and but that for the encouragement that this Stranger has given me this Morning. Come my Children, let us pack up, and be gone to the Gate that leads to the Cœlestial Country, that we may see your Father, and be with him, and his Companions in Peace, according to the Laws of that Land.

Then did her Children burst into Tears for Joy that the Heart of their Mother was so inclined. So their *Visitor* bid them farewell: and they began to prepare to set out for their Journey.

But while they were thus about to be gone, two of the women that were *Christiana's* Neighbors, came up to her House and knocked at her door. To whom she said as before, *If you come in God's name, come in.* At this the Women were stun'd, for this kind of Language, they used not to hear, or to perceive to drop from the Lips of *Christiana.* Yet they came in; but behold they found the good Woman a preparing to be gone from her House.

So they began and said, *Neighbor, pray what is your meaning by this.*

Christiana answered and said to the eldest of them whose name was Mrs. *Timorous*, I am preparing for a Journey. (This *Timorous* was daughter to him that met *Christian* upon the Hill *Difficulty:* and would a had him gone back for fear of the Lions.)

TIMOROUS. For what Journey I pray you?

CHRIS. *Even to go after my good Husband;* and with that she fell a weeping.

TIM. I hope not so, good Neighbor, pray for your poor Children's sakes, do not so unwomanly cast away yourself.

CHRIS. *Nay, my Children shall go with me; not one of them is willing to stay behind.*

TIM. I wonder in my very heart, what, or who has brought you into this mind.

CHRIS. Oh, Neighbor, knew you but as much as I do, I doubt not but that you would go with me.

TIM. *Prithee what new knowledge hast thou got that so worketh off thy mind from thy Friends, and that tempteth thee to go nobody knows where?*

CHRIS. Then *Christiana* reply'd, I have been sorely afflicted since my Husband's departure from me; but specially since he went *over the River*. But that which troubleth me most, is my churlish carriages to him when he was under his distress. Besides, I am *now*, as he was *then;* nothing will serve me but going on Pilgrimage. I was a dreaming last night that I saw him. O that my Soul was with him. He dwelleth in the presence of the King of the Country, he sits and eats with him at his Table, he is become a Companion of *Immortals,* and has a House now given him to dwell in, to which, the best Palaces on Earth, if compared, seem to me to be but as a Dunghill. The Prince of the Place has also sent for me with promise of entertainment if I shall come to him; his messenger was here even now, and has brought me a Letter, which invites me to come. And with that she pluck'd out her Letter, and read it, and said to them, what now will you say to this?

TIM. *Oh the madness that has possessed thee and thy Husband, to run yourselves upon such difficulties! You have heard, I am sure, what your Husband did meet with, even in a manner at the first step, that he took on his way, as our Neighbor* Obstinate *can yet testifie; for he went along with him, yea and* Pliable *too until they, like wise men, were afraid to go any further. We also heard over and above, how he met with the Lions, Apollyon, the Shadow of Death, and many other things. Nor is the danger that he met with at* Vanity-fair *to be forgotten by thee. For if he, tho' a man, was so hard put to it, what canst thou, being but a poor Woman do? Consider also that these four sweet Babes are thy Children, thy Flesh and thy Bones. Wherefore, though thou shouldest be so rash as to cast away thyself: Yet for the sake of the Fruit of thy Body, keep thou at home.*

But *Christiana* said unto her, tempt me not, my Neighbor: I have now a price put into mine hand to get gain, and I should be a Fool of the greatest size, if I should have no heart to strike in with the opportunity. And for that you tell me of all these Troubles that I am like to meet with in the way, they are so far off from being to me a discouragement, that they shew I am in the right. *The bitter must come before the sweet,* and that also will make the sweet the sweeter. Wherefore since you came not to my House *in God's name,* as I said, I pray you to be gone, and not to disquiet me farther.

Then *Timorous* also revil'd her, and said to her Fellow, come Neighbor

Mercy, let's leave her in her own hands, since she scorns our Counsel and Company. But *Mercy* was at a stand, and could not so readily comply with her Neighbor: and that for a two-fold reason. First, her Bowels yearned over *Christiana:* so she said within herself, If my Neighbor will needs be gone, I will go a little way with her, and help her. Secondly, her Bowels yearned over her own Soul, (for what *Christiana* had said, had taken some hold upon her mind.) Wherefore she said within herself again, I will yet have more talk with this *Christiana*, and if I find Truth and Life in what she shall say, myself with my Heart shall also go with her. Wherefore *Mercy* began thus to reply to her Neighbor *Timorous*.

MERCY. Neighbor, *I did indeed come with you to see* Christiana *this Morning, and since she is, as you see, a taking of her last farewell of her Country, I think to walk this Sunshine Morning, a little way with her to help her on the way*. But she told her not of her second Reason, but kept that to herself.

TIM. Well, I see you have a mind to go a fooling too: but take heed in time, and be wise: while we are out of danger we are out; but when we are in, we are in. So Mrs. *Timorous* returned to her House, and *Christiana* betook herself to her Journey. But when *Timorous* was got home to her House, she sends for some of her Neighbors, to wit, Mrs. *Bats-eyes*, Mrs. *Inconsiderate*, Mrs. *Light-mind* and Mrs. *Know-nothing*. So when they were come to her House, she falls to telling of the story of *Christiana*, and of her intended Journey. And thus she began her Tale.

TIM. Neighbors, having had little to do this morning, I went to give *Christiana* a visit, and when I came at the door, I knocked, as you know 'tis our Custom. And she answered, *If you come in God's name, come in.* So in I went, thinking all was well. But when I came in, I found her preparing herself to depart the Town, she and also her Children. So I asked her what was her meaning by that, and she told me in short, that she was now of a mind to go on Pilgrimage, as did her Husband. She told me also a Dream that she had, and how the King of the Country where her Husband was, had sent her an inviting Letter to come thither.

Then said Mrs. Know-nothing, *and what do you think she will go?*

TIM. Ay, go she will, what ever come on't; and methinks I know it by this, for that which was my great Argument to perswade her to stay at home, (to wit, the Troubles she was like to meet with in the way) is one great Argument with her to put her forward on her Journey. For she told me in so many words, *The bitter goes before the sweet.* Yea, and for as much as it so doth, it makes the sweet the sweeter.

MRS. BATS-EYES. Oh this blind and foolish Woman, said she, will she not take warning by her Husband's Afflictions? For my part, I see if he was here again he would rest him content in a whole Skin, and never run so many hazards for nothing.

MRS. *Inconsiderate* also replied, saying, Away with such Fantastical Fools from the Town, a good riddance, for my part, I say, of her. Should she stay where she dwells, and retain this her mind, who could live quietly by her?

for she will either be dumpish or unneighborly, or talk of such matters as no wise body can abide. Wherefore for my part I shall never be sorry for her departure, let her go and let better come in her room; 'twas never a good World since these whimsical Fools dwelt in it.

Then Mrs. *Light-mind* added as followeth. Come put this kind of Talk away. I was Yesterday at Madame *Wanton's*, where we were as merry as the Maids. For who do you think should be there, but I, and Mrs. *Love-the-flesh*, and three or four more with Mr. *Lechery*, Mrs. *Filth*, and some others. So there we had Musick and dancing, and what else was meet to fill up the pleasure. And I dare say my Lady herself is an admirably well bred Gentlewoman, and Mr. *Lechery* is as pretty a fellow.

Christiana Would Have Her Neighbor with Her

By this time *Christiana* was got on her way, and *Mercy* went along with her. So as they went, her Children being there also, *Christiana* began to discourse. And, *Mercy*, said *Christiana*, I take this as an unexpected favour, that thou shouldest set foot out of Doors with me to accompany me a little in my way.

Mercy. *Then said young* Mercy *(for she was but young,) If I thought it would be to purpose to go with you, I would never go near the Town any more.*

Chris. Well *Mercy*, said *Christiana*, cast in thy Lot with me. I well know what will be the end of our Pilgrimage, my Husband is where he would not but be, for all the Gold in the *Spanish* Mines. Nor shalt thou be rejected, tho' thou goest but upon *my Invitation*. The King who hath sent for me and my Children, is one that delighteth in *Mercy*. Besides, if thou wilt, I will hire thee, and thou shalt go along with me as my servant. Yet we will have all things in common betwixt thee and me; only go along with me.

Mercy. *But how shall I be ascertained that I also shall be entertained? Had I this hope, but from one that can tell, I would make no stick at all, but would go being helped by him that can help, tho' the way was never so tedious.*

Chris. Well, loving *Mercy*, I will tell thee what thou shalt do; go with me to the *Wicket Gate*, and there I will further enquire for thee, and if there thou shalt not meet with encouragement, I will be content that thou shalt return to thy place. I also will pay thee for thy Kindness which thou shewest to me and my Children in thy accompanying of us in our way as thou doest.

Mercy. *Then will I go thither, and will take what shall follow, and the Lord grant that my Lot may there fall even as the King of Heaven shall have his heart upon me.*

Christiana, then was glad at her heart, not only that she had a Companion, but also for that she had prevailed with this poor Maid to fall in love with her own Salvation. So they went on together, and *Mercy* began to weep. Then said *Christiana*, wherefore weepeth my Sister so?

Mercy. *Alas! said she, who can but lament that shall but rightly consider what a State and Condition my poor Relations are in, that yet remain in our sinful Town? and that which makes my grief the more heavy, is because they have no Instructor, nor any to tell them what is to come.*

Chris. Bowels becometh Pilgrims. And thou dost for thy Friends, as my good *Christian* did for me when he left me; he mourned for that I would not heed nor regard him, but his Lord and ours did gather up his Tears, and put them into his Bottle, and now both I, and thou, and these my sweet Babes, are reaping the Fruit and benefit of them. I hope, *Mercy*, these Tears of thine will not be lost, for the truth hath said; *That they that sow in Tears shall reap in Joy, in singing. And he that goeth forth and weepeth, bearing precious seed, shall doubtless come again with rejoicing, bringing his Sheaves with him.*

Then said *Mercy*,

> *Let the most blessed be my guide,*
> *If't be his blessed Will,*
> Unto *his Gate*, into *his fold,*
> Up to *his Holy Hill.*
> *And let him never suffer me,*
> *To swerve, or turn aside*
> *From his free grace, and Holy ways,*
> *What ere shall me betide.*
> *And let him gather them of mine,*
> *That I have left behind.*
> *Lord make them pray they may be thine,*
> *With all their heart and mind.*

The Slough of Dispond

Now my old Friend proceeded and said, But when *Christiana* came up to the Slough of *Dispond*, she began to be at a stand: For, said she, This is the place in which my dear Husband had like to a been smothered with Mud. She perceived also, that notwithstanding the Command of the King to make this place for Pilgrims good, yet it was rather worse than formerly. So I asked if that was true? Yes, said the Old Gentleman, too true. For that many there be that pretend to be the King's Labourers; and that say they are for mending the King's Highway, that bring *Dirt* and *Dung* instead of Stones, and so mar instead of mending. Here *Christiana* therefore with her Boys, did make a stand: but said *Mercy*, come let us venture, only let us be wary. Then they looked well to the *Steps*, and made a shift to get staggeringly over.

Yet *Christiana* had like to a been in, and that not once nor twice. Now they had no sooner got over, but they thought they heard words that said unto them, *Blessed is she that believeth, for there shall be a performance of the things that have been told her from the Lord.*

Then they went on again; and said *Mercy* to *Christiana*, Had I as good ground to hope for a loving reception at the *Wicket-Gate*, as you, I think no Slough of *Dispond* would discourage me.

Well, said the other, you know *your sore*, and I know *mine;* and good friend, we shall all have enough evil before we come at our Journey's end.

For can it be imagined, that the people that design to attain such excellent Glories *as we do,* and that are so envied that Happiness *as we are;* but that we shall meet with what Fears and Scares, with what troubles and afflictions they can possibly assault us with, that hate us?

And now Mr. *Sagacity* left me to Dream out my Dream by my self. Wherefore me-thought I saw *Christiana,* and *Mercy* and the *Boys* go all of them up to the Gate. To which when they were come, they betook themselves to a short debate, about *how* they must manage their calling at the Gate, and what should be said to him that did open to them. So it was concluded, since *Christiana* was the eldest, that she should knock for entrance, and that she should speak to him that did open, for the rest. So *Christiana* began to knock, and as her poor Husband did, she *knocked,* and *knocked* again. But instead of any that answered, they all thought that they heard, as if a Dog came barking upon them. A Dog and a great one too, and this made the Women and Children afraid. Nor durst they for a while to knock any more, for fear the *Mastiff* should fly upon them. Now therefore they were greatly tumbled up and down in their minds, and knew not what to do. Knock they durst not, for fear of the Dog: go back they durst not for fear that the Keeper of that Gate should espy them, as they so went, and should be offended with them. At last they thought of knocking again, and knocked more vehemently than they did at the first. Then said the Keeper of the Gate, who is there? So the *Dog* left off to bark and he opened unto them.

Then *Christiana* made low obeisance, and said, Let not our Lord be offended with his Handmaidens for that we have knocked at his Princely Gate. Then said the Keeper, Whence come ye, and what is that you would have?

Christiana answered, we are come from whence *Christian* did come, and upon the same *Errand* as he; to wit, to be, if it shall please you, graciously admitted by this Gate, into the way that leads to the Cœlestial City. And I answer, my Lord in the next place, that I am *Christiana* once the Wife of *Christian,* that now is gotten above.

With that the Keeper of the Gate did marvel, saying, *What is she become now a Pilgrim, that but a while ago abhorred that Life?* Then she bowed her Head, and said, Yes; and so are these my sweet Babes also.

Then he took her by the hand, and let her in and said also, *Suffer the little Children to come unto me,* and with that he shut up the Gate. This done, he called to a Trumpeter that was above over the Gate, to entertain *Christiana* with shouting and sound of Trumpet for joy. So he obeyed and sounded, and filled the Air with his Melodious Notes.

Now all this while, poor *Mercy* did stand without, trembling and crying for fear that she was rejected. But when *Christiana* had gotten admittance for herself and her Boys, then she began to make intercession for Mercy.

CHRIS. *And she said, my Lord, I have a Companion of mine that stands yet without, that is come hither upon the same account as myself. One that is much dejected in her mind, for that she comes, as she thinks, without sending for, whereas I was sent to by my Husband's King to come.*

Now *Mercy* began to be very impatient, for each *Minute* was as long to her as an hour, Wherefore she prevented *Christiana* from a fuller interceding for her, by knocking at the Gate herself. And she knocked *then* so loud, that she made *Christiana* to start. Then said the Keeper of the Gate who is there? And said *Christiana*, it is my Friend.

So he opened the Gate, and looked out; but *Mercy* was fallen down without in a Swoon, for she fainted and was afraid that no Gate would be opened to her.

Then he took her by the hand, and said, *Damsel*, I bid thee arise.

O Sir, said she, I am faint, there is scarce Life left in me. But he answered, That one once said, *When my soul fainted within me, I remembered the Lord, and my prayer came in unto thee, into thy Holy Temple.* Fear not, but stand upon thy Feet, and tell me wherefore thou art come.

MERCY. I am come, for *that*, unto which I was never invited, as my Friend *Christiana* was. *Hers* was from the King, and *mine* was but from *her:* Wherefore I fear I presume.

Did she desire thee to come with her to this Place?

MERCY. Yes. And as my Lord sees, I am come. And if there is any Grace or forgiveness of Sins to spare, I beseech that I thy poor Handmaid may be partaker thereof.

Then he took her again by the Hand, and led her gently in, and said, I pray for all them that believe on me, by what means soever they come unto me. Then said he to those that stood by, Fetch something, and give it *Mercy* to smell on, thereby to stay her fainting. So they fetcht her a *Bundle* of *Myrrh*, and awhile after she was revived.

And now was *Christiana* and her Boys and *Mercy* received of the Lord at the head of the way, and spoke kindly unto by him.

Then said they yet further unto him, We are sorry for our Sins, and beg of our Lord his Pardon, and further information what we must do.

I grant Pardon, said he, by word, and deed; by word in the promise of forgiveness: by deed in the way I obtained it. Take the first from my Lips with a Kiss, and the other, as it shall be revealed.

Now I saw in my Dream that he spake many good words unto them, whereby they were greatly gladded. He also had them up to the top of the Gate and shewed them by what *deed* they were saved, and told them withal, that that sight they would have again as they went along in the way, to their comfort.

So he left them awhile in a Summer Parlor below, where they entred into talk by themselves. And thus *Christiana* began, *O Lord! How glad am I, that we are got in hither!*

MERCY. So you well may; but I, of all, have cause to leap for joy.

CHRIS. *I thought, one time, as I stood at the Gate (because I had knocked and none did answer) that all our Labour had been lost. Specially when that ugly Cur made such a heavy barking against us.*

MERCY. But my worst Fears was after I saw that you was taken in to his favour, and that I was left behind. Now thought I, 'tis fulfilled which is written. *Two women shall be Grinding together, the one shall be taken, and the other left.* I had much ado to forbear crying out, Undone, Undone.

And afraid I was to knock any more; but when I looked up to what was written over the Gate, I took Courage. I also thought that I must either knock again or die. So I knocked; but I cannot tell how, for my spirit now *struggled* betwixt life and death.

CHRIS. *Can you not tell how you knocked? I am sure your knocks were so earnest, that the very sound of them made me start, I thought I never heard such knocking in all my Life. I thought you would a come in by violent hands, or a took the Kingdom by storm.*

MERCY. Alas, to be in my Case, who that so was, could but a done so? You saw that the Door was shut upon me, and that there was a most cruel *Dog* thereabout. Who, I say, that was so faint hearted as I, that would not a knocked with all their might? But pray what said my Lord to my rudeness, was he not angry with me?

CHRIS. *When he heard your lumbring noise, he gave a wonderful innocent smile. I believe what you did pleas'd him well enough. For he shewed no sign to the contrary. But I marvel in my heart why he keeps such a Dog; had I known that afore, I fear I should not have had heart enough to have ventured myself in this manner. But now we are in, we are in, and I am glad with all my heart.*

MERCY. I will ask if you please next time he comes down, why he keeps such a filthy Cur in his Yard. I hope he will not take it amiss.

Ay, do, said the Children, and perswade him to hang him, for we are afraid he will bite us when we go hence.

So at last he came down to them again, and *Mercy* fell to the Ground on her Face before him and worshipped, and said, Let my Lord accept of the Sacrifice of praise which I now offer unto him, with the calves of my lips.

So he said unto her, Peace be to thee, stand up.

But she continued upon her Face and said, *Righteous art thou O Lord when I plead with thee, yet let me talk with thee of thy Judgments, Wherefore dost thou keep so cruel a Dog in thy Yard, at the sight of which, such Women and Children as we, are ready to fly from thy Gate for fear?*

He answered, and said; *That Dog* has another Owner, he also is kept close in another man's ground; only my Pilgrims hear his barking. He belongs to the Castle which you see there at a distance, but can come up to the walls of this place. He has frighted many an honest Pilgrim from worse to better, by the great voice of his roaring. Indeed he that owneth him, doth not keep him of any good will to me or mine; but with intent to keep the Pilgrims from coming to me, and that they may be afraid to knock at this Gate for entrance. Sometimes also he has broken out, and has *worried* some that I love; but I take all at present patiently. I also give my Pilgrims timely help; so they are not delivered up to his power to do to them what his Doggish nature would prompt him to. But what! My purchased one, I tro, hadst thou known never so much before hand, thou wouldst not a been afraid of a Dog.

The Beggars that go from Door to Door, will, rather than they will lose a supposed Alms, run the hazard of the bawling, barking, and biting too of a Dog: and shall a Dog, a Dog in another Man's Yard, a Dog whose barking I turn to the profit of Pilgrims, keep any from coming to me? I deliver them from the *Lions,* their Darling from the power of the Dog.

MERCY. Then said *Mercy, I confess my Ignorance: I spake what I understood not: I acknowledge* that *thou doest all things well.*

CHRIS. Then *Christiana* began to talk of their Journey, and to enquire after the way. So he fed them, and washed their feet, and set them in the way of his Steps, according as he had dealt with her Husband before.

So I saw in my Dream, that they walkt on in their way, and had the weather very comfortable to them.

Then *Christiana* began to sing, saying:

Bless't be the Day that I began,
A Pilgrim for to be.
And blessed also be that man,
That thereto moved me.
'Tis true, 'twas long ere I began
To seek to live for ever:
But now I run fast as I can,
'Tis better late, *than* never.
Our Tears *to joy, our* fears *to Faith*
Are turned, as we see:
Thus our beginning (*as one saith*)
Shews, what our end will be.

THE DEVIL'S GARDEN

Now there was, on the other side of the Wall that fenced in the way up which *Christiana* and her Companions was to go, a Garden; and that Garden belonged to him whose was that *Barking Dog* of whom mention was made before. And some of the Fruit-Trees that grew in that Garden shot their branches over the Wall, and being mellow, they that found them did gather them up and oft eat of them to their hurt. So *Christiana's* Boys, as Boys are apt to do, being pleas'd with the Trees, and with the fruit that did hang thereon, did *plash* them and began to eat. Their Mother did also chide them for so doing; but still the Boys went on.

Well, said she, my Sons, you Transgress, for that fruit is none of ours: but she did not know that they did belong to the Enemy. *I'll* warrant you if she had, she would a been ready to die for fear. But that passed, and they went on their way. Now by that they were gone about two Bow's-shot from the place that let them into the way, they espyed two very *ill-favoured ones* coming down apace to meet them. With that *Christiana,* and *Mercy* her Friend covered themselves with their Vails, and so kept on their Journey: the Children also went on before, so that at last they met together. Then they that came down to meet them, came just up to the Women, as if they would embrace them: but *Christiana* said, Stand back, or go peaceably by as you should. Yet these two, as men that are deaf, regarded not *Christiana's* words; but began to lay hands upon them; at that *Christiana* waxing very wroth, spurned at them with her feet. *Mercy* also, as well as she could, did what she could to shift them. *Christiana* again, said to them, Stand back and be gone, for we have no Money to lose, being Pilgrims as ye see, and such too as live upon the Charity of our Friends.

ILL-FA. Then said one of the two of the Men, we make no assault upon you for Money, but are come out to tell you, that if you will but grant one small request which we shall ask, we will make Women of you for ever.

CHRIS. Now *Christiana* imagining what they should mean, made answer again, *We will neither hear nor regard, nor yield to what you shall ask. We are in haste, cannot stay, our Business is a Business of Life and Death.* So again she and her Companions made a fresh assay to go past them. But they letted them in their way.

ILL-FA. And they said, we intend no hurt to your lives, 'tis another thing we would have.

CHRIS. Ay, quoth *Christiana,* you would have us Body and Soul, for I know 'tis for that you are come; but we will die rather upon the spot, than suffer ourselves to be brought into such Snares as shall hazard our wellbeing hereafter. And with that they both *Shrieked* out, and cryed Murder, Murder: and so put themselves under those Laws that are provided for the Protection of Women. But the men still made their approach upon them, with design to prevail against them: They therefore cryed out again.

Now they being, as I said, not far from the Gate in at which they came, their voice was heard from where they was, thither. Wherefore some of the House came out, and knowing that it was *Christiana's* Tongue, they made haste to her relief. But by that they was got within sight of them, the Women was in a very great scuffle, the Children also stood crying by. Then did he that came in for their relief, call out to the Ruffians saying, What is that thing that you do? Would you make my Lord's People to transgress? He also attempted to take them: but they did make their escape over the Wall into the Garden of the Man, to whom the great Dog belonged, so the Dog became their Protector. This *Reliever* then came up to the Women, and asked them how they did. So they answered, we thank thy Prince, pretty well, only we have been somewhat affrighted, we thank thee also for that thou camest in to our help, for otherwise we had been overcome.

RELIEVER. So after a few more words, this *Reliever* said, as followeth: *I marvelled much when you was entertained at the Gate above, being ye knew that ye were but weak Women, that you petitioned not the Lord there for a Conductor. Then might you have avoided these Troubles, and Dangers; for he would have granted you one.*

CHRIS. Alas said *Christiana,* we were so taken with our present blessing, that Dangers to come were forgotten by us; besides, who could have thought that so near the King's Palace there should have lurked such naughty ones? Indeed it had been well for us had we asked our Lord for one; but since our Lord knew 'twould be for our profit I wonder he sent not one along with us.

RELIEVER. *It is not always necessary to grant things not asked for, lest by so doing they become of little esteem; but when the want of a thing is felt, it then comes under, in the Eyes of him that feels it, that estimate that properly is its due, and so consequently will be thereafter used. Had my Lord granted you a Conductor, you would not neither so have bewailed that oversight of yours in not asking for one, as now you have occasion to do. So all things work for good, and tend to make you more wary.*

CHRIS. Shall we go back again to my Lord, and confess our folly and ask one?

RELIEVER. *Your Confession of your folly, I will present him with: to go back again, you need not. For in all places where you shall come, you will find no want at all, for in every of my Lord's Lodgings which he has prepared for the reception of his Pilgrims, there is sufficient to furnish them against all attempts whatsoever. But, as I said, he will be inquired of by them to do it for them; and 'tis a poor thing that is not worth asking for.* When he had thus said, he went back to his place, and the Pilgrims went on their way.

MERCY. Then said *Mercy*, what a sudden blank is here? I made account we had now been past all danger, and that we should never see sorrow more.

CHRIS. Thy *Innocency*, my Sister, said *Christiana* to *Mercy*, may excuse thee much; but as for me, my fault is so much the greater, for that I saw this danger before I came out of the Doors, and yet did not provide for it, where Provision might a been had. I am therefore much to be blamed.

MERCY. *Then said* Mercy, *how knew you this before you came from home? pray open to me this Riddle.*

CHRIS. Why, I will tell you. Before I set Foot out of Doors, one Night, as I lay in my Bed, I had a Dream about this. For methought I saw two men, as like these as ever the World they could look, stand at my *Bed's-feet*, plotting how they might prevent my Salvation. I will tell you their very words. They said, ('twas when I was in my Troubles,) *What shall we do with this Woman? For she cries out waking and sleeping for forgiveness: if she be suffered to go on as she begins, we shall lose her as we have lost her Husband.* This you know might have made me take heed, and have provided when Provision might a been had.

MERCY. *Well*, said *Mercy*, *as by this neglect, we have an occasion ministred unto us, to behold our own imperfections: so our Lord has taken occasion thereby, to make manifest the Riches of his Grace. For he, as we see, has followed us with an unasked kindness, and has delivered us from their hands that were stronger than we, of his mere good pleasure.*

Thus now when they had talked away a little more time, they drew nigh to an House which stood in the way, which House was built for the relief of Pilgrims, as you will find more fully related in the first part of these Records of the *Pilgrim's Progress.*

TALK IN THE INTERPRETER'S HOUSE

So they drew on towards the House, (the House of the Interpreter) and when they came to the Door they heard a great talk in the House, they then gave ear, and heard, as they thought, *Christiana* mentioned by name. For you must know that there went along, even before her, a talk of her and her Children's going on Pilgrimage. And this thing was the more pleasing to them, because they had heard that she was *Christian's* Wife; that Woman who was some time ago, so unwilling to hear of going on Pilgrimage. Thus therefore they stood still and heard the good people within commending her, who they little thought stood at the Door. At last *Christiana* knocked as she had done at the Gate before. Now when she had knocked, there came to the Door a young Damsel, and opened the Door and looked, and behold two Women was there.

DAMS. *Then said the Damsel to them, With whom would you speak in this place?*

CHRIS. *Christiana* answered, we understand that this is a privileged place for those that are become Pilgrims, and we now at this Door are such. Wherefore we pray that we may be partakers of that for which we at this time are come; for the day, as thou seest, is very far spent, and we are loath to night to go any further.

DAMS. Pray what may I call your name, that I may tell it to my Lord within?

CHRIS. My name is *Christiana,* I was the Wife of that Pilgrim that some years ago did travel this way, and these be his four Children. This Maiden also is my Companion, and is going on Pilgrimage too.

INNOCENT. Then ran *Innocent* in (for that was her name) and said to those within, Can you think who is at the Door! There is *Christiana* and her Children, and her Companion, all waiting for entertainment here. Then they leaped for Joy, and went and told their Master. So he came to the Door, and looking upon her, he said, *Art thou that* Christiana *whom* Christian *the Good-man, left behind him, when he betook himself to a Pilgrim's Life.*

CHRIS. I am that Woman that was so hard-hearted as to slight my Husband's troubles, and that left him to go on in his Journey alone, and these are his four Children; but now I also am come, for I am convinced that no way is right but this.

INTER. *Then is fulfilled that which also is written of the Man that said to his Son, go work to day in my Vineyard, and he said to his Father, I will not; but afterwards repented and went.*

CHRIS. Then said *Christiana,* So be it, *Amen.* God made it a true saying upon me, and grant that I may be found at the last of him, in peace without spot and blameless.

INTER. *But why standest thou thus at the Door? Come in thou Daughter of* Abraham, *we was talking of thee but now: for tidings have come to us before, how thou art become a Pilgrim. Come Children, come in; come Maiden, come in;* so he had them all into the House.

So when they were within, they were bidden sit down and rest them, the which when they had done, those that attended upon the Pilgrims in the House came into the Room to see them. And one smiled, and another smiled, and they all smiled for Joy that *Christiana* was become a Pilgrim. They also looked upon the Boys, they stroaked them over the Faces with the Hand, in token of their kind reception of them: they also carried it lovingly to *Mercy*, and bid them all welcome into their Master's House.

After a while, because Supper was not ready, the *Interpreter* took them into his *Significant* Rooms, and shewed them what *Christian*, *Christiana's* Husband had seen sometime before. Here therefore they saw the *Man* in the *Cage*, the *Man* and his Dream, the man that cuts his ways thorough his Enemies, and the Picture of the biggest of them all: together with the rest of those things that were then so profitable to *Christian*.

This done, and after these things had been somewhat digested by *Christiana*, and her company, the *Interpreter* takes them apart again, and has them first into a Room, *where was a man that could look no way but downwards, with a Muckrake in his hand. There stood also one over his head with a Cœlestial Crown in his Hand, and proffered to give him that Crown for his Muckrake; but the man did neither look up, nor regard; but raked to himself the Straws, the small Sticks, and Dust of the Floor.*

Then said *Christiana*, *I perswade myself that I know somewhat the meaning of this: For this is a Figure of a man of this World: Is it not, good Sir?*

INTER. Thou hast said the right, said he, and his *Muckrake*, doth shew his Carnal mind. And whereas thou seest him rather give heed to rake up Straws and Sticks, and the Dust of the Floor, than to what he says that calls to him from above with the Cœlestial Crown in his Hand; it is to show, that Heaven is but as a Fable to some, and that things here are counted the only things substantial. Now whereas it was also shewed thee, that the man could look no way but downwards, it is to let thee know that earthly things when they are with Power upon Men's minds, quite carry their hearts away from God.

CHRIS. *Then said* Christiana, *O! deliver me from this Muckrake.*

INTER. That Prayer, said the *Interpreter*, has lain by till 'tis almost rusty: *Give me not Riches*, is scarce the Prayer of one of ten thousand. Straws, and Sticks, and Dust, with most, are the great things now looked after.

With that *Mercy*, and *Christiana* wept, and said, It is alas! too true.

When the *Interpreter* had shewed them this, he has them into the very best Room in the House, (a very brave Room it was) so he bid them look round about, and see if they could find anything profitable there. Then they looked round and round, for there was nothing there to be seen but a very great *Spider* on the Wall, and that they overlookt.

MERCY. *Then said* Mercy, *Sir, I see nothing; but* Christiana *held her peace.*

INTER. But said the *Interpreter*, look again: she therefore lookt again and said, Here is not any thing, but an *ugly Spider*, who hangs by her Hands upon the Wall. Then said he, Is there but one *Spider* in all this spacious room? Then the water stood in *Christiana's* Eyes, for she was a Woman quick of apprehension: and she said, Yes, Lord, there is here more than one. Yea, and *Spiders* whose Venom is far more destructive than that which is in her. The *Interpreter* then looked pleasantly upon her, and said, Thou hast said the Truth. This made *Mercy* blush, and the Boys to cover their Faces: For they all began now to understand the Riddle.

Then said the *Interpreter* again, *The Spider taketh hold with her hands as you see, and is in King's Palaces*. And wherefore is this recorded, but to shew you, that how full of the Venom of Sin soever you be, yet you may by the hand of Faith lay hold of, and dwell in the best Room that belongs to the King's House above?

CHRIS. I thought, said *Christiana*, of something of this; but I could not imagine it all. I thought that we were like *Spiders*, and that we looked like ugly Creatures, in what fine Room soever we were. But that by this *Spider*, this venomous and ill-favoured Creature, we were to learn *how to act Faith*, that came not into my mind. And yet she has taken hold with her hands, as I see, and dwells in the best Room in the House. God has made nothing in vain.

Then they seemed all to be glad; but the water stood in their Eyes. Yet they looked one upon another, and also bowed before the *Interpreter*.

He had them then into another Room where was a Hen and Chickens, and bid them observe a while. So one of the Chickens went to the Trough to drink, and every time she drank she lift up her head and her eyes towards Heaven. See, said he, what this little Chick doth, and learn of her to acknowledge whence your Mercies come, by receiving them with looking up. Yet again, said he, observe and look: So they gave heed, and perceived that the Hen did walk in a fourfold Method towards her Chickens. 1. She had a *common call*, and that she hath all day long. 2. She had a *special call*, and that she had but sometimes. 3. She had a *brooding note*, and 4. she had an *out-cry*.

Now, said he, compare this *Hen* to your King, and these Chickens to his obedient ones. For answerable to her, himself has his Methods, which he walketh in towards his People. By his common call, *he gives nothing;* by his special call, he always *has something to give;* he has also a brooding voice, *for them that are under his Wing;* and he has an out-cry, to give *the Alarm when he seeth the Enemy come*. I chose, my Darlings, to lead you into the Room where such things are because you are Women and they are easy for you.

CHRIS. And Sir, said *Christiana*, pray let us see some more: So he had them into the Slaughter-house, where was a *Butcher* a killing of a Sheep: and behold the Sheep was quiet, and took her Death patiently. Then said the *Interpreter:* you must learn of this Sheep, to suffer, and to put up wrongs without murmurings and complaints. Behold how quietly she takes her Death, and without objecting she suffereth her Skin to be pulled over her Ears. Your King doth call you his Sheep.

After this, he led them into his Garden, where was great variety of Flowers; and he said, do you see all these? So *Christiana* said, yes. Then said he again, Behold the Flowers are divers in *Stature*, in *Quality*, and *Colour*, and *Smell*, and *Virtue*, and some are better than some: also where the Gardener has set them, there they stand, and quarrel not one with another.

Again, he had them into his Field, which he had sowed with Wheat, and

Corn: but when they beheld, the tops of all was cut off, only the Straw remained. He said again, This Ground was Dunged, and Plowed, and Sowed; but what shall we do with the Crop? Then said *Christiana*, burn some and make muck of the rest. Then said the *Interpreter* again, Fruit you see is that thing you look for, and for want of that you condemn it to the Fire, and to be trodden under foot of men. Beware that in this you condemn not yourselves.

Of the Robin and the Spider

Then, as they were coming in from abroad, they espied a little *Robin* with a great *Spider* in his mouth. So the Interpreter said, look here. So they looked, and *Mercy* wondred; but *Christiana* said, what a disparagement is it to such a little pretty Bird as the *Robin-red-breast* is, he being also a Bird above many, that loveth to maintain a kind of Sociableness with Man? I had thought they had lived upon crumbs of Bread, or upon other such harmless matter. I like him worse than I did.

The *Interpreter* then replied, This *Robin* is an Emblem very apt to set forth some Professors by; for to sight they are as this *Robin*, pretty of Note, Colour and Carriage, they seem also to have a very great Love for Professors that are sincere; and above all other to desire to associate with, and to be in their Company, as if they could live upon the good Man's Crumbs. They pretend also that therefore it is, that they frequent the House of the Godly, and the appointments of the Lord: but when they are by themselves, *as the Robin*, they can catch and gobble up *Spiders*, they can change their Diet, drink *Iniquity*, and swallow down *Sin* like Water.

So when they were come again into the House, because Supper as yet was not ready, *Christiana* again desired that the *Interpreter* would either *shew* or *tell* of some other things that are Profitable.

Then the *Interpreter* began and said, *The fatter the Sow is, the more she desires the Mire; the fatter the Ox is, the more gamesomly he goes to the Slaughter; and the more healthy the lusty man is, the more prone he is unto Evil.*

There is a desire in Women to go neat and fine, and it is a comely thing to be adorned with that, that in God's sight is of great price.

'Tis easier watching a night or two, than to sit up a whole year together: So 'tis easier for one to begin to profess well, than to hold out as he should to the end.

Every Ship-Master, when in a Storm, will willingly cast that overboard that is of the smallest value in the Vessel; but who will throw the best out first? none but he that feareth not God.

One leak will sink a Ship, and one Sin will destroy a Sinner.

He that forgets his Friend is ungrateful unto him: but he that forgets his Saviour is unmerciful to himself.

He that lives in Sin, and looks for Happiness hereafter, is like him that soweth Cockle, and thinks to fill his Barn with Wheat or Barley.

If a man would live well, let him fetch his last day to him, and make it always his company-Keeper.

Whispering and change of thoughts, proves that Sin is in the World.

If the World, which God sets light by, is counted a thing of that worth with men: what is Heaven which God commendeth?

If the life that is attended with so many troubles, is so loth to be let go by us, What is the life above?

Every Body will cry up the goodness of Men; but who is there that is, as he should, affected with the Goodness of God?

We seldom sit down to Meat, but we eat, and leave: So there is in Jesus Christ more Merit and Righteousness than the whole World has need of.

When the *Interpreter* had done, he takes them out into his Garden again, and had them to a Tree whose *inside* was Rotten, and gone, and yet it grew and had Leaves. Then said *Mercy*, what means this? This Tree, said he, whose *outside* is fair, and whose *inside* is rotten; it is to which many may be compared that are in the Garden of God: who with their mouths speak high in behalf of God, but indeed will do nothing for him: whose Leaves are fair, but their heart Good for nothing but to be *Tinder* for the Devil's *Tinder-Box.*

Now supper was ready, the Table spread, and all things set on the Board; so they sate down and did eat when one had given thanks. And the *Interpreter* did usually entertain those that lodged with him with Musick at Meals, so the Minstrels played. There was also one that did Sing. And a very fine voice he had.

His song was this.

The Lord is only my Support,
And he that doth me feed:
How can I then want anything,
Whereof I stand in need?

When the Song and Musick was ended, the *Interpreter* asked *Christiana*, *What it was that at first did move her to betake herself to a Pilgrim's Life?*

Christiana answered: *First*, the loss of my Husband came into my mind, at which I was heartily grieved: but all that was but natural Affection. Then after that, came the Troubles, and Pilgrimage of my Husband's into my mind, and also how like a Churl I had carried it to him as to that. So guilt took hold of my mind, and would have drawn me into the *Pond;* but that opportunely I had a Dream of the well-being of my Husband, and a Letter sent me by the King of that Country where my Husband dwells, to come to him. The Dream and the Letter together so wrought upon my mind, that they forced me to this way.

INTER. *But met you with no opposition afore you set out of Doors?*

CHRIS. Yes, a Neighbor of mine one Mrs. *Timorous.* (She was akin to him that would have perswaded my Husband to go back for fear of the Lions.) She all-to-be-fooled me for, as she called it, my intended desperate adventure; she also urged what she could, to dishearten me to it, the hardship and

Troubles that my Husband met with in the way; but all this I got over pretty well. But a Dream that I had of two ill-lookt ones, that I thought did plot how to make me miscarry in my Journey, that hath troubled me much: Yea, it still runs in my mind, and makes me afraid of every one that I meet, lest they should meet me to do me a mischief, and to turn me out of the way. Yea, I may tell my Lord, tho' I would not have everybody know it, that between this and the Gate by which we got into the way, we were both so sorely assaulted, that we were made to cry out Murder, and the two that made this assault upon us, were like the two that I saw in my Dream.

A Question Put to Mercy

Then said the *Interpreter*, Thy beginning is good, thy latter end shall greatly increase. So he addressed himself to *Mercy*, and said unto her, *And what moved thee to come hither, sweet-heart?*

Mercy. Then *Mercy* blushed and trembled, and for a while continued silent.

Inter. *Then said he, be not afraid, only believe, and speak thy mind.*

Mercy. So she began and said. Truly Sir, my want of Experience, is that that makes me covet to be in silence, and that also that fills me with fears of coming short at last. I cannot tell of Visions, and Dreams, as my friend *Christiana* can; nor know I what it is to mourn for my refusing of the Counsel of those that were good Relations.

Inter. *What was it then, dear-heart, that hath prevailed with thee to do as thou hast done?*

Mercy. Why, when our friend here, was packing up to go from our Town, I and another went accidentally to see her. So we knocked at the Door and went in. When we were within, and seeing what she was doing, we asked what was her meaning. She said she was sent for to go to her Husband, and then she up and told us, how she had seen him in a Dream, dwelling in a curious place among *Immortals* wearing a Crown, playing upon a Harp, eating and drinking at his Prince's Table, and singing Praises to him for bringing him thither, &c. Now methought, while she was telling these things unto us, my heart burned within me. And I said in my Heart, if this be true, I will leave my Father and my Mother, and the land of my Nativity, and will, if I may, go along with *Christiana*.

So I asked her further of the truth of these things, and if she would let me go with her? For I saw now that there was no dwelling, but with the danger of ruin, any longer in our Town. But yet I came away with a heavy heart, not for that I was unwilling to come away; but for that so many of my Relations were left behind. And I am come with all the desire of my heart, and will go, if I may, with *Christiana* unto her Husband, and his King.

Inter. Thy setting out is good, for thou hast given credit to the truth. Thou art a *Ruth*, who did for the love that she bore to *Naomi*, and to the Lord her God, leave Father and Mother, and the land of her Nativity to come out, and go with a People that she knew not heretofore, *The Lord recompence thy work, and a full reward be given thee of the Lord God of* Israel, *under whose wings thou art come to trust.*

Now Supper was ended, and Preparations was made for Bed, the Women were laid singly alone, and the Boys by themselves. Now when *Mercy* was in Bed, she could not sleep for joy, for that now her doubts of missing at last were removed further from her than ever they were before. So she lay blessing and praising God who had had such favour for her.

In the Morning they arose with the *Sun*, and prepared themselves for their departure: but the *Interpreter* would have them tarry awhile, for, said he, you must orderly go from hence. Then said he to the Damsel that had first opened unto them, Take them and have them into the Garden to the *Bath*, and there wash them, and make them clean from the soil which they have gathered by travelling. Then *Innocent* the Damsel took them and had them into the Garden, and brought them to the *Bath:* so she told them that there they must wash and be clean, for so her Master would have the Women to do that called at his House as they were going on *Pilgrimage*. They then went in and washed, yea they and the Boys and all, and they came out of that *Bath* not only sweet, and clean; but also much enlivened and strengthened in their Joints. So when they came in they looked fairer a deal, than when they went out to the washing.

When they were returned out of the Garden from the *Bath*, the *Interpreter* took them and looked upon them and said unto them, *fair as the Moon*. Then he called for the *Seal* wherewith they used to be *Sealed* that were washed in his *Bath*. So the *Seal* was brought, and he set his Mark upon them, that they might be known in the Places whither they were yet to go: Now the seal was the contents and sum of the Passover which the Children of *Israel* did eat when they came out from the Land of *Egypt*, and the mark was set between their Eyes. This seal greatly added to their Beauty, for it was an Ornament to their Faces. It also added to their gravity and made their Countenances more like them of Angels.

Then said the *Interpreter* again to the Damsel that waited upon these Women, Go into the Vestry and fetch out Garments for these People: so she went and fetched out white Raiment, and laid it down before him; so he commanded them to put it on. *It was fine Linen, white and clean.* When the Women were thus adorned they seemed to be a Terror one to the other. For that they could not see that glory each one on herself, which they could see in each other. Now therefore they began to esteem each other better than themselves. For you are fairer than I am, said one, and you are more comely than I am, said another. The Children also stood amazed to see into what fashion they were brought.

The *Interpreter* then called for a *Man-Servant* of his, one *Great-heart*, and bid him take *Sword*, and *Helmet*, and *Shield*, and take these my Daughters, said he, and conduct them to the House called *Beautiful*, at which place they will rest next. So he took his Weapons, and went before them, and the *Interpreter* said, God speed. Those also that belonged to the Family sent them away with many a good wish. So they went on their way, and sung,

This place has been our second Stage,
Here we have heard and seen
Those good things that from Age to Age,
To others hid have been.
The Dunghill-raker, Spider, Hen,
The Chicken too to me
Hath taught a Lesson, let me then
Conformed to it be.
The Butcher, Garden, and the Field,
The Robin, and his bait,
Also the Rotten-tree doth yield
Me Argument of Weight;
To move me for to watch and pray,
To strive to be sincere,
To take my Cross up day by day,
And serve the Lord with fear.

Now I saw in my Dream that they went on, and *Great-heart* went before them, so they went and came to the place where *Christian's* Burthen fell off his Back, and tumbled into a Sepulchre. Here then they made a pause, and here also they blessed God. Now said *Christiana*, it comes to my mind what was said to us at the Gate, to wit, that we should have Pardon, by *Word* and *Deed;* by *Word*, that is, by the promise; by *Deed*, to wit, in the way it was obtained. What the promise is, of that I know something: but what is it to have Pardon by deed, or in the way that it was obtained, Mr. *Great-heart*, I suppose you know; wherefore if you please let us hear your discourse thereof.

GREAT-HEART. Pardon by the deed done, is Pardon obtained by some one for another that hath need thereof. Not by the Person pardoned, but in the way, *saith another*, in which I have obtained it. So then, to speak to the question more large, the pardon that you and *Mercy* and these Boys have attained was *obtained* by another, to wit, by him that let you in at the Gate. And he hath obtain'd it in this double way. He has performed Righteousness to cover you, and spilt blood to wash you in.

CHRIS. *But if he parts with his Righteousness to us, what will he have for himself?*

GREAT-HEART. He has more Righteousness than you have need of, or than he needeth himself.

CHRIS. *Pray make that appear.*

GREAT-HEART. With all my heart; but first I must premise that he of whom we are now about to speak, is one that has not his Fellow. He has two Natures in one Person, *plain* to be *distinguished*, *impossible* to be *divided*. Unto each of these Natures a Righteousness belongeth, and each Righteousness is essential to that Nature. So that one may as easily cause the nature to be extinct, as to separate its Justice or Righteousness from it. Of *these* Righteousnesses therefore, we are not made partakers so as that they or any of them should be put upon us that we might be made just, and live thereby. Besides these there is a Righteousness which this Person has as these two Natures are joyned in one. And this is not the Righteousness of the *Godhead*, as distinguished from the *Manhood;* nor the Righteousness of the *Manhood*, as distinguished from the *Godhead;* but a Righteousness which standeth in the Union of both Natures; and may properly be called the Righteousness that is essential to his being prepared of God to the capacity of the Mediatory Office which he was to be intrusted with. If he parts with his first Righteousness, he parts with his *Godhead;* if he parts with his second Righteousness, he parts with the purity of his *Manhood;* if he parts with this third, he parts with that perfection that capacitates him to the Office of Mediation. He has therefore another Righteousness which standeth in *performance*, or obedience to a revealed Will; and that is it that he puts upon Sinners, and that by which their Sins are covered. Wherefore he saith, *as by one man's disobedience many were made Sinners: so by the obedience of one shall many be made Righteous.*

CHRIS. *But are the other Righteousnesses of no use to us?*

GREAT-HEART. Yes, for though they are essential to his Natures and Office, and so cannot be communicated unto another, yet it is by Virtue of them, that the Righteousness that justifies is for that purpose efficacious. The *Righteousness* of his *Godhead* gives *Virtue* to his Obedience; the *Righteousness* of his *Manhood* giveth capability to his obedience to justify, and the Righteousness that standeth in the Union of these two Natures to his Office, giveth Authority to that Righteousness to do the work for which it is ordained.

So then, here is a Righteousness that Christ, as God, has no need of, for he is God without it: here is a Righteousness that Christ, as Man, has no need of to make him so, for he is perfect man without it. Again, here is a Righteousness that Christ as God-man has no need of, for he is perfectly so without it. Here then is a Righteousness that Christ, as God, as Man, as God-man has no need of, with Reference to himself, and therefore he can spare it, a justifying Righteousness, that he for himself wanteth not, and therefore he giveth it away. Hence 'tis called the *gift of Righteousness.* This Righteousness, since Christ Jesus the Lord, has made himself under the Law, *must* be given away. For the Law doth not only bind him that is under it *to do justly*, but to use Charity. Wherefore he *must*, he *ought* by the Law, if he hath two Coats, to give one to him that hath none. Now our Lord indeed hath two *Coats*, one for himself, and one to spare. Wherefore he freely bestows one upon those that have none. And thus *Christiana*, and *Mercy*, and the rest of you that are here, doth your Pardon come by *deed*, or by the work of another man? Your Lord Christ is he that has worked, and has given away what he wrought for to the next poor Beggar he meets.

But again, in order to pardon by *deed*, there must something be paid to God as a price, as well as something prepared to cover us withal. Sin has delivered us up to the just curse of a Righteous Law. Now from this curse we must be justified by way of Redemption, a price being paid for the harms we have done, and this is by the Blood of your Lord, who came and stood in your place and stead, and died your death for your Transgressions. Thus has he ransomed you from your Transgressions, by Blood, and covered your polluted and deformed Souls with Righteousness: for the sake of which, God passeth by you, and will not hurt you, when he comes to Judge the World.

CHRIS. *This is brave. Now I see that there was something to be learnt by our being pardoned by* word *and* deed. *Good* Mercy, *let us labour to keep this in mind, and my Children do you remember it also. But, Sir, was not this it that made my good* Christian's *Burden fall from off his Shoulder, and that made him give three leaps for Joy?*

GREAT-HEART. Yes, 'twas the belief of this that cut those Strings that could not be cut by other means, and 'twas to give him a proof of the Virtue of this, that he was suffered to carry his burden to the Cross.

CHRIS. *I thought so, for tho' my heart was lightful and joyous before, yet it is ten times more lightsome and joyous now. And I am perswaded by what I have felt, tho' I have felt but little as yet, that if the most burdened Man in the World was here, and did see and believe, as I now do, 'twould make his heart the more merry and blithe.*

GREAT-HEART. There is not only comfort, and the ease of a Burden brought to us, by the sight and Consideration of these; but an indeared Affection begot in us by it. For who can, if he doth but once think that Pardon comes not only by promise but thus, but be affected with the way and means of his Redemption, and so with the man that hath wrought it for him?

CHRIS. *True, methinks it makes my Heart bleed to think that he should bleed for me. Oh! thou loving one, Oh! thou Blessed one. Thou deservest to have me, thou hast bought me: Thou deservest to have me all, thou hast paid for me ten thousand times more than I am worth. No marvel that this made the water stand in my Husband's Eyes, and that it made him trudge so nimbly on. I am perswaded he wished me with him; but vile Wretch, that I was, I let him come all alone. O* Mercy, *that thy Father and Mother were here, yea, and Mrs.* Timorous *also. Nay, I wish now with all my Heart, that here was Madam* Wanton *too. Surely, surely, their Hearts would be affected, nor could the fear of the one, nor the powerful Lusts of the other, prevail with them to go home again, and to refuse to become good Pilgrims.*

GREAT-HEART. You speak now in the warmth of your Affections: will it, think you, be always thus with you? Besides, this is not communicated to every one, nor to every one that did see your Jesus bleed. There was that stood by, and that saw the Blood run from his heart to the Ground, and yet were so far off this, that instead of lamenting, they laughed at him, and instead of becoming his Disciples, did harden their hearts against him. So that all that you have, my Daughters, you have by a peculiar impression made by a Divine contemplating upon what I have spoken to you. Remember that 'twas told you, that the *Hen* by her common call, gives no meat to her *Chickens.* This you have therefore by a special Grace.

Now I saw still in my Dream, that they went on until they were come to the place, that *Simple,* and *Sloth,* and *Presumption* lay and slept in, when

Christian went by on Pilgrimage. And behold they were hanged up in Irons a little way off on the other-side.

MERCY. *Then said* Mercy *to him that was their Guide and Conductor, What are those three men? and for what are they hanged there?*

GREAT-HEART. These three men, were Men of very bad Qualities: they had no mind to be Pilgrims themselves, and whosoever they could they hindered; they were for sloth and folly themselves, and whoever they could perswade with, they made so too, and withal taught them to presume that they should do well at last. They were asleep when *Christian* went by, and now you go by they are hanged.

MERCY. *But could they perswade any to be of their Opinion?*

GREAT-HEART. Yes, they turned several out of the way. There was *Slow-pace* that they perswaded to do as they. They also prevailed with one *Short-wind*, with one *No-heart*, with one *Linger-after-lust*, and with one *Sleepy-head*, and with a young Woman her name was *Dull*, to turn out of the way and become as they. Besides, they brought up an ill-report of your Lord, perswading others that he was a task-Master. They also brought up an evil report of the good Land, saying, 'twas not half so good as some pretend it was. They also began to vilify his Servants, and to count the very best of them meddlesome, troublesome busy-Bodies. Further, they would call the Bread of God *Husks;* the *Comforts* of his Children *Fancies;* the Travel and Labour of Pilgrims things to no Purpose.

CHRIS. *Nay, said* Christiana, *if they were such, they shall never be bewailed by me; they have but what they deserve, and I think it is well that they hang so near the High-way that others may see and take warning. But had it not been well if their Crimes had been ingraven in some Plate of Iron or Brass, and left here, even where they did their Mischiefs, for a caution to other bad Men.*

GREAT-HEART. So it is, as you well may perceive if you will go a little to the Wall.

MERCY. *No, no, let them hang, and their Names Rot, and their Crimes live for ever against them. I think it a high favour that they were hanged afore we came hither, who knows else what they might a done to such poor women as we are?* Then she turned it into a Song, saying,

> *Now then you three, hang there and be a Sign*
> *To all that shall against the Truth combine:*
> *And let him that comes after fear this end,*
> *If unto Pilgrims he is not a Friend.*
> *And thou my Soul of all such men beware,*
> *That unto Holiness Opposers are.*

THE HILL DIFFICULTY

Thus they went in till they came at the foot of the Hill *Difficulty*. Where again their good Friend, Mr. *Great-heart* took an occasion to tell them of what happened there when *Christian* himself went by. So he had them first to the Spring. Lo, saith he, *This is the Spring that* Christian *drank of* before he went up this Hill, and then 'twas clear, and good; but now 'tis Dirty with the feet of some that are not desirous that Pilgrims here should quench their Thirst. Thereat *Mercy* said, *And why so envious tro?* But said their Guide, It will do, if taken up, and put into a Vessel that is sweet and good; for then the Dirt will sink to the bottom, and the Water come out by itself more clear. Thus therefore *Christiana* and her Companions were compelled to do. They took it up, and put it into an Earthen-pot, and so let it stand till the Dirt was gone to the bottom, and then they drank thereof.

Next he shewed them the two *by-ways* that were at the foot of the Hill, where *Formality* and *Hypocrisy*, lost themselves. And, said he, these are dangerous Paths. Two were here cast away when *Christian* came by. And although, as you see, these ways are since stopt up with *Chains, Posts,* and a *Ditch*, yet there are that will chuse to adventure here, rather than take the pains to go up this Hill.

CHRIS. *The Way of Transgressors is hard. 'Tis a wonder that they can get into those ways, without danger of breaking their Necks.*

GREAT-HEART. They will venture; yea, if at any time any of the King's Servants doth happen to see them, and doth call unto them, and tell them that *they* are in the wrong ways, and do bid them beware the danger; then they will railingly return them answer and say, *As for the Word that thou hast spoken unto us in the name of the King, we will not hearken unto thee; but we will certainly do whatsoever thing goeth out of our own Mouths,* &c. Nay if you look a little farther, you shall see that these ways, are made cautionary enough, not only by these *Posts,* and *Ditch* and *Chain;* but also by being hedged up. Yet they will chuse to go there.

CHRIS. *They are Idle, they love not to take Pains, up-hill-way is unpleasant to them. So it is fulfilled unto them as it is Written. The way of the slothful man is a Hedge of Thorns. Yea, they will rather chuse to walk upon a Snare than to go up this Hill, and the rest of this way to the City.*

Then they set forward, and began to go up the Hill, and up the Hill they went; but before they got to the top, *Christiana* began to *Pant*, and said, I daresay this is a breathing Hill; no marvel if they that love their ease more than their Souls, chuse to themselves a smoother way. Then said *Mercy*, I must sit down; also the least of the Children began to cry. Come, come, said *Great-heart*, sit not down here, for a little above is the Prince's *Arbor*. Then took he the little Boy by the Hand, and led him up thereto.

When they were come to the *Arbor*, they were very willing to sit down, for they were all in a pelting heat. Then said *Mercy, How sweet is rest to them that Labour?* And how good is the Prince of Pilgrims, to provide such resting places for them? Of *this Arbor* I have heard much; but I never saw it before. But here let us beware of sleeping: for as I have heard, for that it cost poor *Christian* dear.

Then said Mr. *Great-heart* to the little ones, Come my pretty *Boys*, how do you do? what think you now of going on Pilgrimage? Sir, said the least, I was almost beat out of heart; but I thank you for lending me a hand at my need. And I remember now what my Mother has told me, namely, That the way to Heaven is as up a Ladder, and the way to Hell is as down a Hill. But I had rather go up the Ladder to Life, than down the Hill to Death.

Then said *Mercy*, But the Proverb is, *To go down the Hill is easy*. But *James* said (for that was his Name), The day is coming when in my Opinion, *going down Hill will be the hardest of all.* 'Tis a good Boy, said his Master, thou hast given her a right answer. Then *Mercy* smiled, but the little Boy did blush.

CHRIS. Come, said *Christiana*, will you eat a bit, a little to sweeten your Mouths, while you sit here to rest your Legs? For I have here a piece of Pomgranate which Mr. *Interpreter* put in my Hand, just when I came out of his Doors; he gave me also a piece of an Honey-comb, and a little Bottle of Spirits. I thought he gave you something, said *Mercy*, because he called you a to-side. Yes, so he did, said the other. But *Mercy*, it shall still be as I said it should, when at first we came from home: thou shalt be a sharer in all the good that I have, because thou so willingly didst become my Companion. Then she gave to them, and they did eat, both *Mercy*, and the Boys. And said *Christiana* to Mr. *Great-heart*, Sir will you do as we? But he answered, You are going on Pilgrimage, and presently I shall return; much Good may what you have, do to you. At home I eat the same every day. Now when they had eaten and drank, and had chatted a little longer, their guide said to them, The day wears away, if you think good, let us prepare to be going. So they got up to go, and the little Boys went before; But *Christiana* forgat to take her Bottle of Spirits with her, so she sent her little Boy back to fetch it. Then said *Mercy*, I think this is a *losing* Place. Here *Christian* lost his *Roll*, and here *Christiana* left her Bottle behind her; Sir, what is the cause of this? so their guide made answer and said, The cause is *sleep* or *forgetfulness;* some *sleep*, when they should keep *awake;* and some *forget*, when they should *remember;* and this is the very cause why often at the resting places some Pilgrims in some things come off losers. Pilgrims should watch and remember what they have already received under their greatest enjoyments. But for want of doing so, oft times their rejoicing ends in Tears, and their Sunshine in a Cloud: witness the story of *Christian* at this place.

When they were come to the place where *Mistrust* and *Timorous* met *Christian* to perswade him to go back for fear of the Lions, they perceived as it were a Stage, and before it towards the Road, a broad plate with a Copy of Verses written thereon, and underneath, the reason of raising up of that Stage in that place, rendered. The Verses were these.

Let him that sees this Stage take heed
Unto his Heart and Tongue:
Lest, if he do not, here he speed
As some have long agone.

The words underneath the Verses were, *This Stage was built to punish such upon who through* Timorousness *or* Mistrust, *shall be afraid to go further on Pilgrimage. Also on this Stage both* Mistrust *and* Timorous *were burned thorough the Tongue with an hot Iron, for endeavouring to hinder* Christian *in his Journey.*

Then said *Mercy.* This is much like to the saying of the beloved, *What shall be given unto thee? or what shall be done unto thee thou false Tongue? sharp Arrows of the mighty, with Coals of* Juniper.

So they went on, till they came within sight of the Lions. Now Mr. *Great-heart* was a strong man, so he was not afraid of a Lion. But yet when they were come up to the place where the Lions were, the Boys that went before were glad to cringe behind, for they were afraid of the Lions, so they stept back and went behind. At this their guide smiled, and said, How now my Boys, do you love to go before when no danger doth approach, and love to come behind so soon as the Lions appear?

Now as they went up, Mr. *Great-heart* drew his Sword with intent to make a way for the Pilgrims in spite of the Lions. Then there appeared one, that it seems, had taken upon him to back the Lions. And he said to the Pilgrims' guide, What is the cause of your coming hither? Now the name of that man was *Grim*, or *Bloody-man*, because of his slaying of Pilgrims, and he was of the race of the *Giants.*

GREAT-HEART. Then said the *Pilgrims'* guide, These Women and Children are going on Pilgrimage, and this is the way they must go, and go it they shall in spite of thee and the Lions.

GRIM. This is not their way, neither shall they go therein. I am come forth to withstand them, and to that end will back the Lions.

Now to say truth, by reason of the fierceness of the Lions, and of the *Grim* Carriage of him that did back them, this way had of late lain much unoccupied, and was almost all grown over with Grass.

CHRIS. Then said *Christiana*, tho' the High-ways have been unoccupied heretofore, and tho' the Travellers have been made in time past to walk thorough by-Paths, it must not be so now I am risen, *Now I am risen a Mother in* Israel.

GRIM. Then he swore *by the Lions*, but it should; and therefore bid them turn aside, for they should not have passage there.

GREAT-HEART. But their guide made first his Approach unto *Grim*, and laid so heavily at him with his Sword, that he forced him to a retreat.

GRIM. Then said he (that attempted to back the Lions) will you slay me upon mine own Ground?

GREAT-HEART. 'Tis the King's High-way that we are in, and in his way it is that thou hast placed thy Lions; but these Women, and these Children, tho' weak, shall hold on their way in spite of thy Lions. And with that he gave him again a down-right blow, and brought him upon his Knees. With this blow he also broke his Helmet, and with the next he cut off an Arm. Then did the *Giant Roar* so hideously, that his Voice frighted the Women, and yet they were glad to see him lie sprawling upon the Ground. Now the Lions were chained, and so of themselves could do nothing. Wherefore when old *Grim* that intended to back them was dead, Mr. *Great-heart* said to the Pilgrims, Come now and follow me, and no hurt shall happen to you from the Lions. They therefore went on; but the Women trembled as they passed by them, the Boys also look't as if they would die; but they all got by without further hurt.

The Porter's Lodge

Now then they were within Sight of the *Porter's* Lodge, and they soon came up unto it; but they made the more haste after this to go thither, because 'tis dangerous travelling there in the Night. So when they were come to the Gate, the Guide knocked, and the Porter cried, *who is there?* but as soon as the Guide had said, *it is I*, he knew his Voice and came down. (For the Guide had oft before that come thither as a Conductor of Pilgrims.) When he was come down, he opened the Gate, and seeing the Guide standing just before it (for he saw not the Women, for they were behind him) he said unto him, How now, Mr. *Great-heart*, what is your business here so late to Night? I have brought, said he, some Pilgrims hither, where by my Lord's Commandment, they must Lodge. I had been here some time ago, had I not been opposed by the Giant that did use to back the Lions. But I after a long and tedious combat with him, have cut him off, and have brought the Pilgrims hither in safety.

Porter. *Will you not go in, and stay till Morning?*

Great-heart. No, I will return to my Lord to night.

Chris. Oh Sir, I know not how to be willing you should leave us in our Pilgrimage, you have been so faithful, and so loving to us, you have fought so stoutly for us, you have been so hearty in counselling of us, that I shall never forget your favour towards us.

Mercy. Then said *Mercy*, O that we might have thy Company to our Journey's end! How can such poor Women as we hold out in a way so full of Troubles as this way is, without a Friend and Defender?

James. Then said *James*, the youngest of the Boys, Pray Sir, be perswaded to go with us, and help us, because we are so weak, and the way so dangerous as it is.

Great-heart. I am at my Lord's Commandment. If he shall allot me to be your guide quite thorough, I will willingly wait upon you. But here you failed at first; for when he bid me come thus far with you, then you should have begged me of him to have gone quite thorough with you, and he would have granted your request. However, at present I must withdraw, and so good *Christiana, Mercy*, and my brave Children, Adieu.

Then the Porter, Mr. *Watchful*, asked *Christiana* of her Country, and of her Kindred, and she said, *I came from the City of* Destruction, *I am a Widow Woman, and my Husband is dead, his Name was* Christian *the Pilgrim*. How, said the Porter, was he your Husband? Yes, said she, and these are his Children; and this, pointing to *Mercy*, is one of my Town's-Women. Then the Porter rang his Bell, as at such times he is wont, and there came to the Door one of the Damsels whose Name was *Humble-mind*. And to her the Porter said, Go tell it within that *Christiana* the Wife of *Christian* and her Children are come hither on Pilgrimage. She went in therefore and told it. But Oh, what a Noise for gladness was there within, when the Damsel did but drop that word out of her Mouth?

So they came with haste to the Porter, for *Christiana* stood still at the Door. Then some of the most grave said unto her, *Come in* Christiana, *come in thou Wife of that Good Man, come in thou Blessed Woman, come in with all that are with thee.* So she went in, and they followed her that were her Children, and her Companions. Now when they were gone in, they were had into a very large Room, where they were bidden to sit down. So they sat down, and the chief of the House was called to see, and welcome the Guests. Then they came in, and, understanding who they were, did salute each other with a kiss, and said, Welcome ye Vessels of the Grace of God, welcome to us your Friends.

Now because it was somewhat late, and because the Pilgrims were weary with their Journey, and also made faint with the sight of the fight, and of the terrible Lions; therefore they desired as soon as might be, to prepare to go to Rest. Nay, said those of the Family, refresh yourselves first with a morsel of Meat. For they had prepared for them a Lamb, with the accustomed Sauce belonging thereto. For the Porter had heard before of their coming, and had told it to them within. So when they had supped, and ended their Prayer with a Psalm, they desired they might go to rest. But let us, said *Christiana*, if we may be so bold as to chuse, be in that Chamber that was my Husband's, when he was here. So they had them up thither, and they lay all in a Room. When they were at Rest, *Christiana* and *Mercy* entred into discourse about things that were convenient.

CHRIS. *Little did I think once, that when my Husband went on Pilgrimage, I should ever a followed.*

MERCY. And you as little thought of lying in his Bed, and in his Chamber to Rest, as you do now.

CHRIS. *And much less did I ever think of seeing his Face with Comfort, and of worshipping the Lord the King with him, and yet now I believe I shall.*

MERCY. Hark, don't you hear a Noise?

CHRIS. *Yes, 'tis as I believe, a Noise of Musick, for joy that we are here.*

MERCY. Wonderful! Musick in the House, Musick in the Heart, and Musick also in Heaven, for joy that we are here.

Thus they talked a while, and then betook themselves to sleep; so in the Morning, when they were awake, *Christiana* said to *Mercy*.

CHRIS. *What was the matter that you did laugh in your sleep to Night? I suppose you was in a Dream?*

MERCY. So I was, and a sweet Dream it was; but are you sure I laughed?

CHRIS. *Yes, you laughed heartily; but prithee* Mercy *tell me thy Dream?*

MERCY. I was a dreamed that I sat all alone in a solitary place, and was bemoaning of the hardness of my Heart.

Now I had not sat there long, but methought many were gathered about me, to see me, and to hear what it was that I said. So they hearkened, and

I went on bemoaning the hardness of my Heart. At this, some of them laughed at me, some called me Fool, and some began to thrust me about. With that, methought I looked up, and saw one coming with Wings towards me. So he came directly to me, and said, *Mercy*, what aileth thee? Now when he had heard me make my complaint, he said, *Peace be to thee:* he also wiped mine Eyes with his Handkerchief, and *clad* me in *Silver and Gold;* he put a chain about my Neck, and Ear-rings in mine Ears, and a beautiful Crown upon my Head. Then he took me by the Hand, and said, *Mercy*, come after me. So he went up, and I followed, till we came at a Golden Gate. Then he knocked, and when they within had opened, the man went in and I followed him up to a Throne, upon which one sat, and he said to me, *welcome Daughter*. The place looked bright, and twinkling like the Stars, or rather like the *Sun*, and I thought that I saw your Husband there, so I awoke from my Dream. But did I laugh?

CHRIS. *Laugh! Ay, and well you might to see yourself so well. For you must give me leave to tell you, that I believe it was a good Dream, and that as you have begun to find the first part true, so you shall find the second at last.* God speaks once, yea twice, yet Man perceiveth it not. In a Dream, in a Vision of the Night, when deep Sleep falleth upon Men, in slumbring upon the Bed. *We need not, when a-Bed, lie awake to talk with God. He can visit us while we sleep, and cause us then to hear his Voice. Our Heart oft times wakes when we sleep, and God can speak to that, either by Words, by Proverbs, by Signs, and Similitudes, as well as if one was awake.*

MERCY. Well, I am glad of my Dream, for I hope ere long to see it fulfilled, to the making of me laugh again.

CHRIS. *I think it is now high time to rise, and to know what we must do?*

MERCY. Pray, if they invite us to stay a while, let us willingly accept of the proffer. I am the willinger to stay a while here, to grow better acquainted with these Maids; methinks *Prudence, Piety* and *Charity*, have very comely and sober Countenances.

CHRIS. *We shall see what they will do.* So when they were up and ready, they came down. And they asked one another of their rest, and if it was comfortable, or not?

MERCY. *Very good, said* Mercy, *it was one of the best Night's Lodging that ever I had in my Life.*

Then said *Prudence*, and *Piety*, if you will be perswaded to stay here a while, you shall have what the House will afford.

CHARITY. *Ay, and that with a very good will, said* Charity. So they consented, and stayed there about a Month or above, and became very Profitable one to another. And because *Prudence* would see how *Christiana* had brought up her Children, she asked leave of her to catechise them? So she gave her free consent. Then she began at the youngest whose Name was *James*.

PRUDENCE. *And she said, Come* James, *canst thou tell who made thee?*

JAMES. God the Father, God the Son, and God the Holy Ghost.

PRUD. *Good Boy. And canst thou tell who saves thee?*

JAM. God the Father, God the Son, and God the Holy Ghost.

PRUD. *Good Boy still. But how doth God the Father save thee?*

JAM. By his Grace.

PRUD. *How doth God the Son save thee?*

JAM. By his Righteousness, Death, and Blood, and Life.

PRUD. *And how doth God the Holy Ghost save thee?*

JAM. By his *Illumination*, by his *Renovation*, and by his *Preservation.*

Then said *Prudence* to *Christiana*, You are to be commended for thus bringing up your Children. I suppose I need not ask the rest these Questions, since the youngest of them can answer them so well. I will therefore now apply myself to the youngest next.

PRUD. Then she said, Come *Joseph* (for his Name was *Joseph*), will you let me Catechise you?

JOSEPH. With all my Heart.

PRUD. What is Man?

JOSEPH. A Reasonable Creature, so made by God, as my Brother said.

PRUD. *What is supposed by this Word, saved?*

JOSEPH. That man by Sin has brought himself into a State of Captivity and Misery.

PRUD. *What is supposed by his being saved by the Trinity?*

JOSEPH. That Sin is so great and mighty a Tyrant, that none can pull us out of its clutches but God, and that God is so good and loving to man, as to pull him indeed out of this Miserable State.

PRUD. *What is God's design in saving of poor Men?*

JOSEPH. The glorifying of his Name, of his Grace, and Justice, &c. And the everlasting Happiness of his Creature.

PRUD. *Who are they that must be saved?*

JOSEPH. Those that accept of his Salvation.

GOOD BOY, *Joseph*, thy Mother has taught thee well, and thou hast hearkened to what she has said unto thee.

Then said *Prudence* to *Samuel*, who was the eldest but one.

PRUD. Come *Samuel*, are you willing that I should Catechise you also?

SAMUEL. Yes, forsooth, if you please.

PRUD. *What is Heaven?*

SAM. A Place and State most blessed, because God dwelleth there.

PRUD. *What is Hell?*

SAM. A Place and State most woful, because it is the dwelling place of Sin, the Devil, and Death.

PRUD. *Why wouldest thou go to Heaven?*

SAM. That I may see God, and serve him without weariness; that I may see Christ, and love him everlastingly; that I may have that fulness of the Holy Spirit in me that I can by no means here enjoy.

PRUD. *A very good Boy also, and one that has learned well.*

Then she addressed herself to the eldest, whose name was *Matthew*, and she said to him, Come *Matthew*, shall I also Catechise you?

MAT. *With a very good Will.*

PRUD. *I ask then, if there was ever any thing that had a being antecedent to, or before God?*

MAT. No, for God is Eternal, nor is there any thing excepting himself that had a being until the beginning of the first day. *For in six days the Lord made Heaven and Earth, the Sea and all that in them is.*

PRUD. *What do you think of the Bible?*

MAT. It is the Holy Word of God.

PRUD. *Is there nothing written therein but what you understand?*

MAT. Yes, a great deal.

PRUD. *What do you do when you meet with such places therein that you do not understand?*

MAT. I think God is wiser than I. I pray also that he will please to let me know all therein that he knows will be for my good.

PRUD. *How believe you as touching the Resurrection of the Dead?*

MAT. I believe they shall rise, the same that was buried: the same in *Nature*, tho' not in Corruption. And I believe this upon a double account. First because God has promised it. Secondly, because he is able to perform it.

Then said *Prudence* to the Boys, You must still hearken to your Mother, for she can learn you more. You must also diligently give ear to what good talk you shall hear from others, for for your sakes do they speak good things. Observe also and that with carefulness, what the Heavens and the Earth do teach you; but especially be much in the meditation of that Book that was the cause of your Father's becoming a Pilgrim. I for my part, my Children, will teach you what I can while you are here, and shall be glad if you will ask me Questions that tend to godly edifying.

Now by that these Pilgrims had been at this place a week, *Mercy* had a Visitor that pretended some good will unto her, and his name was Mr. *Brisk*. A man of some breeding, and that pretended to Religion; but a man that stuck very close to the World. So he came once or twice or more, to *Mercy*, and offered love unto her. Now *Mercy* was of a fair Countenance, and therefore the more alluring.

Her mind also was, to be always busying of herself in doing, for when she had nothing to do for herself, she would be making of Hose and Garments for others, and would bestow them upon them that had need. And Mr. *Brisk* not knowing where or how she disposed of what she made, seemed to be greatly taken for that he found her never idle. I will warrant her a good Huswife, quoth he to himself.

MERCY ENQUIRES CONCERNING MR. BRISK

Mercy then revealed the business to the Maidens that were of the House, and enquired of them concerning him, for they did know him better than she. So they told her that he was a very busy young man, and one that pretended to Religion; but was as they feared, a stranger to the Power of that which was good.

Nay then, said Mercy, *I will look no more on him, for I purpose never to have a clog to my Soul.*

Prudence then replied, That there needed no great matter of discouragement to be given to him, her continuing so as she had began to do for the Poor, would quickly cool his Courage.

So the next time he comes, he finds her at her old work, a making of things for the Poor. Then said he, What, always at it? Yes, said she, either for myself or for others. And what canst thee *earn* a day, quoth he? I do these things, said she, *That I may be Rich in good Works, laying up in store a good Foundation against the time to come, that I may lay hold on Eternal Life.* Why prithee what dost thou with them? said he. Cloath the naked, said she. With that his Countenance fell. So he forbore to come at her again. And when he was asked the reason why, he said, *That* Mercy *was a pretty lass, but troubled with ill Conditions.*

When he had left her, *Prudence* said, Did I not tell thee that Mr. *Brisk* would soon forsake thee? yea he will raise up an ill report of thee; for notwithstanding his pretence to Religion, and his seeming love to *Mercy*, yet *Mercy* and he are of tempers so different, that I believe they will never come together.

MERCY. *I might a had Husbands afore now, tho' I spake not of it to any; but they were such as did not like my Conditions, tho' never did any of them find fault with my Person. So they and I could not agree.*

PRUD. *Mercy* in our days is little set by, any further than as to its Name: the Practice, which is set forth by thy Conditions, there are but few that can abide.

MERCY. *Well, said* Mercy, *if nobody will have me, I will die a Maid, or my Conditions shall be to me as a Husband. For I cannot change my Nature, and to have one that lies cross to me in this, that I purpose never to admit of as long as I live. I had a Sister named* Bountiful, *that was married to one of these Churls; but he and she could never agree; but because my Sister was resolved to do as she had began, that is, to shew Kindness to the Poor, therefore her Husband first cried her down at the Cross, and then turned her out of his Doors.*

PRUD. And yet he was a Professor, I warrant you?

MERCY. *Yes, such a one as he was, and of such as he, the World is now full; but I am for none of them all.*

Now *Matthew* the eldest Son of *Christiana* fell Sick, and his Sickness was sore upon him, for he was much pained in his Bowels, so that he was with it, at times, pulled as 'twere both ends together. There dwelt also not far from thence one Mr. *Skill*, an antient and well approved Physician. So *Christiana* desired it, and they sent for him, and he came. When he was entered the Room, and had a little observed the Boy, he concluded that he was sick of the Gripes. Then he said to his Mother, *What Diet has* Matthew *of late fed upon?* Diet, said *Christiana*, Nothing but that which is wholesome. The Physician answered, *This Boy has been tampering with something that lies in his Maw undigested, and that will not away without means. And I tell you he must be purged, or else he will die.*

SAMUEL. Then said *Samuel, Mother, Mother, what was that which my Brother did gather up and eat, so soon as we were come from the gate that is at the head of this way? You know that there was an Orchard on the left hand, on the other side of the Wall, and some of the Trees hung over the Wall, and my Brother did plash and did eat.*

CHRIS. True my Child, said *Christiana*, he did take thereof and did eat; naughty Boy as he was, I did chide him, and yet he would eat thereof.

SKILL. *I knew he had eaten something that was not wholesome Food. And that Food, to wit, that Fruit, is even the most hurtful of all. It is the Fruit of* Beelzebub's *Orchard. I do marvel that none did warn you of it; many have died thereof.*

CHRIS. Then *Christiana* began to cry, and she said, O naughty Boy, and O careless Mother what shall I do for my Son?

SKILL. *Come, do not be too much Dejected; the Boy may do well again; but he must purge and vomit.*

CHRIS. Pray Sir try the utmost of your Skill with him whatever it costs.

SKILL. *Nay, I hope I shall be reasonable.* So he made him a Purge; but it was too weak. 'Twas said, it was made of the Blood of a Goat, the Ashes of an Heifer, and with some of the Juice of Hyssop, *&c.* When Mr. *Skill* had seen that that Purge was too weak, he made him one to the Purpose, 'Twas made *Ex Carne & Sanguine Christi.* (You know Physicians give strange Medicines to their Patients.) And it was made up into Pills with a Promise or two, and a proportionable quantity of Salt. Now he was to take them three at a time fasting, in half a quarter of a Pint of the Tears of Repentance. When this potion was prepared, and brought to the Boy, he was loth to take it, tho' torn with the Gripes, as if he should be pulled in pieces. *Come, come, said the Physician, you must take it.* It goes against my Stomach, said the Boy. *I must have you take it, said his Mother.* I shall vomit it up again, said the Boy. Pray Sir, said *Christiana* to Mr. *Skill*, how does it taste? It has no ill taste, said the Doctor, and with that she touched one of the pills with the tip of her Tongue. Oh, *Matthew*, said she, this potion is sweeter than Hony. If thou lovest thy Mother, if thou lovest thy Brothers, if thou lovest *Mercy*, if thou lovest thy Life, take it. So with much ado, after a short Prayer for the Blessing of God upon it, he took it, and it wrought kindly with him. It caused him to purge, it caused him to sleep and rest quietly, it put him into a fine heat and breathing sweat, and did quite rid him of his Gripes.

So in little time he got up, and walked about with a Staff, and would go from Room to Room, and talk with *Prudence, Piety,* and *Charity* of his Distemper, and how he was healed.

So when the Boy was healed, *Christiana* asked Mr. *Skill*, saying, Sir, what will content you for your pains and care to and of my Child? And he said, you must pay the *Master of the College* of Physicians, according to rules made in that case and provided.

CHRIS. *But Sir, said she, what is this Pill good for else?*

SKILL. It is an universal Pill, 'tis good against all the Diseases that Pilgrims are incident to, and when it is well prepared, it will keep good, *time* out of *mind.*

CHRIS. Pray Sir, make me up twelve Boxes of them: for if I can get these, I will never take other Physick.

SKILL. These *Pills* are good to prevent Diseases, as well as to *cure* when one is Sick. Yea, I dare say it, and stand to it, that if a man will but use this Physick as he should, *it will make him live for ever.* But, good *Christiana,* thou must give these Pills, *no other way* but as I have prescribed: for if you do, they will do no good. So he gave unto *Christiana* Physick for herself, and her Boys, and for *Mercy:* and bid *Matthew* take heed how he eat any more *Green Plums,* and kist them and went his way.

It was told you before that *Prudence* bid the Boys that if at any time they would, they should ask her some Questions that might be profitable, and she would say something to them.

MAT. Then *Matthew* who had been sick, asked her, *Why for the most part Physick should be bitter to our Palates?*

PRUD. To shew how unwelcome the word of God and the Effects thereof are to a Carnal Heart.

MAT. *Why does Physick, if it does good, purge, and cause that we vomit?*

PRUD. To shew that the Word when it works effectually, cleanseth the Heart and Mind. For look what the one doth to the Body, the other doth to the Soul.

MAT. *What should we learn by seeing the Flame of our Fire go upwards? and by seeing the Beams and sweet Influences of the Sun strike downwards?*

PRUD. By the going up of the Fire, we are taught to ascend to Heaven, by fervent and hot desires. And by the Sun his sending his Heat, Beams, and sweet Influences downwards, we are taught, that the Saviour of the World, tho' high, reaches down with his Grace and Love to us below.

MAT. *Where have the Clouds their Water?*

PRUD. Out of the Sea.

MAT. *What may we learn from that?*

PRUD. That Ministers should fetch their Doctrine from God.

MAT. *Why do they empty themselves upon the Earth?*

PRUD. To shew that Ministers should give out what they know of God to the World.

MAT. *Why is the Rainbow caused by the Sun?*

PRUD. To shew that the Covenant of God's Grace is confirmed to us in Christ.

MAT. *Why do the Springs come from the Sea to us through the Earth?*

PRUD. To shew that the Grace of God comes to us through the Body of Christ.

MAT. *Why do some of the Springs rise out of the tops of high Hills?*

PRUD. To shew that the Spirit of Grace shall spring up in *some* that are Great, and Mighty, as well as in *many* that are poor and Low.

MAT. *Why doth the Fire fasten upon the Candlewick?*

PRUD. To shew that unless Grace doth kindle upon the Heart there will be no true Light of Life in us.

MAT. *Why is the Wick and Tallow and all spent to maintain the light of the Candle?*

PRUD. To shew that Body and Soul and all, should be at the Service of, and spend themselves to maintain in good Condition that Grace of God that is in us.

MAT. *Why doth the Pelican pierce her own Breast with her Bill?*

PRUD. To nourish her Young ones with her Blood, and thereby to shew that Christ the blessed so loveth his Young, his People, as to save them from Death by his Blood.

MAT. *What may one learn by hearing the Cock to Crow?*

PRUD. Learn to remember *Peter's* Sin, and *Peter's* Repentance. The Cock's crowing shews also that day is coming on; let then the crowing of the Cock put thee in mind of that last and terrible Day of Judgment.

Now about this time their Month was out, wherefore they signified to those of the House that 'twas convenient for them to up and be going. Then said *Joseph* to his Mother, It is convenient that you forget not to send to the House of Mr. *Interpreter,* to pray him to grant that Mr. *Great-heart* should be sent unto us, that he may be our Conductor the rest of our way. Good *Boy,* said she, I had almost forgot. So she drew up a Petition and prayed Mr. *Watchful* the Porter to send it by some fit man to her good Friend Mr. *Interpreter;* who when it was come and he had seen the contents of the Petition, said to the Messenger, Go tell them that I will send him.

THE APPLE OF EVE

When the Family where *Christiana* was, saw that they had a purpose to go forward, they called the whole House together to give thanks to their King, for sending of them such profitable Guests as these. Which done they said to *Christiana,* And shall we not shew thee something, according as our Custom is to do to Pilgrims, on which thou mayest meditate when thou art upon the way? So they took *Christiana,* her Children, and *Mercy* into the Closet, and shewed them one of the *Apples* that *Eve* did eat of, and that she also did give to her Husband, and that for the eating of which they both were turned out of Paradise, and asked her what she thought that was? Then *Christiana* said, *'Tis Food or Poison, I know not which.* So they opened the matter to her, and she held up her hands and wondered?

Then they had her to a Place, and shewed her *Jacob's Ladder.* Now at that time there were some Angels ascending upon it. So *Christiana* looked and looked, to see the Angels go up, and so did the rest of the Company. Then they were going into another place to shew them something else: but *James* said to his Mother, Pray bid them stay here a little longer, for this is a curious sight. So they turned again, and stood feeding their Eyes with this *so pleasant a prospect.* After this they had them into a Place where did hang up a *Golden Anchor,* so they bid *Christiana* take it down; For, said they, you shall have it with you, for 'tis of absolute necessity that you should, that you may lay hold of that within the vail, and stand stedfast, in case you should meet with turbulent weather. So they were glad thereof. Then they took them, and had them to the mount upon which *Abraham* our Father had offered up *Isaac* his Son, and shewed them the *Altar*, the *Wood*, the *Fire*, and the *Knife*, for they remain to be seen to this very Day. When they had seen it, they held up their hands and blest themselves, and said, Oh! What a man, for love to his Master, and for denial to himself was *Abraham?* After they had shewed them all these things, *Prudence* took them into the Dining-Room, where stood a pair of excellent Virginals: so she played upon them, and turned what she had shewed them into this excellent song, saying,

Eve's *Apple we have shewed you,*
Of that be you aware:
You have seen Jacob's *Ladder too,*
Upon which Angels are.
An Anchor you received have;
But let not these suffice,
Until with Abra'm *you have gave*
Your best a Sacrifice.

Mr. Great-heart Comes Again

Now about this time one knocked at the Door: So the Porter opened, and behold Mr. *Great-heart* was there; but when he was come in, what Joy was there? For it came now fresh again into their minds, how but a little while ago he had slain old *Grim Bloody-man*, the Giant, and had delivered them from the Lions.

Then said Mr. *Great-heart* to *Christiana* and to *Mercy*, My Lord has sent each of you a Bottle of Wine, and also some parched Corn, together with a couple of Pomegranates. He has also sent the Boys some Figs and Raisins to refresh you in your way.

Then they addressed themselves to their Journey, and *Prudence* and *Piety* went along with them. When they came at the Gate *Christiana* asked the Porter, if any of late went by. He said, No, only one some time since: who also told me that of late there had been a great Robbery committed on the Kings High-way, as you go. But he saith, the Thieves are taken, and will shortly be tried for their Lives. Then *Christiana* and *Mercy* was afraid; but *Matthew* said, Mother fear nothing, as long as Mr. *Great-heart* is to go with us, and to be our Conductor.

Then said *Christiana* to the Porter, Sir, I am much obliged to you for all the Kindnesses that you have shewed me since I came hither; and also for that you have been so loving and kind to my Children. I know not how to gratify your Kindness. Wherefore pray as a token of my respects to you accept of this small mite. So she put a Gold Angel in his Hand, and he made her a low obeisance, and said, Let thy Garments be always White, and let thy Head want no Ointment. Let *Mercy* live and not die, and let not her Works be few. And to the Boys he said, Do you fly Youthful lusts, and follow after Godliness with them that are Grave, and Wise, so shall you put Gladness into your Mother's Heart, and obtain Praise of all that are sober-minded. So they thanked the Porter and departed.

Now I saw in my Dream, that they went forward until they were come to the Brow of the Hill, where *Piety* bethinking herself cried out, *Alas!* I have forgot what I intended to bestow upon *Christiana*, and her Companions. I will go back and fetch it. So she ran, and fetched it. While she was gone, *Christiana* thought she heard in a Grove a little way off on the Right-hand, a most curious melodious Note, with words much like these,

Through all my Life thy favour is,
So frankly shew'd to me.
That in thy House for evermore
My dwelling-place shall be.

And listening still she thought she heard another answer it, saying,

For why, The Lord our God is good,
His Mercy is for ever sure:
His Truth at all times firmly stood:
And shall from Age to Age endure.

So *Christiana* asked *Prudence*, what 'twas that made those curious Notes? They are, said she, our Country Birds: they sing these Notes but seldom except it be at the Spring, when the Flowers appear, and the Sun shines warm, and then you may hear them all day long. I often, said she, go out to hear them, we also oft times keep them tame in our House. They are very fine Company for us when we are *Melancholy*, also they make the Woods, and Groves, and Solitary places places desirous to be in.

By this Time *Piety* was come again, so she said to *Christiana*, look here, I have brought thee a *Scheme* of all those things that thou hast seen at our House, upon which thou mayest look when thou findest thyself forgetful, and call those things again to remembrance for thy Edification and Comfort.

Now they began to go down the Hill into the Valley of *Humiliation*. It was a steep Hill, and the way was slippery; but they were very careful, so they got down pretty well. When they were down in the Valley, *Piety* said to *Christiana*, This is the place where *Christian* your Husband met with the foul Fiend, *Apollyon*, and where they had that dreadful fight that they had. I know you cannot but have heard thereof. But be of good Courage, as long you have here Mr. *Great-heart* to be your Guide and Conductor, we hope you will fare the better. So when these two had committed the Pilgrims unto the Conduct of their Guide, he went forward and they went after.

GREAT-HEART. Then said Mr. *Great-heart*, We need not to be so afraid of this Valley: for here is nothing to hurt us unless we procure it to ourselves. 'Tis true, *Christian* did here meet with *Apollyon*, with whom he also had a sore Combat; but that *fray* was the fruit of those slips that he got in his going down the Hill. For they that get *slips* there, must look for *Combats* here.

And hence it is that this Valley has got so hard a name. For the common People when they hear that some frightful thing has befallen such an one in such a place, are of an Opinion that that place is haunted with some foul Fiend, or evil Spirit; when alas it is for the fruit of their doing, that such things do befall them there.

This Valley of *Humiliation* is of itself as fruitful a place as any the Crow flies over; and I am perswaded if we could hit upon it, we might find somewhere hereabouts something that might give us an account why *Christian* was so hardly beset in this place.

Then *James* said to his Mother, Lo, yonder stands a Pillar, and it looks as if something was written thereon: let us go and see what it is. So they went, and found there written, *Let* Christian's *slips before he came hither, and the Battles that he met with in this place, be a warning to those that come after.* Lo, said their Guide, did not I tell you, that there was something hereabouts that would give Intimation of the reason why *Christian* was so hard beset in this place? Then turning himself to *Christiana*, he said: No disparagement to *Christian* more than to many others, whose Hap and Lot his was. For 'tis easier going *up*, than *down this* Hill; and that can be said but of few Hills in all these parts of the World. But we will leave the good Man, he is at rest, he also had a brave Victory over his Enemy; let him grant that dwelleth above, that we fare no worse when we come to be tried than he.

Men Thrive in the Valley of Humiliation

But we will come again to this Valley of *Humiliation*. It is the best, and most fruitful piece of Ground in all those parts. It is fat Ground, and as you see consisteth much in Meadows; and if a man was to come here in the Summertime as we do now, if he knew not anything before thereof, and if he also delighted himself in the sight of his Eyes, he might see that that would be delightful to him. Behold, how green this Valley is, also how beautified *with Lilies*. I have also known many labouring men that have got good Estates in this Valley of *Humiliation* (For God resisteth the Proud; but gives *more, more* Grace to the Humble). For indeed it is a very fruitful Soil, and doth bring forth by handfuls. Some also have wished that the next way to their Father's House were here, that they might be troubled no more with either Hills or Mountains to go over; but the way is the way, and there's an end.

Now as they were going along and talking, they espied a Boy feeding his Father's Sheep. The Boy was in very mean Cloaths, but of a very fresh and well-favoured Countenance, and as he sate by himself he sung. Hark, said Mr. *Great-heart*, to what the Shepherd's Boy saith. So they hearkened, and he said,

He that is down, needs fear no fall,
He that is low, no Pride:
He that is humble, ever shall
Have God to be his Guide.

I am content with what I have,
Little be it, or much:
And, Lord, contentment still I crave,
Because thou savest such.
Fulness to such a burden is
That go on Pilgrimage:
Here little, and hereafter Bliss,
Is best from Age to Age.

Then said their *Guide*, do you hear him? I will dare to say, that this Boy lives a merrier Life, and wears more of that Herb called *Hearts-ease* in his Bosom, than he that is clad in Silk and Velvet; but we will proceed in our Discourse.

In this Valley, our Lord formerly had his Country-house, he loved much to be here. He loved also to walk these Meadows, for he found the Air was pleasant. Besides here a man shall be free from the Noise, and from the hurryings of this Life. All States are full of Noise and Confusion, only the Valley of *Humiliation*, is that empty and solitary Place. Here a man shall not be so let and hindred in his Contemplation, as in other places he is apt to be. This is a Valley that nobody walks in, but those that love a Pilgrim's Life. And tho' *Christian* had the hard hap to meet here with *Apollyon*, and to enter with him a brisk encounter, yet I must tell you, that in former times men have met with Angels here, have found Pearls here, and have in this place found the words of Life.

Did I say, our Lord had here in former Days his Country-house, and that he loved here to walk? I will add, in this Place, and to the People that live and trace these Grounds he has left a yearly revenue to be faithfully paid them at certain Seasons, for their maintenance by the way, and for their further incouragement to go on in their Pilgrimage.

SAMUEL. Now as they went on, *Samuel* said to Mr. *Great-heart, Sir, I perceive that in this Valley my Father and* Apollyon *had their Battle; but whereabout was the Fight, for I perceive this Valley is large?*

GREAT-HEART. Your Father had that Battle with *Apollyon* at a place yonder, before us, in a narrow Passage just beyond *Forgetful-Green*. And indeed that place is the most dangerous place in all these Parts. For if at any time the Pilgrims meet with any brunt, it is when they forget what Favours they have received, and how unworthy they are of them. This is the Place also where others have been hard put to it. But more of the place when we are come to it; for I perswade myself, that to this day there remains either some sign of the Battle, or some Monument to testify that such a Battle there was fought.

MERCY. Then said *Mercy*, I think I am as well in this Valley, as I have been anywhere else in all our Journey. The place methinks suits with my Spirit. I love to be in such places where there is no rattling with Coaches, nor rumbling with Wheels. Methinks here one may without much Molestation, be thinking what he is, whence he came, what he has done, and to what the King has called him. Here one may think, and break at Heart, and melt in one's Spirit until one's Eyes become like the *Fish Pools of Heshbon.* They that go rightly through this Valley of *Baca* make it a Well, the Rain that God sends down from Heaven upon them that are here also *filleth the Pools.* This Valley is that from whence also the King will give to them Vineyards, and they that go through it, shall sing, (as *Christian* did, for all he met with *Apollyon*).

GREAT-HEART. 'Tis true, said their Guide, I have gone through this Valley many a time, and never was better than when here.

I have also been a Conductor to several Pilgrims, and they have confessed the same, *To this man will I look,* saith the King, *even to him that is Poor, and of a contrite Spirit, and that trembles at my Word.*

Now they were come to the place where the afore-mentioned Battle was fought. Then said the Guide to *Christiana* her Children and *Mercy:* This is the place, on this Ground *Christian* stood, and up there came *Apollyon* against him. And look, did not I tell you, here is some of your Husband's Blood upon these Stones to this day. Behold also how here and there are yet to be seen upon the place some of the Shivers of *Apollyon's* broken *Darts.* See also how they did beat the Ground with their Feet, as they fought to make good their Places against each other, how also with their by-blows, they did split the very Stones in pieces. Verily *Christian* did here play the Man, and shewed himself as stout, as could, had he been there, even *Hercules* himself. When *Apollyon* was beat, he made his retreat to the next Valley, that is called the Valley of the Shadow of Death, unto which we shall come anon.

Lo, yonder also stands a Monument on which is engraven this Battle, and *Christian's* Victory to his Fame, throughout all Ages. So because it stood just on the way-side before them, they stept to it and read this Writing, which word for word was this,

Hard by, here was a Battle fought,
Most strange, and yet most true.
Christian *and* Apollyon *sought*
Each other to subdue.
The Man so bravely play'd the Man,
He made the Fiend *to fly:*
Of which a Monument I stand,
The same to testify.

When they had passed by this place, they came upon the Borders of the Shadow of Death, and this Valley was longer than the other; a place also most strangely haunted with Evil things, as many are able to testify. But these Women and Children went the better through it, because they had day-light, and because Mr. *Great-heart* was their Conductor.

When they were entered upon this Valley they thought that they heard a groaning as of dead men, a very great groaning. They thought also they did hear Words of Lamentation spoken, as of some in extream Torment.

These things made the Boys to quake, the Women also looked pale and wan; but their guide bid them be of good Comfort.

So they went on a little further, and they thought that they felt the Ground begin to shake under them, as if some hollow Place was there; they heard also a kind of a hissing as of Serpents; but nothing as yet appeared. Then said the Boys, Are we not yet at the end of this doleful place? But the Guide also bid them be of good Courage, and look well to their Feet, lest haply, said he, you be taken in some Snare.

The Sickness of Fear

Now *James* began to be Sick; but I think the cause thereof was Fear; so his Mother gave him some of that Glass of Spirits that she had given her at the *Interpreter's* House, and three of the Pills that Mr. *Skill* had prepared, and the Boy began to revive. Thus they went on till they came to about the middle of the Valley, and then *Christiana* said, Methinks I see something yonder upon the Road before us, a thing of such a shape such as I have not seen. Then said *Joseph*, Mother, what is it? An ugly thing, Child; an ugly thing, said she. But Mother, what is it like, said he? 'Tis like I cannot tell what, said she. And now it was but a little way off. Then said she, it is nigh.

Well, well, said Mr. *Great-heart*, let them that are most afraid keep close to me. So the *Fiend* came on, and the Conductor met it; but when it was just come to him, it vanished to all their sights. Then remembered they what had been said sometime ago, *Resist the Devil, and he will fly from you.*

They went therefore on, as being a little refreshed; but they had not gone far, before *Mercy* looking behind her saw, as she thought, something most like a Lion, and it came a great padding pace after; and it had a hollow Voice of Roaring, and at every Roar that it gave, it made all the Valley echo, and their Hearts to ake, save the Heart of him that was their Guide. So it came up, and Mr. *Great-heart* went behind, and put the Pilgrims all before him. The Lion also came on apace, and Mr. *Great-heart* addressed himself to give him Battle. But when he saw that it was determined that resistance should be made, he also drew back and came no further.

Then they went on again, and their Conductor did go before them, till they came at a place where was cast up a pit, the whole breadth of the way, and before they could be prepared to go over that, a great mist and a darkness fell upon them, so that they could not see. Then said the Pilgrims, alas! now what shall we do? But their *Guide* made answer, Fear not, stand still and see what an end will be put to this also. So they stayed there because their Path was marr'd. They then also thought that they did hear more apparently the noise and rushing of the Enemies, the fire also and the smoke of the Pit was much easier to be discerned. Then said *Christiana* to *Mercy*, now I see what my poor Husband went through. I have heard much of this place, but I never was here afore now; poor man, he went here all alone in the night; he had night almost quite through the way; also these Fiends were busy about him, as if they would have torn him in pieces. Many have spoke of it, but none can tell what the Valley of the Shadow of Death should mean, until they come in it themselves. *The heart knows its own bitterness, and a stranger intermeddleth not with its Joy*. To be here is a fearful thing.

GREATH. This is like doing business in great Waters, or like going down into the deep; this is like being in the heart of the Sea, and like going down to the Bottoms of the Mountains. Now it seems as if the Earth with its bars were about us for ever. *But let them that walk in darkness and have no light, trust in the name of the Lord, and stay upon their God*. For my Part, as I have told you already, I have gone often through this Valley, and have been much harder put to it than now I am, and yet you see I am alive. I would not boast, for that I am not mine own Saviour. But I trust we shall have a good deliverance. Come let us pray for light to him that can lighten our darkness, and that can rebuke, not only these, but all the Satans in Hell.

So they cried and prayed, and God sent light, and deliverance, for there was now no let in their way, no not there where but now they were stopt with a pit:

Yet they were not got through the Valley; so they went on still, and behold great stinks and loathsome smells, to the great annoyance of them. Then said *Mercy* to *Christiana*, There is not such pleasant being here, as at the *Gate*, or at the Interpreter's, or at the House where we lay last.

O but, said one of the Boys, *it is not so bad to go through here, as it is to* abide *here always, and for ought I know, one reason why we must go this way to the House prepared for us, is, that our home might be made the sweeter to us*.

Well said, *Samuel*, quoth the *Guide*, thou hast now spoke like a man. Why, if ever I get out here again, said the *Boy*, I think I shall prize light, and good way better than ever I did in all my life. Then said the *Guide*, we shall be out by and by.

HEEDLESS IS SLAIN

So on they went, and *Joseph* said, *Cannot we see to the end of this Valley as yet?* Then said the *Guide*, Look to your feet, for you shall presently be among the Snares. So they looked to their feet and went on; but they were troubled much with the Snares. Now when they were come among the Snares, they espied a man cast into the Ditch on the left hand, with his flesh all rent and torn. Then said the *Guide*, That is one *Heedless*, that was a going this way; he has lain there a great while. There was one *Takeheed* with him when he was taken and slain, but *he* escaped their hands. You cannot imagine, how many are killed here about, and yet men are so foolishly venturous, as to set out lightly on Pilgrimage, and to come without a *Guide*. Poor *Christian*, it was a wonder that he here escaped, but he was beloved of his God, also he had a good heart of his own, or else he could never a done it. Now they drew towards the end of the way, and just there where *Christian* had seen the Cave when he went by, out thence came forth *Maul* a Giant. This *Maul* did use to spoil young Pilgrims with Sophistry, and he called *Great-heart* by his name, and said unto him, how many times have you been forbidden to do these things? Then said Mr. *Great-heart*, what things? What things, quoth the *Giant*, you know what things; but I will put an end to your trade. But pray, said Mr. *Great-heart*, before we fall to it, let us understand wherefore we must fight (now the Women and Children stood trembling, and know not what to do) quoth the *Giant*, you rob the Country, and rob it with the worst of Thefts. These are but generals, said Mr. *Great-heart*, come to particulars, man.

Then said the *Giant*, Thou practisest the craft of a *Kidnapper*, thou gatherest up Women, and Children, and carriest them into a strange Country, to the weakning of my Master's Kingdom. But now *Great-heart* replied, I am a Servant of the God of Heaven, my business is to perswade sinners to Repentance; I am commanded to do my endeavour to turn Men, Women, and Children, from darkness to light, and from the power of Satan to God, and if this be indeed the ground of thy quarrel, let us fall to it as soon as thou wilt.

Then the *Giant*, came up and Mr. *Great-heart* went to meet him, and as he went he drew his *Sword;* but the *Giant* had a *Club*. So with out more ado they fell to it, and at the first blow the *Giant* stroke Mr. *Great-heart* down upon one of his knees; with that the Women, and Children cried out. So Mr. *Great-heart* recovering himself, laid about him in full lusty manner, and gave the *Giant* a wound in his arm; thus he fought for the space of an hour to that height of heat, that the breath came out of the *Giant's* nostrils, as the heat doth out of a boiling Caldron.

Then they sat down to rest them, but Mr. *Great-heart* betook him to prayer; also the Women and Children did nothing but sigh and cry all the time that the Battle did last.

The Giant Struck Down

When they had rested them, and taken breath, they both fell to it again, and Mr. *Great-heart* with a full blow fetcht the *Giant* down to the ground. Nay hold, and let me recover, quoth he. So Mr. *Great-heart* fairly let him get up; so to it they went again; and the *Giant* mist but little of all-to-breaking Mr. *Great-heart's* Scull with his Club.

Mr. *Great-heart* seeing that, runs to him in the full heat of his Spirit, and pierceth him under the fifth rib; with that the *Giant* began to faint, and could hold up his Club no longer. Then Mr. *Great-heart* seconded his blow, and smit the head of the *Giant* from his shoulders. Then the Women and Children rejoyced, and Mr. *Great-heart* also praised God, for the deliverance he had wrought.

When this was done, they amongst them erected a Pillar, and fastned the *Giant's* head thereon, and wrote underneath in Letters that Passengers might read.

He that did wear this head was one
That Pilgrims did misuse;
He stopt their way, he spared none,
But did them all abuse;

Until that I, Great-heart, *arose,*
The Pilgrims' Guide *to be;*
Until that I did him oppose,
That was their Enemy.

Now I saw, that they went to the Ascent that was a little way off cast up to be a Prospect for Pilgrims (that was the place from whence *Christian* had the first sight of *Faithful* his Brother). Wherefore here they sat down, and rested, they also here did eat and drink, and make merry; for that they had gotten deliverance from this so dangerous an Enemy. As they sat thus and did eat, *Christiana* asked the *Guide, If he had caught no hurt in the battle.* Then said Mr. *Great-heart, no,* save a little on my flesh; yet that also shall be so far from being to my Determent, that it is at present a proof of my love to my Master and you, and shall be a means by Grace to encrease my reward at last.

But was you not afraid, good Sir, when you see him come out with his Club?

It is my Duty, said he, to distrust mine own ability, that I may have reliance on him that is stronger than all. *But what did you think when he fetched you down to the ground at the first blow?* Why I thought, quoth he, that so my Master himself was served, and yet he it was that conquered at the last.

MATT. *When you all have thought what you please, I think God has been wonderful good unto us, both in bringing us out of this Valley, and in delivering us out of the hand of this Enemy; for my part I see no reason why we should distrust our God any more, since he has* now, *and in* such *a place as this, given us such testimony of his love as this.*

Then they got up and went forward, now a little before them stood an Oak, and under it when they came to it, they found an old *Pilgrim* fast asleep; they knew that he was a *Pilgrim* by his *Clothes,* and his *Staff* and his *Girdle.*

So the *Guide* Mr. *Great-heart* awaked him, and the old Gentleman, as he lift up his eyes, cried out; What's the matter? who are you? and what is your business here?

GREATH. *Come man be not so hot, here is none but Friends;* yet the old man gets up and stands upon his guard, and will know of them what they were. Then said the *Guide,* my name is *Great-heart,* I am the guide of these Pilgrims which are going to the Cœlestial Country.

HONEST. Then said Mr. *Honest,* I cry you mercy; I fear'd that you had been of the Company of those that some time ago did rob *Little-faith* of his money; but now I look better about me, I perceive you are honester People.

GREATH. *Why what would, or could you a done, to a helped yourself, if we indeed had been of that Company?*

HON. Done! Why, I would a fought as long as Breath had been in me; and had I so done, I am sure you could never have given me the worst on't; for a *Christian* can never be overcome, unless he shall yield of himself.

GREATH. *Well said,* Father Honest, *quoth the Guide, for by this I know thou art a Cock of the right kind, for thou hast said the Truth.*

HON. And by this also I know that thou knowest what true Pilgrimage is; for all others do think that we are the soonest overcome of any.

GREATH. *Well, now we are so happily met, pray let me crave your Name, and the name of the Place you came from?*

HON. My Name I cannot, but I came from the Town of *Stupidity;* it lieth about four Degrees beyond the City of *Destruction.*

GREATH. *Oh! Are you that Countryman then? I deem I have half a guess of you, your name is old* Honesty, *is it not?* So the old Gentleman blushed, and said, Not Honesty in the *abstract,* but *Honest* is my Name, and I wish that my *Nature* shall agree to what I am called.

HON. But Sir, said the old Gentleman, how could you guess that I am such a Man, since I came from such a place?

GREATH. *I had heard of you before, by my Master, for he knows all things that are done on the Earth: But I have often wondered that any should come from your place; for your Town is worse than is the City of* Destruction *itself.*

HON. Yes, we lie more off from the Sun, and so are more cold and senseless; but was a Man in a Mountain of Ice, yet if the Sun of Righteousness will arise upon him, his frozen Heart shall feel a Thaw; and thus it hath been with me.

GREATH. I believe it, Father *Honest,* I believe it, for I know the thing is true.

Then the old Gentleman saluted all the Pilgrims with a holy Kiss of Charity, and asked them of their Names, and how they had fared since they set out on their Pilgrimage.

CHRIS. Then said *Christiana,* My Name I suppose you have heard of, good *Christian* was my Husband, and these four were his Children. But can you think how the old Gentleman was taken, when she told them who she was! He skipp'd, he smiled, and blessed them with a thousand good Wishes, saying,

HON. *I have heard much of your Husband, and of his Travels and Wars which he underwent in his days. Be it spoken to your Comfort, the Name of your Husband rings all over these parts of the World. His Faith, his Courage, his Enduring, and his Sincerity under all, has made his Name Famous.* Then he turned him to the Boys, and asked them of their Names, which they told him: and then said he unto them, *Matthew,* be thou like *Matthew* the Publican, not in Vice, but in Virtue. *Samuel,* said he, be thou like *Samuel* the Prophet, a Man of Faith and Prayer. *Joseph,* said he, be thou like *Joseph* in *Potiphar's* House, Chaste, and one that flies from Temptation. And, *James,* be thou like *James* the *Just,* and like *James* the Brother of our Lord.

Honesty Blesses Mercy

Then they told him of *Mercy*, and how she had left her Town and her Kindred to come along with *Christiana*, and with her Sons. At that the old *Honest* Man said, *Mercy* is thy Name? by *Mercy* shalt thou be sustained, and carried thorough all those Difficulties that shall assault thee in thy way; till thou shalt come thither where thou shalt look the Fountain of Mercy in the Face with Comfort.

All this while the Guide Mr. *Great-heart*, was very much pleased, and smiled upon his Companion.

Now as they walked along together, the Guide asked the old Gentleman, *if he did not know one Mr.* Fearing *that came on Pilgrimage out of his Parts.*

Hon. Yes, very well, said he; he was a Man that had the Root of the Matter in him, but he was one of the most troublesome Pilgrims that ever I met with in all my days.

Greath. *I perceive you knew him, for you have given a very right Character of him.*

Hon. Knew him! I was a great Companion of his, I was with him most an end; when he first began to think of what would come upon us hereafter, I was with him.

Greath. *I was his guide from my Master's House, to the Gates of the Cœlestial City.*

Hon. Then you knew him to be a troublesome one.

Greath. *I did so, but I could very well bear it: for Men of my Calling, are oftentimes intrusted with the Conduct of such as he was.*

Hon. Well then, pray let us hear a little of him, and how he managed himself under your Conduct?

Mr. Fearing's Pilgrimage

Greath. Why he was always afraid that he should come short of whither he had a desire to go. Every thing frightned him that he heard any body speak of, that had but the least appearance of Opposition in it. I hear that he lay roaring at the *Slough of Dispond* for above a Month together, nor durst he, for all he saw several go over before him, venture, tho' they, many of them, offered to lend him their Hand. *He would not go back again neither.* The Cœlestial City, he said he should die if he came not to it, and yet was dejected at every Difficulty, and stumbled at every Straw that any body cast in his way. Well, after he had lain at the *Slough of Dispond* a great while, as I have told you; one sunshine Morning, I do not know how, he ventured, and so got over. But when he was over, he would scarce believe it. He had, I think, a *Slough of Dispond* in his mind, a *Slough* that he carried every where with him, or else he could never have been as he was. So he came up to the Gate, you know what I mean, that stands at the head of this way, and there also he stood a good while before he would adventure to knock. When the Gate was opened he would give back, and give place to others, and say that he was not worthy. For, for all he gat before some to the Gate, yet many of them went in before him. There the poor Man would stand shaking and shrinking: I dare say it would have pitied one's Heart to have seen him: *Nor would he go back again.* At last he took the Hammer that hanged on the Gate in his hand, and gave a small Rap or two; then one opened to him, but he shrunk back as before. He that opened stept out after him, and said, Thou trembling one, what wantest thou? with that he fell down to the Ground. He that spoke to him wondered to see him so faint. So he said to him, Peace be to thee, up, for I have set open the Door to thee; come in, for thou art blest. With that he gat up, and went in trembling, and when he was in, he was ashamed to shew his Face. Well, after he had been entertained there a while, as you know how the manner is, he was bid to go on his way, and also told the way he should take. So he came till he came to our House, but as he behaved himself at the Gate, so he did at my Master the *Interpreter's* Door. He lay thereabout in the Cold a good while, before he would adventure to call; *Yet he would not go back.* And the nights were long and cold then. Nay he had a Note of *Necessity* in his Bosom to my Master, to receive him, and grant him the Comfort of his House, and also to allow him a stout and valiant Conduct, because he was himself so *Chicken-hearted* a Man; and yet for all that he was afraid to call at the Door. So he lay up and down thereabouts till, poor man, he was almost starved; yea so great was his Dejection, that tho' he saw several others for knocking got in, yet he was afraid to venture. At last, I think I looked out of the Window, and perceiving a man to be up and down about the Door, I went out to him, and asked what he was; but, poor man, the water stood in his Eyes. So I perceived what he wanted. I went therefore in, and told it in the House, and we shewed the thing to our Lord. So he sent me out again, to entreat him to come in, but I dare say I had hard work to do it. At last he came in, and I will say that for my Lord, he carried it wonderful lovingly to him. There were but a few good bits at the Table but some of it was laid upon his Trencher. Then he presented the *Note*, and my Lord looked thereon and said his Desire should be granted. So when he had been there a good while, he seemed to get some Heart, and to be a little more Comfortable. For my Master, you must know, is one of very tender Bowels, specially to them that are afraid, wherefore he carried it so towards him, as might tend most to his Incouragement. Well, when he had had a sight of the things of the place, and was ready to take his Journey to go to the City, my Lord, as he did to *Christian* before, gave him a Bottle of Spirits, and some comfortable things to eat. Thus we set forward, and I went before him; but the man was of few Words, only he would sigh aloud.

When we were come to where the three Fellows were hanged, he said, that he doubted that that would be his end also. Only he seemed glad when he saw the Cross and the Sepulchre. There I confess he desired to stay a little to look; and he seemed for a while after to be a little *Cheery*. When we came at the Hill *Difficulty*, he made no stick at that, nor did he much fear the Lions: for you must know that his Trouble *was not about such things as those*, his Fear was about his Acceptance at last.

I got him in at the House *Beautiful*, I think before he was willing; also when he was in, I brought him acquainted with the Damsels that were of the Place, but he was ashamed to make himself much for Company; he desired much to be alone, yet he always loved good talk, and often would get behind the *Screen* to hear it; he also loved much to see *antient* Things, and to be *pondering* them in his Mind. He told me afterwards, that he loved to be in those two Houses from which he came last, to wit, at the Gate, and that of the *Interpreters*, but that he durst not be so bold to ask.

When we went also from the House *Beautiful*, down the Hill, into the Valley of *Humiliation*, he went down as well as ever I saw man in my Life, for he cared not how mean he was, so he might be happy at last. Yea, I think there was a kind of a Sympathy betwixt that Valley and him. For I never saw him better in all his Pilgrimage, than when he was in that Valley.

Here he would lie down, embrace the Ground, and kiss the very Flowers that grew in this Valley. He would now be up every Morning by break of Day, tracing, and walking to and fro in this Valley.

But when he was come to the entrance of the Valley of the Shadow of Death, I thought I should have lost my Man; not for that he had any Inclination to go back, that he always abhorred, but he was ready to die for Fear. O, the *Hobgoblins* will have me, the *Hobgoblins* will have me, cried he; and I could not beat him out on't. He made such a noise, and such an outcry here, that, had they but heard him, 'twas enough to encourage them to come and fall upon us.

But this I took very great notice of, that this Valley was as quiet while he went thorough it, as ever I knew it before or since. I suppose, those Enemies here, had now a special Check from our Lord, and a Command not to meddle until Mr. *Fearing* was past over it.

It would be too tedious to tell you of all; we will therefore only mention a Passage or two more. When he was come at *Vanity Fair*, I thought he would have fought with all the men in the Fair, I feared there we should both have been knock'd o' th' Head, so hot was he against their Fooleries; upon the inchanted Ground, he was also very wakeful. But when he was come at the *River* where was no Bridge, there again he was in a heavy Case; now, now he said he should be drowned for ever, and so never see that Face with Comfort, that he had come so many miles to behold.

And here also I took notice of what was very remarkable, the Water of that River was lower at this time, than ever I saw it in all my Life; so he went over at last, not much above wet-shod. When he was going up to the Gate, Mr. *Great-heart* began to take his Leave of him, and to wish him a good Reception above; So he said, *I shall, I shall.* Then parted we asunder, and I saw him no more.

HON. *Then it seems he was well at last.*

GREATH. Yes, yes, I never had doubt about him, he was a man of a choice Spirit, only he was always kept very low, and that made his Life so burthensome to himself, and so troublesome to others. He was above many, tender of Sin; he was so afraid of doing injuries to others, that he often would deny himself of that which was lawful, because he would not offend.

HON. *But what should be the reason that such a good Man should be all his days so much in the dark?*

GREATH. There are two sorts of Reasons for it; one is, The wise God will have it so, Some must *Pipe*, and some must *Weep:* Now Mr. *Fearing* was one that played upon *this Base*. He and his Fellows sound the *Sackbut*, whose Notes are more doleful, than the Notes of other Musick are. Tho' indeed some say, The Base is the Ground of Musick. And for my part I care not at all for that Profession, that begins not in heaviness of Mind. The first string that the Musician usually touches, *is the Base*, when he intends to put all in tune. God also plays upon this string first, when he sets the Soul in tune for himself. Only here was the imperfection of Mr. *Fearing*, he could play upon no other Musick but this till towards his latter end.

I make bold to talk thus Metaphorically, for the ripening of the Wits of young Readers, and because in the Book of the Revelations, the Saved are compared to a company of Musicians that play upon their *Trumpets* and Harps, and sing their Songs before the Throne.

HON. *He was a very zealous man, as one may see by what Relation you have given of him. Difficulties, Lions, or Vanity Fair, he feared not at all: 'Twas only Sin, Death, and Hell, that was to him a Terror;* because he had some Doubts about his Interest in that Cœlestial Country.

GREATH. You say right. *Those* were the things that were his Troublers, and they, as you have well observed, arose from the weakness of his Mind thereabout, not from weakness of Spirit as to the practical part of a Pilgrim's Life. I dare believe that as the Proverb is, he could have bit a Firebrand, had it stood in his Way. But the things with which he was oppressed, no man ever yet could shake off with ease.

CHRIS. *Then said* Christiana, *This relation of Mr.* Fearing *has done me good. I thought no body had been like me, but I see there was some Semblance 'twixt this good man and I, only we differed in two things. His Troubles were so great they brake out, but mine I kept within. His also lay so hard upon him, they made him that he could not knock at the Houses provided for Entertainment; but my Trouble was always such, as made me knock the louder.*

MERCY. If I might also speak my Heart, I must say that something of him has also dwelt in me. For I have ever been more afraid of the Lake and the loss of a place in *Paradise*, than I have been of the loss of other things. Oh, thought I, may I have the Happiness to have a Habitation *there*, 'tis enough, though I part with all the World to win it.

MATT. *Then said* Matthew, *Fear was one thing that made me think that I was far from having that within me, that accompanies Salvation; but if it was so with such a good man as he, why may it not also go well with me?*

JAMES. No fears, no Grace, said *James*. Tho' there is not always Grace where there is the fear of Hell; yet to be sure there is no Grace where there is no fear of God.

GREATH. *Well said,* James, *thou hast hit the Mark, for the fear of God is the beginning of Wisdom; and to be sure they that want the* beginning, *have neither* middle, *nor* end. *But we will here conclude our discourse of Mr.* Fearing, *after we have sent after him this Farewell.*

> *Well, Master* Fearing, *thou didst fear*
> *Thy God, and wast afraid*
> *Of doing any thing, while here,*
> *That would have thee betray'd.*
> *And didst thou fear the Lake and Pit?*
> *Would others did so too:*
> *For, as for them that want thy Wit,*
> *They do themselves undo.*

OF MR. SELFWILL

Now I saw, that they still went on in their Talk. For after Mr. *Great-heart* had made an end with Mr. *Fearing,* Mr. *Honest* began to tell them of another, but his Name was Mr. *Selfwill.* He pretended himself to be a *Pilgrim,* said Mr. *Honest;* But I perswade my self, he never came in at the Gate that stands at the head of the way.

GREATH. *Had you ever any talk with him about it?*

HON. Yes, more than once or twice; but he would always be like himself, *self-willed.* He neither cared for man, nor Argument, nor yet Example; what his Mind prompted him to, that he would do, and nothing else could he be got to.

GREATH. *Pray what Principles did he hold, for I suppose you can tell?*

HON. He held that a Man might follow the Vices, as well as the Virtues of the Pilgrims, and that if he did both, he should be certainly saved.

GREATH. *How? If he had said, 'tis possible for the best to be guilty of the Vices, as well as to partake of the Virtues of Pilgrims, he could not much a been blamed. For indeed we are exempted from no Vice absolutely, but on condition that we Watch and Strive. But this I perceive is not the thing. But if I understand you right, your meaning is, that he was of that Opinion, that it was allowable so to be?*

HON. Ay, ay, so I mean, and so he believed and practised.

GREATH. *But what Ground had he for his so saying?*

HON. Why, he said he had the Scripture for his Warrant.

GREATH. *Prithee, Mr.* Honest, *present us with a few Particulars.*

HON. So I will, He said To have to do with other men's Wives, had been practised by *David,* God's Beloved, and therefore he could do it. He said to have more Women than one, was a thing that *Solomon* practised, and therefore he could do it. He said that *Sarah,* and the godly Midwives of *Egypt* lied, and so did saved *Rahab,* and therefore he could do it. He said that the

Disciples went at the bidding of their Master, and took away the Owner's *Ass*, and therefore he could do so too. He said that *Jacob* got the Inheritance of his Father in a way of Guile and Dissimulation, and therefore he could do so too.

GREATH. *High base! indeed, and you are sure he was of this Opinion?*

HON. I have heard him plead for it, bring Scripture for it, bring Argument for it, *&c.*

GREATH. *An opinion that is not fit to be, with any Allowance, in the World.*

HON. You must understand me rightly. He did not say that any man might do this; but, that those that had the Virtues of those that did such things, might also do the same.

GREATH. *But what more false than such a Conclusion? For this is as much to say, that because good men heretofore have sinned of Infirmity, therefore he had allowance to do it of a presumptuous Mind. Or if because a Child, by the blast of the Wind, or for that it stumbled at a stone, fell down and defiled it self in Mire, therefore he might wilfully lie down and wallow like a Boar therein. Who could a thought that any one could so far a been blinded by the power of Lust? But what is written must be true. They stumble at the Word, being disobedient, whereunto also they were appointed.*

His supposing that such may have the godly Man's Virtues, who addict themselves to their Vices, is also a Delusion as strong as the other. 'Tis just as if the Dog *should say, I have, or may have the* Qualities *of the* Child, *because I lick up its stinking Excrements. To eat up the Sin of God's People, is no sign of one that is possessed with their Virtues. Nor can I believe that one that is of this Opinion, can at present have Faith or Love in him. But I know you have made strong Objections against him, prithee what can he say for himself?*

HON. Why, he says, to do this by way of Opinion, seems abundance more honest, than to do it, and yet hold contrary to it in Opinion.

GREATH. *A very wicked Answer, for tho' to let loose the Bridle to Lusts, while our Opinions are against such things, is bad; yet to sin and plead a Toleration so to do, is worse; the one stumbles Beholders accidentally, the other pleads them into the Snare.*

HON. There are many of this man's mind, that have not this man's mouth, and *that* makes going on Pilgrimage of so little esteem as it is.

GREATH. *You have said the Truth, and it is to be lamented. But he that feareth the King of Paradise shall come out of them all.*

CHRIS. There are strange Opinions in the World. I know one that said, 'twas time enough to repent when they come to die.

GREATH. *Such are not over wise. That man would a been loth, might he have had a week to run twenty mile in for his Life, to have deferred that Journey to the last hour of that Week.*

HON. You say right, and yet the generality of them that count themselves Pilgrims, do indeed do thus. I am, as you see, an old Man, and have been a Traveller in this Road many a day; and I have taken notice of many things.

I have seen some that have set out as if they would drive all the World afore them, who yet have in few days died as they in the Wilderness, and so never gat sight of the promised Land.

I have seen some that have promised nothing at first setting out to be Pilgrims, and that one would a thought could not have lived a day, that have yet proved very good Pilgrims.

I have seen some, that have run hastily forward, that again have after a little time, run as fast just back again.

I have seen some who have spoke very well of a Pilgrim's Life at first, that after a while, have spoken as much against it.

I have heard some, when they first set out for Paradise, say positively, there is such a place, who when they have been almost there, have come back again, and said there is none.

I have heard some vaunt what they would do in case they should be opposed, that have even at a false Alarm fled Faith, the Pilgrim's way, and all.

Now as they were thus in their way, there came one running to meet them, and said, Gentlemen, and you of the weaker sort, if you love Life, shift for your selves, for the Robbers are before you.

GREATH. Then said Mr. *Great-heart,* They be the three that set upon *Little-faith* heretofore. Well, said he, we are ready for them; So they went on their way. Now they looked at every Turning when they should a met with the Villains. But whether they heard of Mr. *Great-heart,* or whether they had some other Game, they came not up to the Pilgrims.

CHRIS. *Christiana* then wished for an Inn for herself and her Children, because they were weary. Then said Mr. *Honest,* there is one a little before us, where a very honorable Disciple, one *Gaius,* dwells. So they all concluded to turn in thither; and the rather, because the old Gentleman gave him so good a Report. So when they came to the Door, they went in, not knocking, for Folks use not to knock at the Door of an Inn. Then they called for the Master of the House, and he came to them. *So they asked if they might lie there that Night?*

GAIUS. Yes Gentlemen, if you be true Men, for my House is for none but Pilgrims. Then was *Christiana, Mercy,* and the *Boys,* the more glad, for that the Innkeeper was a Lover of Pilgrims. So they called for Rooms; and he shewed them one for *Christiana* and her Children and *Mercy,* and another for Mr. *Great-heart* and the old Gentleman.

GREATH. *Then said Mr.* Great-heart, *Good* Gaius, *what hast thou for Supper? for these Pilgrims have come far to day and are weary.*

GAIUS. It is late, said *Gaius;* so we cannot conveniently go out to seek Food; but such as we have you shall be welcome to, if that will content.

GREATH. *We will be content with what thou hast in the House; for, as much as I have proved thee, thou art never destitute of that which is convenient.*

Then he went down, and spake to the Cook, whose Name was *Taste-that-which-is-good,* to get ready Supper for so many Pilgrims. This done, he comes up again, saying, Come my good Friends, you are welcome to me, and

I am glad that I have an House to entertain you; and while Supper is making ready, if you please, let us entertain one another with some good Discourse. So they all said, Content.

GAIUS. Then said *Gaius, whose Wife is this aged Matron, and whose Daughter is this young Damsel?*

GREATH. The Woman is the Wife of one *Christian*, a Pilgrim of former times, and these are his four Children. The Maid is one of her Acquaintance; one that she hath perswaded to come with her on Pilgrimage. The Boys take all after their Father, and covet to tread in his Steps. Yea, if they do but see any place where the old Pilgrim hath lain, or any print of his Foot, it ministreth Joy to their Hearts, and they covet to lie or tread in the same.

GAIUS. Then said *Gaius,* Is this *Christian's* Wife, and are these *Christian's* Children? I knew your Husband's Father, yea, also, his Father's Father. Many have been good of this stock, their Ancestors dwelt first at *Antioch. Christian's* Progenitors (I suppose you have heard your Husband talk of them) were very worthy men. They have above any that I know, shewed themselves men of great Virtue and Courage for the Lord of the Pilgrims, his ways, and them that loved him. I have heard of many of your Husband's Relations that have stood all Trials for the sake of the Truth. *Stephen* that was one of the first of the Family from whence your Husband sprang, was knocked o' th' Head with Stones. *James*, another of this Generation, was slain with the edge of the Sword. To say nothing of *Paul* and *Peter*, men antiently of the Family from whence your Husband came, there was *Ignatius*, who was cast to the Lions; *Romanus*, whose Flesh was cut by pieces from his Bones; and *Polycarp*, that played the man in the Fire. There was he that was hanged up in a Basket in the Sun, for the Wasps to eat; and he who they put into a Sack and cast him into the Sea, to be drowned. 'Twould be impossible, utterly to count up all of that Family that have suffered Injuries and Death, for the love of a Pilgrim's Life. Nor can I but be glad to see that thy Husband has left behind him four such Boys as these. I hope they will bear up their Father's Name, and tread in their Father's Steps, and come to their Father's End.

GREATH. *Indeed Sir, they are likely Lads; they seem to chuse heartily their Father's Ways.*

GAIUS. That is it that I said, wherefore *Christian's* Family is like still to spread abroad upon the face of the Ground, and yet to be numerous upon the face of the Earth. Wherefore let *Christiana* look out some Damsels for her Sons, to whom they may be betrothed, *&c.* that the Name of their Father, and the House of his Progenitors may never be forgotten in the World.

HON. *'Tis pity this Family should fall, and be extinct.*

GAIUS. Fall it cannot, but be diminished it may. But let *Christiana* take my Advice, and that's the way to uphold it.

And *Christiana*, Said this Innkeeper, I am glad to see thee and thy Friend *Mercy* together here, a lovely Couple. And may I advise, take *Mercy* into a nearer Relation to thee. If she will, let her be given to *Matthew* thy eldest

Son. 'Tis the way to preserve you a Posterity in the Earth. So this Match was concluded, and in process of time they were married. But more of that hereafter.

Gaius also proceeded, and said, I will now speak on the behalf of Women, to take away their Reproach. For as Death and the Curse came into the World by a Woman, so also did Life and Health; *God sent forth his Son, made of a Woman.* Yea, to shew how much those that came after did abhor the Act of their Mother, this Sex, in the old Testament, coveted Children, if happily this or that Woman might be the Mother of the Saviour of the World. I will say again, that when the Saviour was come, Women rejoyced in him, before either Man or Angel. I read not that ever any man did give unto Christ so much as one Groat, but the Women followed him, and ministred to him of their Substance. 'Twas a Woman that washed his Feet with Tears, and a Woman that anointed his Body to the Burial. They were Women that wept, when he was going to the Cross; and Women that followed him from the Cross, and that sat by his Sepulchre when he was buried. They were Women that was first with him at his Resurrection-morn, and Women that brought Tiding first to his Disciples that he was risen from the Dead. Women therefore are highly favoured, and shew by these things that they are sharers with us in the Grace of Life.

Now the Cook sent up to signify that Supper was almost ready, and sent one to lay the Cloth, the Trenchers, and to set the Salt and Bread in order.

Then said *Matthew, the sight of this Cloth, and of this Forerunner of a Supper, begetteth in me a greater Appetite to my Food than I had before.*

GAIUS. So let all ministring Doctrines *to* thee in this Life, beget *in* thee a greater desire to sit at the Supper of the great King in his Kingdom; for all Preaching, Books and Ordinances here, are but as the laying of the Trenchers, and as setting of Salt upon the Board, when compared with the Feast that our Lord will make for us when we come to his House.

So Supper came up, and first a *Heave-shoulder* and a *Wave-Breast* was set on the Table before them, to shew that they must begin their *Meal* with Prayer and Praise to God. The *heave-shoulder David* lifted his Heart up to God with, and with the *wave-Breast, where his Heart lay,* with that he used to lean upon his Harp when he played. These two Dishes were very fresh and good, and they all eat heartily-well thereof.

The next they brought up, was a Bottle of Wine, red as Blood. So *Gaius* said to them, Drink freely, this is the Juice of the true Vine, that makes glad the Heart of God and Man. So they drank and were merry.

The next was a Dish of Milk well crumbed. But *Gaius* said, *Let the Boys have that, that they may grow thereby.*

Then they brought up in course a dish of *Butter* and *Hony.* Then said *Gaius,* Eat freely of *this,* for this is good to cheer up, and strengthen your Judgments and Understandings. This was our Lord's Dish when he was a Child. *Butter and Hony shall he eat, that he may know to refuse the Evil, and chuse the Good.*

Then they brought them up a dish of Apples, and they were very good tasted Fruit. Then said *Matthew*, May we eat Apples, since they were such, by, and with which, the Serpent beguiled our first Mother?

Then said *Gaius*,

> *Apples were they* with *which we were beguil'd,*
> *Yet* Sin, *not Apples hath our Souls defil'd.*
> *Apples forbid, if eat, corrupts the Blood.*
> *To eat such, when commanded, does us good.*
> *Drink of his Flagons then, thou Church, his Dove,*
> *And eat* his *Apples, who are sick of Love.*

Then said *Matthew, I made the Scruple, because I awhile since, was sick with eating of Fruit.*

Gaius. Forbidden Fruit will make you sick; but not what our Lord has tolerated.

While they were thus talking, they were presented with an other Dish; and 'twas a dish of *Nuts*. Then said some at the Table, *Nuts* spoil tender Teeth; specially the Teeth of Children. Which when *Gaius* heard, he said,

> *Hard* Texts *are* Nuts (*I will not call them* Cheaters),
> *Whose* Shells *do keep their* Kernels *from the* Eaters.
> *Ope then the Shells, and you shall have the Meat,*
> *They here are brought, for you to crack and eat.*

Then were they very Merry, and sat at the Table a long time, talking of many Things. Then said the Old Gentleman, My good Landlord, while we are cracking your *Nuts*, if you please, do you open this Riddle.

> *A man there was, tho' some did count him mad,*
> *The more he cast away, the more he had.*

Then they all gave good heed, wondring what good *Gaius* would say, so he sat still a while, and then thus replied:

> *He that bestows his Goods upon the Poor,*
> *Shall have as much again, and ten times more.*

Then said *Joseph*, I dare say Sir, I did not think you could a found it out.

Oh! Said *Gaius*, I have been trained up in this way a great while. Nothing teaches like Experience. I have learned of my Lord to be kind, and have found by experience, that I have gained thereby. *There is that scattereth, yet increaseth, and there is that witholdeth more than is meet, but it tendeth to Poverty. There is that maketh himself Rich, yet hath nothing. There is that maketh himself poor, yet hath great Riches.*

Then *Samuel* whispered to *Christiana* his Mother, and said, Mother, this is a very good man's House, let us stay here a good while, and let my Brother *Matthew* be married here to *Mercy*, before we go any further.

The which *Gaius* the Host overhearing, said, *With a very good Will, my Child.*

So they staid there more than a Month, and *Mercy* was given to *Matthew* to Wife.

While they stayed here, *Mercy* as her Custom was, would be making Coats and Garments to give to the Poor, by which she brought up a very good Report upon the Pilgrims.

The Riddle

But to return again to our Story. After Supper, the lads desired a Bed, for that they were weary with Travelling. Then *Gaius* called to shew them their Chamber, but said *Mercy*, I will have them to Bed. So she had them to Bed, and they slept well, but the rest sat up all Night. For *Gaius* and they were such suitable Company, that they could not tell how to part. Then after much talk of their Lord, themselves, and their Journey, old Mr. *Honest*, he that put forth the Riddle to *Gaius*, began to *nod*. Then said *Great-heart*, What Sir, you begin to be drowzy, come, rub up, now here's a *Riddle* for you. Then said Mr. *Honest*, let's hear it.

Then said Mr. *Great-heart*,

He that will kill, must first be overcome:
Who live abroad would, first must die at home.

Hah, said Mr. *Honest*, it is a hard one, hard to expound, and harder to practise. But come Landlord, said he, I will if you please, leave my part to you; do you expound it, and I will hear what you say.

No said *Gaius*, 'twas put to you, and 'tis expected that you should answer it.

Then said the Old Gentleman,

He first by Grace must conquer'd be,
That Sin would mortify.
And who, that lives, would convince me,
Unto himself must die.

It is right, said *Gaius*, good Doctrine and Experience teaches this. For first, until Grace displays itself, and overcomes the Soul with its Glory, it is altogether without Heart to oppose Sin. Besides, if Sin is Satan's Cords, by which the Soul lies bound, how should it make Resistance, before it is loosed from that Infirmity?

Secondly, Nor will any that knows either Reason or Grace, believe that such a man can be a living Monument of Grace, that is a Slave to his own Corruptions.

And now it comes in my Mind, I will tell you a Story, worth the hearing. There were two Men that went on Pilgrimage, the one began when he was young, the other when he was old. The young Man had strong Corruptions to grapple with, the old Man's were decayed with the decays of Nature. The young man trod his steps as even as did the old one, and was every way as light as he; who now, or which of them, had their Graces shining clearest, since both seemed to be alike?

Hon. *The young Man's doubtless. For that which heads it against the greatest Opposition, gives best demonstration that it is strongest. Specially when it also holdeth pace with that that meets not with half so much; as to be sure old Age does not.*

Besides, I have observed that old men have blessed themselves with this mistake; Namely, taking the decays of Nature, for a gracious Conquest over Corruptions, and so have been apt to beguile themselves. Indeed old men that are gracious, are best able to give Advice to them that are young, because they have seen most of the emptiness of things. But yet, for an old and a young to set out both together, the young one has the advantage of the fairest discovery of a work of Grace within him, tho' the old Man's Corruptions are naturally the weakest.

Thus they sat talking till break of Day. Now when the Family was up, *Christiana* bid her Son *James* that he should read a Chapter; so he read the 53rd of *Isaiah*. When he had done, Mr. *Honest* asked why it was said, *That the Saviour is said to come out of a dry ground, and also that he had no Form nor Comeliness in him?*

GREATH. Then said Mr. *Great-heart,* To the first I answer, because, The Church of the Jews, of which Christ came, had then lost almost all the Sap and Spirit of Religion. To the second I say, The Words are spoken in the Person of the Unbelievers, who because they want that Eye, that can see into our Prince's Heart, therefore they judge of him by the meanness of his Outside.

Just like those that know not that precious Stones are covered over with a homely *Crust;* who when they have found one, because they know not what they have found, cast it again away as men do a common Stone.

Well, said *Gaius,* Now you are here, and since, as I know, Mr. *Great-heart* is good at his Weapons, if you please, after we have refreshed ourselves, we will walk into the Fields, to see if we can do any good. About a mile from hence, there is one *Slay-good,* a *Giant,* that doth much annoy the King's High-way in these parts. And I know whereabout his Haunt is. He is Master of a number of Thieves; 'twould be well if we could clear these Parts of him.

So they consented and went, Mr. *Great-heart* with his *Sword, Helmet,* and *Shield;* and the rest with Spears and Staves.

When they came to the place where he was, they found him with one *Feeble-mind* in his Hands, whom his Servants had brought unto him, having taken him in the Way; now the Giant was rifling of him, with a purpose after that to pick his Bones. For he was of the nature of *Flesh-eaters.*

Well, so soon as he saw Mr. *Great-heart* and his Friends at the Mouth of his Cave with their Weapons, he demanded what they wanted?

GREATH. We want thee; for we are come to revenge the Quarrel of the many that thou hast slain of the Pilgrims, when thou hast dragged them out of the King's High-way; wherefore come out of thy Cave. So he armed himself and came out, and to a Battle they went, and fought for above an Hour, and then stood still to take Wind.

SLAY-GOOD. *Then said the Giant, why are you here on my Ground?*

GREATH. To revenge the Blood of Pilgrims, as I also told thee before; so they went to it again, and the Giant made Mr. *Great-heart* give back, but he came up again, and in the greatness of his Mind, he let fly with such stoutness at the Giant's Head and Sides, that he made him let his Weapon fall out of his Hand. So he smote him and slew him, and cut off his Head, and brought it away to the *Inn.* He also took *Feeble-mind* the Pilgrim, and brought him with him to his Lodgings. When they were come home, they shewed his Head to the Family, and then set it up as they had done others before, for a Terror to those that should attempt to do as he, hereafter.

Then they asked Mr. *Feeble-mind* how he fell into his hands?

Mr. Feeble-mind as Pilgrim

Feeblem. Then said the poor man, I am a sickly man, as you see, and because *Death* did usually once a day *knock at my Door*, I thought I should never be well at home. So I betook myself to a Pilgrim's Life; and have travelled hither from the Town of *Uncertain*, where I and my Father were born. I am a man of no strength at all of Body, nor yet of Mind, but would, if I could, tho' I can but *crawl*, spend my Life in the Pilgrim's way. When I came at the Gate that is at the head of the Way, the Lord of that place did entertain me freely. Neither objected he against my weakly Looks, nor against my *Feeble Mind;* but gave me such things that were necessary for my Journey, and bid me hope to the end. When I came to the House of the *Interpreter*, I received much Kindness there, and because the Hill *Difficulty* was judged too hard for me, I was carried up that by one of his Servants. Indeed I have found much Relief from Pilgrims, tho' none was willing to go so softly as I am forced to do. Yet still as they came on, they bid me be of good Cheer, and said, that it was the will of their Lord that Comfort should be given to the *feeble-minded*, and so went on their *own* pace. When I was come up to *Assault-Lane*, then this *Giant* met with me, and bid me prepare for an *encounter;* but alas, feeble one that I was, I had more need of a *Cordial.* So he came up and took me; I conceited he should not kill me; also when he had got me into his Den, since I went not with him *willingly*, I believed I should come out alive again. For I have heard, that not any Pilgrim that is taken Captive by violent Hands, if he keeps Heart-whole towards his Master, is by the Laws of Providence to die by the Hand of the Enemy. *Robbed*, I looked to be, and Robbed to be sure I am; but I am as you see escaped with Life, for the which I thank my King as Author, and you, as the Means. Other Brunts I also look for, but this I have resolved on, to wit, to *run* when I can, to *go* when I cannot *run*, and to *creep* when I cannot *go.* As to the main, I thank him that loves me, I am fixed; my way is before me, my mind is beyond the *River* that has no Bridge, tho' I am, as you see, but of a *feeble Mind.*

Hon. *Then said old Mr.* Honest, *Have not you some time ago, been acquainted with one Mr.* Fearing, *a* Pilgrim?

Feeblem. Acquainted with him; Yes. He came from the Town of *Stupidity*, which lieth *four Degrees* to the Northward of the City of *Destruction*, and as many off, of where I was born; Yet we were well acquainted, for indeed he was mine Uncle, my Father's Brother; he and I have been much of a Temper, he was a little shorter than I, but yet we were much of a Complexion.

HON. *I perceive you know him, and I am apt to believe also that you were related one to another; for you have his whitely Look, a Cast like his with your Eye, and your Speech is much alike.*

FEEBLEM. Most have said so, that have known us both, and besides, what I have read in him, I have for the most part, found in my self.

GAIUS. *Come Sir, said good* Gaius, *be of good Cheer, you are welcome to me, and to my House; and what thou hast a mind to, call for freely; and what thou would'st have my Servants do for thee, they will do it with a ready Mind.*

FEEBLEM. Then said Mr. *Feeble-mind*, This is unexpected Favor, and as the Sun, shining out of a very dark Cloud. Did Giant *Slay-good* intend me this Favor when he stop'd me, and resolved to let me go no further? Did he intend that after he had rifled my Pockets, I should go to *Gaius mine Host!* Yet so it is.

Now, just as Mr. *Feeble-mind* and *Gaius* was thus in talk, there comes one running and called at the Door, and told, That about a Mile and an half off, there was one Mr. *Not-right*, a Pilgrim, struck dead upon the place where he was, with a *Thunder-bolt.*

FEEBLEM. Alas! said Mr. *Feeble-mind*, is he slain? He overtook me some days before I came so far as hither, and would be my Company-keeper. He also was with me when *Slay-good* the Giant took me, but he was nimble of his Heels, and escaped. But it seems, he escaped to die, and I was took to live.

> *What, one would think, doth seek to slay* outright
> *Ofttimes delivers from the saddest* Plight.
> *That very* Providence, *whose Face is* Death,
> *Doth ofttimes, to the Lowly, Life* bequeath.
> *I taken was, he did escape and flee,*
> *Hands Crost, gives Death to him, and Life to me.*

Now about this time *Matthew* and *Mercy* was Married; also *Gaius* gave his Daughter *Phœbe* to *James, Matthew's* Brother, to Wife; after which time, they yet stayed above ten days, at *Gaius's* House, spending their time and the Seasons, like as Pilgrims use to do.

THE PILGRIMS PREPARE TO GO FORWARD

When they were to depart, *Gaius* made them a Feast, and they did eat and drink, and were merry. Now the Hour was come that they must be gone, wherefore Mr. *Great-heart* called for a Reckoning. But *Gaius* told him that at his House, it was not the Custom for *Pilgrims* to pay for their Entertainment. He boarded them by the year, but looked for his Pay from the good *Samaritan*, who had promised him at his return, whatsoever Charge he was at with them, faithfully to repay him. Then said Mr. *Great-heart* to him.

GREATH. *Beloved, thou dost faithfully, whatsoever thou dost, to the Breth-*

ren and to Strangers, which have borne Witness of thy Charity before the Church, whom if thou (yet) bring forward on their Journey after a Godly sort, thou shalt do well.

Then *Gaius* took his Leave of them all and of his Children, and particularly of Mr. *Feeble-mind*. He also gave him something to drink by the way.

Now Mr. *Feeble-mind*, when they were going out of the door, made as if he intended to linger. The which, when Mr. *Great-heart* espied, he said, Come, Mr. *Feeble-mind*, Pray do you go along with us, I will be your *Conductor*, and you shall fair as the rest.

FEEBLEM. *Alas, I want a suitable Companion, you are all lusty and strong, but I, as you see, am weak. I chuse therefore rather to come behind, lest, by reason of my many Infirmities, I should be both a Burthen to myself and to you. I am, as I said, a man of a weak and feeble Mind, and shall be offended and made weak at that which others can bear. I shall like no Laughing; I shall like no gay Attire, I shall like no unprofitable Questions. Nay, I am so weak a Man, as to be offended with that which others have a liberty to do. I do not yet know all the Truth; I am a very ignorant* Christian man; *sometimes if I hear some rejoice in the Lord, it troubles me because I cannot do so too. It is with me as it is with a weak Man among the strong, or as with a sick Man among the healthy, or as a Lamp despised, (He that is ready to slip with his Feet, is as a Lamp despised in the Thought of him that is at ease.)* So that I know not what to do.

GREATH. But Brother, said Mr. *Great-heart*, I have it in Commission, to comfort the *feeble-minded*, and to support the weak. You must needs go along with us; we will wait for you, we will lend you our help, we will deny ourselves of some things, both *Opinionative* and *Practical*, for your sake; we will not enter into Doubtful Disputations before you, we will be made all things to you rather than you shall be left behind.

Now, all this while they were at *Gaius's* Door; and behold as they were thus in the heat of their Discourse, Mr. *Ready-to-halt* came by, with his *Crutches* in his hand, and he also was going on Pilgrimage.

FEEBLEM. *Then said Mr.* Feeble-mind *to him, Man! How comest thou hither? I was but just now complaining that I had not a suitable Companion, but thou art according to my wish. Welcome, welcome, good Mr.* Ready-to-halt, *I hope thee and I may be some help.*

READY-TO-HALT. I shall be glad of thy Company, said the other; and good Mr. *Feeble-mind*, rather than we will part, since we are thus happily met, I will lend thee one of my Crutches.

FEEBLEM. *Nay, said he, tho' I thank thee for thy good Will, I am not inclined to halt afore I am Lame. How be it, I think when occasion is, it may help me against a Dog.*

READYTO. If either *myself*, or my *Crutches* can do thee a pleasure, we are both at thy Command, good Mr. *Feeble-mind.*

Thus therefore they went on, Mr. *Great-heart*, and Mr. *Honest* went before, *Christiana* and her Children went next, and Mr. *Feeble-mind*, and Mr. *Ready-to-halt* came behind with his Crutches. Then said Mr. *Honest*,

HON. *Pray Sir, now we are upon the Road, tell us some profitable things of some that have gone on Pilgrimage before us.*

GREATH. With a good Will. I suppose you have heard how *Christian* of old, did meet with *Apollyon* in the Valley of *Humiliation,* and also what hard work he had to go thorow the Valley of the Shadow of Death. Also I think you cannot but have heard how *Faithful* was put to it with *Madam Wanton,* with *Adam* the first, with one *Discontent,* and *Shame;* four as deceitful Villains, as a man can meet with upon the Road.

HON. *Yes, I have heard of all this; but indeed good* Faithful *was hardest put to it with Shame; he was an unwearied one.*

GREATH. Ay, for as the Pilgrim well said, He of all men had the wrong Name.

HON. *But pray Sir where was it that* Christian *and* Faithful *met* Talkative? *that same was also a notable one.*

GREATH. He was a confident Fool, yet many follow his ways.

HON. *He had like to a beguiled* Faithful.

GREATH. Ay, but *Christian* put him into a way quickly to find him out. Thus they went on till they came at the place where *Evangelist* met with *Christian* and *Faithful,* and prophesied to them of what should befall them at Vanity-Fair.

GREATH. Then said their *Guide,* Hereabouts did *Christian* and *Faithful* meet with *Evangelist,* who prophesied to them of what Troubles they should meet with at Vanity-Fair.

HON. *Say you so! I dare say it was a hard Chapter that then he did read unto them?*

GREATH. 'Twas so, but he gave them encouragement withal. But what do we talk of them, they were a couple of Lion-like Men; they had set their Faces like Flint. Don't you remember how undaunted they were when they stood before the Judge?

HON. *Well* Faithful *bravely Suffered?*

GREATH. So he did, and as brave things came on't. For *Hopeful* and some others, as the Story relates it, were Converted by his Death.

HON. *Well, but pray go on; for you are well acquainted with things.*

GREATH. Above all that *Christian* met with after he had past thorow Vanity-Fair, one *By-Ends* was the arch one.

HON. *By-Ends; What was he?*

GREATH. A very arch Fellow, a down-right Hypocrite; one that would be Religious, which way ever the World went, but so cunning, that he would be sure neither to lose, nor suffer for it.

He had his *Mode* of Religion for every fresh Occasion, and his Wife was as good at it as he. He would turn and change from Opinion to Opinion; yea, and plead for so doing too. But so far as I could learn, he came to an ill End with his *By-Ends,* nor did I ever hear that any of his Children was ever of any Esteem with any that truly feared God.

Now by this Time, they were come within sight of the Town of *Vanity,* where Vanity-Fair is kept. So when they saw that they were so near the

Town, they consulted with one another how they should pass thorow the Town, and some said one thing, and some another. At last Mr. *Great-heart*, said, I have, as you may understand, often been a *Conductor* of Pilgrims thorow *this* Town. Now I am acquainted with one Mr. *Mnason*, a *Cyprusian* by Nation, an old Disciple, at whose House we may Lodge. If you think good, said he, we will turn in there?

Content, said Old *Honest;* Content, said *Christiana;* Content, said Mr. *Feeble-mind;* and so they said all. Now you must think it was *Even-tide*, by that they got to the outside of the Town, but Mr. *Great-heart* knew the way to the Old Man's House. So thither they came; and he called at the Door, and the old Man within knew his Tongue so soon as ever he heard it. So he opened, and they all came in. Then said *Mnason* their Host, How far have ye come to day? so they said, from the House of *Gaius* our Friend. I promise you, said he, you have gone a good stitch, you may well be a weary; sit down. So they sat down.

GREATH. *Then said their Guide, Come, what Cheer Sirs, I dare say you are welcome to my Friend.*

MNASON. I also, said Mr. *Mnason,* do bid you Welcome; and what ever you want, do but say, and we will do what we can to get it for you.

HON. *Our great Want, a while since, was Harbor, and good Company, and now I hope we have both.*

MNA. For Harbor you see what it is, but for good Company, that will appear in the Trial.

GREATH. *Well, said Mr.* Great-heart, *will you have the Pilgrims up into their Lodging?*

MNA. I will, said Mr. *Mnason.* So he had them to their respective Places; and also shewed them a very fair Dining-Room where they might be and sup together, until time was come to go to Rest.

PEOPLE OF VANITY TOWN

Now when they were set in their places, and were a little cheery after their Journey, Mr. *Honest* asked his Landlord if there were any store of good People in the Town?

MNA. We have a few, for indeed they are but a few, when compared with them on the other Side.

HON. *But how shall we do to see some of them? for the Sight of good Men to them that are going on Pilgrimage, is like to the appearing of the Moon and the Stars to them that are sailing upon the Seas.*

MNA. Then Mr. *Mnason* stamped with his Foot, and his Daughter *Grace* came up; so he said unto her, *Grace* go you, tell my Friends, Mr. *Contrite*, Mr. *Holy-man*, Mr. *Love-saint*, Mr. *Dare-not-lie*, and Mr. *Penitent*, that I have a Friend or two at my House, that have a mind this Evening to see them.

So *Grace* went to call them, and they came, and after Salutation made, they sat down together at the Table.

Then said Mr. *Mnason*, their Landlord, My Neighbours, I have, as you see, a company of *Strangers* come to my House, they are *Pilgrims:* they come from afar, and are going to Mount *Sion*. But who, quoth he, do you think this is? pointing with his Finger to *Christiana*. It is *Christiana*, the Wife of *Christian*, that famous Pilgrim, who with *Faithful* his Brother were so shamefully handled in our Town. At that they stood amazed, saying, we little thought to see *Christiana*, when *Grace* came to call us, wherefore this is a very comfortable Surprize. Then they asked her of her welfare, and if these young Men were her Husband's Sons. And when she had told them they were; they said, The King whom you love, and serve, make you as your Father, and bring you where he is in Peace.

HON. Then Mr. *Honest* (*when they were all sat down*) *asked Mr.* Contrite *and the rest, in what posture their Town was at present.*

CONTRITE. You may be sure we are full of Hurry in Fair time. 'Tis hard keeping our Hearts and Spirits in any good Order, when we are in a cumbred Condition. He that lives in such a place as this is, and that has to do with such as we have, has Need of an Item, to caution him to take heed, every Moment of the Day.

HON. *But how are your Neighbors for quietness?*

CONT. They are much more moderate now than formerly. You know how *Christian* and *Faithful* were used at our Town; but of late, I say, they have been far more moderate. I think the Blood of *Faithful* lieth with load upon them till now; for since they burned him, they have been ashamed to burn any more. In those Days we were afraid to walk the Streets, but *now* we can shew our Heads. *Then* the Name of a Professor was odious, *now* specially in some parts of our Town (for you know our Town is large) Religion is counted Honourable.

Then said Mr. Contrite *to them, Pray how fareth it with you in your Pilgrimage, how stands the Country affected towards you?*

HON. It happens to us, as it happeneth to Wayfaring men; sometimes our way is clean, sometimes foul; sometimes up hill, sometimes down hill; we are seldom at a Certainty. The Wind is not always on our Backs, nor is every one a Friend that we meet with in the Way. We have met with some notable Rubs already; and what are yet behind we know not, but for the most part we find it true, that has been talked of of old: *A good Man must suffer Trouble.*

CONT. *You talk of Rubs, what Rubs have you met withal?*

HON. Nay, ask Mr. *Great-heart*, our Guide, for he can give the best Account of that.

GREATH. We have been beset three or four times already: First *Christiana* and her Children were beset with two Ruffians, that they feared would a took away their Lives; We was beset with Giant *Bloody-Man*, Giant *Maul*, and Giant *Slay-good*. Indeed we did rather beset the last, than were beset of him. And thus it was: After we had been some time at the House of *Gaius, mine Host and of the whole Church*, we were minded upon a time to take our Weapons with us, and so go see if we could light upon any of those that were Enemies to Pilgrims (for we heard that there was a notable one thereabouts). Now *Gaius* knew his *Haunt* better than I, because he dwelt thereabout, so we looked and looked, till at last we discerned the Mouth of his Cave; then we were glad and pluck'd up our Spirits. So we approached up to his *Den*, and lo when we came there, he had dragged by mere force into his Net, this *poor man*, Mr. *Feeble-mind*, and was about to bring him to his End. But when he saw us, supposing, as we thought, he had had another Prey, he left the poor man in his Hole, and came out. So we fell to it full sore, and he lustily laid about him; but, in conclusion, he was brought down to the Ground, and his Head cut off, and set up by the Way side for a Terror to such as should after practise such Ungodliness. That I tell you the Truth, here is the man himself to affirm it, who was as a Lamb taken out of the Mouth of the Lion.

FEEBLEM. *Then said Mr.* Feeble-mind, *I found this true to my Cost, and Comfort. To my Cost, when he threatned to pick my Bones every Moment, and to my Comfort, when I saw Mr.* Great-heart *and his Friends with their Weapons approach so near for my Deliverance.*

HOLY-MAN. Then said Mr. *Holy-man*, there are two things that they have need to be possessed with that go on Pilgrimage, *Courage*, and an *unspotted Life*. If they have not *Courage*, they can never hold on their way; and if their Lives be *loose*, they will make the very name of a *Pilgrim* stink.

LOVES. Then said Mr. *Love-saint;* I hope this Caution is not needful amongst you. But truly there are many that go upon the Road, that rather declare themselves Strangers to Pilgrimage, than Strangers and Pilgrims in the Earth.

DARENOT. *Then said Mr.* Dare-not-lie, *'Tis true; they neither have the Pilgrim's* Weed, *nor the Pilgrim's Courage; they go not uprightly, but all* awry *with their Feet; one shoe goes* inward, *another* outward, *and their Hosen out behind; there a Rag, and there a Rent,* to *the Disparagement of their Lord.*

PENIT. These things said Mr. *Penitent*, they ought to be troubled for, nor are the Pilgrims like to have that Grace put upon them and their Pilgrim's Progress, as they desire, until the way is cleared of such Spots and Blemishes.

Thus they sat talking and spending the time, until Supper was set upon the Table. Unto which they went and refreshed their weary Bodies, so they went to Rest. Now they stayed in this Fair a great while, at the House of this Mr. *Mnason*, who in process of time, gave his Daughter *Grace* unto *Samuel*, *Christiana's* Son, to Wife, and his Daughter *Martha* to *Joseph*.

The time, as I said, that they lay here, was long (for it was not now as in former times.) Wherefore the *Pilgrims* grew acquainted with many of the good People of the Town, and did them what Service they could. *Mercy*, as she was wont, laboured much for the Poor, wherefore their Bellys and Backs blessed her, and she was there an Ornament to her Profession. And to say the truth for *Grace*, *Phœbe*, and *Martha*, they were all of a very good Nature, and did much good in their place. They were all also of them very

Fruitful, so that *Christian's* Name, as was said before, was like to live in the World.

While they lay here, there came a *Monster* out of the Woods, and slew many of the People of the Town. It would also carry away their Children, and teach them to suck its Whelps. Now no Man in the Town durst so much as face this *Monster;* but all Men fled when they heard of the noise of his coming.

The *Monster* was like unto no one Beast upon the Earth. Its Body was like a Dragon, and it had seven Heads and ten Horns. *It made great havock of Children, and yet it was governed by a Woman.* This *Monster* propounded Conditions to men; and such men as loved their Lives more than their Souls, accepted of those Conditions. So they came under.

Now this Mr. *Great-heart*, together with these that came to visit the Pilgrims at Mr. *Mnason's* House, entered into a Covenant to go and engage this Beast, if perhaps they might deliver the People of this Town from the Paw and Mouths of this so devouring a Serpent.

Then did Mr. *Great-heart*, Mr. *Contrite*, Mr. *Holy-man*, Mr. *Dare-not-lie*, and Mr. *Penitent*, with their Weapons go forth to meet him. Now the *Monster* at first was very Rampant, and looked upon these Enemies with great Disdain; but they so belabored him, being sturdy men at Arms, that they made him make a Retreat; so they came home to Mr. *Mnason's* House again.

The *Monster*, you must know had his certain Seasons to come out in, and to make his Attempts upon the Children of the People of the Town; also these Seasons did these valiant Worthies watch him in, and did still continually assault him; in so much, that in process of time, he became not only wounded, but lame; also he has not made that havock of the Towns-men's Children, as formerly he has done. And it is verily believed by some, that this Beast will die of his Wounds.

This therefore made Mr. *Great-heart* and his Fellows of great Fame in this Town, so that many of the People that wanted their taste of things, yet had a reverend Esteem and Respect for them. Upon this account therefore it was that these Pilgrims got not much hurt there. True, there were some of the baser sort that could see no more than a *Mole*, nor understand more than a *Beast*, these had no reverence for these men, nor took they notice of their Valour or Adventures.

Well, the time grew on that the Pilgrims must go on their way, wherefore they prepared for their Journey. They sent for their Friends, they conferred with them, they had some time set apart therein to commit each other to the protection of their Prince. There was again that brought them of such things as they had, that was fit for the weak and the strong, for the Women and the men; and so *laded* them with such things as was necessary.

Then they set forwards on their way, and their Friends accompanying them so far as was convenient, they again committed each other to the Protection of their King, and parted.

They therefore that were of the Pilgrims' Company went on, and Mr.

Great-heart went before them. Now the Women and Children being weakly, they were forced to go as they could bear, by this means Mr. *Ready-to-halt* and Mr. *Feeble-mind* had more to sympathize with their Condition.

When they were gone from the Townsmen, and when their Friends had bid them farewell, they quickly came to the place where *Faithful* was put to Death. There therefore they made a stand, and thanked him that had enabled him to bear his Cross so well, and the rather, because they now found that they had a benefit by such a manly Suffering as his was.

They went on therefore after this a good way further, talking of *Christian* and *Faithful*, and how *Hopeful* joined himself to *Christian* after that *Faithful* was dead.

Now they were come up with the *Hill Lucre*, where the *Silver-mine* was, which took *Demas* off from his Pilgrimage, and into which, as some think, *By-ends* fell and perished; wherefore they considered that. But when they were come to the old Monument that stood over against the *Hill Lucre*, to wit, to the Pillar of Salt that stood also within view of *Sodom*, and its stinking Lake, they marvelled, as did *Christian* before, that men of that Knowledge and ripeness of Wit as they was, should be so blinded as to turn aside here. Only they considered again, that Nature is not affected with the Harms that others have met with, specially if that thing upon which they look has an attracting Virtue upon the foolish Eye.

I saw now that they went on till they came at the River that was on this Side of the Delectable Mountains. To the River where the fine Trees grow on both sides, and whose Leaves, if taken inwardly, are good against Surfeits; where the Meadows are green all the year long, and where they might lie down safely.

By this River-side in the Meadow, there were Cotes and Folds for Sheep, an House built for the *nourishing*, and bringing up of those Lambs, the Babes of those Women that go on Pilgrimage. Also there was here one that was intrusted with them, who could have compassion, and that could gather these Lambs with his Arm, and carry them in his Bosom, and that could gently lead those that were with young. Now to the Care of *this Man*, *Christiana* admonished her four Daughters to commit their little ones; that by these Waters they might be housed, harbored, succoured, and nourished, and that none of them might *be lacking in time to come*. This *man*, if any of them go astray or be lost, he will bring them again, he will also bind up that which was broken, and will strengthen them that are sick. Here they will never want Meat and Drink and Cloathing, here they will be kept from Thieves and Robbers, for this man will die before one of those committed to his Trust shall be lost. Besides, here they shall be sure to have good *Nurture* and *Admonition*, and shall be taught to walk in right Paths, and that you know is a Favour of no small account. Also here, as you see, are delicate *Waters*, pleasant *Meadows*, dainty *Flowers*, Variety of *Trees*, and such as bear *wholsome Fruit*. Fruit, not like that that *Matthew* eat of, that fell over the Wall out of *Beelzebub's* Garden, but Fruit that procureth Health where there is none, and that continueth and increaseth it where it is.

So they were content to commit their little Ones to him; and that which was also an encouragement to them so to do was for that all this was to be at the Charge of the King, and so was as an Hospital to young Children, and *Orphans*.

Now they went on: and when they were come to *By-path* Meadow, to the Stile over which *Christian* went with his Fellow *Hopeful*, when they were taken by *Giant Despair*, and put into *Doubting* Castle, they sat down and consulted what was best to be done, to wit, now they were so strong, and had got such a man as Mr. *Great-heart* for their Conductor; whether they had not best to make an Attempt upon the Giant, demolish his Castle, and if there were any Pilgrims in it, to set them at liberty before they went any further. So one said one thing, and another said the contrary. One questioned if it was lawful to go upon *unconsecrated* Ground, another said they might, provided their end was good; but Mr. *Great-heart* said, Though that assertion offered last, cannot be universally true, yet I have a Commandment to resist Sin, to overcome Evil, to fight the good Fight of Faith. And I pray, with whom should I fight this good Fight, if not with *Giant Despair?* I will therefore attempt the taking away of his Life, and the demolishing of *Doubting* Castle. Then said he, who will go with me? Then said old *Honest*, I will, and so will we too, said Christian's four Sons, *Matthew, Samuel, James*, and *Joseph*, for they were young men and strong.

So they left the Women in the Road, and with them Mr. *Feeble-mind*, and Mr. *Ready-to-halt*, with his Crutches, to be their Guard, until they came back, for in that place tho' *Giant Despair* dwelt so near, they keeping in the Road, *a little Child might lead them*.

So Mr. *Great-heart*, old *Honest*, and the four young men, went to go up to *Doubting* Castle to look for *Giant Despair*. When they came at the Castle Gate they knocked for Entrance with an unusual Noise. At that the old *Giant* comes to the Gate, and *Diffidence* his Wife follows. Then said he, Who, and what is he, that is so hardy, as after this manner to molest the *Giant Despair?* Mr. *Great-heart* replied, It is I, *Great-heart*, one of the King of the Cœlestial Country's Conductors of Pilgrims to their Place. And I demand of thee that thou open thy Gates for my Entrance, prepare thyself also to fight, for I am come to take away thy Head, and to demolish *Doubting* Castle.

Now *Giant Despair*, because he was a *Giant*, thought no man could overcome him, and again, thought he, since heretofore I have made a Conquest of Angels, shall *Great-heart* make me afraid? So he harnessed himself and went out. He had a Cap of Steel upon his Head, a Breast-plate of Fire girded to him, and he came out in Iron-Shoes, with a great Club in his Hand. Then these six men made up to him, and beset him behind and before; also when *Diffidence*, the *Giantess*, came up to help him, old Mr. *Honest* cut her down at one Blow. Then they fought for their Lives, and *Giant Despair* was brought down to the Ground, *but was very loth to die*. He struggled hard, and had, as they say, as many Lives as a Cat, but *Great-heart* was his death, for he left him not till he had severed his Head from his shoulders.

Doubting Castle Demolished

Then they fell to demolishing *Doubting* Castle, and that you know might with ease be done, since *Giant Despair* was dead. They was seven Days in destroying of that; and in it of Pilgrims they found one Mr. *Dispondency*, almost starved to Death, and one *Much-afraid* his Daughter; these two they saved alive. But it would a made you a wondered to have seen the dead Bodies that lay here and there in the Castle Yard, and how full of dead men's Bones the Dungeon was.

When Mr. *Great-heart* and his Companions had performed this Exploit, they took Mr. *Dispondency*, and his Daughter *Much-afraid* into their Protection, for they were honest People, tho' they were Prisoners in *Doubting Castle* to that Tyrant *Giant Despair*. They therefore I say, took with them the Head of the Giant (for his Body they had buried under a heap of Stones) and down to the Road and to their Companions they came, and shewed them what they had done. Now when *Feeble-mind* and *Ready-to-halt* saw that it was the Head of *Giant Despair* indeed, they were very jocund and merry. Now *Christiana*, if need was, could play upon the *Viol*, and her Daughter *Mercy* upon the *Lute;* so, since they were so merry disposed, she plaid them a Lesson, and *Ready-to-halt* would Dance. So he took *Dispondency's* Daughter, named *Much-afraid*, by the Hand, and to dancing they went in the Road. True he could not dance without one Crutch in his Hand, but I promise you, he footed it well; also the Girl was to be commended, for she answered the Musick handsomely.

As for Mr. *Dispondency*, the Musick was not much to him; he was for feeding rather than dancing, for that he was almost starved. So *Christiana* gave him some of her Bottle of Spirits for present Relief, and then prepared him something to eat; and in little time the old Gentleman came to himself, and began to be finely revived.

Now I saw in my Dream, when all these things were finished, Mr. *Great-heart* took the Head of *Giant Despair*, and set it upon a Pole by the Highway-side, right over against the Pillar that *Christian* erected for a *Caution* to Pilgrims that came after, to take heed of entering into his Grounds.

Then he writ under it upon a *Marble*-stone, these Verses following.

This is the Head *of* him, *Whose* Name *only*
In former times, did Pilgrims *terrify.*
His Castle's *down, and* Diffidence *his Wife,*
Brave Master Great-heart *has bereft of Life.*
Dispondency, *his Daughter* Much-afraid,
Great-heart *for them also the Man has plaid.*
Who hereof doubts, if he'll but cast his Eye
Up hither, may his Scruples satisfy.
This Head also, when doubting Cripples dance,
Doth shew from Fears they have Deliverance.

When these men had thus bravely shewed themselves against *Doubting Castle*, and had slain *Giant Despair*, they went forward, and went on till they came to the *Delectable* Mountains, where *Christian* and *Hopeful* refreshed themselves with the Varieties of the Place. They also acquainted themselves with the Shepherds there, who welcomed them as they had done *Christian* before, unto the Delectable Mountains.

Now the Shepherds seeing so great a train follow Mr. *Great-heart* (for with him they were well acquainted;) they said unto him, Good Sir, you have got a goodly Company here; pray where did you find all these?

Then Mr. *Great-heart* replyed,

> *First here's* Christiana *and her train,*
> *Her Sons, and her Sons' Wives, who like the Wain,*
> *Keep by the Pole, and do by Compass steer,*
> *From Sin to Grace, else they had not been here.*
> *Next here's old* Honest *come on Pilgrimage,*
> Ready-to-halt *too, who, I dare engage,*
> *True hearted is, and so is* Feeble-mind,
> *Who willing was not to be left behind.*
> Dispondency, *good-man, is coming after,*
> *And so also is* Much-afraid, *his Daughter.*
> *May we have Entertainment here, or must*
> *We further go? let's know whereon to trust?*

Then said the Shepherds, This is a comfortable Company. You are welcome to us, for we have for the *Feeble*, as for the *Strong;* our Prince has an Eye to what is done to the least of these. Therefore Infirmity must not be a block to our Entertainment. So they had them to the Palace Door, and then said unto them, Come in Mr. *Feeble-mind*, come in Mr. *Ready-to-halt*, come in Mr. *Dispondency*, and Mrs. *Much-afraid* his Daughter. *These* Mr. *Great-heart*, said the Shepherds to the Guide, we call in by name, for that they are most subject to draw back; but as for you, and the rest that are *strong*, we leave you to your wonted Liberty. Then said Mr. *Great-heart*, This day I see that Grace doth shine in your Faces, and that you are my Lord's Shepherds indeed; for that you have not *pushed* these Diseased neither with Side nor Shoulder, but have rather strewed their way into the Palace with Flowers, as you should.

So the Feeble and Weak went in, and Mr. *Great-heart* and the rest did follow. When they were also set down, the Shepherds said to those of the weakest sort, What is it that you would have? For, said they, all things must be managed here to the supporting of the Weak, as well as the warning of the Unruly.

So they made them a Feast of things easy of Digestion, and that were pleasant to the Palate, and nourishing; the which when they had received, they went to their Rest, each one respectively unto his proper place. When Morning was come, because the mountains were high, and the day clear; and because it was the Custom of the Shepherds to shew to the Pilgrims before their Departure some Rarities; therefore after they were ready, and had refreshed themselves, the Shepherds took them out into the Fields, and shewed them first what they had shewed to *Christian* before.

Then they had them to some new places. The first was to *Mount-Marvel*, where they looked, and beheld a man at a Distance, *that tumbled the Hills about with Words*. Then they asked the Shepherds what that should mean? So they told him, that that man was the Son of one *Great-grace*, of whom you read in the first part of the Records of the *Pilgrim's Progress*. And he is set there to teach Pilgrims how to believe down, or to tumble out of their ways what Difficulties they shall meet with, by Faith. Then said Mr. *Great-heart*, I know him, he is a man above many.

Then they had them to another place, called *Mount Innocent*. And there they saw a man cloathed all in White; and two men, *Prejudice*, and *Ill-will*, continually casting Dirt upon him. Now behold the Dirt, whatsoever they cast at him, would in little time fall off again, and his Garment would look as clear as if no Dirt had been cast thereat.

Then said the Pilgrims what means this? The Shepherds answered, This man is named *Godly-man*, and this Garment is to shew the Innocency of his Life. Now those that throw Dirt at him, are such as hate his *Well-doing;* but as you see the Dirt will not stick upon his Cloaths, so it shall be with him that liveth truly innocently in the World. Whoever they be that would make such men dirty, they labor all in vain; for God, by that a little time is spent, will cause that their *Innocence* shall break forth as the Light, and their Righteousness as the Noon day.

Then they took them, and had them to *Mount-Charity*, where they shewed them a man that had a bundle of Cloth lying before him, out of which he cut Coats and Garments for the Poor that stood about him; yet his Bundle or Roll of Cloth was never the less.

Then said they, what should this be? This is, said the Shepherds, to shew you, that he that has a Heart to give of his Labor to the Poor, shall never want where-withal. He that watereth shall be watered himself. And the Cake that the Widow gave to the Prophet, did not cause that she had ever the less in her Barrel.

They had them also to a place where they saw one *Fool*, and one *Want-wit*, washing of an *Ethiopian* with intention to make him white, but the more they washed him, the blacker he was. They then asked the Shepherds what that should mean. So they told them, saying, Thus shall it be with the vile Person; all means used to get such an one a good Name, shall in conclusion tend but to make him more abominable. Thus it was with the *Pharisees*, and so shall it be with all Hypocrites.

Then said *Mercy* the Wife of *Matthew*, to *Christiana* her Mother, Mother, I would, if it might be, see the hole in the Hill; or that, commonly called, the *By-way* to Hell. So her Mother brake her mind to the Shepherds. Then they went to the Door. It was in the side of an Hill, and they opened it, and bid *Mercy* hearken awhile. So she hearkened, and heard one saying, *Cursed be my Father for holding of my Feet back from the way of Peace and Life;* and another said, *O that I had been torn in pieces before I had, to save my Life, lost my Soul;* and another said, *If I were to live again, how would I deny myself rather than come to this place.* Then there was as if the very Earth had groaned, and quaked under the Feet of this young Woman for fear; so she looked white, and came trembling away, saying, Blessed be he and she that is delivered from this Place.

Now when the Shepherds had shewed them all these things, then they had them back to the Palace, and entertained them with what the House would afford. But *Mercy*, being a young and breeding Woman, longed for something that she saw there, but was ashamed to ask. Her Mother-in-law then asked her what she ailed, for she looked as one not well. Then said *Mercy*, There is a Looking-glass hangs up in the Dining-room, off of which I cannot take my mind; if therefore I have it not, I think I shall miscarry. Then said her Mother, I will mention thy Wants to the Shepherds, and they will not deny it thee. But she said, I am ashamed that these men should know that I longed. Nay my Daughter, said she, it is no Shame, but a Virtue, to long for such a thing as that. So *Mercy* said, Then Mother, if you please, ask the Shepherds if they are willing to sell it.

Now the Glass was one of a thousand. It would present a man, one way, with his own Feature exactly, and turn it but another way, and it would shew one the very Face and Similitude of the Prince of Pilgrims himself. Yea I have talked with them that can tell, and they have said that they have seen the very Crown of Thorns upon his Head, by looking in that Glass, they have therein also seen the holes in his Hands, in his Feet, and his Side. Yea such an excellency is there in that Glass, that it will shew him to one where they have a mind to see him; whether living or dead, whether in Earth or Heaven, whether in a State of Humiliation or in his Exaltation, whether coming to Suffer, or coming to Reign.

Christiana therefore went to the Shepherds apart. (Now the Names of the Shepherds are *Knowledge*, *Experience*, *Watchful*, and *Sincere*) and said unto them, There is one of my Daughters a breeding Woman, that I think doth long for something that she hath seen in this House, and she thinks she shall miscarry if she should by you be denyed.

EXPERIENCE. Call her, call her, she shall assuredly have what we can help her to. So they called her, and said to her, *Mercy*, what is that thing thou wouldest have? Then she blushed and said, The great Glass that hangs up in the Dining-room. So *Sincere* ran and fetched it, and with a joyful Consent it was given her. Then she bowed her Head and gave Thanks, and said, By this I know that I have obtained Favor in your Eyes.

They also gave to the other young Women such things as they desired, and to their Husbands great Commendations for that they joined with Mr. *Great-heart* to the slaying of *Giant Despair*, and the demolishing of *Doubting Castle*.

About *Christiana's* Neck, the Shepherds put a Bracelet, and so they did about the Necks of her four Daughters, also they put Ear-rings in their Ears, and Jewels on their Foreheads.

When they were minded to go hence, they let them go in Peace, but gave not to them those certain Cautions which before was given to *Christian* and his Companion. The Reason was for that these had *Great-heart* to be their Guide, who was one that was well acquainted with things, and so could give them their Cautions more seasonably, to wit, even then when the Danger was nigh the approaching.

What Cautions *Christian* and his Companions had received of the Shepherds, they had also lost by that the time was come that they had need to put them in practise. Wherefore here was the Advantage that this Company had over the other.

They Go Singing

From hence they went on Singing, and they said,

> *Behold, how* fitly *are the Stages set!*
> *For their Relief that Pilgrims are become;*
> *And how they* us *receive without* one *let,*
> *That make the* other *Life our* Mark *and Home.*
> *What* Novelties *they have, to* us *they give,*
> *That we,* tho' *Pilgrims joyful Lives may Live;*
> *They do upon us too such things bestow,*
> *That shew we Pilgrims are, where'er we go.*

When they were gone from the Shepherds, they quickly came to the place where *Christian* met with one *Turn-away*, that dwelt in the Town of *Apostacy*. Wherefore of him Mr. *Great-heart* their Guide did now put them in mind; saying, This is the place where *Christian* met with one *Turn-away*, who carried with him the Character of his Rebellion at his Back. And this I have to say concerning this man, He would hearken to no Counsel, but once afalling, perswasion could not stop him. When he came to the place where the Cross and the Sepulchre was, he did meet with one that did bid him *look there;* but he gnashed with his Teeth, and stamped, and said, he was resolved to go back to his own Town. Before he came to the Gate, he met with *Evangelist*, who offered to lay Hands on him, to turn him into the way again. But this *Turn-away resisted him*, and having done much *despite* unto him, he got away over the Wall, and so escaped his Hand.

Then they went on, and just at the place where *Little-faith* formerly was Robbed, there stood a man with his Sword drawn, and his Face all bloody. Then said Mr. *Great-heart* What art thou? The man made Answer, saying, I am one whose Name is *Valiant-for-truth*. I am a Pilgrim, and am going to the Cœlestial City. Now as I was in my way, there was three men did beset me, and propounded unto me these three things. 1. Whether I would become one of them? 2. Or go back from whence I came? 3. Or die upon the place? To the first I answered, I had been a true Man a long Season, and therefore, it could not be expected that I now should cast in my Lot with Thieves. Then they demanded what I would say to the second. So I told them that the Place from whence I came, had I not found Incommodity there, I had not forsaken it at all, but finding it altogether unsuitable to me, and very unprofitable for me, I forsook it for this Way. Then they asked me what I said to the third. And I told them, my Life cost more dear far, than that I should lightly give it away. Besides, you have nothing to do thus to put things to my Choice; wherefore at your Peril be it, if you meddle. Then these three, to wit, *Wildhead*, *Inconsiderate*, and *Pragmatick*, drew upon me, and I also drew upon them.

So we fell to it, one against three, for the space of above three Hours. They have left upon me, as you see, some of the Marks of their Valour, and have also carried away with them some of mine. They are but just now gone. I suppose they might, as the saying is, hear your Horse dash, and so they betook them to flight.

Greath. *But here was great Odds, three against one.*

Valiant. 'Tis true, but *little* and *more*, are nothing to him that has the Truth on his side. *Though an Host should encamp against me, said one, my Heart shall not fear. Tho' War should rise against me, in this will I be Confident*, &c. Besides, said he, I have read in some Records, that one man has fought an army; and how many did *Samson* slay with the Jaw-Bone of an Ass?

Greath. *Then said the Guide, Why did you not cry out, that some might a come in for your Succour?*

Valiant. So I did, to my King, who I knew could hear, and afford invisible Help, and that was sufficient for me.

Greath. *Then said* Great-heart *to Mr.* Valiant-for-truth, *Thou hast worthily behaved thyself; let me see thy Sword.* So he shewed it him.

When he had taken it in his Hand, and looked thereon a while, he said, Ha! *It is a right* Jerusalem *Blade.*

Valiant. It is so. Let a man have one of *these Blades*, with a Hand to wield it, and skill to use it, and he may venture upon an Angel with it. He need not fear its holding, if he can but tell how to lay on. Its Edges will never blunt. It will cut *Flesh*, and *Bones*, and *Soul*, and *Spirit*, and all.

Greath. *But you fought a great while, I wonder you was not weary?*

Valiant. I fought till my Sword did cleave to my Hand; and when they were joined together, as if a Sword grew out of my Arm, and when the Blood run thorow my Fingers, then I fought with most Courage.

Greath. *Thou hast done well. Thou hast resisted unto Blood, striving against Sin. Thou shalt abide by us, come in, and go out with us; for we are thy Companions.*

Then they took him and washed his Wounds, and gave him of what they had, to refresh him, and so they went on together. Now as they went on, because Mr. *Great-heart* was delighted in him (for he loved one greatly that he found to be a man of his Hands) and because there was with his Company them that was feeble and weak, therefore he questioned with him about many things; as first, *what Country-man he was?*

Valiant. I am of *Dark-land*, for there I was born, and there my Father and Mother are still.

GREATH. *Dark-land*, said the Guide, *Doth not that lie upon the same Coast with the City of* Destruction?

VALIANT. Yes it doth. Now that which caused me to come on Pilgrimage, was this. We had one Mr. *Tell-true* came into our parts, and he told it about what *Christian* had done, that went from the City of *Destruction.* Namely, how he had forsaken his *Wife* and *Children,* and had betaken himself to a *Pilgrim's* Life. It was also confidently reported how he had killed a *Serpent* that did come out to resist him in his Journey, and how he got thorow to whither he intended. It was also told what Welcome he had at all his Lord's Lodgings; specially when he came to the Gates of the Cœlestial City. For there, said the man, He was received with sound of Trumpet by a company of shining ones. He told it also, how all the Bells in the City did ring for Joy at his Reception, and what Golden Garments he was cloathed with; with many other things that now I shall forbear to relate. In a word, that man so told the Story of *Christian* and his Travels, that my Heart fell into a burning haste to be gone after him, nor could Father or Mother stay me, so I got from them, and am come thus far on my Way.

GREATH. *You came in at the Gate, did you not?*

VALIANT. Yes, yes. For the same man also told us, that all would be nothing, if we did not begin to enter this way at the Gate.

GREATH. *Look you, said the Guide, to* Christiana, *The Pilgrimage of your Husband, and what he has gotten thereby, is spread abroad far and near.*

VALIANT. Why, is this *Christian's* Wife?

GREATH. *Yes, that it is; and these are also her four Sons.*

VALIANT. What! and going on Pilgrimage too?

GREATH. *Yes verily, they are following after.*

VALIANT. It glads me at Heart! Good man! How Joyful will he be, when he shall see them that would not go with him, yet to enter after him in at the Gates into the City?

GREATH. *Without doubt it will be a Comfort to him. For next to the Joy of seeing himself there, it will be a Joy to meet there his Wife and his Children.*

VALIANT. But now you are upon that, pray let me hear your Opinion about it. Some make a Question whether we shall know one another when we are there?

GREATH. *Do they think they shall know themselves then? Or that they shall rejoyce to see themselves in that Bliss? And if they think they shall know and do these, why not know others, and rejoyce in their Welfare also?*

Again, since Relations are our second self, tho' that State will be dissolved there, yet why may it not be rationally concluded that we shall be more glad to see them there, than to see they are wanting?

VALIANT. Well, I perceive whereabouts you are as to this. Have you any more things to ask me about my beginning to come on Pilgrimage?

GREATH. *Yes. Was your Father and Mother willing that you should become a Pilgrim?*

VALIANT. Oh, no. They used all means imaginable to perswade me to stay at Home.

GREATH. *Why, what could they say against it?*

VALIANT. They said it was an idle Life, and if I myself were not inclined to Sloth and Laziness, I would never countenance a Pilgrim's Condition.

GREATH. *And what did they say else?*

VALIANT. Why, They told me, That it was a dangerous Way; yea the most dangerous Way in the World, said they, is that which the Pilgrims go.

GREATH. *Did they show wherein this way is so dangerous?*

VALIANT. Yes, and that in many Particulars.

GREATH. *Name some of them.*

VALIANT. They told me of the Slough of *Dispond*, where *Christian* was well-nigh smothered. They told me that there were Archers standing ready in *Beelzebub-Castle,* to shoot them that should knock at the *Wicket*-Gate for Entrance. They told me also of the Wood and dark Mountains, of the Hill *Difficulty*, of the Lions, and also of the three Giants, *Bloody-Man*, *Maul*, and *Slay-good*. They said moreover, that there was a foul *Fiend* haunted the Valley of *Humiliation*, and that *Christian* was, by him, almost bereft of Life. Besides, said they, you must go over the *Valley of the Shadow of Death*, where the *Hobgoblins* are, where the Light is Darkness, where the way is full of Snares, Pits, Traps, and Gins. They told me also of *Giant-Despair*, of *Doubting-Castle*, and of the *Ruins* that the Pilgrims met with there. Further, they said, I must go over the enchanted Ground, which was dangerous. And that after all this, I should find a River, over which I should find no Bridge, and that that River did lie betwixt me and the Cœlestial Country.

GREATH. *And was this all?*

VALIANT. No, they also told me that this way was full of *Deceivers*, and of Persons that laid await there, to turn good men out of the Path.

GREATH. *But how did they make that out?*

VALIANT. They told me that Mr. *Worldly-wise-Man* did there lie in wait to deceive. They also said that there was *Formality* and *Hypocrisy* continually on the Road. They said also that *By-ends*, *Talkative*, or *Demas*, would go near to gather me up; that the Flatterer would catch me in his Net; or that with green-headed *Ignorance* I would presume to go on to the Gate, from whence he always was sent back to the Hole that was in the side of the Hill, and made to go the By-way to Hell.

GREATH. *I promise you, this was enough to discourage. But did they make an end here?*

VALIANT. No, stay. They told me also of many that had tried that way of old, and that had gone a great way therein, to see if they could find something of the Glory there that so many had so much talked of from time to time; and how they came back again, and befooled themselves for setting a foot out of Doors in that Path, to the Satisfaction of all the Country. And they named several that did so, as *Obstinate* and *Pliable*, *Mistrust*, and *Timorous*, *Turn-away*, and old *Atheist*, with several more; who, they said, had, some of them, gone far to see if they could find, but not one of them found so much Advantage by going as amounted *to the weight of a Feather*.

GREATH. *Said they any thing more to discourage you?*

VALIANT. Yes, they told me of one Mr. *Fearing*, who was a Pilgrim, and how *he* found this way so solitary, that he never had comfortable Hour therein; also that Mr. *Dispondency* had like to been starved therein; yea, and also, which I had almost forgot, that *Christian* himself, about whom there has been such a Noise, after all his Ventures for a Cœlestial Crown, was certainly drowned in the black River, and never went foot further, however it was smothered up.

GREATH. *And did none of these things discourage you?*

VALIANT. No. They seemed but as so many Nothings to me.

GREATH. *How came that about?*

VALIANT. Why, I still believed what Mr. *Tell-true* had said; and that carried me beyond them all.

GREATH. *Then this was your Victory, even your Faith.*

VALIANT. It was so. I believed and therefore came out, got into the Way, fought all that set themselves against me, and by believing am come to this Place.

Who would true Valour see,
Let him come hither;
One here will constant be,
Come Wind, come Weather.
There's no Discouragement,
Shall make him once Relent,
His first avow'd Intent,
To be a Pilgrim.

Who so beset him round
With dismal Stories,
Do but themselves confound,
His Strength the more is.
No Lion *can him fright,*
He'll with a Giant *Fight,*
But he will have a right,
To be a Pilgrim.

Hobgoblin, *nor foul* Fiend,
Can daunt *his Spirit;*
He knows, he at the end,
Shall Life Inherit.
Then Fancies fly away,
He'll fear not what men say,
He'll labor Night and Day,
To be a Pilgrim.

The Enchanted Ground

By this time they were got to the *enchanted Ground*, where the Air naturally tended to make one *Drowsy*. And that place was all grown over with Briars and Thorns; excepting *here* and *there*, where was an *enchanted Arbor*, upon which, if a Man sits, or in which if a Man sleeps, 'tis a question, say some, whether ever they shall rise or wake again in this World. Over this Forest therefore they went, both one with another, and Mr. *Great-heart* went before, for that he was the Guide, and Mr. *Valiant-for-truth*, he came behind, being there a Guard, for fear lest peradventure some *Fiend*, or *Dragon*, or *Giant*, or *Thief*, should fall upon their Rear, and so do Mischief. They went on here each man with his Sword drawn in his Hand; for they knew it was a dangerous place. Also they cheered up one another as well as they could. *Feeble-mind*, Mr. *Great-heart* commanded should come up after him, and Mr. *Dispondency* was under the Eye of Mr. *Valiant*.

Now they had not gone far, but a great Mist and a Darkness fell upon them all, so that they could scarce, for a great while, see the one the other. Wherefore they were forced for some time, to feel for one another by Words, for they walked not by Sight.

But any one must think that here was but sorry going for the best of them all, but how much worse for the Women and Children, who both of *Feet* and *Heart* were but tender. Yet so it was, that, thorow the incouraging Words of he that led in the Front, and of him that brought them up behind, they made a pretty good shift to wag along.

The Way also was here very wearisome thorow Dirt and Slabbiness. Nor was there on *all* this Ground, so much as one *Inn* or *Victualling-House*, therein to refresh the feebler sort. Here therefore was *grunting*, and *puffing*, and *sighing:* While one tumbleth over a Bush, another sticks fast in the Dirt, and the Children, some of them, lost their Shoes in the Mire. While one crys out, I am down, and another, Ho, where are you? and a third, the Bushes have got such fast hold on me, I think I cannot get away from them.

Then they came at an *Arbor*, warm, and promising much Refreshing to the Pilgrims; for it was finely wrought above-head, beautified with *Greens*, furnished with *Benches* and *Settles*. It also had in it a soft Couch whereon the weary might lean. This, you must think, all things considered, was tempting; for the Pilgrims already began to be foiled with the badness of the way; but there was not one of them that made so much as a motion to stop there. Yea, for ought I could perceive, they continually gave so good heed to the Advice of their Guide, and he did so faithfully tell them of *Dangers*, and of the *Nature* of Dangers when they were at them, that usually when they were nearest to them, they did most pluck up their Spirits, and hearten one another to deny the Flesh. This *Arbor* was called *The Slothful's Friend*, on purpose to allure, if it might be, some of the Pilgrims there, to take up their Rest, when weary.

The Guide Has a Map

I saw then in my Dream, that they went on in this their *solitary* Ground, till they came to a place at which a man is apt to lose his Way. *Now*, tho' when it was light, their Guide could well enough tell how to miss those ways that led wrong, yet in the dark he was put to a stand. But he had in his Pocket a Map of all ways leading to or from the Cœlestial City; wherefore he strook a Light (for he never goes also without his Tinder-box) and takes a view of his Book or Map, which bids him be careful in that place to turn to the right-hand-way. And had he not here been careful to look in his Map, they had all, in probability, been smothered in the Mud, for just a little before them, and that at the end of the cleanest Way too, was a Pit, none knows how deep, full of nothing but Mud, there made on purpose to destroy the Pilgrims in.

Then thought I with myself, who that goeth on Pilgrimage, but would have one of these Maps about him, that he may look when he is at a *stand*, which is the way he must take.

They went on then in this *enchanted* Ground, till they came to where was an other *Arbor*, and it was built by the High-way-side. And in that *Arbor* there lay two men whose Names were *Heedless* and *Too-bold*. These two went thus far on Pilgrimage; but here being wearied with their Journey, they sat down to rest themselves, and so fell fast asleep. When the Pilgrims saw them, they stood still and shook their Heads, for they knew that the Sleepers were in a pitiful Case. Then they consulted what to do, whether to go on and leave them in their Sleep, or to step to them and try to awake them. So they concluded to go to them and wake them; that is, if they could; but with this Caution, namely, to take heed that themselves did not sit down nor embrace the offered Benefit of that *Arbor*.

So they went in and spake to the men, and called each by his Name, (for the Guide, it seems, did know them) but there was no Voice nor Answer. Then the Guide did shake them, and do what he could to disturb them. Then said one of them, *I will pay you when I take my Mony*. At which the Guide shook his Head. *I will fight so long as I can hold my Sword in my Hand*, said the other. At that, one of the Children laughed.

Then said *Christiana*, what is the meaning of this? The Guide said, *They talk in their Sleep*. If you strike them, beat them, or what ever else you do to them, they will answer you after this fashion; or as one of them said in old time, when the Waves of the Sea did beat upon him, and he slept as one upon the Mast of a Ship, *When I awake I will seek it again*. You know when men talk in their Sleeps, they say any thing; but their Words are not governed, either by Faith or Reason. There is an *Incoherency* in their Words *now*, as there was before, betwixt their going on Pilgrimage and sitting down here. This then is the Mischief on't, when *heedless* ones go on Pilgrimage, 'tis twenty to one, but they are served thus. For this *enchanted* Ground is one of the last Refuges that the Enemy to Pilgrims has; wherefore it is as you see, placed almost at the end of the Way, and so it standeth against us with the more Advantage. For when, thinks the Enemy, will these Fools be so desirous to sit down, as when they are weary? and when so like to be weary, as when almost at their Journey's end? Therefore it is, I say, that the *enchanted* Ground is placed so nigh to the Land *Beulah*, and so near the end of their Race. Wherefore let Pilgrims look to themselves, lest it happen to them as it has done to these, that, as you see, are fallen asleep, and none can wake them.

Then the Pilgrims desired with trembling to go forward, only they prayed their Guide to strike a Light, that they might go the rest of their way by the help of the light of a Lanthorn. So he strook a light, and they went by the help of that thorow the rest of this way, tho' the Darkness was very great.

But the Children began to be sorely weary, and they cryed out unto him that loveth Pilgrims, to make their way more Comfortable. So by that they had gone a little further, a Wind arose that drove away the Fog, so the Air became more clear.

Yet they were not off (by much) of the *enchanted* Ground; only now they could see one another better, and the way wherein they should walk.

Now when they were almost at the end of this Ground, they perceived that a little before them, was a *solemn* Noise, as of one that was much concerned. So they went on and looked before them, and behold, they saw, as they thought, *a Man upon his Knees*, with Hands and Eyes lift up, and speaking, as they thought, earnestly to one that was above. They drew nigh, but could not tell what he said; so they went softly till he had done. When he had done, he got up and began to run towards the Cœlestial City. Then Mr. *Great-heart* called after him, saying, Soho, Friend, let us have your Company, if you go, as I suppose you do, to the Cœlestial City. So the man stopped, and they came up to him. But so soon as Mr. *Honest* saw him, he said, I know this man. Then said Mr. *Valiant-for-truth*, Prithee, who is it? 'Tis one, said he, that comes from whereabouts I dwelt; his Name is *Stand-fast*, he is certainly a right good Pilgrim.

So they came up one to another and presently *Stand-fast* said to old *Honest*, Ho, Father *Honest*, are you there? Ay, said he, that I am, as sure as you are there. Right glad am I, said Mr. *Stand-fast*, that I have found you on this Road. And as glad am I, said the other, that I espied you upon your Knees. Then Mr. *Stand-fast* blushed, and said, But why? did you see me? Yes, that I did, quoth the other, and with my Heart was glad at the Sight. Why, what did you think, said *Stand-fast?* Think, said old *Honest*, what should I think? I thought we had an honest Man upon the Road, and therefore should have his Company by and by. If you thought not amiss, how happy am I? But if I be not as I should, I alone must bear it. That is true, said the other. But your fear doth further confirm me that things are right betwixt the Prince of Pilgrims and your Soul. For he saith, *Blessed is the Man that feareth always.*

VALIANT. Well but Brother, I pray thee tell us what was it that was the cause of thy being upon thy Knees, even now? Was it for that some special Mercy laid Obligations upon thee, or how?

STAND. Why we are as you see, upon the *enchanted Ground*, and as I was coming along, I was musing with myself of what a dangerous Road the Road in this place was, and how many that had come even thus far on Pilgrimage, had here been stopt, and been destroyed. I thought also of the manner of the Death with which this place destroyeth Men. Those that die here, die of no violent Distemper. The Death which such die, is not grievous to them. For he that goeth away in a *Sleep*, begins that Journey with Desire and Pleasure. Yea such acquiesce in the Will of that Disease.

HON. *Then Mr.* Honest *Interrupting of him said, did you see the two Men asleep in the Arbor?*

STAND. Ay, Ay, I saw *Heedless*, and *Too-bold* there; and for ought I know, there they will lie till they Rot. But let me go on in my Tale? As I was thus Musing, as I said, there was one in very pleasant Attire, *but old*, that presented herself unto me, and offered me three things, to wit, her *Body*, her *Purse*, and her *Bed*. Now the Truth is, I was both aweary and sleepy; I am also as poor as a *Howlet*, and that, perhaps, the *Witch* knew. Well, I repulsed her once and twice, but she put by my Repulses, and smiled. Then I began to be angry, but she mattered that nothing at all. Then she made Offers again, and said, If I would be ruled by her, she would make me great and happy. For, said she, I am the Mistress of the World, and men are made happy by me. Then I asked her Name, and she told me it was *Madam Bubble*. This set me further from her; but she still followed me with Intice-ments. Then I betook me, as you see, to my Knees, and with Hands lift up and cries, I pray'd to him that had said, he would help. So just as you came up, the Gentlewoman went her way. Then I continued to give thanks for this my great Deliverance; for I verily believe she intended no good, but rather sought to make stop of me in my Journey.

HON. *Without doubt her Designs were bad. But stay, now you talk of her, methinks I either have seen her, or have read some story of her.*

STAND. Perhaps you have done both.

HON. *Madam Bubble? Is she not a tall comely Dame, something of a swarthy Complexion?*

STAND. Right, you hit it, she is just such an one.

HON. *Doth she not speak very smoothly, and give you a Smile at the end of a Sentence?*

STAND. You fall right upon it again; for these are her very Actions.

HON. *Doth she not wear a great Purse by her Side, and is not her Hand often in it, fingering her Mony, as if that was her Heart's delight?*

STAND. 'Tis just so. Had she stood by all this while, you could not more amply have set her forth before me, nor have better described her Features.

HON. Then he that drew her Picture was a good *Limner*, and he that wrote of her, said true.

GREATH. This Woman is a *Witch*, and it is by Virtue of her *Sorceries* that this Ground is *enchanted.* Whoever doth lay their Head down in *her Lap*, had as good lay it down upon that Block over which the Ax doth hang; and whoever lay their Eyes upon her Beauty are counted the Enemies of God. This is she that maintaineth in their Splendor, all those that are the Enemies of Pilgrims. Yea, This is she that has bought off many a man from a Pilgrim's Life. She is a great *Gossiper*, she is always, both she and her Daughters, at one Pilgrim's Heels or other, now commending, and then preferring the excellencies of this Life. She is a bold and impudent Slut; she will talk with any Man. She always laugheth poor Pilgrims to scorn, but highly commends the Rich. If there be one cunning to get Mony in a Place, she will speak well of him from House to House. She loveth Banqueting, and Feasting, mainly well, she is always at one full Table or another. She has given it out in some places, that she is a Goddess, and therefore some do Worship her. She has her times and open places of Cheating, and she will say and avow it, that none can shew a Good comparable to hers. She promiseth to dwell with Children's Children, if they will but love and make much of her. She will cast out of her Purse Gold like Dust, in some places, and to some Persons. She loves to be sought after, spoken well of, and to lie in the Bosoms of Men. She is never weary of commending her Commodities, and she loves them most that think best of her. She will promise to some Crowns and Kingdoms, if they will but take her Advice; yet many has she brought to the Halter, and ten thousand times more to Hell.

STAND. *O! said* Stand-fast, *What a Mercy is it that I did resist her: for whither might she a drawn me?*

GREATH. Whither! Nay, none but God knows whither. But in general to be sure, she would a drawn thee *into many foolish and hurtful Lusts, which drown men in Destruction and Perdition.*

'Twas she that set *Absalom* against his Father, and *Jeroboam* against his Master. 'Twas she that persuaded *Judas* to sell his Lord, and that prevailed with *Demas* to forsake the godly Pilgrim's Life. None can tell of the Mischief that she doth. She makes Variance betwixt Rulers and Subjects, betwixt Parents and Children, 'twixt Neighbor and Neighbor, 'twixt a Man and his Wife, 'twixt a Man and himself, 'twixt the Flesh and the Heart.

Wherefore good Master *Stand-fast*, be as your Name is, and when you have done all *stand.*

At this Discourse there was among the Pilgrims a mixture of Joy and Trembling, but at length *they brake* out and Sang.

What Danger is the Pilgrim in,
How many are his Foes,
How many ways there are to Sin,
No living Mortal knows.
Some of the Ditch shy are, yet can
Lie tumbling on the Mire.
Some tho' they shun the Frying-pan,
Do leap into the Fire.

After this I beheld, until they were come unto the Land of *Beulah*, where the Sun shineth Night and Day. Here, because they was weary, they betook themselves a while to Rest. And because this Country was common for Pilgrims, and because the Orchards and Vineyards that were here, belonged to the King of the Cœlestial Country, therefore they were licensed to make bold with any of his things.

But a little while soon refreshed them here, for the Bells did so ring, and the Trumpets continually sound so melodiously, that they could not sleep, and yet they received as much refreshing as if they had slept their Sleep never so soundly. Here also all the noise of them that walked the Streets, was, *More Pilgrims are come to Town.* And another would answer, saying, And so many went over the Water, and were let in at the Golden Gates to Day. They would cry again, There is now a Legion of Shining ones, just come to Town; by which we know that there are more Pilgrims upon the Road, for here they come to wait for them, and to comfort them after all their Sorrow. Then the Pilgrims got up and walked to and fro. But how were their Ears now filled with heavenly Noises, and their Eyes delighted with Cœlestial Visions? In this Land, they *heard* nothing, *saw* nothing, *felt* nothing, *smelt* nothing, *tasted* nothing, that was offensive to their Stomach or Mind; only when they tasted of the Water of the River over which they were to go, they thought that tasted a little Bitterish to the Palate, but it proved sweeter when 'twas down.

In this place there was a Record kept of the Names of them that had been Pilgrims of old, and a History of all the famous Acts that they had done. It was here also much discoursed how the *River* to some had had its *flowings,* and what *ebbings* it has had while others have gone over. It has been in a manner *dry* for some, while it has overflowed its Banks for others.

In this place, the Children of the Town would go into the King's Gardens and gather Nosegays for the Pilgrims, and bring them to them with much Affection. Here also grew *Camphire* with *Spikenard*, and *Saffron*, *Calamus*, and *Cinamon*, with all its Trees of *Frankincense*, *Myrrh*, and *Aloes*, with all *chief* Spices. With these the Pilgrims' Chambers were perfumed while they stayed here; and with these were their Bodies anointed to prepare them to go over the *River* when the time appointed was come.

Now while they lay here and waited for the good Hour, there was a Noise in the Town, that there was a *Post* come from the Cœlestial City, with Matter of great Importance, to one *Christiana*, the Wife of *Christian* the Pilgrim. So Enquiry was made for her, and the House was found out where she was, so the Post presented her with a Letter. The Contents whereof was, *Hail, Good Woman, I bring thee Tidings that the Master calleth for thee, and expecteth that thou shouldest stand in his Presence, in Cloaths of Immortality, within this ten Days.*

When he had read this Letter to her, he gave her therewith a sure Token that he was a true Messenger, and was come to bid her make haste to be gone. The Token was, *An Arrow with a Point sharpened with Love, let easily into her Heart, which by degrees wrought so effectually with her, that at the time appointed she must be gone.*

When *Christiana* saw that her time was come, and that she was the first of this Company that was to go over, she called for Mr. *Great-heart* her Guide, and told him how Matters were. So he told her he was heartily glad of the News, and could a been glad had the Post came for him. Then she bid that he should give Advice how all things should be prepared for her Journey.

So he told her, saying, Thus and thus it must be, and we that survive will accompany you to the River-side.

Then she called for her Children, and gave them *her Blessing,* and told them that she yet read with Comfort the Mark that was set in their Foreheads, and was glad to see them with her there, and that they had kept their Garments so white. Lastly, she bequeathed to the Poor that little she had, and commanded her Sons and her Daughters to be ready against the Messenger should come for them.

When she had spoken these Words to her Guide and to her Children, she called for Mr. *Valiant-for-truth,* and said unto him, Sir, you have in all places shewed yourself true-hearted; be faithful unto Death, and my King will give you a Crown of Life. I would also intreat you to have an Eye to my Children, and if at any time you see them faint, speak comfortably to them. For my Daughters, my Sons' Wives, they have been faithful, and a fulfilling of the Promise upon them will be their end. But she gave Mr. *Stand-fast* a Ring.

Then she called for old Mr. *Honest,* and said of him, Behold an Israelite indeed, in whom is no Guile. Then said *he,* I wish you a fair Day when you set out for Mount *Sion,* and shall be glad to see that you go over the River dry-shod. But she answered, Come *Wet,* come *Dry,* I long to be gone. For however the Weather is in my Journey, I shall have time enough when I come there to sit down and rest me, and dry me.

Then came in that good Man Mr. *Ready-to-halt* to see her. So she said to him, Thy Travel hither has been with Difficulty, but that will make thy Rest the sweeter. But watch, and be ready, for at an Hour when you think not, the Messenger may come.

After him, came in Mr. *Dispondency,* and his Daughter *Much-afraid.* To whom she said, You ought with Thankfulness for ever, to remember your Deliverance from the Hands of Giant *Despair,* and out of *Doubting-Castle.* The effect of that Mercy is that you are brought with Safety hither. Be ye watchful, and cast away Fear. Be sober, and hope to the End.

Then she said to Mr. *Feeble-Mind,* Thou wast delivered from the Mouth of Giant *Slay-good,* that thou mightest live in the Light of the Living for ever, and see thy King with Comfort. Only I advise thee to repent thee of thy aptness to fear and doubt of his Goodness before he sends for thee, lest thou shouldest when he comes, be forced to stand before him for that Fault with Blushing.

Now the Day drew on that *Christiana* must be gone. So the Road was full of People to see her take her Journey. But behold all the Banks beyond the

River were full of Horses and Chariots, which were come down from above to accompany her to the City-Gate. So she came forth and entered the *River*, with a *Beckon* of Farewell, to those that followed her to the River side. The last word she was heard to say here, was, *I come Lord, to be with thee and bless thee.*

So her Children and Friends returned to their Place, for that those that waited for *Christiana* had carried her out of their Sight. So she went, and called, and entered in at the Gate with all the Ceremonies of Joy that her Husband *Christian* had done before her.

At her Departure her Children wept, but Mr. *Great-heart*, and Mr. *Valiant*, played upon the well-tuned Cymbal and Harp for Joy. So all departed to their respective Places.

Many Are Summoned

In process of time there came a *Post* to the Town again, and his Business was with Mr. *Ready-to-halt*. So he enquired him out and said to him, I am come to thee in the Name of him whom thou hast Loved and Followed, tho' upon *Crutches*. And my Message is to tell thee, that he expects thee at his Table to Sup with him in his Kingdom the next Day after *Easter*. Wherefore prepare thyself for this Journey.

Then he also gave him a Token that he was a true Messenger, saying, *I have broken thy golden Bowl*, and loosed *thy silver Cord*.

After this, Mr. *Ready-to-halt* called for his Fellow Pilgrims, and told them saying, I am sent for, and God shall surely visit you also. So he desired Mr. *Valiant* to make his *Will*. And because he had nothing to bequeath to them that should survive him but his *Crutches* and his good *Wishes*, therefore thus he said. *These Crutches I bequeath to my Son that shall tread in my Steps, with an hundred warm Wishes that he may prove better than I have done.*

Then he thanked Mr. *Great-heart* for his Conduct and Kindness, and so addressed himself to his Journey. When he came at the brink of the River, he said, Now I shall have no more need of these *Crutches*, since yonder are Chariots and Horses for me to ride on. The last words he was heard to say, was, *Welcome Life*. So he went his way.

After this, Mr. *Feeble-mind* had Tidings brought him, that the Post sounded his Horn at his Chamber Door. Then he came in and told him, saying, I am come to tell thee that thy Master has need of thee, and that in very little time thou must behold his Face in Brightness. And take this as a Token of the Truth of my Message. *Those that look out at the Windows shall be darkened.*

Then Mr. *Feeble-mind* called for his Friends, and told them what Errand had been brought unto him, and what Token he had received of the truth of the Message. Then he said, Since I have nothing to bequeath to any, to what purpose should I make a Will? As for my *feeble Mind*, that I will leave behind me, for that I have no need of that in the place whither I go. Nor is it worth bestowing upon the poorest Pilgrim. Wherefore when I am gone I desire that you, Mr. *Valiant*, would bury it in a Dung-hill. This done, and the Day being come, in which he was to depart, he entered the *River* as the rest. His last Words were, *Hold out Faith and Patience*. So he went over to the other Side.

When Days had many of them passed away, Mr. *Dispondency* was sent for. For a *Post* was come and brought this Message to him. *Trembling Man, these are to summon thee to be ready with thy King, by the next Lord's Day, to shout for Joy for thy Deliverance from all thy Doubtings.*

And said the Messenger, That my Message is true, take this for a Proof. So he gave him *The Grasshopper to be a Burthen unto him.* Now Mr. *Dispondency's* Daughter, whose Name was *Much-afraid*, said, when she heard what was done, that she would go with her Father. Then Mr. *Dispondency* said to his Friends, Myself and my Daughter, you know what we have been, and how troublesomely we have behaved ourselves in every Company. My will and my Daughter's is, That our *Disponds* and slavish Fears, be by no man ever received, from the day of our *Departure*, for ever. For I know that after my Death they will offer themselves to others. For, to be plain with you, they are Ghosts, the which we entertained when we first began to be Pilgrims, and could never shake them off after. And they will walk about and seek Entertainment of the Pilgrims; but for our Sakes shut ye the Doors upon them.

When the time was come for them to depart, they went to the Brink of the *River*. The last Words of Mr. *Dispondency*, were, *Farewell Night, Welcome Day*. His Daughter went thorow the River singing, but none could understand what she said.

Then it came to pass, awhile after, that there was a *Post* in the Town that enquired for Mr. *Honest*. So he came to his House where he was, and delivered to his Hand these Lines, *Thou art Commanded to be ready against this Day seven Night, to present thyself before thy Lord, at his Father's House*. And for a Token that my Message is true, *All thy Daughters of Musick shall be brought low*. Then Mr. *Honest* called for his Friends, and said unto them, I Die, but shall make no Will. As for my Honesty, it shall go with me; let him that comes after be told of this. When the Day that he was to be gone was come, he addressed himself to go over the *River*. Now the *River* at that time overflowed the Banks in some places. But Mr. *Honest* in his Life time had spoken to one *Good-conscience* to meet him there, the which he also did, and lent him his Hand, and so helped him over. The last Words of Mr. *Honest* were, *Grace Reigns*. So he left the World.

After this, it was noised abroad that Mr. *Valiant-for-truth* was taken with a Summons, by the same *Post* as the other, and had this for a Token that the Summons was true, *That his Pitcher was broken at the Fountain*. When he understood it, he called for his Friends, and told them of it. Then said he, I am going to my Fathers, and tho' with great Difficulty I am got hither, yet now I do not repent me of all the Trouble I have been at to arrive where I am. *My Sword*, I give to him that shall succeed me in my Pilgrimage, and my *Courage* and *Skill*, to him that can get it. My *Marks* and *Scars* I carry with me, to be a Witness for me, that I have fought his Battles who now will be my Rewarder. When the Day that he must go hence, was come, many accompanied him to the River side, into which, as he went, he said, *Death, where is thy Sting?* And as he went down deeper, he said, *Grave, where is thy Victory?* So he passed over, and all the Trumpets sounded for him on the other side.

End of the Journey

Then there came forth a Summons for Mr. *Stand-fast*. (This Mr. *Stand-fast*, was he that the rest of the Pilgrims found upon his Knees in the *enchanted* Ground.) For the *Post* brought it him open in his Hands. The Contents whereof were, *That he must prepare for a Change of Life, for his Master was not willing that he should be so far from him any longer*. At this Mr. *Stand-fast* was put into a Muse. Nay, said the Messenger, you need not doubt of the Truth of my Message, for here is a Token of the Truth thereof, *Thy Wheel is broken at the Cistern*. Then he called to him Mr. *Great-heart* who was their Guide, and said unto him, Sir, Altho' it was not my hap to be much in your good Company in the Days of my Pilgrimage, yet since the time I knew you, you have been profitable to me. When I came from home, I left behind me a Wife, and five small Children. Let me entreat you, at your Return, (for I know that you will go, and return to your Master's House, in Hopes that you may yet be a Conductor to more of the Holy Pilgrims,) that you send to my Family, and let them be acquainted with all that hath and shall happen unto me. Tell them moreover, of my happy Arrival to this Place, and of the present late blessed Condition that I am in. Tell them also of *Christian* and *Christiana* his Wife, and how *She* and her Children came after her Husband. Tell them also of what a happy End she made, and whither she is gone. I have little or nothing to send to my Family, except it be Prayers and Tears for them. Of which it will suffice, if thou acquaint them, if peradventure they may prevail. When Mr. *Stand-fast* had thus set things in order, and the time being come for him to haste him away, he also went down to the River. Now there was a great Calm at that time in the River, wherefore Mr. *Stand-fast*, when he was about half way in, he stood a while and talked to his Companions that had waited upon him thither. And he said,

This River has been a Terror to many, yea the thoughts of it also have often frighted me. But now methinks I stand easy, my Foot is fixed upon that upon which the Feet of the Priests that bare the Ark of the Covenant stood while *Israel* went over this *Jordan*. The Waters indeed are to the Palate bitter, and to the Stomach cold, yet the thoughts of what I am going to, and of the Conduct that waits for me on the other side, doth lie as a glowing Coal at my Heart.

I see myself now at the *end* of my Journey, my *toilsome* Days are ended. I am going now to see *that* Head that was Crowned with Thorns, and *that* Face that was spit upon, for me.

I have formerly lived by Hear-say, and Faith, but now I go where I shall live by sight, and shall be with him, in whose Company I delight myself.

I have loved to hear my Lord spoken of, and wherever I have seen the print of his Shoe in the Earth, there I have coveted to set my Foot too.

His Name has been to me as a *Civet-Box*, yea, sweeter than all Perfumes. His Voice to me has been most sweet, and his Countenance, I have more desired than they that have most desired the Light of the Sun. His Word I did use to gather for my Food, and for Antidotes against my Faintings. He has held me, and I have kept me from mine Iniquities. Yea, my Steps hath he strengthened in his Way.

Now while he was thus in Discourse, his Countenance changed, his *strong man* bowed under him, and after he had said, *Take me, for I come unto thee*, he ceased to be seen of them.

But Glorious it was, to see how the open Region was filled with Horses and Chariots, with Trumpeters and Pipers, with Singers and Players on stringed Instruments, to welcome the Pilgrims as they went up, and followed one another in at the beautiful Gate of the City.

As for *Christian's* Children, the four Boys that *Christiana* brought with her, with their Wives and Children, I did not stay where I was till they were gone over. Also since I came away, I heard one say, that they were yet alive, and so would be for the Increase of the Church in that Place where they were for a time.

Shall it be my Lot to go that way again I may give those that desire it an Account of what I here am silent about; mean time I bid my Reader *Adieu*.

FINIS.

THE HOLY WAR

Made by Shaddai

upon Diabolus

TO THE READER

'Tis strange to me, that they that love to tell
Things done of old, yea, and that do excel
Their equals in historiology,
Speak not of Mansoul's wars, but let them lie
Dead, like old fables, or such worthless things,
That to the reader no advantage brings:
When men, let them make what they will their own,
Till they know this, are to themselves unknown.
Of stories, I well know, there's divers sorts,
Some foreign, some domestic; and reports
Are thereof made as fancy leads the writers:
(By books a man may guess at the inditers).
Some will again of that which never was,
Nor will be, feign (and that without a cause)
Such matter, raise such mountains, tell such things
Of men, of laws, of countries, and of kings;
And in their story seem to be so sage,
And with such gravity clothe every page,
That though their frontispiece says all is vain,
Yet to their way disciples they obtain.
But, readers, I have somewhat else to do
Than with vain stories thus to trouble you;
What here I say, some men do know so well,
They can with tears and joy the story tell.
The town of Mansoul is well known to many,
Nor are her troubles doubted of by any
That are acquainted with those histories
That, Mansoul and her wars anatomize.
Then lend thine ear to what I do relate,
Touching the town of Mansoul and her state;
How she was lost, took captive, made a slave;
And how against him set, that should her save;
Yea, how by hostile ways she did oppose
Her Lord, and with his enemy did close.

For they are true: he that will them deny
Must needs the best of records vilify.
For my part, I myself was in the town,
Both when 'twas set up, and when pulling down.
I saw Diabolus in his possession,
And Mansoul also under his oppression.
Yea, I was there when she owned him for lord,
And to him did submit with one accord.
When Mansoul trampled upon things divine,
And wallowed in filth as does a swine,
When she betook herself unto her arms,
Fought her Emmanuel, despised his charms,
Then I was there, and did rejoice to see
Diabolus and Mansoul so agree.
Let no men, then, count me a fable-maker,
Nor make my name or credit a partaker
Of their derision: what is here in view,
Of mine own knowledge I dare say is true.
I saw the Prince's armed men come down
By troops, by thousands, to besiege the town;
I saw the captains, heard the trumpets sound,
And how his forces covered all the ground.
Yea, how they set themselves in battle-ray,
I shall remember to my dying day.
I saw the colours waving in the wind,
And they within to mischief how combined
To ruin Mansoul, and to make away
Her primum mobile *without delay.*
I saw the mounts cast up against the town,
And how the slings were placed to beat it down:
I heard the stones fly whizzing by mine ears,
(What longer kept in mind than got in fears?)
I heard them fall, and saw what work they made,
And how old Mors did cover with his shade
The face of Mansoul; and I heard her cry
"Woe worth the day, in dying I shall die!"
I saw the battering-rams, and how they played
To beat ope Ear-gate; and I was afraid
Not only Ear-gate, but the very town
Would by those battering-rams be beaten down.
I saw the fights, and heard the captains shout,
And in each battle saw who faced about;
I saw who wounded were, and who were slain,
And who, when dead, would come to life again.
I heard the cries of those that wounded were,
(While others fought like men bereft of fear),

And while the cry, "Kill, kill," was in mine ears,
The gutters ran, not so with blood as tears.
Indeed, the captains did not always fight,
But then they would molest us day and night;
Their cry, "Up, fall on, let us take the town,"
Kept us from sleeping, or from lying down.
I was there when the gates were broken ope,
And saw how Mansoul then was stripped of hope;
I saw the captains march into the town,
How there they fought, and did their foes cut down.
I heard the Prince bid Boanerges go
Up to the castle, and there seize his foe;
And saw him and his fellows bring him down
In chains of great contempt quite through the town.
I saw Emmanuel, when he possessed
His town of Mansoul; and how greatly blest
A town this gallant town of Mansoul was
When she received his pardon, loved his laws.
When the Diabolonians were caught,
When tried, and when to execution brought,
Then I was there; yea, I was standing by
When Mansoul did the rebels crucify.
I also saw Mansoul clad all in white,
And heard her Prince call her his heart's delight.
I saw him put upon her chains of gold,
And rings and bracelets, goodly to behold.
What shall I say? I heard the people's cries,
And saw the Prince wipe tears from Mansoul's eyes.
I heard the groans, and saw the joy of many:
Tell you of all I neither will, nor can I.
But by what here I say, you well may see
That Mansoul's matchless wars no fables be.
Mansoul, the desire of both princes was:
One keep his gain would, t'other gain his loss.
Diabolus would cry, "The town is mine!"
Emmanuel would plead a right divine
Unto his Mansoul: then to blows they go,
And Mansoul cries, "These wars will me undo."
Mansoul! her wars seemed endless in her eyes:
She's lost by one, becomes another's prize;
And he again that lost her last would swear,
"Have her I will, or her in pieces tear."
Mansoul, it was the very seat of war;
Wherefore her troubles greater were by far
Than only where the noise of war is heard,
Or where the shaking of a sword is feared;

Or only where small skirmishes are fought,
Or where the fancy fighteth with the thought.
She saw the swords of fighting men made red,
And heard the cries of those with them wounded.
Must not her frights, then, be much more by far
Than theirs that to such doings strangers are?
Or theirs that hear the beating of a drum,
But not made fly for fear from house and home!
Mansoul not only heard the trumpet's sound,
But saw her gallants gasping on the ground:
Wherefore we must not think that she could rest
With them, whose greatest earnest is but jest:
Or where the blustering threatening of great wars
Do end in parleys, or in wording jars.
Mansoul! her mighty wars, they did portend
Her weal or woe, and that world without end:
Wherefore she must be more concerned than they
Whose fears begin and end the selfsame day;
Or where none other harm doth come to him
That is engaged, but loss of life or limb,
As all must needs confess that now do dwell
In Universe, and can this story tell.
Count me not, then, with them that, to amaze
The people, set them on the stars to gaze,
Insinuating with much confidence,
That each of them is now the residence
Of some brave creatures: yea, a world they will
Have in each star, though it be past their skill
To make it manifest to any man,
That reason hath, or tell his fingers can.
But I have too long held thee in the porch,
And kept thee from the sunshine with a torch.
Well, now go forward, step within the door,
And there behold five hundred times much more
Of all sorts of such inward rarities
As please the mind will, and will feed the eyes
With those, which, if a Christian, thou wilt see
Not small, but things of greatest moment be.
Nor do thou go to work without my key
(In mysteries men soon do lose their way);
And also turn it right, if thou wouldst know
My riddle, and wouldst with my heifer plough:
It lies there in the window. Fare thee well,
My next may be to ring thy passing-bell.

JOHN BUNYAN.

AN ADVERTISEMENT TO THE READER

Some say the "Pilgrim's Progress" is not mine,
Insinuating as if I would shine
In name and fame by the worth of another,
Like some made rich by robbing of their brother.
Or that so fond I am of being sire,
I'll father bastards; or, if need require,
I'll tell a lie in print to get applause.
I scorn it: John such dirt-heap never was,
Since God converted him. Let this suffice
To show why I my "Pilgrim" patronize.
It came from mine own heart, so to my head,
And thence into my fingers trickled;
Then to my pen, from whence immediately
On paper I did dribble it daintily.
Manner and matter, too, was all mine own;
Nor was it unto any mortal known
Till I had done it; nor did any then
By books, by wits, by tongues, or hand, or pen,
Add five words to it, or wrote half a line
Thereof: the whole and every whit is mine.
Also for THIS, *thine eye is now upon,*
The matter in this manner came from none
But the same heart, and head, fingers, and pen,
As did the other. Witness all good men,
For none in all the world, without a lie,
Can say that this is mine, excepting I.
I write not this of any ostentation,
Nor 'cause I seek of men their commendation;
I do it to keep them from such surmise
As tempt them will my name to scandalize.
Witness my name, if anagram'd to thee,
The letters make—"Nu hony in a B."

JOHN BUNYAN.

A RELATION

OF

THE HOLY WAR, etc.

In my travels, as I walked through many regions and countries, it was my chance to happen into that famous continent of Universe. A very large and spacious country it is: it lieth between the two poles, and just amidst the four points of the heavens. It is a place well watered, and richly adorned with hills and valleys, bravely situate, and for the most part, at least where I was, very fruitful, also well peopled, and a very sweet air.

The people are not all of one complexion, nor yet of one language, mode, or way of religion, but differ as much as ('tis said) do the planets themselves. Some are right, and some are wrong, even as it happeneth to be in lesser regions.

In this country, as I said, it was my lot to travel; and there travel I did, and that so long even till I learned much of their mother tongue, together with the customs and manners of them among whom I was. And, to speak truth, I was much delighted to see and hear many things which I saw and heard among them; yea, I had, to be sure, even lived and died a native among them (so was I taken with them and their doings), had not my master sent for me home to his house, there to do business for him, and to oversee business done.

Now, there is in this gallant country of Universe a fair and delicate town, a corporation, called Mansoul; a town for its building so curious, for its situation so commodious, for its privileges so advantageous (I mean with reference to its original), that I may say of it, as was said before of the continent in which it is placed, There is not its equal under the whole heaven.

As to the situation of this town, it lieth just between the two worlds; and the first founder and builder of it, so far as by the best and most authentic records I can gather, was one Shaddai; and he built it for his own delight. He made it the mirror and glory of all that he made, even the top-piece, beyond anything else that he did in that country. Yea, so goodly a town was Mansoul when first built, that it is said by some, the gods, at the setting up thereof, came down to see it and sang for joy. And as he made it goodly to behold, so also mighty to have dominion over all the country round about. Yea, all were commanded to acknowledge Mansoul for their metropolitan, all were enjoined to do homage to it. Ay, the town itself had positive commission and power from her King to demand service of all, and also to subdue any that anyways denied to do it.

There was reared up in the midst of this town a most famous and stately palace; for strength, it might be called a castle; for pleasantness, a paradise; for largeness, a place so copious as to contain all the world. This palace the King Shaddai intended but for himself alone, and not another with him, partly because of his own delights, and partly because he would not that the terror of strangers should be upon the town. This place Shaddai made also a garrison of, but committed the keeping of it only to the men of the town. The wall of the town was well built, yea, so fast and firm was it knit and compact together, that, had it not been for the townsmen themselves, they could not have been shaken or broken for ever. For here lay the excellent wisdom of him that builded Mansoul, that the walls could never be broken down nor hurt by the most mighty adverse potentate, unless the townsmen gave consent thereto.

This famous town of Mansoul had five gates in at which to come, out at which to go; and these were made likewise answerable to the walls, to wit, impregnable, and such as could never be opened nor forced but by the will and leave of those within. The names of the gates were these: Ear-gate, Eye-gate, Mouth-gate, Nose-gate, and Feel-gate.

Other things there were that belonged to the town of Mansoul, which if you adjoin to these, will yet give further demonstration to all of the glory and strength of the place. It had always a sufficiency of provision within its walls; it had the best, most wholesome, and excellent law that then was extant in the world. There was not a rascal, rogue, or traitorous person then within its walls: they were all true men, and fast joined together: and this, you know, is a great matter. And to all these it had always (so long as it had the goodness to keep true to Shaddai the King) his countenance, his protection, and it was his delight, etc.

Diabolus

Well, upon a time, there was one Diabolus, a mighty giant, made an assault upon this famous town of Mansoul, to take it and make it his own habitation. This giant was king of the blacks, or negroes, and a most raving prince he was. We will, if you please, first discourse of the original of this Diabolus, and then of his taking of this famous town of Mansoul.

This Diabolus is indeed a great and mighty prince, and yet both poor and beggarly. As to his original, he was at first one of the servants of King Shaddai, made and taken and put by him into most high and mighty place; yea, was put into such principalities as belonged to the best of his territories and dominions. This Diabolus was made son of the morning, and a brave place he had of it: it brought him much glory, and gave him much brightness, an income that might have contented his Luciferian heart, had it not been insatiable, and enlarged as hell itself.

Well, he seeing himself thus exalted to greatness and honour, and raging in his mind for higher state and degree, what doth he but begins to think with himself how he might be set up as lord over all, and have the sole power under Shaddai. Now, that did the King reserve for his Son, yea, and had already bestowed it upon him. Wherefore he first consults with himself what had best to be done; and then breaks his mind to some other of his companions, to the which they also agree. So, in fine, they came to this issue, that they should make an attempt upon the King's Son to destroy him, that the inheritance might be theirs. Well, to be short, the treason, as I said, was concluded, the time appointed, the word given, the rebels rendezvoused, and the assault attempted. Now, the King and his Son being ALL and always EYE, could not but discern all passages in his dominions; and he, having always love for his Son as for himself could not at what he saw but be greatly provoked and offended: wherefore what does he, but takes them in the very nick and first trip that they made towards their design, convicts them of the treason, horrid rebellion, and conspiracy that they had devised, and now attempted to put into practice, and casts them altogether out of all place of trust, benefit, honour, and preferment. This done, he banishes them the court, turns them down into the horrible pits, as fast bound in chains, never more to expect the least favour from his hands, but to abide the judgment that he had appointed, and that for ever, and yet.

Now, they being thus cast out of all place of trust, profit, and honour, and also knowing that they had lost their prince's favour for ever (being banished his courts, and cast down to the horrible pits), you may be sure they would now add to their former pride what malice and rage against Shaddai, and against his Son, they could. Wherefore, roving and ranging in much fury from place to place, if, perhaps, they might find something that was the King's, to revenge by spoiling of that, themselves on him; at last they happened into this spacious country of Universe, and steer their course towards the town of Mansoul; and considering that that town was one of the chief works and delights of King Shaddai, what do they, but after counsel taken, make an assault upon that. I say, they knew that Mansoul belonged unto Shaddai; for they were there when he built it and beautified it for himself. So, when they had found the place, they shouted horribly for joy, and roared on it as a lion upon the prey, saying, "Now we have found the prize, and how to be revenged on King Shaddai for what he hath done to us." So they sat down, and called a council of war, and considered with themselves what ways and methods they had best to engage in for the winning to themselves this famous town of Mansoul; and these four things were then propounded to be considered of:—First, Whether they had best all of them to show themselves in this design to the town of Mansoul.

Secondly, Whether they had best to go and sit down against Mansoul in their now ragged and beggarly guise.

Thirdly, Whether they had best show to Mansoul their intentions, and what design they came about, or whether to assault it with words and ways of deceit.

Fourthly, Whether they had not best, to some of their companions, to give out private orders to take the advantage, if they see one or more of the principal townsmen, to shoot them, if thereby they shall judge their cause and design will the better be promoted.

1. It was answered to the first of these proposals in the negative–to wit, that it would not be best that all should show themselves before the town, because the appearance of many of them might alarm and frighten the town; whereas a few or but one of them was not so likely to do it. And to enforce this advice to take place 'twas added further, that if Mansoul was frighted, or did take the alarm, " 'Tis impossible," said Diabolus (for he spake now), "that we should take the town: for that none can enter into it without its own consent. Let, therefore, but few, or but one, assault Mansoul; and in mine opinion," said Diabolus, "let me be he." Wherefore to this they all agreed.

2. And then to the second proposal they came–namely, Whether they had best to go and sit down before Mansoul, in their now ragged and beggarly guise. To which it was answered also in the negative, By no means; and that because, though the town of Mansoul had been made to know, and to have to do, before now, with things that are invisible, they never did as yet see any of their fellow-creatures in so sad and rascally condition as they; and this was the advice of that fierce Alecto. Then said Apollyon, "The advice is pertinent; for even one of us appearing to them as we are now must needs both beget and multiply such thoughts in them, as will both put them into a consternation of spirit, and necessitate them to put themselves upon their guard. And if so," said he then, "as my Lord Alecto said but now, 'tis in vain for us to think of taking the town." Then said that mighty giant Beelzebub, "The advice that is already given is safe; for though the men of Mansoul have seen such things as we once were, yet hitherto they did never behold such things as we now are; and 'tis best, in mine opinion, to come upon them in such a guise as is common to, and most familiar among them." To this when they had consented, the next thing to be considered was in what shape, hue, or guise Diabolus had best to show himself when he went about to make Mansoul his own. Then one said one thing, and another the contrary. At last Lucifer answered, that in his opinion, it was best that his lordship should assume the body of some of those creatures that they of the town had dominion over; "for," quoth he, "these are not only familiar to them, but being under them, they will never imagine that an attempt should by them be made upon the town; and to blind all, let him assume the body of one of those beasts that Mansoul deems to be wiser than any of the rest." This advice was applauded of all: so it was determined that the giant Diabolus should assume the dragon, for that he was in those days as familiar with the town of Mansoul as now is the bird with the boy; for nothing that was in its primitive state was at all amazing to them. Then they proceeded to the third thing, which was–

3. Whether they had best to shew their intentions, or the design of his coming to Mansoul, or no. This also was answered in the negative, because of the weight that was in the former reasons: to wit, for that Mansoul were a strong people, a strong people in a strong town, whose wall and gates were impregnable (to say nothing of their castle), nor can they by any means be

won but by their own consent. "Besides," said Legion (for he gave answer to this), "a discovery of our intentions may make them send to their King for aid; and if that be done, I know quickly what time of day it will be with us. Therefore let us assault them in all pretended fairness covering our intentions with all manner of lies, flatteries, delusive words; feigning things that never will be, and promising that to them, that they shall never find. This is the way to win Mansoul, and to make them of themselves to open their gates to us; yea, and to desire us too, to come in to them. And the reason why I think that this project will do, is because the people of Mansoul now are, every one, simple and innocent, all honest and true; nor do they as yet know what it is to be assaulted with fraud, guile, and hypocrisy. They are strangers to lying and dissembling lips; wherefore we cannot, if thus we be disguised, by them at all be discerned; our lies shall go for true sayings, and our dissimulations for upright dealings. What we promise them, they will in that believe us, especially, if in all our lies and feigned words, we pretend great love to them, and that our design is only their advantage and honour." Now, there was not one bit of a reply against this; this went as current down, as doth the water down a steep descent. Wherefore they go to consider of the last proposal, which was—

4. Whether they had not best to give out orders to some of their company, to shoot some one or more of the principal of the townsmen, if they judge that their cause may be promoted thereby. This was carried in the affirmative, and the man that was designed by this stratagem to be destroyed was one Mr. Resistance, otherwise called Captain Resistance. And a great man in Mansoul this Captain Resistance was, and a man that the giant Diabolus and his band more feared than they feared the whole town of Mansoul besides. Now, who should be the actor to do the murder? That was the next, and they appointed Tisiphone, a fury of the lake, to do it.

Diabolus Demands Audience

They thus having ended their council of war, rose up, and essayed to do as they had determined; they marched towards Mansoul, but all in a manner invisible, save one, only one; nor did he approach the town in his own likeness, but under the shape and in the body of the dragon.

So they drew up, and sat down before Ear-gate, for that was the place of hearing for all without the town, as Eye-gate was the place of perspection. So, as I said, he came up with his train to the gate, and laid his ambuscado for Captain Resistance within bow-shot of the town. This done, the giant ascended up close to the gate, and called to the town of Mansoul for audience. Nor took he any with him, but one Ill-Pause, who was his orator in all difficult matters. Now, as I said, he being come up to the gate (as the manner of those times was), sounded his trumpet for audience; at which the chief of the town of Mansoul, such as my Lord Innocent, my Lord Will-be-will, my Lord Mayor, Mr. Recorder and Captain Resistance, came down to the wall to see who was there, and what was the matter. And my Lord

Will-be-will, when he had looked over and saw who stood at the gate, demanded what he was, wherefore he was come, and why he roused the town of Mansoul with so unusual a sound.

Diabolus, then, as if he had been a lamb, began his oration, and said, "Gentlemen of the famous town of Mansoul, I am, as you may perceive, no far dweller from you, but near, and one that is bound by the King to do you my homage, and what service I can; wherefore, that I may be faithful to myself and to you, I have somewhat of concern to impart unto you. Wherefore, grant me your audience, and hear me patiently. And first, I will assure you, it is not myself, but you; not mine, but your advantage that I seek by what I now do, as will full well be made manifest, by that I have opened my mind unto you. For, gentlemen, I am (to tell you the truth) come to show you how you may obtain great and ample deliverance from a bondage that, unawares to yourselves, you are captivated and enslaved under." At this the town of Mansoul began to prick up its ears. And "What is it? Pray what is it?" thought they. And he said, "I have somewhat to say to you concerning your King, concerning his law, and also touching yourselves. Touching your King, I know he is great and potent; but yet all that he hath said to you is neither true nor yet for your advantage. 1. 'Tis not true, for that wherewith he hath hitherto awed you shall not come to pass, nor be fulfilled, though you do the thing that he hath forbidden. But if there was danger, what a slavery it is to live always in fear of the greatest of punishments, for doing so small and trivial a thing as eating of a little fruit is! 2. Touching his laws, this I say further, they are both unreasonable, intricate, and intolerable. Unreasonable, as was hinted before; for that the punishment is not proportioned to the offence: there is great difference and disproportion betwixt the life and an apple; yet the one must go for the other by the law of your Shaddai. But it is also intricate, in that he saith, first, you may eat of all; and yet after forbids the eating of one. And then, in the last place, it must needs be intolerable, forasmuch as that fruit which you are forbidden to eat of (if you are forbidden any) is that, and that alone, which is able, by your eating, to minister to you a good as yet unknown by you. This is manifest by the very name of the tree; it is called the tree of knowledge of good and evil; and have you that knowledge as yet? No, no; nor can you conceive how good, how pleasant, and how much to be desired to make one wise it is, so long as you stand by your King's commandment. Why should you be holden in ignorance and blindness? Why should you not be enlarged in knowledge and understanding? And now, O ye inhabitants of the famous town of Mansoul, to speak more particularly to yourselves, you are not a free people! You are kept both in bondage and slavery, and that by a grievous threat; no reason being annexed but 'So I will have it; so it shall be.' And is it not grievous to think on, that that very thing which you are forbidden to do, might you but do it, would yield you both wisdom and honour? for then your eyes will be opened, and you shall be as gods. Now, since this is thus," quoth he, "can you be kept by any prince in more slavery and in greater bondage than you are under this day? You are made underlings, and are wrapped up in inconveniences, as I have well made appear. For what bondage greater than to be kept in blindness? Will not reason tell you, that it is better to have eyes than to be without them? and so to be at liberty to be better than to be shut up in a dark and stinking cave?"

And just now, while Diabolus was speaking these words to Mansoul, Tisiphone shot at Captain Resistance, where he stood on the gate, and mortally wounded him in the head; so that he, to the amazement of the townsmen, and the encouragement of Diabolus, fell down dead quite over the wall.

Speech of Ill-Pause

Now, when Captain Resistance was dead (and he was the only man of war in the town), poor Mansoul was wholly left naked of courage, nor had she now any heart to resist. But this was as the devil would have it. Then stood forth that he, Mr. Ill-Pause, that Diabolus brought with him, who was his orator; and he addressed himself to speak to the town of Mansoul; the tenor of whose speech here follows:—

"Gentlemen," quoth he, "it is my master's happiness that he has this day a quiet and teachable auditory; and it is hoped by us that we shall prevail upon you not to cast off good advice. My master has a very great love for you; and although, as he very well knows, that he runs the hazard of the anger of King Shaddai, yet love to you will make him do more than that. Nor doth there need that a word more should be spoken to confirm for truth what he hath said; there is not a word but carries with it self-evidence in its bowels; the very name of the tree may put an end to all controversy in this matter. I therefore, at this time, shall only add this advice to you, under and by the leave of my lord" (and with that he made Diabolus a very low congee): "consider his words, look on the tree and the promising fruit thereof; remember also that yet you know but little, and that this is the way to know more; and if your reasons be not conquered to accept of such good counsel, you are not the men that I took you to be."

But when the townsfolk saw that the tree was good for food, and that it was pleasant to the eye, and a tree to be desired to make one wise, they did as old Ill-Pause advised: they took and did eat thereof. Now this I should have told you before, that even then, when this Ill-Pause was making of his speech to the townsmen, my Lord Innocent (whether by a shot from the camp of the giant, or from some sinking qualm that suddenly took him, or whether by the stinking breath of that treacherous villain old Ill-Pause, for so I am apt to think), sunk down in the place where he stood, nor could he be brought to life again. Thus these two brave men died; brave men I called them, for they were the beauty and glory of Mansoul, so long as they lived therein; nor did there now remain any more a noble spirit in Mansoul; they all fell down and yielded obedience to Diabolus, and became his slaves and vassals, as you shall hear.

Now these being dead, what do the rest of the townsfolk, but, as men that had found a fool's paradise, they presently, as afore was hinted, fall to prove the truth of the giant's words. And, first, they did as Ill-Pause had taught them: they looked, they considered, they were taken with the forbidden fruit; they took thereof, and did eat; and having eaten, they became immediately drunken therewith. So they opened the gate, both Ear-gate and Eye-gate, and let in Diabolus with all his bands, quite forgetting that their good Shaddai, his law, and the judgment that he had annexed, with solemn threatening, to the breach thereof.

Diabolus, having now obtained entrance in at the gates of the town, marches up to the middle thereof, to make his conquest as sure as he could; and finding, by this time, the affections of the people warmly inclining to him, he, as thinking 'twas best striking while the iron is hot, made this further deceivable speech unto them, saying, "Alas! my poor Mansoul! I have done thee indeed this service, as to promote thee to honour, and to greaten thy liberty; but, alas, alas! poor Mansoul! thou wantest now one to defend thee; for assure thyself that when Shaddai shall hear what is done, he will come; for sorry will he be that thou hast broken his bonds, and cast his cords away from thee. What wilt thou do? Wilt thou, after enlargement, suffer thy privileges to be invaded and taken away? or what wilt resolve with thyself?"

Then they all with one consent said to this bramble, "Do thou reign over us." So he accepted the motion, and became the king of the town of Mansoul. This being done, the next thing was to give him possession of the castle, and so of the whole strength of the town. Wherefore, into the castle he goes: it was that which Shaddai built in Mansoul for his own delight and pleasure; this now was become a den and hold for a giant Diabolus.

Diabolus in Possession

Now, having got possession of this stately palace or castle, what doth he but makes it a garrison for himself, and strengthens and fortifies it with all sorts of provision, against the King Shaddai, or those who should endeavour the regaining of it to him and his obedience again. This done, but not thinking himself yet secure enough, in the next place he bethinks himself of new modelling the town; and so he does, setting up one and putting down another at pleasure. Wherefore my Lord Mayor, whose name was my Lord Understanding, and Mr. Recorder, whose name was Mr. Conscience, these are put out of place and power.

As for my Lord Mayor, though he was an understanding man, and one too that had complied with the rest of the town of Mansoul in admitting of the giant into the town, yet Diabolus thought not fit to let him abide in his former lustre and glory, because he was a seeing man. Wherefore he darkened it, not only by taking from him his office and power, but by building a high and strong tower, just between the sun's reflections and the windows of my lord's palace; by which means this house and all, and the whole of his habitation, were made as dark as darkness itself. And thus, being alienated from the light, he became as one that was born blind. To this his house my lord was confined as to a prison; nor might he, upon his parole, go farther than within his own bounds. And now, had he an heart to do for Mansoul, what could he do for it, or wherein could he be profitable to her? So then, so long as Mansoul was under the power and government of Diabolus (and so long it was under him as it was obedient to him, which was even until by a war it was rescued out of his hand), so long my Lord Mayor was rather an impediment in, than an advantage to, the famous town of Mansoul.

As for Mr. Recorder, before the town was taken he was a man well read in the laws of his King, and also a man of courage and faithfulness to speak truth at every occasion; and he had a tongue as bravely hung as he had an head filled with judgment. Now, this man Diabolus could by no means abide, because, though he gave his consent to his coming into the town, yet he could not, by all the wiles, trials, stratagems, and devices that he could use, make him wholly his own. True, he was much degenerated from his former King, and also much pleased with many of the giant's laws and service; but all this would not do, forasmuch as he was not wholly his. He would now and then think upon Shaddai, and have dread of his law upon him, and then he would speak against Diabolus with a voice as great as when a lion roareth. Yea, he would also at certain times, when his fits were upon him (for you must know that sometimes he had terrible fits), make the whole town of Mansoul shake with his voice; and therefore the now King of Mansoul could not abide him.

Diabolus, therefore, feared the Recorder more than any that was left alive in the town of Mansoul, because, as I said, his words did shake the whole town; they were like the rattling thunder, and also like thunder-claps. Since, therefore, the giant could not make him wholly his own, what doth he do but studies all that he could to debauch the old gentleman, and by debauchery to stupefy his mind, and more harden his heart in ways of vanity. And as he attempted, so he accomplished his design: he debauched the man, and by little and little so drew him into sin and wickedness, that at last he was not only debauched, as at first, and so by consequence defiled, but was almost (at last, I say) past all conscience of sin. And this was the farthest Diabolus could go. Wherefore he bethinks him of another project, and that was, to persuade the men of the town that Mr. Recorder was mad, and so not to be regarded. And for this he urged his fits, and said, "If he be himself, why doth he not do thus always? But," quoth he, "as all mad folks have their fits, and in them their raving language, so hath this old and doting gentleman."

Thus, by one means or another, he quickly got Mansoul to slight, neglect, and despise whatever Mr. Recorder could say. For, besides what already you have heard, Diabolus had a way to make the old gentleman, when he was merry, unsay and deny what he in his fits had affirmed. And, indeed, this was the next way to make himself ridiculous, and to cause that no man should regard him. Also now he never spake freely for King Shaddai, but always by force and constraint. Besides, he would at one time be hot against that at which, at another, he would hold his peace, so uneven was he now in his doings. Sometimes he would be as if fast asleep, and again sometimes as dead; even then, when the whole town of Mansoul was in her career after vanity, and in her dance after the giant's pipe.

Wherefore, sometimes when Mansoul did use to be frightened with the thundering voice of the Recorder that was, and when they did tell Diabolus of it, he would answer, that what the old gentleman said was neither of love to him nor pity to them, but of a foolish fondness that he had to be prating; and so would hush, still, and put all to quiet again. And that he might leave no argument unurged that might tend to make them secure, he said, and said it often, "O Mansoul! consider that, notwithstanding the old gentleman's rage, and the rattle of his high and thundering words, you hear nothing of Shaddai himself;" when liar and deceiver that he was, every outcry of Mr. Recorder against the sin of Mansoul was the voice of God in him to them. But he goes on, and says, "You see that he values not the loss nor rebellion of the town of Mansoul, nor will he trouble himself with calling his town to a reckoning for their giving themselves to me. He knows that though you were his, now you are lawfully mine; so, leaving us to one another, he now hath shaken his hands of us.

"Moreover, O Mansoul!" quoth he, "consider how I have served you, even to the uttermost of my power; and that with the best that I have, could get, or procure for you in all the world: besides, I dare say, that the laws and customs that you now are under, and by which you do homage to me, do yield you more solace and content than did the paradise that at first you possessed. Your liberty also, as yourselves do very well know, has been greatly widened and enlarged by me; whereas I found you a penn'd-up people. I have not laid any restraint upon you; you have no law, statute, or judgment of mine to fright you; I call none of you to account for your doings, except the madman–you know who I mean; I have granted you to live, each man like a prince in his own, even with as little control from me as I myself have from you."

And thus would Diabolus hush up and quiet the town of Mansoul, when the Recorder that was, did at times molest them; yea, and with such cursed orations as these, would set the whole town in a rage and fury against the old gentleman. Yea, the rascal crew at sometimes would be for destroying him. They have often wished, in my hearing, that he had lived a thousand miles off from them; his company, his words, yea, the sight of him, and especially when they remembered how in the old times he did use to threaten and condemn them (for all he was now so debauched), did terrify and afflict them sore.

But all wishes were vain, for I do not know how, unless by the power of Shaddai, and his wisdom, he was preserved in being amongst them. Besides, his house was as strong as a castle, and stood hard by a strong hold of the town: moreover, if at any time any of the crew or rabble attempted to make him away, he could pull up the sluices, and let in such floods as would drown all round about him.

My Lord Will-be-will

But to leave Mr. Recorder, and to come to my Lord Will-be-will, another of the gentry of the famous town of Mansoul. This Will-be-will was as high-born as any man in Mansoul, and was as much, if not more, a freeholder than many of them were; besides, if I remember my tale aright, he had some privileges peculiar to himself in the famous town of Mansoul. Now, together with these, he was a man of great strength, resolution, and courage, nor in his occasion could any turn him away. But I say, whether he was proud of his estate, privileges, strength, or what (but sure it was through pride of something), he scorns now to be a slave in Mansoul; and therefore resolves to bear office under Diabolus, that he might (such a one as he was) be a petty ruler and governor in Mansoul. And, headstrong man that he was! thus he began betimes; for this man, when Diabolus did make his oration at Ear-gate, was one of the first that was for consenting to his words, and for accepting his counsel as wholesome, and that was for the opening of the gate, and for letting him into the town: wherefore Diabolus had a kindness for him, and therefore he designed for him a place. And perceiving the valour and stoutness of the man, he coveted to have him for one of his great ones, to act and do in matters of the highest concern.

So he sent for him, and talked with him of that secret matter that lay in his breast, but there needed not much persuasion in the case; for as at first he was willing that Diabolus should be let into the town, so now he was as willing to serve him there. When the tyrant, therefore, perceived the willingness of my lord to serve him, and that his mind stood bending that way, he forthwith made him the captain of the castle, governor of the wall, and keeper of the gates of Mansoul; yea, there was a clause in his commission, that nothing without him should be done in all the town of Mansoul. So that now, next to Diabolus himself, who but my Lord Will-be-will in all the town of Mansoul! nor could anything now be done, but at his will and pleasure, throughout the town of Mansoul. He had also one Mr. Mind for his clerk, a man to speak on every way like his master; for he and his lord were in principle one, and in practice not far asunder. And now was Mansoul brought under to purpose, and made to fulfil the lusts of the will and of the mind.

But it will not out of my thoughts, what a desperate one this Will-be-will was, when power was put into his hand. First, he flatly denied that he owed any suit or service to his former prince and liege lord. This done, in the next place he took an oath, and swore fidelity to his great master Diabolus, and then, being stated and settled in his places, offices, advancements, and preferments, oh, you cannot think, unless you had seen it, the strange work that this workman made in the town of Mansoul!

First, he maligned Mr. Recorder to death; he would neither endure to see him, nor to hear the words of his mouth; he would shut his eyes when he saw him, and stop his ears when he heard him speak. Also he could not endure that so much as a fragment of the law of Shaddai should be anywhere seen in the town. For example, his clerk, Mr. Mind, had some old, rent, and torn parchments of the law of good Shaddai in his house, but when Will-be-will saw them, he cast them behind his back. True, Mr. Recorder had some of the laws in his study; but my lord could by no means come at them. He also thought, and said, that the windows of my old Lord Mayor's house were always too light for the profit of the town of Mansoul. The light of a candle he could not endure. Now nothing at all pleased Will-be-will but what pleased Diabolus his lord. There was none like him to trumpet about the streets the brave nature, the wise conduct, and great glory of the King Diabolus. He would range and rove throughout all the streets of Mansoul to cry up his illustrious lord, and would make himself even as an abject, among the base and rascal crew, to cry up his valiant prince. And I say, when and wheresoever he found these vassals, he would even make himself as one of them. In all ill courses he would act without bidding, and do mischief without commandment.

The Lord Will-be-will also had a deputy under him, and his name was Mr. Affection: one that was also greatly debauched in his principles, and answerable thereto in his life: he was wholly given to the flesh, and therefore they called him Vile-Affection. Now there was he and one Carnal-Lust, the daughter of Mr. Mind (like to like, quoth the devil to the collier), that fell in love, and made a match, and were married; and, as I take it, they had several children, as Impudent, Black-mouth, and Hate-Reproof. These three were black boys. And besides these they had three daughters, as Scorn-Truth, and Slight-God, and the name of the youngest was Revenge. These were all married in the town, and also begot and yielded many bad brats; too many to be here inserted. But to pass by this.

When the giant had thus ingarrisoned himself in the town of Mansoul, and had put down and set up whom he thought good, he betakes himself to defacing. Now, there was in the market-place in Mansoul, and also upon the gates of the castle, an image of the blessed King Shaddai. This image was so exactly ingraven (and it was ingraven in gold), that it did most resemble Shaddai himself of anything that then was extant in the world. This he basely commanded to be defaced, and it was as basely done by the hand of Mr. No-Truth. Now, you must know, that as Diabolus had commanded, and that by the hand of Mr. No-Truth, the image of Shaddai was defaced, he likewise gave order that the same Mr. No-Truth should set up in its stead the horrid and formidable image of Diabolus; to the great contempt of the former King, and debasing of his town of Mansoul.

Moreover, Diabolus made havoc of all remains of the laws and statutes of Shaddai that could be found in the town of Mansoul; to wit, such as contained either the doctrines of morals, with all civil and natural documents. Also relative severities he sought to extinguish. To be short, there was nothing of the remains of good in Mansoul which he and Will-be-will sought not to destroy; for their desire was to turn Mansoul into a brute, and to make it like to the sensual sow, by the hand of Mr. No-Truth.

When he had destroyed what law and good orders he could, then, further to effect his design,—namely, to alienate Mansoul from Shaddai her king,—he commands, and they set up his own vain edicts, statutes, and commandments, in all places of resort or concourse in Mansoul; to wit, such as gave the liberty to the lusts of the flesh, the lusts of the eyes, and the pride of life, which are not of Shaddai, but of the world. He encouraged, countenanced, and promoted lasciviousness and ungodliness there. Yea, much more did Diabolus to encourage wickedness in the town of Mansoul: he promised them peace, content, joy, and bliss, in doing his commands, and that they should never be called to an account for their not doing the contrary. And let this serve to give a taste to them that love to hear tell of what is done beyond their knowledge afar off in other countries.

Now, Mansoul being wholly at his beck and brought wholly to his bow, nothing was heard or seen therein but that which tended to set up him.

But now he, having disabled the Lord Mayor and Mr. Recorder from bearing of office in Mansoul, and seeing that the town, before he came to it, was the most ancient of corporations in the world; and fearing, if they did not maintain greatness, they at any time should object that he had done them an injury; therefore, I say (that they might see that he did not intend to lessen their grandeur, or to take from them any of their advantageous things), he did choose for them a Lord Mayor and a Recorder himself, and such as contented *them* at the heart, and such also as pleased *him* wondrous well.

The New Lord Mayor

The name of the Mayor that was of Diabolus's making was the Lord Lustings, a man that had neither eyes nor ears. All that he did, whether as a man or an officer, he did it naturally, as doth the beast. And that which made him yet the more ignoble, though not to Mansoul, yet to them that beheld and were grieved for its ruin, was that he never could savour good, but evil.

The Recorder was one whose name was Forget-Good, and a very sorry fellow he was. He could remember nothing but mischief, and to do it with delight. He was naturally prone to do things that were hurtful, even hurtful to the town of Mansoul, and to all the dwellers there. These two, therefore by their power and practice, examples and smiles upon evil, did much more grammar and settle the common people in hurtful ways. For who doth not perceive that when those who sit aloft are vile and corrupt themselves, they corrupt the whole region and country where they are?

Besides these, Diabolus made several burgesses and aldermen in Mansoul, such as out of whom the town, when it needed, might choose them officers, governors, and magistrates. And these are the names of the chief of them:— Mr. Incredulity, Mr. Haughty, Mr. Swearing, Mr. Whoring, Mr. Hard-Heart, Mr. Pitiless, Mr. Fury, Mr. No-Truth, Mr. Stand-to-Lies, Mr. False-Peace, Mr. Drunkenness, Mr. Cheating, Mr. Atheism—thirteen in all. Mr. Incredulity is the eldest, and Mr. Atheism the youngest of the Company.

There was also an election of common councilmen and others, as bailiffs, sergeants, constables, and others; but all of them alike to those aforenamed, being either fathers, brothers, cousins, or nephews to them; whose names, for brevity's sake I omit to mention.

When the giant had thus far proceeded in his work, in the next place he betook him to build some strongholds in the town, and he built three that seemed to be impregnable. The first he called the Hold of Defiance, because it was made to command the whole town, and to keep it from the knowledge of its ancient King. The second he called Midnight Hold, because it was builded on purpose to keep Mansoul from the true knowledge of itself. The third was called Sweet-sin Hold, because by that he fortified Mansoul against all desires of good. The first of these holds stood close by Eye-gate, that, as much as might be, light might be darkened there; the second was builded hard by the old castle, to the end that that might be made more blind, if possible; and the third stood in the market-place.

He that Diabolus made governor over the first of these was one Spite-God, a most blasphemous wretch: he came with the whole rabble of them that came against Mansoul at first, and was himself one of themselves. He that was made the governor of Midnight Hold was one Love-no-Light: he was also of them that came first against the town. And he that was made the governor of the hold called Sweet-sin Hold was one whose name was Love-Flesh: he was also a very lewd fellow, but not of that country where the other are bound. This fellow could find more sweetness when he stood sucking of a lust, than he did in all the paradise of God.

And now Diabolus thought himself safe. He had taken Mansoul, he had ingarrisoned himself therein: he had put down the old officers, and had set up new ones; he had defaced the image of Shaddai, and had set up his own; he had spoiled the old law-books, and had promoted his own vain lies; he had made him new magistrates, and set up new aldermen; he had built him new holds, and had manned them for himself; and all this he did to make himself secure, in case the good Shaddai, or his Son, should come to make an incursion upon him.

Now you may well think, that long before this time, word, by some or other, could not but be carried to the good King Shaddai, how his Mansoul, in the continent of Universe, was lost; and that the runagate giant Diabolus, once one of his Majesty's servants, had, in rebellion against the King, made sure thereof for himself. Yea, tidings were carried and brought to the King thereof, and that to a very circumstance.

As first, how Diabolus came upon Mansoul (they being a simple people and innocent) with craft, subtlety, lies, and guile. Item, that he had treacherously slain the right noble and valiant captain, their Captain Resistance, as he stood upon the gate with the rest of the townsmen. Item, how my brave Lord Innocent fell down dead (with grief, some say, or with being poisoned with the stinking breath of one Ill-Pause, as say others) at the hearing of his just lord and rightful prince, Shaddai, so abused by the mouth of so filthy a Diabolonian as that varlet Ill-Pause was. The messenger further told, that after this Ill-Pause had made a short oration to the townsmen on behalf of Diabolus, his master, the simple town, believing that what was said was true, with one consent did open Ear-gate, the chief gate of the corporation, and did let him, with his crew, into a possession of the famous town of Mansoul. He further showed how Diabolus had served the Lord Mayor and Mr. Recorder; to wit, that he had put them from all place of power and trust. Item, he showed also that my Lord Will-be-will was turned a very rebel and runagate, and that so was one Mr. Mind, his clerk; and that they two did range and revel it all the town over, and teach the wicked ones their ways. He said, moreover, that this Will-be-will was put into great trust, and particularly that Diabolus had put into Will-be-will's hand all the strong places in Mansoul, and that Mr. Affection was made my Lord Will-be-will's deputy in his most rebellious affairs. "Yea," said the messenger, "this monster, Lord Will-be-will, has openly disavowed his King Shaddai, and hath horribly given his faith and plighted his troth to Diabolus.

"Also," said the messenger, "besides all this, the new king, or rather rebellious tyrant, over the once famous but now perishing town of Mansoul, has set up a Lord Mayor and a Recorder of his own. For Mayor, he has set up one Mr. Lustings; and for Recorder, Mr. Forget-Good; two of the vilest of all the town of Mansoul." This faithful messenger also proceeded, and told what a sort of new burgesses Diabolus had made; also that he had built several strong forts, towers, and strongholds in Mansoul. He told, too (the which I had almost forgot), how Diabolus had put the town of Mansoul into arms, the better to capacitate them, on his behalf, to make resistance against Shaddai their King, should he come to reduce them to their former obedience.

Now, this tidings-teller did not deliver his relation of things in private, but in open court, the King and his Son, high lords, chief captains, and nobles, being all there present to hear. But by that they had heard the whole of the story, it would have amazed one to have seen, had he been there to behold it, what sorrow and grief and compunction of spirit there was among all sorts, to think that famous Mansoul was now taken: only the King and his Son foresaw all this long before, yea, and sufficiently provided for the relief of Mansoul, though they told not everybody thereof. Yet because they also would have a share in condoling of the misery of Mansoul, therefore they also did, and that at the rate of the highest degree, bewail the losing of Mansoul. The King said plainly that it grieved him at his heart, and you may be sure that his Son was not a whit behind him. Thus gave they conviction to all about them that they had love and compassion for the famous town of Mansoul. Well, when the King and his Son were retired into the privy chamber, there they again consulted about what they had designed before: to wit, That as Mansoul should in time be suffered to be lost, so as certainly it should be recovered again; recovered, I say, in such a way as that both the King and his Son would get themselves eternal fame and glory thereby. Wherefore, after this consult, the Son of Shaddai (a sweet and comely person, and one that had always great affection for those that were in affliction, but one that had mortal enmity in his heart against Diabolus, because he was designed for it, and because he sought his crown and dignity)—this Son of Shaddai, I say, having stricken hands with his Father, and promised that he would be his servant to recover his Mansoul again, stood by his resolution, nor would he repent of the same. The purport of which agreement was this: to wit, That at a certain time, prefixed by both, the King's Son should take a journey into the country of Universe, and there, in a way of justice and equity, by making amends for the follies of Mansoul, he should lay a foundation of her perfect deliverance from Diabolus and from his tyranny.

Moreover, Emmanuel resolved to make, at a time convenient, a war upon the giant Diabolus, even while he was possessed of the town of Mansoul; and that he would fairly, by strength of hand, drive him out of his hold, his nest, and take it to himself to be his habitation.

A Brave Design for the Town of Mansoul

This now being resolved upon, order was given to the Lord Chief Secretary to draw up a fair record of what was determined, and to cause that it should be published in all the corners of the kingdom of Universe. A short breviat of the contents thereof you may, if you please, take here as follows:—

"Let all men know who are concerned, that the Son of Shaddai, the great King, is engaged by covenant to his Father to bring his Mansoul to him again; yea, and to put Mansoul too, through the power of his matchless love, into a far better and more happy condition than it was in before it was taken by Diabolus."

These papers, therefore, were published in several places, to the no little molestation of the tyrant Diabolus; "for now," thought he, "I shall be molested, and my habitation will be taken from me."

But when this matter, I mean this purpose of the King and his Son, did at first take air at court, who can tell how the high lords, chief captains, and noble princes that were there, were taken with the business! First, they whispered it one to another, and after that it began to ring out throughout the King's palace, all wondering at the glorious design that between the King and his Son was on foot for the miserable town of Mansoul. Yea, the courtiers could scarce do anything either for the King or kingdom, but they would mix with the doing thereof a noise of the love of the King and his Son, that they had for the town of Mansoul.

Nor could these lords, high captains, and princes be content to keep this news at court; yea, before the records thereof were perfected, themselves came down and told it in Universe. At last, it came to the ears, as I said, of Diabolus, to his no little discontent; for you must think it would perplex him to hear of such a design against him. Well, but after a few casts in his mind, he concluded upon these four things:—

First, That this news, this good tidings, if possible, should be kept from the ears of the town of Mansoul; "for," said he, "if they should once come to the knowledge that Shaddai, their former King, and Emmanuel, his Son, are contriving good for the town of Mansoul, what can be expected by me but that Mansoul will make a revolt from under my hand and government, and return again to him?"

Now, to accomplish this his design, he renews his flattery with my Lord Will-be-will, and also gives him strict charge and command, that he should keep watch by day and by night at all the gates of the town, especially Ear-gate and Eye-gate; "for I hear of a design," quoth he, "a design to make us all traitors, and that Mansoul must be reduced to its first bondage again. I hope they are but flying stories," quoth he; "however, let no such news by any means be let into Mansoul, lest the people be dejected thereat. I think, my lord, it can be no welcome news to you; I am sure it is none to me; and I think that, at this time, it should be all our wisdom and care to nip the head of all such rumours as shall tend to trouble our people. Wherefore, I desire, my lord, that you will in this matter do as I say. Let there be strong guards daily kept at every gate of the town. Stop also and examine from whence such come that you perceive do from far come hither to trade, nor let them by any means be admitted into Mansoul, unless you shall plainly perceive that they are favourers of our excellent government. I command, moreover," said Diabolus, "that there be spies continually walking up and down the town of Mansoul, and let them have power to suppress and destroy any that they shall perceive to be plotting against us, or that shall prate of what by Shaddai and Emmanuel is intended."

This, therefore, was accordingly done: my Lord Will-be-will hearkened to his lord and master, went willingly after the commandment and, with all the diligence he could, kept any that would from going out abroad, or that sought to bring this tidings to Mansoul, from coming into the town.

Secondly, this done, in the next place, Diabolus, that he might make Mansoul as sure as he could, frames and imposes a new oath and horrible covenant upon the townsfolk:—To wit, That they should never desert him nor his government, nor yet betray him, nor seek to alter his laws; but that they should own, confess, stand by, and acknowledge him for their rightful king, in defiance to any that do or hereafter shall, by any pretence, law, or title whatever, lay claim to the town of Mansoul; thinking, belike, that Shaddai had not power to absolve them from this covenant with death, and agreement with hell. Nor did the silly Mansoul stick or boggle at all at this most monstrous engagement; but, as if it had been a sprat in the mouth of a whale, they swallowed it without any chewing. Were they troubled at it? Nay, they rather bragged and boasted of their so brave fidelity to the tyrant, their pretended king, swearing that they would never be changelings, nor forsake their old lord for a new. Thus did Diabolus tie poor Mansoul fast.

Thirdly, But jealousy, that never thinks itself strong enough, put him, in the next place, upon another exploit, which was yet more, if possible, to debauch this town of Mansoul. Wherefore he caused, by the hand of one Mr. Filth, an odious, nasty, lascivious piece of beastliness to be drawn up in writing, and to be set upon the castle gates; whereby he granted and gave licence to all his true and trusty sons in Mansoul to do whatsoever their lustful appetites prompted them to do; and that no man was to let, hinder, or control them, upon pain of incurring the displeasure of their prince.

Now this he did for these reasons:—

1. That the town of Mansoul might be yet made weaker and weaker, and so more unable, should tidings come that their redemption was designed, to believe, hope, or consent to the truth thereof; for reason says, the bigger the sinner, the less grounds of hopes of mercy.

2. The second reason was, if perhaps Emmanuel, the Son of Shaddai their King, by seeing the horrible and profane doings of the town of Mansoul, might repent, though entered into a covenant of redeeming them, of pursuing that covenant of their redemption; for he knew that Shaddai was holy, and that his Son Emmanuel was holy; yea, he knew it by woeful experience; for, for the iniquity and sin of Diabolus was he cast from the highest orbs. Wherefore what more rational than for him to conclude that thus, for sin, it might fare with Mansoul? But fearing also lest this knot should break, he bethinks himself of another, to wit:—

Fourthly, To endeavour to possess all hearts in the town of Mansoul that Shaddai was raising an army, to come to overthrow and utterly to destroy this town of Mansoul. And this he did to forestall any tidings that might come to their ears of their deliverance; "for," thought he, "if I first bruit this, the tidings that shall come after will all be swallowed up of this; for what else will Mansoul say, when they shall hear that they must be delivered, but that the true meaning is, Shaddai intends to destroy them?" Wherefore he summons the whole town into the market-place, and there with deceitful tongue, thus he addresses himself unto them:—

"Gentlemen, and my very good friends, you are all, as you know, my legal subjects, and men of the famous town of Mansoul. You know how, from the first day that I have been with you until now, I have behaved myself among you, and what liberty and great privileges you have enjoyed under my government, I hope to your honour and mine, and also to your content and delight. Now, my famous Mansoul, a noise of trouble there is abroad, of trouble to the town of Mansoul; sorry I am thereof for your sakes: for I have received but now by the post from my Lord Lucifer (and he useth to have good intelligence), that your old King Shaddai is raising an army to come against you, to destroy you root and branch; and this, O Mansoul, is now the cause that at this time I have called you together, namely, to advise what in this juncture is best to be done. For my part, I am but one, and can with ease shift for myself, did I list to seek my own ease, and to leave my Mansoul in all the danger; but my heart is so firmly united to you, and so unwilling am I to leave you, that I am willing to stand and fall with you, to the utmost hazard that shall befall me. What say you, O my Mansoul? Will you now desert your old friend, or do you think of standing by me?" Then, as one man, with one mouth, they cried out together, "Let him die the death that will not."

Then said Diabolus again, "It is in vain for us to hope for quarter, for this

King knows not how to show it. True, perhaps, he, at his first sitting down before us, will talk of and pretend to mercy, that thereby with the more ease, and less trouble, he may again make himself the master of Mansoul. Whatever, therefore, he shall say, believe not one syllable or tittle of it; for all such language is but to overcome us, and to make us, while we wallow in our blood, the trophies of his merciless victory. My mind is, therefore, that we resolve to the last man to resist him, and not to believe him upon any terms; for in at that door will come our danger. But shall we be flattered out of our lives? I hope you know more of the rudiments of politics than to suffer yourselves so pitifully to be served.

"But suppose he should, if he gets us to yield, save some of our lives, or the lives of some of them that are underlings in Mansoul, what help will that be to you that are the chief of the town, especially you whom I have set up, and whose greatness has been procured by you through your faithful sticking to me? And suppose, again, that he should give quarter to every one of you: be sure he will bring you into that bondage under which you were captivated before, or a worse, and then what good will your lives do you? Shall you with him live in pleasure as you do now? No, no; you must be bound by laws that will pinch you, and be made to do that which at present is hateful to you. I am for you, if you are for me; and it is better to die valiantly than to live like pitiful slaves. But, I say, the life of a slave will be counted too good for Mansoul now. Blood, blood, nothing but blood, is in every blast of Shaddai's trumpet against poor Mansoul now. Pray, be concerned; I hear he is coming. Up, and stand to your arms, that now, while you have any leisure, I may learn you some feats of war. Armour for you I have, and by me it is; yea, and it is sufficient for Mansoul from top to toe; nor can you be hurt by what his force can do, if you shall keep it well girt and fastened about you. Come, therefore, to my castle, and welcome, and harness yourselves for the war. There is helmet, breastplate, sword, and shield, and what not, that will make you fight like men.

"1. My helmet, otherwise called a head-piece, is hope of doing well at last, what lives soever you live. This is that which they had who said that they should have peace, though they walked in the wickedness of their heart, to add drunkenness to thirst. A piece of approved armour this is, and whoever has it, and can hold it, so long no arrow, dart, sword, or shield can hurt him. This therefore keep on, and thou wilt keep off many a blow, my Mansoul.

"2. My breastplate is a breastplate of iron. I had it forged in mine own country, and all my soldiers are armed therewith. In plain language, it is a hard heart, a heart as hard as iron, and as much past feeling as a stone; the which if you get and keep, neither mercy shall win you, nor judgment fright you. This therefore is a piece of armour most necessary for all to put on that hate Shaddai, and that would fight against him under my banner.

"3. My sword is a tongue that is set on fire of hell, and that can bend itself to speak evil of Shaddai, his Son, his ways, and people. Use this; it has been tried a thousand times twice told. Whoever hath it, keeps it, and makes that use of it as I would have him, can never be conquered by mine enemy.

"4. My shield is unbelief, or calling into question the truth of the word, or all the sayings that speak of the judgment that Shaddai has appointed for wicked men. Use this shield: many attempts he has made upon it, and sometimes, it is true, it has been bruised; but they that have writ of the wars of Emmanuel against my servants, have testified that he could do no mighty work there because of their unbelief. Now, to handle this weapon of mine aright, it is not to believe things because they are true, of what sort or by whomsoever asserted. If he speaks of judgment, care not for it; if he speaks of mercy, care not for it; if he promises, if he swears that he would do to Mansoul, if it turn, no hurt, but good, regard not what is said, question the truth of all, for this is to wield the shield of unbelief aright, and as my servants ought to do; and he that doth otherwise loves me not, nor do I count him but an enemy to me.

"5. Another part or piece," said Diabolus, "of mine excellent armour is a dumb and prayerless spirit, a spirit that scorns to cry for mercy: wherefore be you, my Mansoul, sure that you make use of this. What! cry for quarter! Never do that, if you would be mine. I know you are stout men, and am sure that I have clad you with that which is armour of proof. Wherefore, to cry to Shaddai for mercy, let that be far from you. Besides all this, I have a good maul, firebrands, arrows, and death, all good hand-weapons, and such as will do execution."

After he had thus furnished his men with armour and arms, he addressed himself to them in such like words as these:—"Remember," quoth he, "that I am your rightful king, and that you have taken an oath and entered into covenant to be true to me and my cause: I say, remember this, and show yourselves stout and valiant men of Mansoul. Remember also the kindness that I have always showed to you, and that without your petition I have granted to you external things; wherefore the privileges, grants, immunities, profits, and honours wherewith I have endowed you, do call for, at your hands, returns of loyalty, my lion-like men of Mansoul; and when so fit a time to show it, as when another shall seek to take my dominion over you into his own hands? One word more, and I have done. Can we but stand, and overcome this one shock or brunt, I doubt not but in little time all the world will be ours; and when that day comes, my true hearts, I will make you kings, princes, and captains, and what brave days shall we have then!"

Diabolus having thus armed and forearmed his servants and vassals in Mansoul against their good and lawful King Shaddai, in the next place, he doubleth his guards at the gates of the town, and he takes himself to the castle, which was his stronghold. His vassals also, to show their wills, and supposed (but ignoble) gallantry, exercise themselves in their arms every day, and teach one another feats of war; they also defied their enemies, and sang up the praises of their tyrant; they threatened also what men they would be, if ever things should rise so high as a war between Shaddai and their king.

Shaddai Prepares an Army

Now, all this time the good King, the King Shaddai, was preparing to send an army to recover the town of Mansoul again from under the tyranny of their pretended King Diabolus; but he thought good at the first, not to send them by the hand and conduct of brave Emmanuel his Son, but under the hand of some of his servants, to see first by them the temper of Mansoul, and whether by them they would be won to the obedience of their King. The army consisted of above forty thousand, all true men, for they came from the King's own court, and were those of his own choosing.

They came up to Mansoul under the conduct of four stout generals, each man being a captain of ten thousand men, and these are their names and their ensigns. The name of the first was Boanerges, the name of the second was Captain Conviction, and the name of the third was Captain Judgment, and the name of the fourth was Captain Execution. These were the Captains that Shaddai sent to regain Mansoul.

These four captains, as was said, the King thought fit, in the first place, to send to Mansoul, to make an attempt upon it; for, indeed, generally in all his wars he did use to send these four captains in the van, for they were very stout and rough-hewn men, men that were fit to break the ice, and to make their way by dint of sword, and their men were like themselves.

To each of these captains the King gave a banner, that it might be displayed, because of the goodness of his cause, and because of the right that he had to Mansoul.

First, to Captain Boanerges, for he was the chief, to him, I say, were given ten thousand men. His ensign was Mr. Thunder; he bare the black colours, and his scutcheon was the three burning thunderbolts.

The second captain was Captain Conviction; to him also were given ten thousand men. His ensign's name was Mr. Sorrow; he did bear the pale colours, and his scutcheon was the book of the law wide open, from whence issued a flame of fire.

The third captain was Captain Judgment; to him were given ten thousand men. His ensign's name was Mr. Terror; he bare the red colours, and his scutcheon was a burning fiery furnace.

The fourth captain was Captain Execution; to him were given ten thousand men. His ensign was one Mr. Justice; he also bare the red colours, and his scutcheon was a fruitless tree, with an axe lying at the root thereof.

These four captains, as I said, had every one of them under his command ten thousand men, all of good fidelity to the King, and stout at their military actions.

Well, the captains and their forces, their men and under officers, being had upon a day by Shaddai into the field, and there called all over by their names, were then and there put into such harness as became their degree and that service which now they were going about for their King.

Now, when the King had mustered his forces (for it is he that mustereth the host to the battle), he gave unto the captains their several commissions, with charge and commandment in the audience of all the soldiers, that they should take heed faithfully and courageously to do and execute the same. Their commissions were, for the substance of them, the same in form, though, as to name, title, place, and degree of the captains, there might be some, but very small variation. And here let me give you an account of the matter and sum contained in their commission.

A Commission from the great Shaddai, King of Mansoul, to his trusty and noble Captain, the Captain Boanerges, for his making War upon the town of Mansoul.

"O thou, Boanerges, one of my stout and thundering captains over one ten thousand of my valiant and faithful servants, go thou in my name, with this thy force, to the miserable town of Mansoul; and when thou comest thither, offer them first conditions of peace; and command them that, casting off the yoke and tyranny of the wicked Diabolus, they return to me, their rightful Prince and Lord. Command them also that they cleanse themselves from all that is his in the town of Mansoul, and look to thyself, that thou hast good satisfaction touching the truth of their obedience. Thus when thou hast commanded them (if they in truth submit thereto), then do thou, to the uttermost of thy power, what in thee lies to set up for me a garrison in the famous town of Mansoul; nor do thou hurt the least native that moveth or breatheth therein, if they will submit themselves to me, but treat thou such as if they were thy friend or brother; for all such I love, and they shall be dear unto me, and tell them that I will take a time to come unto them, and to let them know that I am merciful.

"But if they shall, notwithstanding thy summons and the producing of thy authority, resist, stand out against thee, and rebel, then do I command thee to make use of all thy cunning, power, might, and force, to bring them under by strength of hand. Farewell."

Thus you see the sum of their commissions; for, as I said before, for the substance of them, they were the same that the rest of the noble captains had.

Wherefore they, having received each commander his authority at the hand of their King, the day being appointed and the place of their rendezvous prefixed, each commander appeared in such gallantry, as became his cause and calling. So, after a new entertainment from Shaddai, with flying colours they set forward to march towards the famous town of Mansoul. Captain Boanerges led the van, Captain Conviction and Captain Judgment made up the main body, and Captain Execution brought up the rear. They then, having a great way to go (for the town of Mansoul was far off from the court of Shaddai), marched through the regions and countries of many people, not hurting or abusing any, but blessing wherever they came. They also lived upon the King's cost in all the way they went.

Having travelled thus for many days, at last they came within sight of

Mansoul; the which when they saw, the captains could for their hearts do no less than for a while bewail the condition of the town; for they quickly saw how that it was prostrate to the will of Diabolus, and to his ways and designs.

Well, to be short, the captains came up before the town, march up to Ear-gate, sit down there (for that was the place of hearing). So, when they had pitched their tents and entrenched themselves, they addressed themselves to make their assault.

Now the townsfolk at first beholding so gallant a company, so bravely accoutred, and so excellently disciplined, having on their glittering armour, and displaying of their flying colours, could not but come out of their houses and gaze. But the cunning fox Diabolus, fearing that the people, after this sight, should on a sudden summons, open the gates to the captains, came down with all haste from the castle and made them retire into the body of the town, who, when he had them there, made this lying and deceivable speech unto them:—

"Gentlemen," quoth he, "although you are my trusty and well-beloved friends, yet I cannot but a little chide you for your late uncircumspect action, in going out to gaze on that great and mighty force that but yesterday sat down before, and have now entrenched themselves in order to the maintaining of a siege against the famous town of Mansoul. Do you know who they are, whence they come, and what is their purpose in sitting down before the town of Mansoul? They are they of whom I have told you long ago, that they would come to destroy this town, and against whom I have been at the cost to arm you with cap-a-pe for your body, besides great fortifications for your mind. Wherefore, then, did you not rather, even at the first appearance of them, cry out, 'Fire the beacons!' and give the whole town an alarm concerning them, that we might all have been in a posture of defence, and been ready to have received them with the highest acts of defiance? Then had you shown yourselves men to my liking; whereas, by what you have done, you have made me half afraid; I say, half afraid, that when they and we shall come to push a pike, I shall find you want courage to stand it out any longer. Wherefore have I commanded a watch, and that you should double your guards at the gates? Wherefore have I endeavoured to make you as hard as iron, and your hearts as a piece of the nether millstone? Was it, think you, that you might show yourselves women, and that you might go out like a company of innocents to gaze on your mortal foes? Fie, fie! put yourselves into a posture of defence, beat up the drum, gather together in warlike manner, that our foes may know that, before they shall conquer this corporation, there are valiant men in the town of Mansoul.

"I will leave off now to chide, and will not further rebuke you; but I charge you that henceforwards you let me see no more such actions. Let not henceforward a man of you, without order first obtained from me, so much as show his head over the wall of the town of Mansoul. You have now heard me: do as I have commanded, and you shall cause me that I dwell securely with you, and that I take care, as for myself, so for your safety and honour also. Farewell."

Now were the townsmen strangely altered: they were as men stricken with a panic fear; they ran to and fro through the streets of the town of Mansoul, crying out, "Help, help! the men that turn the world upside down are come hither also." Nor could any of them be quiet after; but still, as men bereft of wit, they cried out, "The destroyers of our peace and people are come." This went down with Diabolus. "Ay," quoth he to himself, "this I like well: now it is as I would have it; now you show your obedience to your prince. Hold you but here, and then let them take the town if they can."

The King's Trumpet Sounded at Ear-gate

Well, before the King's forces had sat before Mansoul three days, Captain Boanerges commanded his trumpeter to go down to Ear-gate, and there, in the name of the great Shaddai, to summon Mansoul to give audience to the message that he, in his Master's name, was to them commanded to deliver. So the trumpeter, whose name was Take-heed-what-you-hear, went up, as he was commanded, to Ear-gate, and there sounded his trumpet for a hearing; but there was none that appeared that gave answer or regard, for so had Diabolus commanded. So the trumpeter returned to his captain, and told him what he had done, and also how he had sped; whereat the captain was grieved, but bid the trumpeter go to his tent.

Again Captain Boanerges sendeth his trumpeter to Ear-gate, to sound as before for a hearing; but they again kept close, came not out, nor would they give him an answer, so observant were they of the command of Diabolus their king.

Then the captains and other field-officers called a council of war, to consider what further was to be done for the gaining of the town of Mansoul; and, after some close and thorough debate upon the contents of their commissions, they concluded yet to give to the town, by the hand of the fore-named trumpeter, another summons to hear; but if that shall be refused, said they, and that the town shall stand it out still, then they determined, and bid the trumpeter tell them so, that they would endeavour, by what means they could, to compel them by force to the obedience of their King.

So Captain Boanerges commanded his trumpeter to go up to Ear-gate again, and, in the name of the great King Shaddai, to give it a very loud summons to come down without delay to Ear-gate, there to give audience to the King's most noble captains. So the trumpeter went, and did as he was commanded: he went up to Ear-gate and sounded his trumpet, and gave a third summons to Mansoul. He said, moreover, that if this they should still refuse to do, the captains of his Prince would with might come down upon them, and endeavour to reduce them to their obedience by force.

Then stood up my Lord Will-be-will, who was the governor of the town (this Will-be-will was that apostate of whom mention was made before), and the keeper of the gates of Mansoul. He therefore, with big and ruffling words, demanded of the trumpeter who he was, whence he came, and what was the cause of his making so hideous a noise at the gate, and speaking such insufferable words against the town of Mansoul.

The trumpeter answered, "I am servant to the most noble captain, Captain Boanerges, general of the forces of the great King Shaddai, against whom both myself, with the whole town of Mansoul, have rebelled, and lift up the heel; and my master, the captain, hath a special message to this town, and to thee as a member thereof; the which if you of Mansoul shall peaceably hear, so; and if not, you must take what follows."

Then said the Lord Will-be-will, "I will carry thy words to my lord, and will know what he will say."

But the trumpeter soon replied, saying, "Our message is not to the giant Diabolus, but to the miserable town of Mansoul; nor shall we at all regard what answer by him is made, nor yet by any for him. We are sent to this town to recover it from under his cruel tyranny, and to persuade it to submit, as in former times it did, to the most excellent King Shaddai."

Then said the Lord Will-be-will, "I will do your errand to the town."

The trumpeter then replied, "Sir, do not deceive us, lest, in so doing, you deceive yourselves much more." He added, moreover, "For we are resolved, if in peaceable manner you do not submit yourselves, then to make a war upon you, and to bring you under by force. And of the truth of what I now say, this shall be a sign unto you—you shall see the black flag, with its hot, burning thunderbolts, set upon the mount to-morrow, as a token of defiance against your prince, and of our resolutions to reduce you to your Lord and rightful King."

So the said Lord Will-be-will returned from off the wall, and the trumpeter came into the camp. When the trumpeter was come into the camp, the captains and officers of the mighty King Shaddai came together to know if he had obtained a hearing, and what was the effect of his errand. So the trumpeter told, saying, "When I had sounded my trumpet, and had called aloud to the town for a hearing, my Lord Will-be-will, the governor of the town, and he that hath charge of the gates, came up when he heard me sound, and, looking over the wall, he asked me what I was, whence I came, and what was the cause of my making this noise. So I told him my errand and by whose authority I brought it. 'Then,' said he, 'I will tell it to the governor and to Mansoul;' and then I returned to my lords."

Then said the brave Boanerges, "Let us yet for a while lie still in our trenches, and see what these rebels will do."

Now, when the time drew nigh that audience by Mansoul must be given to the brave Boanerges and his companions, it was commanded that all the men of war throughout the whole camp of Shaddai should as one man stand to their arms, and make themselves ready, if the town of Mansoul shall hear, to receive it forthwith to mercy; but if not, to force a subjection. So the day being come, the trumpeters sounded, and that throughout the whole camp, that the men of war might be in readiness for that which then should be the work of the day. But when they that were in the town of Mansoul heard the sound of the trumpets throughout the camp of Shaddai, and thinking no other but that it must be in order to storm the corporation, they at first were put to great consternation of spirit; but after they were a little settled again they also made what preparation they could for war, if they did storm; else, to secure themselves.

Well, when the utmost time was come, Boanerges was resolved to hear their answer; wherefore he sent out his trumpeter again to summon Mansoul to a hearing of the message that they had brought from Shaddai. So he went up and sounded, and the townsmen came up, but made Ear-gate as sure as they could. Now, when they were come up to the top of the wall, Captain Boanerges desired to see the Lord Mayor; but my Lord Incredulity was then Lord Mayor, for he came in the room of my Lord Lustings. So Incredulity came up and showed himself over the wall; but when the Captain Boanerges had set his eyes upon him, he cried out aloud, "This is not he: where is my Lord Understanding, the ancient Lord Mayor of the town of Mansoul? for to him I would deliver my message."

Then said the giant (for Diabolus was also come down) to the captain, "Mr. Captain, you have by your boldness given to Mansoul at least four summonses to subject herself to your King, by whose authority I know not, nor will I dispute that now. I ask therefore what is the reason of all this ado, or what would you be at, if you know yourselves?"

The Captain Boanerges, whose were the black colours, and whose scutcheon was the three burning thunderbolts, taking no notice of the giant or of his speech, thus addressed himself to the town of Mansoul: "Be it known unto you, O unhappy and rebellious Mansoul, that the most gracious King, the great King Shaddai, my Master, has sent me unto you with commission" (and so he showed to the town his broad seal) "to reduce you to his obedience; and he hath commanded me, in case you yield upon my summons, to carry it to you as if you were my friends or brethren; but he also hath bid, that if after summons to submit you still stand out and rebel, we should endeavour to take you by force."

Then stood forth Captain Conviction, and said (his were the pale colours, and for a scutcheon he had the book of the law wide open, &c.), "Hear, O Mansoul! Thou, O Mansoul, wast once famous for innocency, but now thou art degenerated into lies and deceit. Thou hast heard what my brother, the Captain Boanerges, hath said; and it is your wisdom, and will be your happiness, to stoop to and accept of conditions of peace and mercy when offered, specially when offered by one against whom thou hast rebelled, and one who is of power to tear thee in pieces; for so is Shaddai, our King; nor, when he is angry, can anything stand before him. If you say you have not sinned, or acted rebellion against our King, the whole of your doings since the day that you cast off his service (and there was the beginning of your sin) will sufficiently testify against you. What else means your hearkening to the tyrant, and your receiving him for your king? What means else your rejecting of the laws of Shaddai, and your obeying of Diabolus? Yea, what means this your taking up of arms against, and the shutting of your gates upon us, the faithful servants of your King? Be ruled, then, and accept of my brother's invitation, and overstand not the time of mercy, but agree with thine adversary quickly. Ah, Mansoul, suffer not thyself to be kept from mercy, and to be run into a thousand miseries by the flattering wiles of Diabolus. Perhaps that piece of deceit may attempt to make you believe that we seek our own profit in this our service; but know it is obedience to our King, and love to your happiness, that is the cause of this undertaking of ours.

"Again I say to thee, O Mansoul, consider if it be not amazing grace that Shaddai should so humble himself as he doth: now he, by us, reasons with you, in a way of entreaty and sweet persuasions, that you would subject yourselves to him. Has he that need of you, that we are sure you have of him? No, no; but he is merciful, and will not that Mansoul should die, but turn to him and live."

Then stood forth Captain Judgment, whose were the red colours, and for a scutcheon he had the burning fiery furnace, and he said: "O ye, the inhabitants of the town of Mansoul, that have lived so long in rebellion and acts of treason against the King Shaddai, know that we have come not today to this place, in this manner, with our message of our own minds, or to revenge our own quarrel; it is the King, my Master, that hath sent us to reduce you to your obedience to him; the which if you refuse in a peaceable way to yield, we have commission to compel you thereto. And never think of yourselves, nor yet suffer the tyrant Diabolus to persuade you to think, that our King, by his power, is not able to bring you down, and to lay you under his feet; for he is the former of all things, and if he touches the mountains they smoke. Nor will the gate of the King's clemency stand always open; for the day that shall burn like an oven is before him; yea, it hasteth greatly, it slumbereth not.

"O Mansoul, is it little in thine eyes that our King doth offer thee mercy, and that after so many provocations? Yea, he still holdeth out his golden sceptre to thee, and will not yet suffer his gate to be shut against thee: wilt thou provoke him to do it? If so, consider of what I say: to thee it is opened no more for ever. If thou sayest thou shalt not see him, yet judgment is before him; therefore trust thou in him. Yea, because there is wrath, beware lest he take thee away with his stroke; then a great ransom cannot deliver thee. Will he esteem thy riches? no, not gold, nor all the forces of strength. He hath prepared his throne for judgment; for he will come with fire, and with his chariots like a whirlwind, to render his anger with fury, and his rebuke with flames of fire. Therefore, O Mansoul, take heed lest, after thou hast fulfilled the judgment of the wicked, justice and judgment should take hold of thee."

Now, while the Captain Judgment was making this oration to the town of Mansoul, it was observed by some that Diabolus trembled; but he proceeded in his parable and said, "O thou woeful town of Mansoul, wilt thou not yet set open thy gate to receive us, the deputies of thy King, and those that would rejoice to see thee live? Can thine heart endure, or can thine hands be strong, in the day that he shall deal in judgment with thee? I say, canst thou endure to be forced to drink, as one would drink sweet wine, the sea of wrath that our King has prepared for Diabolus and his angels? Consider, betimes consider."

The Speech of Captain Execution

Then stood forth the fourth captain, the noble Captain Execution, and said, "O town of Mansoul, once famous, but now like the fruitless bough; once the delight of the high ones, but now a den of Diabolus: hearken also to me, and to the words that I shall speak to thee in the name of the great Shaddai. Behold, the axe is laid to the root of the tree; every tree, therefore, that bringeth not forth good fruit, is hewn down, and cast into the fire.

"Thou, O town of Mansoul, hast hitherto been this fruitless tree; thou barest nought but thorns and briers. The evil fruit fore-bespeaks thee not to be a good tree; thy grapes are grapes of gall, their clusters are bitter. Thou hast rebelled against thy King; and, lo! we, the power and force of Shaddai, are the axe that is laid to thy roots. What sayest thou, wilt thou turn? I say again, tell me, before the first blow is given, wilt thou turn? Our axe must first be laid *to* thy root before it be laid *at* thy root: it must first be laid *to* thy root in a way of threatening, before it is laid *at* thy root by way of execution; and between these two is required thy repentance, and this is all the time that thou hast. What wilt thou do? Wilt thou turn, or shall I smite? If I fetch my blow, Mansoul, down you go; for I have commission to lay my axe *at* as well as *to* thy roots, nor will anything but yielding to our King prevent doing of execution. What art thou fit for, O Mansoul, if mercy preventeth not, but to be hewn down, and cast into the fire and burned?

"O Mansoul, patience and forbearance do not act for ever: a year, or two, or three, they may; but if thou provoke by a three years' rebellion (and thou hast already done more than this), then what follows but, Cut it down? nay, After that thou shalt cut it down. And dost thou think that these are but threatenings, or that our King has not power to execute his words? O Mansoul, thou wilt find that in the words of our King, when they are by sinners made little or light of, there is not only threatning, but burning coals of fire.

"Thou hast been a cumber-ground long already, and wilt thou continue so still? Thy sin has brought this army to thy walls, and shall it bring it in judgment to do execution into thy town? Thou hast heard what the captains have said, but as yet thou shuttest thy gates. Speak out, Mansoul: wilt thou do so still, or wilt thou accept of conditions of peace?"

These brave speeches of these four noble captains the town of Mansoul refused to hear; yet a sound thereof did beat against Ear-gate, though the force thereof could not break it open. In fine, the town desired a time to prepare their answer to these demands. The captains then told them, that if they would throw out to them one Ill-Pause that was in the town, that they might reward him according to his works, then they would give them time to consider; but, if they would not cast him to them over the wall of Mansoul, then they would give them none; "for," said they, "we know that so long as Ill-Pause draws breath in Mansoul, all good consideration will be confounded, and nothing but mischief will come thereon."

Then Diabolus, who was there present, being loth to lose his Ill-Pause, because he was his orator (and yet be sure he had, could the captains have laid their fingers on him), was resolved at this instant to give them answer by himself; but then changing his mind, he commanded the then Lord Mayor, the Lord Incredulity, to do it, saying, "My lord, do you give these runagates an answer, and speak out, that Mansoul may hear and understand you."

So Incredulity, at Diabolus's command, began and said, "Gentlemen, you have here, as we do behold, to the disturbance of our prince and the molestation of the town of Mansoul, camped against it: but from whence you come, we will not know; and what you are, we will not believe. Indeed, you tell us in your terrible speech that you have this authority from Shaddai; but by what right he commands you to do it, of that we shall yet be ignorant.

"You have also, by the authority aforesaid, summoned this town to desert her lord, and, for protection, to yield herself up to the great Shaddai, your King; flatteringly telling her, that if she will do it, he will pass by and not charge her with her past offences.

"Further, you have also, to the terror of the town of Mansoul, threatened with great and sore destructions to punish this corporation, if she consents not to do as your wills would have her.

"Now, captains, from whence soever you come, and though your designs be never so right, yet know ye that neither my Lord Diabolus, nor I, his servant, Incredulity, nor yet our brave Mansoul doth regard either your persons, message, or the King that you say hath sent you. His power, his greatness, his vengeance we fear not; nor will we yield at all to your summons.

"As for the war that you threaten to make upon us, we must therein defend ourselves as well as we can; and know ye, that we are not without wherewithal to bid defiance to you; and in short (for I will not be tedious), I tell you, that we take you to be some vagabond runagate crew, that, having shaken off all obedience to your King, have gotten together in tumultuous manner, and are ranging from place to place to see if, through the flatteries you are skilled to make on the one side, and threats wherewith you think to fright on the other, to make some silly town, city, or country desert their place, and leave it to you; but Mansoul is none of them.

"To conclude: we dread you not, we fear you not, nor will we obey your summons. Our gates we keep shut upon you, our place we will keep you out of. Nor will we long thus suffer you to sit down before us: our people must live in quiet: your appearance doth disturb them. Wherefore arise with bag and baggage, and begone, or we will let fly from the walls against you."

This oration, made by old Incredulity, was seconded by desperate Will-be-will, in words to this effect:—"Gentlemen, we have heard your demands, and the noise of your threats, and have heard the sound of your summons; but we fear not your force, we regard not your threats, but will still abide as you found us. And we command you, that in three days' time you cease to appear in these parts, or you shall know what it is once to dare offer to rouse the lion Diabolus when asleep in his town of Mansoul."

The Recorder, whose name was Forget-Good, he also added as followeth: —"Gentlemen, my lords, as you see, have with mild and gentle words answered your rough and angry speeches; they have, moreover, in my hearing, given you leave quietly to depart as you came: wherefore, take your kindness and be gone. We might have come out with force upon you, and have caused you to feel the dint of our swords; but as we love ease and quiet ourselves, so we love not to hurt or molest others."

Then did the town of Mansoul shout for joy, as if by Diabolus and his crew some great advantage had been gotten of the captains. They also rang the bells and made merry, and danced upon the walls.

Diabolus also returned to the castle, and the Lord Mayor and Recorder to their place; but the Lord Will-be-will took special care that the gates should be secured with double guards, double bolts, and double locks and bars; and that Ear-gate especially might the better be looked to, for that was the gate in at which the King's forces sought most to enter. The Lord Will-be-will made one old Mr. Prejudice, an angry and ill-conditioned fellow, captain of the ward at that gate, and put under his power sixty men, called Deaf-men; men advantageous for that service, forasmuch as they mattered no words of the captains, nor of the soldiers.

Now, when the captains saw the answer of the great ones, and that they could not get a hearing from the old natives of the town, and that Mansoul was resolved to give the King's army battle, they prepared themselves to receive them, and to try it out by the power of the arm. And, first, they made their force more formidable against Ear-gate; for they knew that unless they could penetrate that, no good could be done upon the town. This done, they put the rest of their men in their places; after which they gave out the word, which was, "YE MUST BE BORN AGAIN." Then they sounded the trumpet; then they in the town made them answer, with shout against shout, charge against charge, and so the battle began. Now, they in the town had planted upon the tower over Ear-gate two great guns, the one called Highmind, and the other Heady. Unto these two guns they trusted much: they were cast in the castle by Diabolus's founder, whose name was Mr. Puff-up, and mischievous pieces they were. But so vigilant and watchful, when the captains saw them, were they, that though sometimes their shot would go by their ears with a whiz, yet they did them no harm. By these two guns the townsfolk made no question but greatly to annoy the camp of Shaddai, and well enough to secure the gate; but they had not much cause to boast of what execution they did, as by what follows will be gathered.

The famous Mansoul had also some other small pieces in it, of the which they made use against the camp of Shaddai.

The Battle Begun

They from the camp also did as stoutly, and with as much of that as may in truth be called valour, let fly as fast at the town and at Ear-gate; for they saw that, unless they could break open Ear-gate, it would be but in vain to batter the wall. Now, the King's captains had brought with them several slings, and two or three battering-rams; with their slings, therefore, they battered the houses and people of the town, and with their rams they sought to break Ear-gate open.

The camp and the town had several skirmishes and brisk encounters, while the captains with their engines made many brave attempts to break open or beat down the tower that was over Ear-gate, and at the said gate to make their entrance; but Mansoul stood it out so lustily, through the rage of Diabolus, the valour of the Lord Will-be-will, and the conduct of old Incredulity, the Mayor, and Mr. Forget-Good, the Recorder, that the charge and expense of that summer's wars, on the King's side, seemed to be almost quite lost, and the advantage to return to Mansoul. But when the captains saw how it was, they made a fair retreat, and intrenched themselves in their winter quarters. Now, in this war, you must needs think there was much loss on both sides, of which he pleased to accept of this brief account following.

The King's captains, when they marched from the court to come up against Mansoul to war, as they came crossing over the country, they happened to light upon three young fellows that had a mind to go for soldiers; proper men they were, and men of courage and skill, to appearance. Their names were Mr. Tradition, Mr. Human-Wisdom, and Mr. Man's-Invention. So they came up to the captains, and proffered their services to Shaddai. The captains then told them of their design, and bid them not to be rash in their offers; but the young men told them that they had considered the thing before, and that hearing they were upon their march for such a design, came hither on purpose to meet them, that they might be listed under their excellencies. Then Captain Boanerges, for that they were men of courage, listed them into his company, and so away they went to the war.

Now, when the war was begun, in one of the briskest skirmishes, so it was that a company of the Lord Will-be-will's men sallied out at the sally-port or postern of the town, and fell in upon the rear of Captain Boanerges' men, where these three fellows happened to be; so they took them prisoners, and away they carried them into the town; where they had not lain long in durance, but it began to be noised about the streets of the town what three notable prisoners the Lord Will-be-will's men had taken and brought in prisoners out of the camp of Shaddai. At length tidings thereof were carried to Diabolus to the castle; to wit, what my Lord Will-be-will's men had done, and whom they had taken prisoners.

Then Diabolus called for Will-be-will, to know the certainty of this matter. So he asked him, and he told him. Then did the giant send for the prisoners, who, when they were come, demanded of them who they were, whence they came, and what they did in the camp of Shaddai; and they told him. Then he sent them to ward again. Not many days after, he sent for them to him again, and then asked them if they would be willing to serve him against their former captains. They then told him that they did not so much live by religion as by the fates of fortune; and that since his lordship was willing to entertain them, they should be willing to serve him. Now, while things were thus in hand, there was one Captain Anything, a great doer in the town of Mansoul; and to this Captain Anything did Diabolus send these men, with a note under his hand to receive them into his company: the contents of which letter were thus:—

"ANYTHING, MY DARLING,—The three men that are the bearers of this letter have a desire to serve me in the war; nor know I better to whose conduct to commit them than to thine. Receive them, therefore, in my name, and, as need shall require, make use of them against Shaddai and his men. Farewell."

So they came, and he received them; and he made two of them sergeants; but he made Mr. Man's-Invention his ancient-bearer. But thus much for this; and now to return to the camp.

They of the camp did also some execution upon the town; for they did beat down the roof of the Lord Mayor's house, and so laid him more open than he was before. They had almost, with a sling slain my Lord Will-be-will outright; but he made a shift to recover again. But they made a notable slaughter among the aldermen, for with only one shot they cut off six of them; to wit Mr. Swearing, Mr. Whoring, Mr. Fury, Mr. Stand-to-Lies, Mr. Drunkenness, and Mr. Cheating.

They also dismounted the two guns that stood upon the tower over Ear-gate, and laid them flat in the dirt. I told you before that the King's noble captains had drawn off to their winter quarters, and had there intrenched themselves and their carriages, so as with the best advantage to their King, and the greatest annoyance to the enemy, they might give seasonable and warm alarms to the town of Mansoul. And this design of them did so hit, that I may say they did almost what they would to the molestation of the corporation. For now could not Mansoul sleep securely as before, nor could they now go to their debaucheries with that quietness as in times past; for they had from the camp of Shaddai such frequent, warm, and terrifying alarms, first at one gate and then at another, and again at all the gates at once, that they were broken as to former peace. Yea, they had their alarms so frequently, and that when the nights were at longest, the weather coldest, and so consequently the season most unseasonable, that that winter was to the town of Mansoul a winter by itself. Sometimes the trumpets would sound, and sometimes the slings would whorl the stones into the town. Sometimes ten thousand of the King's soldiers would be running round the walls of Mansoul at midnight, shouting and lifting up the voice for the battle. Sometimes, again, some of them in the town would be wounded, and their cry and lamentable voice would be heard, to the great molestation of the now languishing town of Mansoul. Yea, so distressed with those that laid siege against them were they, that, I daresay, Diabolus, their king, had in these days his rest much broken.

In these days, as I was informed, new thoughts, and thoughts that began to run counter one to another, began to possess the minds of the men of the town of Mansoul. Some would say, "There is no living thus." Others would then reply, "This will be over shortly." Then would a third stand up and answer, "Let us turn to the King Shaddai, and so put an end to these troubles." And a fourth would come in with a fear, saying, "I doubt he will not receive us." The old gentleman, too, the Recorder, that was so before Diabolus took Mansoul, he also began to talk aloud, and his words were now to the town of Mansoul as if they were great claps of thunder. No noise now so terrible to Mansoul as was his, with the noise of the soldiers and shoutings of the captains.

Also things began to grow scarce in Mansoul; now the things that her soul lusted after were departing from her. Upon all her pleasant things there was a blast, and burning instead of beauty. Wrinkles now, and some shows of the shadow of death, were upon the inhabitants of Mansoul. And now, oh, how glad would Mansoul have been to have enjoyed quietness and satisfaction of mind, though joined with the meanest condition in the world!

The captains also, in the deep of this winter, did send by the mouth of Boanerges' trumpeter a summons to Mansoul to yield up herself to the King, the great King Shaddai. They sent it once, and twice, and thrice; not knowing but that at some times there might be in Mansoul some willingness to surrender up themselves unto them, might they have but the colour of an invitation to do it under. Yea, so far as I could gather, the town had been surrendered up to them before now, had it not been for the opposition of old Incredulity, and the fickleness of the thoughts of my Lord Will-be-will. Diabolus also began to rave; wherefore Mansoul, as to yielding, was not yet all of one mind; therefore they still lay distressed under these perplexing fears.

I told you but now that they of the King's army had this winter sent three times to Mansoul to submit herself.

The first time the trumpeter went, he went with words of peace, telling them that the captains, the noble captains of Shaddai, did pity and bewail the misery of the now perishing town of Mansoul, and were troubled to see them so much to stand in the way of their own deliverance. He said, moreover, that the captains bid him tell them, that if now poor Mansoul would humble herself and turn, her former rebellions and most notorious treasons should, by their merciful King, be forgiven them, yea, and forgotten too. And having bid them beware that they stood not in their own way, that they opposed not themselves, nor made themselves their own losers, he returned again into the camp.

Secondly: The second time the trumpeter went, he did treat them a little more roughly; for, after sound of trumpet, he told them that their continuing in their rebellion did but chafe and heat the spirit of the captains, and that they were resolved to make a conquest of Mansoul, or to lay their bones before the town walls.

Thirdly: He went again the third time, and dealt with them yet more roughly; telling them, that now, since they had been so horribly profane, he did not know, not certainly know, whether the captains were inclining to mercy or judgment. "Only," said he, "they commanded me to give you a summons to open the gates unto them." So he returned, and went into the camp.

These three summons, and especially the two last, did so distress the town, that they presently call a consultation, the result of which was this—That my Lord Will-be-will should go up to Ear-gate, and there, with sound of trumpet, call to the captains of the camp for a parley. Well, the Lord Will-be-will sounded upon the wall; so the captains came up in their harness, with their ten thousands at their feet. The townsmen then told the captains that they had heard and considered their summons, and would come to an agreement with them, and with their King Shaddai, upon such certain terms, articles, and propositions as, with and by the order of their prince, they to them were appointed to propound; to wit, they would agree upon these grounds to be one people with them:—

"1. If that those of their own company, as the now Lord Mayor and their Mr. Forget-Good, with their brave Lord Will-be-will, might, under Shaddai, be still the governors of the town, castle, and gates of Mansoul.

"2. Provided that no man that now serveth under their great giant Diabolus be by Shaddai cast out of house, harbour, or the freedom that he hath hitherto enjoyed in the famous town of Mansoul.

"3. That it shall be granted them, that they of the town of Mansoul shall enjoy certain of their rights and privileges; to wit, such as have formerly been granted them, and that they have long lived in the enjoyment of, under the reign of their King Diabolus, that now is, and long has been, their only lord and great defender.

"4. That no new law, officer, or executioner of law or office, shall have any power over them, without their own choice and consent.

"These be our propositions or conditions of peace; and upon these terms," said they, "we will submit to your King."

But when the captains had heard this week and feeble offer of the town of Mansoul, and their high and bold demands, they made to them again, by their noble captain, the Captain Boanerges, this speech following:—

"O ye inhabitants of the town of Mansoul, when I heard your trumpet sound for a parley with us, I can truly say I was glad; but when you said you were willing to submit yourselves to our King and Lord, then I was yet more glad; but when, by your silly provisoes and foolish cavils, you laid the stumbling-block of your iniquity before your own faces, then was my gladness turned into sorrows, and my hopeful beginnings of your return into languishing fainting fears.

"I count that old Ill-Pause, the ancient enemy of Mansoul, did draw up those proposals that now you present us with as terms of an agreement; but they deserve not to be admitted to sound in the ear of any man that pretends to have service for Shaddai. We do therefore jointly, and that with the highest disdain, refuse and reject such things, as the greatest of iniquities.

"But, O Mansoul, if you will give yourselves into our hands, or rather into the hands of our King, and will trust him to make such terms with and for you as shall seem good in his eyes (and I dare say they shall be such as you shall find to be most profitable to you), then we will receive you, and be at peace with you; but if you like not to trust yourselves in the arms of Shaddai our King, then things are but where they were before, and we know also what we have to do."

Then cried out old Incredulity, the Lord Mayor, and said, "And who, being out of the hands of their enemies, as you see we are now, will be so foolish as to put the staff out of their own hands into the hands of they know not who? I, for my part, will never yield to so unlimited a proposition. Do we know the manner and temper of their King? It is said by some that he will be angry with his subjects if but the breadth of an hair they chance to step out of the way; and by others, that he requireth of them much more than they can perform. Wherefore, it seems, O Mansoul, to be thy wisdom to take good heed what thou dost in this matter; for if you once yield, you give up yourselves to another, and so you are no more your own. Wherefore, to give up yourselves to an unlimited power is the greatest folly in the world; for now you indeed may repent, but can never justly complain. But do you indeed know, when you are his, which of you he will kill, and which of you he will save alive? or whether he will not cut off every one of us, and send out of his own country another new people, and cause them to inhabit this town?"

This speech of the Lord Mayor undid all, and threw flat to the ground their hopes of an accord. Wherefore the captains returned to their trenches, to their tents, and to their men, as they were; and the Mayor to the castle and to his king.

Now, Diabolus had waited for his return, for he had heard that they had been at their point. So, when he was come into the chamber of state, Diabolus saluted him with—"Welcome, my lord. How went matters betwixt you to-day?" So the Lord Incredulity, with a low congee, told him the whole of the matter, saying, "Thus and thus said the captains of Shaddai, and thus and thus said I." The which when 'twas told to Diabolus, he was very glad to hear it, and said, "My Lord Mayor, my faithful Incredulity, I have proved thy fidelity above ten times already, but never yet found thee false. I do promise thee, if we rub over this brunt, to prefer thee to a place of honour, a place far better than to be Lord Mayor of Mansoul. I will make thee my universal deputy, and thou shalt, next to me, have all nations under thy hand; yea, and thou shalt lay bands upon them, that they may not resist thee; nor shall any of our vassals walk more at liberty, but those that shall be content to walk in thy fetters."

Now came the Lord Mayor out from Diabolus, as if he had obtained a favour indeed. Wherefore to his habitation he goes in great state, and thinks to feed himself well enough with hopes, until the time came that his greatness should be enlarged.

A Mutiny in Mansoul

But now, though the Lord Mayor and Diabolus did thus well agree, yet this repulse to the brave captains put Mansoul into a mutiny. For while old Incredulity went into the castle to congratulate his lord with what had passed, the old Lord Mayor, that was so before Diabolus came to the town, to wit, my Lord Understanding, and the old Recorder, Mr. Conscience, getting intelligence of what had passed at Ear-gate (for you must know that they might not be suffered to be at that debate, lest they should then have mutinied for the captains; but, I say, they got intelligence of what had passed there, and were much concerned therewith), wherefore they, getting some of the town together, began to possess them with the reasonableness of the noble captains' demands, and with the bad consequences that would follow upon the speech of old Incredulity, the Lord Mayor; to wit, how little reverence he showed therein either to the captains or to their King; also how he implicitly charged them with unfaithfulness and treachery. "For what less," quoth they, "could be made of his words, when he said he would not yield to their proposition, and added, moreover, a supposition that he would destroy us, when before he had sent us word that he would show us mercy?" The multitude, being now possessed with the conviction of the evil that old Incredulity had done, began to run together by companies in all places, and in every corner of the streets of Mansoul; and first they began to mutter, then to talk openly, and after that they ran to and fro, and cried as they ran, "Oh, the brave captains of Shaddai! would we were under the government of the captains, and of Shaddai their King!" When the Lord Mayor had intelligence that Mansoul was in an uproar, down he comes to appease the people, and thought to have quashed their heat with the bigness and the show of his countenance; but when they saw him, they came running upon him, and had doubtless done him a mischief, had he not betaken himself to house. However, they strongly assaulted the house where he was, to have pulled it down about his ears; but the place was too strong, so they failed of that. So he, taking some courage, addressed himself out at a window to the people in this manner:—

"Gentlemen, what is the reason that there is here such an uproar to-day?"

Then answered my Lord Understanding, "It is even because that thou and thy master have carried it not rightly, and as you should, to the captains of Shaddai; for in three things you are faulty. First, in that you would not let Mr. Conscience and myself be at the hearing of your discourse. Secondly, in that you propounded such terms of peace to the captains that by no means could be granted, unless they had intended that their Shaddai should have been only a titular prince, and that Mansoul should still have had power by law to have lived in all lewdness and vanity before him, and so by consequence Diabolus should still here be king in power, and the other only king in name. Thirdly, for that thou didst thyself, after the captains had showed us upon what conditions they would have received us to mercy, even undo all again with thy unsavoury, unseasonable, and ungodly speech."

When old Incredulity had heard this speech he cried out, "Treason! treason! To your arms! to your arms! O ye, the trusty friends of Diabolus in Mansoul!"

Und. "Sir, you may put upon my words what meaning you please; but I am sure that the captains of such a high lord as theirs is, deserves a better treatment at your hands."

Then said old Incredulity, "This is but little better. But, Sir," quoth he, "what I spake I spake for my prince, for his government, and the quieting of the people, whom by your unlawful actions you have this day set to mutiny against us."

Then replied the old Recorder, whose name was Mr. Conscience, and said, "Sir, you ought not thus to retort upon what my Lord Understanding hath said. It is evident enough that he hath spoken the truth, and that you are an enemy to Mansoul. Be convinced, then, of the evil of your saucy and malapert language, and of the grief that you have put the captains to; yea, and of the damages that you have done to Mansoul thereby. Had you accepted of the conditions, the sound of the trumpet and the alarm of war had now ceased about the town of Mansoul; but that dreadful sound abides, and your want of wisdom in your speech has been the cause of it."

Then said old Incredulity, "Sir, if I live, I will do your errand to Diabolus, and there you shall have an answer to your words. Meanwhile we will seek the good of the town, and not ask counsel of you."

Und. "Sir, your prince and you are both foreigners to Mansoul, and not the natives thereof; and who can tell but that when you have brought us into greater straits (when you also shall see that yourselves can be safe by no other means than by flight), you may leave us and shift for yourselves, or set us on fire, and go away in the smoke, or by the light of our burning, and so leave us in our ruins?"

Incred. "Sir, you forget that you are under a governor, and that you ought to demean yourself like a subject; and know thee, when my lord and king shall hear of this day's work, he will give you but little thanks for your labour."

Now, while these gentlemen were thus in their chiding words, down came from the walls and gates of the town the Lord Will-be-will, Mr. Prejudice, old Ill-Pause, and several of the new-made aldermen and burgesses, and they asked the reason of the hubbub and tumult; and with that every man began to tell his own tale, so that nothing could be heard distinctly. Then was a silence commanded, and the old fox Incredulity began to speak. "My Lord," quoth he, "here are a couple of peevish gentlemen, that have, as a fruit of their bad dispositions, and, as I fear, through the advice of one Mr. Discontent, tumultuously gathered this company against me this day, and also attempted to run the town into acts of rebellion against our prince."

Then stood up all the Diabolonians that were present, and affirmed these things to be true.

Now, when they that took part with my Lord Understanding and with Mr. Conscience perceived that they were like to come to the worst, for that force and power was on the other side, they came in for their help and relief: so a great company was on both sides. Then they on Incredulity's side would have had the two old gentlemen presently away to prison; but they on the other side said they should not. Then they began to cry up parties again: the Diabolonians cried up old Incredulity, Forget-Good, the new aldermen, and their great one Diabolus; and the other party, they also cried up Shaddai, the captains, his laws, their mercifulness, and applauded their conditions and ways. Thus the bickerment went a while; at last they passed from words to blows, and now there were knocks on both sides. The good old gentleman, Mr. Conscience, was knocked down twice by one of the Diabolonians, whose name was Mr. Benumbing; and my Lord Understanding had like to have been slain with an arquebus, but that he that shot did not take his aim aright. Nor did the other side wholly escape; for there was one Mr. Rashhead, a Diabolonian, that had his brains beaten out by Mr. Mind, the Lord Will-be-will's servant; and it made me laugh to see how old Mr. Prejudice was kicked and tumbled about in the dirt; for though, awhile since, he was made captain of a company of the Diabolonians, to the hurt and damage of the town, yet now they had got him under their feet, and, I'll assure you, he had, by some of the Lord Understanding's party, his crown soundly cracked to boot. Mr. Anything also, he became a brisk man in the broil; but both sides were against him, because he was true to none. Yet he had, for his malapertness, one of his legs broken, and he that did it wished it had been his neck. Much harm more was done on both sides, but this must not be forgotten: it was now a wonder to see my Lord Will-be-will so indifferent as he was: he did not seem to take one side more than another, only it was perceived that he smiled to see how old Prejudice was tumbled up and down in the dirt. Also, when Captain Anything came halting up before him, he seemed to take but little notice of him.

Now, when the uproar was over, Diabolus sends for my Lord Understanding and Mr. Conscience, and claps them both up in prison as the ringleaders and managers of this most heavy riotous rout in Mansoul. So now the town began to be quiet again, and the prisoners were used hardly; yea, he thought to have made them away, but that the present juncture did not serve for that purpose, for that war was in all their gates.

But let us return again to our story. The captains, when they were gone back from the gate, and were come into the camp again, called a council of war, to consult what was further for them to do. Now, said some, "Let us go up presently, and fall upon the town;" but the greatest part thought rather better 'twould be to give them another summons to yield; and the reason why they thought this to be best was, because that, so far as could be perceived, the town of Mansoul now was more inclinable than heretofore. "And if," said they, "while some of them are in a way of inclination, we should by ruggedness give them distaste, we may set them further from closing with our summons than we would be willing they should."

Wherefore to this advice they agreed, and called a trumpeter, put words into his mouth, set him his time, and bid him God speed. Well, many hours were not expired before the trumpeter addressed himself to his journey. Wherefore, coming up to the wall of the town he steereth his course to Ear-gate, and there sounded as he was commanded. Then they that were within came out to see what was the matter, and the trumpeter made them this speech following:—

"O hard-hearted and deplorable town of Mansoul, how long wilt thou love thy sinful, sinful simplicity? and, ye fools, delight in your scorning? As yet despise you the offers of peace and deliverance? As yet will ye refuse the golden offers of Shaddai, and trust to the lies and falsehoods of Diabolus? Think you, when Shaddai shall have conquered you, that the remembrances of these your carriages towards him will yield you peace and comfort, or that by ruffling language you can make him afraid as a grasshopper? Doth he entreat you for fear of you? Do you think that you are stronger than he? Look to the heavens, and behold and consider the stars, how high are they? Can you stop the sun from running his course, and hinder the moon from giving her light? Can you count the number of the stars, or stay the bottles of heaven? Can you call for the waters of the sea and cause them to cover the face of the ground? Can you behold everyone that is proud, and abase him, and bind their faces in secret? Yet these are some of the works of our King, in whose name this day we come up unto you, that you may be brought under his authority. In his name, therefore I summon you again to yield up yourselves to his captains."

At this summons the Mansoulians seemed to be at a stand, and knew not what answer to make. Wherefore Diabolus forthwith appeared, and took upon him to do it himself; and thus he begins, but turns his speech to them of Mansoul:—

"Gentlemen," quoth he, "and my faithful subjects, if it is true that this summoner hath said concerning the greatness of their King, by his terror you will always be kept in bondage, and so be made to sneak. Yea, how can you now, though he is at a distance, endure to think of such a mighty one? And if not to think of him while at a distance, how can you endure to be in his presence? I, your prince, am familiar with you, and you may play with me as you would with a grasshopper. Consider, therefore, what is for your profit, and remember the immunities that I have granted you.

"Further, if all be true that this man hath said, how comes it to pass that the subjects of Shaddai are so enslaved in all places where they come? None in the universe so unhappy as they, none so trampled upon as they.

"Consider, my Mansoul;—would thou wert as loth to leave me as I am loth to leave thee!—But consider, I say, the ball is yet at thy foot; liberty you have, if you know how to use it; yea, a king you have too, if you can tell how to love and obey him."

Mansoul Grows Worse

Upon this speech, the town of Mansoul did again harden their hearts yet more against the captains of Shaddai. The thoughts of his greatness did quite quash them, and the thoughts of his holiness sank them in despair. Wherefore, after a short consultation, they (of the Diabolonian party they were) sent back this word by the trumpeter: That, for their parts, they were resolved to stick to their king, but never yield to Shaddai; so it was but in vain to give them any further summons, for they had rather die upon the place than yield. And now things seemed to be gone quite back, and Mansoul to be out of reach or call; yet the captains, who knew what their Lord could do, would not yet be beat out of heart; they therefore send them another summons, more sharp and severe than the last; but the oftener they were sent to, to be reconciled to Shaddai, the further off they were. As they called them, so they went from them; yea, though they called them to the Most High.

So they ceased that way to deal with them any more, and inclined to think of another way. The captains, therefore, did gather themselves together, to have free conference among themselves, to know what was yet to be done to gain the town, and to deliver it from the tyranny of Diabolus; and one said after this manner, and another after that. Then stood up the right noble the Captain Conviction, and said, "My brethren, mine opinion is this:—

"First, that we continually play our slings into the town, and keep it in a continual alarm, molesting them day and night. By thus doing, we shall stop the growth of their rampant spirit; for a lion may be tamed by continual molestation.

"Secondly, this done, I advise that in the next place, we with one consent draw up a petition to our Lord Shaddai, by which after we have showed our King the condition of Mansoul and of affairs here, and have begged his pardon for our no better success, we will earnestly implore his Majesty's help, and that he will please to send us more force and power and some gallant and well-spoken commander, to head them, that so his Majesty may not lose the benefit of these his good beginnings, but may complete his conquest upon the town of Mansoul."

To this speech of the noble Captain Conviction they as one man consented, and agreed that a petition should forthwith be drawn up, and sent by a fit man away to Shaddai with speed. The contents of the petition were thus:—

"Most gracious and glorious King, the Lord of the best world, and the builder of the town of Mansoul: we have, dread Sovereign, at thy commandment, put our lives in jeopardy, and at thy bidding made a war upon the famous town of Mansoul. When we went up against it, we did, according to our commission, first offer conditions of peace unto it. But they, great King, set light by our counsel, and would none of our reproof. They were for shutting their gates, and for keeping us out of the town. They also mounted their guns, they sallied out upon us, and have done us what damage they could; but we pursued them with alarm upon alarm, requiting them with such retribution as was meet, and have done some execution upon the town.

"Diabolus, Incredulity, and Will-be-will are the great doers against us. Now we are in our winter quarters, but so as that we do yet with a high hand molest and distress the town.

"Once, as we think, had we had but one substantial friend in the town, such as would but have seconded the sound of our summons as they ought, the people might have yielded themselves; but there were none but enemies there, nor any to speak in behalf of our Lord to the town. Wherefore, though we have done as we could, yet Mansoul abides in a state of rebellion against thee.

"Now, King of kings, let it please thee to pardon the unsuccessfulness of thy servants, who have been no more advantageous in so desirable a work as the conquering of Mansoul is. And send, Lord, as we now desire, more forces to Mansoul, that it may be subdued; and a man to head them, that the town may both love and fear.

"We do not thus speak because we are willing to relinquish the wars (for we are for laying of our bones against the place), but that the town of Mansoul may be won for thy Majesty. We also pray thy Majesty, for expedition in this matter, that, after their conquest, we may be at liberty to be sent about other thy gracious designs. Amen."

The petition, thus drawn up, was sent away with haste to the King by the hand of that good man, Mr. Love-to-Mansoul.

When this petition was come to the palace of the King, who should it be delivered to but to the King's Son? So he took it and read it, and because the contents of it pleased him well, he mended, and also in some things added to the petition himself. So, after he had made such amendments and additions as he thought convenient with his own hand, he carried it in to the King; to whom, when he had with obeisance delivered it, he put on authority, and spake to it himself.

Now, the King, at the sight of the petition, was glad; but how much more, think you, when it was seconded by his Son! It pleased him also to hear that his servants who camped against Mansoul were so hearty in the work, and so steadfast in their resolves, and that they had already got some ground upon the famous town of Mansoul.

Wherefore the King called to him Emmanuel, his Son, who said, "Here am I, my Father." Then said the King, "Thou knowest, as I do myself, the condition of the town of Mansoul, and what we have purposed, and what thou hast done to redeem it. Come now, therefore, my Son, and prepare thyself for the war, for thou shalt go to my camp at Mansoul. Thou shalt also there prosper and prevail, and conquer the town of Mansoul."

Then said the King's Son, "Thy law is within my heart: I delight to do thy will. This is the day that I have longed for, and the work that I have waited for all this while. Grant me, therefore, what force thou shalt in thy wisdom think meet, and I will go and will deliver from Diabolus, and from his power, thy perishing town of Mansoul. My heart has been often pained within me for the miserable town of Mansoul; but now 'tis rejoiced, but now 'tis glad." And with that he leaped over the mountains for joy, saying, "I have not, in my heart, thought anything too dear for Mansoul: the day of vengeance is in mine heart for thee, my Mansoul; and glad am I that thou, my Father, hast made me the Captain of their salvation. And I will now begin to plague all those that have been a plague to my town of Mansoul, and will deliver it from their hand."

When the King's Son had said this to his Father, it presently flew like lightning round about at court; yea, it there became the only talk what Emmanuel was to go to do for the famous town of Mansoul. But you cannot think how the courtiers too were taken with this design of the Prince; yea, so affected were they with this work, and with the justness of the war, that the highest lord and greatest peer of the kingdom did covet to have commission under Emmanuel, to go to help to recover again to Shaddai, the miserable town of Mansoul.

Then it was concluded that some should go and carry tidings to the camp that Emmanuel was to come to recover Mansoul, and that he would bring along with him so mighty, so impregnable a force that he could not be resisted. But, oh, how ready were the high ones at court to run like lacqueys to carry these tidings to the camp that was at Mansoul! Now, when the captains perceived that the King would send Emmanuel, his Son, and that it also delighted the Son to be sent on this errand by the great Shaddai, his Father, they also, to show how they were pleased at the thoughts of his coming, gave a shout that made the earth rend at the sound thereof. Yea, the mountains did answer again by echo, and Diabolus himself did totter and shake.

For you must know that though the town of Mansoul itself was not much if at all concerned with the project (for, alas for them! they were woefully besotted, for they chiefly regarded their pleasure and their lusts), yet Diabolus their governor was; for he had his spies continually abroad, who brought him intelligence of all things, and they told what was doing at court against him, and that Emmanuel would shortly certainly come with a power to invade him. Nor was there any man at court, nor peer of the kingdom, that Diabolus so feared as he feared this Prince; for, if you remember, I showed you before that Diabolus had felt the weight of his hand already; so that, since it was he that was to come, this made him the more afraid.

Well, you see how I have told you that the King's Son was engaged to come from the court to save Mansoul, and that his Father had made him the Captain of the forces. The time therefore of his setting forth being now expired, he addressed himself for his march, and taketh with him, for his power, five noble captains and their forces.

1. The first was that famous captain, the noble Captain Credence. His were the red colours, and Mr. Promise bore them; and for a scutcheon, he had the holy lamb and golden shield; and he had ten thousand men at his feet.

2. The second was that famous captain, the Captain Good-Hope. His were the blue colours: his standard-bearer was Mr. Expectation, and for a scutcheon he had the three golden anchors; and he had ten thousand men at his feet.

3. The third was that valiant captain, the Captain Charity. His standard-bearer was Mr. Pitiful: his were the green colours, and for his scutcheon he had three naked orphans embraced in the bosom; and he had ten thousand men at his feet.

4. The fourth was that gallant commander, the Captain Innocent. His standard-bearer was Mr. Harmless: his were the white colours, and for his scutcheon he had the three golden doves.

5. The fifth was the truly loyal and well-beloved captain, the Captain Patience. His standard-bearer was Mr. Suffer-Long: his were the black colours, and for a scutcheon he had three arrows through the golden heart.

These were Emmanuel's captains, these their standard-bearers, their colours, and their scutcheons; and these the men under their command. So, as was said, the brave Prince took his march to go to the town of Mansoul. Captain Credence led the van, and Captain Patience brought up the rear; so the other three, with their men, made up the main body, the Prince himself riding in his chariot at the head of them.

But when they set out for their march, oh, how the trumpets sounded, their armour glittered, and how the colours waved in the wind! The Prince's armour was all of gold, and it shone like the sun in the firmament; the captains' armour was of proof, and was in appearance like the glittering stars. There were also some from the court that rode reformades for the love that they had to the King Shaddai, and for the happy deliverance of the town of Mansoul.

Emmanuel also, when he had thus set forwards to go to recover the town of Mansoul, took with him, at the commandment of his Father, fifty-four battering-rams and twelve slings, to whirl stones withal. Every one of these was made of pure gold; and these they carried with them, in the heart and body of their army, all along as they went to Mansoul.

Mansoul Beleaguered All Round

So they marched till they came within less than a league of the town; and there they lay till the first four captains came thither to acquaint them with matters. Then they took their journey to go to the town of Mansoul, and unto Mansoul they came; but when the old soldiers that were in the camp saw that they had new forces to join with, they again gave such a shout before the walls of Mansoul, that it put Diabolus into another fright. So they sat down before the town; not now as the other four captains did, to wit, against the gates of Mansoul only, but they environed it round on every side, and beset it behind and before; so that now, let Mansoul look which way it will, it saw force and power lie in siege against it. Besides, there were mounts cast up against it. The Mount Gracious was on the one side, and Mount Justice was on the other. Farther, there were several small banks and advance-grounds, as Plain-Truth Hill and No-Sin Banks, where many of the slings were placed against the town. Upon Mount Gracious were planted four, and upon Mount Justice were planted as many, and the rest were conveniently placed in several parts round about the town. Five of the best battering-rams, that is, of the biggest of them, were placed upon Mount Hearken, a mount cast up hard by Ear-gate, with intent to break that open.

Now, when the men of the town saw the multitude of the soldiers that were come up against the place, and the rams and slings, and the mounts on which they were planted, together with the glittering of the armour and the waving of their colours, they were forced to shift, and shift, and again to shift their thoughts; but they hardly changed for thoughts more stout, but rather for thoughts more faint; for though before they thought themselves sufficiently guarded, yet now they began to think that no man knew what would be their hap or lot.

When the good Prince Emmanuel had thus beleaguered Mansoul, in the first place he hangs out the white flag, which he caused to be set up among the golden slings that were planted upon Mount Gracious. And this he did for two reasons:—1. To give notice to Mansoul that he could and would yet be gracious if they turned to him. 2. And that he might leave them the more without excuse, should he destroy them, they continuing in their rebellion.

So the white flag, with the three golden doves on it, was hung out for two days together, to give them time and space to consider; but they, as was hinted before, as if they were unconcerned, made no reply to the favourable signal of the Prince.

Then he commanded, and they set the red flag upon that mount called Mount Justice. It was the red flag of Captain Judgment, whose scutcheon was the burning fiery furnace; and this also stood waving before them in the wind for several days together. But look, how they carried it under the white flag, when that was hung out, so did they also when the red one was; and yet he took no advantage of them.

Then he commanded again that his servants should hang out the black flag of defiance against them, whose scutcheon was the three burning thunderbolts; but as unconcerned was Mansoul at this as at those that went before. But when the Prince saw that neither mercy, nor judgment, nor execution of judgment, would or could come near the heart of Mansoul, he was touched with much compunction, and said, "Surely this strange carriage of the town of Mansoul doth rather arise from ignorance of the manner and feats of war, than from a secret defiance of us, and abhorrence of their own lives; or if they know the manner of the war of their own, yet not the rites and ceremonies of the wars in which we are concerned, when I make wars upon mine enemy Diabolus."

Therefore he sent to the town of Mansoul, to let them know what he meant by those signs and ceremonies of the flag; and also to know of them which of the things they would choose, whether grace and mercy, or judgment and the execution of judgment. All this while they kept their gates shut with locks, bolts, and bars, as fast as they could. Their guards also were doubled, and their watch made as strong as they could. Diabolus also did pluck up what heart he could, to encourage the town to make resistance.

The townsmen also made answer to the Prince's messenger, in substance according to that which follows:—

"GREAT SIR,—As to what, by your messenger, you have signified to us, whether we will accept of your mercy or fall by your justice, we are bound by the law and custom of this place, and can give you no positive answer; for it is against the law, government, and the prerogative royal of our king, to make either peace or war without him. But this we will do: we will petition that our prince will come down to the wall, and there give you such treatment as he shall think fit and profitable for us."

When the good Prince Emmanuel heard this answer, and saw the slavery and bondage of the people, and how much content they were to abide in the chains of the tyrant Diabolus, it grieved him at the heart; and indeed, when at any time he perceived that any were contented under the slavery of the giant, he would be affected with it.

But to return again to our purpose. After the town had carried this news to Diabolus, and had told him, moreover, that the Prince, that lay in the leaguer without the wall, waited upon them for an answer, he refused, and huffed as well as he could; but in heart he was afraid.

Then said he, "I will go down to the gates myself, and give him such an answer as I think fit."

So he went down to Mouth-gate, and there addressed himself to speak to Emmanuel (but in such language as the town understood not), the contents whereof were as follow:—

"O thou great Emmanuel, Lord of all the world, I know thee, that thou art the Son of the great Shaddai! Wherefore art thou come to torment me, and to cast me out of my possession? This town of Mansoul, as thou very well knowest, is mine, and that by a twofold right. 1. It is mine by right of conquest: I won it in the open field; and shall the prey be taken from the mighty or the lawful captive be delivered? 2. This town of Mansoul is mine also by their subjection. They have opened the gates of their town unto me; they have sworn fidelity to me, and have openly chosen me to be their king; they have also given their castle into my hands; yea, they have put the whole strength of Mansoul under me.

"Moreover, this town of Mansoul hath disavowed thee; yea, they have cast thy law, thy name, thy image, and all that is thine, behind their back, and have accepted and set up in their room my law, my image, and all that ever is mine. Ask else thy captains, and they will tell that Mansoul hath, in answer to all their summons, shown love and loyalty to me, but always disdain, despite, contempt, and scorn to thee and thine. Now, thou art the Just

One and the Holy, and shouldest do no iniquity. Depart, then, I pray thee, therefore, from me, and leave me to my just inheritance peaceably."

This oration was made in the language of Diabolus himself; for although he can, to every man, speak in their own language (else he could not tempt them all as he does,) yet he has a language proper to himself, and it is the language of the infernal cave, or black pit.

Wherefore the town of Mansoul (poor hearts) understood him not; nor did they see how he crouched and cringed while he stood before Emmanuel, their Prince.

Yea, they all this while took him to be one of that power and force that by no means could be resisted. Wherefore, while he was thus entreating that he might yet have his residence there, and that Emmanuel would not take it from him by force, the inhabitants boasted even of his valour, saying, "Who is able to make war with him?"

Well, when this pretended king had made an end of what he would say, Emmanuel, the golden Prince, stood up and spake; the contents of whose words follow:—

"Thou deceiving one," said he, "I have, in my Father's name, in mine own name, and on the behalf and for the good of this wretched town of Mansoul, somewhat to say unto thee. Thou pretendest a right, a lawful right, to the deplorable town of Mansoul, when it is most apparent to all my Father's court that the entrance which thou hast obtained in at the gates of Mansoul was through thy lies and falsehood. Thou beliedst my Father, thou beliedst his law, and so deceivedst the people of Mansoul. Thou pretendest that the people have accepted thee for their king, their captain, and right liege lord; but that also was by the exercise of deceit and guile. Now, if lying, wiliness, sinful craft, and all manner of horrible hypocrisy, will go in my Father's court (in which court thou must be tried) for equity and right, then will I confess unto thee that thou hast made a lawful conquest. But, alas! what thief, what tyrant, what devil is there that may not conquer after this sort? But I can make it appear, O Diabolus, that thou, in all thy pretences to a conquest of Mansoul, hast nothing of truth to say. Thinkest thou this to be right, that thou didst put the lie upon my Father, and madest him (to Mansoul) the greatest deluder in the world? And what sayest thou to thy perverting knowingly the right purport and intent of the law? Was it good also that thou madest a prey of the innocency and simplicity of the now miserable town of Mansoul? Yea, thou didst overcome Mansoul by promising to them happiness in their transgressions, against my Father's law, when thou knewest, and couldest not but know, hadst thou consulted nothing but thine own experience, that that was the way to undo them. Thou hast also thyself, O thou master of enmity, of spite defaced my Father's image in Mansoul, and set up thine own in its place, to the great contempt of my Father, the heightening of thy sin, and to the intolerable damage of the perishing town of Mansoul.

"Thou hast, moreover (as if all these were but little things with thee), not only deluded and undone this place, but by thy lies and fraudulent carriage hast set them against their own deliverance. How hast thou stirred them up against my Father's captains, and made them to fight against those that were sent of him to deliver them from their bondage! All these things, and very many more, thou hast done against thy light, and in contempt of my Father and of his law, yea, and with design to bring under his displeasure for ever the miserable town of Mansoul. I am therefore come to avenge the wrong that thou hast done to my Father, and to deal with thee for the blasphemies wherewith thou hast made poor Mansoul blaspheme his name. Yea, upon thy head, thou prince of the infernal cave, will I requite it.

"As for myself, O Diabolus, I am come against thee by lawful power, and to take, by strength of hand, this town of Mansoul out of thy burning fingers; for this town of Mansoul is mine, O Diabolus, and that by undoubted right, as all shall see that will diligently search the most ancient and most authentic records, and I will plead my title to it, to the confusion of thy face.

"First, for the town of Mansoul, my Father built and did fashion it with his hand. The palace also that is in the midst of that town, he built for his own delight. This town of Mansoul, therefore, is my Father's, and that by the best of titles, and he that gainsays the truth of this must lie against his soul.

"Secondly, O thou master of the lie, this town of Mansoul is mine:—

"1. For that I am my Father's heir, his first-born, and the only delight of his heart. I am therefore come up against thee in mine own right, even to recover mine own inheritance out of thine hand.

"2. But further, as I have a right and title to Mansoul by being my Father's heir, so I have also my Father's donation. His it was, and he gave it me; nor have I at any time offended my Father, that he should take it from me, and give it to thee. Nor have I been forced, by playing the bankrupt, to sell, or set to sale to thee my beloved town of Mansoul. Mansoul is my desire, my delight, and the joy of my heart. But—

"3. Mansoul is mine by right of purchase. I have bought it, O Diabolus, I have bought it to myself. Now, since it was my Father's, and mine, as I was his heir, and since also I have made it mine by virtue of a great purchase, it followeth that, by all lawful right, the town of Mansoul is mine, and that thou art an usurper, a tyrant, and traitor, in thy holding possession thereof. Now, the cause of my purchasing of it was this: Mansoul had trespassed against my Father; now my Father had said, that in the day that they broke his law they should die. Now, it is more possible for heaven and earth to pass away than for my Father to break his word. Wherefore, when Mansoul had sinned indeed by hearkening to thy lie, I put in and became a surety to my Father, body for body, and soul for soul, that I would make amends for Mansoul's transgressions, and my Father did accept thereof. So when the time appointed was come, I gave body for body, soul for soul, life for life, blood for blood, and so redeemed my beloved Mansoul.

"4. Nor did I do this by halves: my Father's law and justice, that were both concerned in the threatening upon transgression, are both now satisfied, and very well content that Mansoul should be delivered.

"5. Nor am I come out this day against thee, but by commandment of my Father; 'twas he that said unto me, 'Go down and deliver Mansoul.'

"Wherefore, be it known unto thee, O thou fountain of deceit, and be it also known to the foolish town of Mansoul, that I am not come against thee this day without my Father.

"And now," said the golden-headed Prince, "I have a word to the town of Mansoul." But so soon as mention was made that he had a word to speak to the besotted town of Mansoul, the gates were double-guarded, and all men commanded not to give him audience. So he proceeded and said, "O unhappy town of Mansoul, I cannot but be touched with pity and compassion for thee. Thou hast accepted of Diabolus for thy king, and art become a nurse and minister of Diabolonians against thy sovereign Lord. Thy gates thou hast opened to him, but hast shut them fast against me; thou hast given him a hearing, but hast stopt thine ears at my cry. He brought to thee thy destruction, and thou didst receive both him and it: I am come to thee bringing salvation, but thou regardest me not. Besides, thou hast, as with sacrilegious hands, taken thyself, with all that was mine in thee, and hast given all to my foe, and to the greatest enemy my Father has. You have bowed and subjected yourselves to him; you have vowed and sworn yourselves to be his. Poor Mansoul! what shall I do unto thee? Shall I save thee?—shall I destroy thee? What shall I do unto thee? Shall I fall upon thee, and grind thee to powder, or make thee a monument of the richest grace? What shall I do unto thee? Hearken, therefore, thou town of Mansoul, hearken to my word, and thou shalt live. I am merciful, Mansoul, and thou shalt find me so. Shut me not out of thy gates.

"O Mansoul, neither is my commission nor inclination at all to do thee hurt. Why fliest thou so fast from thy friend, and stickest so close to thine enemy? Indeed, I would have thee, because it becomes thee, to be sorry for thy sin; but do not despair of life: this great force is not to hurt thee, but to deliver thee from thy bondage, and to reduce thee to thy obedience.

"My commission, indeed, is to make a war upon Diabolus, thy king, and upon all Diabolonians with him; for he is the strong man armed that keeps the house, and I will have him out: his spoils I must divide, his armour I must take from him, his hold I must cast him out of, and must make it a habitation for myself. And this, O Mansoul, shall Diabolus know when he shall be made to follow me in chains, and when Mansoul shall rejoice to see it so.

"I could, would I now put forth my might, cause that forthwith he should leave you and depart; but I have it in my heart so to deal with him, as that the justice of the war that I shall make upon him may be seen and acknowledged by all. He hath taken Mansoul by fraud, and keeps it by violence and deceit, and I will make him bare and naked in the eyes of all observers.

"All my words are true. I am mighty to save, and will deliver my Mansoul out of his hand."

This speech was intended chiefly for Mansoul, but Mansoul would not have the hearing of it. They shut up Ear-gate, they barricaded it up, they kept it lockt and bolted, they set a guard thereat, and commanded that no Mansoulonian should go out to him, nor that any from the camp should be admitted into the town. All this they did, so horribly had Diabolus enchanted them to do, and seek to do for him, against their rightful Lord and Prince; wherefore, no man, nor voice, nor sound of man that belonged to the glorious host, was to come into the town.

Emmanuel Prepares to Make War upon Mansoul

So when Emmanuel saw that Mansoul was thus involved in sin, he calls his army together (since now also his words were despised), and gave out a commandment throughout all his host to be ready against the time appointed. Now, forasmuch as there was no way lawfully to take the town of Mansoul but to get in by the gates, and at the Ear-gate as the chief, therefore he commanded his captains and commanders to bring their rams, their slings, and their men, and place them at the Eye-gate and Ear-gate, in order to his taking the town.

When Emmanuel had put all things in readiness to give Diabolus battle, he sent again to know of the town of Mansoul, if in peaceable manner they would yield themselves, or whether they were yet resolved to put him to try the utmost extremity. They then, together with Diabolus their king, called a council of war, and resolved upon certain propositions that should be offered to Emmanuel, if he will accept thereof, so they agreed; and then the next was, who should be sent on this errand. Now, there was in the town of Mansoul an old man, a Diabolonian, and his name was Mr. Loth-to-Stoop, a stiff man in his way, and a great doer for Diabolus: him, therefore, they sent, and put into his mouth what he should say. So he went, and came to the camp to Emmanuel, and when he was come, a time was appointed to give him audience. So, at the time he came, and after a Diabolonian ceremony or two, he thus began and said, "Great Sir, that it may be known unto all men how good-natured a prince my master is, he hath sent me to tell your Lordship that he is very willing, rather than go to war, to deliver up into your hands one-half of the town of Mansoul. I am therefore to know if your Mightiness will accept of this proposition."

Then said Emmanuel, "The whole is mine by gift and purchase, wherefore I will never lose one-half."

Then said Mr. Loth-to-Stoop, "Sir, my master hath said that he will be content that you shall be the nominal and titular Lord of all, if he may possess but a part."

Then Emmanuel answered, "The whole is mine really, not in name and word only; wherefore I will be the sole lord and possessor of all, or of none at all, of Mansoul."

Then Mr. Loth-to-Stoop said again, "Sir, behold the condescension of my master! He says that he will be content, if he may but have assigned to him some place in Mansoul as a place to live privately in, and you shall be Lord of all the rest."

Then said the golden Prince, "All that the Father giveth me shall come to me; and of all that he giveth me I will lose nothing–no not a hoof nor a hair. I will not, therefore, grant him, no not the least corner in Mansoul to dwell in; I will have all to myself."

Then Loth-to-Stoop said again, "But, Sir, suppose that my Lord should resign the whole town to you, only with this proviso, that he sometimes, when he comes into this country, may, for old acquaintance' sake, be entertained as a wayfaring man for two days, or ten days, or a month, or so: may not this small matter be granted?"

Then said Emmanuel, "No. He came as a wayfaring man to David, nor did he stay long with him, and yet it had like to have cost David his soul. I will not consent that he ever should have any harbour more there."

Then said Mr. Loth-to-Stoop, "Sir, you seem to be very hard. Suppose my master should yield to all that your Lordship hath said, provided that his friends and kindred in Mansoul may have liberty to trade in the town, and to enjoy their present dwellings: may not that be granted, Sir?"

Then said Emmanuel, "No: that is contrary to my Father's will; for all, and all manner of Diabolonians that now are, or that at any time shall be found in Mansoul, shall not only lose their lands and liberties, but also their lives."

Then said Mr. Loth-to-Stoop again, "But, Sir, may not my master and great lord, by letters, by passengers, by accidental opportunities, and the like, maintain, if he shall deliver up all unto thee, some kind of old friendship with Mansoul?"

Emmanuel answered, "No, by no means; forasmuch as any such fellowship, friendship, intimacy, or acquaintance, in what way, sort, or mode soever maintained, will tend to the corrupting of Mansoul, the alienating of their affections from me, and the endangering of their peace with my Father."

Mr. Loth-to-Stoop yet added further, saying, "But, great Sir, since my master hath many friends, and those that are dear to him, in Mansoul, may he not, if he shall depart from them, even of his bounty and good-nature, bestow upon them, as he sees fit, some tokens of his love and kindness that he had for them, to the end that Mansoul, when he is gone, may look upon such tokens of kindness once received from their old friend, and remember him who was once their king, and the merry times that they sometimes enjoyed one with another, while he and they lived in peace together?"

Then said Emmanuel, "No; for if Mansoul come to be mine, I shall not admit of nor consent that there should be the least scrap, shred, or dust of Diabolus left behind, as tokens or gifts bestowed upon any in Mansoul, thereby to call to remembrance the horrible communion that was betwixt them and him."

"Well, Sir," said Mr. Loth-to-Stoop, "I have one thing more to propound, and then I am got to the end of my commission. Suppose that, when my master is gone from Mansoul, any that shall yet live in the town should have such business of high concerns to do, that if they be neglected the party shall be undone; and suppose, Sir, that nobody can help in that case so well as my master and lord, may not now my master be sent for upon so urgent an occasion as this? Or if he may not be admitted into the town, may not he and the person concerned meet in some of the villages near Mansoul, and there lay their heads together, and there consult of matters?"

This was the last of those ensnaring propositions that Mr. Loth-to-Stoop had to propound to Emmanuel on behalf of his master Diabolus; but Emmanuel would not grant it; for he said, "There can be no case, or thing, or matter fall out in Mansoul, when thy master shall be gone, that may not be solved by my Father; besides, it will be a great disparagement to my Father's wisdom and skill to admit any from Mansoul to go out to Diabolus for advice, when they are bid before, in everything, by prayer and supplication, to let their requests be made known to my Father. Further, this, should it be granted, would be to grant that a door should be set open for Diabolus, and the Diabolonians in Mansoul, to hatch, and plot, and bring to pass treasonable designs, to the grief of my Father and me, and to the utter destruction of Mansoul."

When Mr. Loth-to-Stoop had heard this answer, he took his leave of Emmanuel, and departed, saying that he would carry word to his master concerning this whole affair. So he departed, and came to Diabolus to Mansoul, and told him the whole of the matter, and how Emmanuel would not admit, no not by any means, that he when he was once gone out, should for ever have anything more to do either in or with any that are of the town of Mansoul. When Mansoul and Diabolus had heard this relation of things, they with one consent concluded to use their best endeavour to keep Emmanuel out of Mansoul, and sent old Ill-Pause, of whom you have heard before, to tell the Prince and his captains so. So the old gentleman came up to the top of Ear-gate, and called to the camp for a hearing, to whom, when they gave audience, he said, "I have in commandment from my high lord to bid you tell it to your Prince Emmanuel, that Mansoul and their king are resolved to stand and fall together; and that it is in vain for your Prince to think of ever having Mansoul in his hand, unless he can take it by force." So some went and told to Emmanuel what old Ill-Pause, a Diabolonian in Mansoul, had said. Then said the Prince, "I must try the power of my sword, for I will not (for all the rebellions and repulses that Mansoul has made against me) raise my siege and depart, but will assuredly take my Mansoul, and deliver it from the hand of her enemy." And with that he gave out a commandment that Captain Boanerges, Captain Conviction, Captain Judgment, and Captain Execution should forthwith march up to Ear-gate with trumpets sounding, colours flying, and with shouting for the battle. Also he would that Captain Credence should join himself with them. Emmanuel, moreover, gave order that Captain Good-Hope and Captain Charity should draw themselves up before Eye-gate. He bid also that the rest of his captains and their men should place themselves for the best of their advantage against the enemy round about the town; and all was done as he had commanded.

Then he bid that the word should be given forth, and the word was at that time "EMMANUEL." Then was an alarm sounded, and the battering-rams were played, and the slings did whirl stones into the town amain, and thus the battle began. Now Diabolus himself did manage the townsmen in the war, and that at every gate; wherefore their resistance was the more forcible, hellish, and offensive to Emmanuel. Thus was the good Prince engaged and entertained by Diabolus and Mansoul for several days together; and a sight worth seeing it was to behold how the captains of Shaddai behaved themselves in this war.

And first for Captain Boanerges (not to undervalue the rest), he made three most fierce assaults, one after another, upon Ear-gate, to the shaking of the posts thereof. Captain Conviction, he also made up as fast with Boanerges as possibly he could, and both discerning that the gate began to yield, they commanded that the rams should still be played against it. Now, Captain Conviction, going up very near to the gate, was with great force driven back, and received three wounds in the mouth. And those that rode reformades, they went about to encourage the captains.

For the valour of the two captains made mention of before, the Prince sent for them to his pavilion, and commanded that a while they should rest themselves, and that with somewhat they should be refreshed. Care also was taken for Captain Conviction that he should be healed of his wounds. The Prince also gave to each of them a chain of gold, and bid them yet be of good courage.

Nor did Captain Good-Hope nor Captain Charity come behind in this most desperate fight, for they so well did behave themselves at Eye-gate, that they had almost broken it quite open. These also had a reward from their Prince, as also had the rest of the captains, because they did valiantly round about the town.

In this engagement several of the officers of Diabolus were slain, and some of the townsmen wounded. For the officers, there was one Captain Boasting slain. This Boasting thought that nobody could have shaken the posts of Ear-gate, nor have shaken the heart of Diabolus. Next to him there was one Captain Secure slain. This Secure used to say that the blind and lame in Mansoul were able to keep the gates of the town against Emmanuel's army. This Captain Secure did Captain Conviction cleave down the head with a two-handed sword, when he received himself three wounds in his mouth.

Besides these there was one Captain Bragman, a very desperate fellow, and he was captain over a band of those that threw firebrands, arrows, and death; he also received, by the hand of Captain Good-Hope at Eye-gate, a mortal wound in the breast.

There was, moreover, one Mr. Feeling; but he was no captain, but a great stickler to encourage Mansoul to rebellion. He received a wound in the eye by the hand of one of Boanerges' soldiers, and had by the captain himself been slain, but that he made a sudden retreat.

But I never saw Will-be-will so daunted in all my life: he was not able to do as he was wont, and some say that he also received a wound in the leg, and that some of the men in the Prince's army have certainly seen him limp as he afterwards walked on the wall.

I shall not give you a particular account of the names of the soldiers that were slain in the town, for many were maimed and wounded and slain; for when they saw that the posts of Ear-gate did shake, and Eye-gate was well-nigh broken quite open, and also that their captains were slain, this took away the hearts of many of the Diabolonians; they fell also by the force of the shot that were sent by the golden slings into the midst of the town of Mansoul.

Of the townsmen there was one Love-no-Good; he was a townsman, but a Diabolonian; he also received his mortal wound in Mansoul, but he died not very soon.

Mr. Ill-Pause also, who was the man that came along with Diabolus when at first he attempted the taking of Mansoul, he also received a grievous wound in the head; some say that his brain-pan was crackt. This I have taken notice of, that he was never after this able to do that mischief to Mansoul as he had done in times past. Also old Prejudice and Mr. Anything fled.

Now, when the battle was over, the Prince commanded that yet once more the white flag should be set upon Mount Gracious in sight of the town of Mansoul, to show that yet Emmanuel had grace for the wretched town of Mansoul.

When Diabolus saw the white flag hung out again, and knowing that it was not for him, but Mansoul, he cast in his mind to play another prank; to wit, to see if Emmanuel would raise his siege and begone, upon promise of reformation. So he comes down to the gate one evening, a good while after the sun was gone down, and calls to speak with Emmanuel, who presently came down to the gate, and Diabolus saith unto him:—

"Forasmuch as thou makest it appear by thy white flag that thou art wholly given to peace and quiet, I thought meet to acquaint thee that we are ready to accept thereof upon terms which thou mayst admit. I know that thou art given to devotion, and that holiness pleaseth thee; yea, that thy great end in making a war upon Mansoul is, that it may be an holy habitation. Well, draw off thy forces from the town, and I will bend Mansoul to thy bow.

"First, I will lay down all acts of hostility against thee, and will be willing to become thy deputy, and will, as I have formerly been against thee, now serve thee in the town of Mansoul. And more particularly—

"1. I will persuade Mansoul to receive thee for their Lord; and I know that they will do it the sooner when they shall understand that I am thy deputy.

"2. I will show them wherein they have erred, and that transgression stands in the way to life.

"3. I will show them the holy law into which they must conform, even that which they have broken.

"4. I will press upon them the necessity of a reformation according to thy law.

"5. And, moreover, that none of these things may fail, I myself, at my own proper cost and charge, will set up and maintain a sufficient ministry, besides lectures, in Mansoul.

"6. Thou shalt receive, as a token of our subjection to thee continually, year by year, what thou shalt think fit to lay and levy upon us in token of our subjection to thee."

Then said Emmanuel to him, "O full of deceit, how moveable are thy ways! How often hast thou changed and re-changed, if so be thou mightest still keep possession of my Mansoul, though, as has been plainly declared before, I am the right heir thereof! Often hast thou made thy proposals already, nor is this last a whit better than they. And failing to deceive when thou shewedst thyself in thy black, thou hast now transformed thyself into an angel of light, and wouldest, to deceive, be now as a minister of righteousness.

"But know thou, O Diabolus, that nothing must be regarded that thou canst propound, for nothing is done by thee but to deceive. Thou neither hast conscience to God, nor love to the town of Mansoul; whence, then, should these thy sayings arise but from sinful craft and deceit? He that can of list and will propound what he pleases, and that wherewith he may destroy them that believe him, is to be abandoned, with all that he shall say. But if righteousness be such a beauty-spot in thine eyes now, how is it that wickedness was so closely stuck to by thee before? But this is by the by.

"Thou talkest now of a reformation in Mansoul, and that thou thyself, if I will please, wilt be at the head of that reformation; all the while knowing that the greatest proficiency that man can make in the law, and the righteousness thereof, will amount to no more, for the taking away of the curse from Mansoul, than just nothing at all; for a law being broken by Mansoul, that had before, upon a supposition of the breach thereof, a curse pronounced against him for it of God, can never, by his obeying of the law, deliver himself therefrom (to say nothing of what a reformation is like to be set up in Mansoul when the devil is become the corrector of vice). Thou knowest that all that thou hast now said in this matter is nothing but guile and deceit; and is, as it was the first, so it is the last card that thou hast to play. Many there be that do soon discern thee when thou showest them thy cloven foot; but in thy white, thy light, and in thy transformation, thou art seen but of a few. But thou shalt not do thus with my Mansoul, O Diabolus; for I do still love my Mansoul.

"Besides, I am not come to put Mansoul upon works to live thereby: should I do so, I should be like unto thee; but I am come that by me, and by what I have and shall do for Mansoul, they may to my Father be reconciled, though by their sin they have provoked him to anger, and though by the law they cannot obtain mercy.

"Thou talkest of subjecting of this town to good, when none desireth it at thy hands. I am sent by my Father to possess it myself, and to guide it by the skilfulness of my hands into such a conformity to him as shall be pleasing in his sight. I will therefore possess it myself; I will dispossess and cast thee out; I will set up mine own standard in the midst of them; I will also govern them by new laws, new officers, new motives, and new ways; yea, I will pull down this town, and build it again, and it shall be as though it had not been, and it shall then be the glory of the whole universe."

Diabolus Confounded

When Diabolus heard this, and perceived that he was discovered in all his deceits, he was confounded, and utterly put to a nonplus; but having in himself the fountain of iniquity, rage, and malice against both Shaddai and his Son, and the beloved town of Mansoul, what doth he but strengthen himself what he could to give fresh battle to the noble Prince Emmanuel. So, then, now we must have another fight before the town of Mansoul is taken. Come up, then, to the mountains, you that love to see military actions, and behold by both sides how the fatal blow is given, while one seeks to hold, and the other seeks to make himself master of the famous town of Mansoul.

Diabolus, therefore, having withdrawn himself from the wall to his force that was in the heart of the town of Mansoul, Emmanuel also returned to the camp; and both of them, after their divers ways, put themselves into a posture fit to bid battle one to another.

Diabolus, as filled with despair of retaining in his hands the famous town of Mansoul, resolved to do what mischief he could (if, indeed, he could do any) to the army of the Prince and to the famous town of Mansoul; for, alas! it was not the happiness of the silly town of Mansoul that was designed by Diabolus, but the utter ruin and overthrow thereof, as now is enough in view. Wherefore he commands his officers that they should then, when they see that they could hold the town no longer, do it what harm and mischief they could, rending and tearing men, women, and children. "For," said he, "we had better quite demolish the place, and leave it like a ruinous heap, than so leave it that it may be an habitation for Emmanuel."

Emmanuel again, knowing that the next battle would issue in his being made master of the place, gave out a royal commandment to all his officers, high captains, and men of war, to be sure to show themselves men of war against Diabolus and all Diabolonians; but favourable, merciful, and meek to all the old inhabitants of Mansoul. "Bend, therefore," said the noble Prince, "the hottest front of the battle against Diabolus and his men."

So the day being come, the command was given, and the Prince's men did bravely stand to their arms, and did, as before, bend their main force against Ear-gate and Eye-gate. The word was then, "Mansoul is won;" so they made their assault upon the town. Diabolus also, as fast as he could, with the main of his power, made resistance from within; and his high lords and chief captains for a time fought very cruelly against the Prince's army.

But after three or four notable charges by the Prince and his noble captains, Ear-gate was broken open, and the bars and bolts wherewith it was used to be fast shut up against the Prince, were broken into a thousand pieces. Then did the Prince's trumpets sound, the captains shout, the town shake, and Diabolus retreat to his hold. Well, when the Prince's forces had broken open the gate, himself came up and did set his throne in it; also he set his standard thereby, upon a mount that before by his men was cast up to place the mighty slings thereon. The mount was called Mount Hear-well. There, therefore, the Prince abode, to wit, hard by the going in at the gate. He commanded also that the golden slings should yet be played upon the town, especially against the castle, because for shelter thither was Diabolus retreated. Now, from Ear-gate the street was straight even to the house of Mr. Recorder that so was before Diabolus took the town; and hard by his house stood the castle, which Diabolus for a long time had made his irksome den. The captains, therefore, did quickly clear that street by the use of their slings, so that the way was made up to the heart of the town. Then did the Prince command that Captain Boanerges, Captain Conviction, and Captain Judgment, should forthwith march up the town to the old gentleman's gate. Then did the captains in most warlike manner enter into the town of Mansoul, and, marching in with flying colours, they came up to the Recorder's house, and that was almost as strong as was the castle. Battering-rams they took also with them, to plant against the castle gates. When they were come to the house of Mr. Conscience, they knocked and demanded entrance. Now, the old gentleman, not knowing as yet fully their design, kept his gates shut all the time of this fight. Wherefore Boanerges demanded entrance at his gates; and no man making answer, he gave it one stroke with the head of a ram, and this made the old gentleman shake, and his house to tremble and totter. Then came Mr. Recorder down to the gate, and as he could, with quivering lips, he asked who was there? Boanerges answered, "We are the captains and commanders of the great Shaddai, and of the blessed Emmanuel, his Son, and we demand possession of your house for the use of our noble Prince." And with that the battering-ram gave the gate another shake. This made the old gentleman tremble the more, yet durst he not but open the gate: then the King's forces marched in, namely, the three brave captains mentioned before. Now, the Recorder's house was a place of much convenience for Emmanuel, not only because it was near to the castle, and strong, but also because it was large, and fronted the castle, the den where now Diabolus was, for he was now afraid to come out of his hold. As for Mr. Recorder, the captains carried it very reservedly to him; as yet he knew nothing of the great designs of Emmanuel, so that he did not know what judgment to make, nor what would be the end of such thundering beginnings. It was also presently noised in the town how the Recorder's house was possessed, his rooms taken up, and his palace made the seat of the war; and no sooner was it noised abroad, but they took the alarm as warmly, and gave it out to others of his friends; and you know, as a snowball loses nothing by rolling, so in a little time the whole town was possessed that they must expect nothing from the Prince but destruction; and the ground of the business was this, the Recorder was afraid, the Recorder trembled, and the captains carried it strangely to the Recorder. So many came to see; but when they with their own eyes did behold the captains in the palace, and their battering-rams ever playing at the castle gates to beat them down, they were riveted in their fears, and it made them all in amaze. And as I said, the man of the house would increase all this; for whoever came to him, or discoursed with him, nothing would he talk of, tell them, or hear, but that death and destruction now attended Mansoul.

"For," quoth the old gentleman, "you are all of you sensible that we all have been traitors to that once despised, but now famously victorious and glorious Prince Emmanuel; for he now, as you see, doth not only lie in close siege about us, but hath forced his entrance in at our gates. Moreover, Diabolus flees before him; and he hath, as you behold, made of my house a garrison against the castle, where he is. I, for my part, have transgressed greatly, and he that is clean, 'tis well for him. But I say I have transgressed greatly in keeping silence when I should have spoken, and in perverting justice when I should have executed the same. True, I have suffered something at the hand of Diabolus for taking part with the laws of King Shaddai; but that, alas! what will that do? will that make compensation for the rebellions and treasons that I have done, and have suffered without gainsaying to be committed in the town of Mansoul? Oh! I tremble to think what will be the end of this so dreadful and so ireful a beginning!"

Now, while these brave captains were thus busy in the house of the old Recorder, Captain Execution was as busy, in other parts of the town, in securing the back streets and the walls. He also hunted the Lord Will-be-will sorely; he suffered him not to rest in any corner; he pursued him so hard, that he drove his men from him, and made him glad to thrust his head into a hole. Also this mighty warrior did cut three of the Lord Will-be-will's officers down to the ground: one was old Mr. Prejudice, he that had his crown cracked in the mutiny. This man was made by Lord Will-be-will keeper of Ear-gate, and fell by the hand of Captain Execution. There was also one Mr. Backward-to-all-but-naught, and he also was one of Lord Will-be-will's officers, and was the captain of the two guns that once were mounted on the top of Ear-gate; he also was cut down to the ground by the hands of Captain Execution. Besides these two there was another, a third, and his name was Captain Treacherous; a vile man this was, but one that Will-be-will did put a great deal of confidence in: but him also did this Captain Execution cut down to the ground with the rest.

He also made a very great slaughter among my Lord Will-be-will's soldiers, killing many that were stout and sturdy, and wounding many that for Diabolus were nimble and active. But all these were Diabolonians; there was not a man, a native of Mansoul, hurt.

Other feats of war were also performed by other of the captains; as at Eye-gate, where Captain Good-Hope and Captain Charity had a charge, was great execution done; for the Captain Good-Hope with his own hands slew one Captain Blindfold, the keeper of that gate. This Blindfold was captain of a thousand men, and they were they that fought with mauls; he also pursued his men, slew many, and wounded more, and made the rest hide their heads in corners.

There was also at that gate Mr. Ill-Pause, of whom you have heard before. He was an old man, and had a beard that reached down to his girdle: the same was he that was orator to Diabolus: he did much mischief in the town of Mansoul, and fell by the hand of Captain Good-Hope.

What shall I say? The Diabolonians in these days lay dead in every corner, though too many yet were alive in Mansoul.

Now, the old Recorder and my Lord Understanding, with some others of the chief of the town, to wit, such as knew that they must stand and fall with the famous town of Mansoul, came together upon a day, and, after consultation had, did jointly agree to draw up a petition, and to send it to Emmanuel, now while he sat in the gate of Mansoul. So they drew up their petition to Emmanuel, the contents whereof were this:—That they, the old inhabitants of the now deplorable town of Mansoul, confessed their sin, and were sorry that they had offended his princely Majesty, and prayed that he would spare their lives.

Unto this petition he gave no answer at all, and that did trouble them yet so much the more. Now, all this while the captains that were in the Recorder's house were playing with the battering-rams at the gates of the castle, to beat them down. So, after some time, labour, and travel, the gate of the castle that was called Impregnable was beaten open, and broken into several splinters, and so a way made to go up to the hold in which Diabolus had hid himself. Then was tidings sent down to Ear-gate, for Emmanuel still abode there, to let him know that a way was made in at the gates of the castle of Mansoul. But, oh! how the trumpets at the tidings sounded throughout the Prince's camp, for that now the war was so near an end, and Mansoul itself of being set free.

Then the Prince arose from the place where he was, and took with him such of his men of war as were fittest for that expedition, and marched up the street of Mansoul to the old Recorder's house.

Emmanuel Marches into Mansoul

Now the Prince himself was clad all in armour of gold, and so he marched up the town with his standard borne before him; but he kept his countenance much reserved all the way as he went, so that the people could not tell how to gather to themselves love or hatred by his looks. Now, as he marched up the street, the townsfolk came out at every door to see, and could not but be taken with his person and the glory thereof, but wondered at the reservedness of his countenance; for as yet he spake more to them by his actions and works than he did by words or smiles. But also poor Mansoul (as in such cases all are apt to do), they interpreted the carriage of Emmanuel to them as did Joseph's brethren his to them, even all the quite contrary way. "For," thought they, "if Emmanuel loved us, he would show it to us by word or carriage; but none of these he doth, therefore Emmanuel hates us. Now, if Emmanuel hates us, then Mansoul shall be slain, then Mansoul shall become a dunghill." They knew that they had transgressed his

Father's law, and that against him they had been in with Diabolus, his enemy. They also knew that the Prince Emmanuel knew all this; for they were convinced that he was as an angel of God, to know all things that are done in the earth; and this made them think that their condition was miserable, and that the good Prince would make them desolate.

"And," thought they, "what time so fit to do this in as now, when he has the bridle of Mansoul in his hand?" And this I took special notice of, that the inhabitants, notwithstanding all this, could not, no, they could not, when they see him march through the town, but cringe, bow, bend, and were ready to lick the dust of his feet. They also wished a thousand times over that he would become their Prince and Captain, and would become their protection. They would also one to another talk of the comeliness of his person, and how much for glory and valour he outstript the great ones of the world. But, poor hearts, as to themselves, their thoughts would change, and go upon all manner of extremes. Yea, through the working of them backward and forward, Mansoul became as a ball tossed, and as a rolling thing before the whirlwind.

Diabolus Taken Prisoner

Now, when he was come to the castle gates, he commanded Diabolus to appear, and to surrender himself into his hands. But, oh! how loth was the beast to appear! how he stuck at it! how he shrunk! ay, how he cringed! yet out he came to the Prince. Then Emmanuel commanded, and they took Diabolus and bound him fast in chains, the better to reserve him to the judgment that he had appointed for him. But Diabolus stood up to entreat for himself that Emmanuel would not send him into the deep, but suffer him to depart out of Mansoul in peace.

When Emmanuel had taken him and bound him in chains, he led him into the market-place, and there, before Mansoul, stript him of his armour, in which he boasted so much before. This now was one of the acts of triumph of Emmanuel over his enemy; and all the while that the giant was stripping, the trumpets of the golden Prince did sound amain; the captains also shouted, and the soldiers did sing for joy.

Then was Mansoul called upon to behold the beginning of Emmanuel's triumph over him in whom they so much had trusted, and of whom they so much had boasted in the days when he flattered them.

Thus having made Diabolus naked in the eye of Mansoul, and before the commanders of the Prince, in the next place he commands that Diabolus should be bound with chains to his chariot wheels. Then leaving off some of his forces, to wit, Captain Boanerges and Captain Conviction, as a guard for the castle gates, that resistance might be made on his behalf (if any that heretofore followed Diabolus should make an attempt to possess it), he did ride in triumph over him quite through the town of Mansoul, and so out at and before the gate called Ear-gate, to the plain where his camp did lie.

But you cannot think, unless you had been there, as I was, what a shout there was in Emmanuel's camp when they saw the tyrant bound by the hand of their noble Prince, and tied to his chariot wheels!

And they said, "He hath led captivity captive, he hath spoiled principalities and powers. Diabolus is subjected to the powers of his sword, and made the object of all derision."

Those also that rode reformades, and that came down to see the battle, they shouted with that greatness of voice, and sung with such melodious notes, that they caused them that dwell in the highest orbs to open their windows, put out their heads, and look down to see the cause of that glory.

The townsmen also, so many of them as saw this sight, were, as it were, while they looked, betwixt the earth and the heavens. True, they could not tell what would be the issue of things as to them; but all things were done in such excellent methods, and I cannot tell how, but things in the management of them seemed to cast a smile towards the town, so that their eyes, their heads, their hearts, and their minds, and all that they had, were taken and held, while they observed Emmanuel's order.

So, when the brave Prince had finished this part of his triumph over Diabolus, his foe, he turned him up in the midst of his contempt and shame, having given him a charge no more to be a possessor of Mansoul. Then went he from Emmanuel, and out of the midst of his camp, to inherit the parched places in a salt land, seeking rest, but finding none.

Now Captain Boanerges and Captain Conviction were both of them men of very great majesty; their faces were like the faces of lions, and their words like the roaring of the sea; and they still quartered in Mr. Conscience's house, of whom mention was made before. When, therefore, the high and mighty Prince had thus far finished his triumph over Diabolus, the townsmen had more leisure to view and to behold the actions of these most noble captains. But the captains carried it with that terror and dread in all that they did (and you may be sure that they had private instructions so to do), that they kept the town under continual heartaching, and caused (in their apprehension) the well-being of Mansoul for the future to hang in doubt before them, so that for some considerable time they neither knew what rest, or ease, or peace, or hope meant.

Nor did the Prince himself as yet abide in the town of Mansoul, but in his royal pavilion in the camp, and in the midst of his Father's forces. So, at a time convenient, he sent special orders to Captain Boanerges to summon Mansoul, the whole of the townsmen into the castle-yard, and then and there, before their faces, to take my Lord Understanding, Mr. Conscience, and that notable one, the Lord Will-be-will, and put them all three in ward, and that they should set a strong guard upon them there, until his pleasure concerning them was further known; the which orders, when the captains had put them in execution, made no small addition to the fears of the town of Mansoul; for now, to their thinking, were their former fears of the ruin of Mansoul confirmed. Now, what death they should die, and how long they should be in dying, was that which most perplexed their heads and hearts; yea, they were afraid that Emmanuel would command them all into the deep, the place that the Prince Diabolus was afraid of, for they knew that they had deserved it. Also to die by the sword in the face of the town, and in the open way of disgrace, from the hand of so good and so holy a Prince, that, too, troubled them sore. The town was also greatly troubled for the men that were committed to ward, for that they were their stay and their guide, and for that they believed that, if those men were cut off, their execution would be but the beginning of the ruin of the town of Mansoul. Wherefore, what do they, but, together with the men in prison, draw up a petition to the Prince, and sent it to Emmanuel by the hand of Mr. Would-live. So he went, and came to the Prince's quarters, and presented the petition, the sum of which was this:—

"Great and wonderful Potentate, victor over Diabolus, and conqueror of the town of Mansoul, we, the miserable inhabitants of that most woeful corporation, do humbly beg that we may find favour in thy sight, and remember not against us former transgressions, nor yet the sins of the chief of our town; but spare us according to the greatness of thy mercy, and let us not die, but live in thy sight. So shall we be willing to be thy servants, and, if thou shalt think fit, to gather our meat under thy table. Amen."

So the petitioner went, as was said, with his petition to the Prince; and the Prince took it at his hand, but sent him away with silence. This still afflicted the town of Mansoul; but yet, considering that now they must either petition or die, for now they could not do anything else, therefore they consulted again, and sent another petition; and this petition was much after the form and method of the former.

But when the petition was drawn up, By whom should they send it? was the next question; for they would not send this by him by whom they sent the first, for they thought that the Prince had taken some offence at the manner of his deportment before him: so they attempted to make Captain Conviction their messenger with it; but he said he neither durst nor would petition Emmanuel for traitors, nor be to the Prince an advocate for rebels. "Yet withal," said he, "our Prince is good, and you may adventure to send it by the hand of one of your town, provided he went with a rope about his head, and pleaded nothing but mercy."

Well, they made through fear their delays as long as they could, and longer than delays were good; but fearing at last the dangerousness of them, they thought, but with many a fainting in their minds, to send their petition by Mr. Desires-awake; so they sent for Mr. Desires-awake. Now, he dwelt in a very mean cottage in Mansoul, and he came at his neighbours' request. So they told him what they had done, and what they would do, concerning petitioning, and that they did desire of him that he would go therewith to the Prince.

Then said Mr. Desires-awake, "Why should not I do the best I can to save so famous a town as Mansoul from deserved destruction?" They therefore delivered the petition to him, and told him how he must address himself to the Prince, and wished him ten thousand good speeds. So he comes to the Prince's pavilion, as the first, and asked to speak with his Majesty. So word was carried to Emmanuel, and the Prince came out to the man. When Mr. Desires-awake saw the Prince, he fell flat with his face to the ground, and cried out, "Oh that Mansoul might live before thee!" and with that he presented the petition; the which when the Prince had read, he turned away for a while and wept; but refraining himself, he turned again to the man, who all this while lay crying at his feet, as at the first, and said to him, "Go thy way to thy place, and I will consider of thy requests."

Now, you may think that they of Mansoul that had sent him, what with guilt, and what with fear lest their petition should be rejected, could not but look with many a long look, and that, too, with strange workings of heart, to see what would become of their petition. At last they saw their messenger coming back. So, when he was come, they asked him how he fared, what Emmanuel said, and what was become of the petition. But he told them that he would be silent till he came to the prison to my Lord Mayor, my Lord Will-be-will, and Mr. Recorder. So he went forwards towards the prison-house, where the men of Mansoul lay bound. But, oh! what a multitude flocked after, to hear what the messenger said! So, when he was come, and had shown himself at the grate of the prison, my Lord Mayor himself lookt as white as a clout; the Recorder also did quake. But they asked and said, "Come, good sir, what did the great Prince say to you?" Then said Mr. Desires-awake, "When I came to my Lord's pavilion, I called, and he came forth. So I fell prostrate at his feet, and delivered to him my petition; for the greatness of his person, and the glory of his countenance, would not suffer me to stand upon my legs. Now, as he received the petition, I cried, 'Oh that Mansoul might live before thee!' So, when for a while he had looked thereon, he turned him about, and said to his servant, 'Go thy way to thy place again, and I will consider of thy requests.'" The messenger added, moreover, and said, "The Prince to whom you sent me is such a one for beauty and glory, that whoso sees him must both love and fear him. I, for my part, can do no less; but I know not what will be the end of these things."

At this answer they were all at a stand, both they in prison, and they that followed the messenger thither to hear the news; nor knew they what, or what manner of interpretation to put upon what the Prince had said. Now, when the prison was cleared of the throng, the prisoners among themselves began to comment upon Emmanuel's words. My Lord Mayor said, That the answer did not look with a rugged face; but Will-be-will said, it betokened evil; and the Recorder, that it was a messenger of death. Now, they that were left, and that stood behind, and so could not so well hear what the prisoners said, some of them catcht hold of one piece of a sentence, and some on a bit of another; some took hold of what the messenger said, and some of the prisoners' judgment thereon; so none had the right understanding of things. But you cannot imagine what work these people made, and what a confusion there was in Mansoul now.

For presently they that had heard what was said flew about the town, one crying one thing, and another the quite contrary; and both were sure enough they told true; for they did hear, they said, with their ears what was said, and therefore could not be deceived. One would say, "We must all be killed;" another would say, "We must all be saved;" and a third would say that the Prince would not be concerned with Mansoul, and a fourth, that the prisoners must be suddenly put to death. And, as I said, every one stood to it that he told his tale the rightest, and that all others but he were out. Wherefore Mansoul had now molestation upon molestation, nor could any man know on what to rest the sole of his foot; for one would go by now, and as he went, if he heard his neighbour tell his tale, to be sure he would tell the quite contrary, and both would stand in it that he told the truth. Nay, some of them had got this story by the end, that the Prince did intend to put Mansoul to the sword. And now it began to be dark, wherefore poor Mansoul was in sad perplexity all that night until the morning.

But so far as I could gather by the best information that I could get, all this hubbub came through the words that the Recorder said when he told them, That in his judgment, the Prince's answer was a messenger of death. It was this that fired the town, and that began the fright in Mansoul; for Mansoul in former times did use to count that Mr. Recorder was a seer, and that his sentence was equal to the best of oracles; and thus was Mansoul a terror to itself.

And now did they begin to feel what were the effects of stubborn rebellion, and unlawful resistance against their Prince. I say, they now began to feel the effects thereof by guilt and fear, that now had swallowed them up; and who more involved in the one but they that were most in the other, to wit, the chief of the town of Mansoul?

To be brief: when the fame of the fright was out of the town, and the prisoners had a little recovered themselves, they take to themselves some heart, and think to petition the Prince for life again. So they did draw up a third petition, the contents whereof was this:—

"Prince Emmanuel the Great, Lord of all worlds, and Master of Mercy, we, thy poor, wretched, miserable, dying town of Mansoul, do confess unto thy great and glorious Majesty, that we have sinned against thy Father and thee, and are no more worthy to be called thy Mansoul, but rather to be cast into the pit. If thou wilt slay us, we have deserved it. If thou wilt condemn us to the deep, we cannot but say thou art righteous. We cannot complain whatever thou dost, or however thou carriest it towards us. But, oh! let mercy reign, and let it be extended to us! Oh! let mercy take hold upon us, and free us from our transgressions, and we will sing of thy mercy and of thy judgment. Amen."

This petition, when drawn up, was designed to be sent to the Prince as the first; but who should carry it, that was the question. Some said, "Let him do it that went with the first"; but others thought not good to do that, and that because he sped no better. Now, there was an old man in the town, and his name was Mr. Good-Deed; a man that bore only the name, but had nothing of the nature of the thing. Now, some were for sending him; but the Recorder was by no means for that; "for," said he, "we now stand in need of, and are pleading for mercy: wherefore, to send our petition by a man of his name, will seem to cross the petition itself. Should we make Mr. Good-Deed our messenger, when our petition cries for mercy?

"Besides," quoth the old gentleman, "should the Prince now, as he receives the petition, ask him and say, 'What is thy name?'—as nobody knows but he will,—and he should say, 'Old Good-Deed,' what, think you, would Emmanuel say but this? 'Ay! is old Good-Deed yet alive in Mansoul? then let old Good-Deed save you from your distresses.' And if he says so, I am sure we are lost; nor can a thousand of old Good-Deeds save Mansoul."

After the Recorder had given in his reasons why old Good-Deed should not go with this petition to Emmanuel, the rest of the prisoners and chief of Mansoul opposed it also, and so old Good-Deed was laid aside, and they agreed to send Mr. Desires-awake again. So they sent for him, and desired him that he would a second time go with their petition to the Prince, and he readily told them he would. But they bid him that in anywise he would take heed that in no word or carriage he gave offence to the Prince; "for by doing so, for aught we can tell, you may bring Mansoul into utter destruction," said they.

Now, Mr. Desires-awake, when he saw that he must go on this errand, besought that they would grant that Mr. Wet-Eyes might go with him. Now this Wet-Eyes was a near neighbour of Mr. Desires, a poor man, a man of a broken spirit, yet one that could speak well to a petition; so they granted that he should go with him. Wherefore, they address themselves to their business: Mr. Desires put a rope upon his head, and Mr. Wet-Eyes went with his hands wringing together. Thus they went to the Prince's pavilion.

Now, when they went to petition this third time, they were not without thoughts that by often coming they might be a burden to the Prince. Wherefore, when they were come to the door of his pavilion, they first made their apology for themselves, and for their coming to trouble Emmanuel so often; and they said, that they came not hither to-day for that they delighted in being troublesome, or for that they delighted to hear themselves talk, but for that necessity caused them to come to his Majesty. They could, they said, have no rest day nor night because of their transgressions against Shaddai and against Emmanuel his Son. They also thought that some misbehaviour of Mr. Desires-awake the last time might give distaste to his Highness, and so cause that he returned from so merciful a Prince empty, and without countenance. So when they had made this apology, Mr. Desires-awake cast himself prostrate upon the ground, as at the first, at the feet of the mighty Prince saying, "Oh that Mansoul might live before thee!" and so he delivered his petition.

The Prince Talks with the Messengers

The Prince then, having read the petition, turned aside awhile as before, and coming again to the place where the petitioner lay on the ground, he demanded what his name was, and of what esteem in the account of Mansoul, for that he, above all the multitude in Mansoul, should be sent to him upon such an errand. Then said the man to the Prince, "Oh, let not my Lord be angry; and why inquirest thou after the name of such a dead dog as I am? Pass by, I pray thee, and take no notice of who I am, because there is, as thou very well knowest, so great a disproportion between me and thee. Why the townsmen choose to send me on this errand to my Lord is best known to themselves, but it could not be for that they thought that I had favour with my Lord. For my part, I am out of charity with myself; who, then, should be in love with me? Yet live I would, and so would I that my townsmen should; and because both they and myself are guilty of great transgressions, therefore they have sent me, and I am come in their names to beg of my Lord for mercy. Let it please thee, therefore, to incline to mercy; but ask not what thy servants are."

Then said the Prince, "And what is he that is become thy companion in this so weighty a matter?" So Mr. Desires told Emmanuel that he was a poor neighbour of his, and one of his most intimate associates. "And his name," said he, "may it please your most excellent Majesty, is Wet-Eyes, of the town of Mansoul. I know that there are many of that name that are naught; but I hope it will be no offence to my Lord that I have brought my poor neighbour with me."

Then Mr. Wet-Eyes fell on his face to the ground, and made this apology for his coming with his neighbour to his Lord:—

"O my Lord," quoth he, "what I am, I know not myself, nor whether my name be feigned or true, especially when I begin to think what some have said, namely, that this name was given me because Mr. Repentance was my father. Good men have bad children, and the sincere do oftentimes beget hypocrites. My mother also called me by this name from my cradle; but whether because of the moistness of my brain, or because of the softness of my heart, I cannot tell. I see dirt in mine own tears, and filthiness in the bottom of my prayers. But I pray thee (and all this while the gentleman wept) that thou wouldst not remember against us our transgressions, nor take offence at the unqualifiedness of thy servants, but mercifully pass by the sin of Mansoul, and refrain from the glorifying of thy grace no longer."

So at his bidding they arose, and both stood trembling before him, and he spake to them to this purpose:—

"The town of Mansoul hath grievously rebelled against my Father, in that they have rejected him from being their King, and did choose to themselves for their captain a liar, a murderer, and a runagate slave. For this Diabolus, your pretended prince, though once so highly accounted of by you, made rebellion against my Father and me, even in our palace and highest court there, thinking to become a prince and king. But being there timely discovered and apprehended, and for his wickedness bound in chains, and separated to the pit with those that were his companions, he offered himself to you, and you have received him.

"Now, this is, and for a long time hath been, a high affront to my Father;

wherefore my Father sent to you a powerful army to reduce you to your obedience. But you know how these men, their captains and their counsels, were esteemed of you, and what they received at your hand. You rebelled against them, you shut your gates upon them, you bid them battle, you fought them, and fought for Diabolus against them. So they sent to my Father for more power, and I, with my men, are come to subdue you. But as you treated the servants, so you treated their Lord. You stood up in hostile manner against me, you shut up your gates against me, you turned the deaf ear to me, and resisted as long as you could; but now I have made a conquest of you. Did you cry me mercy so long as you had hopes that you might prevail against me? But now I have taken the town, you cry; but why did you not cry before, when the white flag of my mercy, the red flag of justice, and the black flag that threatened execution, were set up to cite you to it? Now I have conquered your Diabolus, you come to me for favour; but why did you not help me against the mighty? Yet I will consider your petition, and will answer it so as will be for my glory.

"Go bid Captain Boanerges and Captain Conviction bring the prisoners out to me into the camp to-morrow, and say you to Captain Judgment and Captain Execution, 'Stay you in the castle, and take good heed to yourselves that you keep all quiet in Mansoul until you shall hear further from me.'" And with that he turned himself from them, and went into his royal pavilion again.

So the petitioners, having received this answer from the Prince, returned, as at the first, to go to their companions again. But they had not gone far, but thoughts began to work in their minds that no mercy as yet was intended by the Prince to Mansoul. So they went to the place where the prisoners lay bound; but these workings of mind about what would become of Mansoul, had such strong power over them, that by that they were come unto them that sent them, they were scarce able to deliver their message.

But they came at length to the gates of the town (now the townsmen with earnestness were waiting for their return), where many met them, to know what answer was made to the petition. Then they cried out to those that were sent, "What news from the Prince? and what hath Emmanuel said?" But they said that they must, as afore, go up to the prison, and there deliver their message. So away they went to the prison, with a multitude at their heels. Now, when they were come to the grates of the prison, they told the first part of Emmanuel's speech to the prisoners, to wit, how he reflected upon their disloyalty to his Father and himself, and how they had chosen and closed with Diabolus, had fought for him, hearkened to him, and been ruled by him; but had despised him and his men. This made the prisoners look pale; but the messengers proceeded and said, "He, the Prince, said, moreover, that yet he would consider your petition, and give such answer thereto as would stand with his glory." And as these words were spoken, Mr. Wet-Eyes gave a great sigh. At this they were all of them struck into their dumps, and could not tell what to say; fear also possest them in a marvellous manner, and death seem'd to sit upon some of their eyebrows. Now, there was in the company a notable, sharp-witted fellow, a mean man of estate, and his name was old Inquisitive. This man asked the petitioners if they had told out every whit of what Emmanuel said, and they answered, "Verily, no." Then said Inquisitive, "I thought so, indeed. Pray, what was it more that he said unto you?" Then they paused a while; but at last they brought out all, saying, "The Prince bade us bid Captain Boanerges and Captain Conviction bring the prisoners down to him to-morrow; and that Captain Judgment and Captain Execution should take charge of the castle and town till they should hear further from him." They said also, that when the Prince had commanded them thus to do, he immediately turned his back upon them, and went into his royal pavilion.

But O! how this return, and especially this last clause of it, that the prisoners must go out to the Prince into the camp, brake all their loins in pieces! Wherefore with one voice they set up a cry that reached up to the heavens. This done, each of the three prepared himself to die (and the Recorder said unto them, "This was the thing that I feared"); for they concluded that to-morrow, by that the sun went down, they should be tumbled out of the world. The whole town also counted of no other, but that, in their time and order, they must all drink of the same cup. Wherefore the town of Mansoul spent that night in mourning, in sackcloth and ashes. The prisoners also, when the time was come for them to go down before the Prince, dressed themselves in mourning attire, with ropes upon their heads. The whole town of Mansoul also showed themselves upon the wall, all clad in mourning weeds, if, perhaps, the Prince with the sight thereof might be moved with compassion. But, oh! how the busy-bodies that were in the town of Mansoul did now concern themselves! They did run here and there through the streets of the town by companies, crying out as they ran in tumultuous wise, one after one manner, and another the quite contrary, to the almost utter distraction of Mansoul.

Well, the time is come that the prisoners must go down to the camp and appear before the Prince. And thus was the manner of their going down: Captain Boanerges went with a guard before them, and Captain Conviction came behind, and the prisoners went down, bound in chains, in the midst. So, I say, the prisoners went in the midst, and the guard went with flying colours behind and before, but the prisoners went with drooping spirits.

Or, more particularly, thus:—The prisoners went down all in mourning; they put ropes upon themselves; they went on, smiting themselves on the breasts, but durst not lift up their eyes to heaven. Thus they went out at the gate of Mansoul, till they came into the midst of the Prince's army, the sight and glory of which did greatly heighten their affliction. Nor could they now longer forbear, but cry aloud, "O unhappy men! O wretched men of Mansoul!" Their chains, still mixing their dolorous notes with the cries of the prisoners, made the noise more lamentable.

So, when they were come to the door of the Prince's pavilion, they cast themselves prostrate upon the place; then one went in and told his Lord that the prisoners were come down. The Prince then ascended a throne of state, and sent for the prisoners in; who, when they came, did tremble before him, also they covered their faces with shame. Now, as they drew near to the place where he sat, they threw themselves down before him. Then said the Prince to the Captain Boanerges, "Bid the prisoners stand upon their feet." Then they stood trembling before him, and he said, "Are you the men that heretofore were the servants of Shaddai?" And they said, "Yes, Lord, yes." Then said the Prince again, "Are you the men that did suffer yourselves to be corrupted and defiled by that abominable one, Diabolus?" And they said, "We did more than suffer it, Lord; for we chose it of our own mind." The Prince asked further, saying, "Could you have been content that your slavery should have continued under his tyranny as long as you had lived?" Then said the prisoners, "Yes, Lord, yes; for his ways were pleasing to our flesh, and we were grown aliens to a better state." "And did you," said he, "when I came up against this town of Mansoul, heartily wish that I might not have the victory over you?" "Yes, Lord, yes," said they. Then said the Prince, "And what punishment is it, think you, that you deserve at my hand, for these and other your high and mighty sins?" And they said, "Both death and the deep, Lord; for we have deserved no less." He asked again, if they had aught to say for themselves why the sentence that they confessed that they had deserved, should not be passed upon them? And they said, "We can say nothing, Lord: thou art just, for we have sinned." Then said the Prince, "And for what are those ropes on your heads?" The prisoners answered, "These ropes are to bind us withal to the place of execution, if mercy be not pleasing in thy sight." So he further asked, if all the men in the town of Mansoul were in this confession, as they? And they answered, "All the natives, Lord; but for the Diabolonians that came into our town when the tyrant got possession of us, we can say nothing for them."

A Victory Proclaimed

Then the Prince commanded that an herald should be called, and that he should, in the midst and throughout the camp of Emmanuel, proclaim, and that with sound of trumpet, that the Prince, the Son of Shaddai, had in his Father's name, and for his Father's glory, gotten a perfect conquest and victory over Mansoul; and that the prisoners should follow him, and say Amen. So this was done as he had commanded. And presently the music that was in the upper region sounded melodiously, the captains that were in the camp shouted, and the soldiers did sing songs of triumph to the Prince; the colours waved in the wind, and great joy was everywhere, only it was wanting as yet in the hearts of the men of Mansoul.

Then the Prince called for the prisoners to come and to stand again before him, and they came and stood trembling. And he said unto them, "The sins, trespasses, iniquities, that you, with the whole town of Mansoul, have from time to time committed against my Father and me, I have power and commandment from my Father to forgive to the town of Mansoul, and do forgive you accordingly;" and having so said, he gave them, written in parchment, and sealed with seven seals, a large and general pardon, commanding my Lord Mayor, my Lord Will-be-will, and Mr. Recorder, to proclaim, and cause it to be proclaimed to-morrow, by that the sun was up, throughout the whole town of Mansoul.

Moreover, the Prince stript the prisoners of their mourning weeds, and gave them beauty for ashes, the oil of joy for mourning, and the garment of praise for the spirit of heaviness.

Then he gave to each of the three jewels of gold and precious stones, and took away their ropes, and put chains of gold about their necks, and earrings in their ears.

Now, the prisoners, when they did hear the gracious words of Prince Emmanuel, and had beheld all that was done unto them, fainted almost quite away; for the grace, the benefit, the pardon, was sudden, glorious, and so big, that they were not able, without staggering, to stand up under it. Yea, my Lord Will-be-will swooned outright; but the Prince stepped to him, put his everlasting arms under him, embraced him, kissed him, and bid him be of good cheer, for all should be performed according to his word. He also did kiss and embrace and smile upon the other two that were Will-be-will's companions, saying, "Take these as further tokens of my love, favour, and compassion to you; and I charge you that you, Mr. Recorder, tell in the town of Mansoul what you have heard and seen."

Then were their fetters broken to pieces before their faces, and cast into the air, and their steps were enlarged under them. Then they fell down at the feet of the Prince, and kissed his feet, and wetted them with tears; also they cried out with a mighty strong voice, saying, "Blessed be the glory of the Lord from this place." So they were bid rise up and go to the town, and tell to Mansoul what the Prince had done. He commanded also that one with a pipe and tabor should go and play before them all the way into the town of Mansoul. Then was fulfilled what they never looked for, and they were made to possess that which they never dreamt of.

The Prince also called for the noble Captain Credence, and commanded that he and some of his officers should march before the noblemen of Mansoul with flying colours into the town. He gave also unto Captain Credence a charge, that about that time that the Recorder did read the general pardon in the town of Mansoul, that at that very time he should with flying colours march in at Eye-gate with his ten thousands at his feet; and that he should so go until he came by the high street of the town, up to the castle gates, and that himself should take possession thereof against his Lord came thither. He commanded, moreover, that he should bid Captain Judgment and Captain Execution to leave the stronghold to him, and to withdraw from Mansoul, and to return into the camp with speed unto the Prince.

And now was the town of Mansoul also delivered from the terror of the first four captains and their men.

Well, I told you before how the prisoners were entertained by the noble Prince Emmanuel, and how they behaved themselves before him, and how he sent them away to their home with pipe and tabor going before them.

And now you must think that those of the town that had all this while waited to hear of their death, could not but be exercised with sadness of mind, and with thoughts that pricked like thorns. Nor could their thoughts be kept to any one point; the wind blew with them all this while at great uncertainties; yea, their hearts were like a balance that had been disquieted with shaking hand. But at last, as they with many a long look looked over the wall of Mansoul, they thought that they saw some returning to the town; and thought again, Who should they be too? Who should they be? At last they discerned that they were the prisoners; but can you imagine how their hearts were surprised with wonder, especially when they perceived also in what equipage and with what honour they were sent home? They went down to the camp in black, but they came back to the town in white; they went down to the camp in ropes, they came back in chains of gold; they went down to the camp with their feet in fetters, but came back with their steps enlarged under them; they went also to the camp looking for death, but they came back from thence with assurance of life; they went down to the camp with heavy hearts, but came back again with pipe and tabor playing before them. So, so soon as they were come to Eye-gate, the poor and tottering town of Mansoul adventured to give a shout; and they gave such a shout as made the captains in the Prince's army leap at the sound thereof. Alas, for them, poor hearts! who could blame them, since their dead friends were come to life again? for it was to them as life from the dead, to see the ancients of the town of Mansoul shine in such splendour. They looked for nothing but the axe and the block; but, behold, joy and gladness, comfort and consolation, and such melodious notes attending them, that was sufficient to make a sick man well.

So, when they came up, they saluted each other with "Welcome, welcome! and blessed be he that has spared you!" They added also, "We see it is well with you; but how must it go with the town of Mansoul? And will it go well with the town of Mansoul?" said they. Then answered them the Recorder and my Lord Mayor, "Oh, tidings! glad tidings! good tidings of good, and of great joy to poor Mansoul!" Then they gave another shout, that made the earth to ring again. After this, they inquired yet more particularly how things went in the camp, and what message they had from Emmanuel to the town. So they told them all passages that had happened to them at the camp, and everything that the Prince did to them. This made Mansoul wonder at the wisdom and grace of the Prince Emmanuel. Then they told them what they had received at his hands for the whole town of Mansoul, and the Recorder delivered it in these words:

"PARDON, PARDON, PARDON for Mansoul! and this shall Mansoul know tomorrow!" Then he commanded, and they went and summoned Mansoul to meet together in the market-place to-morrow, there to hear their general pardon read.

But who can think what a turn, what a change, what an alteration this hint of things did make in the countenance of the town of Mansoul! No man of Mansoul could sleep that night for joy; in every house there was joy and music, singing and making merry: telling and hearing of Mansoul's happiness was then all that Mansoul had to do; and this was the burden of all their song: "Oh! more of this at the rising of the sun; more of this to-morrow!" "Who thought yesterday," would one say, "that this day would have been such a day to us? And who thought, that saw our prisoners go down in irons, that they would have returned in chains of gold? Yea, they that judged themselves as they went to be judged of their judge, were by his mouth acquitted, not for that they were innocent, but of the Prince's mercy, and sent home with pipe and tabor. But is this the common custom of princes? Do they use to show such kind of favours to traitors? No; this is only peculiar to Shaddai, and unto Emmanuel his Son!"

Now morning drew on apace; wherefore the Lord Mayor, the Lord Will-be-will, and Mr. Recorder came down to the market-place at the time that the Prince had appointed, where the townsfolk were waiting for them; and when they came, they came in that attire and in that glory that the Prince had put them into the day before, and the street was lightened with their glory. So the Mayor, Recorder, and my Lord Will-be-will drew down to Mouth-gate, which was at the lower end of the market-place, because that of old time was the place where they used to read public matters. Thither, therefore, they came in their robes, and their tabret went before them. Now, the eagerness of the people to know the full of the matter was great.

Then the Recorder stood up upon his feet, and, first beckoning with his hand for silence, he read out with a loud voice the pardon. But when he came to these words, "The Lord, the Lord God, merciful and gracious, pardoning iniquity, transgressions, and sin;" and to them, "all manner of sin and blasphemy shall be forgiven," &c., they could not forbear leaping for joy. For this you must know, that there was conjoined herewith every man's name in Mansoul; also the seals of the pardon made a brave show.

When the Recorder had made an end of reading the pardon, the townsmen ran up upon the walls of the town, and leaped and skipped thereon for joy, and bowed themselves seven times with their faces towards Emmanuel's pavilion, and shouted out aloud for joy, and said, "Let Emmanuel live for ever!"

Then order was given to the young men in Mansoul that they should ring the bells for joy. So the bells did ring, and the people sing, and the music go in every house in Mansoul.

When the Prince had sent home the three prisoners of Mansoul with joy, and pipe, and tabor, he commanded his captains, with all the field-officers and soldiers throughout his army, to be ready in that morning that the Recorder should read the pardon in Mansoul, to do his further pleasure. So the morning, as I have showed, being come, just as the Recorder had made an end of reading the pardon, Emmanuel commanded that all the trumpets in the camp should sound, that the colours should be displayed, half of them upon Mount Gracious, and half of them upon Mount Justice. He commanded also that all the captains should show themselves in all their harness, and that the soldiers should shout for joy. Nor was Captain

Credence, though in the castle, silent in such a day; but he, from the top of the hold, showed himself with sound of trumpet to Mansoul and to the Prince's camp.

Thus have I showed you the manner and way that Emmanuel took to recover the town of Mansoul from under the hand and power of the tyrant Diabolus.

Now, when the Prince had completed these, the outward ceremonies of his joy, he again commanded that his captains and soldiers should show unto Mansoul some feats of war: so they presently addressed themselves to this work. But, oh! with what agility, nimbleness, dexterity, and bravery did these military men discover their skill in feats of war to the now gazing town of Mansoul!

They marched, they countermarched; they opened to the right and left; they divided and subdivided; they closed, they wheeled, made good their front and rear with their right and left wings, and twenty things more, with that aptness, and then were all as they were again, that they took, yea, ravished the hearts that were in Mansoul to behold it. But add to this, the handling of their arms, the managing of their weapons of war, were marvellously taking to Mansoul and me.

When this action was over, the whole town of Mansoul came out as one man to the Prince in the camp, to thank him and praise him for his abundant favour, and to beg that it would please his grace to come unto Mansoul with his men, and there to take up their quarters for ever; and this they did in most humble manner, bowing themselves seven times to the ground before him. Then said he, "All peace be to you." So the town came nigh, and touched with the hand the top of his golden sceptre; and they said, "Oh that the Prince Emmanuel, with his captains and men of war, would dwell in Mansoul for ever; and that his battering-rams and slings might be lodged in her for the use and service of the Prince, and for the help and strength of Mansoul. For," said they, "we have room for thee, we have room for thy men, we have also room for thy weapons of war, and a place to make a magazine for thy carriages. Do it, Emmanuel, and thou shalt be King and Captain in Mansoul for ever. Yea, govern thou also according to all the desire of thy soul, and make thou governors and princes under thee of thy captains and men of war, and we will become thy servants, and thy laws shall be our direction."

They added moreover, and prayed his Majesty to consider thereof; "For," said they, "if now, after all this grace bestowed upon us, thy miserable town of Mansoul, thou shouldest withdraw, thou and thy captains, from us, the town of Mansoul will die. Yea," said they, "our blessed Emmanuel, if thou shouldest depart from us, now thou hast done so much good for us, and showed so much mercy unto us, what will follow but that our joy will be as if it had not been, and our enemies will a second time come upon us with more rage than at the first? Wherefore, we beseech thee, O thou the desire of our eyes, and the strength and life of our poor town, accept of this motion that now we have made unto our Lord, and come and dwell in the midst of us, and let us be thy people. Besides, Lord, we do not know but that to this day many Diabolonians may yet be lurking in the town of Mansoul, and they will betray us, when thou shalt leave us, into the hand of Diabolus again; and who knows what designs, plots, or contrivances have passed betwixt them about these things already? loth we are to fall again into his horrible hands. Wherefore, let it please thee to accept of our palace for thy place of residence, and of the houses of the best men in our town for the reception of thy soldiers and their furniture."

Then, said the Prince, "If I come to your town, will you suffer me further to prosecute that which is in mine heart against mine enemies and yours? yea, will you help me in such undertakings?"

They answered, "We know not what we shall do; we did not think once that we should have been such traitors to Shaddai as we have proved to be. What then shall we say to our Lord? Let him put no trust in his servants; let the Prince dwell in our castle, and make of our town a garrison; let him set his noble captains and his warlike soldiers over us; yea, let him conquer us with his love, and overcome us with his grace, and then surely shall he be but with us, and help us, as he was and did that morning that our pardon was read unto us. We shall comply with this our Lord, and with his ways, and fall in with his word against the mighty.

"One word more, and thy servants have done, and in this will trouble our Lord no more. We know not the depth of the wisdom of thee, our Prince. Who could have thought, that had been ruled by his reason, that so much sweet as we do now enjoy should have come out of those bitter trials wherewith we were tried at the first? But, Lord, let light go before, and let love come after; yea, take us by the hand, and lead us by thy counsels, and let this always abide upon us, that all things shall be for the best for thy servants, and come to our Mansoul, and do as it pleaseth thee. Or, Lord, come to our Mansoul, do what thou wilt, so thou keepest us from sinning, and makest us serviceable to thy Majesty."

The Prince to Dwell in Mansoul

Then said the Prince to the town of Mansoul again, "Go, return to your houses in peace. I will willingly in this comply with your desires; I will remove my royal pavilion, I will draw up my forces before Eye-gate to-morrow, and so will march forwards into the town of Mansoul. I will possess myself of your castle of Mansoul, and will set my soldiers over you; yea, I will yet do things in Mansoul that cannot be paralleled in any nation, country, or kingdom under heaven."

Then did the men of Mansoul give a shout, and returned unto their houses in peace; they also told to their kindred and friends the good that Emmanuel had promised to Mansoul. "And to-morrow," said they, "he will march into our town, and take up his dwelling, he and his men, in Mansoul."

Then went out the inhabitants of the town of Mansoul with haste to the green trees and to the meadows, to gather boughs and flowers, therewith to strew the streets against their Prince, the Son of Shaddai, should come; they also made garlands and other fine works to betoken how joyful they were and should be to receive their Emmanuel into Mansoul; yea, they strewed the street quite from Eye-gate to the castle gate, the place where the Prince should be. They also prepared for his coming what music the town of Mansoul would afford, that they might play before him to the palace, his habitation.

So, at the time appointed, he makes his approach to Mansoul, and the gates were set open for him; there also the ancients and elders of Mansoul met him to salute him with a thousand welcomes. Then he arose and entered Mansoul, he and all his servants. The elders of Mansoul did also go dancing before him till he came to the castle gates. And this was the manner of his going up thither:—He was clad in his golden armour, he rode in his royal chariot, the trumpets sounded about him, the colours were displayed, his ten thousands went up at his feet, and the elders of Mansoul danced before him. And now were the walls of the famous town of Mansoul filled with the tramplings of the inhabitants thereof, and went up thither to view the approach of the blessed Prince and his royal army. Also the casements, windows, balconies, and tops of the houses, were all now filled with persons of all sorts, to behold how their town was to be filled with good.

Now, when he was come so far into the town as to the Recorder's house, he commanded that one should go to Captain Credence, to know whether the castle of Mansoul was prepared to entertain his royal presence (for the preparation of that was left to that captain), and word was brought that it was. Then was Captain Credence commanded also to come forth with his power to meet the Prince, the which was, as he had commanded, done; and he conducted him into the castle. This done, the Prince that night did lodge in the castle with his mighty captains and men of war, to the joy of the town of Mansoul.

Now, the next care of the townsfolk was how the captains and soldiers of the Prince's army should be quartered among them; and the care was not how they should shut their hands of them, but how they should fill their houses with them; for every man in Mansoul now had that esteem of Emmanuel and his men, that nothing grieved them more than because they were not enlarged enough, every one of them, to receive the whole army of the Prince; yea, they counted it their glory to be waiting upon them, and would, in those days, run at their bidding like lacqueys. At last they came to this result:—

1. That Captain Innocency should quarter at Mr. Reason's.

2. That Captain Patience should quarter at Mr. Mind's. This Mr. Mind was formerly the Lord Will-be-will's clerk in time of the late rebellion.

3. It was ordered that Captain Charity should quarter at Mr. Affection's house.

4. That Captain Good-Hope should quarter at my Lord Mayor's. Now, for the house of the Recorder, himself desired, because his house was next to the castle, and because from him it was ordered by the Prince that, if need

be, the alarm should be given to Mansoul,—it was, I say, desired by him that Captain Boanerges and Captain Conviction should take up their quarters with him, even they and all their men.

5. As for Captain Judgment and Captain Execution, my Lord Will-be-will took them and their men to him, because he was to rule under the Prince for the good of the town of Mansoul now, as he had before under the tyrant Diabolus for the hurt and damage thereof.

6. And throughout the rest of the town were quartered Emmanuel's forces; but Captain Credence, with his men, abode still in the castle. So the Prince, his captains and his soldiers, were lodged in the town of Mansoul.

Now the ancients and elders of the town of Mansoul thought that they never should have enough of the Prince Emmanuel; his person, his actions, his words and behaviour, were so pleasing, so taking, so desirable to them. Wherefore they prayed him, that though the castle of Mansoul was his place of residence (and they desired that he might dwell there for ever), yet that he would often visit the streets, houses, and people of Mansoul. "For," said they, "dread Sovereign, thy presence, thy looks, thy smiles, thy words, are the life, and strength, and sinews of the town of Mansoul."

Besides this, they craved that they might have, without difficulty or interruption, continual access to him (so for that very purpose he commanded that the gates should stand open), that they might there see the manner of his doings, the fortifications of the place, and the royal mansion-house of the Prince.

When he spake, they all stopped their mouths, and gave audience; and when he walked, it was their delight to imitate him in his goings.

Now upon a time Emmanuel made a feast for the town of Mansoul; and upon the feasting-day the townsfolk were come to the castle to partake of his banquet; and he feasted them with all manner of outlandish food, food that grew not in the fields of Mansoul, nor in all the whole kingdom of Universe: it was food that came from his Father's court. And so there was dish after dish set before them, and they were commanded freely to eat. But still, when a fresh dish was set before them, they would whisperingly say to each other, "What is it?" for they wist not what to call it. They drank also of the water that was made wine, and were very merry with him. There was music also all the while at the table; and man did eat angels' food, and had honey given him out of the rock. So Mansoul did eat the food that was peculiar to the court; yea, they had now thereof to the full.

I must not forget to tell you, that as at this table there were musicians, so they were not those of the country nor yet of the town of Mansoul; but they were the masters of the songs that were sung at the court of Shaddai.

Now after the feast was over, Emmanuel was for entertaining the town of Mansoul with some curious riddles of secrets drawn up by his Father's secretary, by the skill and wisdom of Shaddai: the like to these there is not in any kingdom. These riddles were made upon the King Shaddai himself, and upon Emmanuel his Son, and upon his wars and doings with Mansoul.

Emmanuel also expounded unto them some of those riddles himself; but, oh, how they were lightened! They saw what they never saw; they could not have thought that such rarities could have been couched in so few and such ordinary words. I told you before whom these riddles did concern; and as they were opened, the people did evidently see it was so. Yea, they did gather that the things themselves were a kind of portraiture, and that of Emmanuel himself; for when they read in the scheme where the riddles were writ, and looked in the face of the Prince, things looked so like the one to the other, that Mansoul could not forbear but say, "This is the lamb! this is the sacrifice! this is the rock! this is the red cow! this is the door! and this the way!" with a great many other things more.

And thus he dismissed the town of Mansoul. But can you imagine how the people of the corporation were taken with this entertainment? Oh! they were transported with joy, they were drowned with wonderment, while they saw, and understood, and considered what their Emmanuel entertained them withal, and what mysteries he opened to them. And when they were at home in their houses, and in their most retired places, they could not but sing of him and of his actions. Yea, so taken were the townsmen now with their Prince, that they would sing of him in their sleep.

Now, it was in the heart of the Prince Emmanuel to new-model the town of Mansoul, and to put it into such a condition as might be more pleasing to him, and that might best stand with the profit and security of the now flourishing town of Mansoul. He provided also against insurrections at home, and invasions from abroad, such love had he for the famous town of Mansoul.

Wherefore he first of all commanded that the great slings that were brought from his Father's court, when he came to the war of Mansoul, should be mounted, some upon the battlements of the castle, some upon the towers; for there were towers in the town of Mansoul, towers new-built by Emmanuel since he came hither. There was also an instrument, invented by Emmanuel, that was to throw stones from the castle of Mansoul, out at Mouth-gate; an instrument that could not be resisted, nor that would miss of execution. Wherefore, for the wonderful exploits that it did when used, it went without a name; and it was committed to the care of, and to be managed by, the brave captain, the Captain Credence, in case of war.

This done, Emmanuel called the Lord Will-be-will to him, and gave him in commandment to take care of the gates, the wall, and towers in Mansoul; also the Prince gave him the militia into his hand, and a special charge to withstand all insurrections and tumults that might be made in Mansoul against the peace of our Lord the King, and the peace and tranquillity of the town of Mansoul. He also gave him in commission, that if he found any of the Diabolonians lurking in any corner of the famous town of Mansoul, he should forthwith apprehend them and stay them, or commit them to safe custody, that they may be proceeded against according to law.

Then he called unto him the Lord Understanding, who was the old Lord Mayor, he that was put out of place when Diabolus took the town, and put him into his former office again, and it became his place for his lifetime.

He bid him also that he should build him a palace near Eye-gate, and that he should build it in fashion like a tower for defence. He bid him also that he should read in the Revelation of Mysteries all the days of his life, that he might know how to perform his office aright.

He also made Mr. Knowledge the Recorder, not of contempt to old Mr. Conscience, who had been Recorder before, but for that it was in his princely mind to confer upon Mr. Conscience another employ, of which he told the old gentleman he should know more hereafter.

Then he commanded that the image of Diabolus should be taken down from the place where it was set up, and that they should destroy it utterly, beating it into powder, and casting it unto the wind without the town wall; and that the image of Shaddai his Father should be set up again, with his own, upon the castle gates; and that it should be more fairly drawn than ever, forasmuch as both his Father and himself were come to Mansoul in more grace and mercy than heretofore. He would also that his name should be fairly engraven upon the front of the town, and that it should be done in the best of gold, for the honour of the town of Mansoul.

After this was done, Emmanuel gave out a commandment that those three great Diabolonians should be apprehended—namely, the two late Lord Mayors, to wit, Mr. Incredulity, Mr. Lustings, and Mr. Forget-Good, the Recorder. Besides these, there were some of them that Diabolus made burgesses and aldermen in Mansoul, that were committed to ward by the hand of the now valiant and now right noble, the brave Lord Will-be-will.

And these were their names:—Alderman Atheism, Alderman Hard-Heart, and Alderman False-Peace. The burgesses were Mr. No-Truth, Mr. Pitiless, Mr. Haughty, with the like. These were committed to close custody, and the gaoler's name was Mr. True-Man. This True-Man was one of those that Emmanuel brought with him from his Father's court, when at the first he made a war upon Diabolus in the town of Mansoul.

After this, the Prince gave a charge that the three strongholds that at the command of Diabolus the Diabolonians built in Mansoul, should be demolished and utterly pulled down; of which holds and their names, with their captains and governors, you read a little before. But this was long in doing, because of the largeness of the places, and because the stones, the timber, the iron, and all rubbish, were to be carried without the town. When this was done, the Prince gave order that the Lord Mayor and aldermen of Mansoul should call a court of judicature for the trial and execution of the Diabolonians in the corporation now under the charge of Mr. True-Man, the gaoler.

Now when the time was come, and the court set, commandment was sent to Mr. True-Man, the gaoler, to bring the prisoners down to the bar. Then were the prisoners brought down, pinioned and chained together, as the custom of the town of Mansoul was; so when they were presented before the Lord Mayor, the Recorder, and the rest of the honourable bench, first the jury was impanelled, and then the witnesses sworn. The names of the jury were these:—Mr. Belief, Mr. True-Heart, Mr. Upright, Mr. Hate-Bad,

Mr. Love-God, Mr. See-Truth, Mr. Heavenly-Mind, Mr. Moderate, Mr. Thankful, Mr. Good-Work, Mr. Zeal-for-God, and Mr. Humble.

The names of the witnesses were—Mr. Know-All, Mr. Tell-True, Mr. Hate-Lies, with my Lord Will-be-will and his man, if need were.

The Prisoners Brought to the Bar

So the prisoners were set to the bar. Then said Mr. Do-Right (for he was the Town-Clerk), "Set Atheism to the bar, gaoler." So he was set to the bar. Then said the Clerk, "Atheism, hold up thy hand. Thou art here indicted by the name of Atheism (an intruder upon the town of Mansoul), for that thou hast perniciously and doltishly taught and maintained that there is no God, and so no heed to be taken to religion. This thou hast done against the being, honour, and glory of the King, and against the peace and safety of the town of Mansoul. What sayest thou? Art thou guilty of this indictment, or not?"

Atheism. Not guilty.

Crier. Call Mr. Know-All, Mr. Tell-True, and Mr. Hate-Lies into the court.

So they were called, and they appeared.

Then said the Clerk, "You the witnesses for the King, look upon the prisoner at the bar: do you know him?"

Then said Mr. Know-All, "Yes, my lord, we know him: his name is Atheism; he has been a very pestilent fellow for many years in the miserable town of Mansoul."

Clerk. You are sure you know him?

Know. Know him! Yes, my lord; I have heretofore too often been in his company to be at this time ignorant of him. He is a Diabolonian, the son of a Diabolonian: I knew his grandfather and his father.

Clerk. Well said. He standeth here indicted by the name of Atheism, &c., and is charged that he hath maintained and taught that there is no God, and so no heed need be taken to any religion. What say you, the King's witnesses, to this? Is he guilty or not?

Know. My lord, I and he were once in Villain's Lane together, and he at that time did briskly talk of divers opinions; and then and there I heard him say that, for his part, he did believe that there was no God. "But," said he, "I can profess one, and be as religious too, if the company I am in, and the circumstances of other things," said he, "shall put me upon it."

Clerk. You are sure you heard him say thus?

Know. Upon mine oath, I heard him say thus.

Then said the Clerk, "Mr. Tell-True, what say you to the King's judges touching the prisoner at the bar?"

Tell. My lord, I formerly was a great companion of his, for the which I now repent me; and I have often heard him say, and that with very great stomachfulness, that he believed there was neither God, angel, nor spirit.

Clerk. Where did you hear him say so?

Tell. In Blackmouth Lane, and in Blasphemers' Row, and in many other places besides.

Clerk. Have you much knowledge of him?

Tell. I know him to be a Diabolonion, the son of a Diabolonian, and an horrible man to deny a Deity. His father's name was Never-be-Good, and he had more children than this Atheism. I have no more to say.

Clerk. Mr. Hate-Lies, look upon the prisoner at the bar: do you know him?

Hate. My lord, this Atheism is one of the vilest wretches that I ever came near, or had to do with in my life. I have heard him say that there is no God; I have heard him say that there is no world to come, no sin, nor punishment hereafter; and, moreover, I have heard him say that 'twas as good to go to a whore-house as to go to hear a sermon.

Clerk. Where did you hear him say these things?

Hate. In Drunkard's Row, just at Rascal Lane's End, at a house in which Mr. Impiety lived.

Clerk. Set him by, gaoler, and set Mr. Lustings to the bar. Mr. Lustings, thou art here indicted by the name of Lustings (an intruder upon the town of Mansoul), for that thou hast devilishly and traitorously taught, by practice and filthy words, that it is lawful and profitable to man to give way to his carnal desires; and that thou, for thy part, hast not, nor never wilt, deny thyself of any sinful delight as long as thy name is Lustings. How sayest thou? Art thou guilty of this indictment, or not?

Then said Mr. Lustings, "My lord, I am a man of high birth, and have been used to pleasures and pastimes of greatness. I have not been wont to be snub'd for my doings, but have been left to follow my will as if it were law. And it seems strange to me that I should this day be called into question for that, that not only I, but almost all men, do either secretly or openly countenance, love, and approve of."

Clerk. Sir, we concern not ourselves with your greatness (though the higher, the better you should have been); but we are concerned, and so are you now, about an indictment preferred against you. How say you? Are you guilty of it, or not?

Lust. Not guilty.

Clerk. Crier, call upon the witnesses to stand forth and give their evidence.

Crier. Gentlemen, you the witnesses for the King, come in and give in your evidence for our Lord the King against the prisoner at the bar.

Clerk. Come, Mr. Know-All, look upon the prisoner at the bar: do you know him?

Know. Yes, my lord, I know him.

Clerk. What is his name?

Know. His name is Lustings; he was the son of one Beastly, and his mother bare him in Flesh Street: she was one Evil-Concupiscence's daughter. I knew all the generation of them.

Clerk. Well said. You have here heard his indictment; what say you to it? Is he guilty of the things charged against him, or not?

Know. My lord, he has, as he saith, been a great man indeed, and greater in wickedness than by pedigree, more than a thousandfold.

Clerk. But what do you know of his particular actions, and especially with reference to his indictment?

Know. I know him to be a swearer, a liar, a Sabbath-breaker; I know him to be a fornicator and an unclean person; I know him to be guilty of abundance of evils. He has been, to my knowledge, a very filthy man.

Clerk. But where did he use to commit his wickedness? in some private corners, or more open and shamelessly?

Know. All the town over, my lord.

Clerk. Come, Mr. Tell-True, what have you to say for our Lord the King against the prisoner at the bar?

Tell. My lord, all that the first witness has said I know to be true, and a great deal more besides.

Clerk. Mr. Lustings, do you hear what these gentlemen say?

Lust. I was ever of opinion that the happiest life that a man could live on earth was, to keep himself back from nothing that he desired in the world; nor have I been false at any time to this opinion of mine, but have lived in the love of my notions all my days. Nor was I ever so churlish, having found such sweetness in them myself, as to keep the commendations of them from others.

Then said the Court, "There hath proceeded enough from his own mouth to lay him open to condemnation; wherefore set him by, gaoler, and set Mr. Incredulity to the bar."

Incredulity set to the bar.

Clerk. Mr. Incredulity, thou art here indicted by the name of Incredulity (an intruder upon the town of Mansoul), for that thou hast feloniously and wickedly, and that when thou wert an officer in the town of Mansoul, made head, against the captains of the great King Shaddai when they came and demanded possession of Mansoul; yea, thou didst bid defiance to the name, forces, and cause of the King, and didst also, as did Diabolus thy captain, stir up and encourage the town of Mansoul to make head against and resist the said force of the King. What sayest thou to this indictment? Art thou guilty of it, or not?

Then said Incredulity, "I know not Shaddai; I love my old prince; I thought it my duty to be true to my trust, and to do what I could to possess the minds of the men of Mansoul to do their utmost to resist strangers and foreigners, and with might to fight against them. Nor have I, nor shall I change my opinion for fear of trouble, though you at present are possessed of place and power."

Then said the Court, "The man, as you see, is incorrigible; he is for maintaining his villainies by stoutness of words, and his rebellion with impudent confidence; and therefore set him by, gaoler, and set Mr. Forget-Good to the bar."

Forget-Good set to the bar.

Clerk. Mr. Forget-Good, thou art here indicted by the name of Forget-

Good (an intruder upon the town of Mansoul), for that thou, when the whole affairs of the town of Mansoul were in thy hand, didst utterly forget to serve them in what was good, and didst fall in with the tyrant Diabolus against Shaddai the King, against his captains and all his host, to the dishonour of Shaddai, the breach of his law, and the endangering of the destruction of the famous town of Mansoul. What sayest thou to this indictment? Art thou guilty, or not guilty?

Then said Forget-Good, "Gentlemen, and at this time my judges, as to the indictment by which I stand of several crimes accused before you, pray attribute my forgetfulness to mine age, and not to my wilfulness; to the craziness of my brain, and not to the carelessness of my mind; and then I hope I may be by your charity excused from great punishment, though I be guilty."

Then said the Court, "Forget-Good, Forget-Good, thy forgetfulness of good was not simply of frailty, but of purpose, and for that thou didst loathe to keep virtuous things in thy mind. What was bad thou couldst retain, but what was good thou couldst not abide to think of: thy age therefore, and thy pretended craziness, thou makest use of to blind the court withal, and as a cloak to cover thy knavery. But let us hear what the witnesses have to say for the King, against the prisoner at the bar. Is he guilty of this indictment, or not?"

Hate. My lord, I have heard this Forget-Good say, that he could never abide to think of goodness, no, not for a quarter of an hour.

Clerk. Where did you hear him say so?

Hate. In All-base Lane, at a house next door to the sign of the Conscience Seared with a Hot Iron.

Clerk. Mr. Know-All, what can you say for our Lord the King against the prisoner at the bar?

Know. My Lord, I know this man well. He is a Diabolonian, the son of a Diabolonian: his father's name was Love-Naught; and for him, I have often heard him say, that he counted the very thoughts of goodness the most burdensome thing in the world.

Clerk. Where have you heard him say these words?

Know. In Flesh Lane, right opposite to the church.

Then said the Clerk, "Come, Mr. Tell-True, give in your evidence concerning the prisoner at the bar, about that for which he stands here, as you see, indicted before this most honourable Court."

Tell. My lord, I have heard him often say, he had rather think of the vilest thing than of what is contained in the Holy Scriptures.

Clerk. Where did you hear him say such grievous words?

Tell. Where? In a great many places, particularly in Nauseous Street, in the house of one Shameless, and in Filth Lane, at the sign of the Reprobate, next door to the Descent into the Pit.

Court. Gentlemen, you have heard the indictment, his plea, and the testimony of the witnesses. Gaoler, set Mr. Hard-Heart to the bar.

He is set to the bar.

Clerk. Mr. Hard-Heart, thou art here indicted by the name of Hard-Heart (an intruder upon the town of Mansoul), for that thou didst most desperately and wickedly possess the town of Mansoul with impenitency and obdurateness; and didst keep them from remorse and sorrow for their evils, all the time of their apostacy from and rebellion against the blessed King Shaddai. What saist thou to this indictment? Art thou guilty, or not guilty?

Hard. My lord, I never knew what remorse or sorrow meant in all my life. I am impenetrable, I care for no man; nor can I be pierced with men's griefs; their groans will not enter into my heart. Whomever I mischief, whomever I wrong, to me it is music, when to others mourning.

Court. You see the man is a right Diabolonian, and has convicted himself. Set him by, gaoler, and set Mr. False-Peace to the bar.

False-Peace set to the bar.

"Mr. False-Peace, thou art here indicted by the name of False-Peace (an intruder upon the town of Mansoul), for that thou didst most wickedly and satanically bring, hold, and keep the town of Mansoul, both in her apostacy and in her hellish rebellion, in a false, groundless, and dangerous peace, and damnable security, to the dishonour of the King, the transgression of his law, and the great damage of the town of Mansoul. What saist thou? Art thou guilty of this indictment, or not?"

Then said Mr. False-Peace, "Gentlemen, and you now appointed to be my judges, I acknowledge that my name is Mr. Peace; but that my name is False-Peace I utterly deny. If your honours shall please to send for any that do intimately know me, or for the midwife that laid my mother of me, or for the gossips that were at my christening, they will, any or all of them, prove that my name is not False-Peace, but Peace. Wherefore I cannot plead to this indictment, forasmuch as my name is not inserted therein; and as is my true name, so are also my conditions. I was always a man that loved to live at quiet, and what I loved myself, that I thought others might love also. Wherefore, when I saw any of my neighbours to labour under a disquieted mind, I endeavoured to help them what I could; and instances of this good temper of mine many I could give; as—

"1. When, at the beginning, our town of Mansoul did decline the ways of Shaddai, they, some of them, afterwards began to have disquieting reflections upon themselves, for what they had done; but I, as one troubled to see them disquieted, presently sought out means to get them quiet again.

"2. When the ways of the old world, and of Sodom, were in fashion, if anything happened to molest those that were for the customs of the present times, I laboured to make them quiet again, and to cause them to act without molestation.

"3. To come nearer home: when the wars fell out between Shaddai and Diabolus, if at any time I saw any of the town of Mansoul afraid of destruction, I often used, by some way, device, invention, or other, to labour to bring them to peace again. Wherefore, since I have been always a man of so virtuous a temper as some say a peacemaker is, and if a peacemaker be so deserving a man as some have been bold to attest he is, then let me, gentlemen, be accounted by you, who have a great name for justice and equity in Mansoul, for a man that deserveth not this inhuman way of treatment, but liberty, and also a licence to seek damage of those that have been my accusers."

Then said the Clerk, "Crier, make a proclamation."

Crier. O yes! Forasmuch as the prisoner at the bar hath denied his name to be that which is mentioned in the indictment, the Court requireth, that if there be any in this place that can give information to the Court of the original and right name of the prisoner, they would come forth and give in their evidence; for the prisoner stands upon his own innocency.

Then came two into the court, and desired that they might have leave to speak what they knew concerning the prisoner at the bar: the name of the one was Search-Truth, and the name of the other Vouch-Truth. So the Court demanded of these men if they knew the prisoner, and what they could say concerning him, "for he stands," said they, "upon his own vindication."

Then said Mr. Search-Truth, "My lord, I——"

Court. Hold! give him his oath.

Then they sware him. So he proceeded.

Search. My lord, I know and have known this man from a child, and can attest that his name is False-Peace. I knew his father: his name was Mr. Flatter; and his mother, before she was married, was called by the name of Mrs. Soothe-Up; and these two, when they came together, lived not long without this son; and when he was born, they called his name False-Peace. I was his play-fellow, only I was somewhat older than he; and when his mother did use to call him home from his play, she used to say, "False-Peace, False-Peace, come home quick, or I'll fetch you." Yea, I knew him when he sucked; and though I was then but little, yet I can remember, that when his mother did use to sit at the door with him or did play with him in her arms, she would call him, twenty times together, "My little False-Peace! my pretty False-Peace!" and, "Oh, my sweet rogue, False-Peace!" and again, "Oh, my little bird, False-Peace!" and, "How do I love my child!" The gossips also know it is thus, though he has had the face to deny it in open court.

Then Mr. Vouch-Truth was called upon to speak what he knew of him. So they sware him.

Then said Mr. Vouch-Truth, "My lord, all that the former witness hath said is true. His name is False-Peace, the son of Mr. Flatter, and of Mrs. Soothe-Up, his mother; and I have in former times seen him angry with those that have called him anything else but False-Peace, for he would say that all such did mock and nickname him; but this was in the time when Mr. False-Peace was a great man, and when the Diabolonians were the brave men in Mansoul."

The Court Sums Up

Court. Gentlemen, you have heard what these two men have sworn against the prisoner at the bar. And now, Mr. False-Peace, to you: you have denied your name to be False-Peace, yet you see that these honest men have sworn that that is your name. As to your plea, in that you are quite besides the matter of your indictment: you are not by it charged for evil-doing because you are a man of peace, or a peacemaker among your neighbours; but for that you did wickedly and satanically bring, keep, and hold the town of Mansoul, both under its apostacy from and in its rebellion against its King, in a false, lying, and damnable peace, contrary to the law of Shaddai, and to the hazard of the destruction of the then miserable town of Mansoul. All that you have pleaded for yourself is, that you have denied your name, &c.; but here, you see, we have witnesses to prove that you are the man. For the peace that you so much boast of making among your neighbours, know that peace that is not a companion of truth and holiness, but that which is without this foundation, is grounded upon a lie, and is both deceitful and damnable, as also the great Shaddai hath said. Thy plea, therefore, hath not delivered thee from what by the indictment thou art charged with, but rather it doth fasten all upon thee. But thou shalt have very fair play. Let us call the witnesses that are to testify as to matter of fact, and see what they have to say for our Lord the King against the prisoner at the bar.

Clerk. Mr. Know-All, what say you for our Lord the King against the prisoner at the bar?

Know. My lord, this man hath of a long time made it, to my knowledge, his business to keep the town of Mansoul in a sinful quietness in the midst of all her lewdness, filthiness, and turmoils, and hath said, and that in my hearing, "Come, come, let us fly from all trouble, on what ground soever it comes, and let us be for a quiet and peaceable life, though it wanteth a good foundation."

Clerk. Come, Mr. Hate-Lies, what have you to say?

Hate. My lord, I have heard him say, that peace, though in a way of unrighteousness, is better than trouble with truth.

Clerk. Where did you hear him say this?

Hate. I heard him say it in Folly Yard, at the house of one Mr. Simple, next door to the sign of the Self-Deceiver. Yea, he hath said this to my knowledge twenty times in that place.

Clerk. We may spare further witness; this evidence is plain and full. Set him by, gaoler, and set Mr. No-Truth to the bar.

Mr. No-Truth, thou art here indicted by the name of No-Truth (an intruder upon the town of Mansoul), for that thou hast always, to the dishonour of Shaddai, and the endangering of the utter ruin of the famous town of Mansoul, set thyself to deface and utterly to spoil all the remainders of the law and image of Shaddai that have been found in Mansoul after her deep apostacy from her King to Diabolus, the envious tyrant. What saist thou? art thou guilty of this indictment, or not?

No. Not guilty, my lord.

Then the witnesses were called, and Mr. Know-All did first give in his evidence against him.

Know. My lord, this man was at the pulling down of the image of Shaddai; yea, this is he that did it with his own hands. I myself stood by and saw him do it, and he did it at the commandment of Diabolus. Yea, this Mr. No-Truth did more than this, he did also set up the horned image of the beast Diabolus in the same place. This also is he that, at the bidding of Diabolus, did rend and tear, and cause to be consumed, all that he could of the remainders of the law of the King, even whatever he could lay his hands on in Mansoul.

Clerk. Who saw him do this besides yourself?

Hate. I did, my lord, and so did many more besides; for this was not done by stealth, or in a corner, but in the open view of all; yea, he chose himself to do it publicly, for he delighted in the doing of it.

Clerk. Mr. No-Truth, how could you have the face to plead not guilty, when you were so manifestly the doer of all this wickedness?

No. Sir, I thought I must say something, and as my name is, so I speak: I have been advantaged thereby before now, and did not know but by speaking no truth I might have reaped the same benefit now.

Clerk. Set him by, gaoler, and set Mr. Pitiless to the bar.

Mr. Pitiless, thou art here indicted by the name of Pitiless (an intruder upon the town of Mansoul), for that thou didst most traitorously and wickedly shut up all bowels of compassion, and wouldest not suffer poor Mansoul to condole her own misery when she had apostatized from her rightful King, but didst evade and at all times turn her mind awry from those thoughts that had in them a tendency to lead her to repentance. What saist thou to this indictment? guilty or not guilty?

"Not guilty of pitilessness: all I did was to cheer up, according to my name, for my name is not Pitiless, but Cheer-Up; and I could not abide to see Mansoul inclined to melancholy."

Clerk. How! do you deny your name, and say it is not Pitiless, but Cheer-Up? Call for the witnesses. What say you, the witnesses, to this plea?

Know. My lord, his name is Pitiless; so he hath written himself in all papers of concern wherein he has had to do. But these Diabolonians love to counterfeit their names: Mr. Covetousness covers himself with the name of Good-Husbandry, or the like; Mr. Pride can, when need is, call himself Mr. Neat, Mr. Handsome, or the like; and so of all the rest of them.

Clerk. Mr. Tell-True, what say you?

Tell. His name is Pitiless, my lord. I have known him from a child, and he hath done all that wickedness whereof he stands charged in the indictment; but there is a company of them that are not acquainted with the danger of damning, therefore they call all those melancholy that have serious thoughts as to how that state should be shunned by them.

Clerk. Set Mr. Haughty to the bar, gaoler.

Mr. Haughty, thou art here indicted by the name of Haughty (an intruder upon the town of Mansoul), for that thou didst most traitorously and devilishly teach the town of Mansoul to carry it loftily and stoutly against the summons that was given them by the captains of the King Shaddai. Thou didst also teach the town of Mansoul to speak contemptuously and vilifyingly of their great King Shaddai; and didst, moreover, encourage, both by words and example, Mansoul to take up arms both against the King and his Son Emmanuel. How saist thou; art thou guilty of this indictment or not?

Haughty. Gentlemen, I have always been a man of courage and valour, and have not used, when under the greatest clouds, to sneak or hang down the head like a bulrush; nor did it at all at any time please me to see men vail their bonnets to those that have opposed them; yea, though their adversaries seemed to have ten times the advantage of them. I did not use to consider who was my foe, nor what the cause was in which I was engaged. It was enough to me if I carried it bravely, fought like a man, and came off a victor.

Court. Mr. Haughty, you are not here indicted for that you have been a valiant man, nor for your courage and stoutness in time of distress, but for that you have made use of this your pretended valour to draw the town of Mansoul into acts of rebellion, both against the great King and Emmanuel his Son. This is the crime and the thing wherewith thou art charged in and by the indictment.

But he made no answer to that.

Now, when the Court had thus far proceeded against the prisoners at the bar, then they put them over to the verdict of their jury, to whom they did apply themselves after this manner:—

"Gentlemen of the jury, you have been here, and have seen these men; you have heard their indictments, their pleas, and what the witnesses have testified against them: now what remains is, that you do forthwith withdraw yourself to some place, where, without confusion, you may consider of what verdict, in a way of truth and righteousness, you ought to bring in for the King against them, and so bring it in accordingly."

Then the jury—to wit, Mr. Belief, Mr. True-Heart, Mr. Upright, Mr. Hate-Bad, Mr. Love-God, Mr. See-Truth, Mr. Heavenly-Mind, Mr. Moderate, Mr. Thankful, Mr. Humble, Mr. Good-Work, and Mr. Zeal-for-God—withdrew themselves in order to their work. Now, when they were shut up by themselves, they fell to discourse among themselves in order to the drawing up of their verdict.

And thus Mr. Belief (for he was the foreman) began: "Gentlemen," quoth he, "for the men, the prisoners at the bar, for my part I believe that they all deserve death." "Very right," said Mr. True-Heart; "I am wholly of your opinion." "Oh, what a mercy is it," said Mr. Hate-Bad, "that such villains as these are apprehended!" "Ay! ay!" said Mr. Love-God, "this is one of the joyfullest days that ever I saw in my life." Then said Mr. See-Truth, "I know that if we judge them to death, our verdict shall stand before Shaddai himself." "Nor do I at all question it," said Mr. Heavenly-Mind; he said, moreover, "When all such beasts as these are cast out of Mansoul, what a goodly town will it be then!" Then said Mr. Moderate, "It is not my manner to pass my judgment with rashness; but for these, their crimes are so notorious, and the witness so palpable, that that man must be wilfully blind who saith the prisoners ought not to die." "Blessed be God," said Mr. Thankful, "that the traitors are in safe custody!" "And I join with you in this upon my bare knees," said Mr. Humble. "I am glad also," said Mr. Good-Work. Then said the warm man, and true-hearted, Mr. Zeal-for-God, "Cut them off; they have been the plague and have sought the destruction of Mansoul."

Thus, therefore, being all agreed in their verdict, they came instantly into the court.

Clerk. Gentlemen of the jury, answer all to your names:—Mr. Belief, one: Mr. True-Heart, two: Mr. Upright, three: Mr. Hate-Bad, four: Mr. Love-God, five: Mr. See-Truth, six: Mr. Heavenly-Mind, seven: Mr. Moderate, eight: Mr. Thankful, nine: Mr. Humble, ten: Mr. Good-Work, eleven: and Mr. Zeal-for-God, twelve. Good men and true, stand together in your verdict: are you all agreed?

Jury. Yes, my lord.

Clerk. Who shall speak for you?

Jury. Our foreman.

Clerk. You, the gentlemen of the jury, being impanelled for our Lord the King, to serve here in a matter of life and death, have heard the trials of each of these men, the prisoners at the bar: what say you? are they guilty of that, and those crimes for which they stand here indicted, or are they not guilty?

Foreman. Guilty, my lord.

Clerk. Look to your prisoners, gaoler.

This was done in the morning, and in the afternoon they received the sentence of death according to the law.

The gaoler, therefore, having received such a charge, put them all in the inward prison, to preserve them there till the day of execution, which was to be the next day in the morning.

Incredulity Breaks Prison

But now to see how it happened: one of the prisoners, Incredulity by name, in the interim betwixt the sentence and the time of execution, brake prison, and made his escape, and gets him away quite out of the town of Mansoul, and lay lurking in such places and holes as he might, until he should again have opportunity to do the town of Mansoul a mischief for their thus handling of him as they did.

Now when Mr. True-Man, the gaoler, perceived that he had lost his prisoner, he was in a heavy taking, because that prisoner was, to speak on, the very worst of all the gang; wherefore, first he goes and acquaints my Lord Mayor, Mr. Recorder, and my Lord Will-be-will, with the matter, and to get of them an order to make search for him throughout the town of Mansoul. So an order he got, and search was made, but no such man could now be found in all the town of Mansoul.

All that could be gathered was, that he had lurked a while about the outside of the town, and that here and there one or other had a glimpse of him as he did make his escape out of Mansoul; one or two also did affirm that they saw him without the town, going apace quite over the plain. Now when he was quite gone, it was affirmed by one Mr. Did-See, that he ranged all over dry places, till he met with Diabolus his friend; and where should they meet one another but just upon Hell-gate Hill?

But oh! what a lamentable story did the old gentleman tell to Diabolus concerning what sad alteration Emmanuel had made in Mansoul!

As first: how Mansoul had after some delays, received a general pardon at the hands of Emmanuel, and that they had invited him into the town, and that they had given him the castle for his possession. He said, moreover, that they had called his soldiers into the town, coveted who should quarter the most of them; they also entertained him with the timbrel, song, and dance. "But that," said Incredulity, "which is the sorest vexation to me is, that he hath pulled down, O father, thy image, and set up his own; pulled down thy officers, and set up his own. Yea, and Will-be-will, that rebel, who, one would have thought, should never have turned from us, he is now in as great favour with Emmanuel as ever he was with thee. But besides all this, this Will-be-will has received a special commission from his Master to search for, to apprehend, and to put to death all, and all manner of Diabolonians that he shall find in Mansoul; yea, and this Will-be-will has taken and committed to prison already eight of my lord's most trusty friends in Mansoul. Nay, further, my lord, with grief I speak it, they have been all arraigned, condemned, and, I doubt, before this executed in Mansoul. I told my lord of eight, and myself was the ninth, who should assuredly have drunk of the same cup, but that, through craft, I, as thou seest, have made mine escape from them."

When Diabolus had heard this lamentable story, he yelled, and snuffed up the wind like a dragon, and made the sky to look dark with his roaring; he also sware that he would try to be revenged on Mansoul for this. So they, both he and his old friend Incredulity, concluded to enter into great consultation how they might get the town of Mansoul again.

Now before this time, the day was come in which the prisoners in Mansoul were to be executed. So they were brought to the cross, and that by Mansoul, in most solemn manner, for the Prince said that this should be done by the hand of the town of Mansoul, "that I may see," said he, "the forwardness of my now redeemed Mansoul to keep my word, and to do my commandments; and that I may bless Mansoul in doing this deed. Proof of sincerity pleases me well; let Mansoul therefore first lay their hands upon these Diabolonians to destroy them."

So the town of Mansoul slew them, according to the word of their Prince; but when the prisoners were brought to the cross to die, you can hardly believe what troublesome work Mansoul had of it to put the Diabolonians to death; for the men knowing that they must die, and every one of them having implacable enmity in their hearts to Mansoul, what did they but took courage at the cross, and there resisted the men of the town of Mansoul? Wherefore the men of Mansoul were forced to cry out for help to the captains and men of war. Now, the great Shaddai had a secretary in the town, and he was a great lover of the men of Mansoul, and he was at the place of execution also; so he, hearing the men of Mansoul cry out against the strugglings and unruliness of the prisoners, rose up from his place, and came and put his hands upon the hands of the men of Mansoul. So they crucified the Diabolonians that had been a plague, a grief, and an offence to the town of Mansoul.

Now when this good work was done, the Prince came down to see, to visit, and to speak comfortably to the men of Mansoul, and to strengthen their hands in such work. And he said to them, that by this act of theirs he had proved them, and found them to be lovers of his person, observers of his laws, and such as had also respect to his honour. He said, moreover (to show them that they by this should not be losers, nor their town weakened by the loss of them), that he would make them another captain, and that of one of themselves. And that this captain should be the ruler of a thousand, for the good and benefit of the now flourishing town of Mansoul.

So he called one to him whose name was Waiting, and bid him, "Go quickly up to the castle gate, and inquire there for one Mr. Experience, that waiteth upon that noble captain, the Captain Credence, and bid him come hither to me." So the messenger that waited upon the good Prince Emmanuel went and said as he was commanded. Now, the young gentleman was waiting to see the captain train and muster his men in the castle yard. Then said Mr. Waiting to him, "Sir, the Prince would that you should come down to his highness forthwith." So he brought him down to Emmanuel, and he came and made obeisance before him. Now, the men of the town knew Mr. Experience well, for he was born and bred in Mansoul; they also knew him to be a man of conduct, of valour, and a person prudent in matters; he was also a comely person, well spoken, and very successful in his undertakings.

Wherefore the hearts of the townsmen were transported with joy, when they saw that the Prince himself was so taken with Mr. Experience, that he would needs make him a captain over a band of men.

So with one consent they bowed the knee before Emmanuel, and with a shout said, "Let Emmanuel live for ever!" Then said the Prince to the young gentleman whose name was Mr. Experience, "I have thought good to confer upon thee a place of trust and honour in this my town of Mansoul." Then the young man bowed his head and worshipped. "It is," said Emmanuel, "that thou shouldest be a captain, a captain over a thousand men in my beloved town of Mansoul." Then, said the captain, "Let the King live." So the Prince gave out orders forthwith to the King's secretary, that he should draw up for Mr. Experience a commission to make him a captain over a thousand men; "and let it be brought to me," said he, "that I may set to my seal." So it was done as it was commanded. The commission was drawn up, brought to Emmanuel, and he set his seal thereto. Then, by the hand of Mr. Waiting, he sent it away to the captain.

Now, so soon as the captain had received his commission, he sounded his trumpet for volunteers, and young men came to him apace; yea, the greatest and chief men in the town sent their sons to be listed under his command. Thus Captain Experience came under command to Emmanuel, for the good of the town of Mansoul. He had for his lieutenant one Mr. Skilful, and for his cornet one Mr. Memory. His under-officers I need not name. His colours were the white colours for the town of Mansoul, and his scutcheon was the dead lion and dead bear. So the Prince returned to his royal palace again.

Now, when he was returned thither, the elders of the town of Mansoul —to wit, the Lord Mayor, the Recorder, and the Lord Will-be-will—went to congratulate him, and in special way to thank him for his love, care, and the tender compassion which he showed to his ever-obliged town of Mansoul. So, after a while, and some sweet communion between them, the townsmen having solemnly ended their ceremony, returned to their place again.

Emmanuel also at this time appointed them a day wherein he would renew their charter, yea, wherein he would renew and enlarge it, mending several faults therein, that Mansoul's yoke might be yet more easy. And this he did without any desire of theirs, even of his own frankness and noble mind. So when he had sent for and seen their old one, he laid it by, and said, "Now that which decayeth and waxeth old is ready to vanish away." He said, moreover, "The town of Mansoul shall have another, a better, a new one, more steady and firm by far." An epitome hereof take as follows:—

"Emmanuel, Prince of Peace, and a great lover of the town of Mansoul: I do, in the name of my Father, and of mine own clemency, give, grant, and bequeath to my beloved town of Mansoul—

"First: Free, full, and everlasting forgiveness of all wrongs, injuries, and offences done by them against my Father, me, their neighbour, or themselves.

"Secondly: I do give them the holy law and my testament, with all that therein is contained, for their everlasting comfort and consolation.

"Thirdly: I do also give them a portion of the selfsame grace and goodness that dwells in my Father's heart and mine.

"Fourthly: I do give, grant, and bestow upon them freely, the world and what is therein, for their good; and they shall have that power over them, as shall stand with the honour of my Father, my glory, and their comfort; yea, I grant them the benefits of life and death, and of things present and things to come. This privilege no other city, town, or corporation shall have, but my Mansoul only.

"Fifthly: I do give and grant them leave, and free access to me in my palace at all seasons, to my palace above or below, there to make known their wants to me; and I give them, moreover, a promise that I will hear and redress all their grievances.

"Sixthly: I do give, grant to, and invest the town of Mansoul with full power and authority to seek out, take, enslave, and destroy all, and all manner of Diabolonians that at any time, from whence soever, shall be found straggling in or about the town of Mansoul.

"Seventhly: I do further grant to my beloved town of Mansoul that they shall have authority not to suffer any foreigner, or stranger, or their seed, to be free in, and of the blessed town of Mansoul, nor to share in the excellent privileges thereof. But that all the grants, privileges, and immunities that I bestow upon the famous town of Mansoul, shall be for those the old natives, and true inhabitants thereof; to them, I say, and to their right seed after them.

"But all Diabolonians, of what sort, birth, country, or kingdom soever, shall be debarred a share therein."

So when the town of Mansoul had received, at the hand of Emmanuel, their gracious charter (which in itself is infinitely more large than by this lean epitome is set before you), they carried it to audience, that is, to the market-place, and there Mr. Recorder read it in presence of all the people. This being done, it was had back to the castle gates, and there fairly engraven upon the doors thereof, and laid in letters of gold, to the end that the town of Mansoul, with all the people thereof, might have it always in their view, or might go where they might see what a blessed freedom their Prince had bestowed upon them, that their joy might be increased in themselves, and their love renewed to their great and good Emmanuel.

But what joy, what comfort, what consolation think you, did now possess the hearts of the men of Mansoul! The bells ringed, the minstrels played, the people danced, the captains shouted, the colours waved in the wind, and the silver trumpets sounded; and the Diabolonians now were glad to hide their heads, for they looked like them that had been long dead.

A Ministry Established

When this was over, the Prince sent again for the elders of the town of Mansoul, and communed with them about a ministry that he intended to establish among them; such a ministry that might open unto them, and that might instruct them in the things that did concern their present and future state.

"For," said he, "you of yourselves, unless you have teachers and guides, will not be able to know, and, if not to know, to be sure not to do the will of my Father."

At this news, when the elders of Mansoul brought it to the people, the whole town came running together (for it pleased them well, as whatever the Prince now did pleased the people), and all with one consent implored his Majesty that he would forthwith establish such a ministry among them as might teach them both law and judgment, statute and commandment; that they might be documented in all good and wholesome things. So he told them that he would grant them their requests, and would establish two among them: one that was of his Father's court, and one that was a native of Mansoul.

"He that is from the court," said he, "is a person of no less quality and dignity than my Father and I; and he is the Lord Chief Secretary of my Father's house: for he is, and always has been, the chief dictator of my

Father's laws, a person altogether well skilled in all mysteries, and knowledge of mysteries, as is my Father, or as myself is. Indeed he is one with us in nature, and also as to loving of, and being faithful to, and in the eternal concerns of the town of Mansoul.

"And this is he," said the Prince, "that must be your chief teacher; for it is he, and he only, that can teach you clearly in all high and supernatural things. He, and he only, it is that knows the ways and methods of my Father at court, nor can any like him show how the heart of my Father is at all times, in all things, upon all occasions towards Mansoul; for as no man knows the things of a man but that spirit of a man which is in him, so the things of my Father knows no man but this his high and mighty Secretary. Nor can any, as he, tell Mansoul how and what they shall do to keep themselves in the love of my Father. He also it is that can bring lost things to your remembrance, and that can tell you things to come. This teacher, therefore, must of necessity have the pre-eminence, both in your affections and judgment, before your other teacher: his personal dignity, the excellency of his teaching, also the great dexterity that he hath to help you to make and draw up petitions to my Father for your help, and to his pleasing, must lay obligations upon you to love him, fear him, and to take heed that you grieve him not.

"This person can put life and vigour into all he says; yea, and can also put it into your hearts. This person can make seers of you, and can make you tell what shall be hereafter. By this person you must frame all your petitions to my Father and me; and without his advice and counsel first obtained, let nothing enter into the town or castle of Mansoul, for that may disgust and grieve this noble person.

"Take heed, I say, that you do not grieve this minister; for, if you do, he may fight against you; and should he once be moved by you to set himself against you in battle array, that will distress you more than if twelve legions should from my Father's court be sent to make war with you.

"But, as I said, if you shall hearken unto him, and shall love him; if you shall devote yourselves to his teaching, and shall seek to have converse, and to maintain communion with him, you shall find him ten times better than the whole world is to any; yea, he will shed abroad the love of my Father in your hearts, and Mansoul will be the wisest and most blessed of all people."

Then did the Prince call unto him the old gentleman who before had been the Recorder of Mansoul, Mr. Conscience by name, and told him, that forasmuch as he was well skilled in the law and government of the town of Mansoul, and was also well spoken, and could pertinently deliver to them his Master's will in all terrene and domestic matters, therefore he would also make him a minister for, in, and to the goodly town of Mansoul, in all the laws, statutes, and judgments of the famous town of Mansoul. "And thou must," said the Prince, "confine thyself to the teaching of moral virtues, to civil and natural duties; but thou must not attempt to presume to be a revealer of those high and supernatural mysteries that are kept close in the bosom of Shaddai my Father; for those things knows no man, nor can any reveal them but my Father's Secretary only.

"Thou art a native of the town of Mansoul, but the Lord Secretary is a native with my Father; wherefore, as thou hast knowledge of the laws and customs of the corporation, so he of the things and will of my Father.

"Wherefore, O Mr. Conscience, although I have made thee a minister and a preacher in the town of Mansoul, yet as to the things which the Lord Secretary knoweth, and shall teach to this people, there thou must be his scholar and a learner, even as the rest of Mansoul are.

"Thou must therefore, in all high and supernatural things, go to him for information and knowledge; for though there be a spirit in man, this person's inspiration must give him understanding. Wherefore, O thou Mr. Recorder, keep low and be humble, and remember that the Diabolonians that kept not their first charge, but left their own standing, are now made prisoners in the pit. Be therefore content with thy station.

"I have made thee my Father's vicegerent on earth, in such things of which I have made mention before; and thou, take thou power to teach them to Mansoul, yea, and to impose them with whips and chastisements, if they shall not willingly hearken to do thy commandments.

"And, Mr. Recorder, because thou art old, and through many abuses made feeble; therefore I give thee leave and licence to go when thou wilt to my fountain, my conduit, and there to drink freely of the blood of my grape, for my conduit doth always run wine. Thus doing, thou shalt drive from thy heart and stomach all foul, gross, and hurtful humours. It will also lighten thine eyes, and will strengthen thy memory for the reception and keeping of all that the King's most noble Secretary teacheth."

When the Prince had thus put Mr. Recorder (that once so was) into the place and office of a minister to Mansoul, and the man had thankfully accepted thereof, then did Emmanuel address himself in a particular speech to the townsmen themselves.

The Prince's Speech to Mansoul

"Behold," said the Prince to Mansoul, "my love and care towards you; I have added to all that is past this mercy, to appoint you preachers; the most noble Secretary to teach you in all high and sublime mysteries; and this gentleman," pointing to Mr. Conscience, "is to teach you in all things human and domestic, for therein lieth his work. He is not, by what I have said, debarred of telling to Mansoul anything that he hath heard and received at the mouth of the Lord High Secretary; only he shall not attempt to presume to pretend to be a revealer of those high mysteries himself; for the breaking of them up and the discovery of them to Mansoul lieth only in the power, authority, and skill of the Lord High Secretary himself. Talk of them he may, and so may the rest of the town of Mansoul; yea, and may, as occasion gives them opportunity, press them upon each other for the benefit of the whole. These things, therefore, I would have you observe and do, for it is for your life, and the lengthening of your days.

"And one thing more to my beloved Mr. Recorder, and to all the town of Mansoul: You must not dwell in nor stay upon anything of that which he hath in commission to teach you, as to your trust and expectation of the next world (of the next world I say, for I purpose to give another to Mansoul, when this with them is worn out); but for that you must wholly and solely have recourse to and make stay upon his doctrine that is your teacher after the first order. Yea, Mr. Recorder himself must not look for life from that which he himself revealeth; his dependence for that must be founded in the doctrine of the other preacher. Let Mr. Recorder also take heed that he receive not any doctrine, or point of doctrine, that is not communicated to him by his superior teacher, nor yet within the precincts of his own formal knowledge."

Now, after the Prince had thus settled things in the famous town of Mansoul, he proceeded to give to the elders of the corporation a necessary caution, to wit, how they should carry it to the high and noble captains that he had, from his father's court, sent or brought with him, to the famous town of Mansoul.

"These captains," said he, "do love the town of Mansoul, and they are pickt men, pickt out of abundance, as men that best suit, and that will most faithfully serve in the wars of Shaddai against the Diabolonians, for the preservation of the town of Mansoul. I charge you, therefore," said he, "O ye inhabitants of the now flourishing town of Mansoul, that you carry it not ruggedly or untowardly to my captains, or their men; since, as I said, they are picked and choice men, men chosen out of many for the good of the town of Mansoul. I say, I charge you, that you carry it not untowardly to them; for though they have the hearts and faces of lions, when at any time they shall be called forth to engage and fight with the King's foes, and the enemies of the town of Mansoul; yet a little discountenance cast upon them from the town of Mansoul will deject and cast down their faces, will weaken and take away their courage. Do not, therefore, O my beloved, carry it unkindly to my valiant captains and courageous men of war, but love them, nourish them, succour them, and lay them in your bosom; and they will not only fight for you, but cause to fly from you all those the Diabolonians that seek, and will, if possible, be your utter destruction.

"If, therefore, any of them should at any time be sick or weak, and so not able to perform that office of love, which, with all their hearts they are willing to do (and will do also when well and in health), slight them not, nor despise them, but rather strengthen them, and encourage them, though weak and ready to die, for they are your fence, and your guard, your wall, your gates, your locks, and your bars. And although, when they are weak, they can do but little, but rather need to be helped by you, than that you should then expect great things from them, yet, when well, you know what exploits, what feats and warlike achievements they are able to do, and will perform for you.

"Besides, if they be weak, the town of Mansoul cannot be strong; if they be strong, then Mansoul cannot be weak: your safety, therefore, doth lie in their health, and in your countenancing them. Remember also, that if they be sick, they catch that disease of the town of Mansoul itself.

"These things I have said unto you because I love your welfare and your honour: observe, therefore, O my Mansoul, to be punctual in all things that I have given in charge unto you, and that not only as a town corporate, and so to your officers and guard and guides in chief, but to you, as you are a people whose well-being, as single persons, depends on the observation of the orders and commandments of their Lord.

"Next, O my Mansoul, I do warn you of that of which, notwithstanding that reformation that at present is wrought among you, you have need to be warn'd about: wherefore hearken diligently unto me. I am now sure, and you will know hereafter, that there are yet of the Diabolonians remaining in the town of Mansoul,—Diabolonians that are sturdy and implacable, and that do already while I am with you, and that will yet more when I am from you, study, plot, contrive, invent, and jointly attempt to bring you to desolation, and so to a state far worse than that of the Egyptian bondage; they are the avowed friends of Diabolus, therefore look about you. They used heretofore to lodge with their prince in the castle, when Incredulity was the Lord Mayor of this town; but since my coming hither, they lie more in the outsides and walls, and have made themselves dens, and caves, and holes, and strongholds therein. Wherefore, O Mansoul! thy work, as to this, will be so much the more difficult and hard; that is, to take, mortify, and put them to death, according to the will of my Father. Nor can you utterly rid yourselves of them, unless you should pull down the walls of your town, the which I am by no means willing you should. Do you ask me, What shall we do, then? Why, be you diligent, and quit you like men; observe their holds; find out their haunts; assault them, and make no peace with them. Wherever they haunt, lurk, or abide, and what terms of peace soever they offer you, abhor, and all shall be well betwixt you and me. And that you may the better know them from those that are the natives of Mansoul, I will give you this brief schedule of the names of the chief of them; and they are these that follow:—The Lord Fornication, the Lord Adultery, the Lord Murder, the Lord Anger, the Lord Lasciviousness, the Lord Deceit, the Lord Evil-Eye, Mr. Drunkenness, Mr. Revelling, Mr. Idolatry, Mr. Witchcraft, Mr. Variance, Mr. Emulation, Mr. Wrath, Mr. Strife, Mr. Sedition, and Mr. Heresy. These are some of the chief, O Mansoul! of those that will seek to overthrow thee for ever. These, I say, are the skulkers in Mansoul; but look thou well into the law of thy King, and there thou shalt find their physiognomy, and such other characteristical notes of them, by which they certainly may be known.

"These, O my Mansoul (and I would gladly that you should certainly know it), if they be suffered to run and range about the town as they would, will quickly, like vipers, eat out your bowels; yea, poison your captains, cut the sinews of your soldiers, break the bars and bolts of your gates, and turn your now most flourishing Mansoul into a barren and desolate wilderness and ruinous heap. Wherefore, that you may take courage to yourselves to apprehend these villains wherever you find them, I give to you, my Lord Mayor, my Lord Will-be-will, and Mr. Recorder, with all the inhabitants of the town of Mansoul, full power and commission to seek out, to take, and to cause to be put to death by the cross, all and all manner of Diabolonians, when and wherever you shall find them to lurk within or to range without the walls of the town of Mansoul.

"I told you before that I had placed a standing ministry among you; not that you have but these with you, for my first four captains who came against the master and lord of the Diabolonians that was in Mansoul, they can, and if need be, and if they be required, will not only privately inform, but publicly preach to the corporation both good and wholesome doctrine, and such as shall lead you in the way. Yea, they will set up a weekly, yea, if need be, a daily lecture in thee, O Mansoul! and will instruct thee in such profitable lessons that, if heeded, will do thee good at the end. And take good heed that you spare not the men that you have a commission to take and crucify.

"Now as I have set before your eyes the vagrants and runagates by name, so I will tell you, that among yourselves some of them shall creep in to beguile you, even such as would seem, and that in appearance are, very rife and hot for religion. And they, if you watch not, will do you a mischief, such a one as at present you cannot think of.

"These, as I said, will show themselves to you in another hue than those under description before. Wherefore, Mansoul, watch and be sober, and suffer not thyself to be betrayed."

When the Prince had thus far new modelled the town of Mansoul, and had instructed them in such matters as were profitable for them to know, then he appointed another day in which he intended, when the townsfolk came together, to bestow a further badge of honour upon the town of Mansoul–a badge that should distinguish them from all the people, kindreds, and tongues that dwell in the kingdom of Universe. Now it was not long before the day appointed was come, and the Prince and his people met in the King's palace, where first Emmanuel made a short speech unto them, and then did for them as he had said, and unto them as he had promised.

"My Mansoul," said he, "that which I now am about to do is to make you known to the world to be mine, and to distinguish you also in your own eyes from all false traitors that may creep in among you."

Then he commanded that those that waited upon him should go and bring forth out of his treasury those white and glistering robes "that I," said he, "have provided and laid up in store for my Mansoul." So the white garments were fetched out of his treasury, and laid forth to the eyes of the people. Moreover, it was granted to them that they should take them and put them on, "according," said he, "to your size and stature." So the people were put into white, into fine linen, white and clean.

Then said the Prince unto them, "This, O Mansoul is my livery, and the badge by which mine are known from the servants of others. Yea, it is that which I grant to all that are mine, and without which no man is permitted to see my face. Wear them, therefore, for my sake, who gave them unto you; and also if you would be known by the world to be mine."

But now, can you think how Mansoul shone? It was fair as the sun, clear as the moon, and terrible as an army with banners.

The Prince added further, and said, "No prince, potentate, or mighty one of Universe, giveth this livery but myself: behold, therefore, as I said before, you shall be known by it to be mine.

"And now," said he, "I have given you my livery, let me also give you in commandment concerning them; and be sure that you take good heed to my words.

"First, Wear them daily, day by day, lest you should at sometimes appear to others as if you were none of mine.

"Secondly: Keep them always white, for if they be soiled, it is dishonour to me.

"Thirdly: Wherefore, gird them up from the ground, and let them not lag with dust and dirt.

"Fourthly: Take heed that you lose them not, lest you walk naked, and they see your shame.

"Fifthly: But if you should sully them, if you should defile them, the which I am greatly unwilling you should, and the Prince Diabolus will be glad if you would, then speed you to do that which is written in my law, that yet you may stand, and not fall before me and before my throne. Also, this is the way to cause that I may not leave you, nor forsake you while here, but may dwell in this town of Mansoul for ever."

The Glorious State of Mansoul

And now was Mansoul, and the inhabitants of it, as the signet upon Emmanuel's right hand. Where was there now a town, a city, a corporation, that could compare with Mansoul? a town redeemed from the hand and from the power of Diabolus; a town that the King Shaddai loved, and that he sent Emmanuel to regain from the prince of the infernal cave; yea, a town that Emmanuel loved to dwell in, and that he chose for his royal habitation; a town that he fortified for himself, and made strong by the force of his army. What shall I say? Mansoul has now a most excellent Prince, golden captains and men of war, weapons proved, and garments as white as snow. Nor are these benefits to be counted little, but great. Can the town of Mansoul esteem them so, and improve them to that end and purpose for which they are bestowed upon them?

When the prince had thus completed the modelling of the town, to show that he had great delight in the work of his hands, and took pleasure in the good that he had wrought for the famous and flourishing Mansoul, he commanded, and they set his standard upon the battlements of the castle. And then,—

First, he gave them frequent visits; not a day now but the elders of Mansoul must come to him, or he to them, into his palace. Now they must walk and talk together of all the great things that he had done, and yet further promised to do for the town of Mansoul. Thus would he often do with the Lord Mayor, my Lord Will-be-will, and the honest subordinate preacher, Mr. Conscience, and Mr. Recorder. But oh, how graciously, how lovingly, how courteously, and tenderly did this blessed Prince now carry it towards the town of Mansoul! In all the streets, gardens, orchards, and other places where he came, to be sure the poor should have his blessing and benediction; yea, he would kiss them, and if they were ill, he would lay hands on them, and make them well. The captains, also, he would daily, yea, sometimes hourly, encourage with his presence and goodly words. For you must know that a smile from him upon them would put more vigour, more life and stoutness into them than would anything else under heaven.

The Prince would now also feast them, and be with them continually: hardly a week would pass but a banquet must be had betwixt him and them. You may remember that, some pages before, we made mention of one feast that they had together; but now to feast them was a thing more common: every day with Mansoul was a feast-day now. Nor did he, when they returned to their places, send them empty away: either they must have a ring, a gold chain, a bracelet, a white stone, or something, so dear was Mansoul to him now, so lovely was Mansoul in his eyes.

Secondly: When the elders and townsmen did not come to him, he would send in much plenty of provision unto them; meat that came from court, wine and bread that were prepared for his Father's table; yea, such delicates would he send unto them, and therewith would so cover their table, that whoever saw it confessed that the like could not be seen in any kingdom.

Thirdly: if Mansoul did not frequently visit him, as he desired they should, he would walk out to them, knock at their doors, and desire entrance, that amity might be maintained betwixt them and him; if they did hear and open to him, as commonly they would if they were at home, then would he renew his former love, and confirm it too with some new tokens and signs of continued favour.

And was it not now amazing to behold, that in that very place where sometimes Diabolus had his abode, and entertained his Diabolonians, to the almost utter destruction of Mansoul, the Prince of princes should sit eating and drinking with them, while all his mighty captains, men of war, trumpeters, with the singing men and singing women of his Father, stood round about to wait upon them! Now did Mansoul's cup run over, now did her conduits run sweet wine, now did she eat the finest of the wheat, and drink milk and honey out of the rock! Now she said, How great is his goodness! for since I found favour in his eyes, how honourable have I been!

The blessed Prince did also order a new officer in the town, and a goodly person he was; his name was Mr. God's-Peace: this man was set over my Lord Will-be-will, my Lord Mayor, Mr. Recorder, the subordinate preacher, Mr. Mind, and over all the natives of the town of Mansoul. Himself was not a native of it, but came with the Prince Emmanuel from the court. He was a great acquaintance of Captain Credence and Captain Good-Hope:

some say they were kin, and I am of that opinion too. This man, as I said, was made governor of the town in general, especially over the castle, and Captain Credence was to help him there. And I made great observation of it, that so long as all things went in Mansoul as this sweet-natured gentleman would, the town was in most happy condition. Now there were no jars, no chiding, no interferings, no unfaithful doings in all the town of Mansoul; every man in Mansoul kept close to his own employment. The gentry, the officers, the soldiers, and all in place observed their order. And as for the women and children of the town, they followed their business joyfully; they would work and sing, work and sing from morning till night: so that quite through the town of Mansoul now, nothing was to be found but harmony, quietness, joy, and health. And this lasted all that summer.

But there was a man in the town of Mansoul, and his name was Mr. Carnal-Security: this man did, after all this mercy bestowed on this corporation, bring the town of Mansoul into great and grievous slavery and bondage. A brief account of him and of his doings take as followeth.

When Diabolus at first took possession of the town of Mansoul, he brought thither with himself a great number of Diabolonians, men of his own condition. Now, among these there was one whose name was Mr. Self-Conceit, and a notable brisk man he was, as any that in those days did possess the town of Mansoul. Diabolus then, perceiving this man to be active and bold, sent him upon many desperate designs, the which he managed better, and more to the pleasing of his lord, than most that came with him from the dens could do. Wherefore, finding him so fit for his purpose, he preferred him, and made him next to the great Lord Will-be-will, of whom we have written so much before. Now, the Lord Will-be-will being in those days very well pleased with him and with his achievements, gave him his daughter, the Lady Fear-Nothing, to wife. Now, of my Lady Fear-Nothing did this Mr. Self-Conceit beget this gentleman, Mr. Carnal-Security. Wherefore there being then in Mansoul those strange kinds of mixtures, 'twas hard for them, in some cases, to find out who were natives, who not; for Mr. Carnal-Security sprang from my Lord Will-be-will by the mother's side, though he had for his father a Diabolonian by nature.

Well, this Carnal-Security took much after his father and mother; he was self-conceited, he feared nothing, he was also a very busy man; nothing of news, nothing of doctrine, nothing of alteration, or talk of alteration, could at any time be on foot in Mansoul, but be sure Mr. Carnal-Security would be at the head or tail of it; but, to be sure, he would decline those that he deemed the weakest, and stood always with them, in his way of standing, that he supposed was the strongest side.

Now, when Shaddai the mighty, and Emmanuel his Son, made war upon Mansoul, to take it, this Mr. Carnal-Security was then in town, and was a great doer among the people, encouraging them in their rebellion, putting them upon hardening themselves in their resisting the King's forces; but when he saw that the town of Mansoul was taken, and converted to the use of the glorious Prince Emmanuel; and when he also saw what was become of Diabolus, and how he was unroosted, and made to quit the castle in the greatest contempt and scorn; and that the town of Mansoul was well lined with captains, engines of war, and men, and also provision; what doth he but slyly wheel about also; and as he had served Diabolus against the good Prince, so he feigned that he would serve the Prince against his foes.

And having got some little smattering of Emmanuel's things by the end, being bold, he ventures himself into the company of the townsmen, and attempts also to chat among them. Now, he knew that the power and strength of the town of Mansoul was great, and that it could not but be pleasing to the people if he cried up their might and their glory. Wherefore he beginneth his tale with the power and strength of Mansoul, and affirmed that it was impregnable: now magnifying their captains, and their slings, and their rams; then crying up their fortifications and strongholds; and, lastly, the assurances that they had from their Prince, that Mansoul should be happy for ever. But when he saw that some of the men of the town were tickled and taken with his discourse, he makes it his business, and walking from street to street, house to house, and man to man, he at last brought Mansoul to dance after his pipe, and to grow almost as carnally secure as himself: so from talking they went to feasting, and from feasting to sporting; and so to some other matters. Now Emmanuel was yet in the town of Mansoul, and he wisely observed their doings. My Lord Mayor, my Lord Will-be-will, and Mr. Recorder were also all taken with the words of this tattling Diabolonian gentleman, forgetting that their Prince had given them warning before to take heed that they were not beguiled with any Diabolonian sleight; he had further told them that the security of the now flourishing town of Mansoul did not so much lie in her present fortifications and force, as in her so using of what she had, as might oblige her Emmanuel to abide within her castle. For the right doctrine of Emmanuel was, that the town of Mansoul should take heed that they forget not his Father's love and his; also, that they should so demean themselves as to continue to keep themselves therein. Now, this was not the way to do it, namely, to fall in love with one of the Diabolonians, and with such an one too as Mr. Carnal-Security was, and to be led up and down by the nose by him; they should have heard their Prince, feared their Prince, loved their Prince, and have stoned this naughty-pack to death, and took care to have walked in the ways of their Prince's prescribing; for then should their peace have been as a river, then their righteousness had been like the waves of the sea.

Now, when Emmanuel perceived that through the policy of Mr. Carnal-Security the hearts of the men of Mansoul were chilled and abated in their practical love to him,

First, he bemoans them, and condoles their state with the Secretary, saying, "Oh that my people had hearkened unto me, and that Mansoul had walked in my way! I would have fed them with the finest of the wheat; and with honey out of the rock would I have sustained them." This done, he said in his heart, "I will return to the court, and go to my place, till Mansoul shall consider and acknowledge their offence." And he did so, and the cause and manner of his going away from them was, that Mansoul declined him, as is manifest in these particulars:—

The Way of Mansoul's Backsliding

1. They left off their former way of visiting him; they came not to his royal palace as afore.

2. They did not regard, nor yet take notice, that he came or came not to visit them.

3. The love-feasts that had wont to be between their Prince and them, though he made them still, and called them to them, yet they neglected to come to them, or to be delighted with them.

4. They waited not for his counsels, but began to be headstrong and confident in themselves, concluding that now they were strong and invincible, and that Mansoul was secure, and beyond all reach of the foe, and that her state must needs be unalterable for ever.

Now, as was said, Emmanuel perceiving that by the craft of Mr. Carnal-Security the town of Mansoul was taken off from their dependence upon him, and upon his Father by him, and set upon what by them was bestowed upon it; he first, as I said, bemoaned their state, then he used means to make them understand that the way that they went on in was dangerous; for he sent my Lord High Secretary to them, to forbid them such ways; but twice, when he came to them, he found them at dinner in Mr. Carnal-Security's parlour; and perceiving also that they were not willing to reason about matters concerning their good, he took grief and went his way; the which when he had told to the Prince Emmanuel, he took offence, and was grieved also, and so made provision to return to his Father's court.

Now, the methods of his withdrawing, as I was saying before, were thus:—

1. Even while he was yet with them in Mansoul, he kept himself close, and more retired than formerly.

2. His speech was not now, if he came in their company, so pleasant and familiar as formerly.

3. Nor did he, as in times past, send to Mansoul, from his table, those dainty bits which he was wont to do.

4. Nor when they came to visit him, as now and then they would, would he be so easily spoken with as they found him to be in times past. They might now knock once, yea, twice, but he would seem not at all to regard them; whereas formerly at the sound of their feet he would up and run and meet them half-way, and take them to, and lay them in his bosom.

But thus Emmanuel carried it now, and by this his carriage he sought to make them bethink themselves, and return to him. But, alas! they did not consider, they did not know his ways, they regarded not, they were not touched with these, nor with the true remembrance of former favours. Wherefore what does he but in private manner withdraw himself, first from his palace, then to the gate of the town, and so away from Mansoul he goes, till they should acknowledge their offence, and more earnestly seek his face. Mr.

God's-Peace also laid down his commission, and would for the present act no longer in the town of Mansoul.

Thus they walked contrary to him, and he again, by way of retaliation, walked contrary to them. But, alas! by this time they were so hardened in their way, and had so drunk in the doctrine of Mr. Carnal-Security, that the departing of their Prince touched them not, nor was he remembered by them when gone; and so, of consequence, his absence not condoled by them.

Now, there was a day wherein this old gentleman, Mr. Carnal-Security, did again make a feast for the town of Mansoul; and there was at that time in the town one Mr. Godly-Fear, one now but little set by, though formerly one of great request. This man, old Carnal-Security had a mind, if possible, to gull, and debauch, and abuse, as he did the rest, and therefore he now bids him to the feast with his neighbours. So the day being come, they prepare, and he goes and appears with the rest of the guests; and being all set at the table, they did eat and drink, and were merry, even all but this one man; for Mr. Godly-Fear sat like a stranger, and did neither eat nor was merry. The which, when Mr. Carnal-Security perceived, he presently addrest himself in a speech thus to him:—

"Mr. Godly-Fear, are you not well? you seem to be ill of body or mind, or both. I have a cordial of Mr. Forget-Good's making, the which, sir, if you will take a dram of, I hope it may make you bonny and blithe, and so make you more fit for us feasting companions."

Unto whom the good old gentleman discreetly replied, "Sir, I thank you for all things courteous and civil; but for your cordial, I have no list thereto. But a word to the natives of Mansoul: You, the elders and chief of Mansoul, to me it is strange to see you so jocund and merry, when the town of Mansoul is in such woeful case."

Then said Mr. Carnal-Security, "You want sleep, good sir, I doubt. If you please, lie down and take a nap, and we meanwhile will be merry."

Then said the good man as follows: "Sir, if you were not destitute of an honest heart, you could not do as you have done and do."

Then said Mr. Carnal-Security, "Why?"

Godly. Nay, pray interrupt me not. It is true, the town of Mansoul was strong, and, with a proviso, impregnable; but you, the townsmen, have weakened it, and it now lies obnoxious to its foes; nor is it a time to flatter or be silent; it is you, Mr. Carnal-Security, that have wilily stripped Mansoul, and driven her glory from her; you have pulled down her towers, you have broken down her gates, you have spoiled her locks and bars.

And now, to explain myself: from that time that my lords of Mansoul and you, sir, grew so great, from that time the Strength of Mansoul has been offended, and now he is arisen and is gone. If any shall question the truth of my words, I will answer him by this, and suchlike questions: Where is the Prince Emmanuel? When did a man or woman in Mansoul see him? When did you hear from him, or taste any of his dainty bits? You are now a-feasting with this Diabolonian monster, but he is not your Prince. I say, therefore, though enemies from without, had you taken heed, could not have made a prey of you, yet, since you have sinned against your Prince, your enemies within have been too hard for you.

Then said Mr. Carnal-Security, "Fie! fie! Mr. Godly-Fear, fie! will you never shake off your timorousness? Are you afraid of being sparrow-blasted? Who hath hurt you? Behold I am on your side; only you are for doubting, and I am for being confident. Besides, is this a time to be sad in? A feast is made for mirth; why, then, do you now, to your shame and our trouble, break out into such passionate melancholy language when you should eat and drink and be merry?"

Then said Mr. Godly-Fear again, "I may well be sad, for Emmanuel is gone from Mansoul. I say again, he is gone, and you, sir, are the man that has driven him away; yea, he is gone without so much as acquainting the nobles of Mansoul with his going; and if that is not a sign of his anger, I am not acquainted with the methods of godliness.

"And now, my lords and gentlemen, for my speech is still to you, your gradual declining from him did provoke him gradually to depart from you, the which he did for some time, if perhaps you would have been made sensible thereby, and have been renewed by humbling yourselves; but when he saw that none would regard, nor lay these fearful beginnings of his anger and judgment to heart, he went away from this place; and this I saw with mine eye. Wherefore now, while you boast, your strength is gone; you are like the man that had lost his locks that before did wave about his shoulders. You may with this Lord of your feast shake yourselves, and conclude to do as at other times; but since without him you can do nothing, and he is departed from you, turn your feast into a sigh, and your mirth into lamentation."

Then the subordinate preacher, old Mr. Conscience by name, he that of old was Recorder of Mansoul, being startled at what was said, began to second it thus:—

Con. Indeed, my brethren, quoth he, I fear that Mr. Godly-Fear tells us true: I, for my part, have not seen my Prince for a long season. I cannot remember the day, for my part; nor can I answer Mr. Godly-Fear's question. I doubt, I am afraid that all is naught with Mansoul.

Godly. Nay, I know that you shall not find him in Mansoul, for he is departed and gone; yea, and gone for the faults of the elders, and for that they rewarded his grace with unsufferable unkindnesses.

Then did the subordinate preacher look as if he would fall down dead at the table; also all there present, except the man of the house, began to look pale and wan. But having a little recovered themselves, and jointly agreeing to believe Mr. Godly-Fear and his sayings, they began to consult what was best to be done (now Mr. Carnal-Security was gone into his withdrawing-room, for he liked not such dumpish doings), both to the man of the house for drawing them into evil, and also to recover Emmanuel's love.

And with that, that saying of their Prince came very hot into their minds, which he had bidden them to do to such as were false prophets that should arise to delude the town of Mansoul. So they took Mr. Carnal-Security (concluding that he must be he) and burned his house upon him with fire; for he also was a Diabolonian by nature.

So when this was past and over, they bespeed themselves to look for Emmanuel their Prince; and they sought him, but they found him not. Then were they more confirmed in the truth of Mr. Godly-Fear's sayings, and began also severely to reflect upon themselves for their so vile and ungodly doings; for they concluded now that it was through them that their Prince had left them.

Then they agreed and went to my Lord Secretary (him whom before they refused to hear—him whom they had grieved with their doings), to know of him, for he was a seer, and could tell where Emmanuel was, and how they might direct a petition to him. But the Lord Secretary would not admit them to a conference about this matter, nor would admit them to his royal place of abode, nor come out to them to show them his face or intelligence.

And now was it a day gloomy and dark, a day of clouds and of thick darkness with Mansoul. Now they saw that they had been foolish, and began to perceive what the company and prattle of Mr. Carnal-Security had done, and what desperate damage his swaggering words had brought poor Mansoul into. But what further it was like to cost them, that they were ignorant of. Now Mr. Godly-Fear began again to be in repute with the men of the town; yea, they were ready to look upon him as a prophet.

Well, when the Sabbath-day was come, they went to hear their subordinate preacher; but oh, how he did thunder and lighten this day! His text was that in the prophet Jonah: They that observe lying vanities forsake their own mercies. But there was then such power and authority in that sermon, and such a dejection seen in the countenances of the people that day, that the like hath seldom been heard or seen. The people, when sermon was done, were scarce able to go to their homes, or to betake themselves to their imploys the week after; they were so sermon-smitten, and also so sermon-sick by being smitten, that they knew not what to do.

He did not only show to Mansoul their sin, but did tremble before them, under the sense of his own, still crying out of himself, as he preached to them, "Unhappy man that I am! that I should do so wicked a thing! That I, a preacher whom the Prince did set up to teach to Mansoul his law, should myself live senseless and sottishly here, and be one of the first found in transgression! This transgression also fell within my precincts: I should have cried out against the wickedness; but I let Mansoul lie wallowing in it, until it had driven Emmanuel from its borders!" With these things he also charged all the lords and gentry of Mansoul, to the almost distracting of them.

A Great Sickness in Mansoul

About this time, also, there was a great sickness in the town of Mansoul, and most of the inhabitants were greatly afflicted. Yea, the captains also and men of war were brought thereby to a languishing condition, and that for a long time together; so that in case of an invasion, nothing could to purpose now have been done, either by the townsmen or field-officers. Oh, how many pale faces, weak hands, feeble knees, and staggering men were now seen to walk the streets of Mansoul! Here were groans, there pants, and yonder lay those that were ready to faint.

The garments, too, which Emmanuel had given them were but in a sorry case: some were rent, some were torn, and all in a nasty condition; some also did hang so loosely upon them, that the next bush they came at was ready to pluck them off.

After some time spent in this sad and desolate condition, the subordinate preacher called for a day of fasting, and to humble themselves for being so wicked against the great Shaddai and his Son. And he desired that Captain Boanerges would preach. So he consented to do it; and the day being come, his text was this: Cut it down, why cumbereth it the ground? And a very smart sermon he made upon the place. First, he showed what was the occasion of the words, namely, because the fig-tree was barren; then he showed what was contained in the sentence, namely, repentance, or utter desolation. He then showed also by whose authority this sentence was pronounced, and that was by Shaddai himself. And, lastly, he showed the reasons of the point, and then concluded his sermon. But he was very pertinent in the application, insomuch that he made poor Mansoul tremble. For this sermon, as well as the former, wrought much upon the hearts of the men of Mansoul; yea, it greatly helped to keep awake those that were roused by the preaching that went before. So that now, throughout the whole town, there was little or nothing to be heard or seen but sorrow, and mourning, and woe.

Now, after sermon, they got together and consulted what was best to be done. "But," said the subordinate preacher, "I will do nothing of mine own head, without advising with my neighbour, Mr. Godly-Fear. For if he had afore understood more of the mind of our Prince than we, I do not know but he may have it now, even now we are turning again to virtue."

So they called and sent for Mr. Godly-Fear, and he forthwith appeared. Then they desired that he would further show his opinion about what they had best to do. Then said the old gentleman as followeth: "It is my opinion that this town of Mansoul should, in this day of her distress, draw up and send an humble petition to their offended Prince Emmanuel, that he, in his favour and grace, will turn again unto you, and not keep anger for ever."

When the townsmen had heard this speech, they did, with one consent, agree to his advice; so they did presently draw up their request; and the next was, But who shall carry it? At last, they did all agree to send it by my Lord Mayor. So he accepted of the service, and addressed himself to his journey; and went and came to the court of Shaddai, whither Emmanuel, the Prince of Mansoul, was gone. But the gate was shut, and a strict watch kept thereat; so that the petitioner was forced to stand without for a great while together. Then he desired that some would go in to the Prince and tell him who stood at the gate, and what his business was. So one went and told to Shaddai, and to Emmanuel his Son, that the Lord Mayor of the town of Mansoul stood without at the gate of the King's court, desiring to be admitted into the presence of the Prince, the King's Son. He also told what was the Lord Mayor's errand, both to the King and his Son Emmanuel. But the Prince would not come down, nor admit that the gate should be opened to him, but sent him an answer to this effect: "They have turned their back unto me, and not their face; but now, in the time of their trouble, they say to me, Arise, and save us. But can they not now go to Mr. Carnal-Security, to whom they went when they turned from me, and make him their leader, their lord, and their protection now in their trouble? Why now in their trouble do they visit me, since in their prosperity they went astray?"

This answer made my Lord Mayor look black in the face; it troubled, it perplexed, it rent him sore. And now he began again to see what it was to be familiar with Diabolonians, such as Mr. Carnal-Security was. When he saw that at court, as yet, there was little help to be expected, either for himself or friends in Mansoul, he smote upon his breast, and returned weeping, and all the way bewailing the lamentable state of Mansoul.

Well, when he was come within sight of the town, the elders and chief of the people of Mansoul went out at the gate to meet him, and to salute him, and to know how he sped at court. But he told them his tale in so doleful a manner, that they all cried out, and mourned, and wept. Wherefore they threw ashes and dust upon their heads, and put sackcloth upon their loins, and went crying out through the town of Mansoul; the which, when the rest of the townsfolk saw, they all mourned and wept. This, therefore, was a day of rebuke and trouble, and of anguish to the town of Mansoul, and also of great distress.

After some time, when they had somewhat refrained themselves, they came together to consult again what by them was yet to be done; and they asked advice, as they did before, of that reverend Mr. Godly-Fear, who told them that there was no way better than to do as they had done, nor would he that they should be discouraged at all with what they had met with at court; yea, though several of their petitions should be answered with nought but silence or rebuke: "For," said he, "it is the way of the wise Shaddai to make men wait and to exercise patience, and it should be the way of them in want to be willing to stay his leisure."

Then they took courage, and sent again, and again, and again; for there was not now one day, nor an hour, that went over Mansoul's head wherein a man might not have met upon the road one or other riding post, sounding the horn from Mansoul to the court of the King Shaddai; and all with letters petitionary in behalf of and for the Prince's return to Mansoul. The road, I say, was now full of messengers going and returning, and meeting one another; some from the court, and some from Mansoul; and this was the work of the miserable town of Mansoul all that long, that sharp, that cold and tedious winter.

Now, if you have not forgot, you may yet remember that I told you before, that after Emmanuel had taken Mansoul, yea, and after that he had new-modelled the town, there remained in several lurking-places of the corporation many of the old Diabolonians, that either came with the tyrant when he invaded and took the town, or that had there, by reason of unlawful mixtures, their birth, and breeding, and bringing up. And their holes, dens, and lurking-places were in, under, or about the wall of the town. Some of their names are the Lord Fornication, the Lord Adultery, the Lord Murder, the Lord Anger, the Lord Lasciviousness, the Lord Deceit, the Lord Evil-Eye, the Lord Blasphemy, and that horrible villain, the old and dangerous Lord Covetousness. These, as I told you, with many more, had yet their abode in the town of Mansoul, and that after that Emmanuel had driven their Prince Diabolus out of the castle.

Against these the good Prince did grant a commission to the Lord Willbe-will and others, yea, to the whole town of Mansoul, to seek, take, secure, and destroy any or all that they could lay hands on, for that they were Diabolonians by nature, enemies to the Prince, and those that sought to ruin the blessed town of Mansoul. But the town of Mansoul did not pursue this warrant, but neglected to look after, to apprehend, to secure, and to destroy these Diabolonians. Wherefore what do these villains, but by degrees take courage to put forth their heads, and to show themselves to the inhabitants of the town. Yea, and as I was told, some of the men of Mansoul grew too familiar with some of them, to the sorrow of the corporation, as you yet will hear more of in time and place.

Well, when the Diabolonian lords that were left perceived that Mansoul had, through sinning, offended Emmanuel their Prince, and that he had withdrawn himself and was gone, what do they but plot the ruin of the town of Mansoul. So upon a time they met together at the hold of one Mr. Mischief, who was also a Diabolonian, and there consulted how they might deliver up Mansoul into the hands of Diabolus again. Now some advised one way, and some another, every man according to his own liking. At last, my Lord Lasciviousness propounded whether it might not be best, in the first place, for some of those that were Diabolonians in Mansoul to adventure to offer themselves for servants to some of the natives of the town; "for," said he, "if they do so, and Mansoul shall accept of them, they may for us, and for Diabolus our lord, make the taking of the town of Mansoul more easy than otherwise it will be." But then stood up the Lord Murder, and said, "This may not be done at this time; for Mansoul is now in a kind of rage, because, by our friend Mr. Carnal-Security, she hath been once ensnared already, and made to offend against her Prince; and how shall she reconcile herself unto her Lord again, but by the heads of these men? Besides, we know that they have in commission to take and slay us wherever they shall find us; let us therefore be wise as foxes: when we are dead, we can do them no hurt, but while we live we may." Thus, when they had tossed the matter to and fro, they jointly agreed that a letter should forthwith be sent away to Diabolus in their name, by which the state of the town of Mansoul should be showed him, and how much it is under the frowns of their Prince. "We may also," said some, "let him know our intentions, and ask of him his advice in the case."

So a letter was presently framed, the contents of which were these:—

"To our great lord, the Prince Diabolus, dwelling below in the infernal cave:—

"O great father, and mighty Prince Diabolus, we the true Diabolonians yet remaining in the rebellious town of Mansoul, having received our beings from thee, and our nourishment at thy hands, cannot with content and quiet endure to behold, as we do this day, how thou art dispraised, disgraced, and reproached among the inhabitants of this town; nor is thy long absence at all delightful to us, because greatly to our detriment.

"The reason of this our writing unto our lord, is for that we are not altogether without hope that this town may become thy habitation again; for it is greatly declined from its Prince Emmanuel; and he is uprisen, and is departed from them; yea, and though they send, and send, and send, and send after him to return to them, yet can they not prevail, nor get good words from him.

"There has been also of late, and is yet remaining, a very great sickness and fainting among them; and that not only upon the poorer sort of the town, but upon the lords, captains, and chief gentry of the place (we only who are of the Diabolonians by nature remain well, lively, and strong), so that through their great transgression on the one hand, and their dangerous sickness on the other, we judge they lie open to thy hand and power. If, therefore, it shall stand with thy horrible cunning, and with the cunning of the rest of the princes with thee, to come and make an attempt to take Mansoul again, send us word, and we shall to our utmost power be ready to deliver it into thy hand. Or if what we have said shall not by thy fatherhood be thought best and most meet to be done, send us thy mind in a few words, and we are all ready to follow thy counsel to the hazarding of our lives, and what else we have.

"Given under our hands the day and date above written, after a close consultation at the house of Mr. Mischief, who yet is alive, and hath his place in our desirable town of Mansoul."

When Mr. Profane (for he was the carrier) was come with his letter to Hell-gate Hill, he knocked at the brazen gates for entrance. Then did Cerberus, the porter, for he is the keeper of that gate, open to Mr. Profane, to whom he delivered his letter, which he had brought from the Diabolonians in Mansoul. So he carried it in, and presented it to Diabolus his lord, and said, "Tidings, my lord, from Mansoul, from our trusty friends in Mansoul."

Then came together from all places of the den, Beelzebub, Lucifer, Apollyon, with the rest of the rabblement there, to hear what news from Mansoul. So the letter was broken up and read, and Cerberus he stood by. When the letter was openly read, and the contents thereof spread into all the corners of the den, command was given that, without let or stop, Deadman's bell should be rung for joy. So the bell was rung, and the princes rejoiced that Mansoul was likely to come to ruin. Now, the clapper of the bell went, "The town of Mansoul is coming to dwell with us; make room for the town of

Mansoul." This bell therefore they did ring, because they did hope that they should have Mansoul again.

Now, when they had performed this their horrible ceremony, they got together again to consult what answer to send to their friends in Mansoul; and some advised one thing and some another; but at length, because the business required haste, they left the whole business to the Prince Diabolus, judging him the most proper lord of the place. So he drew up a letter as he thought fit, in answer to what Mr. Profane had brought, and sent it to the Diabolonians that did dwell in Mansoul, by the same hand that had brought theirs to him; and these were the contents thereof:—

"To our offspring, the high and mighty Diabolonians that yet dwell in the town of Mansoul, Diabolus, the great prince of Mansoul, wisheth a prosperous issue and conclusion of those many brave enterprises, conspiracies, and designs that you, of your love and respect to our honour, have in your hearts to attempt to do against Mansoul.

"Beloved children and disciples, my Lords Fornication, Adultery, and the rest, we have here, in our desolate den, received, to our high joy and content, your welcome letter, by the hand of our trusty Mr. Profane; and to show how acceptable your tidings were, we rang out our bell for gladness; for we rejoiced as much as we could, when we perceived that yet we had friends in Mansoul, and such as sought our honour and revenge in the ruin of the town of Mansoul. We also rejoice to hear that they are in a degenerated condition, and that they have offended their Prince, and that he is gone. Their sickness also pleaseth us, as does also your health, might, and strength. Glad also would we be, right horribly beloved, could we get this town into our clutches again. Nor will we be sparing of spending our wit, our cunning, our craft, and hellish inventions to bring to a wished conclusion this your brave beginning in order thereto.

"And take this for your comfort (our birth, and our offspring), that shall we again surprise it and take it, we will attempt to put all your foes to the sword, and will make you the great lords and captains of the place. Nor need you fear, if ever we get it again, that we after that shall be cast out any more, for we will come with more strength, and so lay far more fast hold than at first we did. Besides, it is the law of that Prince that now they own, that if we get them a second time, they shall be ours for ever.

"Do you, therefore, our trusty Diabolonians, yet more pry into and endeavour to spy out the weakness of the town of Mansoul. We also would that you yourselves do attempt to weaken them more and more. Send us word also, by what means you think we had best to attempt the regaining thereof: namely, whether by persuasion to a vain and loose life; or whether by tempting them to doubt and despair; or whether by blowing up of the town by the gunpowder of pride and self-conceit. Do you also, O ye brave Diabolonians and true sons of the pit, be always in a readiness to make a most hideous assault within, when we shall be ready to storm it without. Now speed you in your project, and we in our desires, the utmost power of our gates, which is the wish of your great Diabolus, Mansoul's enemy, and him that trembles when he thinks of judgment to come. All the blessings of the pit be upon you, and so we close up our letter.

"Given at the pit's mouth, by the joint consent of all the princes of darkness, to be sent to the force and power that we have yet remaining in Mansoul, by the hand of Mr. Profane, by me, "DIABOLUS."

This letter, as was said, was sent to Mansoul, to the Diabolonians that yet remained there, and that yet inhabited the wall, from the dark dungeon of Diabolus, by the hand of Mr. Profane, by whom they also in Mansoul sent theirs to the pit. Now, when this Mr. Profane had made his return, and was come to Mansoul again, he went and came as he was wont to the house of Mr. Mischief, for there was the conclave, and the place where the contrivers were met. Now, when they saw that their messenger was returned safe and sound, they were greatly gladded thereat. Then he presented them with his letter which he had brought from Diabolus for them; the which, when they had read and considered, did much augment their gladness. They asked him after the welfare of their friends, as how their Lord Diabolus, Lucifer, and Beelzebub did, with the rest of those of the den. To which this Profane made answer, "Well, well, my lords; they are well, even as well as can be in their place. They also," said he, "did ring for joy at the reading of your letter, as you will perceive by this when you read it."

A Plot Against Mansoul

Now, as was said, when they had read their letter, and perceived that it encouraged them in their work, they fell to their way of contriving again, namely, how they might complete their Diabolonian design upon Mansoul. And the first thing that they agreed upon was to keep all things from Mansoul as close as they could. "Let it not be known, let not Mansoul be acquainted with what we design against it." The next thing was, how or by what means they should try to bring to pass the ruin and overthrow of Mansoul; and one said after this manner, and another said after that. Then stood up Mr. Deceit, and said, "My right Diabolonian friends, our lords, and the high ones of the deep dungeon, do propound into us these three ways:—

"1. Whether we had best to seek its ruin by making Mansoul loose and vain.

"2. Or whether by driving them to doubt and despair.

"3. Or whether by endeavouring to blow them up by the gunpowder of pride and self-conceit.

"Now, I think if we shall tempt them to pride, that may do something; and if we tempt them to wantonness, that may help. But, in my mind, if we could drive them into desperation, that would knock the nail on the head; for then we should have them, in the first place, question the truth of the love of the heart of their Prince towards them, and that will disgust him much. This, if it works well, will make them leave off quickly their way of sending petitions to him; then farewell earnest solicitations for help and supply; for then this conclusion lies naturally before them, 'As good do nothing, as do to no purpose.'" So to Mr. Deceit they unanimously did consent.

Then the next question was, But how shall we do to bring this our project to pass? and it was answered by the same gentleman, that this might be the best way to do it: "Even let," quoth he, "so many of our friends as are willing to venture themselves for the promoting of their prince's cause, disguise themselves with apparel, change their names, and go into the market like far-countrymen, and proffer to let themselves for servants to the famous town of Mansoul, and let them pretend to do for their masters as beneficially as may be; for by so doing they may, if Mansoul shall hire them, in little time so corrupt and defile the corporation, that her now Prince shall be not only further offended with them, but in conclusion shall spue them out of his mouth. And when this is done, our prince Diabolus shall prey upon them with ease: yea, of themselves they shall fall into the mouth of the eater."

This project was no sooner propounded, but was as highly accepted, and forward were all Diabolonians now to engage in so delicate an enterprise; but it was not thought fit that all should do thus; wherefore they pitched upon two or three, namely, the Lord Covetousness, the Lord Lasciviousness, and the Lord Anger. The Lord Covetousness called himself by the name of Prudent-Thrifty; the Lord Lasciviousness called himself by the name of Harmless-Mirth; and the Lord Anger called himself by the name of Good-Zeal.

So upon a market day, they came into the market-place, three lusty fellows they were to look on, and they were clothed in sheep's russet, which was also now in a manner as white as were the white robes of the men of Mansoul. Now, the men could speak the language of Mansoul well. So when they were come into the market-place, and had offered to let themselves to the townsmen, they were presently taken up; for they asked but little wages, and promised to do their masters great service.

Mr. Mind hired Prudent-Thrifty, and Mr. Godly-Fear hired Good-Zeal. True, this fellow Harmless-Mirth did hang a little in hand, and could not so soon get him a master as the others did, because the town of Mansoul was now in Lent; but after a while, because Lent was almost out, the Lord Will-be-will hired Harmless-Mirth to be both his waiting-man and his lacquey; and thus they got them masters.

These villains now being got thus far into the houses of the men of Mansoul, quickly began to do great mischief therein; for being filthy, arch, and sly, they quickly corrupted the families where they were; yea, they tainted their masters much, especially this Prudent-Thrifty, and him they call Harmless-Mirth. True, he that went under the visor of Good-Zeal was not so well liked of his master; for he quickly found that he was but a counterfeit rascal; the which when the fellow perceived, with speed he made his escape from the house, or I doubt not but his master had hanged him.

Well, when these vagabonds had thus far carried on their design, and had corrupted the town as much as they could, in the next place they considered with themselves at what time their prince Diabolus without, and themselves within the town, should make an attempt to seize upon Mansoul; and they all agreed upon this, that a market day would be best for that work: for why? then will the townsfolk be busy in their ways. And always take this for a rule, When people are most busy in the world, they least fear a surprise. "We also then," said they, "shall be able with less suspicion to gather ourselves together for the work of our friends and lords; yea, and in such a day, if we shall attempt our work, and miss it, we may, when they shall give us the rout, the better hide ourselves in the crowd, and escape."

These things being thus far agreed upon by them, they wrote another letter to Diabolus, and sent it by the hand of Mr. Profane, the contents of which was this:—

"The Lords of Looseness send to the great and high Diabolus, from our dens, caves, holes, and strongholds, in and about the wall of the town of Mansoul, greeting:

"Our great Lord, and the nourisher of our lives, Diabolus,—how glad we were when we heard of your fatherhood's readiness to comply with us, and help forward our design in our attempts to ruin Mansoul, none can tell but those who, as we do, set themselves against all appearance of good, when and wheresoever we find it.

"Touching the encouragement that your greatness is pleased to give us to continue to devise, contrive, and study the utter desolation of Mansoul, that we are not solicitous about; for we know right well it cannot but be pleasing and profitable to us to see our enemies, and them that seek our lives, die at our feet, or fly before us. We therefore are still contriving, and that to the best of our cunning, to make this work most facile and easy to your lordships and to us.

"First, we considered of that most hellishly cunning, compacted, threefold project, that by you was propounded to us in your last; and have concluded, that though to blow them up with the gunpowder of pride would do well, and to do it by tempting them to be loose and vain will help on, yet to contrive to bring them into the gulf of desperation, we think will do best of all. Now we, who are at your beck, have thought of two ways to do this: first, we, for our parts, will make them as vile as we can, and then you with us, at a time appointed, shall be ready to fall upon them with the utmost force. And of all the nations that are at your whistle, we think that an army of doubters may be the most likely to attack and overcome the town of Mansoul. Thus shall we overcome these enemies, else the pit shall open her mouth upon them, and desperation shall thrust them down into it. We have also, to effect this so much by us desired design, sent already three of our trusty Diabolonians among them: they are disguised in garb, they have changed their names, and are now accepted of them: namely, Covetousness, Lasciviousness, and Anger. The name of Covetousness is changed to Prudent-Thrifty, and him Mr. Mind has hired, and is almost become as bad as our friend. Lasciviousness has changed his name to Harmless-Mirth, and he is got to be the Lord Will-be-will's lacquey; but he has made his master very wanton. Anger changed his name into Good-Zeal, and was entertained by Mr. Godly-Fear; but the peevish old gentleman took pepper in the nose, and turned our companion out of his house. Nay, he has informed us since that he ran away from him, or else his old master had hanged him up for his labour.

"Now, these have much helped forward our work and design upon Mansoul; for notwithstanding the spite and quarrelsome temper of the old gentleman last mentioned, the other two ply their business well, and are likely to ripen the work apace.

"Our next project is, that it be concluded that you come upon the town upon a market day, and that when they are upon the heat of their business; for then, to be sure, they will be most secure, and least think that an assault will be made upon them. They will also at such a time be less able to defend themselves, and to offend you in the prosecution of our design. And we, your trusty (and we are sure your beloved) ones, shall, when you shall make your furious assault without, be ready to second the business within. So shall we, in all likelihood, be able to put Mansoul to utter confusion, and to swallow them up before they can come to themselves. If your serpentine heads, most subtile dragons, and our highly esteemed lords, can find out a better way than this, let us quickly know your minds.

"To the monsters of the infernal cave, from the house of Mr. Mischief in Mansoul, by the hand of Mr. Profane."

Now, all the while that the raging runagates and hellish Diabolonians were thus contriving the ruin of the town of Mansoul, they (namely, the poor town itself) were in a sad and woeful case; partly because they had so grievously offended Shaddai and his Son, and partly because that the enemies thereby got strength within them afresh; and also because, though they had by many petitions made suit to the Prince Emmanuel, and to his Father Shaddai by him, for their pardon and favour, yet hitherto obtained they not one smile; but contrariwise, through the craft and subtilty of the domestic Diabolonians, their cloud was made to grow blacker and blacker, and their Emmanuel to stand at farther distance.

The sickness also did greatly rage in Mansoul, both among the captains and the inhabitants of the town; and their enemies only were now lively and strong, and likely to become the head, whilst Mansoul was made the tail.

Profane Arrives at Hell-gate Hill

By this time the letter last mentioned, that was written by the Diabolonians that yet lurked in the town of Mansoul, was conveyed to Diabolus in the black den, by the hand of Mr. Profane. He carried the letter by Hell-gate Hill as afore, and conveyed it by Cerberus to his lord.

But when Cerberus and Mr. Profane did meet, they were presently as great as beggars, and thus they fell into discourse about Mansoul, and about the project against her.

"Ah! old friend," quoth Cerberus, "art thou come to Hell-gate Hill again? By St. Mary, I am glad to see thee!"

Prof. Yes, my lord, I am come again about the concerns of the town of Mansoul.

Cerb. Prithee, tell me what condition is that town of Mansoul in at present?

Prof. In a brave condition, my lord, for us, and for my lords, the lords of this place, I trow; for they are greatly decayed as to godliness, and that is as well as our heart can wish; their Lord is greatly out with them, and that doth also please us well. We have already, also, a foot in their dish, for our Diabolonian friends are laid in their bosoms, and what do we lack but to be masters of the place? Besides, our trusty friends in Mansoul are daily plotting to betray it to the lords of this town; also the sickness rages bitterly among them; and that which makes up all, we hope at last to prevail."

Then said the dog of Hell-gate, "No time like this to assault them. I wish that the enterprise be followed close, and that the success desired may be soon effected; yea, I wish it for the poor Diabolonians' sakes, that live in the continual fear of their lives in that traitorous town of Mansoul."

Prof. The contrivance is almost finished; the lords in Mansoul that are Diabolonians are at it day and night, and the other are like silly doves: they want heart to be concerned with their state, and to consider that ruin is at hand. Besides, you may, yea must think, when you put all things together, that there are many reasons that prevail with Diabolus to make what haste he can.

Cerb. Thou hast said as it is; I am glad things are at this pass. Go in, my brave Profane, to my lords, they will give thee for thy welcome as good a *coranto* as the whole of this kingdom will afford. I have sent thy letter in already.

Then Mr. Profane went into the den, and his lord Diabolus met him, and saluted him with, "Welcome, my trusty servant: I have been made glad with thy letter." The rest of the lords of the pit gave him also their salutations. Then Profane, after obeisance made to them all, said, "Let Mansoul be given to my lord Diabolus, and let him be her king for ever." And with that the hollow belly and yawning gorge of hell gave so loud and hideous a groan (for that is the music of that place), that it made the mountains about it totter, as if they would fall in pieces.

Now, after they had read and considered the letter, they consulted what answer to return; and the first that did speak to it was Lucifer.

Then said he, "The first project of the Diabolonians in Mansoul is like to be lucky, and to take; namely, that they will, by all the ways and means they can, make Mansoul yet more vile and filthy: no way to destroy a soul like this. Our old friend Balaam went this way and prospered many years ago; let this, therefore, stand with us for a maxim, and be to Diabolonians for a general rule in all ages; for nothing can make this to fail but grace, in which I would hope that this town has no share. But whether to fall upon them on a market day, because of their cumber in business, that I would should be under debate. And there is more reason why this head should be debated, than why some other should; because upon this will turn the whole of what we shall attempt. If we time not our business well, our whole project may fail. Our friends, the Diabolonians, say that a market day is best; for then will Mansoul be most busy, and have fewest thoughts of a surprise. But what if also they should double their guards on those days (and methinks nature and reason should teach them to do it)? and what if they should keep such a watch on those days as the necessity of their present case doth require? yea, what if their men should be always in arms on those days? then you may, my lords, be disappointed in your attempts, and may bring our friends in the town to utter danger of unavoidable ruin."

Then said the great Beelzebub, "There is something in what my lord hath said; but his conjecture may or may not fall out. Nor hath my lord laid it down as that which must not be receded from; for I know that he said it only to provoke to a warm debate thereabout. Therefore we must understand, if we can, whether the town of Mansoul has such sense and knowledge of her decayed state, and of the design that we have on foot against her, as doth provoke her to set watch and ward at her gates, and to double them on market days. But if, after inquiry made, it shall be found that they are asleep, then any day will do, but a market day is best; and this is my judgment in this case."

Then quoth Diabolus, "How should we know this?" and it was answered, "Inquire about it at the mouth of Mr. Profane." So Profane was called in, and asked the question, and he made his answer as follows:—

Prof. My lords, so far as I can gather, this is at present the condition of the town of Mansoul: they are decayed in their faith and love; Emmanuel, their Prince, has given them the back; they send often by petition to fetch him again, but he maketh not haste to answer their request, nor is there much reformation among them.

Diab. I am glad that they are backward to a reformation, but yet I am afraid of their petitioning. However, their looseness of life is a sign that there is not much heart in what they do, and without the heart things are little worth. But go on, my masters; I will divert you, my lords, no longer.

Beel. If the case be so with Mansoul, as Mr. Profane has described it to be, it will be no great matter what day we assault it; not their prayers nor their power will do them much service.

When Beelzebub had ended his oration, then Apollyon did begin. "My opinion," said he, "concerning this matter, is, that we go on fair and softly, not doing things in a hurry. Let our friends in Mansoul go on still to pollute and defile it, by seeking to draw it yet more into sin (for there is nothing like sin to devour Mansoul). If this be done, and it takes effect, Mansoul of itself will leave off to watch, to petition, or anything else that should tend to her security and safety; for she will forget her Emmanuel, she will not desire his company; and can she be gotten thus to live, her Prince will not come to her in haste. Our trusty friend, Mr. Carnal-Security, with one of his tricks did drive him out of the town; and why may not my Lord Covetousness, and my Lord Lasciviousness, by what they may do, keep him out of the town? And this I will tell you (not because you know it not), that two or three Diabolonians, if entertained and countenanced by the town of Mansoul, will do more to the keeping of Emmanuel from them, and towards making the town of Mansoul your own, than can an army of a legion that should be sent out from us to withstand him. Let, therefore, this first project that our friends in Mansoul have set on foot, be strongly and diligently carried on with all cunning and craft imaginable; and let them send continually, under one guise or another, more and other of their men to play with the people of Mansoul; and then, perhaps, we shall not need to be at the charge of making a war upon them; or if that must of necessity be done, yet the more sinful they are, the more unable, to be sure, they will be to resist us, and then the more easily we shall overcome them. And besides, suppose (and that is the worst that can be supposed) that Emmanuel should come to them again, why may not the same means, or the like, drive him from them once more? Yea, why may he not, by their lapse into that sin again, be driven from them for ever, for the sake of which he was at the first driven from them for a season? And if this should happen, then away go with him his rams, his slings, his captains, his soldiers, and he leaveth Mansoul naked and bare. Yea, will not this town, when she sees herself utterly forsaken of her Prince, of her own accord open her gates again unto you, and make of you as in the days of old? But this must be done by time; a few days will not effect so great a work as this."

So soon as Apollyon had made an end of speaking, Diabolus began to blow out his own malice, and to plead his own cause; and he said, "My lords, and powers of the cave, my true and trusty friends, I have with much impatience, as becomes me, given ear to your long and tedious orations. But my furious gorge and empty paunch so lusteth after a repossession of my famous town of Mansoul, that whatever comes out, I can wait no longer to see the events of lingering projects. I must, and that without further delay, seek, by all means I can, to fill my insatiable gulf with the soul and body of the town of Mansoul. Therefore lend me your heads, your hearts, and your help, now I am going to recover my town of Mansoul."

When the lords and princes of the pit saw the flaming desire that was in Diabolus to devour the miserable town of Mansoul, they left off to raise any more objections, but consented to lend him what strength they could; though had Apollyon's advice been taken, they had far more fearfully distressed the town of Mansoul. But, I say, they were willing to lend him what strength they could, not knowing what need they might have of him, when they should engage for themselves, as he. Wherefore they fell to advising about the next thing propounded, namely, what soldiers they were, and also how many, with whom Diabolus should go against the town of Mansoul to take it; and after some debate, it was concluded, according as in the letter the Diabolonians had suggested, that none was more fit for that expedition than an army of terrible Doubters.

An Army of Doubters

They therefore concluded to send against Mansoul an army of sturdy Doubters. The number thought fit to be employed in that service was between twenty and thirty thousand. So, then, the result of that great council of those high and mighty lords was, That Diabolus should even now, out of hand, beat up his drum for men in the land of Doubting, which land lieth upon the confines of the place called Hell-gate Hill, for men that might be employed by him against the miserable town of Mansoul. It was also concluded that these lords themselves should help him in the war, and that they would to that end head and manage his men. So they drew up a letter, and sent back to the Diabolonians that lurked in Mansoul, and that waited for the back-coming of Mr. Profane, to signify to them into what method and forwardness they at present had put their design. The contents whereof now followeth:—

"From the dark and horrible dungeon of hell, Diabolus, with all the society of the princes of darkness, sends to our trusty ones, in and about, the walls of the town of Mansoul, now impatiently waiting for our most devilish answer to their venomous and most poisonous design against the town of Mansoul.

"Our native ones, in whom from day to day we boast, and in whose actions all the year long we do greatly delight ourselves,—we received your welcome, because highly esteemed letter, at the hand of our trusty and greatly beloved, the old gentleman, Mr. Profane. And do give you to understand, that when we had broken it up, and had read the contents thereof, to your amazing memory be it spoken, our yawning, hollow-bellied place, where we are, made so hideous and yelling a noise for joy, that the mountains that stand round about Hell-gate Hill had like to have been shaken to pieces at the sound thereof.

"We could also do no less than admire your faithfulness to us, with the greatness of that subtilty that now hath showed itself to be in your heads to serve us against the town of Mansoul. For you have invented for us so excellent a method for our proceeding against that rebellious people, a more effectual cannot be thought of by all the wits of hell. The proposals, therefore, which now, at last, you have sent us, since we saw them, we have done little less but highly approved and admired them.

"Nay, we shall, to encourage you in the profundity of your craft, let you know that, at a full assembly and conclave of our princes and principalities of this place, your project was discoursed and tossed from one side of our cave to the other by their mightinesses; but a better, and as was by themselves judged, a more fit and proper way by all their wits could not be invented to surprise, take, and make our own, the rebellious town of Mansoul.

"Wherefore, in fine, all that was said that varied from what you had in your letter propounded, fell of itself to the ground, and yours only was stuck to by Diabolus, the prince; yea his gaping gorge and yawning paunch was on fire to put your invention into execution.

"We, therefore, give you to understand that our stout, furious, and unmerciful Diabolus is raising, for your relief, and the ruin of the rebellious town of Mansoul, more than twenty thousand Doubters to come against that people. They are all stout and sturdy men, and men that of old have been accustomed to war, and that can therefore well endure the drum. I say, he is doing this work of his with all the possible speed he can, for his heart and spirit are engaged in it. We desire therefore, that as you have hitherto stuck to us, and given us both advice and encouragement thus far, you still will prosecute our design; nor shall you lose, but be gainers thereby; yea we intend to make you the lords of Mansoul.

"One thing may not by any means be omitted, that is, those with us do desire that every one of you that are in Mansoul would still use all your power, cunning, and skill, with delusive persuasions, yet to draw the town of Mansoul into more sin and wickedness, even that sin may be finished and bring forth death.

"For thus it is concluded with us, that the more vile, sinful, and debauched the town of Mansoul is, the more backward will be their Emmanuel to come to their help, either by presence or other relief; yea, the more sinful, the more weak, and so the more unable will they be to make resistance when we shall make our assault upon them to swallow them up. Yea, that may cause that their mighty Shaddai himself may cast them out of his protection; yea, and send for his captains and soldiers home, with his slings and rams, and leave them naked and bare; and then the town of Mansoul will, of itself, open to us, and fall as the fig into the mouth of the eater. Yea, to be sure that we then with a great deal of ease shall come upon her and overcome her.

"As to the time of our coming upon Mansoul, we, as yet, have not fully resolved upon that, though at present some of us think as you, that a market day, or a market day at night, will certainly be the best. However, do you be ready, and when you shall hear our roaring drum without, do you be as busy to make the most horrible confusion within. So shall Mansoul certainly be distressed before and behind, and shall not know which way to betake herself for help. My Lord Lucifer, my Lord Beezlebub, my Lord Apollyon, my Lord Legion, with the rest salute you, as does also my Lord Diabolus; and we wish both you, with all that you do, or shall possess, the very self-same fruit and success for their doing, as we ourselves at present enjoy for ours.

"From our dreadful confines in the most fearful pit, we salute you, and so do those many legions here with us, wishing you may be as hellishly prosperous as we desire to be ourselves. By the letter-carrier, Mr. Profane."

Then Mr. Profane addressed himself for his return to Mansoul, with his errand from the horrible pit to the Diabolonians that dwelt in that town. So he came up the stairs from the deep to the mouth of the cave where Cerberus was. Now, when Cerberus saw him, he asked how matters did go below, about and against the town of Mansoul.

Prof. Things go as well as we can expect. The letter that I carried thither was highly approved, and well liked by my lords, and I am returning to tell our Diabolonians so. I have an answer to it here in my bosom, that I am sure will make our masters that sent me glad; for the contents thereof are to encourage them to pursue their design to the utmost, and to be ready also to fall on within, when they shall see my Lord Diabolus beleaguering the town of Mansoul.

Cerb. But does he intend to go against them himself?

Prof. Does he! Ay! and he will take along with him more than twenty thousand, all sturdy Doubters, and men of war, picked men, from the land of Doubting, to serve him in the expedition.

Then was Cerberus glad, and said, "And is there such brave preparations a-making to go against the miserable town of Mansoul? And would I might be put at the head of a thousand of them, that I might also show my valour against the famous town of Mansoul."

Prof. Your wish may come to pass: you look like one that has mettle enough, and my lord will have with him those that are valiant and stout. But my business requires haste.

Cerb. Ay, so it does. Speed thee to the town of Mansoul, with all the deepest mischiefs that this place can afford thee. And when thou shalt come to the house of Mr. Mischief, the place where the Diabolonians meet to plot, tell them that Cerberus doth wish them his service, and that if he may he will with the army come up against the famous town of Mansoul.

Prof. That I will. And I know that my lords that are there will be glad to hear it, and to see you also.

So, after a few more such kind of compliments, Mr. Profane took his leave of his friend Cerberus; and Cerberus again, with a thousand of their pit-wishes, bid him haste, with all speed, to his masters. The which when he had heard, he made obeisance, and began to gather up his heels to run.

Thus, therefore, he returned, and went and came to Mansoul; and going, as afore, to the house of Mr. Mischief, there he found the Diabolonians assembled and waiting for his return. Now when he was come, and had presented himself, he also delivered to them his letter, and adjoined this compliment to them therewith: "My lords, from the confines of the pit, the high and mighty principalities and powers of the den salute you here, the true Diabolonians of the town of Mansoul. Wishing you always the most proper of their benedictions, for the great service, high attempts, and brave achievements that you have put yourselves upon, for the restoring to our Prince Diabolus the famous town of Mansoul."

This was, however, the present state of the miserable town of Mansoul: she had offended her Prince, and he was gone; she had encouraged the powers of hell, by her foolishness, to come against her to seek her utter destruction.

True, the town of Mansoul was somewhat made sensible of her sin, but the Diabolonians were gotten into her bowels; she cried, but Emmanuel was gone, and her cries did not fetch him as yet again. Besides, she knew not now whether ever or never he would return and come to his Mansoul again; nor did they know the power and industry of the enemy, nor how forward they were to put in execution that plot of hell that they had devised against her.

They did, indeed, send petition after petition to the Prince, but he answered all with silence. They did neglect reformation, and that was as Diabolus would have it; for he knew, if they regarded iniquity in their hearts, their King would not hear their prayer; they therefore did still grow weaker and weaker, and were as a rolling thing before the whirlwind. They cried to their King for help, and laid Diabolonians in their bosoms: what therefore should a king do to them? Yea, there seemed now to be a mixture in Mansoul: the Diabolonians and the Mansoulians would walk the streets together. Yea, they began to seek their peace; for they thought that, since the sickness had been so mortal in Mansoul, 'twas in vain to go to handygripes with them. Besides, the weakness of Mansoul was the strength of their enemies, and the sins of Mansoul the advantage of the Diabolonians. The foes of Mansoul did also now begin to promise themselves the town for a possession: there was no great difference now betwixt Mansoulians and Diabolonians: both seemed to be masters of Mansoul. Yea, the Diabolonians increased and grew, but the town of Mansoul diminished greatly. There were more than eleven thousand men, women, and children that died by the sickness in Mansoul.

But now, as Shaddai would have it, there was one whose name was Mr. Prywell, a great lover of the people of Mansoul. And he, as his manner was, did go listening up and down in Mansoul to see and to hear, if at any time he might, whether there was any design against it or no. For he was always a jealous man, and feared some mischief sometime would befall it, either from the Diabolonians within, or from some power without. Now, upon a time it so happened, as Mr. Prywell went listening here and there, that he lighted upon a place called Vilehill, in Mansoul, where Diabolonians used to meet; so hearing a muttering (you must know that it was in the night), he softly drew near to hear; nor had he stood long under the house-end (for there stood a house there), but he heard one confidently affirm, that it was not, or would not be long before Diabolus should possess himself again of Mansoul; and that then the Diabolonians did intend to put all Mansoulians to the sword, and would kill and destroy the King's captains, and drive all his soldiers out of the town. He said, moreover, that he knew there were about twenty thousand fighting men prepared by Diabolus for the accomplishment of this design, and that it would not be months before they all should see it.

When Mr. Prywell had heard this story, he did quickly believe it was true; wherefore he went forthwith to my Lord Mayor's house, and acquainted him therewith; who, sending for the subordinate preacher, brake the business to him; and he as soon gave the alarm to the town; for he was now the chief preacher in Mansoul, because, as yet, my Lord Secretary was ill at ease. And this was the way that the subordinate preacher did take to alarm the town therewith. The same hour he caused the lecture-bell to be rung; so the people came together: he gave them then a short exhortation to watchfulness, and made Mr. Prywell's news the argument thereof. "For," said he, "an horrible plot is contrived against Mansoul, even to massacre us all in a day, nor is this story to be slighted; for Mr. Prywell is the author thereof. Mr. Prywell was always a lover of Mansoul, a sober and judicious man, a man that is no tattler, nor raiser of false reports, but one that loves to look into the very bottom of matters, and talks not of news, but by very solid arguments.

"I will call him, and you shall hear him your own selves." So he called him, and he came and told his tale so punctually, and affirmed its truth with such ample grounds, that Mansoul fell presently under a conviction of the truth of what he said. The preacher did also back him, saying, "Sirs, it is not irrational for us to believe it, for we have provoked Shaddai to anger, and have sinned Emmanuel out of the town; we have had too much correspondence with Diabolonians, and have forsaken our former mercies: no marvel, then, if the enemy both within and without should design and plot our ruin; and what time like this to do it? The sickness is now in the town, and we have been made weak thereby. Many a good meaning man is dead, and the Diabolonians of late grow stronger and stronger.

"Besides," quoth the subordinate preacher, "I have received from this good truth-teller this one inkling further, that he understood by those that he overheard, that several letters have lately passed between the furies and of the Diabolonians in order to our destruction." When Mansoul heard all this, and not being able to gainsay it, they lifted up their voice and wept. Mr. Prywell did also, in the presence of the townsmen, confirm all that their subordinate preacher had said. Wherefore they now set afresh to bewail their folly, and to a doubling of petitions to Shaddai and his Son. They also brake the business to the captains, high commanders, and men of war in the town of Mansoul, entreating them to use the means to be strong, and to take good courage; and that they would look after their harness, and make themselves ready to give Diabolus battle by night and by day, should he come, as they are informed he will, to beleaguer the town of Mansoul.

The Captains Consult

When the captains heard this, they being always true lovers of the town of Mansoul, what do they but, like so many Samsons, they shake themselves, and come together to consult and contrive how to defeat those bold and hellish contrivances that were upon the wheel by the means of Diabolus and his friends against the now sickly, weakly, and much impoverished town of Mansoul; and they agreed upon these following particulars:—

1. That the gates of Mansoul should be kept shut, and made fast with bars and locks, and that all persons that went out, or came in, should be very

strictly examined by the captains of the guards, "to the end," said they "that those that are managers of the plot against us, may, either coming or going, be taken; and that we may also find out who are the great contrivers, amongst us, of our ruin."

2. The next thing was, that a strict search should be made for all kind of Diabolonians throughout the whole town of Mansoul; and that every man's house from top to bottom should be looked into, and that, too, house by house, that if possible a further discovery might be made of all such among them as had a hand in these designs.

3. It was further concluded upon, that wheresoever or with whomsoever any of the Diabolonians were found, that even those of the town of Mansoul that had given them house and harbour should, to their shame, and the warning of others, take penance in the open place.

4. It was, moreover, resolved by the famous town of Mansoul that a public fast and a day of humiliation should be kept throughout the whole corporation, to the justifying of their Prince, the abasing of themselves before him for their transgressions against him, and against Shaddai his Father. It was further resolved that all such in Mansoul as did not on that day endeavour to keep that fast, and to humble themselves for their faults, but that should mind their worldly employs, or be found wandering up and down the streets, should be taken for Diabolonians, and should suffer as Diabolonians for such their wicked doings.

5. It was further concluded then that with what speed, and with what warmth of mind they could, they would renew their humiliation for sin, and their petitions to Shaddai for help. They also resolved to send tidings to the court of all that Mr. Prywell had told them.

6. It was also determined that thanks should be given by the town of Mansoul to Mr. Prywell for his diligent seeking of the welfare of their town; and further, that forasmuch as he was so naturally inclined to seek their good, and also to undermine their foes, they gave him a commission of scout-master-general, for the good of the town of Mansoul.

When the corporation, with their captains, had thus concluded, they did as they had said; they shut up their gates, they made for Diabolonians strict search, they made those with whom any were found to take penance in the open place; they kept their fast, and renewed their petitions to their Prince; and Mr. Prywell managed his charge and the trust that Mansoul had put in his hands with great conscience and good fidelity, for he gave himself wholly up to his employ, and that not only within the town, but he went out to pry, to see, and to hear.

And not many days after he provided for his journey and went towards Hell-gate Hill, into the country where the Doubters were, where he heard of all that had been talked of in Mansoul, and he perceived also that Diabolus was almost ready for his march, &c. So he came back with speed, and calling the captains and elders of Mansoul together, he told them where he had been, what he had heard, and what he had seen. Particularly he told them that Diabolus was almost ready for his march, and that he had made old Mr. Incredulity, that once brake prison in Mansoul, the general of his army; that his army consisted all of Doubters, and that their number was above twenty thousand. He told, moreover, that Diabolus did intend to bring with him the chief princes of the infernal pit, and that he would make them chief captains over his Doubters. He told them, moreover, that it was certainly true that several of the black den would, with Diabolus, ride reformades to reduce the town of Mansoul to the obedience of Diabolus their prince.

He said, moreover, that he understood by the Doubters among whom he had been that the reason why old Incredulity was made general of the whole army was because none truer than he to the tyrant, and because he had an implacable spite against the welfare of the town of Mansoul. Besides, said he, he remembers the affronts that Mansoul has given him, and he is resolved to be revenged of them.

But the black princes shall be made high commanders, only Incredulity shall be over them all, because, which I had almost forgot, he can more easily and more dexterously beleaguer the town of Mansoul than can any of the princes besides.

Now, when the captains of Mansoul, with the elders of the town, had heard the tidings that Mr. Prywell did bring, they thought it expedient, without further delay, to put into execution the laws that against the Diabolonians their Prince had made for them and given them in commandment to manage against them. Wherefore, forthwith a diligent and impartial search was made in all houses in Mansoul for all and all manner of Diabolonians. Now, in the house of Mr. Mind, and in the house of the great Lord Will-be-will, were two Diabolonians found. In Mr. Mind's house was one Lord Covetousness found, but he had changed his name to Prudent-Thrifty. In my Lord Will-be-will's house one Lasciviousness was found, but he had changed his name to Harmless-Mirth. These two the captains and elders of the town of Mansoul took, and committed them to custody under the hand of Mr. True-Man, the gaoler; and this man handled them so severely, and loaded them so well with irons, that in time they both fell into a very deep consumption, and died in the prison-house. Their masters also, according to the agreement of the captains and elders, were brought to take penance in the open place to their shame, and for a warning to the rest of the town of Mansoul.

Now, this was the manner of penance in those days: the persons offending, being made sensible of the evil of their doings, were enjoined open confession of their faults, and a strict amendment of their lives.

After this, the captains and elders of Mansoul sought yet to find out more Diabolonians, wherever they lurked, whether in dens, caves, holes, vaults, or where else they could, in or about the wall or town of Mansoul. But though they could plainly see their footing, and so follow them by their track and smell to their holds, even to the mouths of their caves and dens, yet take them, hold them, and do justice upon them, they could not; their ways were so crooked, their holds so strong, and they so quick to take sanctuary there.

But Mansoul did now with so stiff a hand rule over the Diabolonians that were left, that they were glad to shrink into corners: time was when they durst walk openly, and in the day; but now they were forced to embrace privacy and the night; time was when a Mansoulian was their companion; but now they counted them deadly enemies. This good change did Mr. Prywell's intelligence make in the famous town of Mansoul.

By this time Diabolus had finished his army which he intended to bring with him for the ruin of Mansoul; and had set over them captains and other field-officers such as liked his furious stomach best: himself was lord paramount, Incredulity was general of his army, their highest captains shall be named afterwards; but now for their officers, colours, and scutcheons:—

1. Their first captain was Captain Rage: he was captain over the Election-Doubters; his were the red colours; his standard-bearer was Mr. Destructive, and the great red dragon he had for his scutcheon.

2. The second captain was Captain Fury: he was captain over the Vocation-Doubters; his standard-bearer was Mr. Darkness, his colours were those that were pale, and he had for his scutcheon the fiery flying serpent.

3. The third captain was Captain Damnation: he was captain over the Grace-Doubters; his were the red colours, Mr. No-Life bare them, and he had for his scutcheon the black den.

4. The fourth captain was the Captain Insatiable: he was captain over the Faith-Doubters; his were the red colours, Mr. Devourer bare them, and he had for a scutcheon the yawning jaws.

5. The fifth captain was Captain Brimstone: he was captain over the Perseverance-Doubters; his also were the red colours, Mr. Burning bare them, and his scutcheon was the blue and stinking flame.

6. The sixth captain was Captain Torment: he was captain over the Resurrection-Doubters; his colours were those that were pale, Mr. Gnaw was his ancient-bearer, and he had the black worm for his scutcheon.

7. The seventh captain was Captain No-Ease: he was captain over the Salvation-Doubters; his were the red colours, Mr. Restless bare them, and his scutcheon was the ghastly picture of death.

8. The eighth captain was the Captain Sepulchre: he was captain over the Glory-Doubters; his also were the pale colours, Mr. Corruption was his ancient-bearer, and he had for his scutcheon a skull and dead men's bones.

9. The ninth captain was Captain Past-Hope: he was captain of those that are called the Felicity-Doubters; his ancient-bearer was Mr. Despair; his also were the red colours, and his scutcheon was a hot iron and the hard heart.

These were the captains, and these their forces, these were their ancients, these were their colours, and these were their scutcheons. Now, over these did the great Diabolus make superior captains, and they were in number seven: as, namely, the Lord Beelzebub, the Lord Lucifer, the Lord Legion, the Lord Apollyon, the Lord Python, the Lord Cerberus, and the Lord

Belial; these seven he set over the captains, and Incredulity was lord general, and Diabolus was king. The reformades also, such as were like themselves, were made some of them captains of hundreds, and some of them captains of more. And thus was the army of Incredulity completed.

So they set out at Hell-gate Hill, for there they had their rendezvous, from whence they came with a straight course upon their march toward the town of Mansoul. Now, as was hinted before, the town had, as Shaddai would have it, received from the mouth of Mr. Prywell, the alarm of their coming before. Wherefore they set a strong watch at the gates, and had also doubled their guards; they also mounted their slings in good places, where they might conveniently cast out their great stones to the annoyance of the furious enemy.

Nor could those Diabolonians that were in the town do that hurt as was designed they should; for Mansoul was now awake. But alas poor people, they were sorely affrighted at the first appearance of their foes, and at their sitting down before the town, especially when they heard the roaring of their drum. This, to speak truth, was amazingly hideous to hear; it frightened all men seven miles round, if they were but awake and heard it. The streaming of their colours was also terrible and dejecting to behold.

When Diabolus was come up against the town, first he made his approach to Ear-gate, and gave it a furious assault, supposing, as it seems, that his friends in Mansoul had been ready to do the work within; but care was taken of that before, by the vigilance of the captains. Wherefore missing of the help that he expected from them, and finding his army warmly attended with the stones that the slingers did sling (for that I will say for the captains, that considering the weakness that yet was upon them by reason of the long sickness that had annoyed the town of Mansoul, they did gallantly behave themselves), he was forced to make some retreat from Mansoul, and to entrench himself and his men in the field without the reach of the slings of the town.

Now, having entrenched himself, he did cast up four mounts against the town: the first he called Mount Diabolus, putting his own name thereon, the more to affright the town of Mansoul; the other three he called thus—Mount Alecto, Mount Megara, and Mount Tisiphone; for these are the names of the dreadful furies of hell. Thus he began to play his game with Mansoul, and to serve it as doth the lion his prey, even to make it fall before his terror. But, as I said, the captains and soldiers resisted so stoutly, and did do such execution with their stones, that they made him, though against stomach, to retreat; wherefore Mansoul began to take courage.

Now upon Mount Diabolus, which was raised on the north side of the town, there did the tyrant set up his standard, and a fearful thing it was to behold; for he had wrought in it by devilish art, after the manner of a scutcheon, a flaming flame fearful to behold, and the picture of Mansoul burning in it.

When Diabolus had thus done, he commanded that his drummer should every night approach the walls of the town of Mansoul, and so to beat a parley; the command was to do it at nights, for in the day-time they annoyed him with their slings; for the tyrant said, that he had a mind to parley with the now trembling town of Mansoul, and he commanded that the drums should beat every night, that through weariness they might at last, if possible (at the first they were unwilling yet), be forced to do it.

So this drummer did as commanded: he arose, and did beat his drum. But when his drum did go, if one looked toward the town of Mansoul, behold darkness and sorrow, and the light was darkened in the heavens thereof. No noise was ever heard upon earth more terrible, except the voice of Shaddai when he speaketh. But how did Mansoul tremble! it now looked for nothing but forthwith to be swallowed up.

The Drummer Beats for a Parley

When this drummer had beaten for a parley, he made this speech to Mansoul: "My master has bid me tell you, that if you will willingly submit you shall have the good of the earth; but if you shall be stubborn, he is resolved to take you by force." But by that the fugitive had done beating his drum, the people of Mansoul had betaken themselves to the captains that were in the castle, so that there was none to regard nor to give this drummer an answer; so he proceeded no further that night, but returned again to his master to the camp.

When Diabolus saw that by drumming he could not work out Mansoul to his will, the next night he sendeth his drummer without his drum, still to let the townsmen know that he had a mind to parley with them. But when all came to all, his parley was turned into a summons to the town to deliver up themselves: but they gave him neither heed nor hearing, for they remembered what at first it cost them to hear him a few words.

The next night he sends again, and then who should be his messenger to Mansoul but the terrible Captain Sepulchre; so Captain Sepulchre came up to the walls of Mansoul, and made this oration to the town:—

"O ye inhabitants of the rebellious town of Mansoul! I summon you in the name of the Prince Diabolus, that, without any more ado, you set open the gates of your town, and admit the great lord to come in. But if you shall still rebel, when we have taken to us the town by force, we will swallow you up as the grave; wherefore if you will hearken unto my summons, say so, and if not, then let me know.

"The reason of this my summons," quoth he, "is for that my lord is your undoubted prince and lord, as you yourselves have formerly owned. Nor shall that assault that was given to my lord, when Emmanuel dealt so dishonourably by him, prevail with him to lose his right, and to forbear to attempt to recover his own. Consider, then, O Mansoul, with thyself, wilt thou show thyself, peaceable or no? If thou shalt quietly yield up thyself, then our old friendship shall be renewed; but if thou shalt yet refuse and rebel, then expect nothing but fire and sword."

When the languishing town of Mansoul had heard this summoner and his summons, they were yet more put to their dumps, but made to the captain no answer at all; so away he went as he came.

But, after some consultation among themselves, as also with some of their captains, they applied themselves afresh to the Lord Secretary for counsel and advice from him; for this Lord Secretary was their chief preacher (as also is mentioned some pages before), only now he was ill at ease; and of him they begged favour in these two or three things:—

1. That he would look comfortably upon them, and not keep himself so much retired from them as formerly. Also, that he would be prevailed with to give them a hearing, while they should make known their miserable condition to him. But to this he told them as before, "that as yet he was but ill at ease, and therefore could not do as he had formerly done."

2. The second thing that they desired was, that he would be pleased to give them his advice about their now so important affairs, for that Diabolus was come and set down before the town with no less than twenty thousand Doubters. They said, moreover, that both he and his captains were cruel men, and that they were afraid of them. But to this he said, "You must look to the law of the Prince, and there see what is laid upon you to do."

3. Then they desired that his Highness would help them to frame a petition to Shaddai, and unto Emmanuel his Son, and that he would set his own hand thereto as a token that he was one with them in it: "For," said they, "my lord, many a one have we sent, but can get no answer of peace; but now, surely one with thy hand unto it may obtain good for Mansoul."

But all the answer that he gave to this was, "that they had offended their Emmanuel, and had also grieved himself, and that therefore they must as yet partake of their own devices."

This answer of the Lord Secretary fell like a millstone upon them; yea, it crushed them so that they could not tell what to do; yet they durst not comply with the demands of Diabolus, nor with the demands of his captain. So, then, here were the straits that the town of Mansoul was betwixt, when the enemy came upon her; her foes were ready to swallow her up, and her friends did forbear to help her.

Then stood up my Lord Mayor, whose name was my Lord Understanding, and he began to pick and pick, until he had pickt comfort out of that seemingly bitter saying of the Lord Secretary's; for thus he descanted upon it: "First," said he, "this unavoidably follows upon the saying of our Lord, 'that we must yet suffer for our sins.' Secondly, But," quoth he, "the words yet sound as if at last we should be saved from our enemies; and that after a few more sorrows, Emmanuel will come and be our help."

Now, the Lord Mayor was the more critical in his dealing with the Secretary's words, because my lord was more than a prophet, and because none of his words were such but that at all times they were most exactly significant; and the townsmen were allowed to pry into them, and to expound them to their best advantage.

So they took their leaves of my lord, and returned, and went, and came to the captains, to whom they did tell what my Lord High Secretary had said·

who, when they had heard it, were all of the same opinion as was my Lord Mayor himself. The captains, therefore, began to take some courage unto them, and to prepare to make some brave attempt upon the camp of the enemy, and to destroy all that were Diabolonians, with the roving Doubters that the tyrant had brought with him to destroy the poor town of Mansoul.

So all betook themselves forthwith to their places—the captains to theirs, the Lord Mayor to his, the subordinate preacher to his, and my Lord Will-be-will to his. The captains longed to be at some work for their Prince; for they delighted in warlike achievements. The next day, therefore, they came together and consulted; and after consultation had, they resolved to give an answer to the captain of Diabolus with slings; and so they did at the rising of the sun on the morrow; for Diabolus had adventured to come nearer again, but the sling-stones were to him and his like hornets. For as there is nothing to the town of Mansoul so terrible as the roaring of Diabolus's drum, so there is nothing to Diabolus so terrible as the well playing of Emmanuel's slings. Wherefore Diabolus was forced to make another retreat, yet farther off from the famous town of Mansoul. Then did the Lord Mayor of Mansoul cause the bells to be rung, "and that thanks should be sent to the Lord High Secretary by the mouth of the subordinate preacher; for that by his words the captains and elders of Mansoul had been strengthened against Diabolus."

When Diabolus saw that his captains and soldiers, high lords and renowned, were frightened and beaten down by the stones that came from the golden slings of the Prince of the town of Mansoul, he bethought himself, and said, "I will try to catch them by fawning; I will try to flatter them into my net."

Wherefore, after a while he came down again to the wall, not now with his drum, nor with Captain Sepulchre; but having all to-besugared his lips, he seemed to be a very sweet-mouthed, peaceable prince, designing nothing for humour's sake, nor to be revenged on Mansoul for injuries by them done to him; but the welfare and good and advantage of the town and people therein was now, as he said, his only design. Wherefore, after he had called for audience, and desired that the townsfolk would give it to him, he proceeded in his oration, and said:—

"Oh, the desire of my heart, the famous town of Mansoul! how many nights have I watched, and how many weary steps have I taken, if perhaps I might do thee good! Far be it, far be it from me to desire to make a war upon you, if ye will but willingly and quietly deliver up yourselves unto me. You know that you were mine of old. Remember also that so long as you enjoyed me for your lord, and that I enjoyed you for my subjects, you wanted for nothing of all the delights of the earth that I, your lord and prince, could get for you, or that I could invent to make you bonny and blithe withal. Consider you never had so many hard, dark, troublesome and heart-afflicting hours while you were mine as you have had since you revolted from me, nor shall you ever have peace again until you and I become one as before. But be but prevailed with to embrace me again, and I will grant, yea, enlarge your old charter with abundance of privileges, so that your licence and liberty shall be to take, hold, enjoy, and make your own all that is pleasant from the east to the west. Nor shall any of those incivilities wherewith you have offended me be ever charged upon you by me so long as the sun and moon endure. Nor shall any of those dear friends of mine that now, for the fear of you, lie lurking in dens, and holes, and caves in Mansoul, be hurtful to you any more; yea, they shall be your servants, and shall minister unto you of their substance, and of whatever shall come to hand. I need speak no more. You know them, and have some time since been much delighted in their company. Why, then, should we abide at such odds? Let us renew our old acquaintance and friendship again.

"Bear with your friend; I take the liberty at this time to speak thus freely unto you. The love that I have to you presses me to do it, as also does the zeal of my heart for my friends with you. Put me not, therefore, to further trouble, nor yourselves to further fears and frights. Have you I will, in a way of peace or war. Nor do you flatter yourselves with the power and force of your captains, or that your Emmanuel will shortly come in to your help, for such strength will do you no pleasure.

"I am come against you with a stout and valiant army, and all the chief princes of the den are even at the head of it. Besides, my captains are swifter than eagles, stronger than lions, and more greedy of prey than are the evening wolves. What is Og of Bashan? what's Goliath of Gath? and what's an hundred more of them to one of the least of my captains? How, then, shall Mansoul think to escape my hand and force?"

The Lord Mayor's Answer

Diabolus having thus ended his flattering, fawning, deceitful, and lying speech to the famous town of Mansoul, the Lord Mayor replied to him as follows:—

"O Diabolus, prince of darkness, and master of all deceit, thy lying flatteries we have had and made sufficient probation of, and have tasted too deeply of that destructive cup already. Should we therefore again hearken unto thee, and so break the commandments of our great Shaddai to join in affinity with thee, would not our Prince reject us, and cast us off for ever? And, being cast off by him, can the place that he has prepared for thee be a place of rest for us? Besides, O thou that art empty and void of all truth, we are rather ready to die by thy hand than to fall in with thy flattering and lying deceits."

When the tyrant saw that there was little to be got by parleying with my Lord Mayor, he fell into a hellish rage, and resolved that again, with his army of Doubters, he would another time assault the town of Mansoul.

So he called for his drummer, who beat up for his men (and while he did beat, Mansoul did shake) to be in a readiness to give battle to the corporation: then Diabolus drew near with his army, and thus disposed of his men.

Captain Cruel and Captain Torment, these he drew up and placed against Feel-gate, and commanded them to sit down there for the war. And he also appointed that, if need were, Captain No-Ease should come in to their relief. At Nose-gate he placed the Captain Brimstone and Captain Sepulchre, and bid them look well to their ward, on that side of the town of Mansoul. But at Eye-gate he placed that grim-faced one, the Captain Past-Hope, and there also now did he set up his terrible standard.

Now Captain Insatiable, he was to look to the carriage of Diabolus, and was also appointed to take into custody that, or those persons and things, that should at any time as prey be taken from the enemy.

Now Mouth-gate the inhabitants kept for a sally-port; wherefore that they kept strong; for that was it by and out at which the townsfolk did send their petitions to Emmanuel their Prince. That also was the gate from the top of which the captains did play their slings at the enemies; for that gate stood somewhat ascending, so that the placing of them there, and the letting of them fly from that place, did much execution against the tyrant's army. Wherefore, for these causes, with others, Diabolus sought, if possible, to land up Mouth-gate with dirt.

Now, as Diabolus was busy and industrious in preparing to make his assault upon the town of Mansoul without, so the captains and soldiers in the corporation were as busy in preparing within; they mounted their slings, they set up their banners, they sounded their trumpets, and put themselves in such order as was judged most for the annoyance of the enemy, and for the advantage of Mansoul, and gave to their soldiers orders to be ready, at the sound of the trumpet, for war. The Lord Will-be-will also, he took the charge of watching against the rebels within, and to do what he could to take them while without, or to stifle them within their caves, dens, and holes in the town-wall of Mansoul. And, to speak the truth of him, ever since he took penance for his fault, he has showed as much honesty and bravery of spirit as any he in Mansoul; for he took one Jolly, and his brother Griggish, the two sons of his servant Harmless-Mirth (for to that day, though the father was committed to ward, the sons had a dwelling in the house of my lord),—I say, he took them, and with his own hands put them to the cross. And this was the reason why he hanged them up: after their father was put into the hands of Mr. True-Man, the gaoler, they, his sons, began to play his pranks, and to be ticking and toying with the daughters of their lord; nay, it was jealoused that they were too familiar with them, the which was brought to his lordship's ear. Now, his lordship being unwilling unadvisedly to put any man to death, did not suddenly fall upon them, but set watch and spies to see if the thing was true; of the which he was soon informed, for his two servants, whose names were Find-out and Tell-all, catcht them together in uncivil manner more than once or twice, and went and told their lord. So when my Lord Will-be-will had sufficient ground to believe the thing was true, he takes the two young Diabolonians (for such they were, for their father was a Diabolonian born), and has them to Eye-gate, where he raised a very high cross, just in the face of Diabolus and of his army, and there he hanged the young villains, in defiance to Captain Past-Hope, and of the horrible standard of the tyrant.

Now, this Christian act of the brave Lord Will-be-will did greatly abash Captain Past-Hope, discouraged the army of Diabolus, put fear into the Diabolonian runagates in Mansoul, and put strength and courage into the captains that belonged to Emmanuel, the Prince; for they without did gather, and that by this very act of my lord, that Mansoul was resolved to fight, and that the Diabolonians within the town could not do such things as Diabolus had hopes they would. Nor was this the only proof of the brave Lord Will-be-will's honesty to the town, nor of his loyalty to his Prince, as will afterwards appear.

Now, when the children of Prudent-Thrifty, who dwelt with Mr. Mind (for Thrift left children with Mr. Mind, when he was also committed to prison, and their names were Gripe and Rake-all; these he begat of Mr. Mind's bastard daughter, whose name was Mrs. Holdfast-Bad);—I say, when his children perceived how the Lord Will-be-will had served them that dwelt with him, what do they but, lest they should drink of the same cup, endeavour to make their escape. But Mr. Mind, being wary of it, took them and put them in hold in his house till morning (for this was done over night), and remembering that by the law of Mansoul all Diabolonians were to die (and to be sure they were at least by father's side such, and some say by mother's side too), what does he but takes them and puts them in chains, and carries them to the selfsame place where my lord hanged his two before, and there he hanged them.

The townsmen also took great encouragement at this act of Mr. Mind, and did what they could to have taken some more of these Diabolonian troubles of Mansoul; but at that time the rest lay so quiet and close, that they could not be apprehended; so they set against them a very diligent watch and went every man to his place.

I told you a little before, that Diabolus and his army were somewhat abasht and discouraged at the sight of what my Lord Will-be-will did, when he hanged up those two young Diabolonians; but his discouragement quickly turned itself into furious madness and rage against the town of Mansoul, and fight it he would. Also the townsmen and captains within, they had their hopes and their expectations heightened, believing at last the day would be theirs; so they feared them the less. Their subordinate preacher, too, made a sermon about it; and he took that theme for his text, Gad, a troop shall overcome him: but he shall overcome at the last. Whence he showed, that though Mansoul should be sorely put to it at the first, yet the victory should most certainly be Mansoul's at the last.

So Diabolus commanded that his drummer should beat a charge against the town; and the captains also that were in the town sounded a charge against them, but they had no drum: they were trumpets of silver with which they sounded against them. Then they which were of the camp of Diabolus came down to the town to take it, and the captains in the castle, with the slingers at Mouth-gate, played upon them amain. And now there was nothing heard in the camp of Diabolus but horrible rage and blasphemy; but in the town good words, prayer, and singing of psalms. The enemy replied with horrible objections, and the terribleness of their drum; but the town made answer with the slapping of their slings, and the melodious noise of their trumpets. And thus the fight lasted for several days together, only now and then they had some small intermission, in the which the townsmen refreshed themselves, and the captains made ready for another assault.

The captains of Emmanuel were clad in silver armour, and the soldiers in that which was of proof; the soldiers of Diabolus were clad in iron, which was made to give place to Emmanuel's engine-shot. In the town, some were hurt and some were greatly wounded. Now, the worst on't was, a chirurgeon was scarce in Mansoul, for that Emmanuel at present was absent. Howbeit, with the leaves of a tree the wounded were kept from dying; yet their wounds did greatly putrefy, and some did grievously stink. Of the townsmen, these were wounded, to wit, my Lord Reason; he was wounded in the head. Another that was wounded was the brave Lord Mayor; he was wounded in the eye. Another that was wounded was Mr. Mind; he received his wound about the stomach. The honest subordinate preacher also, he received a shot not far off the heart; but none of these were mortal.

Many also of the inferior sort were not only wounded, but slain outright.

Now, in the camp of Diabolus were wounded and slain a considerable number; for instance, Captain Rage, he was wounded, and so was Captain Cruel. Captain Damnation was made to retreat, and to entrench himself farther off at Mansoul. The standard also of Diabolus was beaten down, and his standard-bearer, Captain Much-Hurt, had his brains beat out with a slingstone, to the no little grief and shame of his prince, Diabolus.

Many also of the Doubters were slain outright, though enough of them were left alive to make Mansoul shake and totter. Now the victory that day being turned to Mansoul, did put great valour into the townsmen and captains, and did cover Diabolus's camp with a cloud, but withal it made them far more furious. So the next day Mansoul rested, and commanded that the bells should be rung; the trumpets also joyfully sounded, and the captains shouted round the town.

My Lord Will-be-will also was not idle, but did notable service within against the domestics, or the Diabolonians that were in the town, not only by keeping them in awe, for he lighted on one at last whose name was Mr. Anything, a fellow of whom mention was made before; for 'twas he, if you remember, that brought the three fellows to Diabolus, whom the Diabolonians took out of Captain Boanerges' companies, and that persuaded them to list themselves under the tyrant, to fight against the army of Shaddai. My Lord Will-be-will did also take a notable Diabolonian, whose name was Loose-Foot. This Loose-Foot was a scout to the vagabonds in Mansoul, and that did use to carry tidings out of Mansoul to the camp, and out of the camp to those of the enemies in Mansoul. Both these my lord sent away safe to Mr. True-Man, the gaoler, with a commandment to keep them in irons; for he intended then to have them out to be crucified, when it would be for the best to the corporation, and most for the discouragement of the camp of the enemies.

My Lord Mayor also, though he could not stir about so much as formerly, because of the wound that he lately received, yet gave he out orders to all that were the natives of Mansoul, to look to their watch, and stand upon their guard, and, as occasion should offer, to prove themselves men.

Mr. Conscience, the preacher, he also did his utmost to keep all his good documents alive upon the hearts of the people of Mansoul.

Well, a while after, the captains and stout ones of the town of Mansoul agreed and resolved upon a time to make a sally out upon the camp of Diabolus, and this must be done in the night; and there was the folly of Mansoul (for the night is always the best for the enemy, but the worst for Mansoul to fight in); but yet they would do it, their courage was so high; their last victory also still stuck in their memories.

So the night appointed being come, the Prince's brave captains cast lots who should lead the van in this new and desperate expedition against Diabolus, and against his Diabolonian army; and the lot fell to Captain Credence, to Captain Experience, and to Captain Good-Hope to lead the forlorn hope. (This Captain Experience the Prince created such when himself did reside in the town of Mansoul.) So, as I said, they made their sally out upon the army that lay in the siege against them; and their hap was to fall in with the main body of their enemies. Now, Diabolus and his men being expertly accustomed to night-work, took the alarm presently, and were as ready to give them battle as if they had sent them word of their coming. Wherefore to it they went amain, and blows were hard on every side; the hell-drum also was beat most furiously, while the trumpets of the Prince most sweetly sounded. And thus the battle was joined; and Captain Insatiable looked to the enemy's carriages, and waited when he should receive some prey.

The Prince's captains fought it stoutly, beyond what indeed could be expected they should; they wounded many; they made the whole army of Diabolus to make a retreat. But I cannot tell how, but the brave Captain Credence, Captain Good-Hope, and Captain Experience, as they were upon the pursuit, cutting down, and following hard after the enemy in the rear, Captain Credence stumbled and fell, by which fall he caught so great a hurt, that he could not rise till Captain Experience did help him up, at which their men were put in disorder. The captain also was so full of pain that he could not forbear but aloud to cry out: at this, the other two captains fainted, supposing that Captain Credence had received his mortal wound; their men also were more disordered, and had no list to fight. Now, Diabolus, being very observing, though at this time as yet he was put to the worst, perceiving that a halt was made among the men that were the pursuers, what does he, but taking it for granted that the captains were either wounded or dead, he therefore makes at first a stand, then faces about, and so comes up upon the Prince's army with as much of his fury as hell could help him to; and his hap was to fall in just among the three captains, Captain Credence, Captain Good-Hope, and Captain Experience, and did cut, wound, and pierce them so dreadfully, that what through the wounds that now they had received, and also the loss of much blood, they scarce were able, though they had for their power the three best bands in Mansoul, to get safe into the hold again.

Now, when the body of the Prince's army saw how these three captains were put to the worst, they thought it their wisdom to make as safe and good a retreat as they could, and so returned by the sally-port again; and so there was an end of this present action. But Diabolus was so flushed with this night's work, that he promised himself, in few days, an easy and complete conquest over the town of Mansoul; wherefore, on the day following, he comes up to the sides thereof with great boldness, and demands entrance, and that forthwith they deliver themselves up to his government. The Diabolonians, too, that were within, they began to be somewhat brisk, as we shall show afterward.

But the valiant Lord Mayor replied, That what he got he must get by force; for as long as Emmanuel, their Prince, was alive (though he at present was not so with them as they wished), they should never consent to yield Mansoul up to another.

And with that the Lord Will-be-will stood up, and said, "Diabolus, thou master of the den and enemy to all that is good, we poor inhabitants of the town of Mansoul are too well acquainted with thy rule and government, and with the end of those things that for certain will follow submitting to thee, to do it. Wherefore, though while we were without knowledge we suffered thee to take us (as the bird that saw not the snare fell into the hands of the fowler), yet since we have been turned from darkness to light, we have also been turned from the power of Satan to God. And though through thy subtilty, and also the subtilty of the Diabolonians within, we have sustained much loss, and also plunged ourselves into much perplexity, yet give up ourselves, lay down our arms, and yield to so horrid a tyrant as thou, we shall not; die upon the place we choose rather to do. Besides, we have hopes that in time deliverance will come from court unto us, and therefore we yet will maintain a war against thee."

This brave speech of the Lord Will-be-will, with that also of the Lord Mayor, did somewhat abate the boldness of Diabolus, though it kindled the fury of his rage. It also succoured the townsmen and captains; yea, it was as a plaster to the brave Captain Credence's wound; for you must know that a brave speech now (when the captains of the town with their men of war came home routed, and when the enemy took courage and boldness at the success that he had obtained to draw up to the walls, and demand entrance, as he did) was in season, and also advantageous.

Will-be-will's Gallantry

The Lord Will-be-will did also play the man within; for while the captains and soldiers were in the field, he was in arms in the town, and wherever by him there was a Diabolonian found, they were forced to feel the weight of his heavy hand, and also the edge of his penetrating sword: many therefore of the Diabolonians he wounded, as the Lord Cavil, the Lord Brisk, the Lord Pragmatic, and the Lord Murmur: several also of the meaner sort he did sorely maim; though there cannot at this time an account be given you of any that he slew outright. The cause, or rather the advantage that my Lord Will-be-will had at this time to do thus, was for that the captains were gone out to fight the enemy in the field. "For now," thought the Diabolonians within, "is our time to stir and make an uproar in the town." What do they, therefore, but quickly get themselves into a body, and fall forthwith to hurricaning in Mansoul, as if now nothing but whirlwind and tempest should be there. Wherefore, as I said, he takes this opportunity to fall in among them with his men, cutting and slashing with courage that was undaunted; at which the Diabolonians with all haste dispersed themselves to their holds, and my lord to his place as before.

This brave act of my lord did somewhat revenge the wrong done by Diabolus to the captains, and also did let them know that Mansoul was not to be parted with for the loss of a victory or two; wherefore the wing of the tyrant was clipt again, as to boasting,—I mean in comparison of what he would have done if the Diabolonians had put the town to the same plight to which he had put the captains.

Well, Diabolus yet resolves to have the other bout with Mansoul. "For," thought he, "since I beat them once, I may beat them twice." Wherefore he commanded his men to be ready at such an hour of the night to make a fresh assault upon the town; and he gave it out in special that they should bend all their forces against Feel-gate, and attempt to break into the town through that. The word that then he did give to his officers and soldiers was Hell-fire. "And," said he, "if we break in upon them, as I wish we do, either with some or with all our force, let them that break in look to it that they forget not the word. And let nothing be heard in the town of Mansoul but 'Hell-fire! Hell-fire! Hell-fire!'" The drummer was also to beat without ceasing, and the standard-bearers were to display their colours; the soldiers, too, were to put on what courage they could, and to see that they played manfully their parts against the town.

So when night was come, and all things by the tyrant made ready for the work, he suddenly makes his assault upon Feel-gate, and after he had awhile struggled there, he throws the gate wide open: for the truth is, those gates were but weak, and so most easily made to yield. When Diabolus had thus far made his attempt, he placed his captains (namely, Torment and No-Ease) there; so he attempted to press forward, but the Prince's captains came down upon him, and made his entrance more difficult than he desired. And, to speak truth, they made what resistance they could; but the three of their best and most valiant captains being wounded, and by their wounds made much incapable of doing the town that service they would (and all the rest having more than their hands full of the Doubters, and their captains that did follow Diabolus), they were overpowered with force, nor could they keep them out of the town. Wherefore the Prince's men and their captains betook themselves to the castle, as to the stronghold of the town; and this they did partly for their own security, partly for the security of the town, and partly, or rather chiefly, to preserve to Emmanuel the prerogative royal of Mansoul; for so was the castle of Mansoul.

The captains, therefore, being fled into the castle, the enemy, without much resistance, possess themselves of the rest of the town, and spreading themselves as they went into every corner, they cried out as they marched, according to the command of the tyrant, "Hell-fire! Hell-fire! Hell-fire!" so that nothing for a while throughout the town of Mansoul could be heard but the direful noise of "Hell-fire!" together with the roaring of Diabolus's drum. And now did the clouds hang black over Mansoul, nor to reason did anything but ruin seem to attend it. Diabolus also quartered his soldiers in the houses of the inhabitants of the town of Mansoul. Yea, the subordinate preacher's house was as full of these outlandish Doubters as ever it could hold, and so was my Lord Mayor's, and my Lord Will-be-will's also. Yea, where was there a corner, a cottage, a barn, or a hog-stye, that now was not full of these vermin? Yea, they turned the men of the town out of their houses, and would lie in their beds, and sit at their tables themselves. Ah, poor Mansoul! now thou feelest the fruits of sin, and what venom was in the flattering words of Mr. Carnal-Security! They made great havoc of whatever they laid their hands on: yea, they fired the town in several places; many young children also were by them dashed in pieces; yea, those that were yet unborn they destroyed in their mother's wombs; for you must needs think that it could not now be otherwise; for what conscience, what pity, what bowels of compassion can any expect at the hands of outlandish Doubters? Many in Mansoul that were women, both young and old, they forced, ravished, and beastlike abused, so that they swooned, miscarried, and many of them died, and so lay at the top of every street, and in all by-places of the town.

And now did Mansoul seem to be nothing but a den of dragons, an emblem of hell, and a place of total darkness. Now did Mansoul lie almost like the barren wilderness; nothing but nettles, briars, thorns, weeds, and stinking things seemed now to cover the face of Mansoul. I told you before, how that these Diabolonian Doubters turned the men of Mansoul out of their beds; and now I will add, they wounded them, they mauled them, yea, and almost brained many of them. Many, did I say?—yea most, if not all of them. Mr. Conscience they so wounded, yea, and his wounds so festered, that he could have no ease day or night, but lay as if continually upon a rack; but that Shaddai rules all, certainly they had slain him outright. My Lord Mayor they so abused that they almost put out his eyes; and had not my Lord Will-be-will got into the castle, they intended to have chopt him all to pieces; for they did look upon him, as his heart now stood, to be one of the very worst that was in Mansoul against Diabolus and his crew. And indeed he hath shown himself a man, and more of his exploits you will hear of afterwards.

THE EVIL STATE OF MANSOUL

Now a man might have walked for days together in Mansoul, and scarcely have seen one in the town that looked like a religious man. Oh, the fearful state of Mansoul now! Now every corner swarmed with outlandish Doubters; red-coats and black-coats walked the town by clusters, and filled up all the houses with hideous noises, vain songs, lying stories, and blasphemous language against Shaddai and his Son. Now also these Diabolonians that lurked in the walls and dens and holes that were in the town of Mansoul, came forth and showed themselves; yea, walked with open face in company with the Doubters that were in Mansoul. Yea, they had more boldness now to walk the streets, to haunt the houses, and to show themselves abroad, than had any of the honest inhabitants of the now woeful town of Mansoul.

But Diabolus and his outlandish men were not at peace in Mansoul; for they were not there entertained as were the captains and forces of Emmanuel: the townsmen did browbeat them what they could; nor did they partake or make stroy of any of the necessaries of Mansoul, but that which they seized on against the townsmen's will: what they could, they hid from them, and what they could not, they had with an ill will. They, poor hearts, had rather have had their room than their company; but they were at present their captives, and their captives for the present they were forced to be. But, I say, they discountenanced them as much as they were able, and showed them all the dislike that they could.

The captains also from the castle, did hold them in continual play with their slings, to the chafing and fretting of the minds of the enemies. True, Diabolus made a great many attempts to have broken open the gates of the castle, but Mr. Godly-Fear was made the keeper of that; and he was a man of that courage, conduct, and valour, that it was in vain, as long as life lasted with him, to think to do that work, though mostly desired; wherefore all the attempts that Diabolus made against him were fruitless. I have wished sometimes that the man had had the whole rule of the town of Mansoul.

Well, this was the condition of the town of Mansoul for about two years and a half: the body of the town was the seat of war, the people of the town were driven into holes, and the glory of Mansoul was laid in the dust. What rest, then, could be to the inhabitants, what peace could Mansoul have, and what sun could shine upon it? Had the enemy lain so long without in the plain against the town, it had been enough to have famished them; but now, when they shall be within, when the town shall be their tent, their trench and fort against the castle that was in the town; when the town shall be against the town, and shall serve to be a defence to the enemies of her strength and life; I say, when they shall make use of the forts and town-holds to secure themselves in, even till they shall take, spoil, and demolish the castle,—this was terrible! and yet this was now the state of the town of Mansoul.

After the town of Mansoul had been in this sad and lamentable condition for so long a time as I have told you, and no petitions that they presented their Prince with, all this while, could prevail, the inhabitants of the town, namely, the elders and chief of Mansoul, gathered together, and, after some time spent in condoling their miserable state, and this miserable judgment coming upon them, they agreed together to draw up yet another petition, and to send it away to Emmanuel for relief. But Mr. Godly-Fear stood up and answered, that he knew that his Lord the Prince never did nor ever would receive a petition for these matters, from the hand of any whoever, unless the Lord Secretary's hand was to it. "And this," quoth he, "is the reason that you prevailed not all this while." Then they said they would draw up one, and get the Lord Secretary's hand to it. But Mr. Godly-Fear answered again, that he knew also that the Lord Secretary would not set his hand to any petition that himself had not a hand in composing and drawing up. "And, besides," said he, "the Prince doth know my Lord Secretary's hand from all the hands in the world; wherefore he cannot be deceived by any pretence whatever. Wherefore, my advice is that you go to my Lord, and implore him to lend you his aid." (Now he did yet abide in the castle, where all the captains and men-at-arms were.)

So they heartily thanked Mr. Godly-Fear, took his counsel, and did as he had bidden them. So they went and came to my Lord, and made known the cause of their coming to him; namely, that since Mansoul was in so deplorable a condition, his Highness would be pleased to undertake to draw up a petition from them to Emmanuel, the son of the mighty Shaddai, and to their King and his Father by him.

Then said the Secretary to them, "What petition is it that you would have me draw up for you?" But they said, "Our Lord knows best the state and condition of the town of Mansoul; and how we are backslidden and degenerated from the Prince: thou also knowest who is come up to war against us, and how Mansoul is now the seat of war. My Lord knows, moreover, what barbarous usages our men, women, and children have suffered at their hands; and how our home-bred Diabolonians do walk now with more boldness than dare the townsmen in the streets of Mansoul. Let our Lord, therefore, according to the wisdom of God that is in him, draw up a petition for his poor servants to our Prince Emmanuel." "Well," said the Lord Secretary, "I will draw up a petition for you, and will set my hand thereto." Then said they, "But when shall we call for it at the hands of our Lord?" But he answered, "Yourselves must be present at the doing of it; yea, you must put your desires to it. True, the hand and pen shall be mine, but the ink and paper must be yours; else how can you say it is your petition? Nor have I need to petition for myself, because I have not offended."

He also added as followeth: "No petition goes from me in my name to the Prince, and so to his Father by him, but when the people that are chiefly concerned therein do join in heart and soul in the matter, for that must be inserted therein."

So they did heartily agree with the sentence of the Lord, and a petition was forthwith drawn up for them. But now, who should carry it? that was next. But the Secretary advised that Captain Credence should carry it; for he was a well-spoken man. They therefore called for him, and propounded to him the business. "Well," said the captain, "I gladly accept of the motion; and though I am lame, I will do this business for you with as much speed and as well as I can."

The contents of the petition were to this purpose:—

"O our Lord, and Sovereign Prince Emmanuel, the potent, the long-suffering Prince! grace is poured into thy lips, and to thee belongs mercy and forgiveness, though we have rebelled against thee. We, who are no more worthy to be called thy Mansoul, nor yet fit to partake of common benefits, do beseech thee, and thy Father by thee, to do away our transgressions. We confess that thou mightest cast us away for them; but do it not for thy name's sake; let the Lord rather take an opportunity, at our miserable condition, to let out his bowels and compassions to us. We are compassed on every side, Lord; our own backslidings reprove us; our Diabolonians within our town fright us; and the army of the angel of the bottomless pit distresses us. Thy grace can be our salvation, and whither to go but to thee we know not.

"Furthermore, O gracious Prince, we have weakened our captains, and they are discouraged, sick, and of late some of them grievously worsted and beaten out of the field by the power and force of the tyrant. Yea, even those of our captains in whose valour we did formerly use to put most of our confidence, they are as wounded men. Besides, Lord, our enemies are lively and they are strong; they vaunt and boast themselves, and do threaten to part us among themselves for a booty. They are fallen also upon us, Lord, with many thousand Doubters, such as with whom we cannot tell what to do; they are all grim-looked and unmerciful ones, and they bid defiance to us and thee.

"Our wisdom is gone, our power is gone, because thou art departed from us; nor have we what we may call ours but sin, shame, and confusion of face for sin. Take pity upon us, O Lord, take pity upon us, thy miserable town of Mansoul, and save us out of the hands of our enemies. Amen."

This petition, as was touched afore, was handed by the Lord Secretary, and carried to the court by the brave and most stout Captain Credence. Now, he carried it out at Mouth-gate (for that, as I said, was the sally-port of the town), and he went and came to Emmanuel with it. Now, how it came out I do not know; but for certain it did, and that so far as to reach the ears of Diabolus. Thus I conclude, because that the tyrant had it presently by the end, and charged the town of Mansoul with it, saying, "Thou rebellious and stubborn-hearted Mansoul, I will make thee to leave off petitioning. Art thou yet for petitioning? I will make thee to leave." Yea, he also knew who the messenger was that carried the petition to the Prince, and it made him both to fear and rage.

Wherefore he commanded that his drum should be beat again, a thing that Mansoul could not abide to hear; but when Diabolus will have his drum beat, Mansoul must abide the noise. Well, the drum was beat, and the Diabolonians were gathered together.

The Rage of Diabolus

Then said Diabolus, "O ye stout Diabolonians, be it known unto you that there is treachery hatcht against us in the rebellious town of Mansoul, for albeit the town is in our possession, as you see, yet these miserable Mansoulians have attempted to dare, and have been so hardy as yet to send to the court to Emmanuel for help. This I give you to understand, that ye may yet know how to carry it to the wretched town of Mansoul. Wherefore, O my trusty Diabolonians, I command that yet more and more ye distress this town of Mansoul, and vex it with your wiles, ravish their women, deflower their virgins, slay their children, brain their ancients, fire their town, and what other mischief you can; and let this be the reward of the Mansoulians from me, for their desperate rebellions against me."

This, you see, was the charge; but something stept in betwixt that and execution, for as yet there was but little more done than to rage.

Moreover, when Diabolus had done thus, he went the next way up to the castle gates, and demanded that, upon pain of death, the gates should be opened to him, and that entrance should be given him and his men that followed after. To whom Mr. Godly-Fear replied (for he it was that had the charge of that gate), that the gate should not be opened unto him, nor to the men that followed after him. He said, moreover, that Mansoul, when she had suffered a while, should be made perfect, strengthened, settled.

Then said Diabolus, "Deliver me, then, the men that have petitioned against me, especially Captain Credence, that carried it to your Prince. Deliver that varlet into my hands, and I will depart from the town."

Then up starts a Diabolonian, whose name was Mr. Fooling, and said, "My lord offereth you fair. It is better for you that one man perish than that your whole Mansoul should be undone."

But Mr. Godly-Fear made him this replication: "How long will Mansoul be kept out of the dungeon when she hath given up her faith to Diabolus? As good lose the town as lose Captain Credence, for if one be gone the other must follow." But to that Mr. Fooling said nothing.

Then did my Lord Mayor reply, and said, "O thou devouring tyrant, be it known unto thee, we shall hearken to none of thy words. We are resolved to resist thee as long as a captain, a man, a sling, and a stone to throw at thee shall be found in the town of Mansoul."

But Diabolus answered, "Do you hope, do you wait, do you look for help and deliverance? You have sent to Emmanuel, but your wickedness sticks too close in your skirts to let innocent prayers come out of your lips. Think you that you shall be prevailers and prosper in this design? You will fail in your wish, you will fail in your attempts, for 'tis not only I, but your Emmanuel is against you: yea, it is he that hath sent me against you to subdue you. For what, then, do you hope, or by what means will you escape?"

Then said the Lord Mayor, "We have sinned indeed; but that shall be no help to thee, for our Emmanuel hath said it, and that in great faithfulness, And him that cometh to me I will in no wise cast out. He hath also told us, O our enemy, that all manner of sin and blasphemy shall be forgiven to the sons of men. Therefore we dare not despair, but will look for, wait for, and hope for deliverance still."

Now, by this time Captain Credence was returned and come from the court from Emmanuel to the castle of Mansoul, and he returned to them with a packet. So my Lord Mayor, hearing that Captain Credence was come, withdrew himself from the noise of the roaring of the tyrant, and left him to yell at the wall of the town or against the gates of the castle. So he came up to the captain's lodgings, and, saluting him, he asked him of his welfare, and what was the best news at court. But when he asked Captain Credence that, the water stood in his eyes. Then said the captain, "Cheer up, my lord, for all will be well in time." And with that he first produced his packet, and laid it by; but that the Lord Mayor and the rest of the captains took for a sign of good tidings. Now, a season of grace being come, he sent for all the captains and elders of the town, that were here and there in their lodgings in the castle and upon their guard, to let them know that Captain Credence was returned from the court, and that he had something in general, and something in special, to communicate to them. So they all came up to him and saluted him, and asked him concerning his journey, and what was the best news of the court. And he answered them as he had done the Lord Mayor before, that all would be well at last. Now, when the captain had thus saluted them, he opened his packet, and thence did draw out his several notes for those that he had sent for.

And the first note was for my Lord Mayor, wherein was signified:—That the Prince Emmanuel had taken it well that my Lord Mayor had been so true and trusty in his office, and the great concerns that lay upon him for the town and people of Mansoul. Also he bid him to know that he took it well that he had been so bold for his Prince Emmanuel, and had engaged so faithfully in his cause against Diabolus. He also signified, at the close of his letter, that he should shortly receive his reward.

The second note that came out was for the noble Lord Will-be-will, wherein there was signified:—That his Prince Emmanuel did well understand how valiant and courageous he had been for the honour of his Lord, now in his absence, and when his name was under contempt by Diabolus. There was signified, also, that his Prince had taken it well that he had been so faithful to the town of Mansoul in his keeping of so strict a hand and eye over, and so strict a rein upon, the necks of the Diabolonians that did still lie lurking in their several holes in the famous town of Mansoul. He signified, moreover, how that he understood that my lord had, with his own hand, done great execution upon some of the chief of the rebels there, to the great discouragement of the adverse party, and to the good example of the whole town of Mansoul, and that shortly his lordship should have his reward.

The third note came out for the subordinate preacher, wherein was signified:—That his Prince took it well from him that he had so honestly and so faithfully performed his office and executed the trust committed to him by his Lord, while he exhorted, rebuked, and forewarned Mansoul according to the laws of the town. He signified, moreover, that he took it well at his hand that he called to fasting, to sackcloth and ashes, when Mansoul was under her revolt. Also that he called for the aid of the Captain Boanerges to help in so weighty a work, and that shortly he also should receive his reward.

The fourth note came out for Mr. Godly-Fear, wherein his Lord thus signified:—That his Lordship observed that he was the first of all the men in Mansoul that detected Mr. Carnal-Security as the only one that, through his subtilty and cunning, had obtained for Diabolus a defection and decay of goodness in the blessed town of Mansoul. Moreover, his Lord gave him to understand that he still remembered his tears and mourning for the state of Mansoul. It was also observed, by the same note, that his Lord took notice of his detecting of this Mr. Carnal-Security at his own table among his guests in his own house, and that in the midst of his jolliness, even while he was seeking to perfect his villainies against the town of Mansoul. Emmanuel also took notice that this reverend person, Mr. Godly-Fear, stood stoutly to it, at the gates of the castle, against all the threats and attempts of the tyrant, and that he had put the townsmen in a way to make their petition to their Prince, so as that he might accept thereof, and as that they might obtain an answer of peace, and that therefore shortly he should receive his reward.

After all this there was yet produced a note which was written to the whole town of Mansoul, whereby they perceived:—That their Lord took notice of their so often repeating of petitions to him, and that they should see more of the fruits of such their doings in time to come. Their Prince did also therein tell them that he took it well that their heart and mind now at last abode fixed upon him and his ways, though Diabolus had made such inroads upon them, and that neither flatteries on the one hand, nor hardships on the other, could make them yield to serve his cruel designs. There was also inserted at the bottom of this note—That his Lordship had left the town of Mansoul in the hands of the Lord Secretary and under the conduct of Captain Credence, saying, "Beware that you yet yield yourselves unto their governance, and in due time you shall receive your reward."

So after the brave Captain Credence had delivered his notes to those to whom they belonged, he retired himself to my Lord Secretary's lodgings, and there spends time in conversing with him; for they two were very great one with another, and did indeed know more how things would go with Mansoul than did all the townsmen besides. The Lord Secretary also loved the Captain Credence dearly; yea, many a good bit was sent him from my

Lord's table; also he might have a show of countenance when the rest of Mansoul lay under the clouds. So after some time for converse was spent, the captain betook himself to his chambers to rest. But it was not long after when my Lord did send for the captain again. So the captain came to him, and they greeted one another with usual salutations. Then said the captain to the Lord Secretary, "What hath my Lord to say to his servant?" So the Lord Secretary took him and had him aside, and after a sign or two of more favour, he said, "I have made thee the Lord's lieutenant over all the forces in Mansoul, so that from this day forward all men in Mansoul shall be at thy word; and thou shalt be he that shall lead in, and that shalt lead out Mansoul. Thou shalt therefore manage, according to thy place, the war for thy Prince and for the town of Mansoul against the force and power of Diabolus; and at thy command shall the rest of the captains be."

Captain Credence Made Lieutenant

Now the townsmen began to perceive what interest the captain had, both with the court, and also with the Lord Secretary in Mansoul; for no man before could speed when sent, nor bring such good news from Emmanuel as he. Wherefore what do they, after some lamentation that they made no more use of him in their distresses, but send by their subordinate preacher to the Lord Secretary, to desire him that all that ever they were and had might be put under the government, care, custody, and conduct of Captain Credence.

So their preacher went and did his errand, and received this answer from the mouth of his Lord: that Captain Credence should be the great doer in the King's army, against the King's enemies, and also for the welfare of Mansoul. So he bowed to the ground, and thanked his Lordship, and returned and told his news to the townsfolk. But all this was done with all imaginable secrecy, because the foes had great strength in the town. But to return to our story again.

When Diabolus saw himself thus boldly confronted by the Lord Mayor, and perceived the stoutness of Mr. Godly-Fear, he fell into a rage, and forthwith called a council of war, that he might be revenged on Mansoul. So all the princes of the pit came together, and old Incredulity at the head of them, with all the captains of his army. So they consult what to do. Now, the effect and conclusion of the council that day, was how they might take the castle, because they could not conclude themselves masters of the town so long as that was in the possession of their enemies.

So one advised this way, and another advised that; but when they could not agree in their verdict, Apollyon, that president of the council, stood up, and thus he began:—"My brotherhood," quoth he, "I have two things to propound unto you; and my first is this. Let us withdraw ourselves from the town into the plain again, for our presence here will do us no good, because the castle is yet in our enemy's hands; nor is it possible that we should take that, so long as so many brave captains are in it, and that this bold fellow, Godly-Fear, is made the keeper of the gates of it. Now, when we have withdrawn ourselves into the plain, they, of their own accord, will be glad of some little ease; and it may be, of their own accord, they again may begin to be remiss, and even their so being will give them a bigger blow than we can possibly give them ourselves. But if that should fail, our going forth of the town may draw the captains out after us; and you know what it cost them when we fought them in the field before. Besides, can we but draw them out into the field, we may lay an ambush behind the town, which shall, when they are come forth abroad, rush in and take possession of the castle."

But Beelzebub stood up, and replied, saying, "'Tis impossible to draw them all off from the castle; some, you may be sure, will lie there to keep that; wherefore it will be but in vain thus to attempt, unless we were sure that they will all come out." He therefore concluded that what was done must be done by some other means. And the most likely means that the greatest of their heads could invent, was that which Apollyon had advised to before, to wit, to get the townsmen again to sin. "For," said he, "it is not our being in the town, nor in the field, nor our fighting, nor our killing of their men, that can make us masters of Mansoul; for so long as one in the town is able to lift up his finger against us, Emmanuel will take their parts; and if he shall take their parts, we know what time a-day it will be with us. Wherefore, for my part," quoth he, "there is, in my judgment, no way to bring them into bondage to us like inventing a way to make them sin. Had we," said he, "left all our Doubters at home, we had done as well as we have done now, unless we could have made them the masters and governors of the castle; for Doubters at a distance are but like objections refell'd by arguments. Indeed, can we but get them into the hold, and make them possessors of that, the day will be our own. Let us, therefore, withdraw ourselves into the plain (not expecting that the captains in Mansoul should follow us), but yet, I say, let us do this, and before we so do let us advise again with our trusty Diabolonians that are yet in their holds of Mansoul, and set them to work to betray the town to us; for they indeed must do it, or it will be left undone for ever." By these sayings of Beelzebub (for I think 'twas he that gave this counsel), the whole conclave was forced to be of his opinion, to wit, that the way to get the castle was to get the town to sin. Then they fell to inventing by what means they might do this thing.

Lucifer's Advice

Then Lucifer stood up, and said, "The counsel of Beelzebub is pertinent. Now, the way to bring this to pass, in mine opinion, is this: let us withdraw our force from the town of Mansoul; let us do this, and let us terrify them no more, either with summons, or threats, or with the noise of our drum, or any other awakening means. Only let us lie in the field at a distance, and be as if we regarded them not; for frights, I see, do but awaken them, and make them stand more to their arms. I have also another stratagem in my head: you know Mansoul is a market town, and a town that delights in commerce:

what, therefore, if some of our Diabolonians shall feign themselves far-countrymen, and shall go out and bring to the market of Mansoul some of our wares to sell; and what matter at what rates they sell their wares, though it be but for half the worth? Now, let those that thus shall trade in their market be those that are witty and true to us, and I will lay my crown to pawn it will do. There are two that are come to my thoughts already that I think will be arch at this work, and they are Mr. Penniwise-pound-foolish, and Mr. Get-i'the-hundred-and-lose-i'the-shire; nor is this man with the long name at all inferior to the other. What also if you join with them Mr. Sweet-world and Mr. Present-good? they are men that are civil and cunning, but our true friends and helpers. Let these, with as many more engage in this business for us, and let Mansoul be taken up in much business, and let them grow full and rich, and this is the way to get ground of them. Remember ye not that thus we prevailed upon Laodicea, and how many at present do we hold in this snare? Now, when they begin to grow full, they will forget their misery; and if we shall not affright them, they may happen to fall asleep, and so be got to neglect their town watch, their castle watch, as well as their watch at the gates.

"Yea, may we not, by this means, so cumber Mansoul with abundance, that they shall be forced to make of their castle a warehouse instead of a garrison fortified against it, and a receptacle for men of war? Thus if we get our goods and commodities thither, I reckon that the castle is more than half ours. Besides, could we so order it that it shall be filled with such kind of wares, then if we made a sudden assault upon them, it would be hard for the captains to take shelter there. Do you not know that of the parable, 'The deceitfulness of riches choke the word'? and again, 'When the heart is over-charged with surfeiting and drunkenness, and the cares of this life, all mischief comes upon them at unawares.'

"Furthermore, my lords," quoth he, "you very well know that it is not easy for a people to be filled with our things, and not to have some of our Diabolonians as retainers to their houses and services. Where is a Mansoulian that is full of this world that has not for his servants and waiting men Mr. Profuse, or Mr. Prodigality, or some other of our Diabolonian gang, as Mr. Voluptuous, Mr. Pragmatical, Mr. Ostentation, or the like? Now, these can take the castle of Mansoul, or blow it up, or make it unfit for a garrison for Emmanuel, and any of these will do. Yea, these, for aught I know, may do it for us sooner than an army of twenty thousand men. Wherefore, to end as I began, my advice is that we quietly withdraw ourselves, not offering any further force, or forcible attempts upon the castle, at least at this time; and let us set on foot our new project, and let us see if that will not make them destroy themselves."

This advice was highly applauded by them all, and was accounted the very masterpiece of hell, namely, to choke Mansoul with a fulness of this world, and to surfeit her heart with the good things thereof. But see how things meet together! Just as this Diabolonian council was broken up, Captain Credence received a letter from Emmanuel, the contents of which were these:—That upon the third day he would meet him in the field in the plains about Mansoul. "Meet me in the field!" quoth the captain; "what meaneth my Lord by this? I know not what he meaneth by meeting me in the field." So he took the note in his hand, and did carry it to my Lord Secretary, to ask his thoughts thereupon; for my Lord was a seer in all matters concerning the King, and also for the good and comfort of the town of Mansoul. So he showed my Lord the note, and desired his opinion thereof. "For my part," quoth Captain Credence, "I know not the meaning thereof." So my Lord did take and read it; and, after a little pause, he said, "The Diabolonians have had against Mansoul a great consultation to-day; they have, I say, this day been contriving the utter ruin of the town; and the result of their counsel is to set Mansoul into such a way which, if taken, will surely make her destroy herself. And to this end they are making ready for their own departure out of the town, intending to betake themselves to the field again, and there to lie till they shall see whether this their project will take or no. But be thou ready with the men of thy Lord (for on the third day they will be in the plain), there to fall upon the Diabolonians; for the Prince will by that time be in the field; yea, by that it is break of day, sunrising, or before, and that with a mighty force against them. So he shall be before them, and thou shalt be behind them, and betwixt you both their army shall be destroyed."

When Captain Credence heard this, away goes he to the rest of the captains, and tells them what a note he had a while since received from the hand of Emmanuel. "And," said he, "that which was dark therein has my Lord, the Lord Secretary, expounded unto me." He told them, moreover, what by himself and by them must be done to answer the mind of their Lord. Then were the captains glad; and Captain Credence commanded that all the King's trumpeters should ascend to the battlements of the castle, and there, in the audience of Diabolus, and of the whole town of Mansoul, make the best music that heart could invent. The trumpeters did as they were commanded. They got themselves up to the top of the castle, and thus they began to sound. Then did Diabolus start, and said, "What can be the meaning of this? they neither sound Boot-and-saddle, nor Horse-and-away, nor a charge. What do these madmen mean, that yet they should be so merry and glad?" Then answered him one of themselves, and said, "This is for joy that their Prince Emmanuel is coming to relieve the town of Mansoul; that to this end he is at the head of an army, and that this relief is near."

The men of Mansoul also were greatly concerned at this melodious charm of the trumpets: they said, yea, they answered one another, saying, "This can be no harm to us; surely, this can be no harm to us." Then said the Diabolonians, "What had we best to do?" and it was answered, "It was best to quit the town;" and "that," said one, "ye may do in pursuance of your last counsel, and by so doing also be better able to give the enemy battle, should an army from without come upon us." So, on the second day, they withdrew themselves from Mansoul, and abode in the plains without; but they encamped themselves before Eye-gate, in what terrene and terrible manner they could. The reason why they would not abide in the town (beside the reasons that were debated in their late conclave) was, for that they were not possessed of the stronghold, and "because," said they, "we shall have more convenience to fight, and also to fly, if need be, when we are encamped in the open plains." Besides, the town would have been a pit for them rather than a place of defence, had the Prince come up and enclosed them fast therein. Therefore they betook themselves to the field, that they might also be out of the reach of the slings, by which they were much annoyed all the while that they were in the town.

Well, the time that the captains were to fall upon the Diabolonians being come, they eagerly prepared themselves for action; for Captain Credence had told the captains over-night, that they should meet their Prince in the field to-morrow. This, therefore, made them yet far more desirous to be engaging the enemy; for, "You shall see the Prince in the field to-morrow" was like oil to a flaming fire; for of a long time they had been at a distance: they therefore were for this the more earnest and desirous of the work. So, as I said, the hour being come, Captain Credence, with the rest of the men of war, drew out their forces before it was day by the sally-port of the town. And, being all ready, Captain Credence went up to the head of the army, and gave to the rest of the captains the word, and so they to their under-officers and soldiers: the word was, "The sword of the Prince Emmanuel, and the shield of Captain Credence;" which is in the Mansoulian tongue, "The word of God and faith." Then the captains fell on, and began roundly to front, and flank, and rear Diabolus's camp.

Now they left Captain Experience in the town, because he was yet ill of his wounds, which the Diabolonians had given him in the last fight. But when he perceived that the captains were at it, what does he but, calling for his crutches with haste, gets up, and away he goes to the battle, saying, "Shall I lie here, when my brethren are in the fight, and when Emmanuel the Prince will show himself in the field to his servants?" But when the enemy saw the man come with his crutches, they were daunted yet the more; "for," thought they, "what spirit has possessed these Mansoulians, that they fight us upon their crutches?" Well, the captains, as I said, fell on, and did bravely handle their weapons, still crying out and shouting, as they laid on blows, "The sword of the Prince Emmanuel, and the shield of Captain Credence!"

Now, when Diabolus saw that the captains were come out, and that so valiantly they surrounded his men, he concluded that, for the present, nothing from them was to be looked for but blows, and the dints of their "two-edged sword."

Wherefore he also falls upon the Prince's army with all his deadly force: so the battle was joined. Now, who was it that at first Diabolus met with in the fight, but Captain Credence on the one hand, and the Lord Will-be-will on the other: now Will-be-will's blows were like the blows of a giant, for that man had a strong arm, and he fell in upon the Election-Doubters, for they were the life-guard of Diabolus, and he kept them in play a good while, cutting and battering shrewdly. Now, when Captain Credence saw my Lord engaged, he did stoutly fall on, on the other hand, upon the same company also; so they put them to great disorder. Now Captain Good-Hope had engaged the Vocation-Doubters, and they were sturdy men; but the captain was a valiant man: Captain Experience did also send him some aid; so he made the Vocation-Doubters to retreat. The rest of the armies were hotly engaged, and that on every side, and the Diabolonians did fight stoutly. Then did my Lord Secretary command that the slings from the castle should be played; and his men could throw stones at an hair's-breadth. But, after a little while, those that were made to fly before the captains of the Prince did begin to rally again, and they came up stoutly upon the rear of the Prince's army: wherefore the Prince's army began to faint, but, remembering that they should see the face of their Prince by-and-bye, they took courage, and a very fierce battle was fought. Then shouted the captains, saying, "The sword of the Prince Emmanuel, and the shield of Captain Credence!" and with that Diabolus gave back, thinking that more aid had been come. But no Emmanuel as yet appeared. Moreover, the battle did hang in doubt; and they made a little retreat on both sides. Now, in the time of respite, Captain Credence bravely encouraged his men to stand to it; and Diabolus did the like as well as he could. But Captain Credence made a brave speech to his soldiers, the contents whereof here follow:—

"Gentlemen, soldiers, and my brethren in this design, it rejoiceth me much to see in the field for our Prince, this day, so stout and so valiant an army, and such faithful lovers of Mansoul. You have hitherto, as hath become you, shown yourselves men of truth and courage against the Diabolonian forces; so that, for all their boast, they have not yet much cause to boast of their gettings. Now, take to yourselves your wonted courage, and show yourselves men even this once only; for in a few minutes after the next engagement, this time, you shall see your Prince show himself in the field; for we must make this second assault upon this tyrant Diabolus, and then Emmanuel comes."

No sooner had the captain made this speech to his soldiers, but one Mr. Speedy came post to the captain from the Prince, to tell him that Emmanuel was at hand. This news when the captain had received, he communicated to the other field officers, and they again to their soldiers and men of war. Wherefore, like men raised from the dead, so the captains and their men arose, made up to the enemy, and cried as before, "The sword of the Prince Emmanuel, and the shield of Captain Credence!"

Emmanuel Comes

The Diabolonians also bestirred themselves, and made resistance as well as they could; but in this last engagement the Diabolonians lost their courage, and many of the Doubters fell down dead to the ground. Now, when they had been in heat of battle about an hour or more, Captain Credence lifted up his eyes and saw, and, behold, Emmanuel came; and he came with colours flying, trumpets sounding, and the feet of his men scarce touched the ground, they hasted with that celerity towards the captains that were engaged. Then did Credence wind with his men to the townward, and gave to Diabolus the field: so Emmanuel came upon him on the one side, and the enemies' place was betwixt them both. Then again they fell to it afresh; and now it was but a little while more but Emmanuel and Captain Credence met, still trampling down the slain as they came.

But when the captains saw that the Prince was come, and that he fell upon the Diabolonians on the other side, and that Captain Credence and his Highness had got them up betwixt them, they shouted (they so shouted that the ground rent again), saying, "The sword of Emmanuel, and the shield of Captain Credence!" Now, when Diabolus saw that he and his forces were so hard beset by the Prince and his princely army, what does he, and the lords of the pit that were with him, but make their escape, and forsake their army, and leave them to fall by the hand of Emmanuel and of his noble Captain Credence; so they fell all down slain before them, before the Prince and before his royal army; there was not left so much as one Doubter alive: they lay spread upon the ground dead men, as one would spread dung upon the land.

When the battle was over, all things came into order in the camp. Then the captains and elders of Mansoul came together to salute Emmanuel, while without the corporation; so they saluted him, and welcomed him, and that with a thousand welcomes, for that he was come to the borders of Mansoul again. So he smiled upon them, and said, "Peace be to you." Then they addressed themselves to go to the town; they went then to go up to Mansoul, they, the Prince, with all the new forces that now he had brought with him to the war. All the gates of the town were set open for his reception, so glad were they of his blessed return. And this was the manner and order of this going of his into Mansoul:—

First: As I said, all the gates of the town were set open, yea, the gates of the castle also; the elders, too, of the town of Mansoul placed themselves at the gates of the town, to salute him at his entrance thither: and so they did; for, as he drew near and approached towards the gates, they said, Lift up your heads, O ye gates; and be ye lift up, ye everlasting doors; and the King of glory shall come in. And they answered again, Who is the King of glory? and they made return to themselves, The Lord, strong and mighty; the Lord mighty in battle. Lift up your heads, O ye gates; even lift them up, ye everlasting doors, etc.

Secondly: It was ordered also, by those of Mansoul, that all the way from the town gates to those of the castle, his blessed Majesty should be entertained with the song, by them that had the best of skill in music in all the town of Mansoul; then did the elders, and the rest of the men of Mansoul, answer one another as Emmanuel entered the town, till he came at the castle gates, with songs and sound of trumpets, saying, They have seen thy goings, O God: even the goings of my God, my King, in the sanctuary. So the singers went before, the players on instruments followed after; and among them were the damsels playing with timbrels.

Thirdly: Then the captains (for I would speak a word of them), they in their order waited on the Prince, as he entered into the gates of Mansoul. Captain Credence went before, and Captain Good-Hope with him; Captain Charity came behind with other of his companions, and Captain Patience followed after all; and the rest of the captains, some on the right hand, and some on the left, accompanied Emmanuel into Mansoul. And all the while the colours were displayed, the trumpets sounded, and continual shoutings were among the soldiers. The Prince himself rode into the town in his armour, which was all of beaten gold, and in his chariot—the pillars of it were of silver, the bottom thereof of gold, the covering of it was of purple, the midst thereof being paved with love for the daughters of the town of Mansoul.

Fourthly: When the Prince was come to the entrance of Mansoul, he found all the streets strewed with lilies and flowers, curiously decked with boughs and branches from the green trees that stood round about the town. Every door also was filled with persons who had adorned every one their fore-part against their house with something of variety and singular excellency, to entertain him withal as he passed in the streets; they also themselves, as Emmanuel passed by, did welcome him with shouts and acclamations of joy, saying, "Blessed be the Prince that cometh in the name of his Father Shaddai."

Fifthly: At the castle gates the elders of Mansoul, namely, the Lord Mayor, the Lord Will-be-will, the subordinate preacher, Mr. Knowledge, and Mr. Mind, with other of the gentry of the place, saluted Emmanuel again. They bowed before him, they kissed the dust of his feet, they thanked, they blessed, and praised his Highness, for not taking advantage against them for their sins, but rather had pity upon them in their misery, and returned to them with mercies, and to build up their Mansoul for ever. Thus was he had up straightway to the castle—for that was the royal palace, and the place where his Honour was to dwell—the which was ready prepared for his Highness by the presence of the Lord Secretary and the work of Captain Credence. So he entered in.

Sixthly: Then the people and commonalty of the town of Mansoul came to him into the castle to mourn, and to weep, and to lament for their wickedness, by which they had forced him out of the town. So they, when they were come, bowed themselves to the ground seven times; they also wept, they wept aloud, and asked forgiveness of the Prince, and prayed that he would again, as of old, confirm his love to Mansoul.

To which the great Prince replied, "Weep not, but go your way, eat the fat, and drink the sweet, and send portions to them for whom nought is prepared; for the joy of your lord is your strength. I am returned to Mansoul with mercies, and my name shall be set up, exalted, and magnified by it." He also took these inhabitants, and kissed them, and laid them in his bosom.

Moreover, he gave to the elders of Mansoul, and to each town officer, a chain of gold and a signet. He also sent to their wives ear-rings and jewels, and bracelets, and other things. He also bestowed upon the true-born children of Mansoul many precious things.

When Emmanuel the Prince had done all these things for the famous town of Mansoul, then he said unto them, first, "Wash your garments, then put on your ornaments, and then come to me into the castle of Mansoul." So they went to the fountain that was set open for Judah and Jerusalem to wash in; and there they washed, and there they made their "garments white," and came again to the Prince into the castle, and thus they stood before him.

Music and Dancing

And now there was music and dancing throughout the whole town of Mansoul, and that because their Prince had again granted to them his presence and the light of his countenance; the bells also did ring, and the sun shone comfortably upon them for a great while together.

The town of Mansoul did also now more thoroughly seek the destruction and ruin of all remaining Diabolonians that abode in the walls and the dens that they had in the town of Mansoul; for there was of them that had to this day escaped with life and limb from the hand of their suppressors in the famous town of Mansoul.

But my Lord Will-be-will was a greater terror to them now than ever he had been before; forasmuch as his heart was yet more fully bent to seek, contrive, and pursue them to the death; he pursued them night and day, and did put them now to sore distress, as will afterwards appear.

After things were thus far put into order in the famous town of Mansoul, care was taken, and order given by the blessed Prince Emmanuel, that the townsmen should, without further delay, appoint some to go forth into the plain to bury the dead that were there,—the dead that fell by the sword of Emmanuel and by the shield of the Captain Credence,—lest the fumes and ill savours that would arise from them might infect the air, and so annoy the famous town of Mansoul. This also was a reason of this order, namely, that as much as in Mansoul lay, they might cut off the name, and being, and remembrance of those enemies from the thought of the famous town of Mansoul and its inhabitants.

So order was given out by the Lord Mayor, that wise and trusty friend of the town of Mansoul, that persons should be employed about this necessary business; and Mr. Godly-Fear, and one Mr. Upright, were to be overseers about this matter; so persons were put under them to work in the fields, and to bury the slain that lay dead in the plains. And these were their places of employment: some were to make the graves, some to bury the dead, and some were to go to and fro in the plains, and also round about the borders of Mansoul, to see if a skull, or a bone, or a piece of a bone of a Doubter, was yet to be found aboveground anywhere near the corporation; and if any were found, it was ordered that the searchers that searched should set up a mark thereby, and a sign, that those that were appointed to bury them might find it, and bury it out of sight, that the name and remembrance of a Diabolonian Doubter might be blotted out from under heaven; and that the children and they that were born in Mansoul, might not know, if possible, what a skull, what a bone, or a piece of bone of a Doubter was. So the buriers, and those that were appointed for that purpose, did as they were commanded: they buried the Doubters, and all the skulls and bones, and pieces of bones of Doubters, wherever they found them; and so they cleansed the plains. Now also Mr. God's-Peace took up his commission, and acted again as in former days.

Thus they buried in the plains about Mansoul the Election-Doubters, the Vocation-Doubters, the Grace-Doubters, the Perseverance-Doubters, the Resurrection-Doubters, the Salvation-Doubters, and the Glory-Doubters; whose captains were Captain Rage, Captain Cruel, Captain Damnation, Captain Insatiable, Captain Brimstone, Captain Torment, Captain No-Ease, Captain Sepulchre, and Captain Past-Hope; and old Incredulity was, under Diabolus, their general. There were also the seven heads of their army; and they were the Lord Beelzebub, the Lord Lucifer, the Lord Legion, the Lord Apollyon, the Lord Python, the Lord Cerberus, and the Lord Belial. But the princes and the captains, with old Incredulity, their general, did all of them make their escape: so their men fell down slain by the power of the Prince's forces and by the hands of the men of the town of Mansoul. They also were buried, as before related, to the exceeding great joy of the now famous town of Mansoul. They that buried them buried also with them their arms, which were cruel instruments of death (their weapons were arrows, darts, mauls, firebrands, and the like). They buried also their armour, their colours, banners, with the standard of Diabolus, and what else soever they could find that did smell of a Diabolonian Doubter.

Now, when the tyrant had arrived at Hell-gate Hill, with his old friend Incredulity, they immediately descended the den, and having there with their fellows for a while condoled their misfortune and great loss that they sustained against the town of Mansoul, they fell at length into a passion, and revenged they would be for the loss that they sustained before the town of Mansoul. Wherefore they presently call a council to contrive yet further what was to be done against the famous town of Mansoul; for their yawning paunches could not wait to see the result of their Lord Lucifer's and their Lord Apollyon's counsel that they had given before; for their raging gorge thought every day, even as long as a short for ever, until they were filled with the body and soul, with the flesh and bones, and with all the delicates of Mansoul. They therefore resolve to make another attempt upon the town of Mansoul, and that by an army mixed and made up partly of Doubters, and partly of Blood-men. A more particular account now take of both.

The Doubters are such as have their name from their nature, as well as from the land and kingdom where they are born: their nature is to put a question upon every one of the truths of Emmanuel; and their country is called the Land of Doubting, and that land lieth off, and farthest remote to the north, between the Land of Darkness and that called the Valley of the Shadow of Death. For though the Land of Darkness, and that called the

Valley of the Shadow of Death, be sometimes called as if they were one and the selfsame place, yet, indeed, they are two, lying but a little way asunder, and the Land of Doubting points in, and lieth between them. This is the Land of Doubting; and these that came with Diabolus to ruin the town of Mansoul are the natives of that country.

The Blood-men are a people that have their name derived from the malignity of their nature, and from the fury that is in them to execute it upon the town of Mansoul: their land lieth under the dog-star, and by that they are governed as to their intellectuals. The name of their country is the province of Loathe-Good: the remote parts of it are far distant from the Land of Doubting, yet they do both butt and bound up the hill called Hell-gate Hill. These people are always in league with the Doubters, for they jointly do make question of the faith and fidelity of the men of the town of Mansoul, and so are both alike qualified for the service of their prince.

Another Army

Now, of these two countries did Diabolus, by the beating of his drum, raise another army against the town of Mansoul, of five-and-twenty thousand strong. There were ten thousand Doubters, and fifteen thousand Blood-men, and they were put under several captains for the war; and old Incredulity was again made general of the army.

As for the Doubters, their captains were five of the seven that were heads of the last Diabolonian army, and these are their names: Captain Beelzebub, Captain Lucifer, Captain Apollyon, Captain Legion, and Captain Cerberus; and the captains that they had before were some of them made lieutenants, and some ensigns of the army.

But Diabolus did not count that, in this expedition of his, these Doubters would prove his principal men, for their manhood had been tried before; also the Mansoulians had put them to the worst: only he did bring them to multiply a number, and to help, if need was, at a pinch. But his trust he put in his Blood-men, for that they were all rugged villains, and he knew that they had done feats heretofore.

As for the Blood-men, they also were under command; and the names of their captains were Captain Cain, Captain Nimrod, Captain Ishmael, Captain Esau, Captain Saul, Captain Absalom, Captain Judas, and Captain Pope.

1. Captain Cain was over two bands, namely, the Zealous and the Angry Blood-men; his standard-bearer bare the red colours, and his scutcheon was the murdering club.

2. Captain Nimrod was captain over two bands; namely, the Tyrannical and Encroaching Blood-men: his standard-bearer bare the red colours, and his scutcheon was the great bloodhound.

3. Captain Ishmael was captain over two bands, namely, the Mocking and Scorning Blood-men: his standard-bearer bare the red colours, and his scutcheon was one mocking at Abraham's Isaac.

4. Captain Esau was captain over two bands, namely, the Blood-men that

grudged that another should have the blessing; also over the Blood-men that are for executing their private revenge upon others: his standard-bearer bare the red colours, and his scutcheon was one privately lurking to murder Jacob.

5. Captain Saul was captain over two bands, namely, the groundlessly jealous and the devilishly furious Blood-men: his standard-bearer bare the red colours, and his scutcheon was three bloody darts cast at harmless David.

6. Captain Absalom was captain over two bands, namely, over the Blood-men that will kill a father or a friend for the glory of this world; also, over those Blood-men that will hold one fair in hand with words, till they shall have pierced him with their swords: his standard-bearer did bear the red colours, and his scutcheon was the son pursuing the father's blood.

7. Captain Judas was over two bands, namely, the Blood-men that will sell a man's life for money, and those also that will betray their friend with a kiss: his standard-bearer bare the red colours, and his scutcheon was thirty pieces of silver and the halter.

8. Captain Pope was captain over one band, for all these spirits are joined in one under him: his standard-bearer bare the red colours, and his scutcheon was the stake, the flame, and the good man in it.

Now, the reason why Diabolus did so soon rally another force, after he had been beaten out of the field, was, for that he put mighty confidence in this army of Blood-men; for he put a great deal of more trust in them than he did before in his army of Doubters; though they had also often done great service for him in the strengthening of him in his kingdom. But these Blood-men, he had proved them often, and their sword did seldom return empty. Besides, he knew that these, like mastiffs, would fasten upon any,—upon father, mother, brother, sister, prince, or governor, yea, upon the Prince of princes. And that which encouraged him the more was, for that they once did force Emmanuel out of the kingdom of Universe. "And why," thought he, "may they not also drive him from the town of Mansoul?"

So this army of five-and-twenty thousand strong was, by their general, the great Lord Incredulity, led up against the town of Mansoul. Now, Mr. Prywell, the Scoutmaster-General, did himself go out to spy, and he did bring Mansoul tidings of their coming. Wherefore, they shut up their gates, and put themselves in a posture of defence against these new Diabolonians that came up against the town.

So Diabolus brought up his army, and beleaguered the town of Mansoul; the Doubters were placed about Feel-gate, and the Blood-men set down before Eye-gate and Ear-gate.

Now, when this army had thus encamped themselves, Incredulity did, in the name of Diabolus, his own name, and in the name of the Blood-men and the rest that were with him, send a summons as hot as a red-hot iron to Mansoul, to yield to their demands; threatening that if they still stood it out against them, they would presently burn down Mansoul with fire. For you must know that, as for the Blood-men, they were not so much that Mansoul should be surrendered, as that Mansoul should be destroyed, and cut off out of the land of the living. True, they send to them to surrender; but should they do so, that would not stanch or quench the thirsts of these men. They must have blood, the blood of Mansoul, else they die; and it is from hence that they have their name. Wherefore these Blood-men he reserved, while now that they might, when all his engines proved ineffectual, as his last and sure card, be played against the town of Mansoul.

Now, when the townsmen had received this red-hot summons, it begat in them at present some changing and interchanging thoughts; but they jointly agreed, in less than half an hour, to carry the summons to the Prince, the which they did when they had writ at the bottom of it, "Lord, save Mansoul from bloody men!"

So he took it, and looked upon it, and considered it, and took notice also of that short petition that the men of Mansoul had written at the bottom of it, and called to him the noble Captain Credence, and bid him go and take Captain Patience with him, and go and take care of that side of Mansoul that was beleaguered by the Blood-men. So they went and did as they were commanded; the Captain Credence went and took Captain Patience, and they both secured that side of Mansoul that was besieged by the Blood-men.

Then he commanded that Captain Good-Hope and Captain Charity, and my Lord Will-be-will, should take charge of the other side of the town.

"And I," said the Prince, "will set my standard upon the battlements of your castle, and do you three watch against the Doubters."

This done, he again commanded that the brave captain, Captain Experience, should draw up his men in the market-place, and that there he should exercise them day by day before the people of the town of Mansoul. Now, this siege was long, and many a fierce attempt did the enemy, especially those called the Blood-men, make upon the town of Mansoul; and many a shrewd brush did some of the townsmen meet with from them, especially Captain Self-Denial, who, I should have told you before, was commanded to take the care of Ear-gate and Eye-gate now against the Blood-men. This Captain Self-Denial was a young man, but stout, and a townsman in Mansoul, as Captain Experience also was. And Emmanuel, at his second return to Mansoul, made him a captain over a thousand of the Mansoulians, for the good of the corporation. This captain, therefore, being a hardy man, and a man of great courage, and willing to venture himself for the good of the town of Mansoul, would now and then sally out upon the Blood-men, and give them many notable alarms, and entered several brisk skirmishes with them, and also did some execution upon them; but you must think that this could not easily be done, but he must meet with brushes himself, for he carried several of their marks in his face; yea, and some in some other parts of his body.

So, after some time spent for the trial of the faith, and hope, and love of the town of Mansoul, the Prince Emmanuel upon a day calls his captains and men of war together, and divides them into two companies; this done, he commands them, at a time appointed, and that in the morning very early, to sally out upon the enemy, saying, "Let half of you fall upon the Doubters, and half of you fall upon the Blood-men. Those of you that go out against the Doubters, kill and slay, and cause to perish so many as by any means you can lay hands on; but for you that go out against the Blood-men, slay them not, but take them alive."

So, at the time appointed, betimes in the morning, the captains went out as they were commanded against the enemies. Captain Good-Hope, Captain Charity, and those that were joined with them, as Captain Innocency and Captain Experience, went out against the Doubters; and Captain Credence, and Captain Patience, with Captain Self-Denial, and the rest that were to join them, went out against the Blood-men.

Now, those that went out against the Doubters drew up into a body before the plain, and marched on to bid them battle. But the Doubters, remembering their last success, made a retreat, not daring to stand the shock, but fled from the Prince's men; wherefore they pursued them, and in their pursuit slew many, but they could not catch them all. Now, those that escaped went some of them home; and the rest by fives, nines, and seventeens, like wanderers, went straggling up and down the country, where they upon the barbarous people showed and exercised many of their Diabolonian actions: nor did these people rise up in arms against them, but suffered themselves to be enslaved by them. They would also after this show themselves in companies before the town of Mansoul, but never to abide in it; for if Captain Credence, Captain Good-Hope, or Captain Experience did but show themselves, they fled.

Those that went out against the Blood-men did as they were commanded; they forbore to slay any, but sought to compass them about. But the Blood-men, when they saw that no Emmanuel was in the field, concluded also that no Emmanuel was in Mansoul; wherefore they, looking upon what the captains did to be, as they called it, a fruit of the extravagancy of their wild and foolish fancies, rather despised them than feared them. But the captains, minding their business, at last did compass them round; they also that had routed the Doubters came in amain to their aid; so, in fine, after some little struggling (for the Blood-men also would have run for it, only now it was too late; for though they are mischievous and cruel where they can overcome, yet all Blood-men are chicken-hearted men when they once come to see themselves matcht and equall'd)—so the captains took them, and brought them to the Prince.

Now, when they were taken, had before the Prince, and examined, he found them to be of three several counties, though they all came out of one land.

1. One sort of them came out of Blindman-shire, and they were such as did ignorantly what they did.

2. Another sort of them came out of Blind-zeal-shire, and they did superstitiously what they did.

3. The third sort of them came out of the town of Malice, in the county of Envy, and they did what they did out of spite and implacableness.

For the first of these, namely, they that came out of Blindman-shire, when they saw where they were, and against whom they had fought, they trembled and cried, as they stood before him; and as many of them as asked him mercy, he touched their lips with his golden sceptre.

They that came out of Blind-zeal-shire, they did not as their fellows did; for they pleaded that they had a right to do what they did, because Mansoul was a town whose laws and customs were diverse from all that dwelt thereabout. Very few of these could be brought to see their evil; but those that did, and asked mercy, they also obtained favour.

Now, they that came out of the town of Malice, that is in the county of Envy, they neither wept nor disputed, nor repented, but stood gnawing their tongues before him for anguish and madness, because they could not have their will upon Mansoul. Now, these last, with all those of the two sorts that did not unfeignedly ask pardon for their faults,—those he made to enter into sufficient bond to answer for what they had done against Mansoul, and against her King, at the great and general assizes to be holden for our Lord the King, where himself should appoint, for the county and kingdom of Universe. So they became bound, each man for himself, to come in when called upon to answer before our Lord the King, for what they had done as before.

And thus much concerning this second army that was sent by Diabolus to overthrow Mansoul.

Mr. Evil-Questioning

But there were three of those that came from the Land of Doubting, who, after they had wandered and ranged the country a while, and perceived that they had escaped, were so hardy as to thrust themselves, knowing that yet there were in the town Diabolonians, I say they were so hardy as to thrust themselves into Mansoul among them. (Three, did I say? I think there were four.) Now, to whose house should these Diabolonian Doubters go, but to the house of an old Diabolonian in Mansoul, whose name was Evil-Questioning, a very great enemy he was to Mansoul, and a great doer among the Diabolonians there. Well, to this Evil-Questioning's house, as was said, did these Diabolonians come (you may be sure that they had directions how to find the way thither); so he made them welcome, pitied their misfortune, and succoured them with the best that he had in his house. Now, after a little acquaintance (and it was not long before they had that), this old Evil-Questioning asked the Doubters if they were all of a town (he knew that they were all of one kingdom), and they answered, "No, nor not of one shire neither; for I," said one, "am an Election-Doubter:" "I," said another, "am a Vocation-Doubter:" then said the third, "I am a Salvation-Doubter:" and the fourth said he was a Grace-Doubter. "Well," quoth the old gentleman, "be of what shire you will, I am persuaded that you are down boys: you have the very length of my foot, are one with my heart, and shall be welcome to me."

So they thanked him, and were very glad that they had found themselves a harbour in Mansoul.

Then said Evil-Questioning to them, "How many of your company might there be that came with you to the siege of Mansoul?" And they answered, "There were but ten thousand Doubters in all, for the rest of the army consisted of fifteen thousand Blood-men. These Blood-men," quoth they, "border upon our country; but, poor men! as we hear, they were every one taken by Emmanuel's forces." "Ten thousand!" quoth the old gentleman; "I will promise you, that is a round company. But how came it to pass, since you were so mighty in number, that you fainted, and durst not fight your foes?" "Our general," said they, "was the first man that did run for it." "Pray," quoth their landlord, "who was that, your cowardly general?" "He was once the Lord Mayor of Mansoul," said they; "but pray call him not a cowardly general; for whether any, from the east to the west, has done more service for our prince Diabolus, than has my Lord Incredulity, will be a hard question for you to answer. But had they catched him, they would for certain have hanged him; and we promise you, hanging is but a bad business." Then said the old gentleman, "I would that all the ten thousand Doubters were now well armed in Mansoul, and myself at the head of them; I would see what I could do." "Ay," said they, "that would be well if we could see that; but wishes, alas! what are they?" and these words were spoken aloud. "Well," said old Evil-Questioning, "take heed that you talk not too loud: you must be quiet and close, and must take care of yourselves while you are here, or, I will assure you, you will be snapt." "Why?" quoth the Doubters. "Why!" quoth the old gentleman; "why! because both the Prince and Lord Secretary, and their captains and soldiers, are all at present in town; yea, the town is as full of them as ever it can hold. And besides, there is one whose name is Will-be-will, a most cruel enemy of ours, and him the Prince has made keeper of the gate, and has commanded him that, with all the diligence he can, he should look for, search out, and destroy all and all manner of Diabolonians. And if he lighteth upon you, down you go, though your heads were made of gold."

And now, to see how it happened, one of the Lord Will-be-will's faithful soldiers, whose name was Mr. Diligence, stood all this while listening under old Evil-Questioning's eaves, and heard all the talk that had been betwixt him and the Doubters that he entertained under his roof.

The soldier was a man that my lord had much confidence in, and that he loved dearly; and that both because he was a man of courage, and also a man that was unwearied in seeking after Diabolonians to apprehend them.

Now, this man, as I told you, heard all the talk that was between old Evil-Questioning and these Diabolonians; wherefore what does he but goes to his lord, and tells him what he had heard. "And sayest thou so, my trusty?" quoth my lord. "Ay," quoth Diligence, "that I do; and if your lordship will be pleased to go with me, you shall find it as I have said." "And are they there?" quoth my lord. "I know Evil-Questioning well, for he and I were great in the time of our apostacy; but I know not now where he dwells."

"But I do," said his man, "and if your lordship will go, I will lead you the way to his den." "Go!" quoth my lord, "that I will. Come, my Diligence, let us go find them out."

So my lord and his man went together the direct way to his house. Now this man went before to show him his way, and they went till they came even under old Mr. Evil-Questioning's wall.

Then said Diligence, "Hark, my lord, do you know the old gentleman's tongue when you hear it?" "Yes," said my lord, "I know it well, but I have not seen him many a day. This I know, he is cunning: I wish he doth not give us the slip." "Let me alone for that," said his servant Diligence. "But how shall we find the door?" quoth my lord. "Let me alone for that, too," said his man. So he had my Lord Will-be-will about, and showed him the way to the door. Then my lord, without more ado, broke open the door, rushed into the house, and caught them all five together, even as Diligence his man had told him. So my lord apprehended them, and led them away, and committed them to the hand of Mr. True-Man, the gaoler, and commanded, and he did put them in ward. This done, my Lord Mayor was acquainted in the morning with what my Lord Will-be-will had done overnight, and his lordship rejoiced much at the news, not only because there were Doubters apprehended, but because that old Evil-Questioning was taken; for he had been a very great trouble to Mansoul, and much affliction to my Lord Mayor himself. He had also been sought for often, but no hand could ever be laid upon him till now.

Well, the next thing was to make preparation to try these five that by my lord had been apprehended, and that were in the hands of Mr. True-Man, the gaoler. So the day was set, and the court called, and come together, and the prisoners brought to the bar. My Lord Will-be-will had power to have slain them when at first he took them, and that without any more ado; but he thought it at this time more for the honour of the Prince, the comfort of Mansoul, and the discouragement of the enemy, to bring them forth to public judgment.

But, I say, Mr. True-Man brought them in chains to the bar, to the town-hall, for that was the place of judgment. So, to be short, the jury was pannelled, the witnesses sworn, and the prisoners tried for their lives: the jury was the same that tried Mr. No-Truth, Pitiless, Haughty, and the rest of their companions.

And first old Questioning himself was sent to the bar, for he was the receiver, the entertainer, and comforter of these Doubters, that by nation were outlandish men. Then he was bid to hearken to his charge, and was told that he had liberty to object if he had aught to say for himself. So his indictment was read; the manner and form here follows:—

"Mr. Questioning, thou art here indicted by the name of Evil-Questioning, an intruder upon the town of Mansoul, for that thou art a Diabolonian by nature and also a hater of the Prince Emmanuel, and one that hast studied the ruin of the town of Mansoul. Thou art also here indicted for countenancing the King's enemies after wholesome laws made to the contrary: 1.

Thou hast questioned the truth of her doctrine and state; 2. In wishing that ten thousand Doubters were in her; 3. In receiving, in entertaining, and encouraging of her enemies that came from their army unto thee. What saiest thou to this indictment? Art thou guilty or not guilty?"

"My lord," quoth he, "I know not the meaning of this indictment, forasmuch as I am not the man concerned in it. The man that standeth by this charge accused before this bench is called by the name of Evil-Questioning, which name I deny to be mine, mine being Honest-Inquiry. The one, indeed, sounds like the other, but I trow your lordships know that between these two there is a wide difference, for I hope that a man, even in the worst of times, and that, too, amongst the worst of men, may make an honest inquiry after things without running the danger of death."

Then spake my Lord Will-be-will, for he was one of the witnesses: "My lord, and you the honourable bench and magistrates of the town of Mansoul, you all have heard with your ears that the prisoner at the bar has denied his name, and so thinks to shift from the charge of the indictment. But I know him to be the man concerned, and that his proper name is Evil-Questioning. I have known him, my lord, above these thirty years, for he and I (a shame it is for me to speak it) were great acquaintance when Diabolus, that tyrant, had the government of Mansoul; and I testify that he is a Diabolonian by nature, an enemy to our Prince, and a hater of the blessed town of Mansoul. He has, in times of rebellion, been at and lain in my house, my lord, not so little as twenty nights together, and we did use to talk then, for the substance of talk, as he and his Doubters have talked of late. True, I have not seen him many a day. I suppose that the coming of Emmanuel to Mansoul has made him change his lodgings, as this indictment has driven him to change his name; but this is the man, my lord."

Then said the Court unto him, "Hast thou any more to say?"

"Yes," quoth the old gentleman, "that I have, for all that as yet has been said against me is but by the mouth of one witness; and it is not lawful for the famous town of Mansoul, at the mouth of one witness, to put any man to death."

Then stood forth Mr. Diligence, and said, "My lord, as I was upon my watch such a night at the head of Bad Street, in this town, I chanced to hear a muttering within this gentleman's house. Then thought I, what's to do here? So I went up close, but very softly, to the side of the house to listen, thinking, as indeed it fell out, that there I might light upon some Diabolonian conventicle. So, as I said, I drew nearer and nearer, and when I was got up close to the wall, it was but a while before I perceived that there were outlandish men in the house; but I did well understand their speech, for I have been a traveller myself. Now, hearing such language in such a tottering cottage as this old gentleman dwelt in, I clapt mine ear to a hole in the window, and there heard them talk as followeth. This old Mr. Questioning asked these Doubters what they were, whence they came, and what was their business in these parts, and they told him to all these questions, yet he did entertain them. He also asked what numbers there were of them, and they told him ten thousand men. He then asked them why they made no more manly assault upon Mansoul, and they told him; so he called their general coward for marching off when he should have fought for his prince. Further, this old Evil-Questioning wisht, and I heard him wish, would all the ten thousand Doubters were now in Mansoul, and himself in the head of them. He bid them also to take heed and lie quiet, for if they were taken they must die, although they had heads of gold."

Then said the Court: "Mr. Evil-Questioning, here is now another witness against you, and his testimony is full. 1. He swears that you did receive these men into your house, and that you did nourish them there, though you knew that they were Diabolonians and the King's enemies. 2. He swears that you did wish ten thousand of them in Mansoul. 3. He swears that you did give them advice to be quiet and close, lest they were taken by the King's servants; all which manifesteth that thou art a Diabolonian; but hadst thou been a friend to the King, thou wouldst have apprehended them."

The Prisoner's Plea

Then said Evil-Questioning: "To the first of these I answer, The men that came into mine house were strangers, and I took them in. And is it now become a crime in Mansoul for a man to entertain strangers? That I did also nourish them is true; and why should my charity be blamed? As for the reason why I wished ten thousand of them in Mansoul, I never told it to the witnesses nor to themselves. I might wish them to be taken, and so my wish might mean well to Mansoul for aught that any yet knows. I did also bid them take heed that they fell not into the captain's hands, but that might be because I am unwilling that any man should be slain, and not because I would have the King's enemies as such escape."

My Lord Mayor then replied: "That though it was a virtue to entertain strangers, yet it was treason to entertain the King's enemies. And for what else thou hast said, thou dost by words but labour to evade and defer the execution of judgment. But could there be no more proved against thee but that thou art a Diabolonian, thou must for that die the death by the law; but to be a receiver, a nourisher, a countenancer, and a harbourer of others of them, yea, of outlandish Diabolonians, yea, of them that came from far on purpose to cut off and destroy our Mansoul: this must not be borne."

Then said Evil-Questioning: "I see how the game will go. I must die for my name, and for my charity." And so he held his peace.

Then they called the outlandish Doubters to the bar, and the first of them that was arraigned was the Election-Doubter. So his indictment was read; and because he was an outlandish man the substance of it was told him by an interpreter, namely, "That he was there charged with being an enemy of Emmanuel the Prince, a hater of the town of Mansoul, and an opposer of her most wholesome doctrine."

Then the judge asked him if he would plead, but he said only this: That he confessed that he was an Election-Doubter, and that that was the religion that he had ever been brought up in. And said, moreover, "If I must die for my religion, I trow I shall die a martyr, and so I care the less."

Judge. Then it was replied: "To question election is to overthrow a great doctrine of the Gospel, namely, the omnisciency, and power, and will of God; to take away the liberty of God with his creature, to stumble the faith of the town of Mansoul, and to make salvation to depend upon works, and not upon grace. It also belied the word and disquieted the minds of the men of Mansoul; therefore by the best of laws he must die."

Then was the Vocation-Doubter called, and set to the bar; and his indictment for substance was the same with the other, only he was particularly charged with denying the calling of Mansoul. The judge asked him also what he had to say for himself.

So he replied: "That he never believed that there was any such thing as a distinct and powerful call of God to Mansoul otherwise than by the general voice of the word, nor by that neither, otherwise than as it exhorted them to forbear evil and to do that which is good, and in so doing a promise of happiness is annexed."

Then said the judge: "Thou art a Diabolonian, and hast denied a great part of one of the most experimental truths of the Prince of the town of Mansoul; for he has called, and she has heard, a most distinct and powerful call of her Emmanuel, by which she has been quickened, awakened, and possessed with heavenly grace to desire to have communion with her Prince, to serve him and do his will, and to look for her happiness merely of his good pleasure. And for thine abhorrence of this good doctrine thou must die the death."

Then the Grace-Doubter was called, and his indictment was read, and he replied thereto: "That though he was of the Land of Doubting, his father was the offspring of a Pharisee, and lived in good fashion among his neighbours, and that he taught him to believe, and believe it I do and will, that Mansoul shall never be saved freely by grace."

Then said the judge: "Why, the law of the Prince is plain: 1. Negatively, 'Not of works:' 2. Positively, 'by grace you are saved.' And thy religion settleth in and upon the works of the flesh, for the works of the law are the works of the flesh. Besides, in saying as thou hast done, thou hast robbed God of his glory, and given it to a sinful man; thou hast robbed Christ of the necessity of his undertaking and the sufficiency thereof, and hast given both these to the works of the flesh. Thou hast despised the work of the Holy Ghost, and hast magnified the will of the flesh and of the legal mind. Thou art a Diabolonian, the son of a Diabolonian; and for thy Diabolonian principles thou must die."

The Court then, having proceeded thus far with them, sent out the jury, who forthwith brought them in guilty of death. Then stood up the Recorder, and addressed himself to the prisoners: "You, the prisoners at the bar, you have been here indicted, and proved guilty of high crimes against Emmanuel our Prince, and against the welfare of the famous town of Mansoul, crimes for which you must be put to death, and die ye accordingly."

So they were sentenced to the death of the cross. The place assigned them for execution was that where Diabolus drew up his last army against Mansoul; save only that old Evil-Questioning was hanged at the top of Bad Street, just over against his own door.

When the town of Mansoul had thus far rid themselves of their enemies and of the troublers of their peace, in the next place a strict commandment was given out, that yet my Lord Will-be-will should, with Diligence his man, search for, and do his best to apprehend, what town Diabolonians were yet left alive in Mansoul.

The names of several of them were Mr. Fooling, Mr. Let-Good-Slip, Mr. Slavish-Fear, Mr. No-Love, Mr. Mistrust, Mr. Flesh, and Mr. Sloth. It was also commanded, that he should apprehend Mr. Evil-Questioning's children, that he left behind him, and that they should demolish his house. The children that he left behind him were these: Mr. Doubt, and he was his eldest son; the next to him was Legal-Life, Unbelief, Wrong-Thoughts-of-Christ, Clip-Promise, Carnal-Sense, Live-by-Feeling, Self-Love. All these he had by one wife, and her name was No-Hope; she was the kinswoman of old Incredulity, for he was her uncle; and when her father, old Dark, was dead, he took her and brought her up, and when she was marriageable, he gave her to this old Evil-Questioning to wife.

Now, the Lord Will-be-will did put into execution his commission, with great Diligence, his man. He took Fooling in the streets, and hanged him up in Want-wit Alley, over against his own house. This Fooling was he that would have had the town of Mansoul deliver up Captain Credence into the hands of Diabolus, provided that then he would have withdrawn his force out of the town. He also took Mr. Let-Good-Slip one day as he was busy in the market, and executed him according to law. Now, there was an honest poor man in Mansoul, and his name was Mr. Meditation, one of no great account in the days of apostacy, but now of repute with the best of the town. This man, therefore, they were willing to prefer. Now, Mr. Let-Good-Slip had a great deal of wealth heretofore in Mansoul, and, at Emmanuel's coming, it was sequestered to the use of the Prince; this, therefore, was now given to Mr. Meditation, to improve for the common good, and after him to his son, Mr. Think-Well: this Think-Well he had by Mrs. Piety, his wife, and she was the daughter of Mr. Recorder.

After this, my lord apprehended Clip-Promise: now because he was a notorious villain, for by his doings much of the king's coin was abused, therefore he was made a public example. He was arraigned and judged to be first set in the pillory, then to be whipt by all the children and servants in Mansoul, and then to be hanged till he was dead. Some may wonder at the severity of this man's punishment; but those that are honest traders in Mansoul are sensible of the great abuse that one clipper of promises in little time may do to the town of Mansoul. And truly my judgment is, that all those of his name and life should be served even as he.

Carnal-Sense Escapes

He also apprehended Carnal-Sense, and put him in hold; but how it came about I cannot tell, but he brake prison, and made his escape; yea, and the bold villain will not yet quit the town, but lurks in the Diabolonian dens a-days, and haunts like a ghost honest men's houses a-nights. Wherefore, there was a proclamation set up in the market-place in Mansoul, signifying that whosoever could discover Carnal-Sense, and apprehend him and slay him, should be admitted daily to the Prince's table, and should be made keeper of the treasure of Mansoul. Many, therefore, did bend themselves to do this thing, but take him and slay him they could not, though often he was discovered.

But my lord took Mr. Wrong-Thoughts-of-Christ, and put him in prison, and he died there; though it was long first, for he died of a lingering consumption.

Self-Love was also taken and committed to custody; but there were many that were allied to him in Mansoul, so his judgment was deferred. But at last Mr. Self-Denial stood up and said: "If such villains as these may be winked at in Mansoul, I will lay down my commission." He also took him from the crowd, and had him among his soldiers, and there he was brained. But some in Mansoul muttered at it, though none durst speak plainly, because Emmanuel was in town. But this brave act of Captain Self-Denial came to the Prince's ears; so he sent for him, and made him a lord in Mansoul. My Lord Will-be-will also obtained great commendations of Emmanuel for what he had done for the town of Mansoul.

Then my Lord Self-Denial took courage, and set to the pursuing of the Diabolonians, with my Lord Will-be-will; and they took Live-by-Feeling, and they took Legal-Life, and put them in hold till they died. But Mr. Unbelief was a nimble Jack: him they could never lay hold of, though they attempted to do it often. He, therefore, and some few more of the subtilest of the Diabolonian tribe, did yet remain in Mansoul, to the time that Mansoul left off to dwell any longer in the kingdom of Universe. But they kept them to their dens and holes: if one of them did appear, or happen to be seen in any of the streets of the town of Mansoul, the whole town would be up in arms after them; yea, the very children in Mansoul would cry out after them as after a thief, and would wish that they might stone them to death with stones. And now did Mansoul arrive to some good degree of peace and quiet: her Prince also did abide within her borders; her captains, also, and her soldiers did their duties; and Mansoul minded her trade that she had with the country that was afar off; also she was busy in her manufacture.

When the town of Mansoul had thus far rid themselves of so many of their enemies and the troublers of their peace, the Prince sent to them and appointed a day wherein he would, at the market-place, meet the whole people, and there give them in charge concerning some further matters, that, if observed, would tend to their further safety and comfort, and to the condemnation and destruction of their home-bred Diabolonians. So the day appointed was come, and the townsmen met together; Emmanuel also came down in his chariot, and all his captains in their state attending him on the right hand and on the left. Then was an "Oyes" made for silence, and, after some mutual carriages of love, the Prince began, and thus proceeded:

"You, my dear Mansoul, and the beloved of mine heart, many and great are the privileges that I have bestowed upon you; I have singled you out from others, and have chosen you to myself, not for your worthiness, but for mine own sake. I have also redeemed you, not only from the dread of my Father's law, but from the hand of Diabolus. This I have done because I loved you, and because I have set my heart upon you to do you good. I have also, that all things that might hinder the way to the pleasures of Paradise might be taken out of the way, laid down for thee for thy soul a plenary satisfaction, and have bought thee to myself; a price not of corruptible things, as of silver and gold, but a price of blood, mine own blood, which I have freely spilled upon the ground to make thee mine. So I have reconciled thee, O my Mansoul, to my Father, and entrusted thee in the mansion houses that are with my Father in the royal city, where things are, O my Mansoul, that eye hath not seen, nor hath entered into the heart of man to conceive.

"Besides, O my Mansoul, thou seest what I have done, and how I have taken thee out of the hands of thine enemies; unto whom thou hadst deeply revolted from my Father, and by whom thou wast content to be possessed, and also to be destroyed. I came to thee first by my law, then by my Gospel, to awaken thee, and show thee my glory. And thou knowest what thou wast, what thou saidst, what thou didst, and how many times thou rebelledst against my Father and me; yet I left thee not, as thou seest this day, but came to thee, have borne thy manners, have waited upon thee, and, after all, accepted of thee, even of my mere grace and favour; and would not suffer thee to be lost, as thou most willingly wouldst have been. I also compassed thee about, and afflicted thee on every side, that I might make thee weary of thy ways, and bring down thy heart with molestation to a willingness to close with thy good and happiness. And when I had gotten a complete conquest over thee, I turned it to thy advantage.

"Thou seest, also, what a company of my Father's host I have lodged within thy borders: captains and rulers, soldiers and men of war, engines and excellent devices to subdue and bring down thy foes: thou knowest my meaning, O Mansoul. And they are my servants, and thine, too, Mansoul. Yea, my design of possessing of thee with them, and the natural tendency of each of them, is to defend, purge, strengthen, and sweeten thee for myself, O Mansoul, and to make thee meet for my Father's presence, blessing, and glory; for thou, my Mansoul, art created to be prepared unto these.

"Thou seest, moreover, my Mansoul, how I have passed by thy backslidings, and have healed thee. Indeed, I was angry with thee, but I have turned mine anger away from thee, because I loved thee still, and mine anger and mine indignation is ceased in the destruction of thine enemies, O Mansoul. Nor did thy goodness fetch me again unto thee, after that I for thy transgressions have hid my face and withdrawn my presence from thee. The way of backsliding was thine, but the way and means of thy recovery was mine. I invented the means of thy return; it was I that made a hedge and a wall, when thou wast beginning to turn to things in which I delighted not. 'Twas I that made thy sweet bitter, thy day night, thy smooth ways thorny, and that also confounded all that sought thy destruction. 'Twas I that set Mr. Godly-Fear to work in Mansoul. 'Twas I that stirred up thy conscience and understanding, thy will and thy affections, after thy great and woeful decay. 'Twas I that put life into thee, O Mansoul, to seek me, that thou mightest find me, and in thy finding find thine own health, happiness, and salvation. 'Twas I that fetched the second time the Diabolonians out of Mansoul; and it was I that overcame them, and that destroyed them before thy face.

"And now, my Mansoul, I am returned to thee in peace, and thy transgressions against me are as if they had not been. Nor shall it be with thee as in former days, but I will do better for thee than at thy beginning. For yet a little while, O my Mansoul, even after a few more times are gone over thy head, I will (but be not thou troubled at what I say) take down this famous town of Mansoul, stick and stone, to the ground. And I will carry the stones thereof, and the timber thereof, and the walls thereof, and the dust thereof, and the inhabitants thereof, into mine own country, even into the kingdom of my Father; and will there set it up in such strength and glory as it never did see in the kingdom where now it is placed. I will even there set it up for my Father's habitation; for for that purpose it was at first erected in the kingdom of Universe; and there will I make it a spectacle of wonder, a monument of mercy, and the admirer of its own mercy. There shall the natives of Mansoul see all that of which they have seen nothing here; there shall they be equal to those unto whom they have been inferior here. And there shalt thou, O my Mansoul, have such communion with me, with my Father, and with your Lord Secretary, as it is not possible here to be enjoyed, nor ever could be, shouldest thou live in Universe the space of a thousand years.

"And there, O my Mansoul, thou shalt be afraid of murderers no more; of Diabolonians and their threats no more. There there shall be no more plots, nor contrivances, nor designs against thee, O my Mansoul. There thou shalt no more hear the evil tidings, or the noise of the Diabolonian drum. There thou shalt not see the Diabolonian standard-bearers, nor yet behold Diabolus's standard. No Diabolonian mount shall be cast up against thee there; nor shall there the Diabolonian standard be set up to make thee afraid. There thou shalt not need captains, engines, soldiers, and men of war. There thou shalt meet with no sorrow nor grief; nor shall it be possible that any Diabolonian should again, for ever, be able to creep into thy skirts, burrow in thy walls, or be seen again within thy borders all the days of eternity. Life shall there last longer than here you are able to desire it should; and yet it shall always be sweet and new, nor shall any impediment attend it for ever.

"There, O Mansoul, thou shalt meet with many of those that have been like thee, and that have been partakers of thy sorrows; even such as I have chosen, and redeemed, and set apart, as thou, for my Father's court and city-royal. All they will be glad in thee, and thou, when thou seest them, shalt be glad in thine heart."

Things Never Yet Seen

"There are things, O Mansoul, even things of thy Father's providing and mine, that never were seen since the beginning of the world; and they are laid up with my Father, and sealed up among his treasures for thee, till thou shalt come thither to enjoy them. I told you before, that I would remove my Mansoul, and set it up elsewhere; and where I will set it, there are those that love thee, and those that rejoice in thee now; but how much more when they shall see thee exalted to honour! My father will then send them for you to fetch you; and their bosoms and chariots to put you in. And you, O my Mansoul, shall ride upon the wings of the wind. They will come to convey, conduct, and bring you to that, when your eyes see more, that will be your desired haven.

"And thus, O my Mansoul, I have showed unto thee what shall be done to thee hereafter, if thou canst hear, if thou canst understand; and now I will tell thee what at present must be thy duty and practice, until I come and fetch thee to myself, according as is related in the Scriptures of truth.

"First, I charge thee that thou dost hereafter keep more white and clean the liveries which I gave thee before my last withdrawing from thee. Do it, I say, for this will be thy wisdom. They are in themselves fine linen, but thou must keep them white and clean. This will be your wisdom, your honour, and will be greatly for my glory. When your garments are white, the world will count you mine. Also, when your garments are white, then I am delighted in your ways; for then your goings to and fro will be like a flash of lightning that those that are present must take notice of; also their eyes will be made to dazzle thereat. Deck thyself, therefore, according to my bidding, and make thyself by my law straight steps for thy feet; so shall thy king greatly desire thy beauty, for he is thy Lord, and worship thou him.

"Now, that thou mayest keep them as I bid thee, I have, as I before did tell thee, provided for thee an open fountain to wash thy garments in. Look, therefore, that thou wash often in my fountain, and go not in defiled garments; for as it is to my dishonour and my disgrace, so it will be to thy discomfort, when thou shalt walk in filthy garments. Let not, therefore, my garments, your garments, the garments that I gave thee, be defiled or spotted by the flesh. Keep thy garments always white, and let thy head lack no ointment.

"My Mansoul, I have ofttimes delivered thee from the designs, plots, attempts, and conspiracies of Diabolus; and for all this I ask thee nothing but that thou render not to me evil for my good; but that thou bear in mind my love, and the continuation of my kindness to my beloved Mansoul, so as to provoke thee to walk in thy measure, according to the benefit bestowed on thee. Of old, the sacrifices were bound with cords to the horns of the altar. Consider what is said to thee, O my blessed Mansoul.

"O my Mansoul, I have lived, I have died. I live, and will die no more for thee. I live that thou mayest not die. Because I live, thou shalt live also. I reconciled thee to my Father by the blood of my cross; and being reconciled, thou shalt live through me. I will pray for thee; I will fight for thee; I will yet do thee good.

"Nothing can hurt thee but sin; nothing can grieve thee but sin; nothing can make thee base before thy foes but sin: take heed of sin, my Mansoul.

"And dost thou know why I at first, and do still, suffer Diabolonians to dwell in thy walls, O Mansoul? It is to keep thee wakening, to try thy love, to make thee watchful, and to cause thee yet to prize my noble captains, their soldiers, and my mercy.

"It is also, that yet thou mayest be made to remember what a deplorable condition thou once wast in. I mean when not some, but all, did dwell, not in thy walls, but in thy castle and in thy stronghold, O Mansoul.

"O my Mansoul, should I slay all them within, many there be without that would bring thee into bondage; for were all those within cut off, those without would find thee sleeping; and then, as in a moment, they would swallow up my Mansoul. I therefore left them in thee, not to do thee hurt (the which they yet will, if thou hearken to them and serve them), but to do thee good, the which they must, if thou watch and fight against them. Know, therefore, that whatever they shall tempt thee to, my design is, that they should drive thee, not farther off, but nearer to my Father, to learn thee war, to make petitioning desirable to thee, and to make thee little in thine own eyes. Hearken diligently to this, my Mansoul.

"Shew me, then, thy love, my Mansoul, and let not those that are within thy walls take thy affections off from him that hath redeemed thy soul. Yea, let the sight of a Diabolonian heighten thy love to me. I came once, and twice, and thrice, to save thee from the poison of those arrows that would have wrought thy death: stand for me, thy Friend, my Mansoul, against the Diabolonians, and I will stand for thee before my Father and all his court. Love me against temptation, and I will love thee notwithstanding thine infirmities.

"O my Mansoul, remember what my captains, my soldiers, and mine engines have done for thee. They have fought for thee, they have suffered by thee, they have borne much at thy hands to do thee good, O Mansoul. Hadst thou not had them to help thee, Diabolus had certainly made a hand of thee. Nourish them, therefore, my Mansoul. When thou dost well, they will be well; when thou dost ill, they will be ill, and sick, and weak. Make not my captains sick, O Mansoul; for if they be sick, thou canst not be well; if they be weak, thou canst not be strong; if they be faint, thou canst not be stout and valiant for thy king, O Mansoul. Nor must thou think always to live by sense: thou must live upon my word. Thou must believe, O my Mansoul, when I am from thee, that yet I love thee, and bear thee upon mine heart for ever.

"Remember, therefore, O my Mansoul, that thou art beloved of me; as I have, therefore, taught thee to watch, to fight, to pray, and to make war against my foes; so now I command thee to believe that my love is constant to thee. O my Mansoul, how have I set my heart, my love upon thee! Watch. Behold, I lay none other burden upon thee than what thou hast already. Hold fast, till I come."